HERETICAL FISHING

BOOK 3

HERETICAL FISHING

A Cozy Guide to Annoying the Cults, Outsmarting the Fish, and Alienating Oneself

BOOK 3

Haylock Jobson

Podium

This book goes out to the gang at Millers Espresso, whose caffeine and terrible (read: fun) personalities fueled the words within.

Cover design by Mary Cruz

ISBN: 978-1-0394-5318-0

Published in 2024 by Podium Publishing
www.podiumentertainment.com

Podium

Previously on Heretical Fishing . . .

Corporal Claws, maiden of the pond and cutest otter in all the land, discovers a strange presence dwelling within a tree. After a series of events—enabled by her unparalleled intellect and fine coat of fur—Lieutenant Colonel Lemony Thicket (Lemon) reawakens. Much to Claws's dismay and delight, Lemon is just as fond of pranks as she is.

A procession of cloaked men leaves the capital of Gormona under cover of night, their intentions murky but destination clear: Tropica. When they arrive, they are revealed to be the Fishing Club of Gormona. They have come to start a church with Fischer as the deity. When it's revealed that Barry has already done so, they happily join the Church of Fischer.

George and Geraldine Kraken, the lord and lady of Tropica village, begin following the instructions of the House Kraken manual. They improve their diet, adopt a strict meditation regime, and genuinely regret their previous exploitation of Tropica's villagers.

Through a series of un-bee-lievable circumstances, a lone bumblebee arrives back in Tropica just as flowers bloom on Lemon's namesake trees. Fischer tries to lure honeybees into a hive using a mixture of water and regular sugar (read: not 'pew-pew sand', as Fischer dubbed the chi-filled variety). The bumblebee, henceforth known as Bumblebro, eats the mixture and awakens. Bumblebro thwarts a malicious crew of hornets that invades the neighboring beehive, and to save the queen's life after she is stung by one of the flying war crimes, he feeds her his royal jelly, making her ascend. (Why are you looking at me like that? Royal jelly is a real thing some species of bees make—stop being weird about it, *pervert*.) Fischer comes across the two spirit beast insects, gives Bumblebro his name, and dubs the queen . . . well, *Queen Bee.*

Fischer discovers Rocky stuffing a pelican into a pot, then apologizes by giving the pelican a rather pungent eel, which he happily eats. The pelican awakens, finds out that two *brown* pelicans have stolen his nest, and hits the male with a flying kick from low orbit. The pair retreat, leaving an egg behind. Fischer names the pelican Warrant Officer Williams, aka Bill, who presents the egg to them. He and Cinnamon care for it.

When Lemon creates the fruit she is named after, she recalls her memories and shows them to Fischer. They witness a scene from long ago, revealing a great war that scoured the land as far as the eye could see.

Trent, the crown prince of Gormona, remains a captive of the Church of Fischer. In exchange for sugary pastries and other sweet treats, he readily tells the church everything he knows, including the existence of artifacts that track awakenings. Thus, when the five members of Gormona's fishing club ascend, they choose the names of five imaginary beasts: Lizard Wizard, Bog Dog, Boat Goat, Hurtle the Turtle, and Glare Bear.

A guard, Deklan, searches Gormona's castle for five missing people he'll never find. Instead of humans, he finds the artifacts that track said advancements. The king is informed, and as more and more of these advancements are revealed, he slowly descends into paranoid madness.

Through experimentation, Fischer learns he can manipulate chi using the skill to condense—or remove—chi from food. He puts this skill to various uses. When the king and queen learn of this ability it causes them a great deal of distress, which emphasizes just how significant it is.

Fischer and the gang are sitting on the sand when suddenly a black portal tears into existence. A hellhound that Fischer had previously kicked in a drunken episode of self-defense leaps through it. The spirit beast reads Fischer's mind and transforms into the evilest of all canids from back on Earth—a Chihuahua. The hellhound shares his thoughts with them, revealing that he has been alone for millennia. With that, Brigadier Borks joins the squad.

Over a span of weeks, a small rift forms between Fischer and Maria. She feels him pulling away, yet every time she asks if things are okay, Fischer lies to her . . . and to himself. It eventually builds and becomes something he can no longer ignore. After speaking to Theo and Barry, he has a breakthrough and runs off to find Maria. As the two embrace, Roger attempts to move Fischer and discovers that he is a cultivator. Despite their difference in strength, the enraged father attempts to deliver Fischer the old left-right-goodnight. Maria and Sharon reveal they are also cultivators, which causes Roger to request that he become one, too. Cultivators are what he hates most in the world, yet he would do *anything* to defend his wife and daughter. He chooses the name An Entire Flock of Birds, which wreaks havoc on the king's mental health.

The brown pelican egg hatches and Private Pelly is born. Cinnamon guards her, threatening a low kick to anyone who dares to come close. When she's only a few weeks old, Pelly develops a core, so Fischer gives her chi-filled food to make her awaken.

Fischer notices that Sergeant Snips has been quite absent. Unbeknownst to him, she has been running reconnaissance in the capital, preparing intel for a secret mission known as Operation: Sticky Fingers. As she hides on a rooftop, she sees squads of cultivators roaming the streets. They appear to shoot at any birds they see.

Sturgill, the local baker, awakens of seemingly natural causes. He and his wife Sue decide to join the church, adopting the names The Beetle Boys and Fat Rat Pack in the System. Said names cause the king to faint, and Deklan comforts him. As a result, the king gains a healthy respect for the guard and his calm nature.

When it comes time for the execution of Operation: Sticky Fingers, Barry brings

Fischer into the fold. Though Fischer wants to be a part of neither planning nor logistics, he is all too happy to help if it means his friends will be safer.

Under the guise of a camping trip, Fischer, Maria, and Borks head to the capital. On the way there, they discover a lake with creatures that were *apparently* created by the followers of Ceto, one of the departed gods. With the operation now underway, they resolve to return at a later date. But when they reach Gormona, they split up; Maria retreats into the forest, Borks runs toward the castle, and Fischer drops down into a grove where a trap is waiting for him. He easily defeats Tom Osnan Sr. and the dozens of cultivators there, steals the grove's power, and begins looking for a cart.

With Cinnamon leading an army of beetles, Claws Tokyo-drifting a cart of rats through the streets, and the pelican pals herding thousands of seagulls into the airspace above Tropica, the assault begins. Within the castle, the rest of the attackers— who had been hiding within Borks's dimensional space the entire time—stream out. They steal the royal library and every single artifact, then most of them retreat into Borks's spatial ability. With the express intention of sowing chaos, those who remain get dressed in the costumes of their respective aliases.

When the king catches sight of the horde of seagulls, he accidentally runs through a wall and reveals to Deklan that *he* is a cultivator. The typically lackadaisical guard shows disdain for the king, who leaves to find the attackers. When the king finds them, his worst fears are confirmed: Hurtle the Turtle (Snips), Boat Goat (Rocky), Bog Dog (Borks), Glare Bear (Pistachio), and worst of all, Lizard Wizard (Ellis, wearing a crafted suit of spirit beast scales) launch through a wall and begin battling in a feast hall. The king is then revealed to be a cultivator of flame chi, and though his power is strong, it is nothing compared to the church's forces. They proceed to toy with him.

After Rocky has his fake goat's head burned off, the disgruntled crustacean loses his cool and begins smashing the king over the head with his own tables. The move is as physically ineffective as it is emotionally devastating, and the king gathers his power to launch a deathly blow, which Ellis blocks. The flames burn away the suits that Snips and Rocky have on, but Ellis's scales reflect twenty percent of the physical attack. Combined with twin blasts from Rocky's clackers, the king is ejected from his own castle. At the last moment, Snips latches on to the king's artifact clothing, leaving his royal member exposed as he hurtles through one mountain peak and into another. With their mission complete, they pile back into Borks's portal, Rocky having to be dragged in by Pistachio after Snips refuses to launch him toward the distant horizon.

Down on the street, Fischer walks along with a cart full of cultivators and some passiona bushes. Deklan finds him there, and after a quick chat, he learns that Fischer plans to free his brother—who is currently unconscious in the back of the cart. Claws and Cinnamon arrive. Cinnamon is grabbed by the scruff of her neck to prevent a roundhouse kick from making contact with Deklan's chest. The two girls advise Fischer that they will collect the rest of the cultivators and, with the help of Pelly and Bill, extricate them from Gormona, making particular note of Deklan's brother.

On the way out of Gormona, Fischer begins selling Deklan on the idea of fishing . . .

HERETICAL FISHING

BOOK 3

Prologue

Corporal Claws grinned and puffed out her chest as adrenaline coursed through her tiny little body. She was the most powerful otter in all the lands and seas, and now she had tamed the sky.

She stood atop a mountain of the fallen, their unmoving bodies a monument to her prowess. This was no metaphorical hill, oh no. She quite literally stood atop dozens of the cultivators. They had been bagged up like grains of wheat and were being flown through the sky by her valiant steeds.

Claws unleashed a chittering laugh. She held her forepaws high, projecting the sound out over the moonlit landscape as her cackle grew, drowning out even the howling wind that rushed past her adorable ears.

Her mirth knew no bounds. Her strength was unmatched. Her coat of fur knew no equal. Her . . .

One of her captives was stirring.

Claws whirled, chirping with indignation at the cultivator that had *dared* regain consciousness while she celebrated. Using the giant net for footholds, she skittered around to find the offending human. She revealed her daggerlike teeth to display her displeasure, but when she found the man, she paused.

It was the man her master had told her to take extra good care of.

"Where . . ." he groaned. "Where am . . ." He trailed off as his eyes focused on Corporal Claws.

Understandable, she thought. *My form is magnificent. My fur is immaculate. My teeth—*

"Glaucus's cursed herbs!" he swore, his eyes tracking the treetops below. *"What's happening? Where am I?"*

"Shhhh," she said by blowing air through her pointed teeth, then patted his cheek and cooed reassuringly. Everything was going to be okay.

"Sp-spirit beast!" he yelled.

He reached for his chi, and Claws sighed.

Sorry, Master.

She sent a small jolt of lightning down her arm and into the man's head, temporarily sending him back into oblivion. Fischer, her master, had told her to take good care of him, so when the man's body went still, she readjusted the bow she'd tied to his head as a marker. The least she could do was ensure he was presentable. Scanning the surrounding cultivators, she found them still unconscious, and with a nod to herself, Claws climbed back to the top of the stack.

She cleared her throat, puffed out her chest, and resumed where she'd left off. Maniacal laughter rolled out through the night sky as she broadcast her joy for all to hear.

After only a few seconds, a cinnamon-colored paw tapped her on the back of the head, cutting her off.

Claws scowled at Cinnamon, her amusement morphing to indignation. For what reason did the divergent bunny interrupt her villainous chuckle? Rather than chastise Claws, however, Cinnamon pointed at herself. Balancing on her rear hoppers, the bunny stood tall, puffed out her chest, pointed at her stomach, and let out a slow, quiet laugh.

At first, Claws wondered if Cinnamon was having a medical episode, but then the bunny pointed at her stomach more emphatically. With each peep that came from Cinnamon's throat, her stomach tensed.

Claws cocked her head all the way to the side as she watched, considering. After a moment, she copied Cinnamon's posture. Rather than forced from her lungs, the laugh felt like it was shot forth from her core like a blast from Pistachio's mighty clacker.

Claws trilled with delight and resumed laughing. She stood tall, as did Cinnamon. Together, they cackled their victory over the pile of cultivators they stood atop of.

As Bill soared over the forest while clutching a giant net filled to the brim with cultivators, he wondered, not for the first time, if Claws might be insane.

Her jaw was spread wide as she trilled and chirped with laughter, her needlelike teeth shining in the moonlight. Beside her, Cinnamon peeped along with the same cadence. With each heave of their chests, their laughs only grew louder.

Suddenly, Claws stopped. She turned and spotted another waking cultivator.

Zap.

Claws struck her with a jolt of electricity. Before the poor woman could even hit the net again, Claws was cackling away, arching her back and facing her head skyward.

Bill shared a glance with Pelly, who looked just as concerned as he felt.

They were approaching the meeting place, so Bill let out a warning honk. Claws darted her eyes his way, but when he nodded toward the ground and she saw the incoming clearing, the scowl died on her face.

Claws hunched down low, wiggled her butt, and launched herself.

All Bill could do was shake his head as she flew groundward toward their master like an arrow in flight.

CHAPTER ONE

Home Sweet Home

When I arrived at the meeting place, a blur of blond hair and cute freckles flew at me.

"Oof!" I said, bracing myself as Maria slammed into my chest.

"How did it go? Is everyone okay? Did you get the bushes? What happened? Was that your blast? The big white pillar that lit up the sky?"

"Whoaaa." I laughed, holding up both hands at the barrage of questions. "One at a time."

"Sorry." She squeezed my chest hard enough that I thought she might crack a rib. "I was just anxious without—oof!"

My revenge arrived in the form of a golden retriever. Brigadier Borks slammed into her side, just as excited to see her as she was to see me.

"Borks!" She ran her hands through his hair but quickly regretted the decision. "Why are you covered in mud?"

Too excited to answer, he rained down a barrage of licks on her chin, which she only moderately succeeded in escaping. When Borks had finally calmed down, Maria stood, stretched, and froze.

"Fischer . . ."

"What's up?"

"Who is that?"

"Who, him?" I asked, pointing to the armored guard that had left Gormona with me. "That's Deklan. He's my new friend."

"New . . . friend?"

"Yeah. Might be a best friend in the making, but don't tell Theo that." I spun toward him. "Deklan. Mate. This is my girlfriend, Maria."

"Nice to meet you," Deklan replied, a little too nonchalant considering he'd just witnessed Maria and Borks exhibiting very cultivatory movements.

"A pleasure, Deklan." She strode forward and held out a hand. "So, what did you do to earn best-friend-in-the-making status with Fischer?"

Deklan shook her hand. "I'm not too sure."

"Get this," I said, leaning in close. "Deklan here likes the idea of *fishing*."

Rather than the excitement I expected, Maria narrowed her eyes at me. "How do you do it?"

"Do what?"

"Just live life and find anglers everywhere."

"There are more anglers?" Deklan asked.

"Of course there are more anglers." Maria shook her head, making her hair sway. "Fischer seems to create them out of thin air."

"Hey, you're one of them," I added, nudging her side.

"Huh." Deklan chewed his lip in thought. "You made it sound relaxing, so it's right up my alley, but I thought it wouldn't be too popular." He waved his hands vaguely. "Because of the whole going-against-the-gods thing, you know?"

"And that doesn't bother you?" Maria asked.

"Why should it?" He shrugged. "They're gone. When you really think about it, it's weirder that others *do* care."

"See?" I grinned at Maria. "Best friend in the making."

"Poor Theo is going to be heartbroken." She sighed. "Speaking of—should we check on them?"

"Check on who?" Deklan asked.

"Oh, right." I patted Borks on the head. "Don't be surprised, but Borks kind of has a pocket-dimension-ability thing going on. We have a bunch of people in there right now. Probably a bunch of stolen artifacts, too."

"Oh, did you take the artifacts that listed all your abilities and stuff?"

"Yeah, those ones. That was the whole—" I whirled on him. "Wait, you know about that?"

"Yeah. I was the guard assigned to them."

Maria and I blinked at each other, then burst into laughter.

"This is too good," she said. "I have so many questions to ask you."

"We should wait until we get back. We've already wasted too much time here, and Ellis will *definitely* want to hear the effect our names have had."

A sound like cracking glass came from beside us as Borks tore open his portal.

"Whoa . . ." Deklan said, staring at the purple-and-black void.

"Back in a moment, mate." I stepped through, and the moment I did, an animated conversation came to an abrupt halt.

"Our Domain is far superior—oh. Hello, Fischer," Ellis said, nodding at me. He looked ridiculous in his lizard outfit, but that was neither here nor there.

"Just checking in before we head back to Tropica. Are you guys all good?"

"We are," Barry replied. "Have Pelly and Bill arrived yet?"

"Not yet, mate. We'll leave the moment they do."

Barry nodded. "How about you? No issues?"

"Yeah, no issues," I lied, pointedly not mentioning the dozens of extra cultivators I'd brought along for the ride.

Theo's eyebrow twitched. He'd clearly read the lie but didn't mention it.

Thank you, mate, I thought, grateful for his discretion.

"Okay, I'll leave you to it. See you back in . . ." I trailed off, staring at Pistachio and the crab he was restraining. "You guys, uh, sure everything is okay?"

Rocky hissed a slew of insulting bubbles at me, earning himself a whack from Snips's claw.

"Nothing serious," Barry said. "Rocky is just a little upset he wasn't thrown over the horizon for his crimes against humanity."

"Oh. So nothing new, then?"

"Nothing new," Barry agreed.

"Sweet. See you guys in a few hours."

I turned to leave, but a furious scuttling drew my attention. I spun just in time to catch Snips as she launched herself into my arms.

"I missed you, too, Snips," I said, laughing and rubbing the top of her carapace. "Will I be seeing more of you now that the operation is over?"

She nodded violently, her entire body bobbing up and down.

"Glad to hear. Now that I think about it, how would you like to run back to Tropica with us?"

Her visible eye lit up, and her hiss of approval was basically a roar.

"You all good with Rocky, Pistachio?"

The lobster, still calm despite holding a murderous crab, nodded his head.

"Right. Let's hit it, Snips."

She launched from my arms, sailing through the portal before me.

In the moment it took me to join her, she had discovered Deklan. Snips stared up at him, cocking her head to the side as she took him in.

"Er . . ." Deklan said, looking a little unsure of himself.

"He's a friend, Snips. This is Deklan." I grinned at the curiosity held in her eye. "Deklan, this is Sergeant Snips, my violently capable guard crab turned powerful spirit beast."

I'm pretty sure he said some sort of greeting, but I didn't hear it. My attention was on the far distance, where I saw an unmistakable sight. Between us and the cultivator-filled net, a devious being approached.

I bent my legs and braced my core just in time to catch Corporal Claws as she struck me like a meteor. Even if I hadn't felt the excessive chi she traveled with, her mischievous grin was enough to warn me. I slid backward through the clearing, my feet tearing up grass and soil. When I finally skidded to a stop, I pulled her into a tight hug.

"Good to see you too, Claws. I'm guessing it went well?"

Yes! she chirped, rubbing her cheeks against me.

Pelly and Bill arrived a moment later, lowering their net to the ground. Cinnamon unleashed a mighty peep as she launched herself at Maria, who caught her with ease. Both of their smiles were radiant, but Maria's slowly melted away.

"Uhhh . . . are all those people cultivators?" she asked.

"Yep."

"That's way too many, isn't it?"

"Yep."

She gave me a flat stare. "You couldn't leave them, could you?"

"Nope."

She laughed and strode over, wrapping her arms around me. "I'm proud of you."

"Thanks!" I pulled her into a hug. "Let's hope Barry feels the same way."

Claws hopped down from our cuddle and ran over to Deklan. She held a paw up toward him, and when he hesitantly took it, she dragged him over to the cultivators.

Look! she chirped, gesticulating at a man with long brown hair. There was a new addition to Deklan's brother's hair: a pink bow, meticulously tied.

"You . . . gave him a bow?" Deklan asked.

She nodded vehemently, then arched her head toward him, gazing up expectantly.

"She is demanding pets for her hard work." Maria giggled.

Still staring at his brother, Deklan obliged her demands.

Pelly and Bill were standing off to the side, so I walked over to them. "Come here, you two."

They stared up at me, still looking a little awkward, so I scooped them both up into a hug. With a bird under each arm, I went over to Deklan, nodding for Snips to follow. After introducing them all—and letting Deklan softly pat their heads—I put them down.

"Okay, gang. Here's the plan. Deklan, unless you wanna be carried by me like a princess, I think you should sit on the net and let Pelly and Bill fly you back to Tropica. Claws and Cinnamon, I want you on the net to keep him safe in the off chance he falls off."

" . . . falls off?" Deklan asked, some of his calm demeanor vanishing.

"Don't worry. Pelly and Bill are gonna be going super fast, but any of the four animal pals along for the ride could save you."

"Can't he go in Borks's portal?" Maria asked.

"And subject him to Ellis's nonstop questioning?"

"Huh. Good point."

"For what it's worth," Deklan said, "flying actually sounds pretty cool."

I grinned. "It's sorted, then. You guys get going and we'll follow."

Deklan started climbing the net, but then Cinnamon expedited the process.

Seeing a bunny as big as Deklan's boot carry him to the top of the rigid net in a single bound was just as funny as you'd imagine, and I couldn't help but smirk at the surprise on his face. Pelly and Bill took hold of the net and flew skyward, gaining altitude before they shot off with their empowered wings.

"*Whoooooaaa!*" Deklan yelled as they rocketed through the sky, his voice trailing off the farther away they got.

"He's a lot of fun," Maria said, watching them go.

"Right?" I agreed. Maria, Snips, Borks, and I were the only ones left, and I shot them a wink. "We don't need to hold back on the way home—we'll be getting there as fast as we can."

Their eyes lit up, reflecting just how I felt.

"On your mark, get set—"

Snips *shot* away, water chi roiling from her joints.

"Cheater!" Maria and I both yelled.

Borks let out a shocked growl, too, and all three of us tore off after Snips, chasing her hisses of victorious laughter.

The surrounding forest was a blur as we raced between trunks. We no longer had to keep our passage subtle, so our footfalls boomed through the trees. Barry's planning had been meticulous; Claws was already running distraction. I'd occasionally catch glimpses of her streaking through the sky as a bolt of lightning, misleading anyone that heard our thundering steps into assuming they came from a passing storm.

When we got halfway to Tropica, the night's activities caught up to me.

"Can I ride you, Borks?" I asked.

He skidded to a stop, and I leaped onto his back. The second I had my arms looped around his powerful neck, he was off.

"*Cheaterrr!*" Maria called as we shot past her, both giving her a wide grin.

Of the four of us, Maria had the weakest cultivation level. But that wasn't a reflection of her; it was a reflection of Snips's and Borks's power. Their cores radiated chi as they raced through the forest, and unlike me, they didn't grow tired. Before the first light of day had broken the eastern horizon, I caught sight of a familiar mountain range—*my* mountain range.

A thrill ran through me as I realized we were almost home, and only a couple of minutes later, the ocean came into view. It was lit by the crescent moon above, its surface calm and inviting. The sight of it caused a deep contentment to wash over me and a grin to split my face.

That same grin dropped as I glanced toward Tropica. It was quiet, but it wasn't the actual village that had caught my attention.

Borks, Maria, and Snips all skidded to a stop, too, also noticing the anomaly.

"What the frack?" Maria asked.

All I could do was shake my head as I took in the shape protruding into the sky.

"I have no idea . . ."

CHAPTER TWO

Fantasy-Land Cult

I jumped down to the sandy soil as we crept toward the giant tree. Its trunk was as wide at the base as a house, and its canopy reached high into the sky before fanning out. Large chunks of earth were strewn around, as if the tree had shot down from orbit and landed there. It looked like a giant oak, but with one distinct difference.

Its bark was *blue*.

It was the largest tree I'd ever seen. "Hang on . . ." I said. "Is that the tree that was growing underneath the church?"

"Its position makes sense," Maria whispered back. "Is that why all the dirt is thrown around? It sprouted up from underground?"

"Makes sense . . . but *how?*"

"You're home!" a familiar voice called, poking her head from around a giant lump of dirt at the tree's base.

"Mom!" Maria's face lit up as she jogged over and embraced Sharon.

As they squeezed each other, a veritable crowd came to greet us. It was the entire congregation that had remained in Tropica, and their faces lit up as they saw us. With one exception, of course. Roger glared at me from the back, but his scowl disappeared when Maria wrapped him in a hug.

"I missed you, Dad."

"Missed you, too, sweetie."

"See?" I said, giving Roger a grin. "I promised you I'd bring her back in one piece."

He grumbled under his breath, but Maria tapped him on the forehead, cutting it off. "Be nice, Dad."

"How did it go?" Sharon asked, giving me a knowing smile.

"We planned on letting everyone out beneath the church, but, uh, what's up with the tree? Is that the one from downstairs?"

"It is." Sharon grimaced. "The walls shook so much that I was worried the ceiling would collapse. The room the tree was in . . . Well, let's just say I wouldn't recommend going anywhere near it."

"That bad?"

"Completely destroyed."

"Damn." I gazed up at the tree. Its canopy had to be at least a hundred meters across, and if I didn't know better, I'd assume it had been here for centuries. "Oh well. I guess we should let them out here."

Borks nodded at me.

Cracks formed in the air, and a moment later, the portal opened. The people within flooded out. Wide grins split their faces, but as they noticed where they were, confusion replaced their exuberance. Barry was the last to emerge. He scooped Helen up into a hug and roared with victorious laughter, but it died in his throat as his gaze drifted toward the giant blue trunk next to him.

" . . . Lemon?" he asked, his head swiveling between the tree and me.

"I don't think so," I replied. "But I can check."

I closed my eyes and extended my awareness toward it. I immediately located Lemon, but it was only part of her. She dwelled beneath the surface, listening but not showing herself for some reason.

No, I realized as I felt the chi she sent toward the giant oak beside us. *Not listening. She's feeding it . . .*

I focused my attention more on the tree, and what I found there made my brows fly toward my hairline.

There was a spirit in the tree. It was clearly related to Lemon somehow, yet also entirely different. As I sent my attention further toward it, the spirit noticed me. It thought I was a threat; I could sense its fear and hesitation. But then a stronger emotion rose up as Lemon radiated reassurance toward the newer spirit, telling it I was trustworthy.

Slowly, it came toward my awareness, and as I extended my senses, the spirit didn't shy away. It was . . . young. *Incredibly* young. Perhaps I could only tell because of how well I knew Lemon, but this spirit was essentially a newborn.

"Was this you, Lemon?" I asked, opening my eyes and withdrawing my chi.

I wasn't sure if she'd be able to respond given how far we were from her tree, but a root immediately shot from the ground in response. Lemon nodded with the entire root, but it wasn't necessary. I could feel her pride. She *had* done this. There was a hint of trickery in her emotions, too, dwelling beneath her overwhelming sense of accomplishment.

"Lemon!" I laughed. "How long have you been scheming to do this?"

Long, she sent me. *Very long.*

I wrapped an arm around her thick root. "You did good . . . I think."

I turned to Barry, keen on weighing his reaction, but Barry was occupied.

"Fischer . . ."

"Yeah, mate?"

"What is that?"

I squinted in the direction he pointed, spotting a large shadow drifting over the western mountains. A familiar shape shot from the net, lightning wreathing Claws's body as she rocketed toward me. Halfway to us, her eyes went wide and she changed course. Claws slammed down against the giant blue trunk of the newly grown tree. She climbed up into the canopy, letting out a chirp that I interpreted as, *What in the frack . . . ?*

"Fischer," Barry said, drawing my attention away from Claws's intoxicating curiosity.

"What's up?"

"The plan was to bring back the cultivators from six squads, right? Four times six. Twenty-four cultivators."

"That *was* the plan, wasn't it?"

"It was . . ." He slowly spun, raising both his brows. "That's a lot more than twenty-four cultivators, and there's only one person who could have ordered your animal pals to bring them . . ."

"Uhhhh." I gave him an apologetic smile. "My bad?"

Barry let out a long-suffering sigh. "What happened?"

I gave him a brief rundown as Pelly and Bill closed the distance with the seventy-odd superhumans, then lowered the net to the ground.

"Lord Osnan Sr. was a cultivator, too . . ." Ellis mused as he scribbled in his notepad.

"Okay." Barry ran a hand through his hair. "This significantly changes our plans, but I guess it can't be helped. I have one more question, though."

"What's that?"

Barry pointed at the man Cinnamon helped down to the ground. "Who is that?"

"I'm Deklan," Deklan said.

"That's Deklan," I agreed.

Danny stepped forward, his face smothered with disbelief. "Deklan? Is that really you, lad?"

"Oh. Hey, Danny," he replied, entirely too relaxed considering the events of the night. "Haven't seen you since you went missing. How's it going?"

"You know him?" Barry asked.

"Aye . . ." Danny answered, still staring at the guard. "Deklan was stationed in the castle when we left the capital."

Barry slowly spun my way again. "Fischer . . . Why did you steal one of the castle's guards?"

"I didn't. Deklan wanted to come fishing."

"Is that true?" Theo asked, his eyes pinned to the lackadaisical guard.

Deklan nodded. "Yeah. It sounds relaxing."

"You're telling the truth?" Theo's face turned incredulous. "You're not a spy? You abandoned the kingdom because you wanted to fish?"

"Wellll," I said, drawing the word out, then pointed at the cultivator Claws had tied a pink bow to. "We also might have abducted his brother?"

"Freed," Barry corrected.

"Yeah, that. There's, uh, one more thing you should probably know." I glanced at the Deklan, trying to convey an apology for what I was about to do to him. "Deklan was the guard assigned to watch the relics."

Ellis appeared before Deklan in a blur, moving so fast that a wall of wind blew the guard's hair back.

"Is that true?" Ellis demanded, his notepad and pencil poised to write.

"Uh . . . yeah." Deklan cocked his head to the side, looking Ellis's lizard suit up and down. "Are you a human?"

"With me, Theo!" Ellis called, completely ignoring the question as he led the poor guard away.

Sorry, mate, I thought, watching them go.

"So," Barry said, "about the cultivators . . ."

I winced. "Are you mad?"

He shook his head. "I'm not mad, Fischer. It's on brand, to be honest. I should have known you wouldn't be okay with leaving people behind. You were worried about them being punished, right?"

"Yeahhh. I kinda embarrassed that Lord Osnan Sr. bloke, and he seemed the kind of dickhead to take it out on others."

"Okay. It's not ideal, but we can probably work with this. The issue is that some of them might be mad, if not just outright evil. We stole enough collars from the capital to control any that exhibit such behavior, but that was only assuming we brought the original amount of cultivators back."

Someone groaned among the pile of cultivators as one of them regained consciousness. Barry tilted his head and turned their way, likely intending to ask them some questions, but he was too slow.

"Claws! Wait!" I tried, but it was too late.

She flew into the net and unleashed a jolt of lightning. The cultivator's body went rigid, then slack once more as he fell back, unconscious. Claws turned to Barry with a wide grin, waiting for the praise she no doubt believed was coming her way.

"Claws . . ." Barry said. "Please tell me you haven't been doing that this entire time."

Realizing she wasn't going to be praised, Claws crossed her arms and scowled at Barry, releasing a defensive chirp.

"I know I told you to keep them placid," he said, rubbing his eyes. "I didn't think you'd be electrifying them to do it. Please don't do that anymore—we don't want to cause any permanent damage."

Whatever, Claws chirped back, pretending Barry didn't exist as she marched back to the giant tree haughtily.

On the other side of the net, another cultivator stirred.

"Open the net," Barry ordered.

Pelly, Bill, and Cinnamon burst into action, cutting lengths of rope that held it together. Within a moment, the rigid net's sides fell away, and the cultivators were free. Barry and I stood before the stirring woman, and she let out a groan as she sat up.

"What happened?" she asked, her voice bleary. She looked around in confusion at the surrounding bodies, and when her gaze flicked up to me and Barry, she froze.

I recognized the woman. She was one of the cultivators who had been in the grove. And she, it appeared, also recognized me. Sheer terror crossed her face as she stared up at me, her eyes going wide. She leaned back, getting as far from me as she could without moving her limbs.

"What . . ." She licked her lips. *"What are you?"*

"I'm Fischer. Nice to meet you." I gave her a hopefully disarming smile. "Are you mad, by the way?"

"Mad . . . ?" she asked, the question confusing enough to replace her fear for a moment.

"Yeah. Mad. You know. Crazy. Insane. Do you have a burning desire to kill people and bathe in the blood of the fallen?"

Her eyebrows knitted. "Ew. No."

"See?" I said, grinning at Barry. "Not mad!"

"Right," he drawled, then kneeled down so he was eye level with the woman. "My name is Barry. What's yours?"

She swallowed. "Anna . . ."

"Nice to meet you, Anna." Barry nodded at me. "This is Fischer. He's a traveler from another realm and seems to be the catalyst for chi returning to the world."

"Whoa!" I held up both hands. "Don't you put that evil on me, Ricky Bobby!"

Barry rubbed the bridge of his nose. "Fischer. Stop being weird in front of the new cultivators."

"You're no fun," I said with a pout, then shot a wink at Anna.

She just blinked up at us, not saying a word.

"And this," Barry said, standing and stepping aside so Anna could see everyone. Humans, spirit beasts, and even a sapient root nodded, waved, or smiled at Anna. "This is the Church of Fischer's congregation. We rescued you all from the capital, and when we can confirm you're not *mad*, as Fischer so eloquently put it, we plan to free you."

Shaking, Anna's hand drifted to her neck. With the shock of regaining consciousness around some sort of fantasy-land cult, she hadn't even realized she was no longer wearing a collar. Her other hand joined the first as it felt her bare neck. Her lip trembled, and she slowly took in the other collarless cultivators surrounding her. The tremble spread to her jaw, and she looked down at her hands as tears started flowing down her cheeks.

"I'm . . . *free?*" Her voice broke with the last word, and she wrapped her arms around her legs, curling into a ball as sobs wracked her small body.

Maria appeared at her side.

"Maria!" Roger yelled. "Get back!"

"Oh, shush," Sharon said, flicking her husband's arm. She appeared at Anna's other side and rubbed her back with circular motions.

"It's okay, love," Maria said, doing her best to console the overwhelmed woman.

Barry turned toward the rest of the congregation. "Okay, everyone! We need to move these people. The villagers could come to see what the deal is with the giant blue tree at any moment! Is the church safe to occupy?"

"I wouldn't go farther than the tree room," Sue answered.

"Former tree room, more like," Sturgill answered with a grimace. "It was destroyed."

"Thank you," Barry replied, his voice holding a feeling of authority. "That sounds too dangerous, so I want these cultivators moved to Lemon's clearing. When they wake, let them know about us and our mission. If they cultivate, restrain them.

If they attack—and I do mean only if they attack, Claws—knock them out until Fischer and I are finished."

Claws saluted.

"Dismissed," Barry said, and everyone exploded into motion.

"Uhhh, Barry?" I raised an eyebrow at him. "What did you mean when you said *until Fischer and I are finished?*"

"Sorry, mate," he replied, not at all looking apologetic. "You brought back almost fifty extra cultivators. I'm going to need your help fixing that."

"Yeah, which I'm down for, but . . . *how?*"

"The congregation is getting pretty big, wouldn't you say?"

Sensing a trap, I raised an eyebrow. "It is . . ."

"Well, Fischer . . ." He gave me a wry smile. "I think it's about time we build a bigger church."

CHAPTER THREE

Frack Around and Find Out

B eneath a blanket of stars, I took a deep breath, delighting in the scents of salt spray and fresh air that assaulted me.

"Are you sure this is necessary, Fischer?" Barry asked from behind me.

"Positive, mate. If I don't get an influx of chi, I'll probably pass out the second we try to create something." Not at all sharing his sense of urgency, I smiled as a fish nibbled the bait at the end of my line. "Besides . . . it won't take long."

Barry sighed. "All right. Well, the fire is ready when you are."

I glanced over my shoulder, seeing his campfire roaring. Its flames shone orange light over the surrounding sand, banishing the darkness. As if it sensed my distraction, something took my bait.

"Fish on!" I yelled, reefing the rod and setting the hook.

"Big enough?" Barry asked.

The rod's tip bounced and bent. I grinned. "Feels like it!"

Hand over hand, I wound the fish in. It darted from side to side, but it never stood a chance. Not even a minute later, I bent and grabbed it by the mouth.

Mature Shore Fish
Uncommon
Found along the ocean shores of the Kallis Realm, this fish is a staple source of both food and bait.

"Just what the doctor ordered," I said, dispatching it with a single movement.

Barry rolled his eyes at me, but I caught the hint of amusement on his lips.

With deft cuts of my knife, I prepared the fish, and as I placed it over the fire, I let out a weary sigh. A small silence stretched as the fish cooked. "So, we both know where I stand with the whole 'not wanting to know what's going on with the church' thing. But if I'm gonna be helping you build something, you should probably give me a rundown of the plan."

He nodded. "So you know how you got a bag of gold coins, and you theorized that it was for reaching certain milestones in your skills?"

"I do."

Barry glanced up, his face going serious. "You were right."

"Oh, yeah, we worked that out already. Maria and I got another two bags of them when we were on the way to the capital."

I reached into my backpack, grabbed them, and flung them toward Barry.

He opened each of them, peering down at the golden relics, then shook his head. "You're *really* bad at being left in the dark."

"I know, right? It's infuriating."

"Well, it makes things easier, at least." He closed the bags and set them aside. "We've collected a modest amount of them over the past month since we found out they were rewarded for every twenty-five points in a skill."

I waved one hand and turned the fish with the other. "Yeah, Maria and I guessed that, too. We'll be using them to create more space in the church, right?"

"Right . . ." he replied, narrowing his eyes at me. "I'm starting to think I don't need to explain the plan at all."

"Blame it on Maria. She's as smart as she is cute. Can't get anything by her." I poked the fish with one finger, seeing it was mostly cooked. "I do have one question, though. Where are you expecting the church to expand? I don't think raising a castle like the one in Gormona is too good an idea."

"Why?"

"Because it'll be pretty obvious we're up to some shenanigans."

"You don't think the castle-sized tree is already going to give us away?"

I laughed. "Point taken. Still, though—going down would be better, right?"

Barry gave me an odd smirk. "We're not going down. We're also not going up."

"Across, then? Not bad, I guess, but I don't want it to go toward Tropica. Or toward Lemon's roots."

His smirk turned malicious. "We're not going across, either."

"Okay, I'm well and truly confused, mate. Where is it going?"

"You'll see," he replied simply, schooling his features.

"Ohhh, a little mystery, huh?" I poked the fish again. The flesh was firm, so I removed it from the heat. I raised an eyebrow at Barry. "Want some?"

"I'm fine, thanks. If you don't have enough energy and you faint or something, Maria will have my head."

"Good point." I laughed.

I devoured the fish, not wanting to take too long and give Barry a panic attack or something. Despite wolfing the food down, it was a blissful meal. With each bite, delicious flavors washed over my awareness, and chi poured down into my core. I picked the bones clean, not wasting a single flake of energy. I might be in a rush, but I wasn't about to disrespect the creature.

"Okay," I said, standing and stretching. A small bit of fatigue remained, but my body was brimming with potential energy. "Let's do some building!"

Barry led me back to the church, and when we got to the bottom of the stairs, we both paused.

"Damn . . ." he said, staring down the hallway.

"Couldn't have said it better myself, mate."

The previously clear passage was filled with thick roots, barely leaving enough room for anyone to squeeze past.

Barry strode into the meeting room, whose entrance sat before the tangle of plant matter. He went around the back and slid a chest out from under the table. It made a sound like a boulder scraping across stone.

I raised an eyebrow at Barry. "How many coins are inside that thing? It sounded way too heavy for how big it is."

"It's not just the contents," he replied. "The smiths and woodworkers made the chests so a regular human couldn't steal or open them."

"Hang on, did you just say *chests*?"

In response, he dragged two more out. After a few trips upstairs, we'd moved their contents to the surface.

"Barry . . ."

"Yes, Fischer?"

"Remember how you told me you had a *modest* amount of coins?" I pointed down at the two wheelbarrows absolutely loaded with small System-made bags. "In what world is this a modest amount?"

"There are over a dozen of us now. What did you think we've been up to all this time?"

"I mean, you've got a point, but still . . ." I shook my head. "With only a fraction of this, we built an entire underground building . . ."

"You're leaving out an important ingredient," he replied, wheeling his barrow south.

"What am I forgetting?" I asked, cocking my head as I rushed to keep up with him.

"Iridescent stones. Pearls, as you call them."

"Ohhh! Right. Sorry, mate. It's been a long night."

Barry shared a smile with me. "I know it has, Fischer. We have a substantial amount of coins, yes, but we're not entirely sure how effective they'll be."

"It'll work out."

He nodded. "I think so too. I have a . . . feeling, as dumb as that might sound."

"Not dumb at all, my man. I've learned to trust those instincts in this weird fantasy world you've got going on." I pulled up beside Barry as we continued striding south. "I think I have another question."

"You want to know where we're going?"

"That's the one." We were walking over my property's sandy flats. At first I'd thought we'd turn west and go meet the rest of the church by Lemon, but Barry hadn't changed course. "Where *are* we going, mate?"

"You'll just have to wait and see."

I rolled my eyes. "You know, the whole mystery thing is a lot less fun when I'm on the receiving end."

"Does that mean you'll stop doing it to *literally* everyone?"

I gave him a full-toothed grin. "Nope!"

"In that case, I'll be drawing this out as long as possible."

True to his word, Barry said nothing of where we were going as we crossed sand flats, the river, and sand flats again.

I looked down at my dripping body as we approached the distant forest on the south side of my property. "You know, Barry, you never mentioned getting drenched as part of the plan."

He waggled his eyebrows at me, mimicking one of my favorite gestures. "It's all part of the *mystery*."

I snorted. "Okay, secret keeper. Lead on."

When the barren ground gave way to grassy forest, Barry veered west. Rather than ask why and give him the satisfaction, I trailed silently. Mountains blocked out the sky the farther we got into the trees. Looking up at them, Barry nodded to himself and stopped.

"Everything okay, mate?" I asked.

"We're here."

I pouted, gazing at our surroundings. "It just looks like a regular old forest to me, mate."

"For now, that's all it is." He started unloading his barrow, placing the coin-filled sacks on the ground. "Well? Are you gonna help me?"

"Ooooh, he's mysterious *and* sassy," I replied, grabbing bags and adding them to his pile.

When all of them were sitting in a pile on the grass, Barry took a deep breath and let it out with a sigh. I did the same, stretching my body and enjoying the vigor still radiating through me from the fish I'd eaten.

"Okay, Fischer. Here's the plan." He spun on me, his eyes going serious. "We're not expanding the church. We're creating a village."

I arched a brow. "You're serious, aren't you?"

"I am."

"That's . . . ambitious."

"It is. Any complaints?"

Rather than answer his question, I sat on the ground, crossing my legs and getting comfortable. "Ready when you are, mate."

As he sat on the grass beside me, I closed my eyes, letting my awareness extend toward the pile of coins. Their power was clear. It was like sitting next to the remnant coals of a bonfire, and as Barry exerted strands of chi into them, embers rose from the ashes. Those embers became flames, and the flames became a roaring fire of force under Barry's guidance. I joined my efforts to his. Matching his chi, our wills coalesced around the currency, swirling, combining. *Consuming*.

One by one, the coins started evaporating.

I'd not taken part in building something since my last breakthrough, and it was an entirely different experience with my awareness as it was now. The essence that came from the coins was somehow . . . wrong. Maybe wrong wasn't the right word, but I couldn't think of a better one. The power they held wasn't one that I could wield. I'd sooner be able to draw water into my veins than the chi that came from the coins. What I could do, though, was guide it.

As if he knew my thoughts, Barry pressed his will down on the cloud of essence. I focused my will with his, and to my surprise, I felt what he pictured.

A village large enough to house hundreds of people. Simple. Utilitarian. Sleeping quarters. Crafting spaces. A semicircular theater to hold meetings in. Something . . . caged? A prison, I realized. Barry imagined a *prison*.

Damn, my guy, I thought. *That's pretty dark.*

It made sense, though. I'd brought back dozens of cultivators, all of which were a potential horror film waiting to happen. As I further considered the implications, I got the mental equivalent of a slap across the face.

Sorry, Barry.

I rejoined my awareness to his, helping him mold the coins into something more. Something *better*. We poured the essence into the buildings he envisioned, and now that they were taking shape, I opened up my core. Chi flowed from me in powerful torrents, and as the streams left me, the world began its transformation.

I had expected the process to be exhausting; it was anything but.

My soul seemed to rejoice at the power pouring from me, just as it had done when I unleashed blasts of light in the capital. As I got the sense that it was almost over, something within me stirred. I furrowed my brow, trying to understand what it was, and that's when I realized. It was the essence I'd somehow stolen from the lemon and passiona grove back in Gormona. It sat right beside my core, and it wanted to be free.

Being the kind of guy to frack around and find out, I let it come.

The bubble burst from me, propelled along by my will. Surprise came from Barry, but after a moment's consideration, he pictured another structure. A grove, large enough to house multiple trees. The foreign pocket of chi obeyed us, shooting off to the far side of the village and forming. I returned my attention to the rest of our build, and beneath the weight of our combined wills, the last of the coins were consumed.

Abruptly, I came back to my body. I was no longer sitting in a forest. Hard stones lined the path beneath me, and I put my hands out, running my fingers along their uniform surface. A smile came to my face as I slowly opened my eyes, filled with anticipation for what we'd built.

Instead, lines of text scrolled before me, blocking my field of view.

CHAPTER FOUR

Evolution

blinked to clear my vision, but the words remained.

New Village established!
Scanning . . .

"Scanning?" Barry asked. "What does—"

Scan complete.
Village already exists.
Upgrading existing village: Tropica . . .

I shook my head, but before I could turn to Barry and ask him what the frack was going on, the System spoke up again.

[Tropica has evolved and become a Tier 1 village!]

"Barry?" I asked, slowly spinning his way.

"Yes, Fischer?"

"Any idea what all that means, mate?"

He blinked at me. "No clue."

"Yeah, me neither . . ."

Now that the System was done having its way with my field of view, I gazed out at the surrounding world.

We stood in a giant crossroads, atop smooth stones and surrounded by buildings. Most of the constructions were only a single story, much like the homes and shops that made up Tropica. But unlike those structures, these were made by the System. Though built of simple stone, there was a beauty to their uniformity.

Without realizing what I was doing, I wandered toward the closest building. Just like the church, gilding lined its door. Taking a deep breath, I turned the handle and pulled it open. With Barry at my side, I gazed into the newly constructed smithy. Though it was only slightly larger than the aboveground one in Tropica, six forges lined its walls. Myriad anvils, trenches, and tools were scattered around the room, positioned perfectly to make use of the space.

I ran a hand over the surface of one of the furnaces, pausing as I furrowed my brows. Something was . . . wrong.

"You feel it too?" Barry asked, drawing me from my thoughts.

"Yeah . . . what is it?"

Barry pressed a stone button beside the forge, and unlike the ones within the church, nothing happened. The System's magicy bullshit wasn't working.

"It's incomplete," he replied, pursing his lips.

I reached out with my awareness in search of the power that I expected to find lacing everything around us. My eyes went wide. "It doesn't have any chi . . ."

Since my last breakthrough, I had been able to sense the faint lines of essence running through each brick making up the church. They were particularly strong around the crafters' workshops there, but this smithy had none.

We strode around the village quickly, finding the buildings that we'd poured the coins' power into. There were crafting spaces for every vocation imaginable. A theater large enough to seat hundreds. The prison Barry had insisted on, each of its cells spacious and lavish. And living quarters, constructed like townhouses from back on Earth. They were the only two-story constructions in the village, and I wondered if I'd subconsciously influenced their shape.

Barry and I strode into one of them, and when I tried to turn the shower on, I shook my head. "No hot showers? This village sucks, Barry."

He smirked at me, hearing the joke in my tone. "What ever will we do without *hot water*? The people will revolt."

I nodded along. "You're telling me, mate. They'll have us strung up and lashed for our crimes against humanity."

We lapsed into silence as we walked beneath the sea of stars, both lost in our thoughts. When I felt a pulse of power from ahead of us, I picked up my pace, filled with curiosity. I knew what I'd find there, and as we rounded a short wall, I gazed out into the grove. Its chi signature was unmistakable, feeling exactly like the one I'd sucked the essence out of back in the capital city.

The smell of freshly tilled soil sprang up to greet me, its scents reminiscent of a forest after rain. I breathed deep of its life as I strode between rows of dirt, a small smile coming to my face. I let out a slow sigh, feeling reinvigorated by the chi crisscrossing the very earth beneath us.

The sigh died in my throat as I felt something gathering power. Barry leaped back and took a defensive stance; he'd felt it too.

Unlike Barry, I recognized who it was, and I barked a laugh as a blue sapling sprouted in the grove's center. Its trunk creaked as it thickened, and within a matter of breaths, a mature tree blocked out the night sky.

"Hello, Lemon. Didn't expect to see you here so soon."

"*Lemon?*" Barry demanded, lowering his arms.

Lieutenant Colonel Lemony Thicket shook her leaves in greeting. I'd expected her to sprout a root and nod vigorously, but she was too busy being awestruck. Her emotions radiated from her trunk, wild and ferocious. As Lemon's awareness extended to the mesh of surrounding chi, her curiosity only grew. She was cautious at first, hesitantly extending her essence toward the alien-feeling power.

The moment they touched, the world shuddered.

The entire village shook as her network of roots joined with the grove's life-giving spirit, and when light shone from all around Barry and me, I grinned. In slow motion, luminescent beams shot up from the ground, casting a pillar of solid white into the night sky. A wave of ecstasy washed over me.

Barry's legs buckled, so I reached out, grabbing his shoulder to keep him upright. Within the blink of an eye, the light was gone, and I let out a shaky breath, letting my eyes adjust to the returning darkness of night.

Before I could inspect the grove, words rushed up to meet me.

Domain has evolved!
[Error: Insufficient power.]

I hadn't seen my old nemesis in a while. I waved the error message away, unable to stop myself from frowning. But then I saw Lemon.

"Oh . . ." Barry said, staring up at her canopy.

"Yeah . . ." I agreed, my eyes running over her mighty boughs. "That's something."

Lemon's tree had, for lack of a better word, aged. She'd at least doubled in size, her formerly smooth trunk now covered in thick bark. Knotted roots branched out into the earth, giving her the appearance of a centuries-old oak. Though it was still Lemon within the tree, her chi felt . . . different. When I sent my awareness out toward her, I realized why—she and the alien-feeling power had merged.

No. She had *absorbed* it.

"How are you feeling, Lemon?" I asked, taking a step forward.

Awe, excitement, and joy oozed from her. At my question, she seemed to come back to herself. A giant root sprouted from the ground, so big that it split the earth in giant chunks. It wrapped around me gently, hugging my torso tight.

"I love you, too." I laughed. "What the frack just happened, though? How did you even get here?"

What followed was a conversation between myself and a prehensile root that would have made even the most compassionate of observers assume I was batshit crazy.

"What did she say?" Barry asked, giving me side-eye as I giggled and batted away an attempted tickle from Lemon.

"What? Oh, right." I patted the part of Lemon's root that served as a head. "When she felt us creating the village—or the extension of Tropica, I suppose—she came over to see what we were up to. She trailed us around, inspecting the stones and buildings from underneath, and when she got to the grove . . ." I shrugged. "It was irresistible. She *had* to grow a tree here." I cocked my head. "How long have you been able to do that, by the way? Just grow more trees?"

She sent me the emotional equivalent of no, then pointed me toward the power she'd joined with.

"Oh! It gave you the ability to do so?"

Yes. She nodded.

"Well, there you have it," I said to Barry. "Just your typical tree-spirit shenanigans."

"Yeah. Nothing new." He shook his head and gave us a wry smile. "With the addition of the grove, I think we have almost everything we need until we can gather more coins to finish the village."

I shot him a glance. "About that . . . I was thinking there was something else we could try."

He gave me a questioning look.

"The one thing we were missing from last time was pearls, right?" I answered. "Lucky for us, I have it on good authority that some local weirdos filled a nearby bay with a bunch of oyster cages."

Barry quirked an eyebrow, grinning. "Midnight feast?" he asked.

"Midnight feast," I agreed, delighting in the look on his face.

We split off, Barry running for Lemon's old clearing and me dashing for my shore. When I arrived, I took a minute to stare up at the crescent moon, stealing a moment of peace all for myself. Small waves lapped the shore, their constant susurration making a deep calm wash over me. I lost myself to the sensations of my body.

And was abruptly returned to the present when an otter wreathed in lightning barreled into my back.

"Oof!"

I slid in the sand, stopping myself just before crashing down into the ocean. Before I could ask Claws what that was all about, she climbed around my body like a squirrel, staring up into my eyes.

"Claws?"

She screamed a chirp at me, so loud that I almost didn't catch its meaning.

"Yes, Claws. We're getting the oysters."

How many? she chirp-screamed again.

"How many, huh . . . ?" I tapped my chin in thought, drawing out the moment. "All of them, I suppose—"

She shot from my chest, using me as a platform from which to launch herself out into the bay. I shook my head at her lightning-covered body as it rocketed down next to the cages.

"Little scoundrel . . ."

The rest of my animal pals and Maria arrived a moment later. "Is it true?" Maria asked, skidding to a stop before me.

"Uh, which part?"

"All of it! The village! Lemon's transformation! The Domain! *The oysters!*"

"It's all true," I replied, scooping up Sergeant Snips into a hug, who gazed up at me with affection. "I'll need your help to retrieve the cages, though."

It took less than a half hour to retrieve over a hundred cages from the water, all of which were *filled* with full-grown mollusks. When I emerged from the ocean with the last of them, we immediately started shucking oysters. We were a well-oiled, shell-opening machine, and Borks was a tail-wagging delivery service, constantly bringing us new cages to open.

"Found my fourth!" Maria called.

My second, Pistachio bubbled, his overlarge clackers not the best at handling the tiny things.

Tenth, Snips hissed.

Ten-billionth! Claws lied, shooting me a mischievous grin when I glowered at her.

The pelicans worked together, Pelly holding them, and Bill using his beak's claw to crack them in two. Even Cinnamon helped out, using her little hoppers to kick still-closed oysters our way. By the time we finished, we had an entire pouch of the overwhelmingly valuable stones. I turned, intending to run it back to Barry, but found myself looking at a sea of faces.

All the cultivators had awakened and been led down to the shore. Some looked angry. Others were confused. Some had tear-streaked faces. Most, however, were some mix of the above. They cast every possible emotion over me, my animal pals, and the congregation that was arrayed around them. I gave them a kind smile and flung the pouch at Barry, who caught it with a look of wonder on his face.

When he opened it, he let out a soft whistle. "Yeah. That should do it . . ."

I glanced up at the sky. Though the predawn light was yet to arrive, the sun would rise in the next couple of hours. I walked over toward the cultivators. "Hello, friends. I'm Fischer. I don't really have time for proper introductions or explanations right now, but we've harvested a whole bunch of seafood. You're welcome to try, but chances are you won't like them raw." I turned toward Peter. "Would you be happy to cook some up, mate? I'm a little busy, I'm afraid."

Barry stepped forward with the bag of pearls.

I held up a hand, halting his assumption. "Can I speak to you for a moment?"

Barry raised an eyebrow at me as we walked away, but I waited until we were far enough for no one to hear. "There's something I didn't tell you yet, mate . . ."

As he listened to my explanation, his face grew pensive. "You're sure you want to do this, Fischer?"

I nodded. "Yeah, mate. It needs to be done now. I'm not willing to risk it."

"Who are you taking?"

"Borks, Claws, and Snips."

Barry shook his head. "You need to take more. You're being too reckless."

"Less is more, mate. The sun is about to rise, and the villagers will be lining the street."

He chewed his lip. "Pelly and Bill have to watch from above. If you can't agree to that, I'm not on board."

"Deal!" I said, spinning. "Borks, Claws, Snips! Let's go!" I called. "Pelly, Bill, follow us in the sky!"

They were at my side in a moment, and I raised an eyebrow at the uninvited guest. "Can I help you, young lady?"

"You can." Maria laced her hand in mine. "I'm coming."

"You don't even know where we're going . . ."

"Really?" She gave me a flat look. "You don't think I know you well enough to figure out you're going to speak to some nobles in Tropica?"

I blew air through my lips. "That obvious, huh?"

"To me, you're an open book." She smirked, clearly not willing to relent.

I sighed, accepting my face. "See you soon, Barry."

"Good luck," he replied, turning.

"Cheers, mate!"

"I'll let Roger and Sharon know where you went."

Maria poked me in the side. "Ready when you are."

I looked down at her, staring into her eyes. She wrinkled her nose up at me and made a funny face, doing her best to appear unattractive. It didn't work.

"Come on," I said. "The sooner we get this over with, the sooner we can go fishing."

With a cute girl's hand in mine, my animal pals at my side, and the sun threatening to rise over the eastern horizon, I made my way toward Tropica.

CHAPTER FIVE

Rude Awakening

"To define enlightenment is to shackle the fledgling meditator with an unfair burden. What it means to be enlightened is subjective, and it falls upon each child to traverse this path alone, lest their road be ravaged by false information."

Excerpt from Prologue, House Kraken manual

In the predawn hours, George, the lord of Tropica, let out a slow sigh.

He'd had a terrible sleep, riddled with interruptions that he couldn't explain. The first had pulled at his abdomen just after midnight. Unable to calm his racing heart, he'd remained awake for who knew how long, and just when slumber welcomed him into its open arms once more, the second event occurred. Unlike the first, this one had seemed to constrict his entire body. It'd only lasted for half a breath, but that was plenty of time for anxiety to shoot up his spine and ruin any chance of more sleep.

Which was why he'd decided to meditate instead.

As he traversed his way toward his study, George wondered if he was close to reaching the "enlightenment" his family spoke of. The term was loosely defined, the texts insisting that if explained, it would be harder for one to reach it. What else could these strange occurrences be? After all, they had only begun after he and his wife, Geraldine, started reading House Kraken's manual. The better they got at the meditations listed within, the more frequent and powerful the unexplainable events became.

Realizing he was lost in thought, George shook his head, smiling at himself.

I claim to be getting better at the meditations, yet here I am, lost in past worries and future possibilities.

George sat cross-legged in his study, and he let out his breath, focusing once more on the sensations of his body in space. Just as his family's tome instructed.

The hardwood of his study's floor beneath him. His breaths, cooling each nostril when he inhaled and warming them when he exhaled hot air. The spot where his hands rested on his knees, and the tingling that ran up and down his fingers. Together, they rooted him in the present, an unignorable tether to the here and now.

But then the knock came, three sharp raps of a knuckle on his front door that made adrenaline shoot through George's body.

He took a deep breath, holding it and willing his heart to remain calm. Just when he thought he'd lose the battle, a hand rested softly on his leg. George cracked his eyes and peered over at his beloved wife.

Geraldine gave him a kind smile, rubbing his knee softly with one hand. "Want me to get it, dear?"

"No," he replied, getting to his feet and stretching. "I can handle him."

George bent and kissed the top of her head before striding out the door and heading for the stairs. As he walked down them, he didn't rely on the ornate banisters to either side. House Kraken's manual was strict with one's diet, and George had been following it militantly. Though it had been hard to give up his sugary treats at first, that temporary discomfort was nothing beneath the weight of George's former stressors. Much of his prodigious size had melted away like candle wax, leaving behind a body that could move much more freely.

As George reached the landing, he paused for a moment in front of the door. Taking one last calming breath, he opened it.

Fischer was standing there, his hand upraised and ready to knock again. "Oh. G'day, George. How are ya, mate?"

"I am well, Fischer. And you?"

"I'm great, thanks! You remember Maria, don't you?"

"Of course. Hello."

"Hi!" Maria gave him a brilliant smile. "Good to see you!"

"And this is my doggy pal, Borks," Fischer continued. "I'm not sure you've been introduced."

The golden-colored dog wagged his tail as he stared up at George. Was he expected to greet the dog, too? He decided it was safest to do so. "Hello, Borks."

The dog let out a soft bark, his tail swishing faster.

George pursed his lips, looking back up toward Fischer. The faintest whispers of the day to come shone over the eastern rooftops, the sky there turning a light purple as the sun announced its arrival.

"What can I do for you at this early hour?"

"Sorry about that, mate. I hope I didn't wake you."

"Not at all."

"Good. I came with a request, actually."

"Oh?" George swallowed, hoping he'd hidden the spike of fear that drove into him. "I can do my best to fulfill it. What do you need?"

"I want to see your wedding ring."

George froze, his skin prickling. What did Fischer want with his family's treasure? The rings he and Geraldine wore had been passed down since time immemorial, always going to the heir of House Kraken. Given Fischer's position and how low George's house had fallen in recent years, if Fischer saw fit to confiscate the iridescent-stone-encrusted jewelry, there was nothing George could do about it.

"Everything okay, mate?" Fischer asked, his predatory gaze drilling into George's very soul.

"Yes," he forced out through a suddenly dry mouth. "Of course you can look at it . . ."

As George slipped the ring off, Fischer's eyes never left him. They weren't on George's face or hands, though—they seemed pinned to his abdomen for some reason.

"Here . . ." George said, offering the ring on a shaking palm.

Fischer plucked the ring from George's hand, and as he held it up before his face, Fischer's eyes went distant. They seemed to look through the ring, and as something flashed in Fischer's pupils, George felt a tug at his abdomen.

It was nothing like the strength of those last night. The pull was so faint that George thought he might have imagined it at first, but it continued, his very core getting drawn toward . . . Fischer. George's abdomen started to tingle, and when the tingle became a buzz, sweat sprouted from his pores.

Abruptly, Fischer's eyebrows shot up, and that same weighing gaze drifted to George. There was something in the crown agent's scrutiny that made a primitive part of George's brain want to flee. To get as far away from the threat as possible. Of its own accord, his right foot slid back, ready to sprint.

"Huh . . ." Fischer said, and all at once the ferocity melted away, leaving behind features covered in surprise.

George wiped perspiration from his brow with a shaky movement as he brought his leg forward again. "Is . . ." The word came out strained. He cleared his throat. "Is something wrong?"

Fischer grinned. "Not at all, mate! Thanks for that."

George accepted the offered ring, staring down at it numbly.

"I've been really curious about jewelry lately, and seeing this design was a big help. Could I ask one more favor of you, mate?"

"Of course," George replied, slowly raising his head to look at Fischer.

"Thanks, George. Do you know where Tom Osnan Jr. lives? I wanted to have a peek at his rings, too. He has so many of them!"

He nodded, still half expecting Fischer to attack. He hadn't missed the omission of "Lord" from Tom Osnan Jr.'s name and winced internally at his disrespect of such a powerful family. "If you follow this street and turn right at the intersection, it's three houses down. You'll know it when you see it . . ."

"Cheers, mate." Fischer reached a hand out, and in its approach, George saw his doom. The limb seemed to come in slow motion, but when it reached George, Fischer patted him softly on the shoulder. "Have a good day, yeah? See ya round."

"Bye, George," Maria said, giving him a wave as she turned and followed Fischer's departure.

"Until next time . . ."

George stepped back inside and closed the door, his legs giving way the moment he was alone. He slid down the wall and came to rest on the floor.

"What in Poseidon's salted shaft was that?"

* * *

When my enhanced hearing caught George's whispered curse, I stopped mid-step, turning to raise an eyebrow at Maria.

She covered her mouth, her eyes bugging out as she stifled a laugh.

"Maria!" I whisper-yelled, trying to hide my amusement. "We shouldn't laugh at poor George's social anxiety!"

"I can't help it! I never thought he'd say something so crass!"

I shook my head. "Poor bloke. He's been doing so well, but every time I talk to him, he reverts back to his anxious self."

"Okay, you're right. I shouldn't have laughed." A smile tugged at her lip, betraying her true feelings. "So. Did you learn anything?"

"I did," I replied, chewing my lip as I recalled the ring's description.

Iridescent Ring of the Kraken
Epic
A ring of precious metal, adorned by the most sought-after stones found in the Kallis Realm. More than just a symbol of wealth, this ring has a multitude of purposes for those with the requisite knowledge.

I relayed it to Maria, and it was her turn to pause. "You're serious?"

"I am, but that's not all. I felt chi from George."

"You did?" she asked entirely too loudly, then winced, adopting a quieter tone. "He's a cultivator? Why did we leave, then?"

"Not a cultivator, no. It was weird. He hasn't awakened yet, but there was definitely something there . . ."

"That's . . . troubling."

I shrugged. "We'll have to keep an eye on it, but I'm not worried about him. George is a good bloke."

Maria chewed her cheek. "I'm not too sure about that, but he has been doing better by the villagers lately . . ."

We slipped into silence as we followed the street, only our footfalls and the tapping of Borks's nails interrupting the quiet. As we entered the intersection, I looked up, gazing three doors down to the home of Lord Osnan Jr.

"Holy frack . . ."

"Yeah," Maria agreed. "George wasn't kidding when he said we'd know it when we saw it."

Lord Tom Osnan Jr., heir to House Osnan, woke abruptly.

"What . . . ?" he asked, sitting upright and looking around.

The sky past his silken curtains was still dark, nary a hint of the sun's rays cresting the horizon.

His wife, Joanne, groaned from beside him, rolling over and covering her head with a lush pillow. "Someone at the door," came her muffled voice.

Surely that wasn't the case. What sort of fool would—

Thump. Thump. Thump.

For a moment, Tom was confused, but then fury roiled within him. He'd already had a fitful sleep after being woken twice by waves of chi, and now he had to deal with some idiot—probably a peasant—knocking on his door in the predawn hours.

He shrugged a robe on, adopted his best scowl, and stomped downstairs. Throwing the door open, he cast his displeasure out onto the street. Three smiles met him.

"G'day, mate. Nice to see you again."

It was the upstart who had accosted him the other week. Tom had tried to slap him, but that fool George Kraken caught his hand.

I should have used my full strength, Tom thought. *Then I wouldn't be dealing with this moron right now.*

"Everything okay, mate?" the peasant asked. "You having a medical episode of some sort?"

Tom's lip twitched, and he didn't bother hiding his displeasure. "Knock on my door again and you'll regret it."

He made to close the door, but the man put his foot forward, blocking it. "I'm afraid I must insist, mate. It's important."

"Very important," the woman added, giving him a grin through the crack.

"Why don't you invite them in, Tom?" Joanne asked, striding down the stairs.

He spun on her, confused by her appearance and the suggestion, but then he caught the righteous anger lining her face.

"Maybe you're right, dear," he replied. "Where are my manners?" He swung the door open again. "Would you like to come in and discuss it? We'd be more than happy to hear you out."

"Thanks!" the man replied, leading them in.

As the three sorry souls entered their home, Tom and Joanne Osnan shared a smirk.

CHAPTER SIX

Frack Around and Find Out 2: Electric-Otter Boogaloo

Thanks for your hospitality," I said, not missing the ugly look the two nobles shared as we strode into their home.

"Of course," the woman replied, her voice sickly sweet. "I am Joanne, and this is my husband, Tom. What are your names?"

"I'm Fischer, this is Maria, and that's Borks."

Joanna nodded as she removed a notepad from her pocket and wrote them down. *That's not ominous at all*, I thought, glancing at Maria.

"So," Tom said, resting his hands before himself. "What can we do for you at this early hour?"

"Oh, nothing too major, mate. Just wanted to have a peek at your jewelry."

"Our jewelry?" Joanne asked, raising an eyebrow.

"Yeah! Your rings, specifically. I've been considering making them as a sort of hobby, so I've been going around having a little peep at the nobles' iridescent stones."

"We just came from George's place," Maria said. "His wedding ring was marvelous."

"And insightful," I added.

A vein literally pulsed on Tom's forehead as he forced a smile. "That should be fine. Why don't we let them see *all* of them, Joanne?"

They shared another glance, wordlessly communicating something as they removed a ring each. The moment they did, my suspicions were confirmed.

As Lord Tom Osnan Jr. removed the first of his rings, a fraction of his power stirred, rejoicing at being unshackled. With each metal band that came free, the chains surrounding his core loosened. It had been almost a year since he'd last let his essence out, and his body thrummed in delight, urging him to continue. Joanne matched his pace, and when they removed their second-to-last rings, they shared an ecstatic grin.

The moment the final one came free, he released a shuddering breath.

It would be a challenge for Tom to restrain himself. These foolish sleep interrupters were destined for indentured servitude back in the capital, so it wouldn't do to accidentally smite them from the face of Kallis. With his core unshackled, his senses extended into the surrounding space, making Tom feel free for the first time in a long while.

But what he found in his surroundings made Tom's thoughts die and eyes fly wide open.

The woman and the dog both had cores. *Well-established* cores. Not only that—the woman, Maria, seemed to have *three* of them, one in her abdomen and two in her back. He froze for a fraction of a second, his mind whirling to make sense of what was going on. Neither of their existences were possible. A spirit beast hadn't been seen for centuries, and even the ancient texts said nothing of a cultivator with three nexuses of power.

Joanne was the first to move. "Disgusting creature!" she bellowed, flying forward and aiming a full-strength kick at the golden-furred spirit beast.

Her action broke Tom's moment of confusion. He darted forward, aiming one of his hands at Maria's throat and the other at Fischer's. He'd aim to execute them at the same time, so even if the woman managed to dodge, Fischer would perish, his death driving a spear of anguish into her. As his hands approached, Tom's worry dissipated.

They didn't react. Though she had three cores, she was a newborn cultivator and couldn't hope to match his speed. Satisfaction washed over his entire body, his chi gratified at being unleashed with violent intent. The closer he got to them, the more his core vibrated in pleasure, demanding he end these heretics.

Their fate was sealed. They were as good as dead. They—

The cores in Maria's back shifted.

One of them exploded into motion, shooting from her and for Joanne. Tom followed its passage, unable to stop his enhanced vision from tracking the anomaly. Said anomaly grinned back at him with needle-sharp teeth, giving him a little wave with one lightning-covered paw. Not even looking at her, the otter slammed into his wife. Joanne's body buckled, her limbs tense and pinwheeling as electricity crawled along her skin.

Seeing another spirit beast appear and attack his wife, Tom refocused on his own task. Joanne was still alive, and it would take him only a moment to dispatch these interlopers. He leaned forward, shooting vines from his hands toward both Maria's and Fischer's necks. Before they could reach Maria's, the other core in her back shifted. It darted up and over her shoulder, and an orange claw reached forward, snipping through his vines before grabbing hold of his wrist.

It was another spirit beast, a one-eyed crab covered in spikes and wearing an eye-patch. Blinking, he focused on Fischer. He needed to end the man and destabilize the rest. His vines shot forward, writhing over one another and wrapping around Fischer's neck. Tom snarled and clenched his teeth as he squeezed the vines, severing the foolish man's head from his body. But . . . nothing happened.

Fischer cocked his head to the side and covered a yawn, that small movement snapping some of Tom's bindings. "Is it my turn?" he asked, his eyes drilling into Tom's.

"Wh-what . . . ?"

Power swelled before him, originating in Fischer's stomach. It started as a seed, and with each passing moment, it ebbed outward. In the space of a breath, the presence of a god flooded from the peasant. Tom fell to his knees, his vines withering beneath a blinding light that shone from Fischer, burning away every drop of chi Tom wielded.

He stared up at a visage of annihilation, shrinking back with each step forward Fischer took. When the peasant reached down a hand toward Tom, he flinched back, his entire body trembling.

"Thanks for letting me have a look at them, mate," Fischer said, plucking the rings from Tom's pocket. His hand, still gleaming with light, reached up toward Tom's face.

Tom froze, not daring to take a breath, lest this hidden monster take his head from his shoulders. Fischer opened his palm and Tom closed his eyes. He didn't want to see the blow that would end him. Instead, Fischer dismissed his power and tapped Tom's cheek.

"You've been a naughty boy, Tom Osnan Jr. Just like your old man."

At the mention of his father, Tom's eyes shot open, staring up in confusion.

Just in time to see Fischer's backhand descending. Before the blow could land, a loud trill sounded from Tom's left, and nature chi bloomed. The last thing he felt was a lightning-wreathed otter slamming into his jaw.

Back on the shore of Fischer's property, Barry surveyed the mass of cultivators.

Thankfully, they hadn't been foolish enough to try anything stupid.

"I'm surprised none of them have attacked . . ." his wife, Helen, whispered, soft enough that only he could hear.

"Me too . . ."

Many of the cultivators were casting distrustful glances around, but they were all too aware of the power wielded by the Church of Fischer. It didn't help that there was a spirit beast literally frothing with rage and looking for any excuse to unleash blasts from his twitching claws. Barry shook his head at Rocky. The troublesome crab had returned from his impromptu flight and, knowing he didn't stand a chance against the lobster that had sent him flying, he was looking for someone else to take his anger out on.

When a slight breeze kicked up, it brought a delightful scent to Barry's attention.

Peter had built a massive campfire and was in the process of cooking oysters with savory ingredients. Barry didn't know what they were, but he *did* know they would be delicious. The smell reached the pack of cultivators, and Barry smiled as their faces transformed, instinctual hunger overriding even the most distrusting of them.

The church members had the same reaction. Well, all except for Ellis. The former archivist was pacing on the sand. "They should have left the artifacts behind," he grumbled.

"Borks will be back soon," Barry said.

"Every second we do not know what the Domain does, we—"

"Ellis," Barry warned.

Ellis threw his hands up, acknowledging he'd revealed too much. "Yes, yes. I apologize. I just—"

Suddenly, an immutable pulse of power came from Tropica, cutting Ellis's sentence short. It started small but expanded quickly, the source of it obvious.

Just like when the scent of Peter's cooking hit them, this wave of chi also arrested the cultivators' attention. Every head swiveled to the north, drawn toward the only man that could so casually unleash energy rivaling the sun.

"That . . . that was him, wasn't it?" someone asked.

Barry turned toward the speaker, finding Anna, the first cultivator that had awakened. She faced the north, staring at the point of power as it vanished, sealed once more within Fischer's core.

"Of course it was!" Roger answered, spitting to the side. "What other fool would traipse around, announcing himself for every other cultivator to find?"

"Roger—" Sharon tried.

"Don't you *Roger* me, Sharon! He has our daughter with him!"

Barry shot a warning glare his way, but Sharon had already swooped in. She dragged Roger off to the side, no doubt intent on telling him not to display weakness before the dozens of possibly violent strangers huddled on the sand.

No more pulses of power came, and though some heads remained facing Tropica, others drifted back toward the oysters Peter was cooking. When the chef brought over the first tray of them, none of Gormona's cultivators dared taste one, despite the alluring flavors wafting through the air.

The fishing club held no such compunctions. They rushed forward, even Ellis skulking over to grab a couple before resuming his pacing.

"They're really good," Theo said to the cultivators, then threw one into his mouth. "Mmmm."

"Mmm-hmmm," Danny agreed, closing his eyes as he chewed.

Keith walked over and grabbed a couple, taking one back to Trent. As he watched them eat, Barry raised an eyebrow at the prince's transformation. He looked so different that none of the capital's cultivators had recognized him yet.

The first of said cultivators, a stocky man with thick forearms, stomped forward and took an oyster. He peered down at it for a long moment, then hesitantly scooped it into his mouth. His face immediately shifted, his eyes flying wide and his jaw moving of its own accord.

He swallowed, threw the shell aside, and grabbed another.

"Help yourselves," Barry said. "We didn't save you from the capital just to try and poison you in some roundabout way. Seafood is the basis of our power." He raised an eyebrow at the stocky man as he ate his second oyster and reached for a third. "How was the chi content?"

"Huh?" he replied, blinking for a second before he registered the question. "It's unbelievable! They're so small, but they *fill* you with power!"

Following his endorsement, more came forward to try them. Each and every reaction was the same, and as they feasted and spoke to each other in hushed tones, a small smile crossed Barry's face. Helen squeezed his arm, feeling the exact same way. They peered on, content to let the former slaves enjoy their first moment of freedom.

The vibe was immediately ruined when an otter, wreathed in lightning and unleashing a mighty chirp, slammed down nearby. She dashed for the oysters, all the cultivators taking defensive stances.

"Corporal Claws!" Barry chastised, but all he got in return was a mischievous grin as she started downing mollusks.

Borks arrived a moment later, and when his portal tore open, Maria, Fischer, and Snips came through, carrying two limp bodies.

Barry raised both brows as he felt the noble couple's cores. "So, they *were* cultivators, huh?"

"Yuuup," Fischer replied, bending down to steal an oyster. "Mmmm. Really good, Peter."

Peter grinned back, but before he could reply, Anna stepped forward.

"Is that Tom Osnan Jr?" Her eyebrows narrowed. "And his wife?"

"You know them? And yeah," Fischer replied. "Pretty fracked up, right? You guys were slaves, but these noble pricks have been running around hiding their power with these."

Fischer threw a pouch to Ellis. Its contents clinked when he caught it, and as he pulled open the drawstring, his eyes went distant.

"Ceto's monstrous offspring!" he yelled, his eyes clearing. "These are their rings?"

"Yup. They had ten each." Taking one more oyster, Fischer strode toward Barry. "So, mate, looks like we might need that prison." He pointed to Barry's belt and the pouch that hung there. "What do you say we get up to some more fantasy-land shenanigans?"

Barry shook his head, letting out a soft laugh at Fischer's casual return.

"I'd love to. Let's go fix New Tropica."

Fischer paused mid-turn. "New Tropica, huh?"

"You don't like it?"

He tilted his head, then grinned. "Nah, mate, I love it."

Barry returned the smile as they took off, heading for New Tropica.

CHAPTER SEVEN

The Alchemist

With the sun's approach, the sky's color was starting to change. As Barry and I crossed the sand flats on the south side of the river, I marveled at the sea of stars above us. They'd soon be banished, replaced by a brilliant blue. I tried to burn their image into my mind as I breathed deep of the night air.

The moment we entered the forest near New Tropica, an odd sensation shattered my mindfulness.

The bag of pearls on Barry's belt thrummed with power, and we both froze, staring down at them. As if in protest of our hesitation, the leather container shifted, moving subtly toward the west where we'd find the System-built buildings. Sharing a smirk, we resumed our passage, racing through the trees.

By the time we stood within the main crossroads, the pearls *demanded* that we use them. Without a word, Barry and I sat cross-legged. He removed the bag from his belt and set it down between us as we closed our eyes.

"Ready?" he asked.

"Ready," I confirmed, extending my awareness toward the pouch of potential chi right beside me.

The pearls drew me in, and just like the coins, they began dissolving into clouds of power. Unlike the gold coins, however, they didn't all dissipate at once. The moment two of them had become chi, their essence shot off to my left, entering the building I knew to be the smithy. Another two went off to the tailoring building. Three tunneled to my right and sank into the theater, permeating its stone bricks. A full thirty of them accumulated before winding through the streets and entering the prison; I followed their passage, watching in my mind's eye as the entire structure was reinforced, becoming impervious to cultivators.

Barry was right there beside me, helping guide the pearls to where they wanted to go. The entire time we worked, a sense of supreme ease washed over me. With each building we reinforced, the world seemed . . . better. Like this was exactly what was supposed to happen. It reminded me of the way my chi had flown out of control back in the capital, but I banished that thought when Barry gave me the mental equivalent of a flick on the nose.

Sorry, I sent back, returning my attention to the task at hand.

I had no idea how long it took, but when I opened my eyes again, the sky had shifted to a lighter shade of purple. I released a slow breath, feeling the life that now filled every building of New Tropica. Even the streets had chi flowing through them, seeming to connect the entire village. I peered down at the leather bag between Barry and me, and when I hefted it, the clink of pearls rang out.

"We didn't use them all?" Barry asked, his eyes narrowing.

"Nah, mate." I stood and stretched, groaning slightly at how stiff my body felt. "Man, last night is catching up to me."

"I can imagine. I feel exhausted, and I didn't do a fraction of what you did." He chewed his cheek for a moment before giving me a questioning glance. "I don't suppose you're up to talking about how it felt taking a more active role in the church?"

"You're a force of nature, Barry." I let out a weak laugh. "I'll need to sleep on it first, but I promise I'll talk to you about it tomorrow. Or later today? Whenever I wake up. I can't even think straight right now."

"Deal. Should we get back, then?"

"What do you mean?" I asked, raising an eyebrow.

"What do *you* mean? Don't you wanna rest?"

"When there's a perfectly good village and some fantasy creations just waiting to be explored? Do you even know me, Barry?"

"And I suppose if I ask you to walk and talk about the church, you'll say something along the lines of, 'It would be downright negligent for a bloke to speak while inspecting creations of vast, cosmic importance, mate.' Am I right?"

"Hey!" I laughed, enjoying his exaggerated hand movements way too much. "You *do* know me!" I clapped him on the shoulder and led us toward the smithy. "Come on. We'll just check if everything is in running order and won't accidentally isekai someone."

Barry shook his head at me and rolled his eyes as we set off to inspect the village's structures.

Hidden in a squat room within the bounds of Tropica, a man stood very, *very* still.

With each breath he took, the acidic haze suffusing his workspace made him want to cough. Solomon, Tropica's resident Cult of the Alchemist representative, knew that making a noise could mean his death, so he tried to ignore his scratchy throat.

Of late, there had been numerous surges of chi. Either they'd been getting stronger or Solomon's detection of them had grown more refined as his ascension drew close. One thing was clear: each pulse had to have been caused by his patron, Lord Tom Osnan Jr.

It rankled Solomon that he had to be beholden to another, even if it was only temporary. Being under the watch of a cultivator allowed him a certain level of protection while conducting his experiments, though, so it was worth it.

Not that the foolish Osnan boy knew the extent of Solomon's work.

The Cult of the Alchemist had long worked with Gormona's hidden cultivators, and as far as Soloman knew, they were the only group outside of the royals to know the truth. Not all the cultists knew, of course—only the highest of their order were brought into the fold. Solomon was one such member, having climbed the cult's ranks over his many decades of life.

A disagreement with the other leaders had seen him relegated to this backwater village. He'd spent many a day fantasizing about the moment he returned to Gormona as a cultivator; he couldn't wait to rub in their faces that he had become *the* Alchemist spoken of in their scriptures. He'd have to ascend first, but with how much his body had been changing of late, it was only a matter of time.

His frail frame had filled out, and he didn't cough nearly as much as he used to when inhaling the chi-suppressing smoke that always floated around his workspace. The recipe for said concoction was a relic of ancient times, the manuscripts for its creation having survived the gods' departure because of his cult's meticulous record-keeping. At first, Solomon had assumed the recent bursts of power had been able to penetrate his brew's shielding properties because of how close he was to awakening. After all, *of course* his awareness of chi would increase as he approached ascension.

But then the explosion of chi had happened.

Solomon had been working on some pills at the time, having decided to stay up after being woken by the Osnan boy doing something just outside the village earlier that night. The moment the chi had burst from almost on top of him, he'd frozen, which was the position he still remained in now, over an hour later.

It was widely known among the Cult of the Alchemist's leadership that the nobles of Gormona, those hidden cultivators that thought themselves the pinnacle of power, were just children that saw themselves as warriors. That they needed to rely on mortal alchemists for their pills was proof enough. That blast, though, had told Solomon a different story.

If that was the level of chi they wielded, he had wildly underestimated the nobles' capabilities. They all had.

It told of a level of control that would shred through Solomon's plans. The obscuring haze was a defensive measure, designed to protect the prophesied Alchemist from prying eyes when he awakened. With the level of control that Osnan had just shown, Solomon's shielding would do nothing.

Despite not having awakened his core yet, that burst of raw, overwhelming power had struck Solomon a physical blow. Even if his body hadn't been sent reeling, he instinctively *knew* that he stood no chance against such a being. Whether it was his base instincts or the knowledge that Osnan would snuff out Solomon's life if he discovered the whispers of chi flowing through him, the result was the same: Solomon wasn't going to move until the time was right.

He was nothing if not a cautious man, and he had already charted his escape route for just such an event. The door was hidden behind and to his left, obscured by a clever system of hinges. It led to a tunnel he'd painstakingly dug through the earth, a practice that caused part of the scorn the other cult leaders felt for him. It had taken him months to dig, his aged frame no longer built for such labor. It was all worth it, though—he may just survive this ordeal because of it. Normally, he'd have relished in that fact, rejoiced that he had another thing to throw in the cultists' faces when he made it back to Gormona as the Alchemist.

Now, though, all he felt was terror.

Abruptly, another pulse of energy shot out into the world. It had the same feel as the blast that rocked him an hour ago, and a spike of glacial ice drove itself into Solomon's spine. As his knees wobbled with the knowledge he was about to die, he realized where the pulse had come from. Its source was far away, perhaps over a kilometer from the shed behind the Osnan household that Solomon now occupied.

Tom Osnan Jr. wasn't close by.

Taking one last breath of the acrid air, Solomon whirled, heading for his secret door. He pressed its right side, causing it to swing inward on the hinges. Solomon slid it back into place and lowered the barricade, sealing the door off forevermore.

He scrambled along the passage, his mind fighting his body's instinct to sprint through the pitch-black tunnels. He kept his footfalls as silent as he could, still worried about being discovered despite how far away Tom Osnan Jr. was. As he approached the exit point, his hopes rose. If he could make his getaway, nothing was lost. Solomon could retreat into the mountains to finish his ascension, and once he became the Alchemist, he would grow in power with the help of his alchemical creations, just as the prophecy foretold.

Light peeked down from ahead, and Solomon finally allowed himself to sprint toward it. When he got there, he threw the trapdoor open, poking his head out to ensure he was alone. The only things surrounding him were grass, trees, and bird-song, the feathered creatures calling out to each other as the light of day shone over the eastern horizon. He climbed out and closed the door to his tunnel, pausing to spare one last glance at Tropica.

What he saw there made the blood freeze in his veins.

To the southeast of the village, a *giant* tree grew from the ground, its vast canopy reaching for the heavens. Even if Solomon wasn't aware of House Osnan's plant affinity, he'd have known it was created by Tom. The tree rose in the exact spot he'd felt a pulse of chi from earlier that night, its impossible mass having sprung up from literally nowhere.

"Persephone's luscious growths," he swore, not even realizing he'd spoken aloud as he fell to his knees. "Just how strong is he . . . ?"

Solomon scrambled to his feet and fled, focusing only on the forest before him.

CHAPTER EIGHT

Fatigue

With the sun threatening to breach the eastern horizon, I gazed upward. ". . . Barry?"

"Yes, Fischer?" he replied, standing right beside me and also staring skyward.

"Have you thought about how the frack we're going to explain this giant bloody tree?" My eyes roamed over its branches high above. "It's taller than the big pineapple."

"What's the big pineapple?"

"Pretty self-explanatory, mate. Picture a pineapple, but it's *really* big."

"Yeah, I gathered that part, but what's a pineapple?"

I turned toward him, raising a brow. "You don't have pineapples?"

"Nope."

"Huh. I guess that settles the pineapple-on-pizza debate."

Barry just nodded along, knowing me well enough to not take the bait.

"Whoa!" came Sturgill's overly projected voice from toward Tropica. "It's even bigger up close!"

I glanced over at him, seeing the baker and his wife, Sue, leading a party of villagers toward the giant tree.

Sue locked eyes with me, a gleam of amusement on her face. She was clearly enjoying her acting role. "Barry! Fischer! Do you two have any idea how this got here?"

"No clue!" I replied, shrugging. "It was here when we woke up!"

The villagers fanned out around the trunk, their steps hesitant and eyes awe-filled as they stared up at the canopy's shifting leaves. Toward the back of the mob, I saw two familiar faces, one white with shock, the other casting a worried glance at her husband. George and Geraldine. The former was panicked, and the latter rested a comforting hand on George's shoulder. I gave them a wincing smile. Poor George's social anxiety was back with a vengeance.

They strode over to me and Barry, their eyes constantly flickering between us and the tree.

"Fischer . . ." George said, pausing to swallow. "You didn't see this tree earlier? When you came to see me?"

"Nah, mate. It might have been here, though—I was fixated on seeing your jewelry, so I didn't really look this way."

"What about last night?" Geraldine asked. "Did you two feel anything?"

"I felt nothing," I replied.

Barry tossed his head side to side. "I might have felt something. I recall waking in the middle of the night, but I didn't know why."

The longer George stared up at the tree, the more his features seemed to pale. Geraldine squeezed his shoulder, and he took a steadying breath, closing his eyes as he exhaled.

Poor bloke, I thought. *Just when his anxiety was starting to get better, we hit him with this curveball . . .*

I cleared my throat. "Well, I'd better get going. Lots to do today. See you all later."

Barry gave me a nod, and the two nobles muttered goodbye, both still staring up.

As I strode between fields of sugarcane, the events of the last twenty-four hours caught up to me. Weariness settled into my bones, making my steps feel sluggish. Even my core was fatigued, its usually buzzing power dull and flat.

My mind, too, felt lethargic. It was as if molasses filled my noggin, making it hard for the simplest of thoughts to traverse my head.

Before I knew it, the surrounding fields were replaced by a desert landscape. I ambled over the sand flats, ever heading toward the river mouth and the comfy bed I knew I'd find there. As I rounded the back of the headland, a many-limbed form launched itself at me. I had neither the strength nor inclination to brace my legs, so I caught Sergeant Snips's happily hissing body, letting her throw me backward into the cold sand.

She blew loving bubbles at me from atop my chest, shimmying her body in excitement.

"Hi, Snips." I rubbed the top of her head, the sensation of her sturdy carapace giving me a modicum of energy. "How are you?"

Good, she hissed. *Tired.*

"Yeah, I know how you feel." I replied, sitting up and cradling her in one arm. "You looking for a nap, too?"

She nodded softly, so I stood and strode toward my front door.

But then I caught sight of the sun. It peeked its head over the horizon, beaming its light and warmth over us and washing away some of my fatigue.

I paused on the spot, soaking it in. "You know, Snips, we haven't had much time together because of all your scouting in Gormona." I lifted her up so we were eye to eyestalk. "Do you wanna watch the sunrise with me?"

She blew affirmative bubbles and nuzzled my hand, so I took us down to the bay and sat where sand met rocky shore. As I settled down to the ground, more of my weariness leached away, seeming to flow into the sand below me. Snips sat in my lap, her eye closed and body going still. Some of the fog clouding my mind drifted away with the breeze, allowing thoughts to enter my consciousness.

There was so much to reflect on.

Most pressing was that my chi had released itself in the capital during Operation Sticky Fingers. With everything going on, I hadn't found the opportunity to process it.

"Are you awake, Snips?"

She spun in my lap and nodded, giving me a curious glance.

"Would you be okay if I spoke my thoughts aloud for a bit?"

She blew a stream of happy bubbles that floated away in the morning air, sparkling under the rising sun.

I rubbed her head, beyond thankful for her companionship. Without pause, I launched right into it. I told her of the rings and their suppressing properties. She'd clearly already been told, because she wasn't at all surprised by the revelation.

"I'm guessing that's what the ring I made does. Its description said, 'This ring has a multitude of purposes for those with the requisite knowledge.'"

Next, I told her how it had felt to release my chi. How I had begun by letting a controlled amount out, but my core had taken over, widening the essence that flowed from me. I relayed the feeling of ecstasy—of rightness—that had smothered me, demanding I let even more out.

Snips listened to me intently, her eye sparkling with intelligence as she mulled over the implications.

"It's kinda worrying, right? What happens if someone with less control unleashes too much power? If I had unleashed everything I had on the cultivators in the capital, I'm pretty sure they wouldn't have survived."

Snips shrugged.

"Yeah, I know I'm more powerful than everyone else, but what happens if I can't control my power?"

She waved a dismissive claw, blowing bubbles that meant: *That won't happen.*

I gave a weak smile. "I'm glad you have so much faith in me, but it's still a troubling possibility."

We slipped into silence, me staring out at the churning ocean and Snips gazing up at me, waiting for me to continue.

"The last thing . . ." I shook my head. "It's stupid."

Negative bubbles.

I took a deep breath, exhaling it slowly as I considered. "It's about taking a more active role in the church. I agreed to help in the capital with stealing the artifacts because it was the safest choice. Not only did it make sense to steal the source of intel from the king, but my presence there meant I could intervene if something crazy had happened. The king being a cultivator, for example. Who the *frack* would have seen that coming?"

She hissed her agreement, preening as she recalled her role in launching the naked bloke from the castle and through a mountain or two.

I laughed, replaying the scene in my mind. "We knew from your intel that we were more powerful than Gormona's cultivators. Luckily, you guys were way more powerful than the nobles, too. If they'd been monsters, though, I was close by. I could have been there in an instant and spanked the king's booty. In the worst-case scenario, I could've stalled him, letting you all escape."

Her body went rigid, and she bolted upright, spewing angry bubbles.

"Don't give me that, Snips. I'd never let you sacrifice yourself for me."

She crossed her claws and turned away, trying to appear disgruntled but only succeeding in looking cute.

I rubbed the top of her head. "You're a good girl, Snips. The *best* of girls."

Her tsundere facade melted away under my praise. And she spun back toward me, hissing her affection as I scooped her up into a hug.

"Thanks for listening to my ramblings, Snips. I'm too tired to make a decision about anything, but I feel a lot better after letting them out."

She wiggled closer to me, then closed her eye and went limp. The chi in her core felt as sluggish as mine, and all at once, my bone-weary tiredness returned. I yawned, turning my face toward the now-risen sun.

"Let's go get some rest."

She didn't reply, and when I glanced down, I saw her taking shallow breaths. She'd already fallen asleep.

I stood up with a smile and strode toward my house, heading for bed.

Despite the evening gone, Ellis's body was filled with vigor.

The moment Borks reopened his portal, Ellis strode inside and grabbed the first of the artifacts. The rest of the fishing club followed close, picking up a relic each. When Ellis stepped from the portal once more, he gazed around the headquarters. Located in the heart of New Tropica, the room was bare save for the giant table in its center. Unlike the meeting room back at the underground church, this building had copious amounts of space, and Ellis took his artifact over to one corner, setting it down.

"How are you feeling, Ellis?" Theo asked, placing a relic beside Ellis's.

"I am well. How are you?"

"Are you sure?" Theo gave him an odd look. "How are you not tired after last night? I'm ready for a nap, and I wasn't involved in a fight with the king."

Ellis shrugged and gazed at his surroundings. As Peter and Danny placed their loads down in the wrong places, he shook his head. "Let me take care of the artifacts' positioning. You've done it all wrong."

Peter opened his mouth, likely to complain, but Danny stepped in. "Come on. Let Ellis take care of the layout."

"Thank you." Ellis removed his notepad, checking the floor plan he'd created.

Most would see the organization as frivolous, but Ellis was nothing if not thorough. They were cataloged by size, purpose, and whether they were functional. One was of particular note, and as the rest of the fishing club brought them out, they were placed in their charted positions. Ellis's eyes lingered on that one screen, but he tore his gaze away. He could look at the Domain information after the relics were placed.

"Where is Keith?" he asked, turning toward Theo as the former auditor stepped from the portal with another artifact.

"Are you sure you're all right, Ellis? He's with the prince . . ."

Ellis frowned. How had he forgotten that? "Maybe I am a little fatigued . . ."

"Duh," Danny replied over his shoulder as he strode for the portal. "Even Borks is dead tired, and he's a millennia-old hellhound."

Ruff, Borks agreed, not lifting his head from where he lay on the stone floor.

Keith had told them of Trent's outburst while Operation Sticky Fingers was underway in the capital. The prince had erupted in flames, having some sort of breakthrough and/or breakdown. Ellis couldn't wait to document the event from Trent's point of view, but Keith had expressly forbidden it for now.

Ellis sighed, shaking his head at himself. Now that he looked for them, he *was* exhibiting some signs of exhaustion. Being a cultivator gave his body an unrivaled level of stamina, but his brain still required sleep to function at its highest potential. He would need to rest for a few hours after the relics were placed. With each delivery from his friends, Ellis seemed to grow more tired, even his excessive stamina beginning to strain.

Finally, Danny and Peter strode into the room with one last object.

"All done, Borks," Peter called over his shoulder.

Borks stood, dismissing the portal. He walked under the table, flopped to the ground, and let out a deep huff of air.

"Place it here, if you please," Ellis said.

Danny and Peter put the relic down where indicated, and Ellis stretched, his mission finally complete. He made to leave for his new apartment in the housing quarter, but his eyes lingered on the screen from earlier. He ambled over to it, peering down at the words printed. Thankfully, it still worked after being transported.

"Pretty impressive, right?" Theo asked, stepping up beside him.

Danny snorted. "That's an understatement. I'm surprised you aren't still losing your mind about it, Ellis."

"He's more fatigued than he's letting on." Theo patted Ellis on the shoulder. "You'll be back to your frantic self after some sleep, I'm sure."

"I really should go get some rest . . ."

Despite his words, Ellis's eyes remained fixed on the screen. He read the words over one last time.

Warning! Foreign Domain detected.
Effect: 5% Suppression, 5% Bolstering, 10% Defense, 5% Growth

When he'd read it in Gormona when they stole the artifact, this one had been listed as the "Local Domain." Its effects were astounding.

Compared to theirs, though . . .

Local Domain detected.
Effect: 20% Suppression, 20% Bolstering, 20% Growth
Evolution: All effects doubled

"Forty percent growth, huh?" Peter mused, shooting a meaningful glance at Ellis. "That beard of yours is going to grow out of control, Ellis."

Ellis leveled a flat glare at them, but that only made their laughter grow more fierce.

CHAPTER NINE

Town Meeting

Beneath a star-filled sky, I ran. Humanoid shapes crawled along the ground, trailing and staring after me. Their eyes seemed to peer into my soul.

Pitch-black sand passed by under my feet, but no matter how many steps I took, the distant horizon remained the same. There were no features, nothing to break up the dark monotony of the desert landscape.

Except for the apparitions. They tracked me, reaching out with ethereal fingers that failed to find purchase. With each touch, though, my steps slowed. It was like I ran through mud, the power of my enhanced body no match for the ground's consistency.

Though aware I was dreaming, I couldn't escape it.

I tried to force my eyes open. Tried to return to the waking world. But I was trapped. The more I wanted to leave, the more numerous the apparitions became. Their bodies stretched, necks elongating so that every set of judgmental eyes stared into my soul, their faces a horrifying collage. I came to a complete stop, trapped by their icy stares.

Knock. Knock. Knock.

My burden increased, even more of the apparitions grabbing hold. Anxiety coursed through me as I realized I couldn't breathe. Their attention was too much for me. It forced me down into the black sand, my chest constricting as their gazes followed.

Knock. Knock. Knock.

My eyes flew wide, and I took a deep, shuddering inhalation, staring at the ceiling of my bedroom. I focused on the cold sheets touching me, willing the adrenaline pumping through my veins to leave. With each breath I took, part of my panic fled. Seeking further comfort, I rolled over to wrap my arm around Maria.

When I patted her hard carapace, she hissed at me.

Huh . . . ?

I cracked an eye to find a rather pleased crab staring back. Snips hissed again, blowing happy bubbles as she scooted closer.

"Fischer!" called a beautiful voice from outside my room. "I'm coming in. Barry needs—" Maria cut off as she opened my bedroom door and caught sight of us. "Snips! You man-thief!"

Sergeant Snips, my longest companion and the cutest crustacean I'd ever met, shimmied up on my chest, lowering her body to mine and hissing taunting bubbles at Maria.

"Oh-ho-ho!" she replied, stepping closer. "You dare?" Maria *launched* herself at us, sailing through the air and crashing down with her arms spread wide.

I grunted as my girlfriend body-slammed us, wrapping Snips and me in a hug.

"Lucky you're cute, Snips," Maria said, rubbing her carapace. "Otherwise, I might need to take you out."

"What time is it?" I asked, resting a hand on Maria's head, thankful for her arrival.

"Midday." She squeezed me tight, then extracted herself from the cuddle puddle. "Come on. It's time to go."

"It is . . . ?"

"Yep! Everyone is waiting for you back in New Tropica."

I raised an eyebrow at her. "Define *everyone*."

"Oh, you know, just a few people. Barry, the church, the dozens of cultivators that you freed from slavery and brought back to Tropica." She shot me a wink. "Nothing major."

I groaned. "Town meeting?"

"Yep. Let's get it over with, then we can come back here and . . ." She leaned in close and bit her lip, staring up at me as she whispered in a husky voice, " . . . *go fishing*."

I gasped. "Maria! You brazen hussy!"

She giggled as I threw a shirt on.

"Let's go, then," I said. "The sooner it's over, the sooner we can fish."

When we arrived in New Tropica, we strode hand in hand across the stone street. Myriad voices came from ahead, projecting out across the village. We followed them, finding the source of the commotion when we entered the theater. It was semi-circular, with a stage on the far side and sloped seating that the stairs descended through. The members of my church's congregation—which now included Trent, apparently—all stood on the stage, while Gormona's cultivators occupied the seats.

Someone in the far-left section noticed me first.

The cultivators' eyes went wide as we entered and walked down the steps. One by one, the conversations trailed off, and every head darted our way. Some averted their gaze, but more remained pinned to us, watching our passage carefully as we descended toward the congregation. Unlike those we'd freed from Gormona, everyone on the stage was happy to see Maria and me arrive. Snips scuttled past us, going to join the rest of my animal pals.

Rather than the stage, I chose a spot on the sloped seating, far enough from any of Gormona's cultivators that they wouldn't have an impromptu panic attack.

"Okay!" Barry called, giving me a slight smirk. "Now that Fischer and Maria are here, we can begin!"

Most turned to look at him, but some gazes remained on me, making my skin prickle a little under their attention.

"I should address the elephant in the room," Barry continued, his voice booming out. "I see hesitation, perhaps even fear in your eyes when some of you look at Fischer." He visually weighed the crowd, taking a moment to let those words sink in. "Good."

Everyone turned to look at me again, their stares just as oppressive as the apparitions in the dream I'd woken from earlier.

"Thanks, Barry," I whispered to Maria, who squeezed my hand.

Barry cleared his throat. "Most of you—those who were protecting the grove in Gormona—have experienced his power first hand. The rest of you—the cultivators that were assigned to the squads—have also felt his power. The pillar of light in the capital? That was Fischer. The surge of power earlier that hit all of your cores? That was us creating this village. Which, again, was mostly Fischer."

"Yeah, right," someone muttered from the other side of the seating, loud enough for all of our enhanced ears to hear. "Like you created this village in a single morning. How stupid do you think we are?"

"Oh, shut up, Zeke," a female cultivator replied from beside the man, rolling her eyes. "You felt the power too. Tell me you can't feel the essence flowing through the very stones beneath us."

"That doesn't mean they made it—"

"There will be plenty of time to talk later," Barry's booming voice interrupted, chi flowing from him and over the crowd. "You're free to believe what you like, but for now, understand *this*." He took another moment, letting anticipation swell. Then he spread his arms wide, gesturing at the congregation on the stage. "Any single one of us alone could have ended the king of Gormona's life, who was the most powerful cultivator we've ever come across. As followers of Fischer, we have far exceeded any of you."

Zeke, the man from earlier, snorted. "You really expect us to believe that the king is a cultivator?"

"Coalemus's stupidity, Zeke," the same woman responded. "Osnan was a cultivator. Why is it so shocking that the king would be too?"

A soft wave of oppressing power came from Barry's core, forcing every mouth closed.

"The king is, yes, but that's not what you should take from my statement." His eyes roamed over them. "Despite how potent we of the congregation are, each powerful enough to defeat your strongest cultivator, Fischer could end every single one of us in an instant. In one move, he could annihilate every cultivator, spirit beast, and building in the immediate vicinity. Even if we attacked together, you cultivators from Gormona included . . . we'd stand no chance."

The tone of his declaration held a finality to it, and despite no chi radiating from Barry's core, the crowd remained quiet. Again, every head turned toward me, but this time, none of them looked away. I could see fear, awe, respect, a wink . . . Wait, why had someone winked?

I squinted at the man on the far side of the seats. It was Deklan. I hadn't recognized him without his armor. As I blinked at him dumbly, he gave me a silly little wave.

The dozens of gazes brought me back to the present. They seemed to drill into me, making me feel like a bug under a microscope. Sweat sprouted from my neck, and just as I was beginning to grow uncomfortable, Maria squeezed my hand. Her touch was a port in the storm, and I leaned into it, lifting my chin under the continued scrutiny of so many people.

The silence was so thick you could cut it with a knife, and the air grew tenser by the moment.

Before it grew too stifling, Barry cleared his throat. "However . . . Fischer is also the reason you're all here. Some of you by his very existence, but most of you by his direct intervention."

This statement caused confusion on the surrounding faces.

Barry nodded. "Our mission in the capital was called Operation Sticky Fingers. The main goal was to steal ancient artifacts from the royal family. We only planned to rescue a small number of you originally, but when Fischer agreed to accompany us, we decided to free every cultivator that was part of the roaming squads." He paused, letting his meaning sink in. "I can see most of you understand. If we had followed the plan, those of you that were defending the grove with Tom Osnan would have been left behind."

Most of the cultivators shared glances with one another as the implications hit them.

"It was through no fault of your own," Barry continued. "We simply didn't have the necessary infrastructure. To be blunt, a cultivator that we previously came across was as mad as a rabid dog. No offense, Borks."

Ruff, he replied, not looking at all bothered as he wagged his tail down on the stage.

Barry reached over and scratched Borks's neck before looking back up at everyone. "Fischer, of his own volition, brought the cultivators in the grove with him. In his words, he didn't want to leave you behind and subject you to punishment or torture for your inability to stop us—a task that was impossible given our difference in power. He wanted you to be free."

Zeke stood abruptly, clenching his jaw. "You keep saying free, yet you threaten us with death."

Rocky stepped forward, raising his clackers in threat, but Snips dashed over and held him back.

Zeke had tried to take a step back and half stumbled on his seat, but as Snips got a hold of Rocky, he firmed his shoulders and stood tall. "You removed our physical collars, yes, but how can people like us ever live free? Our very existence goes against the rules of this world. There are no gods to contain us, no beings that can keep our unparalleled power in check."

There was more than a little self-loathing in his words. I grimaced, feeling sorry for what he'd been through.

"Simple," Barry replied, his voice soft yet carrying over the entire crowd. "We, including all of you, are going to raise Fischer to godhood."

At this, every face turned my way again. Their visages held the same mix of emotions as earlier, but this time, they were much more visceral. Deklan's former joviality was nowhere to be seen. As before, anxiety threatened to wash over me, but I knew what Barry was going for here. He'd given them the stick, and now he was showing them the carrot. Providing a path, a way forward. I swept my misgivings aside and grinned at the sea of faces.

"How you accomplish this is up to you," Barry said. A few faces lingered on me, but they slowly turned his way. "You can craft. You can train. If you like, you can even go fishing. All we ask is that you contribute enough to support yourself, and if we ever need to defend the village, you *will* be expected to help. Besides that, as long as you do nothing to harm anyone or our mission, you're free to do as you please. First, though, we need to ensure that you won't betray us . . ."

A pulse of power washed out of Barry's core as he trailed off. It vibrated the air, making everyone around me sink down into their chairs. It pressed into me, seeming to wage a war with my will.

"Damn," I whispered to Maria. "Barry's getting strong . . ."

"If any of you reach for your chi from this moment on," he continued, "you'll be neutralized. Don't give me that look, Zeke. We're not going to kill you, but any of us can have you unconscious before you even know what happened."

Rocky clacked his claws, daring anyone to give him a reason.

"Some of you might recognize this man." Barry pointed to the side. "This is Theo, a former crown auditor."

Muttered conversation erupted from the crowd, but Barry's chi pulsed out again, smothering the noise.

"You're going to answer his questions. If any of you hold ill intent for us or our cause, you'll be confined. You'll be neither injured nor harmed, but—"

A man at the rear of the theater stood and ran, but before he took his second step, a lightning-covered otter shot from the stage and tapped him on the back of the head, making him go limp. A woman behind me took that opportunity to flee, only to be descended upon and roundhouse-kicked by a coconut-sized bunny. Cinnamon gave me a thumbs-up and a wink from atop her unconscious body. I shook my head at her enthusiasm.

"As I said." Barry's voice shattered the silence. *"Neutralized."* He gave the crowd a smile. "The moment you pass Theo's questioning, you'll be one of us. If any of you have misgivings about our purpose here, I highly encourage you to consider what we offer. If you had doubts or ill intent before hearing my words, you won't be punished. As long as your goals are aligned with us in the future, you are *free*. Now, I know this is a lot to ask, but is anyone willing to volunteer to be questioned first? I'd like to avoid having to pick—"

"I'll do it," someone at the front interrupted, standing.

It was Anna, the first cultivator that had regained consciousness upon arriving back in Tropica. Theo hopped down from the stage and met her, giving her a kind smile and ushering her to the side of the theater. As they started conversing, an unfriendly face jumped from the stage and approached.

"Dad . . . ?" Maria said. "Is everything okay?"

He gave her a second's worth of a smile before frowning again as he looked at me. "I need to speak with you."

Maria sighed. "Alone, I'm guessing?"

"Yes."

"Okay. I'll be around here when you're done doing . . ." She waved her hands vaguely. "Whatever you're doing. Don't take too long, though. I still wanna go fishing today."

"All right, Roger. Where to, mate?"

He turned and strode up the stairs, pointedly not replying.

I shrugged, then gave Maria a quick kiss before jogging after him.

CHAPTER TEN

Blade

As I trailed Roger up the stairs from the theater, I glanced back toward the stage. From the looks on the congregation's faces, they knew the subject of the conversation I was about to have. Sharon waved at me, giving me a reassuring smile that did wonders for my racing imagination. If she was happy about our little chat to come, it couldn't be too bad . . . right?

Sergeant Snips blew me a kiss from the far end of the stage, and I mimed catching it and shoving it into my top pocket. Roger hadn't slowed for my little moment of friendship, so I hustled to catch up. He was marching across the street, headed for the main crossroads.

"Where are we going, mate?" I asked, trying to sound relaxed as I came up beside him.

"Smithy."

I waited for more of an explanation, but it didn't come.

I focused on the warm rays of sun beaming down from above, doing my best to not overthink. When we strode into the smithy, I gazed around at the tool-filled room. It was just as I'd left it last time, except for a few additions. A pile of metal ingots sat beside each furnace, waiting to be used. There were metal bins of coal beside the stacks of metal, ready to fuel the fire necessary for smelting. And on the other side of each coal container, there were sealed sacks of gods knew what.

"So . . . what are we doing here?" I asked.

Roger walked over to a furnace, checking it over. "I tried every profession we could think of when we were trying to make Gormona think I was actually a flock of birds. Blacksmithing was the one I found I had the most affinity for."

I could tell that was all the answer I was going to get, so I just watched as he pressed a button on the wall. Chi moved beneath me, circulating around the stone floor. As it passed the furnace by Roger, it flowed through it, then transformed into fire-aspected essence via some Xianxia-land shenanigans that I had no hope of comprehending despite my enhanced awareness.

"Make yourself useful," Roger grumbled as he shoveled coal into the furnace. "Place ten ingots in a large crucible."

I retrieved said crucible and took it to the blazing forge, pausing a moment to stare at the mostly translucent flames flickering within.

Roger was at a metal bench on the side of the room, and with his back to me, he cleared his throat. "I realize that I've been . . . adversarial. I also realize that, without context, my actions likely don't make sense."

I considered how to reply as I placed the ingots into the crucible, deciding that it was best to let him continue when he was ready. I was starting to infer the reason for Roger bringing me here; the grizzled veteran seemed ready to open up, even if only a little.

"Add two scoops of carbon," he said, his back still to me.

"Right. Carbon. Which is . . . ?"

"The charcoal dust in the sacks over there." He waved with one hand. "It's carbon. Add two scoops to the crucible, then put it in the furnace."

"Oh . . . right."

A few moments later, I shot a glance at Roger before placing the raw materials into the forge. He was doing something with thick strips of metal, seeming to build a frame. I put the crucible into the furnace, and Roger fetched a bag from under his bench. As he opened it and started pouring, words ground out from him.

"I've told you before that I was in the army, right?"

"You did, yeah," I replied, watching the glowing coals before me. "When I first got here, you gave me a vague rundown of the different campaigns you were in."

"Right. The thing is, I'm not sure you entirely understand what war means."

"You're right." I poked at a stray coal that seemed too far from the others, the world itself demanding I return it to the center of the furnace. "I don't."

I stared into the crucible, seeing the ingots within still dark and cold.

"I was a career soldier," Roger began. "I enlisted as soon as I was of age. I was proud to serve my kingdom. Proud to fight for my loved ones and preserve their way of life. It wasn't all sunshine and glory, but I never regretted my choice. War . . ." He let out a long sigh. "As horrific as war is, the bonds forged there are incomparable. I made lifelong friends while a soldier. Family, really."

He shook his head, lines of sadness seeming to linger on his face.

"Over the years, I made my way up the ranks. From infantry to squad leader, and eventually captain. Our lack of losses far exceeded the rest of the army, and at the end of the day, that's all that really matters. War is a numbers game. It hinges on your ability to remove their pieces from the board while keeping your own. Because of our effectiveness, my original squad all transitioned to leadership underneath me. Awards, accolades, and each other. We had it all . . ."

He trailed off, and I chewed my cheek as I glanced at his slumped back. I'd guessed he'd had some sort of responsibility in the army just based on his attitude, but I had no idea he was a captain. He continued staring forward, his body frozen.

"I don't know if this is a rude question, mate, but who were you at war with . . . ?" I asked, hoping to draw him from his memories. "I've barely heard mention of another kingdom, let alone an army."

He let out a slow breath and resumed pouring. "Not really surprising that you haven't heard about it. We're at peace now, and this village is far from any of the battlefields. The kingdom we fought was called Theogonia.

"Oh! Maria mentioned that to me when we went camping. I— Wait, *was?*"

"Aye. Was." He upended the sack and shook the last of its contents out into the metal frame, then bent and grabbed another. "The war with them lasted over a decade and was fought by regular humans. Cultivators were employed by both sides, but they were only ever unleashed in isolated areas. They'd destroy supply lines or make terrain impassable for the other side. But they were never used in battle . . . at first, anyway."

"So it was like a ceasefire?" I asked, watching as the metal within the crucible started to glow red. "Neither side wanted to attack with cultivators because the other would retaliate." I grimaced, realizing it wasn't so far from the threat of nuclear war back on Earth. Countries threatened it, sure, but no one was willing to be the first one to drop a nuke and open Pandora's box.

Except in this war with Theogonia, someone had pressed the big red button.

"Something like that," Roger replied, his voice haggard. He picked up a wooden block and used it to flatten whatever material he'd poured into his metal frame.

I clenched my jaw, my mind imagining the havoc a cultivator could wreak on regular humans. I watched the flickering fire and glowing coals of the furnace, having caught whispers of the king's and prince's flame-based cultivation. If such destructive chi were unleashed on civilians . . . the damage would be catastrophic. This wasn't a long time ago, either. It was within Roger's lifetime.

While I was lost in thought, the farmer-turned-heretic had continued working. He let out a bone-weary sigh, grabbing my attention. "Come here a moment."

I strode over and finally got a look at the bench before him. The massive metal frame was filled with black powder, the same color as the carbon I'd added to the ingots, but slightly coarser. Using his wooden block, he'd created a gigantic rectangular impression that almost went all the way to the edge of his mold.

"What's the black stuff?" I asked.

"Graphite carbon. It's the material Fergus suggested for casting."

"Right . . ." I raised an eyebrow at him. "What's the cast for? A big rectangle . . . ?"

"Fergus intended for it to be a surprise but agreed to let us make it together when I told him I needed to speak with you."

He didn't continue, so I cocked my head in question.

Roger remained staring forward as he smoothed the graphite with one hand, fixing imperfections that didn't exist. "It's a . . . what did he call it?" Roger waved his hand vaguely. "It's something you've wanted for a while but haven't had the chance to make. It's for cooking."

My eyes went wide as I looked at the rectangular cast. "Oh! It's a barbecue plate!"

"Yeah. That. Before we pour the iron in, do you want to make any adjustments?"

Normally, being surprised by the prospect of a barbecue plate to cook on would have filled me with joy, but the shadows of Roger's tale lingered fresh in my mind.

"It looks almost perfect, mate. I might make one change . . ." I retrieved the smallest chisel I could find and started shaping a lip around the rectangular indentation Roger had already made. I took my time making the impression uniform, hoping that Roger would continue his story without being prompted. When I stole a glance, he was staring at the wall, his eyes distant.

After I'd already completed one side, he finally spoke.

"As you can imagine, the cultivators joining the battle had dire consequences. No one can truly say who weaponized them first. Gormona's propaganda machine told us that the enemy had leveled a village unprovoked. The enemy accused us of doing the same, of sending a squad of cultivators after their king's head. In the end, it doesn't matter who made the initial attack. The result was the same . . ."

After he trailed off, a long silence stretched between us. I concentrated on the etching I was making in the graphite carbon, trying and failing to focus my will toward creation.

Roger grunted. "There's no way to properly describe what happened when the cultivators joined the battle. The devastation was unparalleled. They were forces of nature." Roger clenched his fists at his side. "In a single attack, I lost my squad. My *family*. The person that attacked them—"

He turned his back to me, clearing his throat and averting his eyes as he took a steadying breath.

My heart dropped in my chest. "Roger . . . I'm so sorry." I put my chisel down and fumbled for the right words to say. "I can understand your hatred for cultivators. I—"

"No, Fischer," he interrupted, his words hoarse. "You can't."

His core vibrated with fury, small whispers of chi radiating from it. Just like the flame-aspected essence roaring within the furnace, his power had a feel to it, but I didn't recognize it. I sent my awareness out, finding his chi . . . *sharp*. It had a deadly edge to it, and my instincts screamed to get away. Instead, I remained, sensing the odd fluctuations coming from his core.

"We were having a meeting when *he* arrived," Roger said, his words quiet yet just as razor-edged as his chi. "We were discussing what to do about the cultivator threat when a single man arrived in our midst. I threw myself to the ground immediately, which is the only reason I yet breathe. Everyone else, though . . ."

Roger's power ebbed, and I thought it might return to his abdomen, but then it rushed back out even stronger than before. My body took a step back, my instincts screaming to get away from his chi.

"In the blink of an eye, they were torn apart," he continued. So much essence flowed from Roger that he seemed to glow to my senses. "There was the sound of a whirling blade, and where my friends had stood, only pieces remained. There was *nothing* I could have done to protect them."

"How did you escape . . . ?" I asked, not sure of what else to say.

"The cultivator took a single step toward me, arm raised and ready to finish me off. He looked at my outfit and said, 'Oh, we're on the same team.'" Roger's upper lip twitched, his body and core tensing. "That psycho *grinned* at me. That cold smile he wore . . ." He clenched his fists so hard that his arms shook and muscles bulged. "I still see it most nights."

I wanted to reach out and place a comforting hand on his shoulder, but my senses still screamed not to get close to the bladelike chi coursing from him. "He's not here in Tropica, is he? That cultivator?"

"No," he replied simply. "He went mad in the battle. He was put down."

"Are . . . are you sure? You're positive he isn't among those we saved from Gormona?"

"I'm not an idiot, Fischer," he spat, whirling on me. "Even if he changed his face entirely, I'd recognize that smile anywhere."

I thought I'd find tears welling in his eyes when he turned my way, but they held only rage. A fire hotter than any forge roared within his gaze, threatening to burn away everything in sight.

"Cultivators are monsters, Fischer." The air around the room stirred. "They tear through humans and rip lives asunder. It's in their nature to destroy."

I wanted to tell him that wasn't the case. That we'd be different. But then I recalled the feeling of ecstasy that had rolled through me back in the capital. My chi had wanted to roar free of my core. It *needed* to be expended, paying zero regard for the surrounding lives that would have been taken as a result. I believed I could control myself—was it possible for me to make that promise for everyone else? I trusted my friends in Tropica too, but what of the cultivators we'd just rescued?

I swallowed, my throat dry. "I can't believe that of you, Roger. You're a cultivator too, and no matter how strong you get, you're way too stubborn a prick to let it control you."

I hoped my joke would bring a grin to his face, but the curl of his lip held no mirth. "You're right on that front, at least. My power will be used to protect—a blade to strike down those that would threaten anyone I love." The essence running through the room seemed to respond to Roger's declaration. "I won't lose anyone again. I *can't* lose anyone again."

The chi retreated, sinking down into the stones to get as far from him as possible. I lowered my brows as I felt it rush back up, but then I realized the truth.

It wasn't the smithy's power; it was the world's. It swelled up from all sides, growing into an immense cloud.

Without warning, it slammed into Roger.

CHAPTER ELEVEN

Apprentices

The cloud of power flew into Roger's core, expanding its bounds. When the foreign essence joined with his, it took on the same bladelike aspect. I knew what would come next, so I dashed forward, letting my own chi spew from my abdomen. A pure bubble of white wrapped around Roger and me just in time. Uncountable arcs of power shot out from him, slamming into my shield and doing their best to tear it apart. I raised another layer of chi between Roger and me, my eyes going wide as I felt the strength of each blow.

If I hadn't been here, the smithy would have been ripped apart. No matter how reinforced the building was, the myriad waves of essence shooting from Roger's core were too numerous. Too *sharp*. Each projection's blade was sharper than a scalpel and stronger than forged steel. More still flew from him, striking the barriers I'd raised and threatening to shred them. I clenched my jaw and focused my will on keeping them contained, but some slipped through beneath his feet, hitting the stone bricks there and cutting deep into them.

Finally, his reserves died out, and the hail of blades came to an end. Roger slumped, his body going limp and dropping to the floor.

I released my shields and appeared at his side in an instant, catching him before his head struck the ground. I sat him upright, holding his back so he couldn't fall over. He came to abruptly, and he blinked as he looked around, stopping only when his gaze landed on the bricks below. His swords of chi had sliced into the stone, leaving a flowerlike pattern in the area beneath him.

"Was . . . was that me?"

"Yup," I replied. "I did my best to shield the workshop, but I couldn't get the barrier close enough to—" My head darted toward the doorway as I felt nature chi approaching.

Corporal Claws skidded to a stop, lightning still wreathing her body as she peered into the workshop. I gave her a thumbs-up and a small shooing gesture. She grinned, waved, and dashed from sight.

"What happened?" Roger asked, still staring down.

"You had a breakthrough, mate. You'll feel chi better now, and you might be able to extend your abilities along objects. It could only be System-made items, though . . . ? I'm not really sure. I've only managed to do it with my fishing rod."

"Breakthrough . . ." Roger repeated, tasting the words. "You mean that time you lost control like a moron and almost blew up Theo, Barry, and the hellhound?"

"Hey! First, his name is Borks. You know that. Second, you almost did the same! If not for me being here, you would have . . ." I narrowed my eyes at the—was that a spark of amusement in his eye? "You're messing with me, aren't you?"

Before he could reply, another source of chi approached. Ellis appeared in the doorway with Sergeant Snips's claw hooked around his leg, trying to stop him from entering.

"I just need to speak to them for a moment. I will not take up much of their—"

A mass of fur slammed into him. Claws rode Borks's bulldog form into battle, giving me a wide grin as they took out Ellis's legs. Before he could fall to the ground, Cinnamon appeared. She was as fast as a bullet, and she struck Ellis's airborne body with a vicious flying kick. He flew from sight, and half a second later, I heard the sound of him striking something in the far distance.

Claws gave me a thumbs-up, scooped Cinnamon out of the air, and smacked Borks on his rotund rump. Her noble steed took off, his paws scrambling for purchase on the stone street for a moment before they disappeared from view. I shook my head, grateful for their intervention and not at all surprised by their methods.

When I turned back to Roger, he was staring at his hands, somehow blissfully unaware of Ellis's ejection.

"Well, mate," I said, "it looks like you might get your wish."

"My wish?" he asked, slowly looking up at me.

"To protect everyone. Other than me, you're now the strongest cultivator we know."

"How much stronger . . . ?"

"Your core is still a little weaker than mine, but the next person after you isn't even close."

He pursed his lips, getting lost in his thoughts. "You were right about my increased awareness. I can feel the chi everywhere. It's—" His head shot around to stare at the furnace. "I . . . I can feel the aspect of the essence there. It's fire. It wants to consume . . ."

"Yep. And I can feel your blade aspect. Or maybe it's a sword aspect? I don't really know, to be honest. One thing's for sure: it's sharp as frack."

His hand drifted down to his abdomen, and as he tested his core, he smiled faintly. It was the closest thing to joy I'd ever seen cross his face, other than when he was looking at Maria or Sharon. I knew exactly what he was feeling; I'd felt much the same after my breakthrough. Even now, I could recall how "right" the world had seemed afterward. Like I was closer to who I was meant to be.

"So . . ." I cleared my throat. "You've had a long day. Should we pause the whole barbecue thing? We can pick up where we left off tomorrow or something if you want to go explore your power."

"No," he replied, getting to his feet. "We see it through. I could use the distraction."

I shrugged. "Works for me, mate. I've wanted a bloody barbecue plate forever."

We went back to the mold, finding it mostly undisturbed despite Roger having unleashed an anime finishing move within the confines of the smithy. Roger used the wooden block to flatten the graphite carbon again while I went around the edges with a chisel, using its small surface to create a uniform indent for the lip.

Though I was focused on the plate, part of my awareness felt the surrounding chi. Roger was doing the same, using trickles of his newfound power to taste the outside world. Just as I was making the finishing touches with the chisel, there was a fluctuation in the essence behind me. I turned, pouting as I stared at the furnace. The fire there had dulled, and when I strode over, I found the ingots within melted into a red-hot slag.

"The smithy turned the heat down by itself . . . ?" I asked aloud.

"It does that," Roger grumbled from beside me. "Are you ready to pour?"

I nodded, and with a large prong each, we removed it from the coals.

"Go slowly," Roger said as we arrived at the bench.

I nodded again, matching him as he tilted the crucible to let molten metal stream into the mold.

"I have to admit that I didn't just bring you here to tell you about my past, Fischer."

"Yeah, I figured as much. What else did you wanna say?"

"I'm sure you've noticed my . . . annoyance with you."

"Annoyance?" I raised an eyebrow. "I'd have described it as loathing. Or perhaps the hatred of a thousand Rockys."

Roger gave me a flat look.

I laughed. "Yeah, mate. I've noticed. Why is that? Other than the whole *turning the two people you love into what you hate the most* thing."

"It was about that at first, and you being a heretical fool most of the time didn't help."

"Agreed. Why do I annoy you now, though?"

Roger stared at the mold as we filled it with molten metal. He scrunched his face, letting some of the emotions I was used to seeing show. "It's because you refuse to take control."

"Take control? Of the church?"

He nodded. "You have a responsibility to everyone. All of those that have become cultivators. Especially my daughter." His face further contorted in displeasure, but rather than unleash the verbal tirade no doubt begging to be flung my way, he took a deep breath and sighed. "You say you love her, yet you're not doing everything in your power to protect her."

My skin prickled, and it had nothing to do with the heat radiating from the crucible beside me. "I don't think that's really fair, mate. First, I would do anything to protect Maria. But how much do you expect me to take responsibility for? I had no choice in being sent here, and even if I wasn't in Tropica, cultivators would be popping up. Just look at Sturgill. He—"

"But you *are* here," Roger interrupted, turning to look at me. His eyes held an echo of the flames from earlier, when he'd spoken of the cultivator that had taken his friends' lives. "You have the power and obligation to lead, yet you'd rather sit around and fish, of all things. It pisses me off. When are you going to step up?"

"*Step up . . . ?* What do you think I've been doing?" I let some of my indignation into my voice. "Of course I feel responsible, which is exactly why I went to the capital for Operation whatever-the-frack, then went personally to deal with the Osnan prick in Tropica. I might not want the responsibility of leadership or the burden of knowledge, but it's not like I'm sitting on my hands and letting everyone take on deadly trials."

"You're just proving my point, Fischer." Roger peered into the crucible as we upended it, letting the last of the molten iron pour out into the mold. "You're already helping out sometimes, so why not just be a man and do what you're supposed to?"

"First off, that's sexist. Second, because I don't bloody want to. I've lived that life, Roger. All it brings is misery!" I sighed as we set down the crucible, its contents having been emptied. "I want to spend my time with the woman I love, my friends, and do as much fishing as humanly possible. Why is that so bad?"

Roger shook his head. "I think you'll find your friends more and more unreachable, Fischer. Do you really think all our problems are gone now that you freed the cultivators from Gormona? If you truly believe that, you're more of a fool than you look. It doesn't matter how many people you beat down or defeat—another will come crawling from the woodwork. There is *always* a bigger bully waiting their turn."

"Yeah, well, that might all be true, but we need to set it aside for now." I closed my eyes for a moment, willing my growing frustration to disappear.

"Why?" Roger demanded. "You got somewhere better to be?"

"What? No. We need to pour our will into the barbecue." I pointed down at the cooling metal. "We haven't got long to shape it."

"Oh." Roger's pout looked almost sheepish, and I tried to sear it into my memory. "Fine," he said, staring back down at the mold. "Let's do it."

As I focused on the still-molten iron, my awareness instinctively felt Roger's chi. It still had the same qualities—like it could lash out and cut at any moment—but it was now in control. As he directed it down toward the barbecue plate-to-be, I sent all my attention with it, banishing the concept of him being a threat from my mind.

Roger's challenge left me on edge, but with each passing second, I sank more and more into the present. Essence flowed all around us, the world's reserves swiftly returning after so much of the surrounding strands had rushed into Roger. They wound by, languidly traveling to and fro.

As my chi caressed the metal, I pictured what I wanted to create. A slab of cast iron, large enough to cook meals for all of my pals. I wanted it to be a source of sustenance, community, and friendship. Following my lead, Roger's will joined mine. I felt the mental equivalent of a mocking laugh come from him when he understood the intentions I was guiding the creation with, but he quickly swept his derision aside and reinforced my plans with his intent.

Power pulsed from both of our cores, traveling down into the cooling mold. The stone bricks of the smithy seemed to vibrate, responding to our efforts. The world's essence answered too, oozing in from all sides, almost inquisitively.

Then, it raced toward the metal.

As it had done to Roger, chi slammed into the barbecue plate. I increased the amount coming from my core, letting as much out as the universe demanded. Roger did the same, and after only a few seconds, it began taking shape.

Usually, when the transformation of System-made objects began, the item would blur, becoming impossible to focus on. This time, I saw each adjustment in exacting detail. The barbecue plate . . . *wobbled*, for lack of a better word. It moved like a liquid, rippling and never quite sitting still. The edges slowly expanded, making the thick frame splinter and warp.

Graphite carbon poured out of the mold onto the workbench as the barbecue plate took shape, becoming defined once more. White light exploded from it, bathing me in warmth, and suddenly, even brighter beams shone from Roger, making my core hum.

I exhaled, looking up at our creation as Roger caught the bag of coins that appeared in the air beside him.

I'd thought the original mold he created was big; the thing sitting on the bench before us made it pale by comparison. The plate had almost quadrupled in size, and if it had gotten any larger, it wouldn't have fit out the smithy's door. It was thicker too, having somehow used our chi to add extra metal. More importantly, it was no longer just a plate—it had grown legs. A hollow body sat beneath its cooking surface, perfect for burning wood within. And a chrome button had sprouted on the front, which I suspected was some sort of fire starter.

I couldn't contain my excitement; I had a whole-ass barbecue.

My eyes were drawn into it.

Cast Iron Barbecue of the Ascendant Apprentices
Rare
Created by kindred blacksmith apprentices, this barbecue is a representation of their bond. Food cooked upon its surface receives a boost to chi content and may be granted a random boon.
Requirement: 25 Cooking

A random boon . . . ? I wondered, shaking my head to dismiss the words.

"Damn, Roger," I said, smirking and raising an eyebrow his way. "Looks like we're kindred spirits . . ."

"Shut up, Fischer," he growled, but I didn't miss the hidden smile as he stared down at our creation.

CHAPTER TWELVE

Memories

After Roger and I set the barbecue down, I took a step back, smiling at the sight. We'd carried it all the way back to my home, and now that it sat on my back deck, an immutable sense of joy washed over me.

I *finally* had a barbecue. I would have been content with just a thick slab of cast iron that I could place over a fire, but the System had given me so, *so* much more. I heard voices coming from the river, and I spun, seeing a procession of humans and creatures carrying firewood.

"I still do not see why you had to hit me so hard, Cinnamon," Ellis said, using one hand to rub his backside. "That would have killed a regular human."

"Well, good thing you're a cultivator, then, huh?" Barry replied, shooting me a quick smirk. "It was your own fault for ignoring Corporal Claws's orders, anyway."

Claws nodded fervently from atop Borks's back, chirping and giving a thumb's up to Cinnamon, who was cradled in Maria's arms at the rear of the group.

Ellis sighed. "I will not apologize for getting excited about an advancement. Every second the data is not recorded is a chance for the memory to fade."

While Barry reminded Ellis for the umpteenth time that we had almost perfect recall as cultivators, I turned to Roger. He was staring down at the barbecue, a slight smile on his face as his eyes roamed over its black frame.

"Roger," I said.

"What?" he replied, reluctantly looking at me.

"Thank you, mate."

Clearly not expecting my gratitude, he paused a moment before sniffing. "You're welcome."

We both stared at the barbecue as everyone placed firewood down beside it, providing us with the necessary fuel to cook something amazing.

"You know, Roger, you don't need to eat any seafood if you don't want to." I kept my face as still as possible. "I'd be happy to test out our little creation without you if you'd rather go report your breakthrough to Ellis somewhere else."

I thought I might break if I locked eyes with the disgruntled farmer, so I glanced at Maria instead. Though she was trying to give me a disapproving glare, her eyes danced with humor.

"That would be ideal," Ellis replied. "The fewer distractions, the better. We—"

"All right," Roger boomed, whirling on me. "Cut the shit, Fischer. You want me to admit it out loud?"

A silence stretched over everyone, and I couldn't hide my wry smile any longer. "Pretty much, yeah."

He rolled his eyes. "Fine. Have it your way. We both know I like the godsdamned seafood, okay? I didn't want to give you the satisfaction, but your constant comments are even more annoying."

"Thank you, mate. That admission was everything I needed and more." I spun toward the others. "I'll get the barbie started. Do we have any volunteers to catch us some fish?"

"On it!" Maria yelled, grabbing a rod and sprinting off with Cinnamon still in arm. Borks trailed after her, Claws giving me a sharp-toothed grin from his back as they all disappeared from sight.

Ellis began peppering Roger with questions about the breakthrough he'd experienced. I retrieved my hatchet from nearby and started splitting a log, hacking off different-sized bits of kindling that I placed in the barbecue's tray. When I'd made a nice little teepee shape, I released a content sigh, staring at my work.

"So," Barry said, kneeling down beside me. "How did your conversation go? I tagged along to have that chat you promised me, but if Roger already convinced you . . ."

"Oh, we just spoke about the usual." I waved a hand. "Roger told me I was a bit of a nerd for not taking responsibility."

Roger snorted, having overheard us. "And Fischer was all, 'I'm a moron and would rather waste time relaxing instead of taking responsibility for my actions.'"

"Oh," Barry said, deflating. "There's no point in me trying to convince you to take control of the church, then?"

"Nope! Still more than happy to step in if anyone is in danger, though."

I pressed down on the metal button on the front of the barbecue. Just as I'd suspected, it caused sparks to fly out. They caught on the tinder I'd placed in the bottom of the tray, and within the space of a few breaths, the flames spread to the smaller bits of kindling. The sounds of crackling wood and Ellis's scrawling pencil blanketed me in a sense of ease.

Barry chewed his cheek beside me, his eyes distant as they stared into the building fire. "I'd hoped that you being willing to go confront Tom Osnan Jr. meant you'd enjoyed taking part in Operation Sticky Fingers . . ."

"Don't get me wrong, mate. I did enjoy it—especially being able to release so much chi. That damned stuff wants to be used. It was like finally scratching an itch that had been bothering me for way too long."

"So why don't you want to take a more active role? It would give you much more of a chance to use it. Plus, we don't know when the next threat will pop up. We could really use you as the visible head of the church, especially as a show of strength for the cultivators you rescued."

"I already tried, Barry," Roger replied for me, turning from Ellis. "He doesn't care. Save your breath."

"Can you really blame me?" I held my hands out, bathing in the warmth radiating from the fire. "My life in Tropica is kind of amazing as is."

"Okay. I won't harp on about it, but I hope you reconsider." Barry stood and stretched. "I meant what I said about threats. You never know . . ."

"If there's a threat, just let me know." I gave him a reassuring smile. "Point me at it, and I'll be there."

"Fischer!" came Maria's voice from far away. A moment later, she skidded around the corner with a giant shore fish in hand. "We caught lunch!"

"Good job!" I held my hand over the barbecue, feeling the heat coming from it. "Barbie's almost ready to go!" I clapped Barry on the shoulder. "I appreciate your concern, mate. Really—I do. I doubt we'll be encountering a threat any time soon, though . . ."

Within the capital city of Gormona, a broken man sat atop a meaningless throne. Sunlight shone in from above, painting his throne room in the beautiful colors of myriad stained-glass windows. Usually, the opulence of his surroundings made Augustus Reginald Gormona feel on top of the world. Made him feel like the king he was.

Today, all the windows did was illuminate his failure.

Their defeat—*his* defeat—had been spectacular in its thoroughness. All but a handful of their cultivators had been taken. Their grove, the very source of Gormona's entrenched power, had been destroyed. Their artifacts, which were the treasure of uncountable kingdoms, had been stolen. Despite his and Tom Osnan's lifetime of cultivation, they'd not stood a chance. Tom's shame was much greater, though. The foolish lord had tried to claim the man he'd met was the true leader of the enemy forces.

Augustus Reginald Gormona knew the truth, though.

It was Lizard Wizard. It had *always* been Lizard Wizard. Ever since the king had been shot from his own castle like a pebble thrown by a child, he'd not been able to stop replaying the encounter. Even upon waking within a crater atop a mountain, his first thought had been of the spirit beasts as they watched his departure. As he'd trudged back to the capital, naked as the day he was born, he recalled the strike he'd landed on Lizard Wizard's side.

The blow should have cracked ribs and torn ligaments. It should have ended the reptile's life then and there. Instead, the energy had been reflected somehow, striking Augustus hard enough to turn him into a cannonball. The reality of the spirit beasts' abilities defied even the secret records he had. He'd removed Boat Goat's head, yet the fiend had continued attacking, completely unfazed. The king's scorching flames had washed over both Boat Goat and Hurtle the Turtle, but instead of burning to dust like they should have, they'd transformed into crabs, their carapaces somehow impervious to his deadly attack.

The door to his throne room swung open, and two sets of steps entered.

"Is it true, Father?" someone asked, the voice only barely registering.

When Augustus glanced up, he found his wife, Penelope, and his daughter, Tryphena. The former downtrodden, the latter ready to explode.

"Is it true?" Tryphena demanded again, her eyes fierce. "You were defeated?"

"Yes," he replied, his voice weak. "It's true."

She swore, slamming her fist into an open palm. Flames spewed out from her strike, dashing against the stones of the castle before sputtering out. "I wasn't here." She dropped to a knee. "Forgive me, Father. I had no way of getting back in time."

"Rise, Daughter. It is not your fault. The blame rests atop my head."

"Forgive my impudence, but I don't believe that." She raised her head, somehow appearing defiant from her lowered position. "In fact, I *know* that's wrong."

Before Augustus could ask what she meant, his wife spoke up. "I took Tryphena to see Aisa and the rest of the handlers before coming here."

"You *what*?" he yelled, getting to his feet and unleashing waves of chi from his core that demanded to be unleashed. "They are to be ignored until their execution!"

"Father, please. Let me explain."

Tryphena strode forward, and just before she entered the range of his flames, Augustus slammed his channels closed. He slumped down into his chair, his fury smothered by the weight of reality. "I have failed my kingdom. Even my daughter goes against my orders."

"With good reason," she replied, kneeling before the throne. "We took an auditor with us to speak with Aisa."

"To what end?" He shook his head, Gormona's crown feeling as heavy as a mountain. "What could that accomplish?"

Tryphena shared a look with her mother before turning back toward him. "Did you talk to Aisa at all . . . ?"

"Enough to understand that all the handlers were defeated by Fat Rat Pack and The Beetle Boys."

"Well . . . we asked her pointed questions. What we learned was terrifying."

Someone cleared their throat, and when Augustus glanced up, his chi threatened to release itself once more. "What is she doing here?"

Aisa marched into the throne room, averting her eyes. When she got halfway to him, she kowtowed.

"I brought her to explain the situation firsthand," Tryphena said. "We've already had all the information verified by an auditor."

"You go too far, daughter." Augustus's lip twitched, his patience growing thin. "For you to talk to her is one thing, but to allow her in my presence after such a grievous failure . . ."

"It wasn't your fault!" Aisa yelled, still pressing her head to the floor.

Augustus exploded forward, flames burning through the back of his robe. He bent, grabbing her by the hair and lifting her face. "What did you say, girl?"

Aisa clenched her jaw, her eyes staring into his. "It wasn't your fault."

He cocked his fist back, gathering chi there that burned white hot. With each bit he let out, his core demanded he release more. He should eliminate this wretch. Punch her with every ounce of power he possessed, ending her existence on the spot.

Tryphena lay a hand on his shoulder. "Just let her explain, Father. If you still want to strike her down afterward, you can."

"Fine," he replied, dismissing his power with no small amount of effort as he stared down into Aisa's defiant gaze once more. "You have ten seconds."

She swallowed. "The enemy was stronger than we ever could have imagined. There was nothing we could have done—nothing *anyone* could have done. Fat Rat Pack and The Beetle Boys . . . they had leaders . . ." She trailed off, her eyes going distant. When they abruptly shot back toward Augustus, they were resolute. "Either of those leaders could have taken on the entire capital's forces at once."

The king snorted. "Impossible. You're mistaken."

"Yet each of the handlers said the same thing," Tryphena said. "And the auditor confirmed their statements."

"You really suspect that a single beast—one that can't have been ascended for longer than a few months—could have taken on the rest of Gormona's forces? Could have taken on *me?*" He let out a bitter chuckle. "You're even more useless than I suspected."

"They're correct, Augustus," came yet another voice from the entrance to his throne room.

"Really, Tom?" the king asked, making his displeasure clear in his voice as he gave his oldest friend, Tom Osnan, a flat glare. "I'm surprised you'd show your face here after your failure at the grove."

Tom was a proud man. Indignation raged on his face unhidden. "If I recall correctly, you failed, too, Augustus."

The king stood, gathering flames around both fists, preparing to attack the man who knew him best. His core vibrated, demanding that he answer the insult with violence.

"That's enough, Augustus!" his wife yelled.

It was enough to bring the king up short, and he turned toward her, arching an eyebrow.

"How many people need to tell you until you believe them? Tom wasn't lying!" As with the rest of them, she stared at him with unwavering resolve. "Fischer, the one who was at the grove, was the man that learned the Chi Manipulation skill not long ago. We both know how many years it took me to learn. He's no simple cultivator."

"His power, Augustus . . ." Tom said. "It was like nothing we've ever seen. Even compared to the old monsters, his chi was *endless.*"

"Yes, yes. It was unaspected, yet supremely powerful. You've already said so, and I've already told you that's *impossible.*"

"The auditor vouched for his words too, Father," Tryphena said.

"That's . . ." Augustus licked his lips, a thorn of uncertainty pricking his awareness. "He did?"

"Yes!" his wife replied. "That's what we've been telling you!"

He took them all in, seeing conviction etched on each of their faces. They were all so sure, but it wasn't possible. None of it made any sense . . . But then he recalled his fight with Lizard Wizard once more.

Even that defied belief. Unlike the information everyone else provided, he'd seen it with his own eyes. Felt it with his own body. Boat Goat, sans head, slamming him with his own tables. Lizard Wizard's immunity to attacks, despite not using elemental chi. Bog Dog's portals, used too often for such a powerful ability. Hurtle the Turtle and the headless goat, who had both transformed into fireproof crabs when he unleashed an inferno. Glare Bear's unnerving eye contact and the way the creature moved—what kind of self-respecting bear would slither around on the ground like a centipede?

If it were all true, though . . . "Ares's rigid spear . . ." Augustus stumbled, his flame chi retreating back into his abdomen. "If you're correct . . ."

"We are," Tryphena said, helping hold him upright. "But we have an answer."

"An answer . . . ?" Laughter bubbled up from within. "What, to swear fealty? What answer could there possibly be?"

Tryphena looked at her mother, who nodded back reassuringly.

"We've thought this over, Father. Weighed the cost, risk, and benefit. There is only one way out of this . . ." His daughter looked into his eyes for a long moment, the air growing thick with tension. Eventually, she spoke a single word.

"Theogonia."

CHAPTER THIRTEEN

Fusion

"You might recall that one of the first lines of this manual is: 'Do not share this work with anyone other than the Kraken bloodline or their immediate family.' But since then, I have repeatedly stressed the importance of helping others. Selflessness lies at the core of our philosophy, and yet, these instructions are to be kept secret, given only to those we deem worthy.

I am sure that you, a descendant of the great Kraken Rider, see the hypocritical nature of this expectation.

It is an unfortunate necessity. The meditations contained within the House Kraken manual are a path to knowledge—a road to power. If they were to fall into the wrong hands, great destruction could follow. So what is a Kraken meditator to do? Where is the line between sharing enlightenment and endangering the world? If you were hoping for a black-and-white answer, I'm afraid I must disappoint. It is up to you to decide.

Fortunately, the guiding question is rather simple.

Which choice is better for your soul?"

Excerpt from Chapter 13, House Kraken manual

Beneath the shade of a colossal tree, the lord of Tropica village took deep, calming breaths.

George and Geraldine Kraken had both returned home, intent on resting after such a fraught twenty-four hours. Upon arriving there, however, sleep had eluded them both. They'd even tried meditating, but neither of them could focus. So they'd wandered the streets instead, trying to overwhelm their racing thoughts with exercise. They had stared up at the giant canopy stretching above the surrounding roofs as they walked, and without realizing what they were doing, they'd arrived back at its base.

Though the sun had beamed down on them, the air was frosty, the night's chill lingering. Exhausted and overwhelmed, George had sat and closed his eyes. The moment he had, he'd understood the magic of this place. It was like nothing he'd ever felt before, and within the space of a few breaths, he slipped into his meditation deeper than he thought possible. The world seemed to caress his very being, as if he was supposed to be here. It was an alien yet wonderful experience.

He focused on his breathing, each inhalation seeming to reinvigorate and fill George with power. Geraldine squeezed his hand from her position on the grass beside him, also lost within herself. Villagers milled around, no doubt giving them odd looks. George cracked an eye, his curiosity getting the better of him.

In his wildest dreams, he'd never have guessed he'd find what he did.

The common folk were arrayed around them, but they weren't staring. Their eyes were closed, their faces peaceful as they also sat on the grass. Most didn't have the cross-legged posture that the House Kraken manual instructed, but some did, having either copied them or found it to be a comfortable position.

Though he couldn't say why, the sight filled him with hope. He cast his gaze over the dozens of common folk, unable to stop himself from smiling. Movement caught his attention from one side of the trunk, and when he focused that way, he saw something that made his smile disappear.

What in Triton's thundering conch . . . ? he thought, gazing at the new arrivals.

Five robed individuals came scuttling into view. They had their hands held up in the approximation of crab claws, walking sideways to mimic the movement of the small crustaceans one could see milling on rocks by the shore. Hissing sounds came from them, and when one accidentally bumped another, the assaulted individual spun on the spot, lashing out with his claw hands. They postured, hissing at each other before turning and following the other three crab walkers.

When they reached the rest of the villagers, they arranged themselves in a circle and crouched low. With his legs approaching of their own accord, George found himself standing above them. Geraldine had followed, also staring down at the confusing congregation.

George squatted down beside one of the men. "Excuse me . . ."

The man's eyes shot open, glaring up at him. "What do you—oh! Lord and Lady . . ." His mouth moved inaudibly, clearly regretting his choice to lash out.

"It's okay," George replied, keeping his voice low. "I wanted to know what you're doing. I find your posture . . ."

"Unique," Geraldine finished, also whispering.

The explanation seemed to mollify the robed man, and his posture relaxed. "We are the members of Tropica's Cult of Carcinization. We are performing the duties of our faith."

Carcinization . . . ? George wondered.

At their muttered conversation, a few of the surrounding commoners glanced their way. Upon seeing the Cult of Carcinization imitating crabs, none of the common folk seemed surprised. Some smiled before closing their eyes once more.

The cult must do this often, then.

Following an impulse, he turned back to the man. "What is your name?"

"Joel, Lord."

"Please—just George is fine. Are you the cult's local leader?"

"I am," Joel replied, somehow appearing proud while folded like an uncooked pretzel.

"Do you . . . mind if we join you?"

Joel's eyes went wide, as did the rest of the cultists'. "We would be honored, George." Joel turned to Geraldine. "Will you be joining us, too, er . . . my lady?"

"Geraldine," she corrected, giving him a kind smile. "I would love to."

"Is that okay . . . ?" the female cultist asked, giving Joel a meaningful look. "It's our *secret* doctrine . . ."

Joel waved his hand. "We've already shared it with Fischer. The more the merrier, I say."

The mention of Fischer made George pause, but then the crab folk scuttled aside, making room for them in their circle.

Sweeping troubling thoughts away, George copied their posture as best he could. Remarkably, it was comfortable. The moment he closed his eyes, he felt the world blanketing him once more. But the metaphorical covering felt . . . different. It was hard to explain, almost like it was made from a different material—which made exactly *zero* sense because it wasn't a physical object. Still, his body's senses didn't lie. As he slipped deeper into his meditation, he imagined energy flowing around him and pouring into his abdomen, just as House Kraken's manual instructed.

The moment he did, something within him vibrated. It was the same sensation that had occurred the previous night, but this time, outside events weren't the cause. *He* was.

Geraldine took a shuddering gasp beside him. A spear of worry drove through George's awareness, shattering his meditation. He reached over, grabbing her arm as his eyes flew open. "Geraldine?" he whispered. "Are you okay?"

She licked her lips, her eyes staring into the far distance before focusing on him. "I . . ." She leaned closer to him, replying under her breath, "I did the meditation practice from the Kraken manual . . ."

"Is everything okay?" Joel asked, looking a little annoyed at being interrupted.

"Everything is fine," George replied. "We just need a moment."

They stood and walked to the side, only stopping when they were outside of hearing range.

"I did, too," George said, his gaze meeting hers. "My core . . ."

"Vibrated?"

"Yes . . ." He glanced back at the cult, seeing them already slipping back into a Zen state. "There is something about that form they use. It reacted with our meditation . . ."

"They said it was part of their doctrine, right?" Her eyes searched his. "What do we do . . . ?"

He knew the meaning behind Geraldine's question. Neither of them had given thought to the claim that the Cult of Carcinization's crab form was some sort of secret, but it had definitely reacted with his family's technique. It placed George in a moral dilemma.

He had been given access to the cult's secret, and it had reacted to his own family's secret—something he was under direct instruction not to share with anyone other than the Kraken bloodline or their immediate family. He glanced back at the cultists, his morality torn in two directions.

"Poseidon's backwash," he hissed. "What *do* we do?"

She chewed her lip, turning to ponder the cultists. Abruptly, she let out a light giggle.

"What's so funny?" he asked, unable to stop himself from smiling at her beautiful laugh.

"The manual literally tells us, George."

" . . . it does?"

Her returned glance was filled with meaning. "*What is better for your soul?*" she quoted.

"What is better for my soul . . ." he repeated, tasting its implications. He didn't have to consider long. "I love you, you know that?"

"I do, dear." She got up on her tiptoes and pecked him on the cheek. "I love you too."

George and Geraldine returned to the circle hand in hand, and when they took up their crab-like form once more, George cleared his throat.

Joel cracked an eye, raising an annoyed brow at them.

"I have something to share," George said, keeping his voice low. "It is something passed down by my family, and though I ask you to keep it a secret among your branch, it may help your meditation . . ."

If any of them had already taken steps on the path of ascension, they'd have felt a great curiosity radiating from the tree that towered above them, shielding them from the midday sun.

It was a *beautiful* day. The sun was high in the sky, my girlfriend was by my side, Corporal Claws was only being *a little* annoying, and two fillets of fish sizzled on the barbecue before me.

My barbecue, I thought, shimmying in glee.

"Are you feeling okay?" Maria asked, smirking at me.

"Feeling great, thanks! I was just trying to shake Claws free."

With an indignant chirp, an otter's head appeared before me, lowered from her position atop my head.

"Just kidding," I replied, scratching the soft fur behind her ear.

She chirped again, her eyes rolling into the back of her head as I scritched just the right place.

A wonderful aroma rose from the barbecue. The scents of fish and wood smoke made my stomach growl. I stared down at the cooking fillets, watching bubbles form around the tallow I'd oiled the surface with. Just as the meal was almost ready, I heard a new arrival scuttling across the front deck and heading our way.

Sergeant Snips slid into view, blowing a stream of happy bubbles that abruptly stopped when she caught sight of Claws smacking my forehead with both paws. Snips pointed an accusatory clacker her way, hissing a demand that she get down. Claws leaped to the ground in response, chirping back a downright rude insult.

They stared at each other for a long moment, everyone going silent as we watched the standoff.

Claws made the first move.

Lightning erupted, wreathing her body as she shot for Snips. Ready for the ambush, Snips batted her aside, sending Claws flying into the sand. Before she stopped moving, Snips was on her, blue chi oozing from her carapace and powering her passage. Claws retreated into the river in the blink of an eye, pausing only to give Snips the same rude gesture with one paw.

I smiled as Snips dove into the water after her.

"Never a dull day, huh?" Theo asked, walking into view.

"Never, mate," I agreed. "How did it go with the cultivators?"

"Good! I got through them faster than I thought, and we only had to imprison three more."

"Five in total?" Barry asked. "Those are better numbers than we expected."

"Agreed! Even better, it was the newer cultivators that subdued them. They took it upon themselves to help."

"See?" I asked, winking at Barry. "You don't need me in control! It's all in hand!"

Theo laughed. "I told you Fischer wouldn't go for it."

Barry sighed. "You were right, unfortunately."

I grinned at Theo. "Did you come to try some barbecue-cooked fish?"

"Well, I'd be lying if I said I wasn't interested, but I actually came to tell you something."

"Hold that thought." I removed the now-cooked fish from the heat with a pair of tongs. "It's ready."

I gazed around at my friends, seeing hunger reflected in their eyes. With practiced moves, I cut the fish into equal portions. Steam escaped as I broke the fillets apart, making an irresistible scent waft over my back deck. The outside of the fish was crispy and had turned golden brown, a stark contrast to the white flesh within. I grabbed a bowl of salt, sprinkling it liberally over the meal.

"I think we should try it with just salt at first. We have plenty of time to experiment with our other seasonings . . ." I picked up the board and held it out to everyone. "Help yourselves."

Maria strode to the end of the deck. "Snips! Claws!" she yelled, cupping her hands around her mouth.

Before she'd made it back to me, the animal pals in question were racing across the sand. Everyone took a piece of fish, and I waited for Claws and Snips to claim theirs before grabbing one myself. I threw Borks a piece, and as it sailed through the air, we all bit down.

My teeth crunched through the skin, easily parting the thin golden-brown layer. The flavor was subtle, yet undeniably changed from being cooked on a barbecue. The umami notes were deeper than only the salt should have made it, and I closed my eyes as the tastes washed over me. I lost track of my other senses, the delicate flesh melting in my mouth.

An *mmmm* escaped Roger's throat.

I stole a peek, smiling at his unveiled enjoyment of the seafood.

"Mmmm," Maria agreed, leaning her head against my shoulder.

I ate slowly, yet all too soon, the meal was finished. It definitely had stronger chi than regular shore fish, just as the barbecue's description said, but I was fairly sure the food hadn't been granted a boon.

"Roger," I said, "thank you for helping me build this beauty." I gestured emphatically at the barbecue. "I needed this in my life."

"I wish you'd made it sooner," Theo added.

"Me too, mate. Me too." I took a deep breath, willing the fish's flavor to linger. "All right, Theo. What did you come to tell me?"

"Oh. Right. When we went to the cells with the five that tried to escape or failed my questioning, the Osnans were awake."

"I guess one more adult job for the day won't hurt . . ." I waggled my eyebrows at Barry. "See? I can take part without being the actual leader of a cult."

"Church."

I waved a hand. "Semantics. Let's go have a chat with some noble pricks."

CHAPTER FOURTEEN

The Seed of Rebellion

With chi-filled food powering our stride, we made it back to New Tropica in no time at all.

The moment we caught sight of the village, I stopped walking and leaned down toward Maria. "Are you seeing this too?"

"Yeah. Why?"

"I was just wondering if the barbecue gave the food a hallucinogenic boon or something . . ."

"You're not imagining it, Fischer," Theo said, assessing the movement on the street. "You'd be excited too if you'd just been granted your freedom."

A dozen or so people were visible, all cultivators that we'd brought back from Gormona. Most were by themselves, but four stood in a loose circle, animatedly discussing something.

"What are they doing . . . ?" I asked.

"Crafting," he replied. "Or planning what to work on? They're doing whatever they please, basically."

"Huh. Neat."

We resumed our passage. As people caught sight of us, they waved, nodded, or outright stared. I returned every nod and wave. By the time we reached the next street—and the next wave of cultivators—I sighed. "My head might topple off if I nod back at everyone."

"You know you don't have to return them, right?" Maria asked, smiling up at me.

"Yeah, but that would just be downright rude."

"If I didn't know any better," Barry said, "I'd think they see you as some kind of god or something."

"Yeahhhh," I drawled. "I wonder how *that* happened."

Though I put on a show of being bothered, seeing them act under their own autonomy—and the purpose with which they moved—filled my metaphorical cup to the brim. I had brought them back to Tropica out of necessity; I couldn't live with leaving them behind and subjecting them to the crown's cruelty. I'd wanted them to find meaning here just as I and the rest of the congregation had, but I hadn't thought they'd find it so soon.

"It's amazing, isn't it?" I whispered to Maria.

"It is." She swept a strand of sun-bleached hair behind her ear. "And it's all thanks to you."

I made a so-so gesture. "Not *all* me. We might not have gone so far in the capital if it wasn't for Barry asking for our help."

She blew air from her lips.

I raised an eyebrow at her. "Did you just blow a raspberry at me?"

"I did," she replied. "And I'll do it every time you say something silly. Are you telling me you'd have gone to the capital and not come back with all the grove's cultivators? Our plan was to go and steal some passiona bushes. You'd have gotten there, knocked them all out and defeated Tom Osnan Sr., and then just left them there? I seriously doubt it."

"Okay, you might be right, but it would have been much harder to bring them back without Pelly and Bill airlifting them here."

"Yet you'd have worked it out." She squeezed my arm. "You always do."

"We always do," I corrected, resting my hand on hers.

I peered into the smithy as we walked past, seeing at least ten of the new arrivals within. Duncan was instructing them while Fergus watched on. The head smith gave me a grin and wave, making the rest of the class turn and either wave or blanch. One lady did both.

As we walked from view, Maria giggled, covering her mouth. "Everyone showing you so much veneration will take some getting used to."

"Right? I'm gonna have to embarrass myself often and flagrantly to make them lose a bit of respect for me. All this admiration is uncomfortable."

Each building we passed had at least a handful of cultivators. Ruby and Steven were instructing their group together, showing them around a massive loom. Roger, upon seeing a group hefting farming tools like weapons, split off and marched toward them, grumbling something about "foolish cultivators" under his breath. A man and woman were set up in the new tannery. I raised an eyebrow at Ellis, curious if he'd go instruct them, but he studiously ignored their presence, clearly wanting to witness the conversation to come.

A pair of shadows passed over me, and I craned my head back, smiling at the two forms gliding on unseen winds high above. "They're keeping watch?"

"Just so," Barry replied. "At least for the first couple of weeks, we'll need to rely on Bill and Pelly to ensure we have no runaways."

I waved up at them, and twin honks boomed back, loud enough to be heard from hundreds of meters above. With my head casting a smile up at them, we arrived at the prison. Someone yelled from inside. I shared a glance with Maria, then dashed in, following the words. As we passed the cells, I couldn't help but marvel at their construction.

Even calling it a prison felt like a lie.

Though each room was made of solid stone and had a barrier of bars blocking any escape, the walls opposite had reinforced windows, letting in the light of day and allowing the captives to see the forest beyond. Sconces sat between each window, magical flames burning within that cast an orange glow. Each cell had a plush bed, a table and chair, and plumbing, making the penitentiaries back on Earth look like gulags.

When we passed the first prisoner, I found him reading a book. It was the man who had tried to run, and I wondered why he'd attempted to flee. Did he have some Stockholm Syndrome going on, still holding allegiance to the crown despite their treatment of him and his fellow cultivators? Was it more simple, and the man had just been looking for a chance to betray us and escape? Noticing us, the man looked up, scowled, then spat to the side.

Maria and I raised our eyebrows at each other, but our amusement was cut short.

"How long did you know?" a voice demanded from up the hall. "Stop playing games!"

We sprinted up the corridor and around a corner. Keith stood with a reassuring hand on Trent's shoulder, who was shaking with rage as he stared into a cell.

"I don't know what you're talking about," the voice of Tom Osnan Jr. replied, holding as much condescension as usual.

Trent's fist lashed out, slamming into the bars. When it struck, chi rushed from his core and out of his extended limb. A gout of fire raged against the metal bars, but their power was absorbed and sucked into the streams of essence suffusing the entire building. If my awareness wasn't so advanced, I might have dashed forward and blocked the blow, but even if the bars weren't there to negate the attack, there was no killing intent in the flames that Trent unleashed. He was evidently pissed but wasn't trying to assassinate the troublesome Osnan.

Claws let out a trill I took to mean, *Ooo, very grumpy.*

Snips, however, wasn't so jovial. She flew forward on her jets of water-aspected chi, sliding to a stop between Trent and the prison. She held her claws open, ready to defend the captive cultivator if need be.

"It's okay, Snips," Keith said, crouching down so they were eye to eyestalk. "He won't hurt him."

Snips blew hesitant bubbles, unsure of her next move, so I intervened. "It's all good, Snips." I strode over and scooped her up into a hug. "You can trust Keith." I turned a grin Tom Osnan Jr.'s way. "Besides, it's not like this bloke is going anywhere."

The formerly secret cultivator's bluster was entirely gone, and he stared at me and Snips with open-mouthed panic.

"How are you doing, mate?" I asked Trent, hoping I could assuage some of his hatred.

When his eyes met mine, a war waged across his face. I struggled to comprehend the complicated emotions.

Before I could understand what had him so conflicted, Keith put a hand on Trent's shoulder again. "Come on, cousin. I think Fischer has some business here."

They both made to leave, but before they could get past, Ellis stepped in the way.

"One moment, if you please, Keith." He had his pen and paper ready. "What were you and Osnan talking about, Trent?"

"Not now, Ellis," Keith replied, taking a step past him.

But Ellis blocked his passage again. "I am afraid it is reaching the point that I must insist, Keith. I trust you, but your behavior since we returned has been troublesome . . ."

Unbridled fury crossed Keith's face, but as he looked down, I got the impression it wasn't entirely because of Ellis.

"Not. Now. Ellis." He clenched his jaw and took a deep breath, then spun on Theo. "I swear that neither of us have any intention of hurting Tropica, New Tropica, any of you, or your interests. We also have no intention of leaving."

"True," Theo replied, cocking his head slightly. "I didn't think you did, though, Keith . . ."

"Trent." Keith nudged his cousin softly in the side. "Tell them."

Trent repeated the same message, his eyes somewhat distant.

It was the first time I'd had an up-close look at Trent since he'd awakened. He had changed dramatically. His face, once looking like a thrice-stubbed toe, was now handsome. A defined jaw and severe eyes stared unrepentantly, darting between Ellis and Theo. His voice, too, had altered. I didn't even recognize it when I heard it from around the corner earlier. Before, it had been nasally. Petulant. Now, it was deep and commanding, as if he expected the world itself to bend before him.

"Also true," Theo replied, giving Ellis a meaningful look. "I think it's best that we let our friend pass."

"*Friends*," Keith stressed, stepping past Ellis and giving us a challenging glance.

"Right." Theo nodded. "Friends."

Trent didn't reply, looking at the ground as he followed Keith down the corridor.

"Hey!" I called. "Prince!"

Trent spun, my raised voice having pulled him from his thoughts.

I grinned at him. "I can't imagine what you're going through. If you ever want a relaxing afternoon, feel free to come for a fish. No questions asked—just the ocean, fresh air, and a good time."

His brow furrowed, but from behind Trent, Keith gave me a small smile, nodding his thanks.

"Sure . . ." Trent replied, his voice once more catching me off guard with its timbre.

The moment they rounded the corner, I spun on Tom Osnan Jr. An odd combination of fear and sheer incredulity covered his face.

"What *are* you . . . ?" he asked.

"I'm your friendly neighborhood fisherman, here to make friends, pat cute animals, and have a good time."

Corporal Claws leaped up to my shoulder, rubbing her cheek against mine as she let out a loving coo.

Tom Osnan Jr's eyes flew wide as she came into view, no doubt recalling the way she'd slammed into his wife and turned her into an abstract windmill. "*You!*"

I suspected he'd have reached for his chi and attacked us if he had the ability to. Fortunately for all of us, the bars wouldn't allow it.

"So, Tom. Can I call you Tom? Good. Anyway, here's the thing—I know you're kind of an evil prick, but if you have a change of heart and want to become one of us, I'm sure we can arrange to—" I cut off as Tom gathered chi and slammed his fist into the ground. I raised an eyebrow, curious if he was trying to attack us anyway, but then the vines sprouted.

They flew from him, writhing over the floor and creating a wall between himself and us.

"Huh . . ." I said. "I think he found a neat little loophole, Barry."

Barry shrugged again. "He's still stuck in there; we just can't see him. Want to talk to his wife instead?"

I bellowed a laugh. "Sure. Assuming she doesn't do the same thing."

We walked seven cells down the hall, and when we reached her, she was already staring a hate-filled gaze our way.

"Nice to meet you, Lady Osnan, I'm—"

"Leave me be."

"What's the matter? Do you not have some ability to wall yourself off like your *cowardly husband?*" I projected the last two words, making sure they made it through the vines Tom had erected. "If you ask me, it was pretty messed up of him to leave you alone to deal with our questioning."

Her mouth bunched at the corners for a moment, quickly replaced by bureaucratic stillness. "My husband is a brave and trusting man. He knows I'll stand strong, no matter what despicable methods of torture you use." She turned to meet my eyes in an attempt to show an unyielding front.

Theo snorted, shattering the facade. "Lie. You think he's a coward too."

"Yeah," I added. "I could tell that, and I'm not even a crown auditor."

"Crown auditor . . . ?" she asked, her eyes widening.

"*Former* crown auditor," Theo corrected.

"Traitor!" She moved in a blur, striking out at the bars with an honestly impressive kick. Her strike was no match for the chi-enhanced metal.

I shook my head. "I don't suppose you'll answer some questions for us?"

After a few heaving breaths, she straightened her clothes, turned on her heel, and strode to sit at a small chair beside a writing desk. "No."

"Truth." Theo shrugged. "It was worth a shot, I guess."

"Well, our offer stands for you too, Lady Osnan." I turned to leave. "If you want to live free, you just need to decide to be one of us. Theo will obviously vet your answer, but—"

"I would *never* betray the crown. I—" She abruptly cut off, her eyes widening on Theo. Before she could continue, she swiveled her chair to face the far wall.

As we walked away from the captives, Theo smirked at me. "Partial truth."

"Ooooooh," Maria said. "*Spicy.*"

Ellis stopped mid-step, hunching to scratch notes in his notepad.

I grinned. "Surprising, to be honest. She was all too keen on attacking us when she thought we were regular humans. She even tried to kick Borks!"

I leaned down to rub his head, the golden-retriever-shaped hellhound appearing not at all bothered by my mention of it. I took a deep breath as we stepped out onto the sunny street. "Now that we've planted the seed of rebellion in their minds, what are you guys gonna get up to?"

"I suppose I will go help those fledgling leatherworkers," Ellis replied, still scribbling as he wandered away.

"Barry and I have some things to attend to." Theo patted Barry on the back. "Let's go, yeah?"

Claws saluted, kissed Maria and me on the cheek, and leaped on Borks's back. She stood proud and tall, puffing her chest out like she was riding a horse into battle as she directed him to follow Barry.

"Godspeed, you little weirdo," I said, causing her to cast a needle-sharp grin my way.

"So." I pursed my lips as I looked at Maria and Sergeant Snips. "Can I take it you two are . . ." I looked around. "Wait, where's Cinnamon?"

Movement caught my attention to my right, and I turned just in time to see Pelly swoop down and collect the miscreant bunny. She gave me a wink as Pelly flapped her wings and returned to the sky.

I shook my head. "They're all as weird as each other."

"I'm sorry, did you just say *they're* weird?" Maria asked.

"All right, you've got a point there. We're all as weird as each other. Better?"

"Much."

"Where was I? Oh yeah—are you two free?"

Snips nodded up and down, blowing happy little bubbles.

"Hmmm," Maria said. "I *suppose* I could spend some time with you . . ."

"Really? You would grace this lowly one with your presence?" I bowed at the waist and pressed my fists together. "This one thanks you, elder sister."

"Please never say that again."

"You started it," I replied, straightening.

"Truce, then." She wove her fingers with mine. "What did you have planned?"

"I want to go see some old friends." I cast my gaze toward the forest to the north. "I'm sure they've been busy little bees since I last saw them . . ."

CHAPTER FIFTEEN

Hivemind

For the first time in the last twenty-four hours, we moved leisurely. Our fight, flight, and general tomfoolery within Gormona had been adrenaline pumping and surprisingly enjoyable. But now that I was walking hand in hand with Maria and had a genial crab riding my shoulder, I was reminded of what I truly enjoyed in life. The canopy above filtered out most of the sun's light, and as I looked up, a gust blew, making the leaves and branches dance languidly.

When we reached the river, we leaped right over it, landing on the bank upstream from my home. We walked in comfortable silence, all content with watching and listening to the world around us. As we drew closer to Lemon's clearing, an unmistakable buzz washed over the grass, calling us forward.

"Is it just me," Maria said, "or is that louder than usual?"

I cocked my head, letting my hearing extend past the self-imposed suppression I enacted by default.

"Huh . . . it certainly sounds louder."

Snips nodded along, an inquisitive bubble floating away from her cute little mouth.

A blanket of movement met us the moment we entered Lemon's original clearing. There were definitely more bees than usual. They practically swarmed the lemon trees. Individually, they were only tiny insects, barely noticeable among the shifting leaves. Together, they were an absolute sea of chaos, churning in every direction at the same time.

Distracted as we were by the sight, Maria didn't notice a thin root extending from the ground behind her. Lieutenant Colonel Lemony Thicket whacked her on the bum, making her jump.

"Lemon! You scared me!"

Lemon's tree swayed with laughter.

"I thought you were in the new grove . . ." Maria bit the inside of her lip as she stared up at the blue trunk. "Are you here right now or . . . ?"

Both, the wind seemed to whisper as it flowed past Lemon's leaves.

I sent my awareness down into the ground, feeling what could only be described as a tunnel of chi running under our feet. It sped south toward New Tropica in one direction and northeast in the other, connecting her with the giant tree that had popped up overnight.

"You're amazing, Lemon," Maria said, marching forward and wrapping her trunk in a hug.

I joined her, one hand resting on Maria's back and one on Lemon's bark. Even Snips took part, patting Lemon and blowing bubbles of praise. Meanwhile, the bees continued visiting flowers above us, unaware of anything other than their purpose. I looked up, tracking an insect's passage as it left the tree closest to us and flew off into the forest.

Its legs were laden with yellow pollen, and as it moved farther and farther away, I pursed my lips. "Where is that bee going . . . ?"

Following my gaze, Maria and Snips tracked the subject of my wonder.

"Uhhh . . . back to the hive?" Maria flicked me lightly on the arm. "Are you feeling okay?"

"Yeah, but that's not the direction of the hive . . ."

I followed the bee's lumbering flight as it headed west toward the mountains. As we got farther away, other insects joined it, heading in the same direction. Finally, we found their destination. They flew into a deformed knot at the base of an ancient tree, crawling down through a bee-sized entrance and out of sight.

Snips scuttled forward slowly, her entire carapace cocking from side to side as she watched more of them disappear into the hive.

"I guess we know why there are more bees," I whispered to Maria. "Another hive has found the clearing."

"At least one more," she corrected. "There were *a lot* of them."

Snips continued creeping up to the hive. A bee in the entrance made an odd buzz with its wings as she leaned in close and peered into the hole.

"Umm, Snips. You might be a bit—"

A few bees emerged, repeating the same buzz as the first. Within a few breaths, they were streaming from the hive. Snips watched them curiously, her contemplation only stopping when one tried to sting her sturdy carapace. She retreated a step, her movement drawing the rest toward her.

"Time to go!" I yelled, trying not to grin at the look of betrayal on Snips's face.

We jogged back to the clearing, easily outpacing the riled-up insects. "Did you know there were more bee hives visiting, Lemon?"

Yes, her pulse of chi told me, tinged with amusement.

"Do you know how many hives there are?"

She sprung a root from the ground and grew four strands of fiber from it. One of them was shorter than the others.

"Three . . . and a half?"

Yes. She nodded.

"Lemon . . ." Maria smirked at her. "How is there half a hive?"

Rather than respond directly, she shimmied her canopy in delight, making passing bees avoid her general vicinity.

Maria narrowed her eyes, but I just laughed. "Looks like we're gonna have to find out on our own. Come on." I gestured for Snips and Maria to follow as I strode from the clearing. "We'll see you soon, Lemon!"

Her shimmying only increased as we left, making me wonder why a half hive had brought her so much enjoyment. But I quickly forgot all about it. Twin rivers of bees flowed to and fro above us, those heading home covered in pollen, the others looking eager and ready to harvest.

As always, Sergeant Snips was mystified by the little creatures.

At one particularly crowded spot, she froze, simply watching their movement and blowing bubbles of awe. It reminded me of when we'd originally encountered the bee hive all those months ago, just after arriving in Tropica. Snips had been awakened for a matter of days at the time, and I'd never have guessed I'd grow to love her as much as I did. Since then, she'd become an irreplaceable part of my life, and I couldn't imagine Tropica without her.

"What's up?" Maria asked, her eyes searching mine.

"Just remembering the first time Sergeant Snips and I found the hive. Even then, she was transfixed by them."

Snips nodded, fervently agreeing with a slew of bubbles.

As we continued following the bees, Snips never once tore her gaze from them. There was an honestly ridiculous number of insects—so many that, if I didn't know better, I might have assumed all the pollinators in the clearing were from Queen Bee's hive. When we reached the tree they called home, I paused, raising an eyebrow.

"That's . . . different," Maria said, sounding just as curious.

"Looks like Queen Bee and Bumblebro have been busy . . ."

The hive had been extended.

Where it previously had a single hole for the denizens to come and go from, a patchwork of sticks had been glued together with a yellow substance. Multiple entrances led into the additional construction, letting the sea of bees enter freely. I crept around the side of the bulbous shape, lightly poking some of the yellow stuff holding it together. It was as hard as stone and not at all sticky to the touch.

"Weird . . ." I said, returning to Maria. "I'd guess it was Bumblebro . . . ? I'm not sure a queen bee could make that stuff, awakened or not."

Remembering my purpose in coming here, I approached the hive Bumblebro called home. I could have sworn I saw a pair of compound eyes staring out at me from within, but they dashed away, hiding from sight.

I hope he's not still pissed off from the last time I was here.

"Bumblebro . . ." I softly called. "Are you in there?"

No reply came.

"I'm sorry for what happened last time," I continued. "I should have knocked. It was super rude of me, and I hope you can forgive me for being such a goof."

Again, there was no answer.

"I could have sworn I saw him peeping from inside," Maria whispered.

"I saw that too . . ."

A soft hum came from within, sounding almost hesitant.

Snips jumped down from my arms and crawled forward. She tilted her body, peering inside from different angles. Another hum came from the box, and Bumblebro appeared in the entrance, only his head visible. I couldn't verbalize it if anyone asked how I knew, but his little face seemed troubled.

"Bumblebro?" I asked, crouching down. "Is everything okay, buddy?"

He took a long moment to respond, eventually letting out a morose buzz, his head low like I was going to hit him.

"What's going on, my man? Is everything okay? Where's Queen Bee?"

With his head still lowered, he crawled outside.

I took a knee, looking at him closely. "Mate. What is it? You're starting to worry me."

He made a tone with his wings that meant *come*, which confused the hell out of me until someone else appeared in the entrance. Queen Bee, looking just as brow beaten, emerged. She came to a stop beside Bumblebro, somehow getting even lower than he was.

"That's it!" I threw my hands high. "What the frack is going on? You guys are gonna give me a panic attack!"

They kowtowed—*actually kowtowed*—pressing their foreheads to the floor.

"Look, if you did something bad, please just tell me. I promise I won't get mad unless you hurt someone. Wait, you didn't sting anyone, did you?"

No! they both buzzed.

"Okay. Good." I sighed. "Tell me what it is, then."

They looked at each other, paused, then both made the same tone Bumblebro had earlier.

Come . . .

Confusion shattered my frustration, and I looked around, waiting for some sort of creature that had gotten into their honey to come barreling through the forest. Instead, another buzz came from within the hive.

"Wait . . ." Maria said. "Don't tell me . . ."

"What?" I asked, not understanding.

Lacking any of Queen Bee's and Bumblebro's humility, another bee zipped outside. It hovered before me, giving me a single nod and waving a forelimb in greeting.

"Er . . . hello?"

I inspected the new arrival.

It had a bulbous body, thicker around than that of a regular honeybee. Its stripes were a deep black and bright yellow, making it stand out against the verdant green forest. Unlike Bumblebro and whatever species he had originally been, a sharp stinger protruded from the tip of its abdomen.

His abdomen, I realized. *It's a bloke bee.*

His jaws were closer to a bumblebee's, the chompers looking designed to chew through even the hardest of woods.

Given his features, the bee's lineage was immediately clear.

"Guys! You had a kid! I—"

Another buzz came from within the hive, cutting me off. It wasn't the quiet drone of a single bee; it was a cacophony of wings, all beating with joy as they headed toward the hive's entrance. In a blurred stream moving faster than any unawakened creature could muster, the rest of the hive emerged. One by one, they came to fly beside their brothers.

Each of them nodded and waved, their procession growing so fast that I just left my hand raised in an eternal greeting. The last of them finally joined the others, hovering on the spot in a cloud of yellow and black. Though there were so many of them, they were completely silent, the beats of their cute little wings not making a sound even to my enhanced ears.

"You're . . . all awakened?"

The cloud nodded, every single one of the dozens of bees bobbing up and down.

"No way . . ." Maria said.

I turned toward Bumblebro and Queen Bee with a wide smile on my face. Instead of congratulating them, however, I narrowed my eyes at their positions. They were still kowtowing, pressing their entire bodies as low as they could.

Sorry, they buzzed. *Sorry. Sorry. Sorry.*

"Why . . . ?"

Bumblebro darted up toward me, coming to hover before my face. Showing a complete disregard for my understanding of insectoid anatomy, a tear swelled beneath one of his compound eyes.

Orders, he buzzed. *I disobeyed.*

"Huh? What orders?"

He made a complicated series of tones that I had to listen to thrice before understanding.

"Oooh! My order to not make more awakened bees!" I raised my hand in realization, and he flinched away, fearing I'd strike him down. Queen Bee threw herself at my feet, making a deep tone that I was pretty sure meant, *Take me instead.*

"You . . . thought I'd be mad at you for having little bee babies?"

Yes, he buzzed.

Sorry, she added.

Sorry, their children echoed, their drone so loud that I could feel it in my chest.

All I could do was blink at them for a long moment. A low squeak came from beside me, drawing all of our attention. Sergeant Snips squealed like a boiling-over kettle, and with our gazes on her, she completely lost it. Her body collapsed to the ground as laughter hissed and bubbled from her. Queen Bee took umbrage and made a warning tone with her wings. Snips paused for a moment before laughing even harder, her legs spasming out to the side uncontrollably.

Maria shook her head, smirking at the misunderstanding.

I bent and picked up Queen Bee, placing her on my hand beside Bumblebro. "I'm not upset at either of you, and you're not in trouble."

Sorry, Bumblebro started to buzz, but stopped. His eyes darted up, staring into mine.

I laughed at the confusion coloring his face. "You heard me, you silly little goose. How could I be mad?"

The two lovers stared up at me hesitantly, shocked into stillness by my words.

Then, as one, the tension left their bodies. They released great sighs, which I'm pretty sure was just a copied movement because of their distinct lack of lungs. As both of them vibrated with sheer relief, their literal army of children joined in, the happy tones infectious and making my core sing.

Maria leaned in close to the cloud of bees, her face beaming as she took them in. "Wow. You guys are *super* cute!"

They danced in response, making her lilting giggle roll over our surroundings. I thought Maria's appreciation of them would be unmatched, but Snips immediately proved me wrong. The adorable crustacean circled them, her lone eye sparkling in the light filtering from above. Maria picked her up, holding her out so she could get a closer look. They nodded in greeting, and Bumblebro let out a sharp buzz that I took to mean *superior*, causing them to nod again before giving her a synchronized salute.

She returned it, preening under their attention.

"Everyone, this is Snips. Snips, this is . . ." I tilted my head to the side. "Er . . . do they have names, Bumblebro?"

No, he buzzed.

"Hmm. It's gonna take me forever to think of names for you all. Any ideas, Maria? I'm—"

No, they interrupted, loud enough for the sound to reverberate in my chest.

"Huh?" Maria asked. "What do you mean, *no?*"

"You . . . don't want individual names?"

They buzzed so hard in the affirmative that I thought they might spontaneously combust.

"Huh. Well, if that's what you want. I'll have to think on it, though. A name is even more important if it applies to all of you!"

Yes, they agreed happily.

"Perfect. I'll let you know the moment I decide. Until then . . ." I glanced at the construction added onto the regular honeybee hive. "Did you guys make that?"

When they confirmed it, I smiled. "Do you guys make honey?"

Bumblebro and Queen Bee shook their heads, making my grin spread even wider.

"Well, if you're open to suggestions, I might have the perfect job for you guys . . ."

They let out a curious buzz, and I launched right into my sales pitch.

CHAPTER SIXTEEN

Fashion

Maria's hand was once more in mine as we strode through the lush forest. She rested a watermelon-sized rock atop her other hand that was so big I'd almost call it a boulder. Bumblebro and Queen Bee sat on my shoulder, their wings twitching nervously. I reached up and patted the top of their heads with a finger, trying to reassure them.

"Sure you don't want me to carry that?" I asked Maria, pointing at the mass of stone she carried.

"Are you calling me weak, Fischer?"

I gave her some audacious side-eye, only for her to wiggle her eyebrows back and shoulder-press the rock with her enhanced muscles.

"Point taken," I replied.

Shooting a glance back at Snips and her layer of shifting clothes, I recalled my conversation with Bumblebro and Queen Bee's children before we'd left. Because I'd mentioned their renovation of the honeybee's hive, they'd originally thought I wanted them to build some things for New Tropica. While they could surely help on that front in the future, I'd had something else in mind. Thankfully, they'd been happy to go along with my plans—ecstatic, even. It had been at least a quarter hour since they'd agreed, and they still buzzed their wings in excitement, making a pleasant hum wash over the surrounding trees.

When we arrived back at New Tropica, the cultivators who noticed us showed the same level of respect they had earlier. This time, though, their gazes, one and all, drifted toward Sergeant Snips. She walked with her carapace held high, pride radiating from her. Eyebrows rose, muttered conversation sprung up, and all eyes remained mostly pinned to Snips, completely fixated on my guard crab and her enthralling outfit.

Extending my senses, I found Barry.

"This way, guys," I said, turning left at the main crossroads and striding for the new headquarters.

As we entered, Theo and Barry turned my way. Borks, who was sleeping beneath an artifact, lifted his head, yawned, wagged his tail, and made to relax again. But then he saw Snips. He did a double take, his ears going alert as he stared at her noisy outfit.

"Oh, hello," Barry said, smiling at us. "I thought you'd be off fishing by now. To what do we owe the . . ." He trailed off, his forehead creasing as he caught sight of Snips.

"Snips . . ." Theo pursed his lips for a long moment before continuing. "Are you aware that you're wearing *bees*?"

She blew affirmative bubbles, bobbing her head happily.

Said bees, who'd been churning over one another atop their crabby steed since we left their hive, finally stilled. They turned their heads toward Barry and Theo, moving with perfect synchronization as they nodded and buzzed their wings in greeting.

"*Bees*?" I demanded, adopting the air of an indignant noble. "Not mere *bees*, my well-intentioned yet misinformed friend! These humble insects are the progeny of one Bumblebro!"

He puffed up on my shoulder, unable to hide his satisfaction with my words.

"And that's not all!" I continued. "Their blood— Wait, do insects have blood?" I shook my head. "Their lineage is so regal, so powerful, that I find my thoughts addled! I ask that you brace yourselves, dear friends! When I reveal their mother, you might need to pick up your jaws from the floor! In your wildest dreams, you would never guess—"

"So Queen Bee and Bumblebro had kids, huh?" Theo asked, projecting his voice to cut me off.

"Congratulations," Barry said, smiling at Bumblebro and Queen Bee as they took flight from my shoulder. "Are they all awakened . . . ?" Barry's chi spread out, and when it reached the army of bees Snips was currently wearing as a hat, his eyes flew wide. "They *are*! Amazing . . ."

I'd begun scowling when my monologue was *rudely* interrupted, and it had only deepened as they continued ignoring me.

"They feel strong for their size. How powerful are they?" Theo asked. "Ellis is going to absolutely lose his—"

"Hey!" I yelled, hamming up my petulance. "I was mid-diatribe, you devious disciples!"

Barry snorted, giving me a smirk. "Disciples would imply that you were the leader of this church. Are you sure about that terminology?"

"Psh!" I waved both hands dismissively. "I'm busy improving my dao. Consider yourself lucky that I haven't left for some closed-door cultivation."

"Okay," Barry replied. "You lost me."

I grinned. "Good. Anyway, I brought them here for introductions, but they can also perform an important role. I was thinking—"

"Do they have names?" Theo interrupted, yelling over me and pointedly looking at Barry.

"Yeah!" Barry boomed, also ignoring me as he stared at the bees. "Do you have names?"

"See what I have to deal with, Maria?" I asked, sighing and shaking my head. "These lowly villagers vex me intentionally. *Me*, of all people."

Her eyes danced with amusement as she faced Theo and Barry. "They don't have names yet!" she yelled. "They said they wanted to be named together, so we'll have to—"

"They're going to be the scouts that protect our shores!" I bellowed, infusing my words with chi.

Evidently, I had released a little too much.

A pulse of pressure shot from me, slamming into the walls and sending any loose objects in the headquarters flying. Maria stumbled to the side, gripping her rock with both hands so she didn't drop it. Bumblebro and Queen Bee shot back a full foot, the former catching the latter on his back before they both stabilized.

When the walls finally stopped vibrating, I grimaced. "Too much?"

"Note to self," Theo said, opening his jaw wide and rubbing an ear. "Keep the messing with Fischer to a minimum."

Barry, rather than being bothered by my whoopsie, faced the bees atop Snips's head. "I can see their number being a boon for intel, but are they strong enough to protect against cultivators . . . ?"

"Thanks for asking! If you'll follow us outside . . ."

They exchanged a look as we led them out, coming to a stop in the middle of the street.

I grinned at Maria. "When you're ready."

She shot me a beautiful smile and cocked her arm back, the boulder resting atop her open palm. She took a deep breath, then absolutely launched the rock into the sky as she exhaled. It sailed to the west, spinning slowly in the wind. Power swelled from the bees, and a susurration of buzzes sprang to life. I'd already assessed their individual power when we were back in the forest, and I enjoyed Barry and Theo's similarly impressed looks. The bees took off as a blur, impossible for anyone but a cultivator to see. The first reached the boulder in less than a second, and when he struck the spherical stone, it shattered. Hundreds of stone pieces were ejected from the impact, sailing in every direction.

Before they could go more than a few meters, the rest of the bees struck.

Those rocks that survived the first volley were swiftly dealt with when the yellow-and-black attackers zipped back around and shot through them. Within the space of a breath, anything larger than a pebble was obliterated. A cloud of dust and debris bloomed in the western sky, still spreading out as the bees returned. They landed on Snips's carapace, all looking rather chuffed with themselves and wiggling into position.

Theo whistled. "Yeah. That should do . . ."

I nodded. "Even if they couldn't stand toe to toe with a cultivator, they're fast and agile. They could easily escape and warn us that someone has fled."

Suddenly, a rhythmic tapping drew all of our attention. I whirled, facing the street it was coming from. I extended my awareness, intent on discovering the source, but the cause of the sound came sprinting around the corner a moment later. Ellis's feet never stopped moving, even as he skidded around the corner like a panicked cat on polished tiles.

"Who are they?" he screamed, his eyes pinned on mine.

His arms and knees pumped as he sprinted for me at full speed. I had to step aside at the last moment, lest he barrel into me and knock me down.

I grabbed his arm, swinging him around and bringing him to a stop. "Who are—"

"The scouts!" he yelled, not even letting me finish my sentence. "Who are the scouts?"

My brain short-circuited for a moment, but then I realized he was talking about the bees. He must have heard me when I'd projected my chi earlier, and as I considered him, his eyes only grew more intense. Ellis had always been thirsty for knowledge, but of late, he'd seemed almost manic in his information gathering. He visibly fought down the urge to demand an answer again, shivering as he stared at me.

"Ellis . . . are you all right, mate?" I asked, holding his shoulders. "You seem . . ."

"Batshit crazy?" Maria suggested, quirking an eyebrow at the former archivist's shaking form.

I laughed. "I was going to say intense, but that's not far off."

"What? I am fine." He took a steadying breath, his composure seeming to return. "I just wish to learn who the scouts are. Has someone else ascended?"

"Uh, kind of?" I pointed at Snips and the carpet of bees lining her carapace. "It's no big deal. Bumblebro and Queen Bee had a bunch of children. They're all spirit beasts or whatever."

"They're *what*?" Ellis dashed over to them and leaned in close. "Remarkable . . ." He removed his pad and began scribbling notes, muttering something under his breath about their features.

"For what it's worth," Theo said, "Ellis has always been so . . . passionate. It's likely just the fact that he's learning secrets he's dreamed about his entire life that has him being even more, er, *him*."

"I can hear you," Ellis replied, not looking up from his note-taking. "But I agree. You are the *batshit-crazy* ones, as Maria so eloquently put it, for not being excited about everything we are learning." He turned his back to us, adding a physical element to his verbal dismissal. "Perhaps you should reassess how blessed we are."

I raised a finger and opened my mouth to reply but came up short. "Huh. He might have a point . . ."

Bumblebro nodded sagely, landing on my shoulder and giving me a reassuring pat.

"Ah well." I shrugged at Barry. "That's all I really wanted to show you guys. Is it okay to leave the planning in your hands?"

"Absolutely."

"Wonderful. Snips, are you gonna stay with our new bee pals or come with me and Maria?"

She blew questioning bubbles.

"Agreed," Maria said, looking at me in confusion. "Where are we going?"

"Fishing, of course. I thought we could invite a new friend to try out our heretical lifestyle . . ."

Snips nodded fervently, shaking some of the bees loose.

"Oh! I'm in!" Maria said. "Who are we inviting, though? I'm not sure if you've looked around recently, but we have *a lot* of new friends."

"Deklan." I gave her a wide grin before turning toward Barry. "Do you know where he is?"

"Why am I not surprised?" Barry shook his head with a smile. "Last I saw him, he was at the smithy."

"Perfect. Catch you guys later."

The sound of Borks's claws scrabbling on the stones came from the headquarters, having somehow slept through the demonstration but never one to miss out on a little fishing. Bumblebro and Queen Bee chose to come along too, riding on my shoulder.

With Maria's hand in mine and a handful of my animal pals along for the ride, we headed off toward the smithy.

CHAPTER SEVENTEEN

Oh Baby, a Triple

When the sand beneath my feet turned to rocky headland, I took a deep breath of the salt-filled air. I had all the things I could need: an armful of rods, a smattering of friends with me, and Maria. As a stiff breeze blew past, Bumblebro and Queen Bee crawled down from my shoulder to take refuge in my pocket. Their cute little heads poked out, gazing at the surrounding landscape in the afternoon light.

Deklan, Maria, Snips, and Borks followed right behind me. I stole a glance at Deklan. As with every other time we'd interacted, the man was a walking contradiction. When I'd invited him to come fishing, he seemed excited. Filled with anticipation. He'd grown up in Gormona, so he'd been well and truly indoctrinated to believe that anything water related was going against the gods, yet that didn't deter him.

But then I'd mentioned that I also invited the crown prince to come fishing.

A dark cloud had crossed Deklan's face, and even now he remained somber, simply staring at the ground as we crossed the slick rocks. I shared a glance with Maria, both of us subtly wincing at my misstep. Refocusing, I took a deep breath, tasting the salty air once more.

If he's anything like me, I thought, *a little fishing will do wonders for his worries.*

As we stepped onto the section of rock wall that was System generated, I set down my armful of rods. Maria placed the tackle box beside them, squeezing my arm before stepping back.

"Okay," I said, smiling at Deklan. "I think it's best we start with the basics, so I'll show you how to tie the knots. Would you mind catching us some bait, Maria?"

"Of course!" She flicked open the tackle box and removed a sabiki rig, not wasting a moment in tying it to her rod. "One eel coming right up—hopefully a stinky one."

As she walked over to the side of the rock wall and cast out, I ran Deklan through making a paternoster rig. His hands were rough and calloused despite his often lackadaisical nature, reflective of the training he'd done as a member of the capital's guard forces, and though he wasn't yet a cultivator, he emulated the knot expertly on the first attempt.

"How does it look?" he asked, holding it up.

"Perfect, mate. Now all we need is some bait."

"Working on it!" Maria called, staring calmly at the water.

I watched her for a long moment, lost in the way her hair swayed in the soft breeze, but then I felt someone approaching.

I recognized the chi signature, and as I turned Keith's way, I spotted the man walking beside him. Trent, the crown prince of Gormona, had a pensive expression.

"G'day, guys!" I said, standing. "Deklan, you've met Keith and Trent?"

"Trent . . . ?" Deklan asked, his eyes narrowing. "Fischer . . ." He leaned in close, whispering, "That's the Trent you were talking about? He's not the prince . . ."

I rubbed the back of my head. "Er, they can hear you, mate. Cultivator hearing and all that. It's a long story, but that's *definitely* the prince."

Deklan's frown deepened. "I don't mean to offend, but I'd recognize him. I've seen him countless—"

"Hello, Deklan," Trent replied, the sadness in his eyes betraying the fake smile he gave. "You once told me that only my opinion of myself mattered, and that I should ignore my family's insults. I believe I threw a jug of wine and a half-eaten pastry at you for your kindness."

Deklan froze. "It . . . *what?*" His eyes widened as he looked Trent over. "It's . . . really you?"

"It is. I'm sorry for how I treated you previously. It . . ." He clenched his jaw, a hint of fire entering his eyes. "I wasn't myself."

"Uh, I mean . . . that's . . . *okay?*" Deklan asked, looking at me, then back to Trent, clearly flummoxed. "I'm surprised you remember me . . ."

"Cultivator," Trent replied, pointing at his chest. "I remember pretty much everything, unfortunately."

A silence stretched between us, and I let it linger for a moment, making sure they weren't going to continue. Borks slid over and licked my leg, wagging his tail up at me and calming my racing mind.

"Okay," I said, patting Borks's head and giving him a smile. "Now that everyone has been reintroduced, do you need my help setting up?"

"No," Keith replied, "I've got it. Trent only wants to watch for now."

"No worries! I brought all the spare rods in case you change your mind. I might go help Deklan cast out, then."

Keith nodded at me and started setting up his rod. I led Deklan down the stone walkway, smiling at Snips, who had crawled across the rocks and was resting in the tidal zone, blowing happy little bubbles. As we approached Maria, her rod's tip twitched. She braced her body, and the moment the fish bit down on her hook, she struck. Pulling up softly, she set the hook and kept tension on the line. She wound the reel in slowly, seeing if any more fish would take the bait.

Her patience and technique were rewarded.

Something much larger struck, making the rod bend down under its weight. Maria's face lit up and a gust of wind blew past her, making her hair sweep back in a chaotic tangle. She paid no mind to the strands whipping around her face as she reeled the line in, grinning at the churning water beneath her. We came to a stop beside her, both Deklan and I leaning forward to try and catch sight of what she'd hooked.

A flash of silver shone, reflecting the sunlight as the bait fish tried to escape. Maria lifted it out of the water, and when I saw what was attached to the bottom hook of her rig, I beamed a grin. I glanced at Deklan, whose face was showing sheer confusion, tinged with a little disgust.

"What. Is. *That?*" he demanded, gesturing with both hands.

Maria and I both cackled, our amusement mixing with excitement.

"A monkeyface eel of the pungent variety," Maria replied. "If you think it looks bad, wait until you smell it."

As if responding to her comment, the universe sent another gust of wind our way, bringing with it the eel's horrific scent.

"Philyra's blessed odors," he swore, covering his mouth. "That's something."

I let out a laugh as I gazed at the eel, letting it draw my eyes in.

Pungent Monkeyface Eel
Rare
Found in the brackish waters of the Kallis Realm, this mature variation of the Common Eel has high oil content and a pungent scent, making it unpalatable food but excellent bait.

I shook my head, clearing my vision. Maria lobbed the juvenile shore fish she'd hooked, and the small creature landed back in the water with a soft splash. She grabbed a spike from her hip and moved to dispatch the eel, but Snips scuttled forward, hissing to wait. My trusty crab was on it in an instant. Her clacker slammed down, making the eel go immediately still. Using meticulous bursts of her chi, she sliced it into hook-sized chunks.

Both my eyebrows flew high. "Dang, Snips. Your control is getting better . . ."

She shimmied under the praise, blowing a stream of content bubbles. I bent to pat her head, and she leaned into my touch, making me scratch her even harder. When the scritches were complete, she returned to the waterline, settling in between two rocks and closing her eye as a small wave washed over her.

"That's our bait sorted," I said. "Ready for your first taste of fishing, Deklan?"

"Yeah . . ." He nodded, his lips slightly pursed as he stared at Snips. "I can't believe you have so many spirit beasts."

"Right? I'm a lucky bloke." I reached up into my pocket and softly patted the heads of the two insects there. Bumblebro and Queen Bee buzzed their wings happily, returning my affection.

I bent and picked up a chunk of fish, then slipped my hook through it, showing Deklan the best way to present the bait. He mimicked my movement expertly, sliding his bait just as I had.

"Well done. Let's get these lines in the water."

I led him down the rock wall, and when we reached the end of the walkway, I stood tall, assessing the ocean's movement. It seemed the tide was coming in, so I faced north, not wanting the lines to get dragged toward the river mouth.

"Flick your reel over like this, mate, then hold your finger to the line so it stays taut and doesn't unwind."

Deklan watched my hands, doing just as I did.

"Perfect," I continued. "Cock the rod back, and when you flick it forward, take your finger off the line."

I sent my sinker and bait flying at a forty-five degree angle. It made a quiet plop when it hit the water a few moments later, sending a splash of water up that reflected the afternoon light. I wound the reel in a few times so my line was taut, then rested a finger on it, waiting for a bite.

"Think you can do that, mate?" I asked. "I cast to the left, so send yours out to the right. It's a whole thing if our lines get tangled."

"I think I can," Deklan replied, stepping forward. He held his rod over his shoulder, watched the hook and sinker for a long moment, then lobbed it out to sea.

The angle was a bit off, and it sailed higher than intended. When it hit the water, it hadn't gone as far as mine.

He gave me a grimace. "Should I try again?"

"Nah, that's good! That was outstanding for a first cast. Wind your line in like I did, then rest your finger on the line. You'll feel it when a fish bites."

He nodded, an intense look of focus on his face that made me smile.

I sat down on the rocks, getting comfy as I leaned into the sensations of my body. The wind blew fitfully, washing over me in small bursts that made my clothes ripple, tickling my skin. Though the breeze was cold, the afternoon sun shone down from above, a perfect counterpoint that canceled out winter's chill. Small waves crashed on the rocks beneath us, causing droplets of water to hit my legs. The longer I focused on the myriad sensations peppering me, the deeper I sank into the moment.

I slipped into a meditative state without even realizing it, the shape of my body melting away and becoming a cloud of feeling.

The chi coursed through the world all around me, sweeping this way and that. It reminded me of the ocean's churning waves, the lines of essence a part of something greater, something *whole*. There was a kernel of truth in that realization, my core seeming to hum its agreement. I felt at the boundary of my core, marveling at how far it had come in my short time in this world.

Something tugged at my attention, and I tried to sweep it away, content with being lost within myself.

It came again, and I shook my head, slowly returning to the world.

"Fischer!" Maria called.

"What's up?" I asked, turning toward her voice.

She was beside me, her rod in hand and line out between Trent and I. She gave me an exasperated look. "Your rod, you goose!"

"What?" I turned forward, seeing my rod was bent almost in half, its tip twitching. "Oh!" I shot to my feet. "Fish on!"

"No kidding!" she replied, a laugh bubbling up from her throat. "Lucky it hooked itself, you peanut!"

"O-oh!" Deklan yelled. His eyes were pinned to his rod. "I think I had a bite—"

With all our gazes on his rod, it bent fully in half, cutting his sentence short. "F-Fish on?" he yelled, sounding more like a question than a statement.

"Double hookup!" Maria beamed at us. "Keep your line tight, Deklan. Fischer doesn't use barbed hooks, so if it goes slack, the fish can—"

She cut off as something massive struck her line. "Whoa! Fish on!" She laughed uproariously. "Triple hookup!"

All three of the fish fought valiantly, never once tiring as we dragged them toward the rocks. Unlike other creatures I'd battled on the end of my line, whatever these fish were, they never changed tack; they fought to escape with everything they had the *entire* time. With my enhanced body, I brought my fish to the rocks first.

When I caught sight of its body, my forehead creased. It was smaller than I'd expected, the fish having put up a fight that belied its size. But adrenaline quickly swept my confusion away—it was a new species. I lifted it up from the water by holding the line and got a good look at it. The first thing I noticed was the razor-sharp teeth lining its mouth. It flopped around in the air, just as energetic without the water as it was within.

As Maria and Deklan pulled theirs from the water, my fish drew my vision in.

As I shook my head, clearing my field of view of the description, my eyes went wide. I looked over at Maria, seeing her vision distant as she inspected hers. The moment they cleared, her head darted toward me.

"Does that mean what I think it does . . . ?"

I nodded, grinning. "It does. Looks like we—"

Light exploded from behind Maria, illuminating our surroundings as a pulse of chi almost knocked me off my feet.

CHAPTER EIGHTEEN

Seasonal

With Maria at my side, a fish flopping around at the end of my hook, and the afternoon sun high above, a brilliant blast exploded from Deklan.

I closed my eyes as a pulse of chi trailed the luminescence flying from Deklan's forming core. It slammed into me, almost knocking me from my feet on the slick rocks. A large portion of the surrounding world's power poured into Deklan, solidifying into a container before drawing more essence in to fill the newly created void. Distracted as he was, Deklan's hands fell to his side.

The fish he'd caught didn't waste the opportunity.

The creature's razor-toothed jaw lashed out, slicing through his line. It flicked off a rock and sailed right back into the ocean, immediately disappearing from sight as it swam into the depths. My new pal couldn't have cared less.

"Whoa . . ." Deklan said, blinking at the world.

Before anything else, I swiftly dispatched the fish I'd caught with a single jab of a nail. Maria had the same idea, brain-spiking her fish and causing it to go limp on her line. When we turned back to Deklan, he was staring at his hands, having set his rod down on the rock wall.

"How do you feel?" I asked, grinning at the awe in his eyes.

"I'm a . . . cultivator?" He blinked rapidly, his gaze drifting up to me.

"Looks like it, mate."

"Huh . . ." He flexed his hands. "Feels pretty good."

I belly laughed. "It does, doesn't it?"

Maria's jaw dropped open. "*Pretty good?* That's all?"

"Yeah, why?" he asked, his relaxed demeanor well and truly shining through.

"Congratulations!" Keith called from farther down the pathway, giving a thumbs-up and a wide grin as he held his rod in another hand.

Trent was beside him, and he gave Deklan a single nod.

"Thanks . . ." Deklan replied. "Oh. I lost my fish? Sorry."

"Don't mention it, mate. Maria and I kept ours."

Maria held hers up toward him. "Here. Now that you're a cultivator, try looking at this."

He did so, his eyes going distant as they were drawn in by the System. When they cleared once more, he frowned at the fish, then at Maria and me.

"Seasonal fish? What does that mean?"

I grinned, staring down at my fish again and letting the words flash in my vision.

Juvenile Bluefish
Rare
The arrival of this seasonal fish has long been seen as a good omen for the coastal villages of the Kallis Realm. They school in large numbers, meaning when you find one, you will most certainly find more. Their strong-flavored flesh contains a higher level of chi than most fish.

The implications of the description weren't lost on me. Maria, either, based on her earlier reaction. More important, though, was Deklan's awakening. The former guard was once more staring down at his hands, no doubt feeling the strength now flowing through them. It had been becoming easier and easier for people to ascend, but never before had someone done so by catching a single fish.

As with every other revelation lately, Ellis was going to lose his mind.

Hopefully the fact it was from fishing, as well as my proximity, had something to do with it. Otherwise, we might be seeing more regular people ascend over the coming weeks. It was bound to happen eventually considering how Sturgill had become a cultivator, but I'd hoped it would take months at least. We barely had the infrastructure for the cultivators we'd saved, let alone if *everyone* started taking steps on the path of ascension.

Realizing I was worrying about things outside of my control, I shifted my thoughts. But just when I started considering the seasonal fish again and what their arrival meant for our little coastal village, Keith let out an excited noise.

"Fish on!" he yelled, arching his back and holding his rod high.

Deklan's training rod had bent almost in half with the fish he hooked earlier; Keith's was bent over all the way, looking like it might snap at any moment.

"*Big* fish on!" I replied. Seeing Deklan still staring down at his hands, I patted him on the back and led him over, knowing this was going to be a battle he wouldn't want to miss.

Maria came to my side, looping her arm through mine. At first, I assumed that the creature Keith had on the end of his line was a different species, but as I watched the way it swam, I started to doubt that assumption. It tried to escape with the same unerring ferocity, darting this way and that with never-ending kicks of its powerful tail.

I glanced at Trent, curious how the fight was affecting him. What I found there made a grin spread over my face. Gone was his pervasive anger and melancholy. His jaw clenched slightly, his nostrils flaring as he took deep breaths. His eyes were on the surface of the bay, tracking the line as it tore through the water. Seeing that stare of his, I was certain.

It was only a matter of time until Trent fell in love with fishing—assuming he wasn't already.

All the while, Keith fought. His muscles bulged as he lifted the rod, slowly bringing the hooked creature closer. Abruptly, the fish made its first blunder. The line went slack as it darted toward us. Keith was ready. He wound the line in so rapidly that his hand would be a blur to the unascended. When his quarry reached the shore, it hustled left, heading farther out to sea. As it changed direction, its silvery scales reflected the sun.

It. Was. *Huge.*

"Poseidon's salted sack," Trent swore. "They get that big?"

I chortled at the string of words, Maria making a similar choking noise from beside me.

"They do!" Keith replied, running along the walkway in the same direction as the fish, not wanting to give up any line. "You should see some of the things Fischer has caught! This is nothing!"

Despite playing down the fish, it was without a doubt the biggest Keith had ever hooked, and every movement he took broadcast just how pumped he was to have it on his line. He ran all the way to the end of the rock wall, only stopping when there was no more distance to cross. And there, he made his stand. With his feet planted on the stone, he arched his back and started retrieving line as he pumped the rod up and down.

The fish wasn't happy about it.

It thrashed and kicked, doing its best to get away. We all slipped into silence as the fight dragged on, content with watching Keith's battle. As much as my eyes were glued to the water, I couldn't help but steal glances at Deklan and Trent, enjoying their reactions to a degree that I couldn't put into words. Maria put her arm through mine again, squeezing me tight and subtly wiggling her eyebrows when she caught me grinning at Deklan.

Minutes passed as Keith and the fish warred against one another. Finally, the water-bound creature started to tire. Its head shakes grew more lethargic, no longer possessing the stamina to continue as it once had. Keith didn't rush; he brought it to the rock wall meticulously, never putting too much tension on the line.

This, too, brought a smile to my face.

Keith and the rest of the fishing club had only been here for months, but they'd already grown so much. They'd lost plenty of fish since arriving here, and if such a large creature had challenged Keith even a few weeks ago, I was under no delusion that the former royal would have won. As he was now, though, the outcome seemed a foregone conclusion.

When the fish was only meters away, it swam on the water's surface, still expending energy in an attempt to get away. There was a blur of orange underneath it, and a second later, it was flying my way, its razor-toothed mouth leading the charge. I dashed aside and caught it in both arms, turning my head to raise an eyebrow at Snips. I was used to Claws messing with me, but to be pranked by my trusty guard crab was a new experience.

But it wasn't Snips that I found when I peered down into the churning water.

Rocky raised his claw high above the ocean so I could see his decidedly rude gesture. I cocked my head to the side, which only made him raise the other claw and dual wield his animosity.

Suddenly, there was another blur beneath him.

A streak of orange and blue shot up from the ocean floor even faster than he had, and Rocky's pissed-off bubbles trailed after him as he was launched out to sea at terrifying speed, his entire body flipping end over end in a chaotic jumble of limbs.

"Damn, Snips. Nice throw," I said, giving her a smile as she swam back to shore while blowing a series of exasperated hisses. I turned to Keith and held out the fish so large that I had to hold it in both arms. "I believe this is yours, mate."

His eyes sparkled as he approached, going dull as the fish pulled his vision in. I looked down, letting the System's information stream across my field of view.

Mature Bluefish

Rare

The arrival of this seasonal fish has long been seen as a good omen for the coastal villages of the Kallis Realm. They school in large numbers, meaning when you find one, you will most certainly find more. Their strong-flavored flesh contains a higher level of chi than most fish.

"Wow . . ." Keith said, his expression awestruck as he took the mature bluefish. "It's so heavy." His eyes darted up to meet mine. "Can we keep it?"

"That's up to you, mate, but I don't think keeping it will hurt their number. Seasonal fish are usually plentiful when they're around, which is likely why the description says they're seen as a good omen. Well, that and the fact that they have a high level of chi."

Where the juvenile variant was around the length of my forearm, the monster Keith had caught was twice as large. Thick slabs of muscle and fat covered its body, explaining how it had fought so hard for so long. No matter which way you looked at it, this creature was an impressive specimen.

"Thank you for the sustenance, fishy," Keith said, nodding toward it and repeating words I'd previously used. He lowered it down to Snips, who had joined us on the walkway. "Would you mind?"

Snips nodded sharply and darted forward, lashing out with a burst of energy from her claw and ending it in an instant.

"Well," I said, my eyes pinned on the colossal thing, "we've certainly got enough for dinner . . ."

Deklan cleared his throat, and when I glanced his way, he was staring at the fish. "Should we try for more if they're only around for a short time? I feel bad that I lost mine . . ."

There was a hunger in his eyes, but it wasn't for food; it was the thrill of the hunt.

I shot Maria a wolfish grin before sweeping it away and turning to face Deklan. "They'll still be here for quite some time, I believe. Before we catch any more, we have some important testing to do."

"Testing?" Deklan asked, tilting his head slightly.

"Yup!" Maria replied, knowing exactly what I was getting at. "The most critical test of all—we need to make sure they taste good."

I nodded, casting my gaze over everyone. "Before we hunt for more, we should check that they're palatable. How do you all feel about an early dinner?"

CHAPTER NINETEEN

Treachery

The sun approached the western mountains as I crept down the rocks with three fish in my arms. When I reached the water, I set them down and washed them off one by one.

"So," I said, glancing up at Deklan and Trent, "there are a bunch of ways to prepare fish."

Deklan pursed his lips. "How do you choose which method to use?"

"It depends on the size and species, usually. Anything smaller than these bluefish, and it's usually better to cook them whole. It's hard not to waste meat, otherwise." I gestured at the smaller two that Maria and I had caught. "For these, I think filleting is best. It saves us having to gut them."

I grabbed a knife from my belt and ran the dull edge along the fish. "Because we're leaving the skin on, the first step is to scale them."

"You . . . eat the skin?" Deklan asked, his expression dubious. "Isn't that kinda gross?"

"Not at all, mate. They come from the ocean, so they've spent their lives in clean salt water. Their skin shouldn't have any unpleasant flavors, and it adds a nice bit of texture when cooked on a hotplate."

With System-enhanced precision, I ran my knife behind their pectoral fins and down toward their tail, ensuring I got every bit of flesh possible. Setting the four fillets aside on the rocks, I held a fish frame upside down and pointed at it.

"This is a bit advanced, but this cut is referred to as the wings." With four swift slices, I removed the section between the frame's head and body. "There are bones in it, but also a ridiculous amount of tasty meat. I'm not trying to enforce my morality on anyone else, but it's important to me that I waste as little as possible."

"Commendable," Trent said, nodding.

I did my best not to arch an eyebrow off my face—I hadn't expected such a comment from the crown prince.

"Is the rest wasted, then?" he asked, pointing at the remaining frame.

"Not at all! We can cook it on the barbecue for my animal pals—they aren't at all bothered by the bones and cartilage. These, though, I'll be using as bait for my crab pot. With any luck, I'll be cooking you guys some fresh sand crab tomorrow."

"Even if we throw the frame back into the ocean," Maria said, "it won't necessarily be a waste. There are plenty of little creatures that will happily pick it clean."

"Exactly," I agreed as I cut the wings off the other frame. Placing it down next to the fillets, I gestured at the mature bluefish. "I think we should fillet, then cut this one into chunks. Are you up to deep frying it if I cook the others on the barbecue, Maria?"

"On it!" she yelled over her shoulder, already running back to the house.

Smiling at her retreating form, I started filleting the mature bluefish.

A half hour later, Deklan stood beside me as I held my hand over the hotplate. Trent was still here, but he and Keith were talking softly a few meters away. I pointed down at the fillets and looked up at Deklan. "Remember how I said the skin adds texture? It gets lovely and crispy on the grill, but it's the same as cooking steak—you need to remove excess moisture before putting it on the heat." I patted it down with a fresh tea towel. "Do you wanna do it?"

"Er . . . I don't want to mess it up . . ."

"Nonsense, mate! Here. I'll put one down first. Just need to add some fat beforehand."

I put a healthy dollop of beef tallow on the barbecue plate. It melted almost immediately as I spread it around with a spatula, coating the cooking surface. I got one of the fillets and placed it skin down. The tallow immediately hissed and bubbled around the edges, making steam and a delicious scent rise into the air.

I nodded at him. "Your turn."

Deklan bit the inside of his cheek as he picked up a fillet with the care you'd give a newborn baby. With one swift movement, he laid it on the hotplate, taking a swift step back as if it would bite him.

"He's an expert already!" Maria called, watching from the end of the deck. "Just letting you know the oil is hot so we're gonna start shallow-frying the big boy Keith caught."

I smiled my gratitude at her. "We'll bring ours over when we're done. Shouldn't be long."

She grinned, blew me a kiss, and skipped from sight, returning to the campfire. Deklan stared after her, his eyebrows narrowing in thought. When he looked back my way, he gave me an odd look. "You know, you're all, like, *super* nice."

The comment caught me off guard and made a laugh fly free of my throat. "Why does that make you look so confused? Are we supposed to be evil?"

"Well, we were always told back in the capital that the commoners living in the far reaches were, er . . . the king would have said *unsavory*, but the rest of Gormona's citizens would use more colorful words."

"You expected to find us a little more disagreeable, huh?"

"To be honest, yeah. I didn't know what to expect. You seemed like a friendly fellow, but you were also with a gang of cultivators. It could have gone either way, really."

"Yet you still ran away with me?" I asked, placing the last two fillets down on the hotplate.

He shrugged. "Like I said, you seemed like a friendly fellow. Plus, the king had just revealed himself as a bit of a . . ."

"Dickhead?" I suggested.

"Yeah, that works."

Deklan's shoulders held some tension. Now that he was a cultivator, I could feel his core fluctuating, likely responding to troubling thoughts as he recalled his time in the capital.

"Well, mate," I said, "you're here now. More importantly, you're one of us." Seeking to change the subject, I shot a smirk his way. "How is your brother going to respond to you being a cultivator?"

The corners of his mouth tugged up as he slammed a fist into his open palm.

I raised a brow. "Uh . . . you're not going to attack him, are you?"

"Attack him?" He revealed a toothy grin. "Absolutely. I'll finally be able to tussle with him on even footing again."

I laughed again, throwing my head back. "How long has he been a cultivator for?"

"A few years."

"*A few years* . . . You have a fair bit of tussling to make up for, then?"

"Damn right." He flexed his hands, feeling his strength. "That scoundrel has no idea what he's in for."

Seeing that the conversation had drawn out Deklan's playful nature and banished his worries, I let a silence stretch, focusing on the cooking fish. When they were halfway done, I flipped the fillets, revealing golden-brown skin that made my mouth water. Deklan took a deep breath through his nose, a sense of calm crossing his features as the scents assaulted him.

"How do you know when it's done?" he asked.

"See how the flesh turns white? When it's flaky and no longer translucent in the middle, it's ready." I poked the top of a fillet. "You can also tell by feel. Press where I just did."

He gingerly pressed a finger down on it. "It's much more firm than before."

"Exactly," I replied and started to remove them. "They're ready."

"You could tell that just by feel?"

"Yep! You'll be able to as well, but it takes a little practice."

With our contribution ready, we went to meet the others. The moment we approached the campfire, the smell of our fish was blown away. The scent of fried breading, boiling-hot beef tallow, and undertones of cooked seafood were an assault on the senses that drew me on.

"Perfect timing!" Maria dipped her tongs into the tallow and pulled out a palm-sized pocket of golden goodness. "We just fried the last portion."

I set our plate down beside Maria's mountain of fried food and immediately started dishing out servings. Despite the sun still lingering in the sky, my stomach demanded I eat the meal. When I broke the barbecue-cooked fish apart, the skin cracked, letting steam rise in the late-afternoon light.

"Okay, everyone," I said, sitting down after passing out the plates. "Dig in."

Snips was the first to partake, wasting no time in crunching down on a bit of fried fish. She shuddered in delight and sank down into the sand, not making a sound other than chewing the crispy skin.

The rest of us took a bite of the fried fish together, and our reactions were much the same. My shoulders dropping was the last thing I felt before the flavor and texture of the bluefish overwhelmed my awareness. As the description had suggested, the meat had a stronger flavor than most fish. Yet it wasn't at all unpleasant. It mingled with the subtle flavors of beef tallow and golden breadcrumbs, combining to become something otherworldly. When I swallowed, the chi traveled down to my core, warming everything it passed.

Being Deklan's first taste of fried fish, his reaction was *superb*.

"Are you serious?" he asked no one in particular. "Is it always this good? And why is it making me feel so warm?"

"That's the chi, and yeah, it's always this good," Trent confirmed, his eyes closed and a smile crossing his face. "It's even better with seasoning."

"This isn't *seasoned*?"

"Fischer usually cooks new fish without seasoning the first time around," Maria said. "It lets us get a feel of its flavor profile."

I nodded. "And pick the correct herbs and spices to use."

"Does that mean you have some in mind?" Keith asked.

"It does, but we'll have to wait until next time. Until then, should we try the grilled fish?"

Snips jumped to her feet, nodding her entire body in fervent approval.

Letting out a light laugh, I picked some up by hand, the white meat crumbling between my fingers. Wasting no time, I put it on my tongue. Warm, savory juices poured out. I'd half expected the fish to be tough considering its size, but the flesh melted in my mouth, falling apart before I even had to chew. When I bit down, the crispy skin crackled, seeming to release an extra burst of umami that exploded outward.

"How does it taste so . . . *different*?" Deklan asked. "It's the same fish . . ."

"Could be my cooking skill taking effect." I shrugged. "Or Maria's. Her deep-fried fish is always amazing."

She leaned over and pecked me on the cheek. "I learned from the best."

Before they could get cold, I held the wings out to Deklan and Trent. "We've all tried them before, so I think these should be yours."

"You're sure . . . ?" Deklan asked.

"I am, mate. We'll all have a chance to eat it again, so dig in."

I watched them closely as they bit down on the charred meat, their bodies relaxing as the flavors washed over them. No one said a word as we finished the meal, the only sounds surrounding us that of the crackling fire and the occasional crunch of deep-fried breading.

After swallowing the last bite, I let out a slow sigh and shot a look Maria's way. "You know what this means, right?"

She returned a half-lidded gaze, giving me a beautiful smile. "It means we're going to have a fun couple of days, if not weeks."

Keith raised an eyebrow at us, but before he could voice his question, I continued. "The seasonal fish is delicious, mate. That means it's worth targeting."

"It also means we're going to need a *lot* more rods," Maria said.

"Well, that depends on if everyone else is keen. I suppose we should go ask."

"I suppose we should . . ." she answered, but didn't make a move. "Soon, anyway. I need to enjoy the meal first."

I lounged back in the sand, a blanket of contentment settling on my entire body. "Soon," I agreed, watching the last rays of sunlight as they disappeared over the western mountains.

Though the sun had long since set by the time we arrived in New Tropica, the streets were alive.

Rescued cultivators strode along, their steps filled with purpose. Those that I spied within the different crafting buildings were focused on their work, backs hunched and brows knitted. As we passed the smithy, I gave Fergus and Duncan a wave. Only the latter noticed, and he shot me a quick wink before reaching over and adjusting the metal bar an apprentice was working on.

As we approached the woodworkers' domain, I turned toward Maria and Deklan. I'd known Maria would come along for a little rod-making, but Deklan also wanting to try it was a pleasant surprise. Though Trent had also seemed interested in trying his hand at crafting, he and Keith left after the meal had settled, needing to be somewhere else for the evening that they didn't elaborate on.

"Ready?" I asked.

"Yeah," Maria replied, much more enthusiastically than Deklan's answering nod.

Taking one last breath of the night air, I led them into the building.

There were a dozen of the rescued cultivators within, their number having grown since we walked past this morning. Greg saw me first. He elbowed Brad in the side, subtly nodding my way and giving his brother a smirk. I raised an eyebrow, not sure what they were up to.

But then they committed their treachery.

Both men snapped a crisp salute, their bodies going rigid. "Sir!" they said together.

Their apprentice woodworkers spun, and with the speed only cultivators could muster, they copied my treasonous friends.

"Sir!" they chorused, their backs stiff and eyes serious.

I groaned. "Can you believe this, Maria?"

"Believe what, sir?" she responded in a clipped tone.

I slowly spun her way, my eyes narrowed. As I'd feared, she was also saluting, a wide grin plastered on her face. I glared my displeasure at her, making Brad and Greg burst into laughter.

"What can we do for you, Fischer?" Brad asked, leaning back on a bench and crossing his arms.

"Other than not doing . . ." I waved a hand in his general direction. "Whatever *that* was to me ever again? We came to make some rods, mate."

"Rods, huh?" Greg rubbed his chin. "What's the occasion? I thought you had plenty."

"We need enough for everyone," Maria replied, her eyes dancing with glee.

"Everyone?" Brad looked between us. "Define *everyone.*"

"Literally everyone." I laughed, then turned toward the cultivators. "Assuming you guys want to try fishing, that is."

Because of who I was, or possibly because of Brad and Greg's stunt, the former slaves met me with silence.

"We caught some seasonal fish!" Maria bounced on her heels, unable to contain her excitement. "We think there will be a lot of them to catch over the coming days and weeks, so it's the perfect opportunity for everyone who wants to try out our heretical lifestyle."

"Enough for almost a hundred people . . . ?" Greg asked, looking skeptical.

"Yep! They fight super hard, and the *taste*, guys . . ." Maria shimmied. "They're *delicious.*"

She relayed the bluefish's description.

"Boosted chi, huh?" Brad took in his apprentices. "What do you guys say? Would you like to try making some fishing rods? Even if you're not down to fish, following Fischer's instructions will probably be great for both your cultivation and woodworking."

Still speechless, they all nodded, only one of them muttering under his breath that he'd love to. Or maybe he said *I love you,* not *I'd love to.* It was hard to tell.

"Okay," I said, stretching my arms high and smiling at them. "Let's get this party started."

CHAPTER TWENTY

Nexus

O kay, everyone," I said, looking down at the bench before me. "Follow along."
Maria and Deklan were on either side of me, the former grinning and
the latter serious. The rest of the apprentice woodworkers were arrayed around the
room, awaiting instruction behind their benches. We all had a square block of soft
wood with a hole drilled in the center, and as I set mine in a vise, I cut into it with
a jigsaw. When the circular shape was finished, I looked around the room. Everyone
other than Maria, Brad, and Greg were following along much slower, their movements filled with care.

One of them cursed under her breath. Her blade had gotten caught and gone
within the lines, removing a small chunk.

"No stress!" I replied, striding over. "Keep going and just do the best you can. We
can sort out any imperfections when we shave it down."

Grimacing, she nodded and resumed cutting, even slower this time.

It took them all a few minutes, and when the last of them were finished, I smiled
at their collective work. "Well done, everyone. Now, we'll plane them down. Any
advice first, Brad? Greg?"

Greg shook his head, and Brad replied, "Nope! This is your show."

"In that case, follow my movements with this plane." I went slower than usual,
showing them all how I used sweeping arcs to remove slivers of wood. My body wanted
to speed away, to get caught up in the workmanship, but I held the urge at bay.

Their eyes tracked my every movement, paying extra attention when I spun my
block of wood in the vise.

"Okay," I said. "That's pretty much it. We can still sand and shape later on, so
don't be too worried if it isn't perfectly round at the end of this step."

When I finished planing my reel, I cast my gaze around the room. There was,
evidently, a difference in aptitude amongst the apprentices. To my surprise, Deklan
seemed to be the most proficient. Between all of them, he seemed the most relaxed,
his hands easily gliding along as he whistled to himself. Whether it was natural tal-
ent or a calm nature fueling his advance, his block of wood had the least number
of flaws.

He sensed me watching. His eyes darted up to meet mine, and rather than look
bothered by my attention, he gave me a quick thumbs-up before returning to his work.

"He's a natural," Maria said, giving my arm a featherlight touch.

I bathed in her company as I waited for the rest of them to finish. Brad and Greg sat back, content to leave me in control as they assessed their apprentices' work.

"Great job, everyone." I turned to Brad and Greg. "I have a bit of feedback, if you don't mind me doing so?"

They both nodded, so I faced the apprentices. "I'm seeing a fair bit of . . . stiffness, for lack of a better word. I know you're probably feeling some pressure to do everything perfectly, especially after your masters treated me like some sort of respected elder, but being too tense will only hurt the outcome. There's no need to be so rigid. Have *fun* with it! There's no punishment for failing to do everything perfectly. Even if you accidentally set your wood on fire somehow, I'd be more impressed than upset."

I got a few smiles from them, so I continued.

"Next, we're carving out a groove for the line to sit in." I grabbed a crescent-shaped file and ran it along the outside of the reel. "This part is super easy. Keep the file straight and drag it all the way around the edge."

I demonstrated briefly, then gestured for them to go ahead.

As I rotated my reel and filed the different sections, a small smile crossed my face. I hadn't been doing much crafting of late, and I'd forgotten how calming an experience it was. My body flowed of its own accord, the file arcing down across the reel with unerring ease. Before I knew it, the groove was complete. I opened my eyes and took in my surroundings, the magical light of the wall sconces bathing the room in their orange light.

"Are you back with us?" Maria asked, smirking at me. "I was worried you were going to do something silly."

"Something silly?"

"Yeah." She opened her vise and spun the reel within. "Like make your block of wood transform into a house or something out of sheer will. I've learned to expect chaos when you look peaceful."

I snorted. "No magical houses, I'm afraid. Just a supreme sense of calm."

"Maybe next time," she replied, the skin beside her eyes crinkling in amusement. She finished her reel soon after, and we watched the apprentices' progress together.

As we gazed out over the room, satisfaction and pride washed over me.

It hadn't even been a half hour, yet they'd already improved. Before, many of their movements had been stiff. Jarring. It appeared as though my impromptu speech had resonated—they even seemed to be enjoying themselves more. When they were finished and awaiting my next instructions, I beamed at them.

"Exceptional job, gang. Much more relaxed than before. Did it feel better?" I asked the lady who had accidentally cut a portion of her reel off in the first step.

She gave me a shy smile and a nod so slight that I almost thought I'd imagined it.

"I'm glad. We're at the last step for the reel now, guys. Does anyone have any sections they think need more filing?"

A man in the back raised his hand, so I strode over and peered down. It appeared as though his file had slipped, gouging lines in the outside face.

"I think that should be fine, to be honest." I faced Brad and Greg. "It's on the outside, so it shouldn't be an issue, right?"

"Aye," Greg agreed. "Gives it personality."

"There you have it!" I clapped the cultivator on the shoulder. "Sand it so there's no jagged bits, and it should be all good!"

I walked back to my workstation and held up one of the bits of sandpaper Greg and Brad were passing around. "Have you guys used this before?"

They all nodded.

"We showed them sandpaper earlier as part of the introduction to woodworking," Brad said.

"Awesome," I replied, then faced the apprentices again. "All we're doing is running this paper along the reel. Try to make it as uniform as possible. If you have any gouged bits, spend a little extra time there. As long as it's not on the groove where the line goes, it doesn't matter if some sides are a little . . . *unique*."

I walked around the room with a leather sack I'd brought with me. Inside, I had a collection of bearings procured from the merchant, Marcus. "When you're finished sanding, place these into the holes Brad drilled."

I finished passing out the bearings.

"There's one more thing, too. The entire time you're completing this step, I want you to imagine in your head what you want the reel to do. Don't be surprised if the System takes over and makes your reel transform. Whatever is motivating you to create this reel, hone in on that. For example, I'll be imagining something that you, my new friends, can use to catch fish and have a good time. It's a vessel for friendship and fun. I realize I'm a bit of a weirdo in that regard, so if you're motivated by gaining levels in Woodworking or something like that, use that desire."

I grinned at the room. "Any questions?"

"Yeah," Brad said. "Why are you so weird?"

"Any useful and not-insulting questions?" I corrected, shaking my head and trying not to smile at Brad.

"Nope!" Greg replied. "If you want any more insulting ones, though, I can think of a few—"

"Okay!" I interrupted, projecting my voice. "Let's get started!"

After flicking a tiny chunk of wood at Greg's head, I started sanding my reel. It was already close to what I wanted to create, so I did soft passes with the sandpaper, smoothing each of the surfaces down. As with the filing, I lost myself to the process. Motes of wood wafted through the air, tickling my nose when some of them drifted in with my breath. I focused my attention on my will, lasering in on what I'd told the cultivators earlier.

This reel, though not intended for me, had to be perfect.

I wanted it to be functional and reliable, because that was what my new pals needed. I poured whispers of chi down into the wood. Its grains soaked them up hungrily, wanting me to send more out. Hesitantly, I obliged, ensuring I didn't send enough to turn my reel into an accidental pipe bomb.

When the fibers seemed full to bursting, I sent more out into the surrounding room, feeling what everyone else was doing. Surprisingly, some of them were also exuding chi. I expected to find it from Maria, Brad, and Greg, but a few of the apprentices were pouring essence out too, as was Deklan. The streams were a little . . . *wrong*. Like they weren't the correct shape to be properly absorbed.

Instead of adding mine to theirs, I used my will to help shape their chi.

I closed my eyes, uncountable strands weaving all around me to poke and prod different flows into the correct form. After a few moments, it came easy, so I once again focused on what I wanted to create. I pictured every single member of Tropica and New Tropica, all standing on the beach. They had rods in their hands and smiles on their faces, bathing in the sensations of their bodies as they waited for a bite.

I was swimming in the ocean with Maria at my side, her sun-kissed shoulders visible above the water's surface. The scene made my soul thrum as I watched it play out in my mind's eye, and an imaginary breeze kicked up, tickling my skin.

Before I could get lost further in the vista, the essence back in the real world responded. It vibrated, quivering as our joined wills pressed outward. I pictured the dozens of rods again, demanding that the universe create what I yearned for. A smattering of confused awarenesses made themselves known, each belonging to one of the surrounding cultivators.

Maria was first, and though she was shocked for a moment, she recognized me almost immediately and joined her desire with mine. Next came Brad and Greg. They were similarly disoriented, but upon a mental urging from Maria, they joined in. Deklan's consciousness peeked through next, and this time, it was me who felt shocked; the man couldn't have been less unfazed. He gave us the metaphysical equivalent of a respectful nod, as if this was the most normal thing in the world. I could tell he'd pictured something different in mind, but it was the same flavor as the scene I pictured.

I'd felt Barry's will join with mine previously, but having so many present at once was an entirely new experience.

The rest of the cultivators I'd rescued from Gormona appeared at the same time. A different emotion was in the forefront of their minds: fear. It made sense considering how alien it must be for them, and one apprentice noped out immediately, fleeing from the call to action. But the rest remained. Upon a barrage of soothing reassurance from Maria and me, they slowly joined their wills with mine.

With my enhanced awareness of chi, I felt every single event that occurred in the next moment.

The surrounding essence exploded forward, rushing into the room. Some of the chi contained within the smithy's stones came too, the very building and village lending their strength to our creation. Different components around the room were swept up in the thick ropes of power, drawn toward our workstations on invisible torrents. Every single reel blurred, their forms evaporating as the System reshaped them.

A whirlwind of potential sprang to life, spinning around the room in a vortex that grew faster and more insistent with every passing fraction of a second. The barrage of chi, materials, and wills combined, manifesting in a single nexus between us. A blinding orb of creation came into being. It drew on my core, and when I opened the floodgate to my power, the rest of the contributing cultivators followed suit. None of their reserves held a candle to mine, yet they joined in, growing less hesitant by the second, more sure of themselves.

As our purpose became one, the swirling storm took shape.

To a regular human, it would have been as if the rods appeared from nowhere. But I was far from a regular human; I saw everything. Wood grew from thin air, extending in thick lengths that tapered toward the end. The reels we'd been working on split apart, replicating themselves and attaching to poles. Iron coagulated in hundreds, perhaps *thousands* of individual nodes that flew toward the newly formed rods.

Luminescence shone from them, and though I could feel their shape, I had to close my eyes against the light. When the glow disappeared, I blinked, trying to focus on my now-dim surroundings. Instead of seeing our creations, however, I was met with a System notification that filled my field of view.

Despite understanding what the words meant, I struggled to comprehend their meaning.

"Frack me . . ." was all I could say as I dismissed the message and stared down at the dozens of rods sitting neatly piled in the center of the room.

CHAPTER TWENTY-ONE

Path to Power

I licked my lips, my consciousness warring with itself to understand the message I'd just received.

Seeking a distraction, I wandered over to the rods.

"Triton's slick conch," Brad swore.

"Agreed," Greg replied, his gaze distant.

Maria leaned back on her bench, her eyes darting around the room yet focusing on nothing in particular. "That . . . *wow*. You saw it, too, Fischer?"

"I did. I'm not sure if it was because of the significance or the fact that my will was aimed at the rods, but the System saw fit to give me a peek."

One by one, the other cultivators' eyes returned to the present, their jaws slack and faces paling.

"Does that mean what I think it does . . . ?" Deklan asked, appearing the least bothered of everyone in the room. "Pretty neat."

Before anyone could reply, the surrounding chi shuddered once more.

It rushed forward from every direction, slamming into the cores of everyone, myself included. Over a dozen pulses of chi exploded from our abdomens a moment later. They bounced off one another, filling the room with blinding light that I had to squint against. The feeling of ecstasy that came with advancement was more palpable than ever before, the dozens of sources creating an overwhelming barrage of sensation.

Essence swelled behind each of the newer cultivators, culminating in a leather bag. The sacks hit the stones, and the tingle of gold coins rang out through the room, the cacophony nothing compared to the bliss coursing through my veins.

When the waves of light finally dissipated, I let out a shuddering sigh and called for the words the System had shown me, letting them appear once more.

You have successfully taken part in a crafting ritual!
New Quest: Group Project
Objective: [Error. Insufficient Power.]
Reward: [Error. Insufficient Power.]

The System had created a quest.

It was broken—as per usual. But that didn't subtract from how monumental an occasion it was. I'd been at the hands of gamelike shenanigans since my arrival in my new world, but something about a literal *quest* made my body tingle. If the System continued to regain functionality, would I one day be able to see the objective and reward? If it regained power entirely, would the System generate more quests? What were the requirements for one of them to be created . . . ?

I looked up at Maria, intent on bouncing these ideas off of someone, but her attention was elsewhere.

She kneeled down before the pile of rods, holding one up to her face and inspecting it. With the shock of receiving a quest, I'd almost entirely forgotten about my purpose in coming here. I strode over and knelt down beside her, as did everyone else. I picked one up and examined its form. Just like the other rods we'd previously crafted, the System had made them into something we had no hope of creating on our own.

I picked up a rod, letting it draw my eyes in.

Communal Rod of the Fisher
Rare
This fishing rod provides boosts to both Fishing and Luck. The stats provided will increase based on how many of its sibling rods are being used within a one-kilometer radius.
+0.2 Fishing per rod
+0.1 Luck per rod

I'd expected the stats to be insane, but not *that* insane. If there were one hundred people using them, each would provide +20 Fishing and +10 Luck.

Brad turned to face one of the apprentices. "What level did you get in Woodworking?"

The man swallowed. "Thirty-one."

Greg whistled. "What were you before?"

"I was only level two. Is that normal?"

Brad laughed, shaking his head. "Not even a little normal. We have Fischer to thank for that."

I smiled at him. "Happy to help, mate, but I think I'm the one that needs to thank all of you." I gestured before us at our creations. "I couldn't tell you how we did it, but there are at least a hundred rods here."

"Er," Deklan said. "It's because you pictured all of us fishing, right?"

My head darted his way. "Wait, you saw *exactly* what I was picturing . . . ?"

"We did," Maria replied, somehow pursing her lips and smiling at me. "It's nice to know you think so highly of me, but maybe give me more clothes next time."

In my head, she'd been wearing her bathing suit because we were swimming in the ocean. One of the apprentices to my right choked, blushing a furious red and staring up at the ceiling.

"Yeah, well, maybe you shouldn't look so good, then. You ever think about that?"

She snorted and lay her head on my shoulder. "I'm just teasing, you big goof. Though," she added, pulling her head back and raising an eyebrow above a mischievous smirk, "I felt your love for your animal pals, too. I was surprised you felt so much affection for Rocky, despite how much of a prick he can be. If you want to see other people, or crabs, just let me know—"

"Stop," I replied, my face heating as I held up both hands. "Not even a little funny, and everyone else might not know you're joking."

She cackled, the sound so loud it would have been abrasive coming from anyone else.

Hiding my embarrassment with a sigh, I stood and stretched, but froze when I noticed someone still at their workstation. The woman from earlier who had messed up the first step was staring down at her hands. With my attention on her, I recognized her chi signature.

She was the one that had shied away from my will when I led the crafting ritual, or whatever the System called it. Maria and I winced at each other; the woman was probably feeling guilty about backing out. I went to meet her, intending to offer some words of consolation, but then I saw the bench before her.

She wasn't looking at her hands—she was looking at what they held.

Her fingers ran over a massive construct of metal and rope. It was a giant treble hook, so large that it looked better suited for grappling onto rooftops than fishing.

"Did you just make that?" I asked, my eyes narrowing on the three deadly sharp tips.

"Y-yes," she stuttered, shying away from me. "Sorry. I know it isn't what you pictured . . ."

Maria, Brad, and Greg came to look at what we were talking about, all their eyebrows flying skyward when they caught sight of it.

"No need to apologize," I replied. "It's kind of neat. I just don't understand . . . well, *how* you made it. I felt you pull away from my vision, which is totally valid, but how did you end up with this?"

"You're . . . not upset?"

"Not at all. Were you trying to think of a way to escape or something?"

"Escape?" She dropped the hook to the table and held up both hands. "No! Not that!" Realizing she'd spoken above a whisper, she flushed. "I, uh, I saw what you were picturing, and it didn't seem right."

I was getting more and more confused by the second. "Why did what I pictured seem wrong?"

"Because they were all so small. How could tiny little sticks and hooks be used to catch monstrous creatures from the deep?" She gestured down at the hook she'd made. "This is way better, no?"

" . . . monstrous creatures from the deep?" Maria repeated, giving her an odd look.

As realization struck me, I did my best to hold my laughter in. But I failed completely. The more I thought about her throwing the grappling hook at a leviathan sea creature and holding on for dear life, the more my chest heaved. Tears came to my eyes, and I wiped them away with both hands, unable to bottle up my mirth for an uncouth amount of time.

"I'm so sorry," I eventually got out. "I'm not laughing at you. Okay, wait, maybe I'm laughing at you a little bit, but only because I'm imagining you using that thing to ride a giant crab into battle."

"Wait . . ." Maria said. "How big do you think the creatures that we fish for are?"

"My mom always said you had to stay away from the water because the sea creatures are bigger than a house. That's why I was so confused that you were picturing such little sticks . . ."

Maria cackled for the second time tonight. "Okay, that definitely explains it."

"What's your name?" I asked the woman, who was once more blushing.

"I'm Bonnie," she replied, so quiet that I wouldn't have heard her if not for my cultivation.

"It's nice to meet you, Bonnie. Sorry to break the news to you, but the creatures we fish for are way smaller than what you imagined."

" . . . they are?"

"Yeah. Most are smaller than my forearm, but we've caught some as big as I am. Those are pretty rare, though."

Her light-pink cheeks turned crimson, and she hunched her shoulders, making herself as small as possible. "I'm *so* sorry."

"Like I said, no need to apologize." I clapped her on the shoulder. "You have a wonderful imagination, and I'm sure we can find a way to make use of it."

"But I wasted so many materials on something useless . . ."

I shook my head. "Not a waste at all. I'm sure we'll find a use for it, and besides, look how many rods we made! We have more than enough for everyone."

When she finally turned away from the bench, her head shot back in surprise. "You made all of those? Just now?"

"We all did," I replied, gesturing at the rest of the cultivators. "And now that they're made, there's only one thing left to do."

"What's that?"

"Thanks for asking." I gave everyone a wide grin, soaking up their anticipation. "We have to test them out, of course!"

Deep within a forest, a man fled for his life. Since spotting the cultivator-made tree, he hadn't stopped moving.

Though his bones were old and his body was weary, an unnatural stamina pushed Solomon on. He'd suspected as much before his flight from Tropica, but now he *knew*. He was becoming the cultivator his cult had prophesized for untold years. He was the Alchemist.

The farther he got from the coast and that terrifying tree Tom Osnan Jr. had grown, the more sure of himself he became. So what if the young lord was more powerful than Soloman had expected? He was on the path of ascension himself, and it was only a matter of time until he was recognized by the heavens.

He was high in the mountains now, and as he came across a clearing in the forest, his travels came to an abrupt end.

There was something about this place that screamed "power" to him, calling him forward. A lone tree stood in the center of the clearing, its limbs bare of leaves. Despite being absent of life, the black bark urged him on, demanded that he pay it attention. He scraped a nail against the trunk, some of the dark substance coming free. Beneath a layer of black, the tree was *blue*. It wasn't a regular tree. As Solomon ran the colored dust between his fingers, he recalled the tales of such trees.

They were the source of many a children's story, sometimes a source of evil, other times a powerful boon.

Many followers of the Cult of the Alchemist had tried using the material but failed, so Solomon had never paid it much mind. All the records told that the trees were impossible to work with, their fibers too strong to properly distill anything, even when boiled. But this specimen was different. It seemed to have died, its body degrading to the point that he could scrape it away with a single fingernail.

A low chuckle began in his chest, slowly climbing as it made its way to his throat. Solomon roared with laughter, broadcasting his glee out into the world. This was where he would build his base.

He fell to his knees, his cheeks aching as tears welled in his eyes.

This tree was his path to power.

His path to *godhood*.

CHAPTER TWENTY-TWO

Conspiracy

A soft breeze blew at my back, coming from the western mountains. The air sweeping along its currents had a hint of sweetness, my senses also detecting notes of wood, earth, and decaying leaves. The ocean lay before me, its softly lapping waves kicking up sea spray that joined the other aromas.

I closed my eyes and breathed deep, allowing the surrounding fragrances to whisk me away.

When I opened them once more, the moon was high overhead, illuminating my shores. What I saw there made my soul rejoice. Lined up and down the rock wall, dozens of people had rods in hand and anticipation coloring their bodies. Each waited patiently for the next bite, most having already caught a fish.

On our way out of New Tropica, we'd told everyone we came across where we were going. The blacksmiths had been the most excitable, practically ordering their apprentices to tag along. They stood next to Ruby and Steven, whose fledgling tailors were also lining the rock wall.

"Fish on!" Duncan yelled, the following high-pitched giggle at odds with his baritone voice.

As he fought the hooked bluefish, Maria squeezed my hand.

"How are you feeling?" she asked, cocking her head and making a strand of hair fall from behind her ear.

"Wonderful," I replied, sweeping the hair back into place. "It's even better than I imagined."

"One step closer to converting everyone to your heretical ways, huh?"

I grinned, picturing even more people lined up, so numerous that they spilled onto the shore and stretched out toward Tropica. "A few dozen down, the rest of the world to go . . ."

The next few days were a joyous experience.

Each morning, the cultivators returned. A few of the more enterprising would already be fishing when I woke up, smiling out at the world with one finger held to their line. Peter had set up permanently on my back deck, arriving at the crack of dawn to start cooking people's fish as soon as they were caught. He had a few apprentices with him, those keen to learn the craft of Cooking from the most experienced of our number.

On the fourth day, I woke to a crab under one arm, an otter under the other, a rabbit sleeping in the crook of my neck, and a Chihuahua sniffing my chin.

"Good morning, Borks," I said, scooping him into a hug.

He collapsed atop me, rolling on his back and looking at me from upside down. I snorted at how goofy he looked, my smile only growing as the rest of my animal pals slowly woke. Snips blew happy bubbles, peering up at me. Claws leaped atop Borks's belly, lounging on his stomach just as he lounged on mine. Cinnamon, clearly deciding it was too early for all this noise, retreated beneath a pillow, disappearing from sight.

Maria had been staying at her home since we returned. We'd decided not to antagonize Roger for the time being, both of us hoping I could win him over for good in the coming weeks and months.

I stretched my arms high, deciding to stay put and absorb as much physical touch as possible from my animal companions before starting the day, but a rhythmic knock came at the door, making Borks bolt upright, his ears alert.

"Yoohoooo!" a beautiful voice called with singsong intonation. "Anyone home?"

Recognizing who it was, I sat up slowly, extracting myself from the cuddle puddle. "Coming!"

Everyone came with me, even Cinnamon, excited to see the person who had come knocking. When I opened the door, though, Maria wasn't alone.

"Oh! Hey, guys. What can I—"

Maria rushed forward, squeezing me so hard that the words faltered in my throat.

"Hello, Fischer," Sharon said, grinning at her daughter.

Roger grunted by way of greeting, which was, astoundingly, an improvement.

"Hi," Maria said, her voice muffled by my chest before pulling back and looking up at me. "Did you sleep well?"

"We did," I replied.

"Er . . . we?"

Claws and Cinnamon flew past me, slamming into her hard enough to throw her off balance. I grabbed her outstretched hand, keeping her upright.

"Good morning, ladies!" She laughed, hugging them both tight as Borks and Snips joined in, rubbing against her legs.

Sharon's smile only widened, just as Roger's scowl deepened, the inclusion of cute animals somehow souring his mood. Despite his general demeanor, him being here made a ray of hope shine from deep within me.

I took a deep breath and looked past them, soaking in the predawn light. The sun was still a fair way off rising, the sky a brilliant mix of purple and pink.

"So . . ." I said, trying to appear nonchalant. "What are you all doing here so early?"

Maria's eyes danced with amusement as they met mine, making the ray of hope brighten. "Well, seeing as how much fun everyone has been having, Mom and Dad thought they'd come try—"

"Not *fun*," Roger interrupted. "Advancement. From the tales I've heard, everyone has been advancing steadily from fishing."

I beamed, not even attempting to hide how happy that made me. "Of course, mate! The levels have been shooting up, only increasing as more people join in and make the overall boosts to Fishing and Luck spike."

He grunted again, giving the slightest of nods.

I felt a devious desire to stretch the moment out and make Roger squirm now that he actually wanted to try fishing, but knowing that doing so might cause him to either walk away or throw a punch, I grinned and stepped outside, pointing down at the tray Sharon held.

"Are those for me?"

"Of course!" she replied, offering up the coffee and croissant atop it.

"You're too good to me." Unable to wait, I took a bite of croissant and washed it down with a sip of the golden liquid. The pastry was flaky, buttery, and still warm from the oven. The coffee's bitterness mingled with the croissant's subtle sweetness, making a smile cross my face.

"Thank you. I needed that." Taking another sip, I led them toward my back deck. "Let's get right into it, then."

Before we even rounded the corner, the scent of cooking fish wafted out to meet us. Peter had already set up, his two apprentices right there beside him. They were cooking two absolutely *massive* fillets that clearly belonged to a mature bluefish.

Leaning against the rocks that encircled my back deck, Deklan and his brother, Dom, smiled over at us. The two had been among the most keen on fishing, always waking up well before dawn to wet their lines.

"Morning!" Deklan said, then pointed over at the barbecue. "Want some brekkie?"

"I'm good for now, mate!" I held up my half-eaten croissant, then raised an eyebrow at Maria and her parents. "Do you guys want some?"

Maria shook her head. "We had breakfast on the way here."

Claws dashed forward, chirping her assent. Snips and Borks joined her, sniffing at the air, and Cinnamon hopped over to Peter, her cute little nose twitching toward his pocket. Letting out a laugh, Peter pulled out a stalk of sugarcane and gave it to her.

I grinned back at the two brothers. "Well, there you have it. My animal pals will happily join you, but we're gonna get right into fishing."

Dom nodded. "We'll be back out there as soon as we've had the wonderful meal the cooks are making for us."

"Almost ready!" one of Peter's apprentices replied, his eyes watching the barbecue intently.

My eyes lingered on Dom for a moment as I returned his smile.

I'd been getting to know him over the past few days, and though he'd been a little reserved at first, likely because of his enslavement at the hands of Gormona, his personality had slowly been shining through. Just like Deklan, when the cultivator was himself, he had a relaxed nature that couldn't be faked. The two brothers would happily sit in silence for hours, bathing in the sun and the sounds of crashing waves. Even when the fish went off the bite, they'd remain, content with merely being. Much like myself, they'd started keeping only the mature bluefish they caught, letting everything else go to fight another day.

"We'll see you guys out there, then," I said. "Roger and Sharon have finally decided to try their hand at fishing."

Deklan nodded, not opening his eyes as he rested against the rock. "You won't regret it. Plenty of fish around this morning."

Noting that there were already a number of rods in use, I collected four of the communal creations. Maria and I hadn't been using our personal rods lately, wanting to increase the stats of everyone by using the same poles as them.

"Okay, gang. If you'll follow me . . ."

As we rounded the headland and the rock wall came into view, my steps grew energized. Despite the sun not yet having risen over the eastern horizon, there were already five other cultivators there. Two were the smiths, both of which had a fish hooked. They hooted and hollered, Fergus's stoic attitude having been ground down by Duncan's infectious excitement.

As the two smiths fought with what appeared to be mature bluefish, I led Roger and Sharon down to the communal tackle boxes we'd set up. There were four spaced out along the rock wall, all stocked with everything we could possibly need. Well, except for proper sinkers, I admitted to myself, but we could take care of that when the seasonal fish were no longer about. For now, rocks worked just fine.

I passed a rod to Maria, Roger, and Sharon, then opened the tackle box.

"Okay. This is how you set up the line with a hook and sinker . . ."

Back in New Tropica, a man strode between buildings. Though he projected a facade of relaxed indifference, his mind was anything but calm.

Nathan fought down his body's desire to run—to expend energy—relying on almost a decade's worth of intense training to take each measured step. Light bled down into the village, the sun threatening to rise over the trees and rooftops at any moment. It made him feel revealed, his mind accustomed to operating beneath the shadowed cover of night.

Though the building he entered was bathed in magical light, it made his sense of unease partially retreat. The stone walls and iron bars, despite being more confined, reminded him of home. It made his steps come easier and his airways feel clear. Striding farther along the stone corridor, he found his quarry.

Nathan nodded at his fellow cultivator. "Your watch is over."

"Thanks, Nathan." He stifled a yawn. "What time is it . . . ?" When he looked out the window, his eyes went wide. "Dawn? Glaucus's scaled form, I'm missing the golden window for fishing!" He sprinted down the hallway, yelling his thanks.

Nathan shook his head. He'd never understand how most of the cultivators in New Tropica had been so easily convinced that anything water related was a good idea.

"Damned heretics . . ." he muttered, his lip twitching.

"Is that you, Nathan?" came a soft mutter.

Before he replied, Nathan extended his ability. A bubble of silence sprang into being, surrounding him, the corridor, and the opposite cell. "Yes, Lord."

Tom Osnan Jr. raised an eyebrow at him.

"Forgive me, Lord." Nathan averted his eyes, able to do at least that. "Showing the requisite respect could lead to discovery."

Tom Osnan Jr. snorted. "Very well. How is the plan progressing?"

"It's going just as planned. Our number and influence grow by the day."

"How long?"

"If I were to hazard a guess, I'd say weeks—"

"*Weeks?*" the lord bellowed, so loud that Nathan shrank down, expecting the alarm to be raised despite his sound-dampening abilities. "Not good enough. They could change their mind and slay us at any moment. We need to return to the capital within the next few days, not *weeks.*"

"My lord . . ." Nathan licked his lips, not looking forward to the words that would come from his mouth. "If we move too soon, we run the risk of the plan falling apart—"

"So plan better! This is not the time for subtlety!"

Nathan knew that to be objectively wrong, yet it wasn't his place to say so. "Yes, Lord. Of course. You know best in these matters." He gave a swift bow after checking the coast was clear. "I will endeavor to speed things up."

"Good. Now leave me."

"Yes, Lord."

Though serving the younger Osnan chagrined him, it was a means to an end. Nathan had to get back to his master in the capital, and he'd kiss every noble ass on the way there if he had to.

He strode down the hallway toward his imprisoned fellows, intent on relaying the events of the last few days.

CHAPTER TWENTY-THREE

Hooked

As with every other cultivator, Roger and Sharon were fast learners when it came to knots. Their fingers deftly tied the thin lengths of line together, easily replicating my movements.

"How does this look?" Sharon asked, holding up her paternoster rig.

"Perfect, Mom!" Maria gave her a wide grin. "You're a natural."

"Yours is expertly done too, Roger," I added, earning a mild grunt in response. "Usually, I'd say we should catch some bait, but we've already got way too much."

We'd been catching plenty of eels, storing them in buckets of brine to preserve the meat. Wanting to give Roger and Sharon the best experience possible, I went for a bucket marked with a yellow ribbon; it contained the pungent monkeyface variety. Though the brine did a wonderful job of keeping the eels intact, it did nothing to remove the smell.

As soon as I removed it from the salty solution, Sharon covered her nose. "Gods above—is that really okay to use for bait?"

"The smellier it is, the better it is as bait." Not wanting to subject her to the scent for too long, I swiftly cut it into small chunks and threw the excess pieces back into the bucket. "I can put the bait on the hook if you'd like?"

Sharon shook her head. "No. We want the full experience, even if it's the worst thing I've ever smelled."

"Even worse than that time Dad accidentally cooked a rotten hunk of meat for eight hours?"

"Okay," Sharon conceded. "Even if it's the second-worst thing I've ever smelled."

Color rose to Roger's cheeks, and he scowled at the two women he loved most.

I raised an eyebrow at Maria, but decided to ask her about it later when Roger wasn't around to hear.

"Okay, gang. Follow along." I grabbed a piece of eel and slid it onto the hook.

They easily did so, Roger still flushing, Sharon trying to hide a smile.

With all of our rods ready to go, I faced the east.

The tip of the sun was just starting to breach the horizon, shining a reddish light over us. Fergus and Duncan had both won the battle versus their respective fish. Either of the creatures would have made a good meal, yet they let them go, the men sharing a high-five before washing their hands in the waves. A cold breeze blew from behind me, ruffling my clothes and tickling my skin. Though a shiver ran down my back, it was a pleasant sensation, the modicum of wrath coming from the sun enough to take the sting from it.

I turned to take in Maria and her parents, finding them also enjoying the view. Even Roger had a small smile, though it quickly morphed into a frown upon noticing my attention. I led them up the rock wall, waving at the smiths as I passed.

"Did you guys already have brekkie?" I asked. "Those were the perfect size for a meal!"

Duncan grinned up at me. "We're waiting for a larger version to come along!"

"The mature ones taste better anyway," Fergus added, giving us a nod that froze when he caught sight of Roger and Sharon. "You're finally trying fishing!" He bellowed a laugh. "Enjoy!"

"We will!" Sharon called over her shoulder.

We strode to the end of the rock wall, stopping only when there was no more path to traverse. I held my rod forward, flicking the reel open. "Put it in this position to cast. Hold your finger on the line so it doesn't unspool, then let go as you cast the rod forward. Like so . . ."

I sent my sinker out. It arced over the ocean, landing with a soft plop not far away.

Maria repeated the same action, letting them observe it twice. I watched their faces intently, noticing how focused they were on our actions.

"Ready, dear?" Sharon asked.

"Mm-hm," Roger replied, stepping forward, his eyes roaming the small waves between us and the horizon.

They flicked their reels forward, held their fingers to the lines, and cast out. They mimicked our movements perfectly, their bait flying at the perfect angle and splashing down into the bay. They reeled in the slack line just as we had, then rested a fingertip to their lines, waiting for the telltale bump of a fish nibbling their bait.

Though I always found the wait for a bite thrilling, I couldn't help but steal glances at Sharon and Roger—especially the latter. I was entirely too invested in him and his potential enjoyment of fishing. The longer I watched him, the more sure I became.

Roger was enjoying himself.

He did a wonderful job of appearing stoic, but even without my enhanced senses, I'd have noticed the way he held himself—the set of his shoulders, the severity in his gaze, and how his fingers twitched slightly as they waited for a bite. With my awareness of chi, though, his very core screamed his excitement for anyone with the requisite advancement to hear. It pulsed from his abdomen, tasting of anticipation, curiosity, and urgency.

He didn't have to wait long; his line dipped, a fish having a nibble.

"Wait," I hissed, feeling his intent to reef the line and set the hook.

He jolted to a standstill, shooting me an accusatory glare.

"Not yet, mate," I continued. "Wait for it . . ."

He returned his attention to his line, the wooden handle creaking within his empowered grasp. The impatience radiating from him increased, but even so, he waited, not flinching until another bite came. Seconds felt like an eternity, everyone holding their breath as we watched the rod's tip. The creature bit the bait again, this time swallowing it whole.

Roger reacted immediately, reefing the rod upward and setting the hook. He wound and lifted the rod, his eyebrow furrowing. He tugged again and again, but it didn't budge.

"Shit," I said. "It might have swum into coral or spat the hook somehow. Maybe it took it on that first bite?"

Roger's lips formed a line as he shot a venomous glance my way. "You told me to wait . . ."

"It was the right call," Maria tried, her voice soothing. "It seems like you're stuck on a rock to me, but there are plenty more fish in the sea."

I chewed my lip, considering. We'd caught only bluefish since they'd come on, the predatory creatures likely chasing everything else from the bay. Whatever had bitten Roger's line, though, didn't seem to be one of the seasonal fish we'd been targeting. The bluefish were aggressive, always smashing the bait on the first go. If they missed the first bite, they'd return a moment later, slamming into it and swimming off.

A single tug didn't match their behavior—neither did retreating to cover behind a rock or snag.

"I'll go get Snips or Claws," I said, giving Roger a wincing smile as I stepped forward to help. "They can swim down for us and dislodge—"

Roger's rod suddenly bent almost in half, something on the end of his line darting out to sea at incredible speed. His reel whined, the bearing spinning freely.

"Fish on still!" I yelled, pointing at him.

His eyes went wide as he moved in a blur, easily grabbing the wooden handle.

Feeling its tether go taut, the fish changed direction, swimming southeast in a straight line. Roger's mouth parted, revealing the flash of teeth as he grinned despite himself. He kept the tension a little too tight, and I felt the need to correct him, but him being, well, *him*, brought me up short, my need to help warring with my desire for him to enjoy himself.

Thankfully, Maria wasn't held back by such worries. "You're holding it too tight, Dad! Reel backwards!"

"What?" he yelled. "What do you mean real backwards? You told me to keep it taut earlier!"

"Your line is too tight! It's going to snap off!"

He did his best to follow our contradicting instructions, but having not spent any time watching us fish, his mistakes piled up.

He didn't move, instead choosing to hold his ground on one of the rock wall's boulders. His rod was held at the wrong angle, the tip not high enough to let the wooden pole flex and handle the fish's mighty head shakes. And though he reeled backwards and let some of the line out, it was nowhere near enough. If the creature he'd hooked had been a bluefish, he would have likely been fine.

But this was no bluefish.

I had no clue what it was, but the thing tore through the water like a missile, occasionally changing direction before launching off once more. Roger's mistakes compounded, working together to place too much stress on the line, and when he reefed the rod at the wrong time, he lost the battle. His line went slack, Maria having to dash over and stop him from falling ass first onto the rocks.

His core radiated disappointment, the sensation honed by his bladelike chi, so sharp that the edges made my hackles rise. But as he wound in his line, more emotions leaped forth. First and foremost was curiosity, his mind unable to comprehend what kind of creature he'd hooked. Joy, elation, and even a sprinkle of gratitude bubbled up, slowly but surely overwhelming his negativity.

As I felt the switch in attitude, my core sang. I'd hoped he would enjoy fishing, but this was better than any hypothetical scenario I'd entertained. Unfortunately for me, Roger had an increased sense of the world around him after his last breakthrough; he felt my happiness. Still winding his reel's handle, he leveled a glare at me, his eyes narrowed and lips pressing together.

I whistled, rocking on my heels and looking out at the churning ocean and rising sun.

"What *was* that?" Sharon asked, her voice tinged with disbelief.

"Big bloody fish," I replied, still averting my eyes. "I think it was a new species based on how it fought. Never seen anything like it."

Roger finished winding in his line. It had snapped below his leader, the sinker remaining but the hook nowhere to be seen. He watched it for a long moment, contemplative.

"Would you have been able to catch that, Maria?"

"Well, I mean, *maybe*, but only because of my Fishing level. Even then—"

"Maria," he interrupted. "Don't honey your words, young lady."

I blew air from my lips at the way he addressed her like a misbehaving child, but resumed whistling and looking literally anywhere else when they both shot me a look.

"Lovely day, isn't it, Sharon?"

She just laughed at me, shaking her head.

Maria sighed. "Yeah. I probably would have caught it, Dad. You made a lot of mistakes. They were why the line snapped."

"Okay." He nodded to himself, chewing his cheek. "I can accept that. I didn't think that it required any level of skill, if I'm being honest."

Focused as I may have been on the conversation, I couldn't miss my line going tight.

"Whoa! Fish on!"

The bluefish on the end of my line took off, wasting no time in trying to escape.

"Me too!" Maria yelled, setting her hook.

"Oh!" Sharon said, her rod also bent in half.

I shot Roger a quick grin. "Watch what Maria and I do—you too, Sharon!"

My fish swam to the north, and I reeled it in with exaggerated movement, letting line out whenever it took a large run. When it darted to the left and headed toward the shore, I ran along the rocks, keeping my line just tight enough with each step.

"Keep your rod like this!" Maria yelled, also running along the boulders to my right, dipping under Sharon's line. "If it's at a forty-five-degree angle, the wood can flex when the fish shakes its head!"

As if on command, the creature on the end of her line thrashed around, making the tip bounce and absorb the vast majority of the force.

Not wanting to make my fish fight for too long, I ended my exaggerated movements, bringing it in toward the rocks. It was a juvenile bluefish, but one of the biggest ones I'd ever seen, likely only days or weeks from becoming the mature version. Though I was happy with its size, I didn't need any more food. I removed it from the hook and dipped it back underwater, watching as it disappeared with a mighty kick of its silvery tail.

Maria pulled hers up on the rocks too. It was much smaller than mine, so after freeing it, she lobbed it back into the water.

"Bye, fishy!" she called, giving it a wave.

Sharon was still fighting hers, mimicking what we'd done to land ours.

I turned to check on Roger, but he was nowhere to be seen. Raising an eyebrow, I scanned the rock wall, finding him hunched over a tackle box. He was tying another hook in place with rapid movements, darting looks back toward Sharon to check on her progress.

I took a deep breath, sighing it out as I glanced at the water.

"Mission successful." Maria snickered, also sneaking looks back toward her father.

I shot her a wink, nodding. "We've hooked him."

"I can hear you!" he yelled, making us both cackle with laughter.

CHAPTER TWENTY-FOUR

Trust

Beneath a hideously bright sky, Augustus Reginald Gormona squinted toward the rising sun, willing it to retreat behind the horizon.

As with everything lately, it didn't go in his favor, and as the golden orb rose ever higher, taunting him, he turned his back to it, refusing to witness any more insubordination, perceived or otherwise. He let his thoughts wander, imagining what he could have done differently when he'd fought the invading spirit beasts.

"Are you ready, Augustus?" someone asked, shattering the fantasized revenge plot currently playing out against Lizard Wizard.

The king whirled, his chi threatening to fly free with the memory of battle still fresh in mind.

His wife flinched back, her face white and eyes panicked.

Seeing fear replace his wife's beauty, a pang of regret stabbed deep into Augustus's core. Realizing his teeth were bared, he sighed, his body sagging. "Apologies. I was . . . elsewhere."

"It's . . . fine," she replied, smoothing her dress. "We're almost ready to leave."

He nodded stiffly. As they walked down the cobbled streets of Gormona, they easily fell into step, matching each other's pace. With her at his side, his worries receded, his breaths coming easier. Though their marriage had once been one of necessity, they had grown close over their many decades of partnership. They would always be a king and queen first, of course, but he had a rare respect for Penelope.

Her hand drifted over, her fingers seeking to intertwine with his.

"Not in public," he replied, lip twitching as he slapped her hand away.

"Of course." She raised her chin, staring forward. "Sorry."

They continued on in silence, his anger at her breach of decorum slowly receding. Voices came from ahead, and when they caught sight of the king and queen, their conversation died off.

Tom Osnan strode forward, nodding at them. "Good morning, Augustus."

"King," he corrected, looking down his nose at his oldest friend. "I've not yet forgiven your failure, Tom. As you should well know."

"Of course." Despite his words, fury lined Tom's face, but he bowed at the waist to hide it.

Following the lord's lead, Aisa and the rest of the handlers bowed even lower. "Good morning, my king," they chorused, their faces remaining downturned.

"Rise," he said.

As their gazes met his, he let his displeasure show clearly on his face. It mattered not that they didn't stand a chance against the force that had attacked Gormona. One and all, they had failed. Until they could regain his favor, he had no intention of letting them off the hook.

"Hello," came a welcome voice.

Augustus spun toward the rising sun, seeing the only person who hadn't failed him in recent memory.

"Good morning, daughter," he said. "Did you sleep well?"

"Yes, Father." Tryphena gave him a slight smile that didn't reach the rest of her face, making Augustus's appreciation for her presence only increase. "What about you?"

He let out a wry chuckle. "I can't recall the last time I slept well, but that's of little importance."

The sound of hooves clopping and wheels trundling over cobblestones came from the street behind Tryphena. When the merchant's cart rounded the corner into view, the man's face was stricken.

"You're almost late, Marcus," Tom Osnan said, shooting a withering glare at the approaching man. "Endeavor to be earlier in the future."

"Wr . . . I'm sorry. There was little notice and I had to collect a number of supplies early this—"

"Save your excuses," Tom interrupted. "You waste your breath."

The merchant's face went even whiter, the blood draining away as he bowed from his seated position. "Yes, my lord. I apologize."

Tom sniffed. "Well, that's everyone." He turned toward the western gate and began walking.

A smirk came to Augustus Reginald Gormona's face. "Not so fast, Tom. We haven't made all the preparations."

When his friend turned to face Augustus, worry lined the lord's face.

Good, Augustus thought.

He stepped forward, waving dismissively at Aisa and the rest of the handlers. "Unhitch the horses."

"My king?" Marcus replied. "We need all of them to carry the—"

"You dare talk back to your king?" Aisa yelled, marching to the side of the cart. "Explain yourself!"

"I, er, I'm sorry . . ." His Adam's apple bobbed as he swallowed, clenching his jaw. "I merely wish to serve, Your Majesty, and I believe the horses are needed in that regard."

"It isn't your place to question him, *peasant*!" Aisa spat the last word, her eyes fiery.

"That's enough," Augustus said. "Though he spoke out of turn, he is correct. Usually, we *would* need horses."

"Usually . . . ?" his wife asked, but at the venomous look he shot her, she said no more.

"Yes. Usually. This mission is of utter import, so we won't be using horses. Lord Tom Osnan will take their place."

"Augustus." Tom took a step forward, fury oozing from his body as he exerted his plant-like chi. "Surely you jest. I may be out of your favor, but to resort to such punishment—"

"Enough!" Augustus Reginald Gormona, king of these lands, bellowed.

Flames licked from his back and fists, singeing the heat-resistant threads of his robe. He let his rage flow, feeding the fire that consumed his very clothing. It had the desired effect, even the battle-hardened Tom Osnan averting his eyes.

"I expect back talk from the peasantry, Tom. They aren't aware of their position." He shot forward on a stream of super-heated air, grabbing his best friend by the chin and forcing his head upward. As their gazes met, Augustus saw the red chi of his eyes reflected in Tom's. "If you ever wish to repair this friendship, Tom, you. Will. *Obey.*"

Outrage and fear warred across Tom's features, but after a moment, the fear won.

"Yes, my king," he said, dipping his head as Augustus let go.

"Good. Though it is unbecoming of my station to explain myself, I'll do so for the sake of brevity. You. Handlers." He waved a hand in their direction. "You are to get in the cart with the wares. You are to act as a beast of burden, Tom, because that is the fastest way to travel. We don't have time to spare."

Though Augustus's intentional verbiage made Tom's lip twitch, the lord nodded, accepting his task.

"Now, unhitch the horses, Aisa. We leave them here."

Augustus watched the merchant carefully, ready to punish the man if he spoke out against leaving his animals behind, but the peasant showed more intelligence than Tom. He nodded, looking at his feet to hide his emotions.

The handlers removed the horses and tied them to a lamp post, and as they climbed into the cart, Tom took his position at the head of the cart.

Without checking to see if they were ready, Augustus, Penelope, and Tryphena took off, jogging toward the western gate. The guards had been informed of their passage, and as the procession crossed the threshold of the capital, the guards bowed, showing their respect.

A small smile came to Augustus's face. Those that attacked his kingdom thought they had dealt Gormona a death blow, but when he returned from Theogonia, they would show them. No, *he* would show them.

It would be Lizard Wizard and his heretical ilk that perished.

When Nathan's replacement came to relieve him of guard duties, it took every ounce of his strength not to lash out at the fool.

"Sorry I'm late," she said, grinning and twirling her ponytail around a finger. "I got a bit caught up with fishing. Roger and Sharon, two of the founders, were there today! They were *unbelievable*! I'd have thought they'd been at it for years, but apparently it was their first time!"

"Lovely," he replied.

"Have you been yet?"

"I haven't, no."

"Really? You *have* to try it!" Her face lit up, making him want to strike the joy from her countenance. "I can't believe how relaxing it is," she continued. "And exciting!"

He bit back a snarky comment, knowing it wasn't yet time to show his true feelings. "Maybe I will," he lied, striding away to hide his look of disgust.

When he emerged into the night air, he paused for a moment, a modicum of tension leaving his body. To be beneath the cover of night was a wonderful thing after spending all day on guard duty, and he took a few breaths for himself. With his steps feeling lighter, he took off, knowing he was already late for the meeting.

He walked out of the southern side of New Tropica, the night air getting colder the deeper he got into the forest. He kept his steps measured, plodding toward the agreed place. When he arrived, he found everyone already there: his co-leader, Zeke; the other five who had remained true to the crown; and a new face. Nathan immediately extended his ability, wrapping the entire area in a bubble of silence.

The newcomer jolted, her body going stiff as she considered him.

"We were beginning to think you weren't coming," Zeke said.

Nathan waved a hand. "I couldn't leave my post until one of the traitors was done fishing."

"Traitors . . . ?" Anna, the new arrival, asked. "There are traitors? And why do I feel like I'm wrapped in your chi right now . . . ?"

Nathan shot a glance Zeke's way. "I thought you said she was with us . . . ?"

"No, I said she would be on board."

"On board?" Anna's eyes darted around the clearing, scanning everyone's faces. She balled her fists as her gaze came to rest on Zeke. "I think you have some explaining to do."

Zeke held his hands up. "Relax, Anna. No one is going to hurt you unless you lash out with that punch you're considering."

She took a step back, not looking at all mollified by his words, her knuckles going white. "Explain. *Now.*"

"May I?" Nathan asked Zeke, getting a nod in return.

"Okay, I'll cut right to the chase, then. This village, this *haven*, as they call it, is going to end in disaster. We mean to not be here when it does."

Anna merely watched him, her lips pursing as her thoughts raced. When the silence stretched for long enough, he continued.

"Everything they're doing here goes against the will of the gods, and even if we do nothing, it will eventually fall into ruin. We aren't planning on killing them. We aren't even planning on getting in their way. All we mean to do is leave and take the Osnans with us."

It was a lie, of course—they would do everything they could to hurt the village before leaving. But this girl didn't need to know that.

"Why are you telling me this?" she asked. "And what would you do to me if I didn't agree?"

"What would we do to you?" Nathan let out a light laugh. "Nothing, of course," he lied again, having already told everyone but Zeke to strike her down unless she agreed to join them. "Zeke here has vouched for you. He says you will agree with us, and that your show of going along with their plans is just that—*a show*."

"Tell them, Anna," Zeke rushed, gesturing wildly. "I've known you most of my life, and you're not the kind of person to roll over and abandon your ideals."

Her eyes never left Nathan.

She weighed him, the lines of her face shifting as her empowered brain considered their words. The longer the silence stretched, the more convinced Nathan became that they would need to snuff her out.

"How did you fool them?" she asked. "They have an auditor with them."

"A former auditor, you mean." Nathan faked a grin. "My ability. It isn't just a deafening space. It leaves the abilities of others . . . ineffective."

She took an involuntary step back. "You bring me out here into the forest and nullify my powers? Hardly the basis with which to form an alliance, is it?"

He nodded. "You're right. I'm going to drop it for a few seconds. If you agree with us, say nothing. If you don't agree with us, feel free to attack or yell for help. That should be sufficient to trust that we mean you no ill will, yes?"

Without preamble, he retracted his power. But not all of it, of course. He had exaggerated his touch, allowing her to feel it on her skin. Now, he made it something subtle instead. It was the same artful application that even the advanced heretics of this village hadn't noticed. He poised his body to attack, leaning forward in a feint of agreeability.

Contrary to his expectations, she said nothing, merely watching and waiting. After three breaths, he made his power detectable again, pushing it out so she could feel it.

"See?" Zeke demanded. "I *told* you she was trustworthy."

Nathan nodded, not needing to fake his surprise. "I take it you're on board, then?"

She licked her lips, considering her reply. "I am. You know me well, Zeke." Her eyebrow twitched as she cast her gaze in the direction of New Tropica. "I'm not the kind of person to abandon my ideals. I was waiting for the right opportunity, which you seem to have provided."

"Perfect." Zeke rubbed his hands together. "Let me tell you the plan in detail, then. I spoke with Lord Tom Osnan Jr. today, and we may need to expedite our timeline . . ."

CHAPTER TWENTY-FIVE

Revenge

Now that Roger and Sharon had joined our heretical endeavors, the rest of the week sped by in a blur.

Each morning, I'd wake to a knock on the door, then receive a barrage of love from Maria while Roger scowled and Sharon smiled. After having breakfast on my porch, we'd all head down to the rock wall and start fishing.

With the tastes of coffee and croissant lingering on my tongue, I stepped onto the stone walkway and smiled out at the world. It was the seventh day since we'd started targeting the seasonal fish, and the weather was as wonderful as the rest of the week, the first rays of sunlight casting a warm glow over the ocean. The wind was stronger than usual, incessantly blowing from the west. A strong gust kicked up, making goose bumps rise on my skin.

Feeling the same sensation, Maria wrapped her arm around my waist and pulled me into a hug, hiding behind my back until the squall subsided.

"Why is it so windy?" she asked. "There isn't a cloud in the sky."

"Smells like rain," Roger said, staring at the horizon.

"Maria," I whispered.

"Yeah?"

"What the frack is he talking about?"

"Maybe it's a farmer thing?" she suggested, our voices slowly rising.

"Well, yeah, but you're a farmer too. Do you smell rain?"

"Hmmm." She tapped her chin. "Nope. Perhaps it's an old farmer thing?"

"He *is* pretty old, isn't he? Practically ancien—*ow!*" I rubbed my lower back where a rod had struck. We'd been taunting Roger, so I'd kept him in my peripheral vision. What I hadn't anticipated was Sharon taking a swing.

She glared at me. "Before you finish that sentence, Fischer, you should remember that I'm around the same age as my husband."

"You *are*? I could have sworn you were Maria's older sister. You don't look a day over thirty."

"Oooo," Maria cooed, adopting an announcer's voice. "Flattery. Will it be enough to win her back?"

Sharon lowered her eyebrows and pursed her lips, considering me. "A good start," she eventually said, smirking past me as she looked at the distant horizon.

"Wonderful. I'll endeavor not to further antagon—*oof!*" I cut off as something slammed into my back, sending me flying. I soared over the rocks and into the ocean, crashing down into the cold waters. Adrenaline ran through me, banishing any remnants of sleep that remained.

When I returned to the surface, Maria and Sharon were laughing so hard that they'd hunched over, bracing themselves on the stone path. Seeing the hint of a smile on Roger's face as he pretended to inspect his fingernails, I understood the truth. Sharon hadn't been smirking at the horizon; she'd been watching Roger line me up. Now that he'd had his breakthrough, he could manipulate his chi enough to fool me—I hadn't felt his approach at all.

Treading water, I couldn't help but laugh. "All right, fair play."

When I got back to the rocks, Maria helped me up, pulling me from the freezing ocean.

"Well, if you'll excuse me, I need to go get some dry clothes before I turn into a popsicle."

"A what . . . ?" Sharon asked.

"Don't," Maria said. "It's a trap."

I shot a wink back her way. "Maybe I can make some for you if we can work out refrigeration. They'd be a blessing come summer."

Without another word, I returned home and got out of my now-drenched clothing. I briefly considered having a shower to get warm but decided against it, wanting to fish as soon as possible. By the time I returned to the rock wall, their lines were already in the water. I rushed to catch up, and with a bit of eel on the end of my hook, I cast it out into the bay.

The morning passed by in an excitement-fueled blur, all of us reeling in fish after fish. By the time the sun was high overhead, most of New Tropica had joined us on the rock wall, all catching and releasing armfuls of the seasonal creatures. By now, everyone had started returning everything but the mature variants back to the ocean, and though we kept dozens of them each day, their number hadn't reduced. I'd become so used to people reaching level twenty-five in Fishing that I barely noticed the clink of coins when System-generated bags periodically hit the stone pathway beneath our feet.

As I released my fourth fish of the day, I smiled and watched it retreat beneath the waves. Another squall blew across my skin, this time bringing with it small drops of rain. I gazed up just in time to see a giant mass block out the sun, the entire eastern sky smothered in gray clouds.

"Huh, how about that?" I said. "It really did smell like rain."

"Uh-huh," Roger agreed, staring at the incoming rain.

I considered asking if they wanted to leave, to retreat back to my deck now that there seemed to be a storm brewing, but as I looked at them, I realized there was no point. Roger and Sharon were completely unperturbed, swiftly returning their attention to their rods after peering at the gray sky. Maria noticed them too, and she shot me a beautiful smile before closing her eyes and waiting for a fish to strike. Rather than cast my line out again right away, I took a moment to bask in her beauty.

The wind blew strong from the east, causing strands of her sun-bleached hair to dance, my enhanced vision able to witness each languid movement as they flowed in the unseen breeze. Her freckled skin was still a golden color even beneath the blanket of darkness above, her glow refusing to be extinguished. Most of all, I was drawn into her expression, the joy and peace held there enough to make my heart thunder. She was a vision of radiance, and try as I might, I couldn't tear my eyes away.

But then, from the corner of my field of view, I witnessed Roger's rod almost snap in half.

"Whoa!" he yelled, scrambling to keep his footing on the slick rocks as he let some line out. "Fish on!"

Though he would never admit it to Fischer, Roger was thoroughly enjoying his time fishing.

He had always seen it as a fanciful waste of time, something that ran too close to heresy for any sane person to take part in. Even after becoming a cultivator himself, he'd still viewed it as a step too far. Over the past few days, that belief had slowly been eroded away like soil in a summer flood.

The act of fishing seemed to tickle a primal part of his mind. It was somehow exciting and calming at the same time, the sensation impossible to put into words. This, at least, he would admit to himself: Fischer was right. Roger had tried it, expecting nothing out of it besides some extra levels. Instead, he'd been hooked, much the same as the fish they targeted.

A storm was coming in. A normal person—anyone other than a heretical fool—would seek shelter. Short of a crop that desperately needed harvesting before the rains hit, Roger would never have stayed in the field with a tempest on the way. And yet, here he was, standing before a coming storm with nothing on his mind but his wife, his daughter, and the next fish he could do battle with.

Lulled into a state of bliss by the sounds of waves lapping at the rock wall, he almost lost his rod when the fish struck.

"Whoa!" he yelled, leaning back and letting the reel spin. "Fish on!"

He'd caught enough bluefish over the past half week to know that this was a different species. It took off in a straight line, heading for the distant horizon like a bolt fired from a crossbow. When it changed directions and darted toward the shore, his lips curled up into a smile.

"Back for more, are you?" he roared, throwing his face skyward and unleashing a laugh. "Bring it on!"

It was the fish that had bested him the first time he'd gone fishing. Roger had been inexperienced then, leading to the creature's escape. This time, though, he wouldn't lose. Roger ran across the rocks in the direction of the shore, handfuls of cultivators getting themselves and their rods out of his way. The fish changed direction again, heading back out to sea, but Roger was ready. He dashed with it, never allowing his line to go slack. The fish continued its passage out to sea, his reel's bearing whining with how much length he was letting out.

"You'll need to fight it!" Fischer yelled. "It's risky, but the fish will spool you otherwise!"

A few days ago, Roger would have told Fischer to kick rocks. He'd have said something about contradicting information, not comprehending what Fischer meant. After his time fishing, though, Roger knew that the human equivalent of a thorn in his side was correct. He pulled his rod up, cringing internally as its fibers creaked and complained. He wound the reel, gaining back ground. When he'd retrieved half of the line, he let the fish go for another run.

"Perfect!" Maria called. "Let it tire itself out, Dad!"

The grin never left Roger's face, and he nodded, watching as the fish cut through the bay. He danced across the rocks more times than he could count, even running along the river-mouth side of the wall on occasion. After what had to be most of an hour, it started to slow, its seemingly endless reserves finally diminished.

"Almost there, mate!" Fischer yelled, making Roger set his jaw and firm his resolve.

He slowly brought it closer to the rocks, and when he finally caught sight of its body, Roger's jaw dropped open.

"Holy *frack*!" Maria yelled, bouncing on her heels. "It's *huge*!"

Roger barely registered how cold it was as he stepped onto a rock below the water's surface. He leaned down and picked the fish up by the body. It kicked its tail feebly, having already used every bit of strength it had. The thing was taller than he was and wider than his chest, with vicious teeth and a body like an arrow.

With his eyes wide, Roger's vision was drawn into it.

Mature Bluefathom Mackerel
Rare
Found in the deep waters of the Kallis Realm, this fish is prized for both sport and the quality of its flesh. Rarely seen, some say that consuming this creature provides a temporary boost to Luck.

Roger swallowed, his eyes clearing as he looked back up toward the rock wall. He hadn't realized that everyone was watching him, not a single line remaining in the water. He took the dozens of cultivators in, still not able to completely grasp the creature he held.

"Damn, Roger," Fischer said, shaking his head to clear his vision. "Imbued with Luck? That's something . . ."

Roger swallowed again, his mouth feeling dry. "Is . . . is it okay if I let it go?"

Fischer's head rocked backwards. *"What?"*

Roger clenched his jaw, ready to tear into the man if he demanded he kill such a noble creature, but then Fischer continued.

"Of course it is, you silly goose. You caught it, you decide what to do with it. Here, let me help you." Fischer jumped down beside Roger. "Put it back underwater. We need to get oxygen running through its gills. Here. Like this . . ."

With one of them on either side of it, they pushed and pulled it through the small waves, apparently allowing it to breathe. Life slowly returned to it over the following minutes, and not a single word was uttered, everyone lost in its majesty. Without warning, it started kicking, some of its strength returning.

Fischer jumped out of the water. "Looks good, mate! Let it go!"

Roger bent down, running his hand along its muscular body. "You fought well, friend." He pushed it off, and the moment it was free of his grasp, it sailed away, disappearing from sight after only a few kicks of its mighty tail. All he could do was watch, feeling an immense amount of respect for his adversary.

Muttered conversations sprung up from the attending cultivators, all beginning to discuss what they'd just witnessed.

"So, Roger," Fischer said, "do they have any sayings about revenge where you're from . . . ?"

"*Revenge* . . . ?" Roger shook his head, still unable to tear his eyes from the ocean. "I've never heard of any, no."

"Really? Weird. Back on Earth, they say it's a dish best served cold."

"What foolishness are you even saying?" Roger asked, his gaze melding with the churning waves.

"Fischer," Maria warned. "Don't you dare—"

Hearing urgency in his daughter's voice, Roger spun.

Well, he'd intended to spin.

Before he could, a foot lashed out and kicked his backside, sending him sprawling into the freezing-cold waves.

CHAPTER TWENTY-SIX

Escape

Within a dark and humid room, a devout man practiced his craft.

The scents of earth, mildew, and sweet herbs surrounded him, standing in stark contrast to the haze that usually filled his domain. It had taken Solomon most of a week to create this place of worship—the holy ground upon which he would take steps on the stairway of ascension.

For as long as Solomon had been practicing alchemy, he had been inhaling the Cult of the Alchemist's chi-suppressing smoke. Toward the end of his stay in Tropica, the burning qualities of the haze had seemed to decrease, his empowered body somehow withstanding the usually agony-inducing qualities of the cult's greatest creation.

He took a deep breath, marveling at the soothing characteristics his newest concoction seemed to have on his throat. Where his past workspaces made him feel physically ill, the vapors wafting up from his cauldron now caused his body to hum, as if it was healing all the prior punishment he had put it through.

Solomon had no doubt as to the ingredient causing this shift; it was the bark of the blue-trunked tree.

The decomposing plant matter was the basis of the brew he currently worked on, aided by medicinal herbs and plants that he'd found in the surrounding forest. This place of power seemed to make plant life flourish; he hadn't needed to travel far in order to find the ingredients he looked for, and Solomon could think of nowhere else on Kallis that he'd ever witnessed so much diversity.

Despite the wondrous soothing of his throat, Solomon's brow knitted. The bark had irrefutable healing qualities, but it wasn't doing what he'd hoped.

Much like he could feel the suppressing aspect of the haze he usually worked within, he could also sense the potent chi held within his concoction. It was there. He was sure of it. Yet he couldn't harness its power. There had to be something missing—an ingredient, perhaps, but try as he might, Solomon couldn't work out what it was.

Taking a deep breath, he tried to focus his will on the concoction, just as the Cult of the Alchemist's doctrine instructed. He closed his eyes, imagining the outcome he desired. Solomon dressed in golden robes, the garb so rich that he shone as bright as the midday sun. The other members of the Cult of the Alchemist, prostate and bowing before him, their god. A pile of riches laying at his feet, brought forth by the kingdoms trying to gain his favor.

Something resonated within his abdomen as the scene played out in his mind's eye. With exhilaration fueling his efforts, he imagined even more people praising him, and an even greater pile of gold. He strained, his body hunching as he sought to focus every ounce of will he had on that eventuality.

No matter how hard he tried, however, nothing happened. The vibration within remained just that—a vibration.

Despite his efforts, there was something nagging at him in the back of his mind. An immovable blockage that halted his progress. He did his best to ignore it, but the stray thought was like a rock in one's shoe, only growing more agitating the longer it was left unremoved. Unlike the metaphorical stone, however, Solomon couldn't just remove his boot and take it out.

There was something missing from the concoction, and no matter how many times he redoubled his efforts, nothing would change that fact.

He let out a sigh as he looked out at the waking world once more, the scene dissipating like a soluble compound in hot water. He couldn't ascend until he found the missing ingredient.

Standing and stretching, he made for the door, intent on finding it.

A heavy breeze washed over me, flecking my skin with small drops of rain. I'd spent the morning fishing, hanging with my friends, and exacting vengeance. All in all, it left me feeling balanced, which was a good thing, considering the blade of chi currently flying for my head.

Going full matrix, I dodged it.

Springing backward, I took off running toward shore, unable to halt my giggles despite the murder held in Roger's eyes. "I had no choice!"

"There is always a choice!" he roared, standing upright in the waves.

"You were perfectly positioned for a good punting! What was I supposed to do?"

He didn't respond, marching from the water as a drowned mess. He continued his approach, completely silent as he strode toward me. Chi roiled from his core and made the air around him shimmer with violent intent. Maria tried to scowl at me, scrunching her face in order to hide the amusement radiating from her abdomen.

Sharon sighed, rubbing the bridge of her nose. "Please don't kill each other."

It was the last sentence I had the chance of hearing; Roger exploded forward, soaring across the pathway toward me. I turned and fled, still laughing as I zipped side to side, dodging the blades of energy sent flying my way.

Nathan stared up at the incoming clouds, their dark shadow lending his awareness a sense of ease.

As he moved along streets and between the buildings of New Tropica, he took measured breaths. When he felt someone looking his way, he paused to peer up at a building's architecture, letting his gaze wander over its utilitarian design.

Though he attempted to appear ponderous and unhurried to anyone watching, Nathan was anything but.

Sweat beaded at his lower back, his heart pounding as the scene he'd witnessed replayed in his mind. He had been at the edge of the forest not long ago, staring out at the sand flats as rain clouds formed to the east. Though the coming storm granted him a sense of comfort, that wasn't why he'd been there.

He was there waiting for an opportunity, and his foresight had been rewarded.

The only warning he had was a vibration in his core, and then the two cultivators had arrived, exchanging blows that reverberated in his chest. They approached from the north, one trailing the other and unleashing a hail of blade-shaped projectiles. Though Fischer was literally deified by the heretics in this treasonous village, it was the other man who filled Nathan with terror.

The blades flying from his body tore through sand, stone, and everything in between. Before they'd passed through, there was a small outcropping of boulders between the sands and the southern mountains. It was now a smattering of angular rocks, the boulders having been sliced apart when Fischer tried to hide behind them.

The entire time, Fischer had laughed. Despite being pressed by a man who could easily level a mountain, Fischer had stopped mid-fight to smile and wave at Nathan, only resuming the battle when dual arcs of power shot for his chest.

It had all happened so fast, and if not for his cultivation, Nathan wouldn't have seen a thing. Within the space of a few breaths, they were gone again. Only distant booms announced their new position on the other side of the southern mountain range, the very ground quaking with each massive attack.

Though their display of power had unsettled him to his core, it was exactly what he'd been waiting for.

Nathan shook his head, dispelling his thoughts and returning to the present. He strode into the smithy, finding two of the loyal.

"Could I bother you two for a moment?" he asked conversationally, not drawing the attention of the head smiths, who, for once, weren't off fishing.

They nodded in response, following him onto the street.

He, Zeke, and Anna had stepped up their recruiting over the past few days. The latter had proven to be an invaluable asset, her efforts seeing the number of the loyal more than double. There were almost two score of them now, and with the village's heretical protector elsewhere, it was time to strike.

He watched as Anna headed into the tailoring workshop, thankful for Zeke's wisdom in recruiting her.

And to think that I wanted to neutralize her, Nathan thought, smirking to himself. It was a shame she wouldn't be making it out of the village.

He would have to introduce her to his master if she ever returned to the capital— Tom Osnan Sr. could always use more pawns.

As the two tailoring apprentices joined their precession, Nathan nodded at Anna. She set her jaw and nodded back. She had volunteered to lead the distraction, which was another reason to be thankful for her service. Two of the newer members followed her as she headed to the east side of the village. They believed he would immediately come back and rescue them, which was a lie, of course, but trickery was perfectly fine if it meant they succeeded in extracting the nobles and getting them back to Gormona. They could be freed when the capital came and crushed this misguided cult calling itself a church.

After a few minutes, everyone but the three distractors reconvened within the corridor of the prison. Zeke met them there, having relieved the person on watch of their duties. They waited there in silence, every passing second making Nathan's unease grow. Anna should have attacked by now. Had they been caught preemptively? Was she acting as a double agent, only pretending to—

Boom!

The prison walls shook with the force of the explosion, and a wicked grin spread over Nathan's face. He took a deep breath and opened the gate to his core, allowing his ability to pour out and smother the area in stillness. The moment it was in place, Zeke used the keys to open the first cultivator's door.

They moved deeper into the prison, releasing them one by one, and when they reached Tom Osnan Jr.'s cell, they all bowed, averting their eyes. Zeke slid forward and opened the bars. The second the captive was freed, a viselike hand grabbed Nathan's neck, forcing his face up. Tom Osnan's expression was fiery, and he struck Nathan's cheek with a savage blow.

Because of the chi roiling from Nathan's core, Tom Osnan Jr.'s cultivation was sealed. The backhanded slap couldn't have harmed a hair on his body, so he threw his head to the side, making it look as though the blow had devastated him.

A surge of chi bloomed far away as a barrage of abilities collided on the edge of the village, the reverberations from the clash more noticeable than the strike.

"That is for your tardiness, cultivator," Tom Osnan Jr. spat. "Do better next time."

"Yes, Lord," Nathan replied, staring at the ground despite being held by the neck.

Osnan let go, casting his gaze over the arrayed followers. "Release my wife. We've remained chained here for long enough."

Nodding hurriedly, Zeke rushed down the hallway, swiftly unlocking her cell. For his efforts, he received a scowl from Lady Osnan.

"Took you long enough," she said. "Let us leave this place."

Unlike the regular cultivators, the lord and his lady wife didn't control their steps, all but running down the hallway. The entire time they moved, more abilities were unleashed by Anna, the other two followers, and the village heretics who had gone to answer their apparent assault. Each wave of force that hit his protective bubble made his smile spread wider.

The distraction was working.

Nathan was right behind the two Osnans as they stepped out on the street, so when they came to an abrupt stop, he almost barreled into their backs.

"Wh-what?" he asked dumbly, not understanding why they'd paused.

A long silence stretched over the street, the silence growing thick as more of the loyal left the prison.

"You!" Tom Osnan Jr. growled.

Swallowing, Nathan leaned to peer around them.

Who he found there made his skin prickle and stomach drop.

CHAPTER TWENTY-SEVEN

Double-Cross

B eneath a roiling sea of gray clouds, Barry shook his head at the people emerging from the prison. The traitors appeared genuinely shocked, bringing him no small amount of amusement. They'd truly thought their plans were unknown.

He glanced at his lone companion, bending to scratch her soft-furred head. Corporal Claws trilled, leaning into his touch before stretching and hunching down. Crackling lightning leaped from her body as she grinned, waiting for the order to attack.

"How did you know?" Tom Osnan Jr. asked, raising his chin.

"That isn't important. All that matters is that your attempt failed. If you don't mind, it will save a whole lot of violence if you calmly take yourself back to your cell."

Tom Osnan Jr. sneered. "You may have bested us last time, but you no longer have the element of surprise."

"Besides," said Nathan, the ringleader of this little prison break, stepping up beside Tom and standing tall. "You're outnumbered."

"Well, yeah," Barry agreed. "But that doesn't mean you'll win."

"Are you sure about that?" Nathan's face grew serious as a blanket of chi seemed to press down on Barry's body, making his chest tighten. "I wonder how useful your power will be when you can't use it?"

Barry reached for his core, his brow scrunching with the effort. Try as he might, his chi seemed to be locked away, right there, yet impossible to reach.

The lightning covering Corporal Claws sputtered out, her eyes going wide.

Nathan laughed, clearly delighting in her expression. "The person who takes them out will be rewarded back in Gormona."

Three people stepped forward, flexing their hands.

"Call me crazy," Barry said, cocking his head, "but wouldn't activating your ability mean that no one can use their chi?"

"I can see why you'd assume that." Nathan looked down his nose at them, all too happy to keep talking. "But mine is no beginner's ability . . ."

He clicked his fingers, and though Barry's chi was suppressed, he sensed pockets opening up within the dulling sphere. They were centered around the escapees, blooming outward to avoid every inch of their forms. The three that had stepped forward flexed their hands as essence flowed out from their cores to flood their bodies.

"What are you waiting for?" Tom Osnan Jr. asked. *"Go."*

"Kill the otter first," Lady Osnan ordered, a disgusting smile covering her face.

The three obliged, their bodies entirely unaffected by the suppression as they exploded forward.

Though Barry couldn't bring forth his power, his senses were still heightened; he saw the following movements in slow motion.

The first step, sending them launching forward. One cultivator's leg drawing back and the muscles there tightening. The sickening power with which he kicked out, his calf bulging as he aimed his foot for the center of Corporal Claws's body. The other two cocking back arms and looping wide, coming toward Claws from either side. Their torsos leaning forward as their fists lashed out, carrying deadly potential. If they were to hit Claws's body while she was under the effect of the suppression, she wouldn't survive.

Time crawled as the blows descended, yet Barry didn't move to intervene.

Two rows of needle-sharp teeth gleamed out at the world between Claws's parted lips, and lightning chi gathered, bringing with it the scent of ozone. The three attackers also had enhanced senses, and though they carried too much momentum to pull back, Barry witnessed—and enjoyed—the moment of realization crossing the traitors' faces. Smirks disappeared, replaced by sheer confusion.

Before their confusion had a chance to morph into fear, the lightning bolt struck.

It descended from the heavens in the blink of a non-cultivator's eye, striking the street where Claws stood. She held her forepaws high like some sort of storm god, embracing the energy as it engulfed her. Given her very body had mastered lightning-aspected chi, she was completely immune to the attack.

Unfortunately for her attackers, they had no such mastery.

It was too late for them to stop, and when their limbs made contact with Claws, the electricity jumped, traveling through them into the ground and each other. Their bodies went rigid, muscles contracting and keeping them upright for a short moment. As quick as it entered them, the lightning vanished, leaving only twitching bodies, and a moment later, they fell to the ground.

"Are they dead?" Barry asked Claws, already knowing the answer to be no.

Playing along, Claws shrugged and let out an uncertain chirp.

"But . . . my ability . . ." Nathan gulped, his expression matching the Osnans'. With eyes darting around the street, he whirled on the rest of the cultivators, his face lined with panic. "Attack! All of you, attack them!"

No one moved.

Barry shook his head, letting out a soft laugh. "You said your ability wasn't that of a beginner, right? Well, I think you'll find that ours aren't, either."

"Mine is the strongest!" he whined. "How else could I have fooled you?"

"What makes you think you fooled us, friend?" a voice called from a side street. Theo stepped into sight, raising an eyebrow at Nathan. "Did you ever stop to consider that we let you believe you evaded our detection? What better way to flush out those with hearts that could be easily swayed?"

Nathan's nostrils flared. "You're bluffing . . ."

Keith and Trent followed Theo from the side street, both casting disapproving gazes over the traitors.

"You could have atoned for your crimes and joined us, Tom," Trent said. "If not for your hubris."

Tom Osnan Jr. spat to the side, his lip twitching. "You think I care what a whelp like you thinks? I—" The words died in his throat as a group entered the street from farther east. He stared at them for a long moment before spitting again. "I should have known better than to trust *peasants*."

Barry smiled as Anna and her two cultivators returned. Unlike Barry, the three looked morose, not having enjoyed their part in the ruse. Borks, Rocky, and Snips were at their side, looking much more cheerful, Borks with a tongue lolling, Snips waving one of her giant snippers and resting another on Rocky, who looked ready to explode into violence at any moment.

With all the excitement, none of the traitors had noticed the fake battle to the east had ended, and they were now forced to face the truth head on.

"So it was treachery that was our undoing?" Nathan shook his head. "I should have known, you two-faced bit—"

Crack!

A sound like two buildings colliding cut off his words, and a blast of force shot over their heads, so violent that winds whipped up in its passing. Nathan's face went pale as he turned to the west, finding Pistachio with one claw slammed shut, the other cocked and aimed at him.

"Pistachio thinks your words were uncouth," Barry explained. "If I were you, I'd probably reconsider using such colorful language to address his friends."

"*Friends*?" Nathan repeated, indignation returning some of the blood to his face. "Would you also consider that *demon* a friend, Anna? Because that is who you ally yourself with."

"Don't be silly," Theo said. "Pistachio isn't a demon. If any of our animal pals are, that title would belong to Borks."

Ruff, Borks agreed, shifting into his hellhound form and making the sound seem like it came from multiple beasts.

Nathan took an involuntary step backwards, needing a few moments to regather himself this time. "It matters not who you're allied with, Anna. If not for your betrayal, this escape would have succeeded. It will only be a matter of time until—"

"Oh, you were screwed even before Anna infiltrated your ranks," Barry interrupted.

"And," Theo added, "even assuming your ability fooled me—which, to be clear, it didn't—you'd still have failed. We've had eyes on you this entire time."

"Impossible! I'd have felt if my ability was infiltrated." He pointed skyward. "We all knew those damned birds were keeping an eye on us. They're too far away to hear anything, let alone penetrate my nullifying—"

Twin honks cut Nathan off, the calls so loud that they shook Barry's chest. Two blurs descended from above, slamming into the cobbled street and sending a shockwave outward. When the air stilled, Pelly and Bill stared at the group of escapees, somehow looking down at them despite being half their height.

Barry laughed, leaning down to pat both pelicans on the head. "You're right—they've been watching, yet they were too far away to hear your plans . . ." He couldn't hide his amusement as he looked back up at Nathan. "But who said it was the birds watching?"

There was a long moment of silence before a hum came from the surrounding buildings, so low that one might assume it a figment of their imagination. As the bee hybrids came into view, the hum became a cacophonous drone, more than a few flying from within the prison's confines. They formed a loose orb beside Barry, hovering to stare at the traitors. They bobbed once, nodding as they let out a buzzed greeting.

A louder tone cut through the monotonous sound of their flight, and Tom Osnan Jr. spun, turning toward Nathan with a venomous glance. Not understanding, Nathan's body went rigid, holding his hands up in supplication, but then he looked down at his robe. Something darted from his belt, shooting up to hover before his face. Bumblebro gave the man a rude gesture, then zipped away, coming to a stop beside his progeny. The bees buzzed affectionately at him, Bumblebro returning the same vibrations.

Barry watched Nathan intently, enjoying the rapid change of emotions sweeping over his face. Realization, fear, anger, and everything in between cycled across his countenance, growing more intense with each repetition. The rest of the traitors were experiencing the same turmoil, falling to their knees—not that many of them had truly been a part of the revolt. Most of the "traitors," including two of the cultivators that had been imprisoned, remained standing.

Nathan looked their way, perhaps seeking a way out, but when he noticed the guilt, sorrow, or amusement they were displaying, he froze. "You . . . *all of you?*" he demanded. His gaze settled on Zeke, who grimaced. "What did they offer you, Zeke? What price have you sold your soul for, coward?"

"What did they offer me . . . ?" Zeke shook his head, looking down at his co-conspirator with pity. "Look around, Nathan. What fool would willingly go back to slavery?"

"I heard your words in the theater. How fickle is your heart to be swayed so easily, swine?"

"Oh, that?" Barry snorted. "My idea. I asked Anna to play the role, but she said it would be more believable coming from Zeke."

"He was always the best actor at our school," Anna explained, twirling a finger around the end of her ponytail. "Did I not mention that's how we knew each other?"

"You *moron!*" Tom Osnan Jr. screamed, grabbing Nathan by his collar.

As Nathan stared up at the furious lord, he looked like he was going to be sick. Tom Osnan Jr. punched down, and Barry would have moved to intervene, but he felt the shift of Nathan's ability. The bubble of protection around the lord disappeared, the nullifying power rushing in. By the time the fist struck Nathan's chin, it was like a toddler trying to assault a mountain.

Lord Tom Osnan screeched in pain, clutching his broken hand. "You *dare*!"

Nathan responded by spreading his arms wide and drawing in chi. As Barry felt the man gathering power in his core, he prepared to jump in. As much as he detested Tom Osnan Jr.'s existence, he wouldn't let him die. The power in Nathan's core fluctuated, drawing in ever more essence at an incredible rate. It flowed on and on, somehow picking up speed. Barry's stomach dropped when he realized what was about to happen. Corporal Claws realized too; she exploded forward on lightning-wreathed limbs. Rocky, itching for a fight, made it closest to Nathan.

But it was too late.

The power rushed into Nathan's core and exploded outward. Though the breakthrough wasn't as strong as Fischer's, it was still enough to send them all flying. Rocky was hit the worst, getting catapulted skyward because of his proximity and angle. Barry braced himself as Claws slammed into the building behind him, only the fact it was System-made saving the structure from obliteration. He and Claws both rushed to their feet, gathering their wits and preparing to rush at the empowered man.

After the chi expanded outward, however, it poured back into Nathan, coalescing in a smoky orb around him. It held hints of his nullifying ability, but as its shape condensed, so, too, did the power. The air became gray, then black, and in an instant, a loud pop rang out. Both Nathan and the orb were gone, leaving everyone in various stages of recovery across the street.

"Frack me," Barry said. "Can't say I saw that coming."

"What do we do?" Theo asked, getting to his feet.

"Pelly, Bill—go get Fischer. We can't risk letting Nathan escape." Barry spun toward Borks as the two birds honked their approval and tore off through the sky. "Can you sense where he went?"

Borks dashed forward, sniffing the spot he'd disappeared from. After lifting his nose and sniffing the air, he nodded.

Wasting no time, Claws leaped to his back. With her one forepaw gripping his fur, she pointed forward with the other, commanding her steed onward with a shrill chirp.

Borks howled in response, transforming into what Fischer called his "long-boi form." All elbows and incredible speed, Borks dashed away to the north. Snips trailed them, oozing blue chi that shot from the rear of her limbs. All the while, Claws released a battle cry from Borks's back, declaring her violent intent.

Double Trouble

As he strode beneath a forest canopy, Deklan held his hand out, feeling the stray drops of rain that bounced off leaves above and fell toward the forest floor. Every few seconds, a tiny droplet splashed against his upturned palm. It made his smile spread even wider, and he lifted his face, enjoying each fragment of rain that hit him.

Rather than fishing, he and his brother had gone for a walk. Well, it had started out as a walk, anyway. As brothers are wont to do, it quickly devolved into a footrace. Given that they were now cultivators, the sand had sped past, as did trees, grass, and eventually mountains, both men sprinting until they were kilometers inland. After a short break to catch their breath, they'd started walking in silence, both soaking in their surroundings.

Deklan peered toward Dom, shaking his head in amusement as he realized his brother was also walking through the rain with an upturned face, smiling at the sensations of his body.

Somehow able to sense his attention, Dom cracked an eye and raised a brow at him. "Something wrong?"

"Not at all. Can't a man enjoy his younger brother's joy?"

Dom's contentment immediately died on his face. "I am *not* your little brother."

"How could you say such a thing? I was born before you."

"*Five minutes* before me. That makes me your twin, Deklan, not your little brother. Wait, have you been telling everyone in New Tropica that I'm your younger sibling?"

"You *haven't* been?" Deklan raised a hand to his chest. "You wound me, little brother."

Dom held his composure for another few seconds before breaking into laughter. "You are so annoying."

"That's what big brothers are for."

"Yeah, yeah." Dom rolled his eyes, the corners of his lips tugging up.

They slipped back into silence as they strode on. Despite the grounding presence of the surrounding forest and falling rain, Deklan's thoughts strayed toward the day's events.

There was some sort of mission going on back in New Tropica.

Given how little the leadership had informed him of, he assumed it was important.

All Barry had told them was that they were welcome to take part. Deklan had mentioned they'd planned to go for a walk, fully expecting Barry to tell him he couldn't. Instead, Barry had just smiled and told them to have a good time.

"You know," Dom said, his tone musing, "I know they keep telling us we can do what we want, but I'm repeatedly surprised when they actually let us . . ."

Deklan laughed. "I was just thinking the same thing. What is it that Barry keeps calling it? Aunotomy?"

Dom snorted in response. "Autonomy, you goose. An older brother would have known that . . ."

"Or maybe this older brother was only pretending not to know. That way his much-younger baby brother could correct him and gain a sense of self confidence."

"Whatever helps you sleep at night."

They shared a smile, and Deklan shook his head. "Jokes aside, I'm constantly surprised by it too. Don't get me wrong—I knew Fischer was a good person despite his power, but I still expected some of it to be a lie, you know? Like they were selling us on taking part, then we'd have to spend half the time getting ordered around."

"They truly gave us freedom, didn't they?"

Deklan took a deep breath and let it out slowly, grinning at the world. "It would seem so."

They stopped walking as they strode into a clearing, both holding their arms wide. The raindrops hitting him made a pleasant shiver run down Deklan's spine, but before he could completely fall into the moment, something slammed into him.

Both their eyes flew open as a wave of chi shot over the landscape, its resonance strong enough to make Deklan's vision pulse.

He stumbled to the side, barely staying upright. "What was—"

Another pulse came, this time from much closer. The tsunami of essence poured over the land, knocking them both to the forest floor. As the power washed over Deklan, it felt vaguely malignant, making his skin crawl. The brothers got to their feet and stared toward where the pulse had come from. They exchanged a wide-eyed glance and nodded.

They had to investigate.

It would take too long to return to New Tropica and inform someone, and if this was a threat, it was on them to stop it. Not needing to speak the words, they shot off, once more sprinting as they trailed invisible aftershocks of chi radiating from the west. They followed a creek that ran between two peaks, and as they neared the source, Deklan clenched his jaw, preparing for a fight if necessary.

But then he caught sight of the man. Only his upper body protruded from the creek, his lower half limp in the running water.

"Nathan!" Dom yelled, dashing forward.

"You know him?"

"You don't?" Dom shook his head. "He's one of the cultivators from New Tropica. Eris's golden apple—what the frack is he doing here?"

"Dom . . . I don't think we should get too close."

"What? Why? He clearly needs our help."

"Did you not feel his chi? It didn't feel right."

"I felt it, but he might have just had a breakthrough or something. Fischer feels much the same to me, and you think he's a good guy, don't you?"

"I guess . . ."

His brother had a point, but Deklan couldn't shake the feeling of wrongness. He approached warily, *tasting* the chi, for lack of a better word. Dom had pulled Nathan from the stream, and with each soft slap his brother gave to the unconscious man, a small wave of essence flowed out from him. It was . . . dark, reminding Deklan of an alleyway on a moonless night.

The longer he tasted the chi, the more sure he became. "Dom. Get away from him."

The tone of Deklan's voice arrested his brother's attention. "Seriously? What's gotten into—"

An oppressive bubble flew from Nathan as the man inhaled a ragged breath, his ability engulfing them. It pressed down on Deklan, driving him to his knees. It was as though the hazy orb surrounding them entered his very abdomen, smothering his core. The more Deklan reached for his power, the stronger Nathan's will became and the harder it was to pour chi into his limbs.

"Nathan . . ." Dom wheezed, bracing his hands on the ground to stay upright. "We're friendly . . ."

Their attacker's eyes held only hatred and fear, darting around as he oriented himself. He blinked, realization seeming to come to his face. The next moment, he was laughing, shaking his head and rubbing the bridge of his nose, but despite his apparent mirth, the pressure never receded.

"Nathan. Please . . ." Dom tried again.

Nathan grinned. "Wrong place, wrong time, traitors." He went to take a step forward, but slipped, his legs giving out. Letting out a grunt, he raised his eyes, nostrils flaring as he glared at Deklan and Dom.

Somehow, his ability grew stronger, forcing them down with even more pressure. Deklan's fledgling capabilities stood no chance against whatever Nathan had become. Despite this, he never ceased reaching, attempting to open the floodgates to his chi. The more he did, the harder it forced him to the ground. It slammed down on his back, pushing his chest to the grass. He forced his head to the right, looking for his brother. When he found him, Deklan rallied his resolve.

Though Dom was also prone, his eyes were defiant. He hadn't yet given up.

Deklan wouldn't either.

Some would call Deklan a fool. Many fellow guards had done so back in Gormona. Despite appearances, Deklan was always listening. He'd heard all about the breakthroughs people had been having. Gods above, he'd *felt* the one that Roger experienced a week ago. They appeared to be reliant on finding one's purpose and admitting it to themselves.

Rather than look for power, Deklan searched for truth.

Thankfully, it was only his physical power that was suppressed, so his mind remained sharp. It whirled through myriad possibilities, and it only took him a moment to find what he believed to be his purpose. He stared into his brother's eyes, conveying his feelings.

· To finally find a place he and his brother belonged, then to have it taken away so abruptly . . . it was *unacceptable.*

As he and Dom looked into each other, their truth resonated. He could sense his brother's thoughts—they were exactly the same as his. Both men wanted to protect each other and the life they'd found. Chi rushed into them, but this time, it wasn't Nathan's.

It was the world's.

Invisible ropes of it penetrated the hazy bubble surrounding them, forcing their way through the muck and into the brothers' bodies. Their cores remained sealed, yet power coursed through them all the same. They got to their knees, then to their feet, hunching against the oppressive darkness that sought their destruction.

As they stood, bracing their shoulders against the assault, Nathan's eyes grew furious. The pressure coming from the man redoubled, the air growing so dark that it obscured the outside world. The creek's water receded, getting forced from Nathan's sphere of influence and leaving the bed dry.

Unwilling to be subdued, both brothers remained standing, calling forth the world's chi as their breakthrough approached. Deklan's body felt full to bursting, yet the chi continued to swell and build, collecting around his core. He felt the same thing happening within Dom, and they radiated reassurance, letting the other know they weren't alone.

The chi condensed, grew to a fever pitch, and then broke.

All at once, it flowed away, flung from them and returned to the outside world. Deklan and Dom collapsed, both letting out pained cries as their bodies slammed into the ground.

Nathan sighed through his teeth, stumbling and almost falling once more. Some of his power subsided, but what remained was enough to keep them held firmly against the ground. He let out a soft laugh, more relieved than victorious.

"Unfortunately for you heretics, I won't repeat Barry's mistake." He shuffled forward, making his way toward Dom, who was only a meter away. "There will be no monologue."

Deklan tried to rally his power, attempting to beckon the world's essence back to him, but it was futile. His core, and everything around it, felt raw. Even if Nathan's ability wasn't pressing down on him, he wasn't sure he could stand, let alone gather the strength to fight back.

Nathan, still wobbling, stood over Dom. He raised his elbow high, gathering power there and preparing to drop it down into Dom's body. If the blow were to land, his brother would be no more; with their chi locked away, their bodies were those of regular humans.

Despite this, Deklan never gave up hope.

He reached out, making his core feel like it caught flame. His abdomen burned, yet he still grasped outward with metaphorical fingers, attempting to find some-thing—anything—that would give him the strength to save his brother.

Uncaring of his wishes, Nathan's elbow gathered the last whisper of power neces-sary. The muscles surrounding his shoulder bunched, and the elbow raced down-ward, aimed for Dom's back. Deklan tried to cry out, and a sound like a blade shearing through metal tore through the air. The elbow continued its deadly trajec-tory, so fast it would go unnoticed by anyone but a cultivator. Deklan had the barest of moments to be confused by the noise seeming to come from his own throat before something catapulted into view.

A blur of brown, orange, and blue rocketed forward, the metal-on-metal sound so loud that it hurt his eardrums.

Corporal Claws, streaming lightning and grinning maliciously, gave Deklan a thumbs-up in passing. Sergeant Snips was right behind her, blowing greeting bub-bles as rivulets of ocean-blue chi propelled her forward.

The next moment, they both slammed into Nathan's chest. The tangle of man and creature flew through a tree, obliterating its trunk before they tumbled into the forest and out of sight. Borks was there a moment later, giving the brothers a drive-by lick on the cheek before leaping over the shattered stump to join Claws and Snips in their assault on the poor fellow.

"Frack me," Deklan said, rolling onto his back. "That was close."

"Uh-huh," Dom agreed, taking heaving breaths.

CHAPTER TWENTY-NINE

Chekhov's Crab

"You, as a descendant of the great Kraken Rider, should beware of any-one selling directions to the heavens. This does not, however, mean one shouldn't try the techniques and meditations of other sects, churches, and families. Knowledge may be gleaned from the guidance of others, after all, even if your only insight is what not to do.

Though easier described than practiced, one should follow the whispers of their mind and body. There are many roads to enlightenment, and only one's instinct can be relied upon to take the correct path."

Excerpt from Chapter 6, House Kraken manual

Are you serious, Barry?" I asked as I patted Bill and Pelly, the birds crooning and leaning into my touch.

My two trusty pelicans had come and retrieved Roger and me, putting a pause on our battle. The moment we'd seen the panic in their avian eyes, Roger and I had raced back to New Tropica. Finding the gathering outside of the prison had been a surprise, but nowhere near as unexpected as the reaction Barry had to the question I'd just voiced.

He seemed to sink into himself, his expression growing dark. I thought it would be momentary, but he only seemed to become more troubled with each passing second. He stared over at Deklan and Dom, the two men resting against a wall after having been dropped off by Borks.

"Everything okay, mate?" I asked Barry, raising an eyebrow, but he ignored me, his worried gaze locked on the two brothers.

He marched over, stopped before them, and bowed at the waist. "I'm sorry. I let my enjoyment of the plan coming together cloud my judgment. It is my fault you were attacked."

"Huh?" Deklan blurted, putting voice to exactly what I was thinking.

Barry lowered himself to his knees, bending so his forehead almost touched the ground. "I should have neutralized the threat immediately. Instead, I dragged it out for my own amusement. Any number of us could have knocked Nathan out before he had a chance to experience a breakthrough. I can't take it back, but I promise that I will learn from this grievous error."

"Er," Deklan said. "I think you're being a bit too harsh on yourself."

"Agreed, but apology accepted," Dom added. "We've experienced worse, right, Deklan?" He nudged his brother, giving him a meaningful look.

"Oh, yeah. Evil powers are bad and all, but they don't hold a candle to our dear mother's cooking."

Dom guffawed. "Remember the apricot chicken? That woman made meals that could have put the Cult of the Alchemist's vilest concoctions to shame."

"Oh, you bastard. I'd managed to forget the apricot chicken. What about the time she added those flavor bulbs to a stir fry? I swear, I loved that woman like nothing else, but some of the things she came up with . . ."

As the two brothers continued listing off their late mother's crimes against humanity, apparently unaffected by their brush with death, Barry slowly raised his head, utter confusion plastering his face. When it finally dawned on him that they truly weren't bothered, he stood and turned my way, bowing at the waist again. "You were right to chastise me, Fischer. I won't let it happen again."

"Uhhhh, I didn't chastise you?" I leaned toward Maria, who was at my side. "Did I chastise Barry?" I stage whispered. "Because I didn't mean to."

"I don't think so?" she replied, peering between Barry and me consideringly. "You did ask him if he was serious, though, which he maybe took as a reprimand?"

"Ohhhh." I clicked my fingers. "Is that what you meant, mate?"

He blinked at me, apparently unprepared for no one to be angry at him. "Yes . . . ?" he slowly said. "You had every right to call me out on my failure."

"Yeah, nah. I wasn't at all upset about that. Your plan came together wonderfully, considering how complicated it was."

He gave me the same look of confusion he'd given the brothers a moment ago. "What were you talking about, then?"

"You set up a double-cross without me! A crime most foul."

"All right, you lost me," Maria said, narrowing her eyes at me.

Barry, clearly agreeing with the sentiment, stood upright and shook his head. "What on Kallis are you talking about? You told me to keep you out of everything possible, which I've been respecting. You *wanted* to be kept in the dark."

"Well, yeah! I usually want to be kept out of things, but a *double-cross?*" I gestured at Anna and the rest of the allied conspirators. "A double-cross with *undercover agents?*" I let out a sigh. "Frankly, I'm insulted you didn't bring me in on the fun. I missed out on a good time."

Everyone just stared at me, and when no one spoke, I continued yapping.

"You warned me that Roger would start a tussle with me for the purpose of some secret mission, but I had no idea it would be for something so exciting. I thought it would be a boring plan, like showing our new friends how strong we are. Or how grumpy Roger is. Next time you've got some plot right out of a thriller, bring me in, my guy. Also . . ." I turned toward Roger. "I was told you'd start a *tussle* with me, not that you'd try and turn me into deli meat. Show some restraint, you peanut."

"You *did* kick him into the ocean . . ." Maria said. "I think he showed miraculous restraint, considering."

"You . . . kicked him into the ocean?" Barry asked, a smile threatening to shatter his remorse.

Roger, his jaw only growing tighter the longer I talked, rubbed his temples. "If I try not to land a fatal blow, does anyone mind if I attack him again?"

"No," came the answering chorus from almost everyone present.

"Ah, I am surrounded by treacherous souls." I cast an aggrieved look toward Maria, who had answered the loudest.

Before I could continue my diatribe in a no doubt hilarious and endearing manner, Borks came padding into the street.

Nathan, the man who had been spearheading the little escape attempt, lay limp over Borks's shoulders. Bruises covered the man's body, his eyes so swollen that it looked like he'd had an allergic reaction. The two who'd given him the swelling stood atop his back, striking heroic poses.

Corporal Claws's eyes were averted, and as she pretended to notice us, she let out a curious coo, as if to say, *Oh. I didn't see you there.*

Snips was playing along, and she mimicked Claws, blowing little bubbles of surprise.

"Come here, you little scamps," I said, holding out my arms.

With a wiggle of her cute little tooshie, Claws leaped for me, crashing into my chest. Snips landed a moment later, nudging the otter aside and lowering herself to the crook of my arm.

Realizing we were missing a particularly disgruntled crab, I looked up. "You said Rocky got blasted skyward by the breakthrough, right? Has anyone, uh, seen him? Shouldn't he have come back down?"

Snips shrugged, blowing dismissive bubbles and waving a claw.

"Yeah," I replied. "Good point. He'll be fine." I hugged Snips and Claws tight. "More importantly, you did well, girls. You too, Borks."

He let out a yip in response, shrugging the traitor off his back and trotting over to lean against my leg. Maria crouched and fussed him all over, reiterating how good of a boy he was.

With Claws and Snips still in my arms, I strode over and peered down at Nathan, extending my senses. When I felt the power and aspect of his core, I scrunched my face up. "Gross."

Ruff, Borks agreed.

"Gross?" Barry asked. "What do you mean?"

I turned toward Roger. "Can you feel it, too?"

His chi flowed out, joining mine to prod at Nathan's abdomen. "I can. It's disgusting."

"Fascinating," Ellis said, scratching away in his notepad. "Do you think you can discern the intent of cultivators the more powerful they become, Fischer, or do you think it is this man's ability that seems unpleasant?"

"No idea, mate. I only know one thing for certain."

"Oh?" His eyes lifted, sparkling with the possibility of new information. "What is that?"

I grinned, looking at Anna, Zeke, and the rest of the cultivators that had gone undercover to help bring Nathan down. "I reckon the success of this mission calls for a celebratory feast . . ."

Snips and Claws perked up immediately, both leaning toward my face with pleading eyes.

Beneath the canopy of a gigantic tree, a soft breeze blew.

The wind washed over George, making the shape of his body seem to dissolve into a cloud of sensations. Calm as he was, the explosion of chi earlier had hardly affected him, his consciousness becoming more used to them over the past week.

He unleashed a slow, ponderous breath, following its passage with his awareness as it flowed from his mouth. When he opened his eyes, he found Joel, the leader of Tropica's Cult of Carcinization branch, smiling at him.

"I know I'm repeating myself here, George, but I must thank you again."

"You really don't need to—"

"Nonsense," Joel interrupted, gesturing at the rest of the cultists and Geraldine, who were deep in meditation. "The past week, since we exchanged the cult's techniques with your house's manual, has been wondrous and enlightening. To think we've come so far in a mere span of days . . ." He smiled even wider, crow's feet appearing beside his eyes. "I can't help but feel like we are almost taking steps on the path of carcinization."

"We should be the ones thanking you," Geraldine said, opening her eyes and resting a hand on George's leg. "Your insights and techniques have been invaluable."

Joel nodded. "I'm glad we've been of similar benefit to the both of you." He paused, pursing his lips for a moment. "After today's meditation, are you still sure that the superior form of the crab isn't for you . . . ?"

George grimaced. They'd had this same discussion daily. "I'm afraid I have to follow my instincts still, Joel, just as the Kraken manual instructs. I can't speak for my wife, but for me, the form doesn't feel correct."

"You can speak for me, dear," Geraldine said, reaching over and squeezing his hand. "You know it doesn't feel right for me either. Sorry, Joel."

Jess, Joel's second-in-command, groaned as she stood and stretched. "Again, Joel?" She walked over and sat down next to Joel, leaving the other members to their meditation. "I think it might be time to accept our friends' words." She smiled at George and Geraldine. "You're always welcome to join our sessions, regardless of whether or not carcinization feels right to you."

George barely heard her last sentence—he was still tripping over the previous one.

I think it might be time to accept our friends' words, Jess had said, with no hint or deception in her voice.

"Friends . . . ?" Geraldine asked. "Did you call us your . . . friends?"

George glanced to his left, his heart breaking when he saw her face. The statement had impacted her, too, causing tears to swell in her eyes. As he watched, one of them fell, slowly rolling down her cheek.

"Oh dear . . ." George said, reaching out to wipe it away.

Jess inhaled sharply, covering her mouth. "Did I say something wrong? I didn't mean to overstep, my lady."

George smiled at her, his own emotions threatening to boil over. "Not at all. We are grateful for your friendship, and my lady wife's reaction is one of . . ." George trailed off as an odd whistling sound came to his ear, and he cocked his head to the side, trying to discern where it was coming from. "Can you all hear that?"

Geraldine cupped a hand to her ear as she blinked away her tears. "What is it . . . ?"

All too late, he looked up.

A creature of nightmare approached, its form massive and limbs numerous.

"Get back—"

It struck the ground like a boulder, sending sand flying in every direction. George scrambled between Geraldine and the monster, raising his fists in a defensive posture.

"Run!" he ordered, but Geraldine remained at his back, her hands gripping his arm.

"I won't leave you!"

"You must!" he hissed. "I can't stand the idea of— *What the frack?*" he said, inadvertently copying a curse he'd heard thrown around by the common folk.

The sand had cleared enough for him to see, and what he found was enough to reset his thoughts.

The monster remained in the crater it had made, slowly getting to its many legs. Rather than run, the cultists were facedown in the sand, kneeling so low that their foreheads pressed into the sand. The creature stood upright in all its majesty, its beady eyes staring down at the bowing humans with an imperious gaze. It was covered in a hardened shell, with claws big enough to sever a man's leg.

It was a spirit beast. George could *feel* it and the power it held.

"Frack me," Geraldine said from beside him, also borrowing the common folk's vernacular. "Maybe you were right about the crab form, Joel . . ."

CHAPTER THIRTY

Self-Control

As Rocky soared through the darkened sky, he reconsidered his life choices.
He'd been launched dozens of kilometers into the air, the very world turning into a vast circle beneath him. At first, he'd been filled with joy—he had never graced such heights. The moment he began to descend, however, realization washed over him.

Though he'd been flung higher than ever before, it hadn't been by his beloved mistress.

This should have been something they experienced together. Instead, his first time into the stratosphere had been experienced with the help of a human male. He had betrayed his spiky mistress, even going so far as to make his body aerodynamic so he went higher and higher. Rocky, for perhaps the first time in his life, experienced self-disgust.

He was a dirty, disloyal crab, and he knew not how many waves would need to crash over his mighty carapace before his sins were cleansed.

There were no distractions to be found in the sky. Even the wonder of his height was nothing before the weight of his betrayal, and the longer he fell, the more he was propelled into despair. How would he tell her? What could he possibly do to regain her trust? Which evil force had concocted the perfect trap for him to fall into and betray his beloved . . . ?

Tropica came into view below him, so small that he could barely make it out. When he spied the headland, only a portion of Fischer's home poking out from the vast stone formation, Rocky had his third-most devious thought of the day.

This, he decided, was all Fischer's fault.

Though Rocky would never tell him, Fischer was the strongest of them all. If he had been there to combat the one called Nathan, Rocky would never have been tempted by the throw of another. It was *Fischer* who had caused Rocky's betrayal. Something within Rocky's core latched on to this belief. It made him lean into his anger, and he changed course. He angled his body, letting the wind flow past him. Within seconds, he had doubled in speed, rocketing downward.

Fischer's crime demanded retribution; Rocky would deliver it.

Bubbles of justice trailed from his mouth as he pictured the destruction in his mind, even Fischer's System-made house having no hope against his immaculate carapace. A wind flew past, causing him to spin chaotically, but it didn't matter—he would change course again and rocket back toward his target.

In his tail spin, however, he noticed something curious.

There was a group of people sitting beneath the giant tree that Lemon had helped create. It was a gathering he recognized. The cultists that he'd been molding into obedient followers sat in meditation, arrayed in a circle that called to Rocky's very soul, the landing spot too perfect to ignore. It was a grander entrance than he could have ever imagined, and each time he rotated and caught sight of it again, he felt even more drawn in.

He could ignore the call no longer.

As much as Fischer needed to be punished, Rocky would have to find another way to enact retribution. He splayed his legs outward, using them to steer toward the tree. With his worries forgotten, Rocky pulled himself into a ball, streamlining his body and gathering speed once more. He retracted his eyestalks and his vision went black, even those small appendages standing in the way of peak velocity.

When he hit the ground, it was with the force of a meteor, the thump so loud that his *everything* shook.

Fragments of sand and dust flew in all directions, his majestic body leaving a crater in the earth. He sat still for a long moment, the fine hairs within his statocyst not properly detecting sound, leaving only a high-pitched tone that rang through him. As the dust began to settle, Rocky's senses returned, and he unfurled his limbs, standing dramatically slow to give the humans time to show their respect.

The cultists were all prone, pressing their faces into the sand and flattening themselves as much as their weird, fleshy bodies could.

"Holy frack," an unknown voice said, making Rocky turn the speaker's way. "Maybe you were right about the crab form, Joel . . ."

He immediately agreed with the woman's assessment, as Joel had no doubt praised his body. But then he realized the woman was *standing*, as was the man beside her. Indignation boiled within Rocky's shell, and he took a step forward.

"Bow down!" Joel yelled, both desperation and reverence lacing his words.

The two, both blinking their stupid meaty eye coverings, slowly acquiesced—*too* slowly, by Rocky's estimate. He scuttled forward, raising his claws high in preparation for a good whack. When he was before them, though, something reached out and touched his core, halting his claws as they descended. Not comprehending the twin sources of chi, he cocked his carapace to the side, studying them.

The two before him . . . they were close to ascension.

It was a curious find, and he was just considering the implications when someone *dared* interrupt his thoughts.

"Forgive them, Sergeant Snips," Joel said. "They are not aware of your majesty."

Rocky whirled, furious at the cultist for mistaking—nay, *disrespecting*—the name of his spiked mistress, but before his claw lashed out, he recalled that the cultists believed he and Sergeant Snips were the same being. After his fall and the discovery of two soon-to-be cultivators, his thoughts were muddier than a mangrove swamp. Rocky blew slow, calming bubbles, knowing he needed every ounce of his vast intellect to decide what to do with the two humans.

He was just about to turn their way and consider them once more when another source of chi leaped out toward his awareness. He stared at Joel, disbelieving, and he quickly spun in a circle, sensing the abdomens of every other cultist. They were *all* close to ascension. His mouth undulated noiselessly as he tasted their chi.

Their power tasted like his and his spiky mistress's own cores . . .

It wasn't exactly the same, but they definitely held a touch of crab, as if they were the water in which a crabby individual had been living. Now that he knew what to look for, the other strangers had a pinch of it, too. It was even weaker than the cultists, but it was definitely there.

As Rocky continued taking them all in, another devious plan began to form.

He pictured a cast of cultivators under his command, their essence closely aligned with that of a crab. Rather than be loyal to Fischer, they would be loyal to him, and by extension, Sergeant Snips. He could use these weird and ugly creatures to craft a faction of superior form. It could be both the punishment for Fischer that Rocky had been looking for, and something to keep Fischer's growing power in check.

Part of Rocky's core, the same darkness that had urged him toward retribution against Fischer earlier, spoke up. It told him that this was the right move. The *only* move. With a growing sense of self-satisfaction, Rocky stood tall, grand plans playing out in his mind.

Come, he hissed, walking toward the ocean.

After a few steps, he glanced behind himself, not having heard any footsteps.

They were all still prone, pressing their faces to the ground.

Releasing a slew of *very* pissed-off bubbles, he sprayed them with sand. When they looked up, he resorted to using human communication, beckoning them on with a wave of his mighty claw.

The entire time they made their way toward the ocean, Rocky's thoughts of grandeur were the only thing stopping him from hitting one of his foolish followers.

As Lord Tom Osnan Sr. set the cart down, he wiped sweat from his forehead.

"Thank you, Lord," the merchant said, bowing low.

Tom nodded at the man, grateful that at least someone was treating him with the requisite respect. As detestable as it was to drag the cart along like a lowly beast, traversing the worn roadway at speed required precise steps, leaving little room for his thoughts to wander.

Now that he was still, his mind burst into action like a lover scorned, eager to point out every mistake and imperfection.

Fischer's visage, his smirk dripping with self-satisfaction and the surety of a man that knew he would win. The blast that had come from him, pure and unaspected, yet stronger than any other. Tom's slaves, his hand-curated cultivators, had been freed. Worst of all, the decimation of the grove, which his family had watched over for generations. Its nurturing essence had been stolen, never to be returned.

It made his chi boil.

It roiled through his body, growing faster and faster. It demanded an output, something primal within him waking up. He swayed. His fists clenched. His vision blurred as he took a step toward—

Slap.

Lord Tom Osnan Sr. blinked, his cultivation base momentarily stunned.

"You are not a child, Tom," Augustus admonished. "Put your rings on and control yourself."

"Yes, my king."

He reached a shaky hand into his pocket and removed them. With each iridescent-stone ring he returned to his fingers, a fraction of his power was sealed. It made him feel like a caged bird, the sensation unwelcome after having been able to spread his wings and soar.

"Thank you for the reminder," he muttered, lowering his eyes. "You are as wise a friend as ever."

Augustus scoffed. "I am your king and nothing more."

"Yes, my king."

As Augustus walked away, Tom stared back in the direction they'd come from. On the distant horizon, dark clouds milled, standing in stark contrast to the clear skies above. They were already halfway to Theogonia, and loath as he was to admit it, Tom pulling the cart had been a good idea.

Though he was also a revered lord of Gormona, the only other cultivators present were the king, queen, and Princess Tryphena. Looking at it through that lens, rather than seeing it as an unjustified punishment, eased some of the turmoil within Tom. Not all of it, of course, but it helped.

As an added bonus, Augustus had seemed more himself with each passing day. The broken man sitting atop Gormona's throne had been almost as shocking as their utter defeat, and despite Tom feeling victimized by his old friend, he was still glad to see Augustus return to his confident self.

With these conflicting emotions not at all dulled by his rings' suppression, he wandered over to join the others. The merchant Marcus was preparing their lunch as the royals lounged, and Tom sat down near them, taking care not to sit close enough for Augustus to raise an eyebrow at his impropriety.

"So," Penelope said, fingering her wedding ring, "would you mind telling us about the corruption again, Tryphena?"

Tom tried to hide his interest in the question. Despite being the king's closest confidant, he had never been permitted to return to Theogonia after the war.

"Of course, Mother," the princess replied, nodding respectfully. "Which aspect would you like me to elaborate on?"

"As we traveled today, I was thinking over your comments from last night. You said the corruption felt more muted than ever while you were under the effects of the Cult of the Alchemist's new potion, yes?"

Again, Tryphena nodded. She waited for the queen to continue.

Penelope chewed her lip for a moment, considering her words. "How much more muted, would you say? I've experienced Theogonia's corrosive essence before, under an earlier version of the alchemists' concoction, and it was still too much to with-stand after a matter of hours."

"It's . . . not perfect," Tryphena admitted. "But it was *much* better than any other time I've visited. I could stay within the city's bounds for days at a time, and I would only have to leave for an hour for my core to return to normal."

Tom swallowed and examined his fingernails in an attempt to appear indifferent to the conversation he desperately wanted to record. His spies had recovered infor-mation about the Cult of the Alchemist's actions in Theogonia, but he'd never heard something so concrete.

"And you were able to traverse the city center?" the queen asked.

"Yes. As I said, there was nowhere in the capital that I couldn't—"

"Enough," Augustus Reginald Gormona declared. "Leave the rest of the conversa-tion for this evening when present company is no longer listening."

Despite Tom's plant-aspected chi, fire burned within him at the clear disrespect.

"Father . . ." Tryphena said with exaggerated calm. "I think it may be best to include Lord Osnan in our planning. I know that his failure was monumental, but we are essentially challenging the heavens. We might need to rely on him if we—"

"He has nothing of value to add," the king interrupted, then spun toward Tom. "Right, Osnan?"

Tom took a long moment, fighting back his urge to lash out at the continued derision. "As you say, my king," he eventually said, his words clipped.

"There you have it. Until he can atone for his failure, he need not be involved in any planning."

Tryphena's gaze drifted Tom's way, her eyes unreadable before she returned her attention to Augustus. "Yes, Father. Please forgive my impropriety. I didn't intend to question your judgment."

Augustus nodded, and as they slipped into silence, Tom's self-control warred with his desire to attack his oldest friend.

CHAPTER THIRTY-ONE

Feast

Pleasant heat washed over me, making a smile spread over my face. Fragrant steam rose from the barbecue plate, bringing with it the scents of beef tallow, fresh fish, woodsmoke, and myriad herbs and spices. I'd seasoned each slab of mature bluefish with a different combination of seasonings, and my mouth watered as I considered how they'd all taste.

In the few hours the residents of New Tropica and I spent fishing for the celebratory feast, we'd caught more than enough. The entire barbecue was covered in thick slabs of mature bluefish, only thin gaps between them revealing the cooking surface below. Tallow hissed and spat around the edges of the fish, bubbling up and crisping every bit of flesh it touched.

Taking a deep breath, I bathed in the flavors suffusing the air. I exhaled slowly, leaning into the welcome warmth rising up before me.

The fillets were ready to turn.

One by one, I flipped them, revealing perfectly cooked, golden-hued skin.

"All right," Peter said, stepping up beside me. "I agreed to let you help, now go socialize." He waved me away with both hands. "Shoo. It's your feast, after all."

I laughed at him, holding my ground. "You dare *shoo* me? The great and venerable *Fischer*?"

He blew air from his lips, telling me exactly what he thought of that description.

"Besides," I continued, "it's not my feast. It's everyone else's."

"Point taken." He rubbed his chin and frowned, glancing between me and the barbecue plate, a glint in his eye. "Tell you what, since you asked so nicely, I will *allow* you to remain and help me cook the fish."

I bowed theatrically. "Lord Peter is gracious! This lowly one thanks you."

"Oh, stop that." He lifted me up by the shoulders, rolling his eyes. "You'll plant the wrong idea in my apprentices' minds."

I smirked at said apprentices, seeing nervous grins on their faces. "I wouldn't worry about that, mate. They already know I'm a full-blown goose."

"It's true," Maria called, striding around the corner onto my back patio. "It only takes a look to diagnose Fischer as a goose."

"See?" I nodded sagely. "Nothing to worry about."

Maria stepped up beside me, resting an arm on my back. "The food on the fire is almost ready. We've already removed the vegetables."

"Perfect timing." I wrapped my arm around her waist. "These will be done in a moment, too."

As swift and soft as a summer breeze, she darted in to plant a kiss on my cheek. I watched her go, my heart racing as she glanced over her shoulder and gave me what was possibly the most beautiful smile I'd ever seen, then disappeared from sight.

"A good lesson, apprentices," Peter said. "Never let your love enter the kitchen. See how distracted Fischer is? He isn't focused on the food, and it might—"

He cut off as I clacked my tongs in front of his face, threatening to pinch him if he continued. He just laughed at me, showing absolutely no remorse.

In the blink of an eye, his demeanor turned serious. "Jokes aside, Fischer, I want to try something . . ."

"Oh? What's that?"

"Well, you know how we haven't been able to unlock a boon from your barbecue yet? I was thinking we could both try pouring our will into it."

"Ohhh! You want to try brute forcing it? I am *so* down."

He stepped up beside me, and as we both stared down at the almost-cooked fish, I sent my will out into the world. I felt Peter's there too. It was potent, revealing his level of cultivation, but was notably less focused than mine. I sent strands of my chi out, helping shape and guide his strands toward the barbecue. At first, Peter's will railed against my influence. I sensed his surprise, and after only a moment, he lowered his walls, letting our intentions join.

With our wills aligned, I closed my eyes, focusing entirely on the barbecue and the food cooking atop it.

The hotplate had its own chi that ran through it, gathering strongest where the fish touched. It was doing *something*, but I couldn't work out what. Rather than try to comprehend the essence's purpose, I pictured what I wanted. What *we* wanted. The food was for all of our friends and acquaintances, its chi and nutrition an offering.

Peter's consciousness pulsed in protest—he disagreed.

My brow furrowing, I let his intent roll over mine, coloring it. He wasn't content with providing *only* what the fish already held. He dreamed of more. Feeling both embarrassment and understanding, I blew air from my nose. He was completely right. Why should I be happy with what the fish already provided? I wanted to give my pals everything possible. I wanted the world itself to contribute and bestow upon the food whatever it could spare.

Shooting Peter a mental nod of gratitude, I redoubled my efforts, letting chi flow from me in a steady stream.

Peter's will was with me; he opened up the gates to his core, giving everything he had. As we released more and more into the surrounding world, the land noticed. Essence flowed up like groundwater burbling to the surface. It didn't head toward the barbecue, though, instead lingering in the air around waist height. Nonplussed by the anomalous occurrence, Peter and I fortified our intention.

This feast was to be a physical representation of our gratitude. We had brought strangers to our village, and though we had freed them from the shackles of slavery, they were free to do what they wanted. Some had chosen to rebel, and even with that corrupting force allowed to roam free, most of them had instead aligned themselves with New Tropica and the church. They'd even come forward of their own accord to let Barry know what was going on, well and truly passing the test he'd laid for them.

I felt a spark of amusement, imagining their faces when Barry revealed that he knew and had planned for it.

Chi continued rising from the ground, forming into small droplets instead of strands as it so often did. Abruptly, I noticed that it wasn't just in the surrounding patio; it was happening on the sands too, especially toward the ocean just east of us, which was where the feast was to take place. The spherical sources of power were like thousands of glowing orbs in my mind's eye, casting a welcoming light over everything their light touched.

Realizing I'd become distracted, I dismissed the thought, immediately returning to the task at hand.

It had been less than a minute since we'd started, and the fish was nearing its completion. I sent my awareness down into the meat, as did Peter. Someone called my name from the waking world, but I ignored them, knowing the pivotal moment had arrived. The person called again, even louder this time—I paid them no mind. The bubbles of chi wavered as I willed them into the food, ordering them to obey. They shook, condensed, yet held their position. I swept my chi around, trying to corral them forward, but it was like attempting to move boulders with a breeze.

I returned to my body, then sent my awareness toward the barbecue. It was now or never; the fish was cooked, and if they remained any longer, they would start to burn. Something shifted around us, making a pressure build in the air. I sent curiosity toward Peter, getting only elation in return.

Elation . . . ? I wondered. *What are you so—*

His thoughts bulldozed over mine, flattening them. He had gained insight, and given we were mentally joined in a task, his newfound knowledge raced through me. This was what Peter existed for. His goal wasn't the mere act of cooking. His fate, his very purpose in life, was food. Through it, he could communicate . . . *everything.* Love, gratitude, kindness, sorrow, regret. Even anger could be channeled into a dish, turning a regular meal into something passion-filled. In response to his understanding, chi shot up from beneath him in vast ropes, winding out into the world in a complicated mesh.

Oh, I realized all too late. *He's having a breakthrough.*

The chi slammed down into him, rocketing toward his core, and as it did, the orbs of chi finally moved. The closest spheres to us appeared within the barbecue in an instant, their glow transferring to the hotplate. Those on the sand did something else, but I didn't have time to consider what that was.

There was an explosion.

Chi shot from Peter in every direction, and though it wasn't like Roger's blade-like chi, the force was ready to burn everything away. At the last possible instant, I ripped my awareness back and surrounded Peter with it, bottling the detonation.

Well, I tried to, at least. A wave of pressure struck my chest, and though I didn't move, Peter's three apprentices were blasted backward, skidding to a stop just before striking the rock wall.

I dashed forward as I released my chi, catching his unconscious form just in time to stop his head from colliding with the ground. With him secure, I checked on the food, and my heart sank.

The fish was nowhere to be seen; it must have been vaporized by the breakthrough.

"What . . . ?" Peter said, groaning as he sat up. "Did I . . . ?"

I grinned. "You certainly did, mate."

"Fischer!" Maria yelled.

I glanced toward the patio entrance, finding only her head visible as she peeked around the side.

"What's up?" I asked.

"*What's up?*" she repeated, giving me an *are-you-fracking-serious* look. "You *have* to come see this. *Now.*" Without another word, she disappeared from sight, her footfalls growing faint as she jogged back to the rest of our pals.

Peter and I raised an eyebrow at each other. I shrugged. "I guess we should go check out whatever magical shenanigans your breakthrough caused. Can you stand?"

Peter nodded, letting me help him to his feet. He clenched and unclenched his fists, his eyes going wide. "This . . . *wow*. This is *my* power?"

"Certainly is, mate. You feel just as strong as Roger. Nowhere near as sharp, though, which is nice."

I'd already sent a tendril of chi out to feel the aspect he'd taken on. It was interesting, to say the least. There was a steady heat there, but it wasn't like the flames that Trent seemed to command. It was more akin to the heat that radiated off a bed of embers.

"You said Roger feels like a blade, right?" he asked, walking for the exit. "What . . . what do I feel like?"

"Honestly, mate? You feel like a heat source. It might be the perfect power for someone who aspires to create experiences with food."

He missed a step, stumbling to catch himself as his eyes darted toward mine. "You, uh, felt that . . . ?"

"Yeah, mate," I said, laughing at his sheepish expression. "Nothing to be ashamed of—I think it's a grand purpose. And the System clearly agreed."

Though his apprentices followed us, they said not a word, simply trailing and watching their teacher with awed expressions.

The moment we walked around the corner of the patio and onto the sand, a roar of voices reached my ears. It sounded as though every single citizen of New Tropica was fighting to be heard over one another, their conversations only growing louder with our approach.

When I caught sight of them, I froze.

They were crowding around the tables we'd set up, gesturing wildly and yelling to each other to be heard over the din. Atop the tables, where we'd intended to place all the food made for the feast, bubbles of thick, golden chi hid whatever was beneath them. I walked forward on uneasy legs, reaching out with my senses to try and understand what was going on.

"There you are!" Maria called, catching sight of me. She dashed over, excitement held in every line of her face. "What did you guys *do*?"

I blinked at the concealing bubbles, then at Peter. "What the frack *did* we do, mate?"

"I . . . don't know."

I turned back to Maria. "Peter had a breakthrough, and I was too distracted keeping the explosion contained to notice what happened out here. What did you see?"

"Chi rose from the ground and formed little orbs the same color as the ones covering the table. They just floated there. I ran over to try to get your attention, but you were too focused on the barbecue."

"Oh, that was you calling? Sorry, I heard you but had to focus. How did they get onto the table . . . ?" I pointed at the massive line of coals that ran along the sand. "And what happened to the rest of the food?"

There had been dozens of bluefish cooking there, along with stacks of root vegetables, but the pans, and the food within, were gone.

"I was hoping you knew," she said. "The veggies were on the table, but the fish was still cooking. The golden orbs all radiated a blinding light. When I opened my eyes again, they were covering the tables and all the food was hidden."

Taking her hand in mine, I walked forward. The crowd noticed our approach and parted, letting us come up beside the table. The sea of bubbles seemed to call me forward, and my arm reached out of its own accord. I paused for a single moment, my finger mere millimeters from an orb the size of my head. Swallowing, I forged forward.

When my skin made contact, light and chi exploded outward, washing over me.

I stood slack-jawed, staring at the words that appeared in my vision and dulled the blinding glow coming from the feast.

CHAPTER THIRTY-TWO

Congregation

The susurration of voices died down, replaced by the sound of air rushing past my ears. Even after the blinding light of the exploding bubbles dissipated, an invisible current still moved around us, whipping at my clothes and hair.

I barely registered the sensations, instead focused on the System message that had rudely commandeered my field of view.

You have successfully taken part in a crafting ritual!
Quest updated: Group Project
Objective: [Error. Insufficient Power.]
Reward: [Error. Insufficient Power.]

I cleared my vision, intending to roll my eyes at the less-than-useful message, but then I caught sight of what sat atop the tables.

Like a scene right out of a cooking anime, our feast seemed to shine. There were piles and piles of food, all cooked to perfection and radiating a golden light. The shore fish that had been cooking on the coals were sitting in their pans, presented so beautifully that they could give a gourmet chef an existential crisis. Between the pans, plates of roasted vegetables sat, the steam rising from them lit by the ever-present glow. As impressive as they were, neither the vegetables nor the juvenile fish were the centerpiece.

Placed intermittently along the tabletops, the slabs of mature bluefish shone brighter than all the rest. Each was a slightly different color, their unique combination of herbs and spices making them appear like entirely different dishes. I had assumed that they'd been destroyed by Peter's breakthrough and the subsequent explosion.

But I was wrong.

They were skin side up, the silvery surface turned into a golden-brown crust. I took a deep breath through my nose, all too happy to be assaulted by the combination of scents. When my eyes roamed over the closest one, I felt a familiar tug on my senses, and I leaned into the feeling, allowing my vision to get drawn in.

Lucky Angler's Feast of the Journeyman Chefs
Mythic

Created by kindred Cooking journeymen, this feast is a representation of their bond and desires. Taking part in this feast will grant the consumer with the boon: Lucky Angler.
Lucky Angler effect: +20 Luck for the next 24 hours.

I shook my head, my vision clearing as I smiled out at the world. Slowly, everyone else's eyes refocused, their faces amazed, ecstatic, and everything in between.

"Well," I said, glancing at Peter. "Looks like our little experiment was a success, mate."

"Yeah . . ." he replied, staring down at one of the slabs of mature fish.

"All right, everyone," I called, basking in their expressions as they looked my way. "Help yourselves!"

Conversations exploded into life as we started piling our plates with the different foods. There wasn't enough room for everyone at once, so Maria and I quickly scooted out of the way. She leaned against my arm as we watched them all, their happiness unignorable.

When Gormona's collared cultivators had first arrived on the sands of Tropica, they'd been terrified—and rightfully so. They had no idea who we were or what we were about, and even the most trusting of people would've had some reservations about being kidnapped by a cadre of powerful heretics. Though we had said we were freeing them, words alone did nothing to assuage their worries. Over the past weeks, however, we had shown them our intentions. Actions spoke louder than words, and we had proven ourselves time and time again.

The joy with which they plucked food from the feast was proof of that. Because of my enhanced awareness following my breakthrough, I could feel a hint of what they were experiencing. Given how many of them there were, it was like an immutable mass of emotion, their individual experiences combining into a wall of contentment that crashed over me.

Someone sniffed beside me, and I stole a glance at Peter just in time for him to wipe a tear away.

"You all good, mate?"

"Yeah," he replied, sniffing again. "It's just . . . I can sense what they're feeling."

"It's a lot, huh?" I reached over, resting a hand on his shoulder. "Your food is the main cause of it, mate. Looks to me like your purpose is already being fulfilled."

His eyes formed slits as he smiled out at them, gratitude radiating from his core. "It is, isn't it?"

Our tender moment was abruptly interrupted when something orange, pinchy, and supremely rude leaped up onto the far end of the table. People gasped and stepped back, retreating from the unwelcome newcomer.

Rocky, not at all bothering to grab a plate, chowed down on a chunk of fish. He displayed no joy, consuming the meat as if it were a chore. Sergeant Snips, who had already retrieved a full plate of food near my end of the table, stood to her full height, her lone eye staring murderously at her insubordinate crab.

As suddenly as he arrived, Rocky leaped away, jumping in the direction of Tropica and scuttling away as fast as he could. I blinked at the shrinking cloud of sand billowing in his wake, genuinely shocked that the situation had resolved itself so peacefully. Snips hissed to get my attention, and when I turned to look at her, she dipped her head and blew bubbles of apology for her troublesome companion, but I just grinned back at her.

"Honestly," Maria said. "That crab . . ."

"At least he stays on brand." I shrugged. "I'd be more surprised if he acted with decorum. Come on. Let's find a seat."

As we settled down on the logs we'd set up for everyone to sit on, I stared down at the plate on my lap. Steam rose from the different portions, each of them radiating a mouthwatering combination of scents. Even when removed from the table, the fish and vegetables still shone with a faint light, the brightest glow coming from the mature fillets Peter and I had cooked on the barbecue.

It made the surrounding scene otherworldly.

As everyone took a seat and waited for the rest of the cultivators to get a helping, their torsos and faces were lit by the golden glow, revealing just how excited they were to try the food. Rather than order them to go ahead, I bathed in their anticipation, also happy to wait. When the final person sat down with their food, I nodded at Barry.

He stood and cleared his throat. "Before we take part in this delicious meal, I wanted to thank you all again. I'll keep it brief, because I can barely speak with how much my mouth is watering right now."

Soft laughter rose from dozens of people, rolling over the sands.

"So," Barry continued. "Thank you for your hard work, loyalty, and for taking a chance with our little village. You haven't been with us long, but you're all valued members of our congregation."

To show he had no more to say, he sat, stabbed his fork into a chunk of juvenile bluefish, and put it into his mouth. Everyone followed suit, and as a portion of seasoned fish hit my tongue, flavor exploded over my awareness.

At first, a buttery, pleasantly hot fat that was laced with garlic covered my tongue, seeming to come from within the fish. Next, a subtler herb came through, taking the edge off the oppressive garlic. When I bit into the soft fish, the dish's true taste arrived. The bluefish was as strong as ever, its flavor unmistakably unique. Though both the fish and its seasoning might have been overwhelming on their own, together, they were perfectly balanced.

There was another sensation in the mix, something that I'd not experienced before.

It was as if my taste buds registered the light emitting from the dish. It cast a warmth over me that went beyond my mouth, heating my entire jaw. As I chewed, all I could focus on was the flavor, and when I swallowed, the warmth washed down my throat, hitting my abdomen and radiating outward to caress every inch of my body.

I blinked, my vision blurry as I returned to the present. Tears welled, and I wiped them away with a shaky hand, breathing out slowly to steady myself.

Peter whimpered from beside me, his lip quivering.

"Mate . . ." I said, reaching over to pat him on the back.

"Yeah . . ." Maria agreed, also sniffling and unable to form any other words.

I reached my other arm out to grab her shoulder, and their position on either side of me was just as soothing as I hoped my presence was to them.

It was, without a doubt, one of the best things I'd ever tasted. Judging by everyone else's reactions, it was the same for them. Most of the cultivators were wide-eyed, not saying a word as they stared into space. Some were talking animatedly to the people beside them, discussing the bite they'd eaten. The rest, just like Peter, Maria, and me, were emotionally overwhelmed. At least a dozen of them sat teary-eyed, unable to express themselves in any other way.

Rather than stare, I turned to Peter. He'd composed himself, a small grin tugging at his mouth as he glanced around at everyone. His core vibrated with *rightness*, for lack of a better word, his chi celebrating the coming together of so many people to partake of his creation.

Maria and I shared a glance, and she darted in to steal a kiss.

"What was that for?" I asked.

"Everything, I guess." She leaned down to rest her head on my shoulder, our bodies fitting together perfectly.

Realizing my food was going cold, I stabbed a potato and placed it in my mouth. Though I'd expected it to be a nice flavor reset before trying a different portion of fish, the starchy vegetable crunched as I bit down into it, its soft, pillowy interior falling apart. As with the fish, I could almost taste the golden light glowing from it, and it warmed my body just the same.

"Gods above," I said.

Maria let out a halting breath. "The veggies are just as good as the fish . . ."

Peter whimpered in agreement, unable to speak.

As Rocky swam through the bay, his carapace hummed with power.

Though he'd put on a front of indifference, that fish was the best godsdamned thing he had ever tasted. He had felt the explosion of power from his new faction's base and rushed over, intent on determining what had caused it. He'd discovered the entirety of Fischer's followers there, all ready to partake in a chi-filled feast.

He'd not had much time to spare, so he'd quickly helped himself to the chi on offer. He took great delight in the reactions of the surrounding humans, their gasps and terror the correct reaction a mere human should have to his spectacular form. Before his spiky mistress could grab and fling him out to sea, he'd performed a tactical retreat.

After all, he had somewhere to be.

Despite the speed with which he flew through the bay's waters, the glowing chi he'd gotten from those few mouthfuls of fish didn't burn away. The essence seemed bottomless, his rear flippers using the never-ending fuel source to send him skidding over the ocean. Before he knew it, he'd reached the distant headland on the northern side of the bay.

When he leaped up onto the rocks there, his carapace glistening as he scuttled over the shore, he found his followers where he left them. Their clothing was finally starting to dry following their swim through the bay earlier, the process aided by the fire they sat around. As Rocky noticed the pan sitting in the coals, he froze, casting his gaze over the humans.

Perhaps they weren't useless after all . . .

Sitting on a pan he'd requisitioned from Fischer's kitchen, two bluefish sat cooking, their juices bubbling out where flesh touched the hot metal. Rocky looked toward the stack of rods he'd borrowed, seeing they'd all been used. He pointed down at the cooking fish, blowing questioning bubbles.

"Er, I hope it's okay, Sergeant Snips," Joel said, bowing low. "We did our best to follow your instructions . . ."

Before leaving, he had ordered them to catch some food.

Though he had seriously considered stealing a fish from the feast back on Fischer's property and bringing it back to his faction, Rocky had decided it wasn't wise. If they partook of Fischer's food and the chi held within, they may have ended up becoming loyal to the troublesome man. Rocky had doubted they'd catch a fish anytime soon, so was reliant on their eventual starvation to motivate them sufficiently. Whether it was his spiky mistress's influence or his ascended awareness, he wouldn't let them starve, but he would happily bring them to the brink in order to further his goals. The darkness within him affirmed this decision, screaming that the ends justified the means.

But it didn't appear they needed any extra motivation.

Despite having neither previous experience nor proper instruction, they'd worked it out. They had caught enough fish to sustain them until tomorrow at least, and as he looked between the almost-cooked fish and the arrayed humans, a wave of suspicion washed over Rocky. Mere humans shouldn't be so capable. How had they done it?

The more he considered it, the worse his paranoia became. What if they were secretly working for Fischer?

Rocky pointed at the fish, the rods, then them, blowing demanding bubbles.

"I'm sorry, great spirit beast," Joel said. "I don't understand the question . . ."

"I think he's asking how we did it," said George, who Rocky had learned was the village lord. "How we caught the fish, I mean."

Rocky bobbed his carapace in acknowledgment, infuriated that he had to resort to human methods of communication to be understood.

"Oh . . ." Joel said, glancing up, then averting his eyes when he saw the fury on Rocky's face. "We were only able to succeed because of your instruction, great spirit beast."

Liar! Rocky hissed, spittle flying.

Joel's eyes went wide. "I . . . I also had some previous experience fishing. I know it's heretical, but it was the only way for me to gather our offerings for you, and I personally caught each of them." He lowered himself further to the sand. "If I have offended you, I ask that you punish only me."

The words swept in like a strong current, washing away Rocky's suspicion and leaving only grandeur in its place. It was because of their rightful praise for him that they had succeeded. His existence was the sole reason they'd managed to catch fish so soon, because if not for him, the cult would never have practiced fishing and gained the requisite skills.

It was as though the very universe urged Rocky on, telling him that his plans would come to fruition. He puffed himself up, standing to his full height as an invisible weight fell away.

Scuttling forward, he took a pinch of the now-cooked fish, putting it into his mouth. As he chewed, he told himself it was just as good as the fish he'd stolen from Fischer. It was a lie, of course, but that didn't diminish how much chi the seasonal fish held.

His eyes sparkled as he spun, taking in the still-bowing forms of his faction.

Not his faction, he mentally corrected. His *church*. He was creating a *church*.

He blew contented bubbles, knowing it was only a matter of time until his congregation took steps on the path of ascension.

CHAPTER THIRTY-THREE

Crabby

As George watched the spirit beast, he got the inkling that it was suffering from delusions of grandeur. He swallowed, his throat feeling dry.

Something was wrong.

It was hard for him to place exactly what it was, but he got the sense it wasn't the mere existence of a powerful spirit beast. That, surprisingly, didn't seem to bother him much. It was an odd sensation, but the longer he examined his internal state, the more sure he became it was something else worrying him. That he perceived the awakened beast as suffering from delusions of grandeur was just as surprising. It was a fabled beast of legend, a creature that, even in his wildest dreams, he'd never expected to encounter.

This "Sergeant Snips" had every right to see herself as above them. And yet, it still felt wrong, as if the beast was being presumptuous.

George glanced over at Geraldine, seeing his confusing mix of emotions reflected in her gaze. She chewed the inside of her lip, and he gave her the smallest of nods, communicating that he felt the same.

The crab held a claw to its mouth, cleaning the orange appendage with its undulating mouth. The moment it was finished, it stepped back and gestured at the fish they'd caught and cooked.

It blew a stream of bubbles that George somehow understood the meaning of.

Eat.

It wanted them to consume the fish.

George's gaze flicked down to the cooking fish as he turned his attention away from the spirit beast. When they had originally caught it, he'd been disgusted. Joel had encouraged them all to touch it, and when George and Geraldine had done so, George's disgust had only increased.

The thing was covered in a slippery, translucent film.

It had a smell to it, as well, that reminded him of the ocean, but not the pleasant smell of salt spray. It had the same odor as washed-up seaweed left to rot in the sun. As George thought back on the fetid scent, it made the delicious smell now filling the air even more confusing. Savory notes had flooded out from the fish the moment it started cooking, and with each passing second, it seemed to grow even stronger.

Geraldine squeezed his arm, drawing his eyes from the meal. She stared at the pan in the fire, her jaw moving subconsciously.

"Can we . . . ?" she asked, her gaze locked on the fatty liquids bubbling from the fish.

"I don't think we have a choice," he whispered back. "Even if we did, though . . ."

"You want to taste it," she finished.

He grimaced, embarrassed that she had seen through him so easily, but she shook her head. "I also want to. It smells . . ."

"Delicious . . ." Joel said, his tone reverent. He sat up, and George wondered if he was finally done bowing.

He was not.

Joel slammed his body back down to the sand, only having sat upright so he could bow all the way down again. "Thank you, great spirit beast! You have blessed this food with your very essence. There is no other explanation for the scent wafting from this fish. We, your loyal followers, are unworthy of your graciousness."

The spirit beast preened, clearly enjoying the praise. It blew bubbles that were . . . pleased? Then, it pointed back down at the food.

Eat, it demanded again, some of its pride still leaking through.

The members of the cult-turned-church shuffled forward, keeping their heads lowered while pulling themselves closer to the fire. George and Geraldine did the same, not wanting to offend the ascendant creature.

They had gathered fan-shaped shells, and Joel passed them around. As one, every human present used one to cut into the fish. George had thought he'd need to slice through the flesh, expecting it to be as tough as any other animal's meat.

He was wrong.

The moment his shell touched the fish, its flesh fell apart. It sloughed off in small chunks and fell into the juices collecting in the pan. George had thought the scent earlier was good, but the vapor rising from within the fish was heavenly.

All seven of them froze for a moment, as shocked as each other at the fish's texture and the scents coming from it. Joel was the first to snap out of it. He slid his shell under a smattering of the flakey bits, and as he lifted them out of the pan, fatty oil dripped down onto his open palm, positioned so he wasted not a drop. Licking his lips, George copied Joel, as did the others. Their shells scraped softly against the metal pan, and a moment later, all seven of them were ready.

Eat, the spirit beast hissed, more insistent than ever.

It wasn't necessary, though. George's mouth was watering, and based on everyone else's expressions, so were theirs. As one, they raised the shells to their lips and had their first-ever taste of fish. Before the white meat even made it to his tongue, a still-dripping oil found his taste buds. They washed over it, turning his salivary glands into faucets. It was so salty that it was almost unpleasant, right on the borderline of being too much.

But then the fish came.

He bit down into the handful of small chunks, their fibers easily parting as he chewed. More juices came from the meat, hot and pleasant. The flavor contained within was unremarkable on its own, perhaps a little unsavory. Combined with the salty oil, however, the disparate tastes danced over one another, building to become something greater.

George's eyes watered, the flavors assaulting his awareness all-encompassing. The muscles of his mouth twitched as he swallowed, almost as if his body wasn't ready to relinquish the blessed ingredients gracing his tongue. After swallowing, he released a shaky breath, then inhaled through his nose, knowing how to enhance any lingering tastes after a lifetime spent consuming sugary treats.

It was almost as delicious as the mouthful itself, his consciousness crying out for more of the food. Another sensation came then. It was something . . . foreign. He'd definitely never experienced it before, yet something in the back of his mind recognized it. He sat frozen for a long moment, his mind racing to recall where he knew this warm and welcome feeling from.

Try as he might, it didn't come.

Suddenly, it felt like it was coming from all around him, not only from within. It blanketed over his entire body like a hug from a loved one. Even more confused, he opened his eyes, seeking to understand what was happening. The fire was burning brighter than before, casting its light over all those present.

"George!"

The fear in Geraldine's voice made adrenaline course through him, and he spun her way, half expecting the crab to have attacked. She was staring wide-eyed across the fire, whatever she saw there filling her with terror. His heart raced as he whirled back. He had just been looking there and had seen nothing to warrant such a reaction.

The spirit beast had appeared before the former cultists. Its claws were held high above it, slowly opening and closing in what George took for victorious posture. For some reason, the creature seemed . . . dim? He narrowed his eyes, growing more confused by the second. How could a campfire light the cultists, yet not a crab that was closer to it?

"The glow . . ." he said aloud, verbally processing the impossible sight. "It's coming from *them* . . ."

He had assumed the fire's light had grown, but that wasn't it. An orange light shone from the five humans, radiating from their position and illuminating the surrounding sands. George and Geraldine stood up on wobbling legs, getting a better view of the surroundings. She reached out, grasping for his hand, and when she found it, their fingers intertwined. Though she was always his lodestone, their contact did nothing to ease George's mind.

The glow was getting brighter, and as it did, the sensation from earlier returned. It wasn't coming from the outside world—it was coming from five glowing humans sitting before him. The mighty crab, whom Joel had called Sergeant Snips, blew encouraging bubbles, urging them on. Being eager servants, they obeyed, getting brighter and brighter.

The light also got more orange. So dark that it was on the borderline of turning red, it resembled the rising sun, bringing with it just as much warmth as that celestial body. George squeezed Geraldine's hand, completely lost in the miraculous occurrence unfolding before their eyes. He thought it couldn't get any more surprising.

But then the pulse of power flew out from all of them, its wondrous form making a shiver of ecstasy run through his entire body. He shuddered, the sensation making him lose touch with the world. When his body came to, he put a twitching hand down to his side, finding sand. He'd fallen back down to the ground when the wave struck him. Geraldine was right beside him, and they exchanged a glance before staring back at the others.

The spirit beast stood with its claws raised high and held all the way open, frozen as it cast its gaze over Joel and the rest of the former cultists. It seemed to be waiting for something. The glow was gone from Joel and the others now, but that same sensation was there, matching the one coming from George's stomach.

Joel's eyes were distant. All at once, he shook his head, his vision focusing once more and settling on the spirit beast. "Please choose a name? Does that mean . . ."

Two explosions rang out, so strong that George and Geraldine were blown backwards. He braced himself and hunched down so he didn't get sent skidding across the sand.

After the first two, Rocky sent a few more celebratory blasts out for good measure, the darkness within his core rejoicing.

It had *worked*.

A single day was all it had taken. A single glorious day, and his genius plan had already borne fruit. He stared out at the newly awakened, measuring the strength of their cores. They were moderately stronger than others upon ascension, and more importantly, they still held that hint of crabby goodness. Though their touch of crab-like chi was only a fraction of their essence, it was enough. It proved that they were loyal to him.

He momentarily considered going to Fischer and showing off immediately, but then he . . . what was it that Fischer said? Snip it in the butt? Yeah, that sounded right. He snipped the thought in the butt, excising it from his awareness.

Though they were loyal to Rocky, they were still freshly awakened. If he waited even a week, they would have more time to gain power, and that would make the reveal all the sweeter.

"We . . . we are cultivators?" Jess asked, licking her lips.

"Are we truly?" Joel asked, his eyes fervent as he stared at Rocky.

Yes, Rocky hissed.

"Thank you, great spirit beast!" Joel yelled, throwing his forehead to the sand. "This is only the beginning of your church, and I vow that we will assist in your ascension to the heavens!"

The others made the same gesture, echoing his sentiments.

Rocky hissed with laughter, holding his claws high once more. This was exactly what he had wanted—what he deserved. Forget waiting. He wanted to show Fischer *now*. That would show the foolish man. So what if they hadn't gained much power? They were his followers—his *church*—and that fact alone should be enough to drive fear into the spine of Rocky's rival.

Come, he ordered, gesturing back toward the ocean, but froze when he spun.

He'd completely forgotten about the other two humans, the lord and his wife. They hadn't ascended yet, which was why his vastly superior mind had banished them from thought. No matter that they hadn't attained enlightenment yet—it was only a matter of time. Should he leave them here, though?

Nope.

He could show Fischer that he had regular human followers, too. That would only further cement Rocky's position as a rival god.

Come, Rocky ordered again, striding between the two failures. He cut a palm tree down with a single strike on his way to the water, then gestured for the two unascended to grab hold of it. Annoyingly, they looked at each other instead of immediately obeying.

Rocky would have to beat that out of them.

Luckily for them, they nodded to each other and stepped forward, following him down to the water. Rocky leaped in, and the seven humans followed, the lord and his wife grasping the trunk. With the end of a palm tree held in one claw and glee fueling his passage, Rocky took off across the bay, his newly awakened followers easily keeping up.

CHAPTER THIRTY-FOUR

Coincidence

Following the feast, I lay on the sands, one hand holding my stomach and the other resting against Maria.

"I never want to eat again," she said, letting out a half laugh, half groan.

"See how you feel about that tomorrow," I said. "But I get where you're coming from. I don't think I've ever felt so full."

"The feast was a trap," Theo complained from somewhere to my left. "I couldn't stop eating."

"No regrets," Peter said from my right, trying and failing to sound unaffected by the excessive amount he'd eaten.

I knew exactly how they felt; I'd gone full glutton, unable to stop myself from consuming more and more of the warmth-inducing meals. Each was as unique as the last, their flavors complementary in a way that I struggled to put into words. Rather than try to find the right combination of syllables to describe how transcendent an experience it had been, I squeezed Maria's hand, the softness of her skin momentarily distracting me from my discomfort. As I did, a breeze blew past me, its cold touch a pleasant counterpoint to the warmth still radiating from my abdomen.

I took a deep breath, smiling out at the world and everything I had gained since arriving in Tropica. Even my overfull stomach couldn't bring down my mood. Come to think of it, I'm not sure anything could.

As George strode along the streets of Tropica, a cold breeze blew, sending a shiver across his entire body. On the sapient crab's orders, George and Geraldine had gone home and gotten dressed. He knew not why they had to make themselves presentable, but when a creature capable of cutting you in half like a sugared pastry told you to do something, you did it.

Though they were no longer wet, he still felt cold, the single bite of fish he'd had the only thing keeping him warm. Geraldine squeezed his hand tighter, making him amend the previous thought; her love and proximity also brought warmth. As with everything lately, an odd calm settled over him in the face of current events. When his musings turned worrisome, he relied on House Kraken's manuscript, following the breathing and meditative techniques contained within.

No matter how one approached the circumstances, both of them *should* be freaking out.

The five people they'd grown close to in recent days, exchanging tips and pointers with regard to their meditations, had awakened as cultivators. The moment the capital found out—which they always did—all five of his new friends were doomed to a life of servitude. He should be terrified of them, given the madness that was said to come with being chosen by the System.

And yet, he wasn't.

Just like the spirit beast they were returning to, their steps on the path of ascension felt . . . right. Like it was both the correct thing to do and a more accurate representation of who they were within. The former cultists seemed to feel the same and had been nothing but smiles and thankfulness since it happened. The entire sequence of events made George start to question . . . well, *everything*.

By itself, a spirit beast appearing was miraculous, and while he *had* wondered at the implications for the world at large, he hadn't considered what it meant for the poor souls that became cultivators. For the safety of others, it was necessary that they were collared by the capital. Along with the power the System granted, humans on the path of ascension also inherited a high chance of going mad. According to the kingdom's teachings, wielders of chi were as strong as they were unstable.

But how would the arrival of a spirit beast—the very species of beast that the Church of Carcinization deified—change their behavior? Would they be safe from the madness-inducing effects of chi? Would the great crab, this Sergeant Snips, save them from the looming possibility of insanity? If so, would it be a metaphysical protection where the madness was drained away, or would the sapient creature physically correct their behavior? The most terrifying of all possibilities was that they wouldn't be shielded from the detrimental effects, and that the awakened creature would encourage any antisocial activities. Given the crab's inhuman sensibilities, it was a horrible and possible eventuality.

It wasn't lost on George that he had been meditating with the people that ascended, either.

He and Geraldine had been following House Kraken's teachings for months now, and finally listening to the words of his family had been a blessing for them, their marriage, and everyone else in Tropica. It had been the catalyst for a world of change, and George could scarcely believe the person he had been less than a year ago. A lifetime spent doing things that only brought him and his wife misery. If not for his ability to stay grounded in the present because of the manual's guidance, remembrance of who he had been for so long would have brought no end of misery and self-loathing.

Though it had been a blessing, what if the path his family described, this *road to enlightenment*, was something more sinister than they had ever imagined? He'd never before considered that House Kraken's manual would turn you into a cultivator. Now, he did. And it made perfect sense. Because of his position as a noble, exiled or not, he had more knowledge of cultivators than most. He was aware of chi, the essence that provided cultivators with their abilities. Now that he looked at the manual's teachings with that knowledge in mind, the puzzle pieces fit.

Despite this realization, this understanding that his family may have been teaching how to become something so wretched, his steps came easily. His shoulders were high and his breaths steady, his heart rate only slightly elevated, even though he should be, by all rights, beside himself. Was this the madness? He and Geraldine had both thought themselves close to some sort of breakthrough, able to sense their proximity to the fabled *enlightenment* that his family spoke of. If they were almost there, and the destination was the base of the steps to ascension, was he already under the effect of a cultivator's madness?

"George . . . ?"

He stopped walking, turning to face his wife. Geraldine also stopped, and the look of trepidation in her eyes made his chest hurt.

"Are we . . ." She trailed off, looking around and chewing her lip before returning her gaze to his. "Are we going mad?"

Despite his similar train of thought, he smiled at her, ever thankful for her company. "I was just thinking the same thing. We just might be." Looking into her face and the beauty it held, realization struck George like an afternoon sugar crash. He chuckled at himself, shaking his head as he pulled her into a hug.

"Oh, you're mad already?" she asked, amusement clear in her voice. "At least I won't go insane by myself."

"You know, we might be, but I don't think I care."

"Yep. Definitely mad." She rubbed his back, squeezing him tighter. "What has you so carefree?"

"Even if we go mad, we'll do it together."

She pulled back and stared into his eyes. "No offense, but I might not love you as much as I do now if you start murdering people."

"Ah, my lady wife wounds me so." He clutched at his chest, drawing an eye-roll from Geraldine. "But I don't think we'll go mad."

"Oh? What makes you so sure?"

"The fact that we're following the instructions of my ancestors. Even if we become cultivators, I trust all those that passed the manual down to not have gifted us a one-way ticket to servitude and insanity. There has to be more to it. I *know* there is more to it. The same way I know that the Church of Carcinization's crab-like meditation is right for them, I know that the Kraken manual's path is correct for us. Maybe it's only that those chosen at random by the System go mad. Or maybe it's because my family derived a way to become cultivators without the risk of insanity, *if* that's even what we are becoming. All I know is that this feels right to both of us, and I trust myself—and you—to make the right call."

As he had continued to speak, a fire rose in Geraldine's eyes. The moment he finished, she latched a hand around the nape of his neck and pulled herself up. Though her lips and body weren't as plump as they once were, her kiss drew him in, washing away any hint of past worries. They kissed for a long moment, and when they separated, both their breaths came heavy.

"We should hurry along," he said.

"We should," she replied, yet pulled him back into a kiss, picking up where they'd left off.

Another few breaths later, they pulled apart. Geraldine let out a sigh. "Come on, dear. We shouldn't keep our grouchy overlord waiting."

"He does seem rather grouchy, doesn't he?"

They traversed the rest of Tropica in silence, and as they approached the meeting place, they found the rest of the group already present. Their five friends were also in clean garb, having been ordered to go change by the sapient beast.

The awakened crab hissed at them, clearly annoyed at how long they had taken.

"Apologies," George said, gesturing at the others. "We lack the speed of our friends from the church."

The crab's claws opened and closed slowly as it narrowed its eyes at them. After considering them for a long moment, it spun, facing the south. *Come*, it hissed, marching off. Seeing the direction it was leading them, the flicker of a worry returned, sparking to life in the depths of his soul. He swept it away, however, knowing there was no way this Sergeant Snips was leading them *there*.

Geraldine, knowing him better than anyone else in the realm, rested a hand on his lower back. "Come on, dear. It'll be fine."

He nodded, having to half force the smile he gave her. "Of course it will be. I have you."

Hand in hand, they trailed the others. The spirit beast traveled at a much more sustainable pace than the speed it had dragged them through the bay. Its steps were measured as it led them between rows of sugarcane, radiating a hint of the pompousness George associated with most of the creature's actions. When they emerged from between the last crops and continued heading south, the flicker of worry returned, its flame brighter than before.

"A coincidence," Geraldine said, squeezing his hand.

"Yeah . . ." he replied, not sure.

"What's wrong?" Joel asked, waiting for them to catch up to him. "What is a coincidence?"

Any other time, George would have wondered at how Joel's hearing had become enhanced so soon after becoming a cultivator; there was no way a regular human could have heard their comments from so far ahead of them. Now, though, it was all George could do to keep his heart from beating out of his chest.

"It's nothing," George lied, eyeing the fence that came into view across the sandy flat.

As the spirit beast approached it, George prayed it would change course and follow the fence line toward the eastern forest. Gods above, even approaching the ocean and swimming out to sea seemed a much more tenable option. Instead, it pointed up at the wooden gate, demanding that someone open it, then leaped over the wooden barrier to land on the other side.

George's stomach sank, the flame of worry growing into a small fire. He glanced at Geraldine, and though she still held his hand, her jaw was tense. He swept away his climbing dread as much as possible, focusing on his family's teachings. Unlike earlier, his troubled thoughts remained, and as they passed through the gate, the flame within sputtered and flared, finding plenty of fuel to burn.

The spirit beast, unaware or uncaring of George's turmoil, veered to the southwest, heading for the rock formation that housed Fischer's home. It made no sense. Why was the spirit beast leading them toward Fischer's place? Was the crown agent somehow involved? He couldn't be . . . could he? Was it possible that the king was somehow in on this, having harnessed—or caused—the ascendance of the crab? Just how deep did this conspiracy go?

Lost as he was in his thoughts, George wasn't paying attention to the outside world.

"Uhhh," a familiar voice he dreaded said, snapping George from his musings.

Fischer stood alone, his face growing incredulous as his eyes roamed over them, and the crown agent abruptly froze when he caught sight of George. "George? Is that you, mate?"

The words, though friendly on the surface, drove a jagged spear of ice into George's spine.

"H-hello, Fischer . . ."

CHAPTER THIRTY-FIVE

Correction

As Rocky walked the final stretch of sand between the fence and Fischer, he could hardly contain his excitement. The time of Fischer's uncontested reign was finally at an end.

He had five cultivators with him, all of which were loyal to him. On top of that, he had the support of two non-cultivators, and though they were yet to ascend, they were almost there. They were far from regular humans, too; they were the lord and lady of Tropica, their noble blood giving them more authority. Rocky glanced back at the two, scowling when he saw how nervous they appeared. They were timid, but he would change that. Through a combination of violence and delicious treats, he would mold them into something greater. Once they ascended, he could use their influence to convert the rest of Tropica's villagers.

He pictured it in his mind, the lord kneeling before him, the rest of the citizens bowing so low that their foreheads touched the sand, just as his reliable cultists did. It was a wondrous sight, and it was all possible because of Rocky's ingenious planning. He puffed his carapace out even more, feeling as large as Pistachio. The closer he got to the feast, the more his anticipation grew, and when they came into sight, he let out slow, hissing laughter, getting everyone's attention.

But something was wrong. There were only two people sitting on the sand, everyone else having disappeared. Fischer got to his feet first, casting his eyes over them all. Maria stood next, and she studied them, her brow furrowing. Okay, so it was only Fischer and his girlfriend there—that was no matter. Rocky bathed in the confusion his adversary must be feeling right now.

"George? Is that you, mate?" Fischer asked.

The lord, who was supposed to be *his* follower, lowered his eyes. "H-hello, Fischer."

Rocky's blood boiled. Fischer dared ignore him and speak directly with his loyal followers?

Look, he hissed, gesturing at the cultivators loyal to him. *Mine. They are mine.*

Fischer smiled at Rocky's cultivators, but as his essence flowed out toward them, the smile died on his face. "You . . ." Fischer balled his fists at his side and narrowed his eyes at Rocky. "*What did you do?*"

Rocky held his claws high, hissing with manic laughter. Fischer finally understood that Rocky had created his own faction. He stood to the tips of his many legs, his entire body shaking with mirth.

It. Was. *Glorious.*

* * *

I narrowed my eyes at the malignant little crab. The Cult of Carcinization had all become cultivators, which in itself was no big deal—I suspected they'd do so sooner rather than later because of their meditative practice. The problem was that there was something off about their chi. They were tinged with *crab*, and given Rocky's triumphant pose, I suspected I knew the culprit.

Rocky spun toward Joel, leveling a claw at him.

Explain, he hissed.

Joel nodded, bowing low to the little miscreant. "Fischer, things are not as they seem. I'm aware that this great spirit beast was pretending to be a loyal pet to you, but she is an awakened creature. You cannot expect to control such a—"

"She?" I asked, cutting him off. "What are you talking about?"

Joel gave me a quizzical look. "Uhhh, you told me that Sergeant Snips was a female when you introduced us . . . *Oooh*." He snapped his fingers, seemingly realizing something. "I see. You're playing coy because of Maria." He gave us a kind smile that would have seemed condescending on most faces, but not Joel's. "Worry not, Fischer—things have changed, and the time for secrecy is over."

Maria tilted her head to the side, her hair falling free of her ear. "What's changed, Joel? And why would Fischer play coy around me?"

"Because," Jess replied, stepping forward with fervent eyes, "he has been in contact with a spirit beast for the last few months. Our beloved deity, Sergeant Snips, has helped us take steps on the path of ascension." She pointed at Rocky, who still cackled and puffed himself up like a cornered echidna. "Now that she has chosen us as her cast of crabs, there is no longer a need to hide the Cult of Carcinization's evolution to a church."

I raised a finger and opened my mouth to correct her, but I didn't even know where to begin.

Maria started laughing, the sound light and bouncing at first. Before long, she was hanging off my shoulder, relying on my support to stand upright as the laughter took her. I smiled down at her, getting swept up in her enjoyment of the moment.

"All of that is wrong, Jess," she eventually got out, wiping tears from her eyes. "Though I'm starting to understand how you got there."

Jess's eyebrow had arched when Maria first started giggling, and it remained high, punctuated by the occasional twitch. "I understand why you're in denial—it's a lot to take in, but I assure you, Fischer has been cavorting with a spirit beast for most of the time he has been here. Though Sergeant Snips could have ended his life at any time, she spared him, showing just how magnanimous she is."

Figuring it was time to set the record straight, I took a step forward, but Maria squeezed my shoulder.

"I've got it," she said, patting me.

I gestured for her to go ahead, and she took a few steps forward, holding her hands behind her back and looking mighty cute.

"First of all, let me just confirm that you believe *that* crab there to be Sergeant Snips."

Jess's mouth formed a line, but Joel strode forward, laying a calming hand on her lower back. "That is her name, yes. I know that it's a lot to take in, but—"

"Got it," Maria interrupted, nodding. "You've been lied to, but that's not really surprising. That crab's name is Rocky, and he *is* a spirit beast, yes, but he's anything but magnanimous. In fact, he's a bit of a prick."

The entire Cult of Carcinization—or I suppose they were a church now—gasped.

"Watch your tongue, Maria!" Joel warned, seeming genuinely worried about our health. Which was entirely misplaced but still warmed my heart a little.

"Yeah, I'm not finished." Maria shook her head. "You said that Fischer was cavorting with a spirit beast, but that's not exactly true."

"Maria . . ." Joel winced, then gave me a half smile. "Is she okay, Fischer? I worry that this is too much for her."

"Oh?" I raised a brow. "How so?"

He frowned. "Because she says she's aware of Sergeant Snips's existence as a spirit beast, yet she uses the wrong name." His narrowed eyes shifted to Maria. "In the same breath, Maria, you deny that Fischer has been in contact with any spirit beasts."

"Nah, she's right, mate. She got you on a technicality."

"A . . . technicality?"

"Yeah!" I grinned, unable to hide my amusement any longer. "She said that I hadn't been in contact with a spirit *beast*, which is entirely true." My eyes shifted over them, taking in their confusion. "I've been cavorting with way more than one spirit beast." I clapped my hands together. "If you would, everyone!"

On cue, sand erupted behind me. A massive cloud of debris billowed, obscuring every being that had just emerged from the ground.

I spread my arms wide. "Allow me to introduce my animal pals . . ."

Since the arrival of Fischer, all George could do was listen to the exchange of words.

His body felt numb, and no matter how much he relied on the breathing and mindfulness exercises of House Kraken, Fischer's web was too all-encompassing to ignore. He and Geraldine had already discovered that Fischer was an elite among Gormona's auditors, but this . . . this was worse than they ever could have imagined.

With each word spoken, George's dread only grew.

Fischer had apparently been in contact with the spirit beast for months. Joel and Jess clearly knew of this, having been introduced to Sergeant Snips by Fischer. His mind raced, trying to connect the dots.

If Fischer was here and involved in this conspiracy, it had to be under the king's orders. Fischer was high in the command of Gormona, so it was the only possibility. Was that why his house had appeared basically overnight? It made more sense than anything else; for a mission so important, the king would have spared no expense. Dozens of cultivators could have brought the supplies overnight and constructed the building before the sun rose. Thinking of cultivators made George's blood run cold, which was the only sensation making it through the fog that seemed to surround his body.

He and Geraldine might be turning into cultivators.

It was all well and good to trust the instincts of his family, but what would happen when the king found out about it? When another possibility struck him, a shiver ran through George, and it was all he could do to stay upright. The king might already know. What if the spirit beast was working under the king? Every story about ascendant creatures told that they couldn't be controlled, yet the king clearly knew of this crab's existence. He was aware, but hadn't sent his horde of collared cultivators after it. Everyone knew that spirit beasts grew in power insanely fast, so why hadn't the king tried to snuff its life out before it could gain more power?

The more pieces of the puzzle that fell into place, the less George understood.

He glanced to the side, tearing his attention from the conversation to check up on Geraldine. She appeared just as aggrieved as he felt, her face moving minutely as her mind whirled. As ever, her brilliance was a light in the dark, shining a warmth over him that would have calmed him completely in any other circumstance. He decided then and there that no matter what happened, he and Geraldine would escape. They had to find a moment to slip out and disappear. He knew not where they'd go, but it had to be far from the king.

Fischer's next sentence ripped George from his internal resolution.

"I've been cavorting with way more than *one* spirit beast."

George's eyes darted back toward Fischer, and what he found there made George's old terror reignite, burning like a bonfire within him. Fischer was grinning at them, his teeth bared in obvious delight. He was relishing this moment, soaking in their despair after speaking such terrible words.

It had to be a lie, though. There was no way that Fischer had actually—

The man clapped his hands together sharply, the sound so loud that it made the night air quiver. "If you would, everyone!"

The ground behind Fischer exploded, sending sand and dust flying in every direction. Whatever had emerged was obscured by the debris, its body large enough to throw a cloud of sand bigger than the very headland.

Fischer spread his arms wide, his smile growing even more predatory. "Allow me to introduce my animal pals . . ."

George's legs finally gave out, and he fell to his knees as all hope of escape left him.

Rocky was content with the events so far.

Yes, his followers would find out that he wasn't really Sergeant Snips, but it was no matter. They had already pledged themselves to him. They could gaze upon Sergeant Snips's mighty carapace, powerful claws, and beautiful spikes just as he did. Let them experience all the wonder that came with her, and when they learned that Rocky was her sole subordinate, it would only heighten their opinions of him, further cementing their dedication.

The two unascended humans were showing a little too much fear of Fischer. It was grating, but he could correct that behavior later in private. Fischer was as self-important as ever, and when the man spread his arms wide before the cloud of sand the rest of the spirit beasts and cultivators had thrown up, Rocky rolled his eyes.

But then, something unacceptable occurred.

With his eyes still locked on Fischer, George fell to his knees. Beside him, his wife did the same.

Rocky saw red.

He had personally invited them to join his congregation. They had agreed to be his followers. And now they dared fall to their knees in supplication to their master's greatest enemy? Rocky's blood became hot magma, fueling the actions that would have to follow. His pride demanded it, as did the darkness within him. Without a second thought, he launched himself forward, flexing his limbs.

With his claws held open, he descended upon the humans, intent on correcting the behavior *immediately* via violent interjection.

CHAPTER THIRTY-SIX

Introduction

I watched Rocky closely, having sensed a visceral reaction from him when George fell to his knees.

Rocky, for whatever reason, saw it as a betrayal. An egregious insult.

So when Rocky exploded forward with his claws spread wide, I was ready. I flew to intercept him, not bothering to hide my disappointment. "You done fracked up, Rocky."

He wrenched at his limbs, trying to withdraw both claws from my iron grip. It was no use. I squeezed tighter, ensuring he couldn't get free.

"How many times have I told you, Rocky?" I held him up, bringing his thrashing body to eye height. "I put up with so much of your bullshit. We *all* do."

His legs reached up to stab at my arms, so I wrapped him up, holding each of his limbs close to his body. In the scuffle, a claw escaped my grasp. He clamped it down on a finger, trying to sever it, but I strengthened it with chi. A pair of twigs would have more luck trying to cut through stone. I ignored the attempt, staring into his eyes as I subdued the stray claw.

"There's a single rule I gave you, Rocky. One that, if you broke, you'd no longer be welcome here."

"F-Fischer . . ." George gasped, his face white. "You're a . . ."

"A cultivator, mate. Yeah. Sorry for keeping it a secret—it was necessary for the safety of my pals." I returned my attention to Rocky, shaking him until his hateful gaze left George and faced me. "I felt your intentions there, mate. George is an unawakened human, and yet you tried to . . ." I trailed off, slowly turning to blink at George. "Hold up. You're almost awakened . . . ?"

Unbidden, my essence had swirled out to sense the outside world. Earlier, I'd been too distracted by the odd, crab-like chi coming from the cultists to notice George and Geraldine. They were close to ascension, and just like the cultists, their chi wasn't entirely human. Part of it was alien, something I couldn't recognize. It vaguely reminded me of the fathomless depths of the ocean floor.

I wrenched my gaze back to Rocky, fury burning deep within my core. "What did you do to them, Rocky? Why does the Church of Carcinization feel partially like crabs, and why do George and Geraldine feel like a dark abyss?"

George tried to say something, but it came out in a squeak.

"Rest up, mate," I said, giving him a reassuring smile. "I've got this."

"Unhand her!" Joel roared, his eyes wide and a sheen of sweat covering his brow.

"I don't know what trickery this is, Fischer, but you defile our god! Let Sergeant Snips go at once!"

"That's not Sergeant Snips," Maria replied, shaking her head then turning to face the cloud of sand behind us. "Would you mind, Snips? Your subordinate has really put his foot in it."

A low hiss came from within the obscuring debris, and when Snips's crabby form came scuttling into view, jets of blue chi billowed from her joints. She held murder in her eyes, and I could tell it took all of her self-restraint to not fly forward, grab Rocky, and introduce him to the stratosphere via yeeting.

"Everyone, *this* is Sergeant Snips," I said. "Sergeant Snips, you remember Joel and Jess, yeah?"

She nodded sharply, still staring at Rocky.

"This is the rest of the Church of Carcinization, and that's George and Geraldine, the nobles I've told you all about." I arched an eyebrow at Joel. "Notice the spiked carapace and eyepatch, Joel? I have no fracking idea how you got convinced that Rocky was the same crab, but they're clearly different. Rocky is just some bloke that randomly gained sapience somehow, and he's loyal to Snips. We generally let him get away with his shenanigans, but this time, he's gone *way* too far."

I squeezed him, putting pressure on his carapace, but not enough to hurt him. "Now, tell me what you did to them so I can undo it. It can't be healthy for a human to have crab chi."

George cleared his throat, and when he spoke, he sounded as if he was shocked at hearing his own voice. "Their, uh, chi . . ." He cleared his throat again. "It felt like a crab before Sergeant—uh, Rocky—came along. I believe it was because of their meditation method . . ."

I furrowed my brow, staring from George to Rocky to the former cultists. "Really?"

"Y-yes!" Geraldine replied. "We felt it too, which was why we didn't follow their methods."

"How did you guys feel that?" Maria asked. "That's kind of amazing."

"No kidding." I studied their faces, then called over my shoulder, "Is that true?"

"Truth," Theo replied from out of sight.

I nodded. "Neat. I guess there's more to you two than meets the eye. I'll explain everything, but first, you'll have to let me punish this little—"

I cut off as lightning detonated behind me, somewhat muted by the particles of earth smattering the air.

I sighed and spun toward my assailant.

Corporal Claws, absolutely brimming with lightning chi that made her eyes glow white and blue, rocketed toward me. She let out an indignant chirp, displaying her daggerlike teeth.

"I was getting to it, Claws," I said, catching her.

She chirped again, poking an accusatory claw into my chest.

"I didn't want to overwhelm them! I know I said I was going to introduce you, but then Rocky attacked! I had to deal with it first!"

She crossed her arms and harrumphed, raising her nose at me.

I booped it, making her sneeze. "Ah, well. I guess they've seen you now." I spun toward the new arrivals, displaying my bratty otter. "Everyone, this is Corporal Claws. Corporal Claws, this is everyone."

Casting aside her annoyance, she grinned and waved, letting out a happy little chirp of greeting.

"H-hello . . ." Joel said, his eyes darting between her and Snips.

George and Geraldine had somehow gone even paler, and they just stared up at Claws, their shallow breaths and occasional blinks the only signs of life.

More shapes moved within the cloud, their monstrous shadows amorphous.

"This is Private Pistachio, the sharpshooting and ever stoic lobster. He's basically the Great Leviathan that the Cult of the Leviathan have been waiting on."

Pistachio waved a single claw as his massive form came into view.

"Then there's Brigadier Borks, the goodest of boys."

Borks, in his golden-retriever form, trotted out. His tongue lolled and tail wagged, intentionally appearing as friendly as possible. I gave him a smile and mouthed *Thank you*, glad he didn't come tearing out of the debris as a nightmare-inducing hellhound.

"Next, we've got Cinnamon."

The little bunny flew from the cloud, unleashing a roundhouse kick of impressive form. She landed on the sand beside me, hopping side to side and shadow boxing.

"As you can see, she's a student of the martial arts, courtesy of Warrant Officer Williams, or *Bill* for short."

A shadow rose toward the top of the debris, and when Bill sailed into view, his mighty wings were spread wide. He soared down to crash beside Cinnamon, nodding at the new arrivals as he ruffled his feathers.

"Then, we've got the smallest of my animal pals! Though they're tiny, their personalities are large!"

The collar of my shirt vibrated, and two insects crawled out, taking flight and hovering toward George and Geraldine. Queen Bee and Bumblebro buzzed a greeting, making the seven newcomers flinch back.

"Don't worry," I said. "That's them saying hello. Once you taste the honey they make, I'm sure you'll come to appreciate them."

Not waiting for her introduction, Pelly unleashed a mighty honk from above us, circling down through the air so fast that she was clearly a spirit beast. She landed next to Bill and Cinnamon, the former nodding at her, the latter leaping up and hugging her neck.

"This is Private Pelly, the adopted daughter of Cinnamon and the biological daughter of two nest-thieving pelicans that had the audacity to mess with one Warrant Officer Williams's nest."

Bill preened, holding his head high at my recounting of his escapades.

"Last but not least, we have the ones that warned me of your arrival—the Buzzy Boys."

At these words, Rocky flexed in my grasp, his core radiating fury at learning the Buzzy Boys had warned of his arrival, giving us the chance to prepare.

A low droning rose up from within the cloud, and the majority of Bumblebro and Queen Bee's children came flying into view, only some still absent so they could monitor our surroundings.

"Fischer . . ." Maria said.

"What's up?"

She gave me a flat look. "The Buzzy Boys?"

I grinned. "It has a ring to it, no? Bumblebro, Queen Bee, and the Buzzy Boys. Plus, it's a play on words. 'Busy boys,' because *boy*, are they *busy*."

She rubbed the bridge of her nose. "How long have you been sitting on that for?"

"A few days. I was waiting for the right chance to reveal it, and well, the opportunity came."

"If I didn't love you so much, I think I'd hate you."

"Thanks," I replied, laughing. "Love you too!"

She rolled her eyes but couldn't completely hide her smile.

The Buzzy Boys came to a stop in the air between the seven people Rocky had brought along. They let out a loud buzz, broadcasting just how overjoyed they were to meet everyone.

"And then," I said, "there are our human pals."

I turned toward the lingering dust, and with a force of will, pushed chi out of my core. It was like a warm light flowing over the ground, and when it reached the cloud, it sent the sand flying. Finally revealed, a sea of friendly faces smiled and waved. Everyone from the original congregation was there, as were the freed cultivators from Gormona. They struck an impressive pose in their church robes.

One of them stepped forward, beaming. "G'day, George!" Theo called. "How ya been, mate?"

In response, George fainted.

He let out a rather emasculating sound on the way down. I struggled to hold my giggle in, and Maria smacked me on the arm, her eyes warning me not to laugh. The effect was mostly ruined by her own lips curling up, as well as Theo's choked laughter from behind me.

Geraldine caught him, her hands shaking. "George! Can you hear me, George?"

"He's fine," I said, kneeling down. "I can feel his core. He just got a bit overwhelmed."

"You . . ." she said, licking her lips. "What are you going to do to us?"

"Whoa there," Maria said, holding her hands up placatingly as she knelt down. "We're not going to do anything to you. Unlike when you were under the care of this little miscreant . . ." She flicked Rocky's shell lightly, making him squirm in my arms. "You're in no danger. We'll explain *everything* as soon as he's been dealt with."

I nodded, returning my attention to Rocky, who was still tangled up like a pretzel. He blew pissed-off bubbles at me, his eyes filled with the promise of violence.

"You're lucky it wasn't your fault their chi doesn't feel completely human, mate," I said. "That's the only reason I'm not turning you into crab chowder."

Snips hissed her agreement, just as annoyed as I was that he'd tried to attack a defenseless human. She let out a barrage of bubbles and hisses that were downright scandalous in their severity. Maria and I raised our eyebrows at each other as it continued on, a little embarrassed that we were privy to the onslaught.

Rocky tried to complain, tried to defend himself, but Snips was an unstoppable force. Her tones rolled over his every attempt, slowly but surely crushing his spirit. When she was finally finished, she turned her back on him, dismissing him from her mind.

For the first time since his pompous arrival as some sort of upstart faction leader, Rocky seemed remorseful. Tears welled in his eyes, but Snips ignored him.

"Looks like she doesn't even care enough to throw you herself, mate." I hefted his weight and walked toward the shore. "Guess that leaves it up to me."

No! he hissed.

"Yeah, well, you should have thought about that before you tried to hurt someone. Frankly, I don't give a shit if you try to start your own faction. Go for it. What I can't abide is you being a maniac and hurting others. Consider that while you soar."

Noooo! he hissed again, but I was done listening.

I drew my arm back, sending chi flowing up from my core. It all happened in an instant, and as the essence gathered in my muscles, it demanded to be used. My abdomen wanted to open the floodgates and let loose with a blast of light.

For a moment, I considered it, picturing Rocky getting blasted into orbit. But I didn't want to kill him. Heck, I didn't even want to hurt him. I just wanted him to learn his lesson.

I gathered my strength, prepared to send him flying, then froze, twisting my neck to look at him. My chi had felt his, and there was something off about his essence. Just as the Church of Carcinization had a hit of crab in their cores, Rocky had a hint of . . . *human.*

"Huh. That's something . . ."

Rocky cocked his carapace in question.

Instead of answering, I grinned. "Enjoy your flight!"

Chi shot through every fiber of my being, all of my muscle groups working in tandem to send him flying.

"*EEEEEEEEEEEEEEEeeeeeeeeeeeeeeeeeeeeeeeeeeeeeeeeeeeeeeee—*"

Rocky didn't even have time to unfurl his limbs. He was gone in the blink of a cultivator's eye, arcing so high that he disappeared from sight.

"You think he'll learn his lesson?" Maria asked, staring at the patch of sky he'd vanished into.

"Honestly? I have no idea. I felt something off about his core, though."

"Oh? What's that?" she asked, resting a hand on my upper back.

I smiled at her. "I'll tell you all about it while we get our new pals situated . . ."

Her hand drifted down to mine, and I took a moment to dwell in her touch as we strode back toward everyone.

CHAPTER THIRTY-SEVEN

Truth

Geoorge Kraken, lord of Tropica village, ran for his life.

Each turn he took, there his pursuer was, taunting him. The cruel antagonist would snarl and laugh, his predatory eyes tracking every move. Sometimes he'd do nothing at all, merely watching as George turned and fled.

No matter how many times George tried to get away, Fischer was there, always one step ahead.

"George . . ." came a heavenly voice.

He turned, looking for the source of the blessed sound. All he found was Fischer's face, as tall as a building and leering down at him. He yelped and ran, wanting to be free of this place. Needing to escape. Suddenly, something clung to him. Opulent chains of bejeweled gold looped around his limbs, pulling toward the ground. He shrugged them off, but for each he removed, two more appeared. His jewelry, his very symbol of wealth, was to be his downfall.

"George . . ." the voice called again, soft and enticing. It was Geraldine. How had he forgotten her?

Help! George tried to say, but gold coins spewed from his mouth, falling to clink against the floor. He attempted to scream, but only coins came, so many that they started piling up around him. His body sank into them, the sheer mass of them holding him still. Slow footsteps approached, unimpeded by the golden morass.

"Geeeooorge," Fischer taunted.

The footsteps came ever closer, making a muted crunching as they crossed over the carpet of coins.

George was up to his neck now, only his head free of the gilded snare.

"George . . ." Fischer whispered, his smile mocking.

George tried to scream, tried to thrash and escape, but it was no use. The coins engulfed his head, plunging him into darkness. He couldn't breathe. He couldn't move. He—

He sat up, taking a panicked inhalation. Instead of coins, he found soft sheets beneath his hands. He'd clutched them, and as he let go, he couldn't help but frown. They were so soft . . .

"George!" Geraldine wrapped him in a hug. "Oh, dear! I was so worried! You slept most of the night away!"

She squeezed him so tight that he felt constricted, but he relished the moment anyway, soaking up every inch of her. He looked down, seeing bedding so luxurious that it rivaled any other he'd seen. When his gaze drifted to the surrounding room and the materials it was built with, his stomach fell. He would recognize them anywhere. They were within Fischer's home.

Fischer . . .

That single thought made his memories come rushing back. They slammed into him, driving the air from his lungs.

He shot to his feet, heaving for air. "We have to get out of here, Geraldine."

"Nonsense, mate!"

George's hair stood on end. He spun slowly, finding the speaker seated in a chair on the other side of the bed. Fischer had the otter, Corporal Claws, in his lap. She pawed at the air, lost in sleep.

Next to him, Theo sat in another chair. He waved. "G'day."

"George," Geraldine said, gripping his hand. "It's not what you think. We were wrong about Fischer." She laughed, looking almost manic in her glee. "*Completely* wrong."

George swallowed. "What did they do to you . . . ?"

The mirth died on her face, and she gave him an unimpressed glare. "They didn't do anything to me, you big goose. Just sit and listen. They'll explain everything."

George, still expecting a trap, glanced around the room. There was an open door that led to a tiled washroom. The other door was closed, likely the only path to freedom. Seeing that Fischer sat between him and his escape, he tried to calm himself and consider the facts.

Fischer was a cultivator, and he didn't have a collar. George had assumed that the man was working with the king, but it was even worse than that. He'd gone rogue. They *all* had. George had recognized some of the faces of those hidden within the cloud of sand earlier. One was Theo, the crown auditor. Others were cultivators he'd seen years ago in the capital, and not one of them had a collar around their neck.

Poseidon's salted backwash, he thought. *There are* hundreds *of spirit beasts if you count the Buzzy Boys, all of whom appear to follow Fischer.*

The thought made any chance of escape seem impossible. No wonder Geraldine was going along with whatever they said.

"George." Geraldine patted the bed. "Sit."

Knowing he had no hope of getting her out while Fischer was present, George decided it was best to play along for now. He sat and waited for them to speak.

"So . . ." Fischer said after a long moment. "Geraldine told me a pretty funny story while you were out. I was hoping to clear some things up for you."

Geraldine shook her head, smiling at George. "You won't believe it . . ."

Was that code? Was she telling him *not* to believe it?

Fischer cleared his throat. "I suppose I should start at the beginning. I'm not from the capital, and I'm not an auditor."

George snorted, finding it hard to indulge such a blatant lie. "Then how did you come across a coin of the ancients and give it to me when you arrived in Tropica?"

"Easy. The System gave it to me."

"Riiight. The *System*."

"Exactly." Fischer nodded. "I came to you because I wanted to buy some land to fish from, and I used the only currency I had. I worked out after our first interaction that it was worth way more than I'd thought."

"Let's assume that's true. If you didn't know what it was worth, why did you warn me not to spend it?"

"I'm guessing I said something along the lines of *Don't spend it all at once*? That's an idiom where I'm from. It was a joke, referencing the fact that I only gave you a single coin." Fischer shrugged. "A coincidence—a pretty funny one if you ask me."

"Your house, then?"

"System made it."

"The ring you brought to me?"

"The one you threw out in an attempt to hide your embezzlement? Don't give me that look, mate. Geraldine told me about your sordid past."

"Okay, then how did you come to possess it if you weren't having me stalked?"

"Easy. I found it in the ocean."

"You *found it in the ocean*? The ocean is very large, Fischer. I find that hard to believe."

"Yeah, well, the ocean might be vast, but the bay isn't. You basically threw the box of ill-gotten goods on top of Sergeant Snips. That one's on you."

George blinked. "You're telling me that I just happened to throw it on top of her? You didn't have one of those bees following me?"

"Yep. That's exactly what I'm telling you. The Buzzy Boys didn't even exist yet, and none of my other pals were tailing you."

George chewed his cheek. He couldn't say why, but he didn't think Fischer was lying. Not blatantly, anyway. Geraldine squeezed his hand, and when he looked her way, she nodded back, encouraging him. It had the opposite effect. He pushed his easy acceptance away, knowing it was up to him to keep his beautiful wife safe from harm. George took a slow breath, focusing his thoughts.

"If all of this is true, how do you explain Theo, a crown auditor, being here? How do you explain him reporting back to you after he interrogated me?" George narrowed his gaze on Theo. "I thought you were going to chew him out for fishing, but then you showed him your notes, and both of you laughed, no doubt happy with your treachery."

Fischer and Theo looked at each other, then cackled. Geraldine laughed too. He gave her a quizzical look, not understanding why she found humor in their misfortune.

"Snips!" Fischer yelled. "We need you!"

A door was thrown open, and frenzied scuttling rang out, growing louder as the creature approached. Sergeant Snips slid into the room at impossible speed, her many feet scrabbling to find purchase on the wooden floor. She performed a little hop, redirecting herself with jets of what looked like blue liquid. Fischer plucked her from the air, smiling as she blew happy little bubbles.

"We need the picture again, Snips."

She nodded, reached under her carapace, and removed a folded bit of paper. More delicate than two giant claws had any right being, she unfolded it and held it out to show George. It was a sketch of a man fishing by a river. Though somewhat rushed, he could easily make out the trees, leaves, and every other minor detail.

George frowned at it. "That's a lovely drawing, especially considering it was done without opposable thumbs, but I don't see how that answers the questions."

Geraldine giggled, covering her mouth. "These were the 'notes' he shared with Fischer, dear. Theo saw him fishing, and to prove that he also enjoyed the pastime— as heretical as it may be—Theo showed him the sketch he'd just completed. The same sketch he drew while talking to us."

George leaned back, taking that in. "You were drawing? While determining our fate?"

Theo grimaced. "People feel more pressured if they think you're recording their words. I was a little bored to be honest, and there's only so many fake notes you can take before you start to detest the whole mummers' show. Still, it's effective, so I drew what I'd rather be doing."

George recalled the panic—the fear for his life—that he had been experiencing at the time. "Bored . . . ? You were *bored*?"

"Afraid so. That interrogation was pretty standard stuff. You think you're the first noble to siphon funds from the commoners?" Theo shook his head. "I've never found a village without at least *some* corruption."

George furrowed his brow. "It still doesn't make sense. You, a crown auditor, like *fishing*? How did you end up here? How are there cultivators from the capital, and why aren't they wearing collars?"

"Whoa, George." Fischer held his hands up. "One question at a time, mate."

"We can probably answer all of those with our own question, though," Theo said, tossing his head side to side. He leaned forward, his eyes growing fierce. "Do you know what a traveler is, George?"

"Okay, now I know you're lying." George clenched his jaw, watching them intently. "You aren't going to fool me with fairy tales."

"Think about it, dear," Geraldine said. "It is hard to believe at first, yes, but doesn't that explain all our assumptions?" She started listing them off on her fingers. "The ancient coins. His odd manner of speaking. His lack of propriety."

"Okay, ouch," Fischer interrupted.

"You know what I mean," she replied, then resumed listing evidence. "His disinterest in passiona and willingness to share it with the commoners. The fact that he has caused the awakening of multiple spirit beasts and somehow commands their obedience."

"They're more like friends, really," Fischer corrected. "Not my subjects I command."

Geraldine gave him a flat look. "You're not helping."

"Just being honest." He rubbed the top of Sergeant Snips's head, and the crab leaned into it, clearly luxuriating in his touch. "I won't pretend to be something I'm not."

"That is how I ended up here," Theo replied. "Fischer made some hooks for me last time I was here. Because of that, the leader of Gormona's fishing club deduced that Fischer was a traveler. We came here to create a church around him, but we kind of got beaten to the punch. Someone had already started the Church of Fischer."

George had nothing to say to that. He looked back and forth between them, not seeing any hint of trickery.

"Is that my cue?" someone asked, their footsteps approaching.

Not knowing who to expect, George was nonetheless surprised. ". . . you?"

"Afraid so, George," Barry replied, giving him a sheepish smile. "I realized what Fischer was pretty early on."

George's gaze went distant as he considered everything he'd just learned. As unbelievable as it was, it made sense. Still, he sought to find holes in their lies. For Geraldine's sake.

Picking his next line of questioning, he nodded to himself. "You still haven't explained why there are so many uncollared cultivators from Gormona here." He paused, imagining the havoc they could unleash. "There had to be at least five of them."

"Five . . . ?" Fischer winced. "Mate . . ."

Geraldine squeezed his shoulder and gave him a similar expression.

"What?" he asked. "What's that look for?"

"Everyone there was a cultivator," Fischer replied. "All the faces you didn't recognize? Cultivators. We freed every single slave from Gormona. Well, the ones that we didn't have to lock up anyway, but that's a different story."

" . . . what?"

"Yeah, we kind of led an assault on the capital and freed them all. It was a whole thing."

"You *what*?"

"I was just as surprised as you are when they told me the plan, mate. It was a pretty gnarly endeavor, especially considering Tom Osnan Sr. and the king were both hidden cultivators. Pretty powerful, those blokes." Fischer gave a predatory grin. "Nowhere near powerful enough, though. We steamrolled them, freed the cultivators, and stole all of their artifacts. Last I saw of the king, he was shot from the castle and through a mountain, completely starkers."

George's mouth had gone dry. "Starkers?" he asked, suspecting it to be the name of some barbaric torture method.

"Yeah, you know. *Starkers*. Naked as the day he was born. Lacking any pants. Airing his meat and potatoes, if you catch my drift."

George leaned forward, staring into Fischer's clearly amused eyes for a long moment. "You're serious, aren't you . . . ?"

"Serious as a Queensland summer, mate."

George, feeling a weight fall away from his awareness that he hadn't even known was there, glanced around the room. Though everyone smiled at him, there was no hint of deception. They truly meant the words that they were saying.

He might have assumed they'd been poisoned by spoiled food and were halluci-nating or temporarily insane, if not for one simple fact: It all made sense. It explained all the unexplainable occurrences that had been happening of late. And it explained the changes within him since he and Geraldine had started following House Kraken's manual.

Something bubbled up within George, and rather than push it aside, he let it roll out into the world.

George laughed. He *really* laughed. With tears making his vision swim, he pulled Geraldine into a hug.

Everything was going to be okay.

CHAPTER THIRTY-EIGHT

Redemption

I smiled up at the first rays of sunshine, enjoying the warmth it lent my skin.

"Should we rescue them soon?" Maria asked, also facing the blazing orb as it peeked over the distant horizon.

I glanced to the side, checking up on George and Geraldine. After they'd had a few hours' rest, we finally let Ellis out of his metaphorical cage. The former archivist was currently peppering them with questions about the manual they'd been using to cultivate.

"I still can't believe the *drama* you put them through . . ." Maria said, her hair swaying as she shook her head. "The poor things."

"The drama they were putting themselves through, you mean," I replied, unable to completely hide my smile. "I feel like I should have realized earlier that it wasn't just social anxiety making George so nervous."

"To be fair, you'd have to be a mind reader to realize he thought you were an auditor from the capital."

I nodded, craning my neck to face Ellis. "Gonna be much longer, mate?" I called. "We've got fun stuff to be about."

"We just got started!" Ellis replied, not raising his eyes from his notepad.

"It's been twenty minutes!"

He took a deep breath, sighing it out dramatically. "Okay. I will leave you for now. Thank you for your information. Would you be free this evening?"

"Of course!" Geraldine replied, smoothing her dress as she stood.

"Wonderful, do you think I could perhaps peruse House Kraken's manual—"

"Ellis!" I chided. "Enough! They can offer that if they like, but they shouldn't be pressured, *especially* after joining us literally like . . . two hours ago."

He opened his mouth and raised a finger to retort but swiftly shut his trap and lowered the hand. "Fischer is correct. I apologize." He jotted one more thing down, then slammed his notepad closed. "I will see you this evening." He turned on his heel and strode away, power-walking back to New Tropica.

"Sorry," I said to George and Geraldine as they approached. "He's super passionate about information."

"It's okay." George looked out at the ocean, squinting his eyes as he took in the rising sun. "I still suspect I might be dreaming?"

Maria and I shared an amused glance.

"You're awake, I'm afraid," Maria said. "Fischer can be a bit annoying as far as powerful beings go, but I'm sure he'll grow on you. Like a barnacle. Or a particularly resilient weed that just won't stop growing back, no matter how many times—"

"Thanks, Maria," I interrupted, dramatically rolling my eyes at her before turning to the lord and lady of Tropica. "So, I was going to offer you some fishing lessons this morning, but I thought I should share one more piece of information with you first."

"Oh?" George asked, his tone slightly hesitant. "What is it you wish to say?"

I pointed at his wedding ring, then at Geraldine's. "I was thinking about what I felt from your cores. Without overloading you with information, I can get a good sense of people's powers. Both of your cores feel . . . different. I'd assumed Rocky did something weird to your cores, but now that I know about your house's manual, it's safe to say that its influence is why your chi feels so odd. The thing is, your wedding rings are likely suppressing your ability to become cultivators. Without them, you'd probably have done so already."

They both turned to each other, their eyes wide.

"Yeah," I said. "I'm telling you this now because if we go fishing, I'm almost certain you'll become cultivators. But because of how much essence both of you already possess, I'm thinking it's better if you ascend by doing the meditations you've already been doing."

They remained staring at each other, having an unspoken conversation in the way only lifelong partners could. At the same time, smirks formed on their faces, and they gave a slight nod.

"Thank you, Fischer!" Geraldine called, leading her husband across the sands.

"You can use my house if you like!" I yelled. "It's closer, and you can come fishing after you ascend!"

Excited as she was, she didn't even ask her husband if that was okay, instead veering left and jogging for my house as she gave me a wide grin.

"I kinda love them as a couple," Maria mused, watching them go.

"Right? Wholesome as heck."

She scooted up beside me, nestling into the spot between my arm and chest. "Should we go fishing?"

"Soon." The smell of her hair drifted up, filling my lungs and making me feel weightless.

She started shaking, and after a moment, I realized she was giggling.

"What's so funny?" I asked.

"I just remembered what you did to Rocky. Do you think he's still flying?"

I barked a laugh, picturing him sailing through the stratosphere. "You know, I have no idea. With any luck, I sent him to the moon."

She let out a contented sigh. "He'll be back soon, no doubt. Hopefully he learned his lesson."

"Well, he'd better. Snips was even more pissed off than I was. I don't think she's going to forgive him so easily this time."

Rather than dwell any longer on the antisocial crab, I focused on Maria. Her body was just as warm and welcoming as the sun. I patted her hair, and she snuggled in even closer, putting a leg over mine. Beneath the morning sun, we slipped into a comfortable silence, both content to just exist with one another.

"Thank you," she said, rubbing my arm.

"For what?" I asked.

"Oh, you know." She tossed her head from side to side. "Everything."

Fueled by a burning hatred and the prospect of sweet, *sweet* revenge, a lone crustacean skimmed across the ocean's surface like a torpedo—if a torpedo could experience borderline apoplectic fury.

Suddenly, his spiky mistress's turned back flashed through his mind, driving a thorn of rejection deep into his core, his mighty carapace no match for the deadly barb. His flippers slowed as anguish overtook him.

He had failed his beloved matriarch . . .

Just as quick as sadness descended, his fury returned, scouring the anguish from existence.

Fischer. It was *his* fault. None of this would have happened if not for Fischer's existence. George wouldn't have fallen to his knees, so Rocky wouldn't have had to punish anyone.

As his limbs sent him rocketing through the ocean, his thoughts drifted to the flight Fischer had subjected him to. It was one of the best and worst things that Rocky had ever experienced. Loath as he was to admit it, Fischer's strength was unparalleled. The man had held back, yet still sent Rocky higher than ever before. He'd soared so high that the world became a giant orb beneath him. Much to his surprise, there had been multiple land masses visible, their different environments breaking up the ocean's monotony. He flew so high that he thought he may never come back down.

But Rocky hadn't even been able to enjoy it, because it had been Fischer's arm that sent him there.

Rocky's eye twitched in disgust, remembering the way those fleshy fingers had restrained Rocky's superior carapace. Despite his inferior form, Fischer's hands had been like vises, stronger than even his beloved mistress's clackers. It went against everything Rocky held dear, and the more he considered it, the more his anger bloomed.

Until the vision of his mistress's discontent returned, anyway.

Rocky slowed again, melancholy washing over him. How could he go on without his beloved? What was the point in all of this if he didn't have the respect and companionship of his spiky mistress? There had to be something he could do . . . but what?

Before he could consider it long, he cycled back toward fury at Fischer. He remained there for a beat, railing at Fischer, whose fault all of this clearly was. When he arrived back at missing Sergeant Snips, he realized just how circular his thoughts had become.

His emotions were turbulent, sweeping him this way and that like an ocean current. He focused, doing his best to find a solution. He had to not only win back his matriarch but also find a way to overpower Fischer.

There was only one possibility, and as he considered it, a devious grin came over Rocky's face. With a goal in mind, his emotions stabilized. He dreamed of vengeance and winning back Snips's approval, and he knew how to meet both goals.

More *power*.

There was only one place he could go, and though it would take him multiple days to return to Tropica at his current speed, it didn't matter. He had a path now. He would follow it as long as need be.

When the sun was high overhead, an island came into view. Rocky gave it a rude gesture. The thing had dared get in his way, so that was the least it deserved. Determined not to change course, even if it would have been faster to go around it, he leaped up onto a shore of black stone, scuttling sideways toward a darkened peak. If he'd been paying attention to his surroundings instead of cursing the island's very existence, he might have recognized the material the peak was made of. Focused as he may have been, however, even Rocky couldn't miss what he found on top of the mountain.

The temperature had been climbing steadily as he approached the rise, but Rocky just thought that was his outrage becoming manifest. He learned the truth when he skidded to a stop and stared down into the gaping hole. An angry heat flowed from the opening, so vicious that it rivaled Rocky's own internal state. He froze there, transfixed by the sight.

Hundreds of meters below him, gigantic sheets of black rock covered a ground of sorts, outlined by veins of glowing red. They reminded him of the underwater vista he was heading for—the place he'd originally used to ascend. To confirm his suspicions, he found a large black boulder. Hefting it with one claw, he threw it down into the pit. Time seemed to slow as it approached the sheets, and when it struck, it plunged right through.

The dark sheets caved in, the boulder passing through and disappearing into the abyss of magma. He'd expected the red-hot stone there to explode in response, just as the underground version he'd found did when disturbed. He held his breath, waiting for the reaction.

It never came.

Cursing at himself—then Fischer, because really, it was all *his* fault—Rocky scuttled back so he could leap right over the chasm. But that's when it happened.

The ground shook, the very world groaning like Rocky's stomach after a particularly large feast. Hoping it meant what he thought it did, he eased forward and peered down into the pit. The magma there bubbled and churned, and before his eyes, erupted. A gout of molten stone shot up into the sky, almost high enough to clear the cliff he stood atop. He could feel the chi running through each and every drop—it was the same as the pit he'd first ascended in, the very same essence that powered Rocky's body.

He held his claws high, hissing with victory. The world itself had blessed him. It had heard his calls for retribution, and it had answered. Blowing bubbles of impending victory, Rocky leaped from the edge. He sailed down toward the magma, making dual rude gestures at the sky, for not even the heavens would be able to contain Rocky's new form when he emerged once more.

This moment of victory was short-lived, because the second he hit the surface of the active volcano, all Rocky knew was pain.

CHAPTER THIRTY-NINE

Affinity

I was waiting for a fish to bite when two pulses of chi came from many newly awakened cultivators. Maria and I shared a grin. We dashed along the rock wall, over the sand, and through the open front door, our rods discarded.

George and Geraldine sat on the floor of my living room with their backs to the wall. They were staring at each other, their eyes filled with admiration, awe, and a healthy dose of affection.

I cleared my throat, getting their attention.

"We . . ." George said, licking his lips. "We did it."

I nodded. "Felt it all the way from the rock wall, mate. Congratulations."

Geraldine's gaze had already drifted back down to her hands. She moved her fingers slowly, feeling the strength contained within. "This is . . . *wow.*"

"Uh-huh." Maria gave her a knowing smile. "It's like that."

While they continued studying their new bodies, I sent my senses toward them. The last time I'd tasted their chi, they had a hint of something inhuman. Now, that dark aspect was even more prevalent. The longer I felt it, the more drawn in I became. I tried to understand, tried to comprehend, but it was like staring into a pitch-black ravine on the ocean floor. There was no insight to be gained. At least not yet.

"What does your chi feel like to you, George?"

"It feels . . ." His mouth moved inaudibly, then he gave me a sheepish smile. "It feels *right*. Sorry for how vague a description that is."

I laughed, running my fingers through my hair. "My bad. That might have been too hard of a question. I thought that maybe your techniques might have given you a higher sensitivity to chi, especially your own."

"What made you think that?" Geraldine asked, her eyebrows slightly furrowed.

"Because George said he could feel the Church of Carcinization's Chi. Could you feel it, too?"

She nodded slowly. "I could, yeah. It was kind of similar to Sergeant Snip—er, Rocky's." She shook her head. "That's going to take some getting used to."

"Yeah, sorry again about Rocky. He's gonna be on a tighter leash when he returns. So, you could both sense their anomalous chi, but not your own. That's definitely *something*, I just don't know what yet."

"What does ours feel like?" George asked.

"Like an endless pit I can't see the bottom of." I jiggled my eyebrows at their shocked expressions. "Right? Pretty wild. It also seems like it's ocean-adjacent, for lack of a better term. I don't see it as a hole in the earth—I see it as a hole in the ocean floor." I shrugged. "But that could just be my love of the ocean peeking through."

They shared a look, staring at each other for a long moment.

"No," George eventually said. "I admit to feeling an affinity with the sea . . ."

Geraldine laughed, covering her mouth with a hand. "Agreed, though it feels weird to admit that out loud. I suppose it's rather aligned with the rest of the congregation."

I beamed at them. "It certainly is. It would be weirder if your cultivation didn't have something to do with the ocean, to be honest. And speaking of . . ." I arched a brow at Maria, who grinned back, knowing exactly where I was going. I turned back toward Tropica's newest cultivators. "How do you two feel about a little fishing?"

Again, they locked eyes, having an entire conversation in the space of a single breath.

George stood first, then helped Geraldine to her feet.

"We would be honored, Fischer," she said, giving me a wide grin.

Though I could feel their anticipation as Maria and I led them down to the rock wall, I think we were more excited than they were. Now that the denizens of New Tropica had all tried their hand at my heretical pastime, I was closer than ever to my dream of having an entire village of anglers. For some reason, though, George and Geraldine following me down to the waterfront felt monumental. Like a key deliverable in a yearslong project, if I were to use terms from my old life.

They were *the* nobles of Tropica, the lord and lady of the village I had stumbled across and decided to call home. That they were not only willing but actively keen on giving fishing a crack was no small deal, and I hoped it would be the stone that started a landslide of Tropica's original denizens coming down to my shores and wetting a line.

There were plenty of rods already set up, and it took no time at all to run George and Geraldine through the basic knots. Despite their recent awakening, their fingers already showed the deftness of a cultivator's enhanced body and awareness. I offered to put the bait on their hooks, but both declined, displaying a willingness to get their hands a little dirty in the pursuit of leisure.

With Maria on one side and my trainee anglers on the other, we demonstrated how to cast out the lines. I watched as both their baited hooks sailed out into the bay, arcing high and landing with dual splashes.

"Perfect!" Maria said. "That might be the best first casts we've seen! Certainly better than Dad's."

"Yeah, yeah," Roger replied from behind us, not falling for her trap.

"I think you tried your best, dear," Sharon said, patting his shoulder and earning a flat glare for her condescension. She cackled, once more reminding me where Maria got her sense of humor.

We all slipped into comfortable silence while waiting for a bite. As time dragged on, waves of tension rolled out from George. The pulses grew stronger; something was bothering him. Something that would build until he finally addressed it.

Rather than inquire, I muted my senses, feeling like I was doing the cultivation equivalent of eavesdropping. He would voice it when he was ready.

Sure enough, before any fish bit down on our lines, he spoke. "I feel a little . . . conflicted, Fischer."

"Yeah?" I took a deep breath, marveling at the sea spray as it cooled my nostrils. "About what, mate?"

He didn't respond for a long moment, seemingly considering his words. "Never mind, actually. It's foolish."

I spun slowly, still smiling at the world's sensations and the joy they brought me. "Whatever it is, I don't think it's foolish. You're welcome to keep it to yourself, but I reckon it's a good idea to let it out if it's bothering you. It won't make me think any less of you."

He chewed his cheek, and after a nod from Geraldine, he sighed. "I wonder if I'm undeserving of this."

"By this, do you mean fishing? Because even that dick-headed Osnan in our prison deserves a little fishing. I'd happily let him do so if I trusted he wouldn't try to punch a hole through someone."

The face George made brought me so, *so* much happiness.

He blinked at me, processing the words. " . . . come again?"

"I said I'd happily let him fish if I trusted he—ow!" I rubbed the arm Maria had struck with a swift slap. "Watch your strength, missy!"

"Stop teasing," she replied, threatening to smack me again. She leaned past me, peering at George and Geraldine. "Tom Osnan Jr. and his wife are in a building that's magically protected against cultivators and serves as our prison. They tried to hurt us, then tried to organize a coup to escape. It didn't work."

Geraldine gaped at Maria, then her eyes darted to me. "They are cultivators? Since when?"

"Since always, I guess. They were hidden because of their ridiculous number of rings. I confronted them after I checked up on you guys and your wedding rings. Unlike you two, they attacked."

"What happened?" George blurted, worry stealing some of his color.

"*What happened?*" I laughed. "Corporal Claws hit them with the old left-right goodnight. They didn't stand a chance."

He gulped. "I stopped his hand from striking you when Marcus came to Tropica . . . and Tom was a cultivator then?"

"Certainly was, mate. Had his rings on, though, so he was like a regular person."

"That's . . . terrifying. He could have slapped my head clean off my body."

"He certainly could have tried, mate. I wouldn't have let him, though."

"Why didn't you tell us this earlier?" Geraldine asked. "That seems like pretty important information."

"There's heaps I haven't told you guys yet—it just seemed better to space it out."

"Like Lieutenant Colonel Lemony Thicket," Maria said. "The sapient tree spirit. She's the one that caused that giant tree—which we're pretty sure also houses an adolescent tree spirit—to grow from the old church."

"What?" George asked.

"The . . . old church?" Geraldine added.

"Yeah!" I grinned. "The one hidden in Barry's shed."

She frowned. "It fits in the shed?"

"Nah, that's just the entrance. And you haven't even seen New Tropica yet—it's *wild*."

"Okay, stop." George was rubbing his temples with one hand, the other holding the rod. "You were right. Please space out the information."

I shot him a wink. "Told ya. Now that I've sufficiently distracted you, let's get back to the topic at hand."

"Er, which one?" Maria asked.

"George's feeling of inadequacy and/or undeservedness."

"Oh. Right. What about it?"

"It's bullshit. Thoughts?"

"Yup." She nodded sagely. "Definitely bullshit."

I smiled at George and Geraldine. "Well, there you have it! Any other concerns?"

A smile played on Geraldine's lips, and she gave me a coy look. "When you say it's bullshit, I assume you're saying he *should* feel deserving of . . ." She gestured around us. "This?"

"Uh-huh," Maria and I both replied. "Jinx!" we said at the same time, then stared at each other, both breaking into a grin.

"But I did so much," George said, shaking his head. "The impact I had. I feel like I need to be punished for—"

"From what you've told us, you already paid quite price," I interrupted. "From my perspective, you fracked around, found out, then learned from your mistakes and grew as a person. That's more than can be said for the Osnans, who are likely planning their next escape and or murder attempt as we speak."

He sat with that for a long moment, chewing over the words. "That's it? All of my sins are just forgiven?"

I shrugged. "What more is there to say? You're welcome to list them if you think it will help. I'm all for talking out your feelings, but I reckon it isn't necessary."

"Not necessary," Maria agreed. "You'll just be beating yourself up for no reason. If you want to atone for everything, just do better from now on. Easy-peasy, right?"

He opened his mouth to reply, likely a retort, but Geraldine lay a hand on his arm. "How about this, dear—I still feel guilty as well, but I can forgive you." She dipped her chin, leaning slightly closer to him and staring into his eyes. "Can you forgive me?"

"Of course I can. I don't blame you in the least."

"Good." She rubbed his back. "We'll start there and work on forgiving ourselves. In the meantime, we do everything we can to help out."

"Now that's a plan!" I beamed at them. "And I know exactly what your first act of atonement can be!"

"Oh?" He leaned forward, staring at me past Geraldine. "What's that?"

I pointed at the tip of his rod. "Catch the fish nibbling at your bait."

"The *what?*"

His hand wasn't resting on his line, so he hadn't felt the tiny bumps jostling the tip of his rod.

He shifted into full focus immediately, setting both hands in place and preparing to strike. The fish kept nibbling.

Maria leaned in close and whispered, "Must be something other than a bluefish, right?"

"Definitely. They aren't so courteous as to have a little taste first—they just smash the bait."

The small bites suddenly stopped, but before George had a chance to get disappointed, his line tore through the water.

"Now there's a bluefish!" I yelled, laughing. Their fight was unmistakable to me by now. "I'm guessing it either scared off or ate the fish that was testing your eel."

"What do I do?" George yelled, reeling in awkwardly.

"Relax, mate! You've got this!"

He slowed his breathing, his movements going more fluid as he actively calmed himself.

I nodded. "Keep tension and reel it in. Try not to overthink the fight. The fish doesn't look *too* big, and I have full faith in your ability to—*whoa!*"

I set my hook, letting line go as a fish tore out to sea. "Double hookup!"

Just like George's, mine appeared to be smaller. I easily brought it back to shore, but not before George. After my reminder to relax, he'd handedly won his fight.

Maria leaped down to the water line. "These things have crazy-sharp teeth, so be careful where you grab them!" She grasped its body behind the gills and lifted it from the water before passing it to George.

He spun to face Geraldine, letting her get a good look at it. The look on their faces, the mix of sheer wonder and childlike glee, made me blunder. I didn't keep the tension on my line, and with rapid-fire shakes of its head, my fish spat the hook.

"Oh . . ." I said, realizing my line had gone slack.

"Amateur," Maria sighed, playfully rolling her eyes at me.

"Oh, shush." I turned my attention to George. "So, mate, ready for your first taste of fish?"

Though I didn't think it would be possible, his eyes flew even wider. "Is it okay to keep? I thought everyone was trying to only keep the bigger ones?"

"It's more than okay to keep, mate. Your call, though."

George looked down at it for a long moment, then shook his head, smiling. "If we let it go, it'll grow bigger, correct?"

I grinned. "Certainly will, mate."

He crept down to the water and lowered the fish. Before it even touched the surface, it kicked, freeing itself from George's grasp. He grunted as he fell back and sat on a boulder. The fish disappeared from sight in a flash, returning to the depths.

Laughing, George accepted Geraldine's offered hand and let her pull him to his feet.

"So," I said. "Ready to try again?"

"Absolutely!" He grabbed his rod and ran up the rocks, heading for more bait.

CHAPTER FORTY

Return

The days bled into one another on the road to Theogonia, each just as bothersome as the rest.

After weeks and weeks of traveling, the surrounding forests had grown dull. The monotony of brown trunks, green leaves, and the overgrown road grated on Augustus, bothering him to no end. He was a king. His position earned him a life of opulence and luxury. Yet here he was, sprinting through the outside world like a peasant late for the market. At first, the ability to use his chi had been a welcome delight, but even that sense of freedom had faded over time.

As if from nowhere, the landscape began changing. The leaves grew sparse, previously thick canopies becoming patchy the farther into Theogonia's lands they got. Myriad trunks, once straight and proud, wound in random directions. Even the grass was brown and dull, as if part of its vitality had been drained away. A sinking feeling crept into Augustus Reginald Gormona's core. One might expect such a development to be the physiological response to some dreaded realization, or perhaps the impending approach of a life-threatening adversary.

One would be wrong.

Though his core was afflicted by the sensation, his mind experienced the opposite. Anticipation rolled through his awareness, making his hopes soar. The cause was obvious to him: they were almost there.

He rolled his shoulders and slowed, coming to a stop beside a patch of bare ground. "We will rest here for lunch," he declared, smiling down at the deadened grass.

Tom Osnan Sr. grunted. "I cannot say I missed this feeling . . ."

"How long has it been for you, Tom?" Tryphena asked, poking a particularly gnarled tree.

"Since the fall of the city, Princess."

She nodded. "This is actually a noticeable improvement. Wouldn't you agree, Mother?"

"Indeed. I recall the dread sinking in much sooner the last time I was here. Before the trees changed, at any rate."

The merchant Marcus, scurrying around as the unascended common folk were wont to do, climbed into the cart Tom had set down and started fetching supplies to cook their luncheon.

Augustus cleared his throat. "How does it feel within the city, daughter?"

"Much the same as out here, Father." She struck the gnarled tree with a swift kick, snapping it off at the base. "A little stronger, but similarly diminished."

"Good," he replied, pride washing over him as his daughter dragged the entire tree toward them with one hand. "We will need to spend long within its bounds in order to gather enough strength. Are the alchemists still located in the same building?"

"Actually, no." Having dragged the twisted trunk closer, she lashed out with four swift chops of her hand. "Now that the corrupted chi seems to have weakened, they moved farther into the city. They were moving the last of their equipment when I left."

Augustus nodded, accepting then sitting on the section of wood his daughter passed him. "We'll head there immediately after we eat."

As the merchant started heating an assortment of expensive spices over a small fire he'd created, Augustus attempted to luxuriate in their rich scents, but a repetitive sound kept interrupting him. He slowly spun toward Tom, leveling a glare at him.

"If you are going to grind your teeth all day, Tom, just speak whatever is bothering you. As annoying as your voice is, that repugnant habit of yours is worse." His lip twitched at the look Tom gave him. "Don't make that pathetic face. I have known you long enough to understand you do it when something is on your mind."

Fury flashed across his oldest friend's face, but it was swiftly banished. "With your permission, my king," he said, nodding. "I was wondering if we should discuss a plan before heading into the city proper?"

"We have discussed the plan already, Tom," Tryphena said with faux sweetness. "With everyone that my father deemed necessary for its implementation, anyway."

Augustus grinned at the barbed words and the immediate response it drew from Tom. The man's nostrils flared, and he clenched his jaw, making that same abhorrent noise as his molars pressed together.

"It's fine, daughter. We can share the basics of the plan now that we're here. I suppose Tom *might* prove useful."

"As you will, my king." She dipped her head at the perfect level, displaying how extensive her decorum training was. She moved gracefully to face Tom. "Once we arrive in the city, we are to visit the Cult of the Alchemist. After that, we are *immediately* heading for the center of the city."

Augustus raised his hand to halt her. "That should be enough for now. If he cannot deduce the rest of the plan from that information alone, he is of no use to us."

Tom nodded, his face schooled to display uncaring calm. "As you say, my king. And I thank you for the explanation, Princess. I understand the plan."

Augustus smiled, content with Tom's continued display of fealty and remorse. With any luck, the man would regain his position with his actions over the coming days and weeks. Though he'd failed the kingdom, Tom Osnan Sr. was once—and could once more become—a valuable asset for Gormona.

They ate their meal in silence before resuming their passage toward the fallen city of Theogonia. They no longer traveled at speed, the very environment anathema to the expenditure of chi. With each step they drew closer, the more deformed the plants became. Before long, there weren't any leaves to be found, and the trees grew so twisted that they were almost unrecognizable. Branches curved down and into the ground, the earth there completely free of any grass. The air seemed thick and took more effort to breathe. A haze blocked out the sky, casting a gloomy shadow over their surroundings.

With the lack of plant matter blocking out the sky, it was easy to spot the city when it came into view. Well, what was left of it, anyway. Only half of the walls remained, the rest completely leveled, their bricks laying in piles. Most of the city's buildings were in the same state, either half standing or completely gone. The castle, once just as grand as Gormona's, only had a single spire remaining, its pointed roof completely gone. That particular detail was *his* fault—given his distance at the time, his blast of fire had missed the bulk of the castle's mass, instead obliterating the spire in question.

He snorted, recalling his momentary regret at not being closer. After all, if he'd been with the rest of the attacking force at the city's walls, his blast would have hit its intended target. But that distance had been his only saving grace a heartbeat later when the implosion happened.

Echoes of the pain caused by the implosion shot through him, his core not so easily forgetting that searing agony.

"It was a momentous day, was it not, Tom?" Augustus asked, feeling somewhat nostalgic as his mind's eye replayed the blinding blast that had detonated above the city.

"Without a doubt, my king," Tom replied, his voice airy. "Not a week has gone by that I haven't recalled that day. Seeing it in person, though . . ."

"It's something else entirely," Augustus finished.

Despite decades having crawled by, it was as though not a single day had passed within the city. The ground looked as scorched as the day they'd attacked, every inch of stone and dirt blackened by either Gormona's blasts or the subsequent implosion of power. The longer Augustus looked, the more the vista drew him in, each detail as eye-catching as the last.

This fallen city was a monument to both Gormona's power and ruthlessness. Now that they had returned, it would be the stepping stone for further ascension. It wasn't lost on Augustus how fitting that was. Realizing he'd stopped walking, he looked around. Everyone was facing him and waiting for his next move. With a smile, he stood tall and took a deep breath. "To Theogonia, then."

The rest of their passage to the city was done in silence. They entered through the front gate, and an image of its former magnificence flashed through his mind. The gate blocking the entrance to the city had been a marvel of creation. A relic of the past, every line of its wooden surface lined with ancient runes of power. Much like the rest of the city, it hadn't survived the attack.

He ran a fingernail across what remained of the stone wall. The entire structure had been created by the System, so his nail, empowered as it might be, didn't leave a scratch. The stone remained black, the very structure somehow changed by the events that had ended the city. The next breath he took smelled of fire and brim-stone, but he suspected it was a figment of his imagination.

Tryphena stepped ahead of the group, leading the way to the Cult of the Alchemist's new headquarters. As they drew farther into the city, the sinking feeling in Augustus's core grew. Judging by everyone's face, they felt the same. Tryphena led them down what had previously been the main street, only stones and dust remaining of the buildings on either side.

Ahead, a lone building stood. Patches of stone had been blasted away around what had likely been windows, but they'd been patched up with planks of blackened wood, even their fibers somehow changed despite not being present when the implosion happened. Tryphena jogged up the stairs and knocked on the door, which was clearly made with wood from the gnarled trees outside the city.

Footsteps scuffed within, and a moment later, the door eased open a crack.

"Ah," came an aged voice. "Princess Tryphena. I didn't expect to see you so . . ." The man trailed off when he saw the procession behind her. "King! Queen!" The leader of the Cult of the Alchemist lowered himself to the floor, relying on the door-frame for assistance. "Forgive me! I was not made aware of your arrival!" His eye twitched as he stood back up before being permitted to do so. "Damn birds," he muttered to himself, too low for anyone but a cultivator to hear. "What good are they if they can't even warn me that guests are coming? I should turn them into soup one of these days." He turned and started shuffling back inside.

Augustus, all too aware of the man's madness, ignored the impropriety. "May we enter, Francis?"

"What?" he demanded, whirling and casting an imperious gaze down on them. When his eyes landed on Augustus, he gaped. "M-my king! Forgive me! I didn't know you were here! Those damned birds. What good are they if they can't even warn me—"

"Francis," Augustus interrupted. "May we enter?"

"Yes!" He bowed at the waist. "Please come in!"

He held the door open for them, maintaining his bow as they entered.

"Not you!" Francis barked, making Augustus peer behind them. "You think I've forgotten your foolishness so soon, Solomon? Wait outside, you thrice-burnt failure of a concoction!"

Marcus, the merchant, stood flummoxed. He blinked at the gnarled finger currently poking his chest.

"Wait outside," Augustus instructed, knowing better than to engage in debate with a madman.

Marcus nodded, bowed, and retreated.

Francis snorted as he slammed the door. "Damned upstarts. Now, where were we?" He smiled at them, his face freezing when he caught sight of Augustus. "Poseidon's hairy calves! The king!"

He tried to drop into a bow, but Augustus swept forward, catching his arm. "Not necessary, Francis. We're here to collect some of your medicine. Tryphena tells us that you have a new recipe?"

"Oh! You flatter me, Your Majesty. This humble alchemist offers all of his potions to you! One moment!" He ran to a bench covered with alchemical equipment, pulled a crate from beneath it with more strength than his wiry frame should possess, and started rummaging. "Where did I put them . . . ?"

As the man searched, Augustus glanced around the room. Benches lined three of the four walls, almost every inch of their surface covered in alchemy-related equipment. Smoke filled the room, its scent both welcome and nostalgic. No matter which Cult of the Alchemist branch he visited, they always smelled the same.

On the one wall without any benches, a tangle of branches had been attached to the floor. It looked almost like an art installation, constructed out of the twisted branches from beyond the city's gates. Seeing his confused look, Tryphena strode to his side.

"They're for his birds."

Augustus looked at the floor, seeing no droppings, feathers, or any other of the hallmarks that came with keeping creatures of the avian variety. "A sign of the madness?" he asked.

"I believe so. He has been getting progressively worse."

"Ah, there you are!" Francis yelled. Glass clinked as he lifted a crate and walked over. When he straightened, he froze. "Gods above! The king!"

Augustus rubbed the bridge of his nose, steadily losing his patience. "Do you know the dosage, Tryphena?"

"One vial until the effects become overwhelming. When they do, leave the city until symptoms recede, then return and take another dose."

"Wonderful." Augustus strode forward and collected the crate. "Thank you, Francis. We will return if we need any more."

"Of course, my king! I'll start making another batch this second!"

Before he could forget and recognize Augustus again, they left the building, firmly closing the door behind them.

"Here," Augustus said, passing the crate to Marcus, who rushed up to take it. "Everyone, take a dose now." He rubbed his chin when his hands were free. "Not you, merchant, unless you want to be turned inside out. Only the gods know what effect it would have on a regular human."

"Pretty sure we just saw the effect it has," Tryphena said, nodding back to the building they'd just left.

"Birdies!" Francis yelled, as if on cue, his voice muffled by the wooden barricades covering the windows and holes. "Where are you?"

After a shake of his head, Augustus removed a vial, popped the cork, and downed its contents.

Heat ran down his throat, oozing out from his stomach and branching off into his limbs. A dull numbness followed, stronger than any of the previous batches he'd tried. All at once, the numbness mostly faded, withdrawing back into his core. When it settled there, the dread he was feeling dissipated. They all let out a slow sigh, enjoying the reprieve the potion granted.

"He may be mad," Tryphena said, "but he's a wizard with alchemy."

"Truly," Penelope agreed. "He wasn't always so . . . eccentric. He has contributed greatly to Gormona."

Augustus nodded. "Which is why his lack of respect is tolerated. Take heed, Tom—that is how a man serves his kingdom properly."

Tom nodded. "Yes, king."

"Tell me—where do you think we are going now?"

"To the center of the city."

Augustus raised a brow. "Yes. That is what my daughter, the princess, told you. But what are we doing there?"

"I believe we are going to see the prisoners, my king."

Augustus nodded, shooting him an appreciative glance. "It appears you still have your wits about you. That is good." He threw the vial aside, letting it smash on the cobbled street. "Let us go converse with some of our old friends . . ."

CHAPTER FORTY-ONE

Training

It had been almost two weeks since George, Geraldine, and the Church of Carcinization had joined our ranks.

After my repeated reassurance that I didn't mind if they continued worshiping crabs as the Church of Carcinization—as long as it did not run in opposition to our goals, of course—Joel had taken to running their daily crab meditations on my shore.

As for George and Geraldine, they had spent most of the last fortnight fishing, and they'd caught a surprising amount of species. Just as quick as the seasonal fish had arrived, their numbers started to dwindle. You could still catch one here and there, but the variety of fish caught from the rock wall had drastically increased, the other species returning after most of the bluefish had left.

There was still no sign of Rocky, but that was probably for the best. The cantankerous little bugger had a fair bit of self-reflection to do, and his absence was mostly unnoticed. Snips had her claws full; most of her days were spent being praised by the Church of Carcinization. As I watched her showing them her wonderful form, I smiled.

"This will never not be funny," Maria said, smiling at the five humans scuttling sideways into the ocean after Snips, "clacking" their hands together all the way.

"I couldn't agree more."

"We can hear you!" Joel called, scowling but still retaining his crab-like posture.

"Do you speak crab?" Maria asked, turning to me.

"I'm ninety-nine percent sure he called me handsome."

Jess giggled, blowing bubbles from her submerged mouth.

A loud crack like far-off thunder tore through the air. I turned southward, gazing at the distant mountains. "Should we go check up on them?"

"Oh, I'd love to! It's always entertaining!"

"Especially when Claws is involved."

Maria leaped to her feet. "That boom was probably her! Let's go!"

"Coming, Snips?" I asked as I stretched.

Soon, she replied with a quiet hiss before submerging back beneath the ocean's water, only her eye visible.

I smiled and blew her a kiss. Though I knew she didn't care for their praise, she had been more than accommodating for Joel and the rest of his followers, always willing to join their meditations.

With Maria's hand in mine, we ran across the sand and leaped right over the river mouth. I stole a glance at her midair, only to find she was staring back. She poked her tongue out at me, only turning away to spot her landing. No sooner did we hit the sand than we were off again, heading for the southern mountains. We reached the forest in record time, not slowing as we dashed between trunks and over grass. Another boom came, this time close enough for me to feel who it was.

Light streamed through the forest ahead of us, and as we emerged into the sunlight, we skidded to a stop.

Roger had cleared a section of forest. Even the stumps were nowhere to be seen, completely uprooted and replaced by a section of tamped ground as large as a football field. Twenty or so people were scattered around the edges, intently watching the match taking place. In the center of the field, Borks hunched down and launched forward.

Roger stood firm, and as the maw of Borks's hellhound form opened to clamp down on his torso, he cut diagonally through the air with one arm. A sharp blade of chi flew from him, and Borks bit down on it.

Boom!

Air shot outward, reverberating in my core when it struck me.

The attack blew Borks back. He skidded to a stop on the sand.

"See how he neutralized my attack?" Roger instructed the surrounding cultivators. "Though I didn't use my full strength, that would have cut most of you in two. Brigadier Borks nullified it by channeling chi into his jaws and biting down on it. With enough control, you can do that with your bodies."

The cultivators nodded, some even recording the words in notepads that Ellis had provided. Over the past week since the bluefish's numbers had begun to drop, Roger had seen fit to start his very own village-wide training montage. Not everyone took part, but more than a few of the cultivators from Gormona were interested in being a part of New Tropica's defense force. Though I wasn't too keen on participating—mostly for fear of accidentally atomizing someone—Maria and I often came to watch.

"Morning, Fischer!" Deklan called, waving to me from across the clearing.

I'd spotted him immediately—he and his brother were the only two audacious enough to risk Roger's wrath by sitting down while waiting for their turn to spar.

"G'day, mate!" I replied.

Now that they noticed us, most of the others gave us a wave or bow. Thankfully, they'd become a lot less reverential of me since they first arrived, but a few still bent a little too low for my liking.

Twin blurs of movement came from my left. Rather than brace my body for the impending blows, I thought I'd let them have their fun. Corporal Claws and Cinnamon slammed into my chest, both trilling their arrival. My feet left the sand as I sailed through the air and skidded to a stop on my back, my two assailants clutched to my chest.

I groaned, holding a hand to my forehead. "Go on without me. I will never recover from such—" My diatribe was cut off by a choked noise coming from my mouth as Claws rammed her little digits into my neck and started tickling. I squirmed away, fighting off her questing paws. "Mercy! I concede!"

As I held Claws by the scruff of her neck, neutralizing her attack, Cinnamon puffed herself up on my chest. She peered down at me with a victorious smirk, all but saying the word *pathetic* as she accepted my surrender.

"Okay, you two," Maria said, scooping them up in an arm each. "That's enough guerrilla warfare for one morning."

In stark opposition to the violence they'd shown me, both creatures cuddled into Maria, Cinnamon by curling into a little loaf, and Claws by rolling onto her back and settling into the nook of Maria's arm.

I stood and shook myself off, doing my best to dislodge any sand that had made its way into my clothing. "Now that we've said good morning, how has your little experiment been going, Claws?"

She sat bolt upright, her eyes going wider than I've ever seen them. The slow grin that made its way over her face told me that there had been progress. Looking more liquid than otter, she flowed out of Maria's arms and landed gracefully on the ground. Cinnamon hopped down to meet her, and together they raced toward the western side of the training grounds.

Yesterday there had been a stack of boulders there. Now, only one remained, the rest having been blasted into gravel by Claws's experiments. Claws started stretching, looking downright adorable as she limbered up. Cinnamon hopped around the boulder, sniffing, touching, and even slapping it a few times, ostensibly assessing its suitability.

When Cinnamon's head swiveled to face Claws, she gave her an almost lecherous smile. Claws returned it. They started giggling, sounding like high-pitched, much cuter versions of Beavis and Butt-Head. Abruptly, their tone shifted. Both went silent, and after a swift nod to each other, they moved into position. Claws faced the boulder and reached out for her chi, her core softly vibrating in preparation. Cinnamon sat at a right angle to Claws, also facing the boulder.

Both closed their eyes as their power swelled. Cinnamon's flowed into her body and flooded her muscles, waiting there for the moment she called on it. Claws's core hummed and opened up, her chi slowly pouring upward into her chest. From there, her will pulsed out, demanding that it . . . change? Obey? It was hard to distinguish, but she was definitely doing *something*.

Beyond intrigued, I sent my awareness out, focusing entirely on her will.

Her lightning chi resisted. It didn't *want* to be altered. Though Claws was a trickster and might appear flippant to those that didn't really know her, I knew the truth. When she set her mind to something—whether it be defending her friends, messing with someone, or devouring a small village's worth of shellfish—nothing would sway her. Her will demanding that her chi obey was an unstoppable force meeting an immovable object. The struggle likely only took a few seconds; to me, it was a day-long battle, filled with skirmishes and feints and headed by two masters of warfare.

Slowly, her chi's metaphorical forces were defeated, systematically dismantled by her immense will and desire. The chi started to change shape. No, that wasn't entirely correct. It was both the same yet undeniably different. Its *flavor*, for lack of a more-accurate term, had shifted, gaining complexity. Focused as I was on what she was doing, I didn't have the bandwidth to run through the implications. I did, however, have a front-row seat to the moment she won the battle.

Corporal Claws's will washed over her chi in a flash, completing its alteration. From her chest, it wound around her, wreathing her limbs. She stood tall and cocked her arm back, gathering the chi in her fist.

Cinnamon, not missing a beat, launched herself along the ground. With her back to the sand, she wedged herself under the boulder, lifted it up on all four limbs, then lobbed it into the air.

The moment it was before Claws, she struck. Her fist raced forward, too fast for anyone but a cultivator to follow. My curiosity swelled as I tried to comprehend exactly what was going on. Her paw held too much strength and would shatter the boulder into a million pieces. Just like every other rock, judging by the surrounding gravel.

She never once slowed, her fist rocketing forward and promising the annihilation of anything in her path. Just before it hit, though, her chi flared. With mere millimeters between her touch of death and the boulder, her lightning flowed out of her body and into the foreign object. This, too, should have brought destruction.

But it didn't.

The essence not only filled the boulder, it also surrounded it, holding it in one piece. The next moment, her fist collided with the rock. Wreathed in arcs of blue essence, the boulder flew skyward so fast that I almost lost sight of it. Thunder boomed, slamming into my chest as lightning seemed to strike in reverse, originating from Claws and ending on the boulder that was now hundreds of meters above us. The mass continued on, soaring from sight, only flashes of blue chi letting me catch sight of it.

As it sailed far upward and slightly northwest, all I could do was stare, my jaw slack and expectations exceeded. When the world's essence flowed in toward us, I had to cut my amazement short. Faster than ever before, it billowed up and slammed into Claws. Knowing what to expect, I slung chi from my core, surrounding Claws in a protective bubble.

The world rushed into her abdomen, filling it to the brim.

I tried to yell for everyone to get back, but my mouth couldn't move fast enough. Her core detonated, the breakthrough's excess chi rushing out and slamming into my protective bubble. Where Roger's chi was bladelike and Peter's radiated heat like a blazing hearth, Corporal Claws's was electric. It arced over the inside of my shielding, seeking a way out. When it succeeded, my panic surged through me. Barbs of it zapped *through* my protective shielding. I only had a fraction of a second to react before it shot out, and not knowing what effect it would have if it struck any of the weaker cultivators, I made an executive decision.

I turned my shielding into a funnel, aiming it for something it could travel through into the ground. Uncountable fingers of electricity formed a single bolt, and with a crack that made my ears ring, it shot into the makeshift lightning rod.

There was only one problem with the whole plan: I was the lightning rod.

It sent me flying backward, and I tried to curl my limbs into a protective ball, but Claws's power still lingered, my muscles nonresponsive. Suddenly, my flight came to an abrupt end, and I blinked, my vision blurry as I turned to look at my saviors.

"Are you okay?" Maria asked, not at all amused. "Are you hurt?"

"Frack me." Barry laughed, entirely *too* amused. "What did I just stumble upon?"

I groaned as I cracked my neck and tested my limbs. "I think I'm okay . . ." I rubbed my eyes. "Claws. Are you—"

A loud chirp was the only warning I had. She landed on my chest a moment later.

"Are you okay, girl?" I asked, reaching up to support her.

She had tears in her eyes, her lower lip quivering as she stared up at me.

"I'm fine," I said, smoothing the fur atop her head. "Barry, are there any villages to the northwest?"

"You mean in the direction that Claws just launched a lightning-covered meteor?"

"Yeah." I opened my jaw, loosening the muscles there and causing my ears to pop. "That's exactly what I mean."

"Nope," he replied, still sounding all too entertained. "It's only forest and wilderness."

"Good. I was worried someone would have to race off and try to catch it." I returned my attention to Claws. "Are you sure you're okay?"

Yes, she chirped, still giving me a guilty look that broke my heart.

"I'm totally fine. I promise." I scratched behind her ear, reassuring her.

"Okay," Maria said. "Now that we know everyone is safe . . ." She picked up Claws, holding her by the underarms and lifting her high. "What the *frack* was that, Claws? That was so cool!"

Claws shimmied her shoulders, unable to suppress her joy at being praised. Maria pulled her back into a hug, my otter pal melting in her arms.

I smiled at them. "Agreed. Did you know it would do that, Claws?"

She shrugged coyly, letting out a mysterious trill and wiggling her fuzzy little eyebrows at me from atop Maria's arms.

"Regardless of your intent, that was a crazy breakthrough, Claws." I wrapped my arms around Maria's waist, pulling them both into a hug. "Well done."

Cinnamon leaped up to my shoulder, joining in the cuddle puddle. Claws revealing her needlelike teeth with a grin as she shimmied again, jubilation radiating from her core.

CHAPTER FORTY-TWO

Echoes of the Past

With sweat peppering his brow, a lone alchemist trudged up a grassy hill. If not for the exhaustion lingering throughout his entire body, he would be fairly skipping up the slope. He had left his shack yesterday at the crack of dawn, heading deep into the mountains in search of his final ingredient. He glanced down at the thick roots held in his bloodied hand, a smile crossing his face despite the weariness.

With its addition—after proper preparation, of course—his potion of ascension would be complete. Solomon was sure of it.

It had taken him *weeks* to gather everything necessary. Milk of thistle, arrow stem, slimpuff bulbs, dendrod leaves, the decayed bark of the blue true, and finally, his secret ingredient. He held his hand up, staring into the roots he'd found high atop a mountain peak. An odd sensation came over him, as if the plump roots were a lodestone that drew in his vision. The moment he'd first dug them up and caught sight of them, this anomalous feeling was how he'd known they were the missing ingredient. The very thing his potion needed.

Solomon suspected that they'd need to be prepared in a certain way, which was the very reason he'd stayed out all day and night, collecting enough of the sparsely grown weed's roots that he could process some in every way possible. For the umpteenth time since he first discovered the plant, he cursed their appearance.

It was no wonder they'd never been discovered and recorded in the Cult of the Alchemist's books. They were only visible on the surface as a tiny vine-like structure that liked to grow underneath rocks, a pale-green leaf or two poking out into the light of day to absorb the sun's energy. It made them almost impossible to spot, and only Solomon's genius had allowed him to discover them. He'd sat down to catch his breath when he spotted one of the leaves. The moment he did, it tugged on his vision, demanding that he investigate.

Extracting them from the hard earth was the cause of his raw and bloodied fingers. He had his tools, of course, but the soft skin of his hands was no match for wooden handles and repetition. Thankfully he barely felt the numerous cuts and burst blisters through the haze of his tiredness.

The ground grew flat as he approached his place of power, and when he crested the final section of hill, he fell to his knees, smiling at the sight that greeted him. His self-constructed shack all but called his name, beckoning him toward its dark and cool depths. Perhaps he would allow himself some rest before working with the unnamed root.

Solomon's eyes slowly widened as the realization struck him. "By the gods," he said aloud, his voice strained with disuse.

Excited as he had been to find the final piece of his ascension, it hadn't really hit him that he'd discovered a new root. He lifted it once more. What would he name it . . . ?

"Solomon root," he decided, wheezing out a laugh.

The name rolled off his tongue. He sat looking at the collected specimens for a long moment, soaking up the accomplishment. The very world seemed to hiss its approval, an unfelt breeze making a barely audible whistle as it wound through the surrounding trees. When the whistling grew louder, he cast his gaze around, his brow furrowing. The trees weren't moving and the air was completely still. So what was that sound . . . ?

He looked up at the sky, his search coming to an end when he spotted something flickering high above. There was a speck in the sky, a star burning so brightly that it was visible in the light of day.

If he'd been standing, Solomon would have fallen to his knees. He stared up at the sign, completely speechless as it grew more and more visible. The gods had long ago fled this realm, yet he and the rest of the Cult of the Alchemist believed that their influence remained, mere echoes and aftershocks of their power. This had to be one such event.

The wills of alchemists past had witnessed his accomplishment, and they had approved.

He laughed softly at first, but it steadily built, growing louder as the star shone brighter, defying the sun's oppressive rays with its blue brilliance. His throat grew pained, yet Solomon continued cackling, unable to hold back his celebration. The whistling sound was much more noticeable now, seeming to get closer by the second.

Tears welled in Solomon's eyes. He was an ambitious man, and he'd hoped and prayed he would one day become the Alchemist of prophecy. As much as he manifested that eventuality, to have the departed pantheon recognize his efforts was an indescribable experience. The tears fell, rolling down his cheeks as he stared up at the star, its form now large enough that he could see blue flames arcing out from its blue mass.

The whistling grew to a fever pitch, and as the star appeared to shift positions in the sky, he blinked away his tears, not understanding. The shining light was moving subtly, so slight that it was almost imperceptible. But it was definitely moving.

Not moving, he realized. *Falling.*

With his eyes glued to it, he tried to get to his feet. As he stood on wobbly legs, the star robbed him of his strength. His body gave out, and he crashed back down to the floor. The shooting star fell directly toward his clearing, its blue flames flaring out and consuming the sky. The whistle was deafening, and all he could do was watch as his death approached. His hand went limp, the gathered roots falling to the grass before him.

Time seemed to crawl to a freeze as the star descended, hurtling for the center of his place of power, right where his shack sat. The shack that held all the ingredients he was going to use to ascend. A wave of ice-cold comprehension drove into Solomon. The departed gods of alchemy had witnessed his attempted ascension, and they had found him wanting.

They sought not only his destruction, but the annihilation of the means with which he meant to ascend. Solomon clenched his jaw. If he was to die, cast aside by his forebears, the least he could do was stare defiantly at the heavens, challenging them to the very last. He forced his eyes to remain open, tracking the star as it sought to break his spirit. Its flames licked out, barbing through the air like bolts of lightning. An eyebrow arched, climbing high on his forehead. The flames weren't *like* lightning. They *were* lightning.

"Zeus's tempestuous beard!" he screamed, the star's whistling so loud that he barely heard himself.

It wasn't his alchemist ancestors that sought to deny him—it was the will of Zeus himself. Solomon's strength and fear of death returned all at once. He turned and lunged to his feet, unfeeling legs stumbling over the grassy clearing. He had to flee. He had to get away. The very future of the Cult of the Alchemist depended on it. He was *almost* there. If he could just live through this, he could relocate and—

Boooom!

Solomon was thrown forward when the star collided. He hurtled headlong into a tree, only his enhanced reaction time allowing him to cushion the blow with his forearms. He skidded to a stop downhill from his place of power, where he remained for entirely too long, winded and gasping for air. When he could breathe again, he rolled over and got to his feet.

His arms ached where they'd impacted the tree. Thankfully, the bones didn't appear broken.

Cradling them against each other, he trudged back up the hill, his entire body feeling cold. When he crested the peak this time, he found nothing worth celebrating. Where his shack and the blue-barked tree had previously been, only a crater remained. In the center of it, half a giant boulder was visible, the other half lodged firmly in the earth. Broken chunks of what had been his shack were strewn all over, most small enough to be called splinters.

Solomon stumbled to the edge of the hole and knelt down, looking for anything he could salvage. All his ingredients, carefully collected and prepared over the past two weeks—*gone*. He spun, looking for the roots he'd left behind in his flight. They were nowhere to be seen. The only things left in the clearing were the boulder, debris, and him.

Move, a voice seemed to scream from inside of him.

He pushed it away. If he could just find his ingredients, he could make his potion and—

Move! the internal voice screamed again.

This time, he stilled, shaking his head as a fog lifted from his awareness.

What in the Alchemist's blessed concoction was he doing?

The will of Zeus had attacked him. Had tried to *kill* him. As long as he survived, he could gather more ingredients. He fumbled around his neck, finding his pouch still hanging there. His shaking fingers pulled the drawstring open, revealing the handful of blue tree bark he'd squirreled away.

With more than just determination fueling his steps, Solomon fled the former place of power as fast as he could, never once looking back.

With a pleasant numbness radiating from his core, Augustus Reginald Gormona stepped into the ruins of the castle. The grand reception chamber no longer looked so grand. Most of the roof had collapsed, as had the floors beneath it. Augustus climbed over the rubble, heading deeper in.

Everyone followed close behind, likely not wanting to be too far from his power while within the desolate city.

"Torch," Augustus demanded.

"Yes, my king," Marcus replied, immediately lighting one and passing it to Augustus.

The king strode forward, leading them from the reception chamber into a hallway beyond. With flames lighting the walls, visions of his youth flashed by.

Augustus had visited these halls many a time in his adolescence, and though his memory of that time was hazy, flashes of colored tapestries, severe servants, and smiling faces sped by in a confusing stream. He recalled running his fingers along a woolen tapestry that ran the entire length of the hallway, its fibers soft to the touch.

"Augustus?" his wife asked, her tone worried. "Is everything okay?"

He returned to the present, finding his hand pressed to a blackened stone wall where the art had been. It was cold and hard, a far cry from the plush wool it had once worn.

He shot his wife a venomous look for making him look weak. "Remain silent while we travel. That goes for everyone."

He marched the rest of the way, having traversed these halls enough to recall the path. Before long, they reached the stairs. After descending three flights, they arrived. Augustus raised an eyebrow at the door. It should have been barred, as the Cult of the Alchemist well knew. He swallowed his fury. If the prison still needed a caretaker when they were done here, it was time to replace Francis.

Augustus opened the door, and the sound of its hinges creaking shattered the silence of the underground halls. Their boots crunched as they strode over what appeared to be dirt and small stones.

"Dinner already?" someone called. They laughed then, the sound high-pitched, slow, and entirely unnatural.

A chorus of cackles crawled through the air, the other prisoners joining in with the speaker's mirth. The hair on Augustus's neck stood tall and a shiver ran down his spine. Annoyed that they still had this effect on him, he arched his shoulders and stood tall. He strode to the first cell and peered inside, barely recognizing the creature within. He was a far cry from the man he'd put there so long ago, but as Augustus continued to stare at the grime-covered face, the lines formed a pattern he once knew well.

The prisoner crept forward, his head twisting to the side, his eyes wide. "Ah," he said. "I am madder than I thought."

"Hello, Tiberius," Augustus said, giving him a nod. "I'm not a vision. I am truly here."

Tiberius giggled. "That's what they all say." He snapped a salute, then spun on the spot, marched to the back of his cell with an oddly inhuman gait, and sat against the rear wall, his rigid posture melting away. "Be gone, ghost of my past. Go bother some other poor soul—perhaps a sane one."

Tom stepped up beside Augustus, resting his hand on the bar. "We're real, Tiberius."

"Oooooh!" Tiberius called. "Lord Tom Osnan is here, gents!"

"Duh!" another replied from deeper in. "He's sitting right beside me!"

Tiberius nodded knowingly. "You see, spirits mine? You are not real, so leave me be."

"Can you two keep it down!" a female voice snarled. "Princess Tryphena is trying to *sleep*!"

"Daughter," Augustus said, gesturing for Tryphena. "Come here, please."

"Ah," Tiberius said. "Two Toms, a king, *and* two princesses? What a treat the visions provide for us to . . . today . . ." He trailed off as Tryphena strode into view. *"Princess . . . ?"* His odd gait returned as he strode to the bars and grabbed them with shaking hands. "You . . . you've *grown* . . ."

"Hello, Uncle Tiberius." The smile she gave was tinged with sadness. "It has been a long time. Mother is here, too."

Penelope stepped up and curtsied. "It's good to see you, Tiberius. House Ward has been sorely missed in Gormona."

"You're all real . . ." Tiberius Ward fell to his knees, staring at the ground. "You've truly returned . . ."

"Tiberius has gone madder," the feminine voice called. "He thinks they're *real*!"

A chorus of laughter, each as unhinged as the last, bounced off the stone walls and metal bars.

Augustus sighed. "Come, family. Let us show them."

As they walked up the hallway and passed more of the cells, the laughter slowly died.

"Real . . ."

"They're here . . ."

"My king!"

"Real."

"Real."

"Real!"

Tryphena paused before the cell containing the woman's voice. "Hello, Aunt Livia. It's been too long."

"Tryphena . . ." Livia Ward, Tiberius's wife and former matriarch of House Ward, stumbled forward into the light. She cradled a bundle of blankets in her arms, and as she spied the *real* Tryphena, she dropped the bundle to the floor. Tears welled in her eyes as she reached a smudged hand through the bars. *"Tryphena . . ."*

The princess reached out, resting the back of her hand in Livia's palm. Though they were imprisoned here, it wasn't because they presented a threat to the royal family. They clasped hands, and when Tryphena saw how dirty Livia was, unhidden fury crossed her face. "They are *filthy*, Father. Francis told me he provided them with baths."

"Baths?" Livia chortled, withdrawing her hand. "Oh, yes! Dirt baths!" She pointed to the corner, and when Augustus lifted the torch, it revealed a mound of dirt in the corner. "For his birds, you see."

"Birds!"

"Birds!"

"Such *pretty* birds!"

"Cawww!"

The prisoners all laughed at the facsimile of a bird call that came from farther in, sounding even more disjointed given the context.

Tryphena's lip twitched. "I'm going to kill him."

"Now, now, Princess." Livia put her hands on her hips. "That is no way for a noblewoman to talk! Birds *like* dirt baths! Things aren't so bad down here—it's how we serve our king!"

A chorus of agreement bounced down the halls, not a hint of malice or deception seeping into their voices.

"It is good to see you well, Livia," Augustus said, reassured by their loyalty.

"And you, my king." She bowed at the waist, and Augustus finally realized what was off about how Tiberius had strutted.

They *moved* like birds.

Tryphena clearly spotted it, too. She struck out, slamming her closed fist in the metal bars before her.

Livia leaped backwards, her eyes wide as she retreated to a corner.

"Sorry." Tryphena averted her eyes, hiding them. "Let's go, Father."

When they reached Tiberius's cell again, he was waiting for them. "What are you doing here?" His gaze searched each of their faces. "Why have you come back . . . ?"

Augustus nodded, glad they were finally at the heart of it. "You made me an offer once, Tiberius. You said you could teach me to channel the corrupted chi that surrounds Theogonia."

In the blink of an eye, Tiberius prostrated himself. "I apologize again, my king. It was not for me to offer. If you changed your mind and want my life, it is yours to take."

"Oh, I did change my mind, Tiberius. But it wasn't in regard to taking your life as penance."

"Then what . . . ?" Tiberius asked, his head twisting to stare up at them like a curious pigeon.

"After decades of peace, Gormona is once again under threat by a foreign power."

The former lord of Gormona jumped to his feet, his face a vision of fury. "Give me the order, Your Majesty, and I will scour them from Kallis and feast on their bones."

"It may come to that, Tiberius, but I had something else in mind." He grinned, already knowing what Tiberius's answer would be. "I wish to learn how to cultivate corrupted chi."

CHAPTER FORTY-THREE

Intoxication

I woke the next morning to a floral fragrance permeating the room.

It reminded me of Maria and the scents that always drifted up from her hair, never quite the same as the day before. I breathed deep, the thoughts of her making a smile come to my face.

Someone moved on the bed beside me, so I reached over, reaching to try find Borks and rub his belly. Instead of soft fur, I found warm and even softer skin. I opened my eyes, blinking at Maria's sleeping form. She must have fallen asleep before heading home last night.

I knew I should wake her. Should let her get ready and prepare an excuse before her father and mother arrived with our breakfast . . .

But I didn't have the strength.

Her beauty drew me in; her serenity kept me there. She was usually so animated. So vibrant. Lost in sleep was the only time I could catch her in a frozen moment. Only her rising and falling chest betrayed her stillness, shifting with each shallow breath she took.

I ran my fingers along the back of her head, making flashes of last night appear unbidden. Her hair draped down around my face and tickling my skin. The softness of her lips, contrasted by her hunger when they pressed into mine. My own hunger. My need.

Our bodies paired like coffee and croissants. Like butter and flour. And though we were composed of disparate pieces, we fit together as if built for one another.

My heart thumped in my chest as I reached over and ran a hand down her slender arm, unable to stop myself, despite knowing it was a bad idea. She stirred, making my thin linen sheet hug her intoxicating form.

Knowing now was *not* the time, I clenched my jaw and took a deep breath, doing everything I could to banish the thoughts of her. I failed, of course, but I forged onward regardless.

"Maria," I said, my voice gruff with disuse. Clearing my throat and getting up on one elbow, I swept loose strands of hair from her face. "Wakey-wakey, beautiful. It's time to get up."

She peered out at me through sleep-filled eyes, giving me a smile that knocked the wind from me. "Good morning."

"We have to get ready," I said. "You fell asleep before you went home last night, and your dad could be kicking down my door at any moment."

She let out a soft groan as she stretched, arching her back like a cat, making the sheet slide over the lines of her body. "I didn't."

"Huh?" I said, having barely heard her. I furrowed my brow, processing the words. "You didn't what?"

"I didn't fall asleep before going home."

"Then . . . how are you here?"

"Because, silly." She pulled back the sheet and leaned onto my chest, pressing herself against me. "I went home after you fell asleep."

"Oh," I replied mechanically, barely able to think past her contact. "You know, you're making it really difficult to get out of this bed."

She ran a hand through my hair, smirking at me. "I told Mom that I'd been . . ." She moved her hand to my neck, pulled herself up, and pressed her lips into mine. She pulled away a moment later, leaving me breathless. " . . . missing you of late," she continued. "Mom, being the wonderful woman she is, hatched a scheme."

I stared at her stunning eyes and the curve of her lips, and when my brain once more caught up with the conversation, I frowned. "Wait, what? You lost me. What scheme?"

"Well . . ." She ran her hand along my chest. "As we speak, Mom and Dad are off collecting coffee and croissants for the entire church." She trailed a finger up and along the side of my neck, making a pleasant shiver run through me. "I've been led to believe that there will be a delay with the croissants."

"A delay, huh?"

"Indeed." Her eyes twinkled. "A real shame."

"And why would a young lady of such noble disposition stoop to base trickery?"

She smirked at my words and shrugged one shoulder, her heart thumping loud enough for me to hear it. "Because I want you, Fischer."

It was all I could take. When our lips met, every other thought vanished like leaves in the wind.

As we stood on the river's shore, the rising sun cast a golden glow over the land, making Maria's flushed face appear even cuter. I wasn't aware such a thing was possible, so all I could do was stare at her rosy cheeks.

She turned my way, her head tilted and hair falling free of her ear. "Did you know that I love you?"

"You do?" I made a thoughtful face that didn't quite hide my smile. "Would it kill you to show it?"

She tried to slap me, but given how soft her strike was, I easily caught her wrist. She made a startled and somehow-still-cute noise as I pulled her off balance and into my arms. I lifted her by the waist, and as our lips met, she melted in my grasp. She was so, so warm, and just when I was losing myself completely in the moment, something splashed in the shallows nearby.

Corporal Claws, my sometimes reliable—*ah, who was I kidding?* Corporal Claws, my *rarely* reliable otter pal, immediately ruined the moment. She let out an eardrum-splitting wolf whistle.

"Okay, ow," Maria said, flinching as she pulled back.

"Claws," I chided. "Did you have to—"

I trailed off as another creature emerged from the depths. Her body was covered in a hard exoskeleton and deadly spikes, and her eyes never once left Corporal Claws as she approached. Sergeant Snips crawled through the shallows directly to Claws's side, leaning so close they almost touched. There was a tense moment where nobody made a move, both animal pals content with staring the other down.

Abruptly, the violence began.

To the eye of a regular human, it would have been a mere explosion of water, as if both creatures had spontaneously exploded. To my enhanced eyes, I easily saw the perpetrator. Corporal Claws had broadcast her intention, the corner of one lip curling up a split millisecond before she splashed river water. Well, splashed might be the wrong word, because the spray of water that hit Snips's carapace could have peeled paint. Snips responded immediately, both her claws slamming down and shooting arcs of energy through the water. Claws went full matrix, leaning backwards with a grin on her face, easily dodging the strikes.

The initial volley was enough for me to understand who would win this battle; Claws was too powerful—too *quick*—following her recent breakthrough. Snips likely recognized it, too.

But that didn't stop her from trying.

As they zipped through the river and engaged in an underwater dogfight, I was reminded of how they'd been all those months ago, back when we'd first encountered the mischievous otter. With those memories playing through my mind, I smiled, feeling an immense amount of love for both of them despite the interruption.

"Should we go get that coffee?" Maria asked. "This could go on for a while . . ."

No! Snips and Claws bubbled and hissed respectively, enacting an immediate ceasefire to let us know that was unacceptable.

I laughed, shaking my head. "Tell you what, we'll go through the forest so you two can finish your little skirmish unwitnessed. Deal?"

Deal! Claws chirped, then head-butted Snips before she could react.

Maria covered her mouth and giggled as Snips skidded to the far riverbank. Wasting not a moment, Snips launched forward again, spewing a stream of angry bubbles.

Just before we reached the tree line, I felt waves of contemplation coming from Maria, so strong that I couldn't help but look her way. "What's up?"

She chewed her lip. "It's odd that Claws had a breakthrough the way she did . . . isn't it?"

"Oh, yeah. Completely."

She narrowed her eyes at me. "So why are you so chill about it? I know you're as relaxed as they come, but even I'm intrigued by the fact that humans appear to have breakthroughs by realizing something about themselves or admitting an uncomfortable truth, whereas creatures or spirit beasts or whatever seem to have breakthroughs by . . . I don't know. What did Claws even do?"

With perfect timing, Claws kicked off the top of Snips's carapace, wiggling her eyebrows at us as she sailed by.

"I don't think that's correct," I answered, watching Snips regather her wits in the middle of the river and prepare a counterattack. "You're forgetting Borks."

"What do you mean I'm forgetting Borks? I'd never forget . . ." She pursed her lips when she realized what I was talking about. "Oh."

"Uh-huh. Brigadier Borks had a breakthrough too, or at least a mini version of one, when he unlocked his storage ability. I don't necessarily—" I ducked the crustacean launched through the space where my head had been. I shot an unamused glare at Claws, which only caused her to burst into chittering laughter. "Where was I? I don't necessarily think it's one way or the other. I reckon both humans and spirit beasts can have a breakthrough of either kind. That's my assumption, anyway. Ellis is probably the bloke to ask, though."

Stop! Snips hissed, holding up a claw.

Despite her penchant for trickery, Corporal Claws skidded to a halt on the grass, having to engage all four legs as brakes to stop before slamming into the undefended Snips.

She may have been getting trounced by Claws and her new level of power, but Snips wasn't the kind of crab to call a stop to things. I raised an eyebrow at her, curious what had caused it.

Completely ignoring all of us, she watched a lone bee as it zipped around in the canopy above.

"It's just a bee, Snips," I said. "Isn't it?"

She blew negative bubbles back, her eye trailing the furiously buzzing insect.

"What is she seeing that we aren't?" Maria asked, tapping her chin.

Its buzzing seemed a little panicked, sure, but they did that sometimes. I just assumed they'd seen a bird or been surprised by an otter zooming past them at Mach 1. Snips was positive, though, so I sent my awareness outward, trying to understand.

I found . . . nothing.

A few more bees of the same kind came from the surrounding trees, apparently answering the call. They emitted the same tone, and when they all arrived, the original bee took off, heading through the trees. The others followed, and so did Snips, her steps silent as she crept after them along the forest floor. Maria, Claws, and I shared a shrug before trailing after her.

As we continued moving, I recognized that we were heading toward the hive of bees to the southwest of Queen Bee's and Bumblebro's abodes. More and more of the insects appeared, the first insect leading the procession back home. Now that there were dozens of them, or perhaps because I'd been listening to it long enough, I understood what had gotten Snips's attention.

They were *pissed.*

Though it held a touch of panic, it was fervent anger that droned from their wings, the sound only getting more intense as others joined the procession. From a low hum to immutable cacophony, the sound built and built, reverberating off the surrounding trunks. There were hundreds now, all charging back home.

"Smell that?" Maria asked.

"Huh?" With my hearing being assaulted by what felt like a jet engine's worth of buzzing, it took me a moment to parse my sense of smell. The moment I did, I knew exactly what she was talking about. "Honey."

It was thick on the air, its scent making my fasted stomach growl.

Snips was the first to round the trunk ahead and catch sight of the hive's entrance. The moment she did, she froze. Claws was next. Her head jarred backward, her jaw dropping open to reveal her needle-sharp teeth.

"What has you two so . . ." Maria said, trailing off as we caught sight of what had the bees in a tizzy.

Something large, covered in fur, and a little too dangerous for my liking, had broken into the hive.

"No fracking way . . ." Maria continued, stealing the words from my mouth.

CHAPTER FORTY-FOUR

Ambush Predators

Deep within the forest to the west of my property, light streamed down through the canopy. A pleasant breeze flowed past the trees, bringing with it the scents of wet grass, pollen, and something indescribably sweet. I had spent the waking hours with my girlfriend, and we were currently doing a little side quest before going to Tropica and getting Sue's deadly coffee-and-croissant combo.

It was, by all measurable metrics, a pleasant morning. Well, if one was to ignore the one-ton creature currently sleeping off a predawn snack, that is.

"Fischer . . ." Maria whispered, leaning toward me.

"Yeah?"

She opened her mouth to respond but paused, her finger swirling before her as if the movement might help divine the correct words to use. Eventually, it worked. "What the frack is *that*?" she blurted, gesturing at the creature with both hands.

"That, my love, is a bear."

The massive beast had its belly pressed to the ground and buried the vulnerable parts of its head under both of its massive arms. The poor bees were waging a full-on war against their honey-stealing foe. For all their efforts, the bear was having a cheeky little nap, relying on its thick fur and thicker skin to keep them away.

Maria gaped for a long moment before responding. "Is it . . . I don't know. Ascended? A spirit beast? Already a god?"

"Nope. Just a regular bear."

"Then why is it so *big* if it's not a spirit beast?"

I rubbed my chin. "That's valid. It's pretty bloody big."

"So it *is* a spirit beast?"

"What? No. It's big, but still a regular ol' bear. It's not even close to ascension."

Claws and Snips had been slowly creeping forward, getting closer to it one step at a time. I couldn't see their eyes from my position, but I knew for a fact that they would be sparkling with curiosity.

"You've never seen a bear?" I asked.

"No. I've heard about them, though. Dad said he saw plenty of them when he was off at war."

"Did people call them big?"

"Well, yeah, but when your dad gets drunk and tells you there are creatures as big as a cart, you don't really believe him. And even if you do . . ."

"Seeing is different from believing," I finished.

"Yeah . . ."

Claws and Snips were right beside the creature now, leaning as close as they could without drawing the bees' ire. As I focused on the attacking insects again, I noticed an intruder. When I squinted at the larger specimen, it waved at me, and a moment later, came to buzz before my face. Seven more of them came, likely the ones sent to guard this area of the forest.

"Fellas," I said, "why didn't you tell me that there was a whole-ass *bear* out here disturbing the peace?"

The small collection of Buzzy Boys made a confused tone with their wings.

"What? You didn't see it as a threat?"

They made an affirmative buzz, some hanging their heads in shame.

"Huh. I guess you have a point. Would you have done something about it if it became a threat?"

Yes, they buzzed again confidently.

"All right. This one is on me. New orders: if you come across any beings, human or creature, that could threaten the life of a regular human, you come let me know, okay?"

They nodded, saluted, and three of them split off.

"Wait!" I called before they could get too far away. "Tell *Barry*. Not me. Only let me know if you can't find any of the senior congregation or an animal pal to inform."

They saluted again and split off, going to relay the order.

"Those are some good boys," Maria said.

"I know, right? Don't know what we'd do without them."

I caught swift movement in the corner of my eye, and with my enhanced speed, I was able to turn toward the bear in time to see Claws smack its ear.

"Claws! What the—"

A mighty growl cut me off as the bear lifted its head and sniffed the air. Before its eyes even opened, it reached a paw over and dipped it into the exposed honeycomb. The claw tore through it like tissue paper, and the honey-covered limb drifted back to its mouth, the bear still not deigning to open its eyes as it lapped at its paw.

I felt a pang of regret for the bees. They'd put so much hard work into their hive, and the bear was so easily destroying it. It was a fanciful thought, though, because that was just the way of the world. Predators have to eat, too, and I imagine I'd be doing the exact same thing in the bear's position. Still, it was hard not to feel sorry for them.

While I wasted time considering the moral quandaries of creatures with no concept of human sensibilities, the bear finally opened his eyes. His gaze drifted our way but seemed to look right through us. He licked up every drop of honey from his paw, and just as he was about to reach back in for more, he froze.

He blinked at us, his eyes finally focusing.

"Don't hurt it, Claws. Even if it attacks," I said.

She spun to face me, giving a surprisingly human look that said, *Well, duh.*

"That includes slapping, Claws!" Maria chided, crossing her arms.

I expected the bear to lash out with how close Snips and Claws were, but he slowly got to his feet, ignoring both Claws and Snips, instead staring at Maria and me. He dipped a paw toward the open hive once again, making me genuinely respect the thing's audacity. He scooped up a massive clump of comb, placed it on the ground between us, and started backing away.

Never once taking his eyes from us, he nudged the offering closer before continuing his careful retreat. The swarming bees were completely ignored, all of his attention reserved for us. When he got far enough away, he turned and fled, moving with more grace than I expected such a creature to possess.

Claws watched him go, her body language screaming that she wanted to give chase. When his footsteps had receded from our range of hearing, she turned on me, her eyes fierce.

Friend! she chirped, pointing with both forepaws in the direction the bear had fled.

"You want the bear as an animal pal?" I asked.

"Then why did you slap him?" Maria demanded, her voice not so much disappointed as genuinely confused.

She made no noise, instead shrugging at Maria then nodding her head at me, so fast that I worried she might take off.

I put on a conspiratorial face. "I don't know, Maria. What do you think? Should we befriend this bear?"

Her eyes sparkled with amusement when they met mine. "Gee, I don't know, Fischer. It might be a bit dangerous. He was a *really* big bear."

Claws screeched, denying this fact.

"I'm sorry, Claws," I said, making my lips form a line to hide my smile. "It might be too risky, you know? And what about all the food he would need? He might eat as much fish as we catch in a day!"

She pointed at her chest, declaring that she would handle it.

Snips came up beside Claws and patted her on the back. Blowing bubbles of apology, she shook her carapace, only the twinkle in her eye giving away her understanding of the farce.

Claws's little head darted between us all, despair creeping over her face. She took a half step toward me, her mouth downturned and eyes welling with tears. It was too much for me, and just when I was about to cancel the whole act, Maria dashed forward.

"Kidding! We were kidding!" She swept Claws into her arms. "Please stop looking at us like that! I'll get you *two* bear friends if you like!"

Claws sniffed and covered her face with both two paws, her body shaking as she started to . . . *Hang on a second.*

A choked chittering came from her, and though she tried to hide her smile, I couldn't miss the gleam of her needle-sharp pearls.

"We've been had, Maria."

"Claws!" Maria held her overhead, which did nothing to diminish the trilling laughter now coming from the otter.

Claws raised her forearms toward the sky, booming with victorious giggles at having tricked us.

"Yes, yes." Maria sighed. "Your mischief is unmatched. You win this round."

Claws nodded as Maria set her back down, preening with pride.

"Okay," I said, stepping forward to rub behind Claws's ear. "Jokes aside, we'll have to do it right. We can't catch and force him to ascend, but if we can make something tasty enough for him to eat that gives him enough chi, I'll happily accept him into our little family."

"Especially with how polite he is," Maria added, pointing at the honeycomb he'd pushed toward us. "If I didn't know better, I'd assume he was already most of the way toward ascension."

"Yeah. He's a pretty smart fella. Kinda like the drop bears we used to get back home."

"Drop bears? What are those?"

"Nasty things. They're ambush predators closely related to the koala bear. They hide in trees and drop on top of people when they walk underneath."

Maria spun to stare where the bear had gone, then slowly turned back toward me. "Please tell me you're joking."

"Afraid not. If you ever go to Australia, keep your eyes on the treetops."

She shivered. "I'm fine here, thanks."

"Clever girl. But yeah, the bear is clever. As far as I can tell, him pushing the honeycomb our way wasn't so much an offering as it was a distraction for his escape."

Maria peered up at the surrounding treetops, keeping her peepers peeled for any would-be ambush bears. When she saw nothing, she turned her beautiful smile my way. "I seem to recall being promised a full breakfast from Tropica's finest bakery."

I grinned at her. "Of course, my lady. Snips, would you mind covering up the hive as best you can without hurting it? I'd hate if they weren't able to recover from this."

She blew resolute bubbles and snapped a crisp salute before whirling, scuttling closer, and assessing the damage with a keen eye. Claws dashed up too, apparently intent on helping.

"Shall we?" I asked, holding my arm out toward Maria.

She closed the distance with a hop, looped her elbow through mine, and got on her tippy toes to plant a peck on my cheek.

Despite this morning's events, that small contact of her lips made my heart flutter as if it was the first time she'd deigned to kiss me. Arm in arm, we wandered off toward Tropica, leaving our animal pals behind to secure the beehive.

Deeper within the forest, a large creature ran for its very life. Though it traveled near full speed, its steps were almost silent, telling of a life spent keenly aware of its position in the food chain.

Another bear of its species might assume it was an apex predator. Might assume that, given its size, there was nothing and no one in these lands that could hope to match its power. This creature, for better or worse, knew better.

That surety urged it on, fueling its flight from the two-legged adversaries. Their posture, their very stances, were just the same as the first and last time he'd encountered such beings.

It was long ago, and though he was just a cub at the time, the memories would never fade.

The images flashed through his mind. Their feigned weakness. The ambush. The flames. The sharpened sticks. The way their faces shifted, revealing their odd-shaped teeth. *My mother . . .*

The thoughts became too painful, so he pushed them away.

Before long, he came to the entrance of his den. Sparing one last glance back into the forest, he crawled within, winding his way down into the narrow gap between rocks. There, he rested, both happy he'd managed to find a hive and disappointed that he'd had to abandon it.

CHAPTER FORTY-FIVE

Pyre

From the very moment his body made contact with the molten rock, all Rocky knew was pain.

Though the volcano contained the same essence as his explosive chi, it showed him no mercy, doing its very best to burn him away. But even if the world itself thought Rocky would allow himself to be so easily snuffed, it had another thing coming.

The entire time he'd been beneath the surface of the volcano, something within him seemed . . . wrong. It was a part of him, though, so he forced the thought away, knowing that he and his form were flawless, the very pinnacle of evolution.

As soon as he'd felt the magma's searing caress, he'd curled into a ball, protecting his body with a constant barrier of chi. Being surrounded by the same power his core held was a small blessing, but he had to constantly replenish his reserves, recycling the very chi that sought his destruction.

Unlike his boundless source of essence, however, his body was beginning to tire. If he didn't experience a breakthrough soon or find some source of sustenance, he would be in trouble.

That mere heat could threaten Rocky, from a volcano or not, made his blood boil hotter than even the molten rock surrounding him.

This, as with everything else, was Fischer's fault.

His mortal enemy had forced Rocky's claw, and if not for that, Rocky would be back with his beloved mistress right now rather than fighting for his life. The fury built within him, too strong to be denied any longer. Rocky cocked his claws open, gathered power there, and unleashed twin blasts out into the world.

He experienced a brief moment of ecstatic release, which was almost immediately overshadowed by agonizing regret. Using his chi as an attack had diverted power from his shielding, letting the volcano's heat burn his hardened carapace.

His anger at Fischer soared back into his awareness, but he set it aside, needing every ounce of attention to restore the protective bubble around his mighty form. Now that the magma had found an opening, though, it didn't relent so easily. It seemed to fight against his body, the explosive chi no longer seeing him as kin. Primordial fear coursed through Rocky as, for the first time since plunging into the volcano, he truly entertained the fact that he might not make it out.

His life being in danger scoured away any thoughts of Fischer; only images of his spiky mistress remained. Her beautiful face flashed through his mind, her mouth undulating as she blew bubbles of praise for a job well done. When he recalled her turning her back on him the last time he'd seen her, Rocky's resolve started to firm. Though she had made a show of disapproving of his methods, she would be expecting him to come home.

He had to survive. He had to prove himself and return to her.

There was only a single path out of the situation he had mired himself in. He had to make a breakthrough.

With every fiber of his body agreeing with the decision, he delved further into himself, doing his best to ignore the pain searing his carapace. It was nigh impossible, the agony rolling over him too potent to ignore. But Rocky was no mere crab. He was the strongest follower of his magnificent mistress, and with her image rooted firmly in mind, he sent his awareness spiraling down toward his core. The sensations of his body grew numb, as if they were happening to someone else. Smiling internally at his prowess, Rocky sank into his core.

What he found there made his hopes climb. His core was near to bursting, every inch of the space absolutely *filled* with explosive chi. He pressed on the walls with his will, metaphorically puffing his chest out at how easy this was going to be. The outside world froze as he imagined what he wanted his core to do, and just as his fear of death was almost completely banished, his expanding walls hit something . . . solid? A spike of panic rose up from deep within his consciousness, making him double his efforts.

But no matter how hard he pushed, the solid object didn't budge.

Anxiety blossoming, he sent his attention toward the outside of his core, intent on finding whatever it was. Before he could leave the bounds of his spiritual space, however, he came to a stop. It wasn't outside of his core—it was *inside*. Wrapping around the entirety of his core, there was a bubble of black chi, so thin that he'd never noticed it. He focused his immense will on the anomaly, and when a familiar feeling washed over him, he realized his folly. He *had* noticed it before—the black bubble was what had caused the feeling of wrongness ever since he'd jumped into the volcano.

He pictured it dissipating, getting absorbed into the rest of his being, but the bubble rallied against him, parrying each mental blow.

He didn't have time for this. His body could burn away at any moment when the molten rock broke through the thin layer of protection surrounding him. Taking a metaphorical breath, he tried to calm himself, knowing panic wasn't of use in the present moment. Instead of fighting against it, he focused his awareness on melding with the bubble in an attempt to guide it out of his body. Surprisingly, it worked. Convinced that he wasn't a threat, the alien essence allowed him to be a momentary part of it.

Rocky instantly regretted his decision.

It wasn't the chi of a crab. It was the disgusting chi of a *human*. Just as the Church of Carcinization had been tinged with the blessed flavor of crab, he had been afflicted by the rancid stench of humanity. Worse, the chi wasn't explosive, instead feeling like the power Corporal Claws wielded. Abruptly, Rocky knew why the volcano sought to destroy him. It wasn't going after him at all—it was going after this unwelcome bubble that was trying to hijack Rocky's future.

He had to get rid of it. With his awareness melded to it, he pictured its banishment. But the moment he switched up his intent, the power fought back. It focused its electrical chi on him, seeking to send Rocky flying from his own core. They warred for what felt like minutes, and the longer the fight went on, the more indignant Rocky grew. How had he missed this? How had he not been aware that a usurper had taken root within him? He was just as angry at himself as he was at the intruder.

But how had a human spirit crawled its way into his being? What manner of treachery had facilitated this betrayal? All at once, the realization struck him, hard enough to rock his consciousness and make him almost lose his battle against the foreign entity.

It was the human he'd used as fuel to ascend.

Rocky had thought he'd consumed the man's essence entirely, but a remnant echo of the human remained. It had been feeding off of his chi this entire time, growing in power as Rocky gained strength. It was a leech. A parasite. A tumor.

It had to be purged.

Now that he knew what to look for, Rocky felt like a fool. The way it fought back, the way its will felt so different to his own, and the way it seemed to slip away from his grasp each time Rocky almost took hold of it. *Of course* it was human, and *of course* it was one of those troublesome cultivators from the capital. These self-deprecating thoughts rolled through Rocky, making a fury greater than ever before bubble to the surface, more visceral even than his hatred for Fischer.

Prepared to lean into the rage as a means of fighting off this invader, he came up short when he felt the source of his fury. It radiated from his core as it always did, but now that he was within his own soul space, he discovered the true nexus.

The fury wasn't his. It was the human's. The black bubble of will was unstable, and as it cycled through negative emotions, they resonated within Rocky, impacting his consciousness. This interloper wasn't only stealing his life force like some bloodsucking parasite.

It was also poisoning his mind.

A cold hatred simmered low in Rocky's body. And this time, the emotion was entirely his own, so passionate that it drew Rocky from his core for the slightest of moments. When he discovered the state of his wondrous carapace, he should have felt despair. It was burning away, the volcano's molten rock having scorched sections of him in an attempt to seek and destroy the human's chi. Instead of being consumed by despair, his simmering hatred came to a boil.

In an incessant stream, every pivotal experience he'd had since awakening played through his mind. Each moment Rocky chose violence, to the detriment of those around him. Each time he embarrassed and brought shame to his beloved Snips.

Each time Rocky saw his actions as justified, lashing out at anyone who dared anger him. They had all led to this very moment, culminating in Rocky's annihilation. Even now, the invader's poisonous thoughts infected him, fueling the fire that was his hatred.

Though he now knew its origin, Rocky didn't fight off its influence. He let it roll over him, the flames growing ever brighter. His core climbed to a blistering heat, yet his resolve remained cold. Knowing his demise was nigh, Rocky sent himself spiraling down into his core once more. This usurper had sealed his fate, but Rocky wasn't yet dead.

He would use its own toxin to destroy it.

He let the black bubble of fury, hatred, and indignation wash over him. He drew the emotions in, demanding ever more. The bonfire within Rocky grew to an inferno, and just when he felt he was going to explode, he channeled it toward his core's intruder. It crashed into the man's echo, and it tried to parry, tried to fight off Rocky as it had so easily done before. This time, Rocky blew right through the defenses. Fear radiated throughout his body, but he knew it wasn't his.

Urged on by his tormenter's terror, Rocky imagined the inferno exploding from within him. It slammed into the bubble from inside. At first, it held its ground, its black tendrils having had months to root themselves within the interior of Rocky's core. But then Rocky's cold intent lanced into it and tore a hole through the dark influence. The gap was only millimeters thick, and the bubble sought to reform immediately, withdrawing power from its roots to bolster the barrier.

Rocky's chi was faster.

As if his core was sapient, every drop of his essence slammed into that small gap, ripping it wide. In the blink of an eye, the human's remnant soul was forced into a tiny ball, each and every root pulled free of Rocky's core. Even minutes ago, Rocky would have tried to consume it for power. Now, he just wanted it gone. With a final push, he forced it out of his body and into the volcano.

The explosive chi held there descended immediately, the rancorous human's soul screeching like hundreds of beings as it burned away into nothing.

At war with the searing agony of Rocky's body, a wave of elation washed over him. Banishing the human's spirit had taken all of his strength, and though the magma no longer sought his destruction, it was too late. The damage was too severe, and as Rocky felt himself sinking deeper into the volcano that was to be his funeral pyre, he accepted his fate.

His mind felt clear for the first time since his awakening. No longer did hatred and fury afflict him, coloring his decisions. He had been poisoned for so long that to be free of it made triumph radiate throughout him. Despite his life coming to an end, he finally had a taste of who he was.

Rocky wasn't, as Fischer would have said, a prick.

This realization made his body feel light, as if the universe caressed him and eased his pains.

Rocky's only regret was that his spiky mistress wouldn't know what became of him, but she would be okay. She was surrounded by good people, after all. His carapace started to tingle, even his pain receptors beginning to fail as his awareness faded. He got the sense that the magma was swelling up around him, the world intent on witnessing his departure.

When the volcano's chi rushed into Rocky, his vision went black.

CHAPTER FORTY-SIX

Birds on the Wind

Well, good morning!" Sue called across the square. She had at least a dozen people waiting for coffees, yet she took a moment to give Maria and me a scandalous eyebrow wiggle. "Did you two have a pleasant morning?"

Heat rose to my face, and when I glanced Maria's way for assistance, I saw a furious blush climbing to her cheeks.

Sue chortled, throwing her head high as she delighted in our awkwardness.

Letting out a sigh, I grabbed Maria's hand and led her to the back of the line.

"So mean," Maria said, laughing and shaking her head. "I guess she earned that, though, considering her assistance."

"Worth it. Wish she'd been a little less public about it, though. I'm guessing some of the villagers were able to infer her meaning based on the glances we got."

"Why don't you look at me like that anymore?" a woman whispered to her husband a few spots ahead of us in line, nudging him in the ribs and smirking at him. "When was the last time you blushed around me?"

"Oh, you want something to blush about, do you?" he replied. "Just you wait until I'm done with the fields today. I'll show you something that—"

I immediately retracted my hearing, shooting a wide-eyed look at Maria.

She stared back at me, covering her mouth to hold in her laughter. We both lost it.

"Heavens," Maria eventually said, wiping tears from her eyes. "Good for them."

I luxuriated in the sun's warmth beaming down from above as we slipped into a comfortable silence. Maria's soft hand in mine was a grounding presence, sweeping away any lingering embarrassment from Sue's not-so-subtle display. Before I knew it, we were at the front of the line, once more under the traitorous cafe owner's scrutiny.

"You two look positively vibrant!" she said. "Must have been a wonderfully restful evening."

"Dear," Sturgill warned, poking his head around the dividing wall that hid the kitchen. "Are you bothering our friends?"

"Oh, pah!" She brushed flour from her apron. "Just having a little fun. So what can I get for you two?"

"Just the usual, thanks," I replied, giving Sturgill a thankful nod.

Sorry, he mouthed, rolling his eyes and only barely dodging the balled-up tea towel flung toward his head.

Sue shot him a pout as he laughed and retreated back out of sight. "Jokes aside," she said. "I was happy to be of service. That father of yours is as stale as yesterday's pastries."

"Thank you," Maria replied, staring at the ground as her cheeks turned rosy once more.

"Don't mention it." Sue gave us a wide smile as she flowed over toward the coffee machine. "Won't be long!"

We stepped aside, joining the milling common folk waiting for their breakfast.

As we strode around the side of the headland, I took my last bite of croissant. Its flaky, buttery goodness was just as good as ever, and after swallowing, I chased it down with a swig of coffee. The bitterness was perfectly balanced against the croissant's sweetness, making a contented sigh escape my lips.

"Yeah," Maria agreed, holding her cup in both hands. "Same."

The sun heralded our way to the side of my house, and the moment we stepped into view of my back deck, two creatures met us.

Corporal Claws clutched onto Maria's front, scrambling around her torso to sniff at her ear. Giggling, Maria raised her shoulder, trying to protect herself from the barrage of sniffs. I wasn't able to spare much of my attention on the adorable interaction, however, because a crab slammed into my chest, hissing overjoyed bubbles. I caught Snips with one arm, skidding to a stop just before my feet met the sand.

"Whoa!" I laughed. "Good to see you too."

She rubbed the top of her shell into my body, her hisses getting quieter. Through some silent agreement, Snips and Claws abruptly swapped positions, the former leaping toward Maria and the latter sailing for me. Claws landed on my shoulder and wrapped herself around my neck, becoming an extremely warm and cute scarf.

"We were just about to go for a midmorning fish. Are you two keen on coming along?"

Claws grinned at me, grabbed me by the chin, and directed my vision toward my back deck. Apparently they'd been busy doing some fishing of their own after covering the beehive.

There was a mature shore fish sitting on the table beside the barbecue, surrounded by herbs and spices they'd already picked out. Set on top of a plate, a large chunk of honeycomb glistened, its yellow namesake pooling below it. I raised an eyebrow as I peered down at Claws, whose forepaws were steepled.

Yes? she seemed to chirp, giving me a nonchalant look.

"Where did you get that honeycomb, Claws?"

She leaped up onto the barbecue, one paw on her hip and the other tapping her chin as she inspected it, pretending she'd never seen it before.

Stolen, Snips hissed, shrugging.

Claws whirled on her, frowning and unleashing a mighty chirp.

Snips merely shrugged again, and I bent down to pat her head. "Thanks for the honesty, Snips."

Claws crossed her arms, looked skyward, and gave a dismissive sniff, telling me exactly how she felt.

"Oh yeah?" I asked, scooping her up. "Too good for me, huh?" I tickled her underarms until she was struggling to breathe, finally letting her go after she begged for mercy. "I don't mind that you took a little bit of their honey as long as they have enough to sustain the hive. You did leave enough for them to survive, right?"

She gave me an indignant chirp that died halfway through when she realized I was teasing.

"Sorry," I said. "I couldn't help myself." I stroked her head, scratching that spot behind her ear that she always leaned into. "Now, are these ingredients for what I think they are?"

Seeing as Claws was lost in the scritches, Snips blew affirmative bubbles.

I grinned. "Well, we'd better get started then, huh?"

Beneath the former capital city of Theogonia, Augustus Reginald Gormona let out a deep sigh. It was time.

"Before I start," he said, "can you check the locket one last time, wife?"

"Of course." Penelope grabbed the thin chain around her neck, tugging on it to reveal one of the few working relics Gormona still possessed.

Augustus strode forward, and when he reached out, his fingers shook. Clenching his jaw, Augustus balled his fists, beyond angry that his body displayed weakness. After a long moment, he extended them once more. He peered into the locket as he flicked it open, finding a soft blinking light.

"Trent yet lives." Augustus nodded, more to himself than anyone else. "We can begin."

"Please forgive my insolence, my king," Tom Osnan Sr. said, taking a knee. "I would be remiss if I didn't offer one last time—please allow me to take your place."

Augustus fought down his urge to blast the man, knowing if he were to strike out, he might accidentally end his oldest friend's life. His gaze drifted over his ringless fingers, the sight bringing him a modicum of clarity. It was the influence of his chi that encouraged violence, and it was to be ignored. He let out a tense breath that did nothing to calm the fury building in his core.

"If I were to let you cultivate the forbidden chi, Tom, what would stop you from seizing the crown's power for yourself?"

Tom's face bunched in anger. "My king. I would never willingly betray the crown."

"And I wish I could believe that, Tom. I truly do."

"For what it's worth," Tryphena said. "The auditor made it clear that Tom's intentions were aligned with Gormona, even after he lost his battle. Perhaps letting him channel the power is a good idea, Father?"

"Ah, my dear." Augustus placed a hand on her shoulder, always appreciating his daughter's input. "You are wise beyond your years, but this task falls to me. No one can truly know the secrets another's heart holds. There is no one else that can do it."

She bit the inside of her cheek, then swiftly put on a neutral face.

He gave her a loving smile. "Are you having second thoughts now that we are here, daughter?"

She thought for a long moment before speaking. "It's not that I don't believe in you. I merely worry about my father." She bowed at the waist. "I'm sorry. The fault lies entirely within me."

"You need not bow, Tryphena. Your worry is appreciated. In fact, I might question your intentions if you didn't care about my well-being. However . . ." He let a silence stretch, emphasizing the importance of his next words. "Recall our conversations on the way here. I am the correct choice. The correct sacrifice."

She dipped her head, her hair falling to hide her face. "As you say, Father. Forgive my weakness."

He shot a look at Penelope, wordlessly ordering her to comfort their daughter. "And you, Tom . . ."

The lord raised his eyes, still containing some heat.

Augustus gave him the smallest of nods. "You still have a place in the capital, and your family will be a part of the rebuilding process. If your words are true and you are attempting to sacrifice yourself for the good of the kingdom, I thank you."

Tom bowed, biting back any retort. "If you change your mind, Your Majesty, I am ever your humble servant. Give the word and I will join you in cultivating the corrupted chi."

"You'd willingly join me in potential madness?"

"Both for my king, and my oldest friend." Tom raised his head once more, and when his eyes met Augustus's, every hint of anger was gone. "Even if we didn't have the bloodlines we do, and the madness was a sure thing, I would still join you. If for nothing other than the insult to our kingdom, I would happily assist in the destruction of that man."

More than anything else Tom had done since his failure, this statement made Augustus begin to truly forgive him. He nodded, acknowledging Tom Osnan Sr.'s resolve. "I appreciate that, Tom, but I believe our forces will already overwhelm them."

"As you say, my king."

Augustus heard the doubt in his voice, making his fury bubble up anew. "I see you do not believe me. No, don't reply. I believe that is due to ignorance." He looked toward the merchant Marcus. "Fetch them."

"Fetch them?" Tom asked, his brow furrowing. In the blink of an eye, realization struck him. "Oh . . ."

"That is correct." Augustus grinned. "It is not only me that will be attempting to channel."

A moment later, Marcus returned, followed by six sets of footsteps. The handlers' faces were a mix of stricken, excited, and accepting.

"Good," Augustus said. "You're here. Are you aware of your purpose?"

Aisa stepped forward, her eyes alight with possibility. "Yes, my king. We await your instruction."

A manic giggle came from the cell beside them, making each of the handlers' faces dart toward it. To their unawakened eyes, they'd only see a blackened cell. Augustus watched as Tiberius stepped forward into the light of their torch.

"When you are ready, Tiberius."

"Helloooo," Tiberius sang, twisting his head and peering at them with one eye, the orange flame's light giving his face and birdlike posture a horrifying appearance. "A pleasure to meet you, ladies." He giggled again and sat cross-legged, facing them. "I will be your teacher in the ways of cultivation. Copy my posture, if you would."

"Copy."

"Copy!"

"*Copy!*" came the voices from the other cells.

One of them cawed, making a slew of unhinged laughs bounce off the walls.

Augustus sat down cross-legged, as did the rest of the handlers, who were now looking much less sure of themselves.

"Imagine, if you will, that you are birds on the wind," Tiberius said, peering at all of them. "The surrounding air is the essence of Theogonia, the granter of *strength*." He spread his arms wide. "Now draw the winds into your abdomen."

When Augustus did so, his core protested, doing everything it could to keep the foreign chi out. Clenching his muscles, he ignored its complaints, drawing more and more of the forbidden chi toward his navel area.

CHAPTER FORTY-SEVEN

First Contact

When Rocky awoke in what must be the afterlife, he let out a contented sigh. Though he was now in a different realm to his beloved mistress and the rest of Tropica, his body had a weightlessness he hadn't experienced since being a regular crab.

Gone was the influence of the parasitic man, his poisonous guidance nowhere to be seen.

Rocky's awareness was clear, leaving only his thoughts in his consciousness. He sent his attention down toward his core, wanting to see what it felt like now that he was in the afterlife. When he entered it and tasted his chi, Rocky's mouth dropped open. His entire nexus was filled to bursting with explosive essence.

Rocky moved his mouth, then froze, confusion washing through him. He still had a physical body. It was surrounded by what felt like the comfiest blanket imaginable, hugging him tight from every direction. He sent his senses outward, and when he discovered the chi there, his thoughts died in their tracks. It wasn't possible . . . was it?

He unfurled his limbs, no longer needing to protect himself against the molten rock that had been trying to destroy him. His body felt . . . different. As he made to move his rear flippers and ascend skyward, his core reached out, and Rocky instinctively knew of a brand-new capability. He sent tendrils of chi out that melded with the explosive essence surrounding him. The next moment, Rocky was ascending through the column of magma, not needing to move a muscle.

When he breached the surface, he opened his eyes.

The sun above was blinding, and he lifted a claw to shield against its light. When he caught sight of his mighty pincer, astonishment shot through him, brighter even than the celestial body above. It was *massive*, and size wasn't where the changes ended. Most of the shell he could see had turned black, interlaced with magma-colored lines. As he watched, the lines grew brighter and duller, shifting as if it was lava exposed to air. With a single burst of chi, he shot over the top of the wall.

Before, it was hundreds of meters down to the magma. Now, lava poured over the side, the volcano actively erupting. As he sailed high above, Rocky got a wonderful view. The small island had become much larger. Where lava had met the ocean, it cooled and hardened into something solid. As more and more lava poured out, the mass expanded. Rocky landed atop the ridge, his chi-covered body standing on the shifting lava even as it flowed out.

Beneath the midday sun, he finally got a good look at himself. The rest of Rocky's carapace was the same as his claw, mostly black and interlaced with small lines of red. It gave him a deadly appearance, and he wondered what his beloved mistress would think of it. As Sergeant Snips flashed through his mind, butterflies took flight in his stomach. His actions while he was affected by the poison had hurt no one more than her. Though he was now free of it, that didn't make up for all the harm he'd done.

A soft hiss of laughter came from him when he realized he was focusing on the wrong thing.

Rocky was *alive*.

It mattered not how long it took. Rocky would make it up to her. Before that, though, he had to get home. He was still so far away, but perhaps that was for the best; he would have time to learn who he truly was without the parasitic human influencing his every thought. The prospect made happiness well up within him, the emotion so foreign that it felt uncomfortable. He'd felt joy before, but it was usually at the expense of someone else or tinged with an underlying hatred that dulled the edges.

There were so many things he would experience for the first time now that he had earned a second life, the first of which he intended to discover immediately.

With anticipatory bubbles coming from his mouth, he spun, extending his claws to the east.

He gathered power there, his core filling his pincers with chi faster than ever before. A split moment later, he leaped high above the volcano, and with nothing but air beneath him, his claws slammed shut. The dual explosions that resulted were so large that their boundaries blurred, becoming a single blast that was larger than the lava-spewing opening. It left behind a cloud just as black as his body, its plumes lit from within by orange and red light.

Rocky could only see these details with his enhanced vision, because the moment his explosions rang out, he *flew*. Only superseded by Fischer's throw from Tropica, he soared higher than his mistress had ever flung him, an overjoyed smile never leaving his face.

Wait for me, Mistress . . .

Beneath the midmorning sun, a man lounged. Despite lying on packed ground, he couldn't have gotten comfier if he tried. All around him, a battle took place, the exchanges violent enough to reverberate within his core. This would have shattered the calm of the average relaxer, making adrenaline course through their veins.

But Deklan was no average relaxer.

"How do you do that?" his brother, Dom, asked.

Deklan cracked an eye and raised his head from where it rested atop his hands. "Do what?"

"Just lie there while those two are sparring. Every time they clash, my core screams that I'm about to be cut in half or burned alive. Sometimes both."

Deklan got up on one elbow, shielding his eyes from the sun with his other hand. In the center of the clearing, Roger and the prince met again. A solid gout of fire launched from Trent's whirling fist, so strong that a wave of heat washed over Deklan. If such a blast had flown for either him or his brother, it would likely be the end of them.

Roger, the man who had apparently been a regular farmer mere months ago, grinned at the approaching inferno. With a flick of his wrist, his own chi sprang into being. Rather than burn away, his essence sought to cut. It tore the prince's attack into ribbons that dissipated into nothing.

Deklan's core recoiled as it felt the reverberations, just as his brother had said. But that was where his body's innate reactions ended. There was no spike of panic, no wide-eyed stare, and no prickling skin.

It was a different story for Dom. He gave a full-body shudder that started in his abdomen, slowly shaking its way out. "Gods above. I'm glad we're on their side."

"Rather impressive, aren't they?"

"That's an understatement . . ."

Trent had backed off, circling to his left. In the blink of an eye, he rocketed forward again with flames jetting from his legs. Deklan raised an eyebrow; he hadn't seen that move before, and he wondered if it was new.

The prince confirmed it a moment later when he darted too far left and lost his footing, having to plant his arms so he didn't faceplant into the packed earth. He immediately sprang back up, his face contorted in rage.

He whirled in a full circle, and when his fists lashed out, Deklan sensed the power swelling there. It was stronger than anything he'd felt from the prince, and he bolted upright, his instincts screaming that Roger needed help against the impending flames.

He took a half step forward, reaching a hand forward, but there was no need. Trent pulled back, returning some of the chi to his core. Unlike Deklan, Roger hadn't responded to the threat at all. When the column of fire came barreling forward, Roger flicked his wrist again. The flame died on the wind, just as the last had.

"That's enough for now," Roger said. "You need to be more in control of your emotions."

Trent clenched his jaw and gave a sharp nod.

"But," Roger continued, "you did well to pull back that strike. It's not easy to recall the chi after letting it out, especially when you're upset." He turned to leave, then called over his shoulder, "And for what it's worth, I would have been fine if you released all of it. You're strong, Trent. Very strong. But you're still no match for me."

Roger strode away, heading for a group of cultivators that were taking notes. Deklan noticed Anna among them, and he gave her a small wave that she swiftly returned before Roger got there.

"I wish I had that strength," Dom said, staring after Trent's departing form.

"I don't know . . ." Deklan also watched him go. "It seems like it came at a cost."

"What do you mean?"

"Don't worry about it," Deklan replied, getting to his feet.

"Where are you going?"

"Just for a little chat. I'll be back in a moment."

Trent had reached his cousin, Keith. The two were thick as thieves, and Deklan didn't miss the slight loss of tension in Trent's shoulders as they began speaking. As they were cultivators, the two former nobles immediately noticed his approach. Their footsteps halting, they spun and waited for him to close the distance.

"What can we do for you, Deklan?" Keith asked. "If you want to spar, we're unfortunately occupied for the—"

"Nah," Deklan interrupted, shaking his head. "Not that. I just wanted to say g'day."

"Oh." Keith smiled, some of his hesitation disappearing. "Well, hello. I really do have to get going, though. I'm working with the smiths today to—"

"No worries!" Deklan interrupted again, grinning. "I was actually hoping to speak to Trent."

Trent's body language shifted, a hint of hostility joining his impassive facade. "Anything you need to say in front of me, you can say in front of my cousin. We don't keep secrets."

Deklan gave a half shrug. "I didn't mean it like that. It's no secret. But if Keith needs to get going, you can catch up to him, yeah?"

The two cousins studied Deklan a little longer.

"If I leave now," Trent said, "you'll come find me later?"

Deklan's grin grew wider. "I imagine I will."

The prince sighed. "Okay, then. I'll come find you soon, Keith."

His cousin nodded, then turned on Deklan. Keith's eyes bored into him. "Before I go, I want to know what it's about."

Trent opened his mouth to reply, but before he could voice his concern, Deklan spoke.

"Well, here's the thing. I only ever see you two hanging out together, and I wanted to talk to you about being friends. Or mates, to borrow Fischer's terminology and *completely* ignore the other connotations that phrase has."

Keith raised an eyebrow, but Trent barked a laugh. "I thought no one else found his use of 'mate' weird. It's fine, Keith. I'll come find you soon."

Assuaged, Keith gave his cousin a nod, Deklan one last glance, and departed.

"So," Deklan said, not waiting for Keith to leave earshot, "I'll cut right to the chase. I reckon you and your cousin and my brother and I would get along well."

"And what makes you say that?" Trent asked, his face impassive as they started strolling.

"First of all, you and I have a little bit of shared history with your dad." Seeing Trent's nostrils flare and mouth form a line, Deklan held up both hands. "That's not to say that we were equally impacted. I don't know the history, but I do know whatever he did was enough to make you spontaneously combust. I feel like that automatically trumps the bullshit he put my family through. I'm not going to diminish your experience, but you can't deny that there's a slight similarity between us, right?"

Trent stopped walking, spinning to raise an eyebrow at Deklan. "You don't mince your words, do you?"

"Not even a little."

"And you're telling me that my father, despite that, called you a friend?"

"Do you find that hard to believe?"

"Hard to believe?" Trent repeated, a small smile playing on his lips. "I'd find it *impossible* to believe if a former auditor hadn't confirmed your story."

Deklan shrugged. "It was a hard time for him."

"Good," Trent said as his legs started moving once more. "A little turmoil is the least he deserves."

"For what it's worth, I'd call it more than *a little* turmoil. I'm slightly ashamed at how much joy I get from looking back on his overreactions when reading names from the relics' screens."

Trent snorted. "I wish I had seen it."

Deklan made a dramatic groan and clutched his chest as he fell to his knees. *"An . . . an entire flock of birds!"* He fell to his back, splaying his legs out wide. "The gods vex me!"

The laugh that came from Trent's throat was like music to Deklan's ears. He stood up, feigned looking down at a screen, and froze. "The Beetle Boys . . . ? Fat Rat Pack . . . ?" As he fell to his knees again, he let out an exaggerated cry, like you'd hear from a noble lady in a play. *"Lizard Wizard has gone on the attack!"* He fell to his back again, pretending to faint.

"Stop!" Trent wheezed, wiping away tears as he descended further into what was, in Deklan's opinion, a much-needed giggle. "I can't take any more."

Deklan brushed dirt off his clothing as he got back to his feet. "If you ever need a good laugh, come find me. There are plenty more where that came from."

"Okay, maybe I can see why he liked you so much. Even if he is a self-important prick." Trent's gaze went distant, and when his shoulders went tense, Deklan suspected that he was once more lost in the past.

"Can I be blunt with you, Trent?"

"Please do," he replied, still staring forward. "I've had enough political games and lies for a lifetime."

"Good. I think you should rely more on the church—on the people of New Tropica."

"That's easy for you to say." His jaw firmed. "You haven't experienced what I have."

"I know. And like I said before, I'm not trying to diminish that. But you're surrounded by some pretty good people. If you ever need to get what happened off your chest, I'll always have a free ear. Or if you want a fishing partner, hit me up any time of day." He shrugged. "Or night, I suppose. I don't need as much sleep as I used to."

"Still getting used to that myself." Trent smiled again, but it didn't reach his eyes. Swift as a summer storm, his uncaring mask had slipped back into place. "Thanks for letting me know, Deklan. I appreciate it."

"Sure. No worries, as Fischer would say."

Trent looked at him for a moment longer, and just when Deklan thought he'd say something, the prince turned and left.

Exhaling a silent breath, Deklan returned to his brother.

Dom raised an eyebrow at him when he got there. "Did it go according to plan?"

"You're not going to ask what I was doing?"

"Nah. I picked up at least that much from what I overheard." Dom ran a hand through his hair as he closed his eyes and smiled, letting the sun hit his face. "So how did it go?"

"Pretty well." In one smooth motion, Deklan returned to his earlier spot on the cleared ground. Within the blink of an eye, he was lounging once more, also luxuriating in the sun's rays. "Much better than I expected."

"A good first contact, huh?"

Deklan shot a glance his brother's way, and they shared a grin. "Agreed," he said. "A good first contact."

CHAPTER FORTY-EIGHT

The World Itself

O kay, Snips," I said. "When you're ready."
No response came, so I tore my eyes from the barbecue before me, casting a glance her way. "Snips? You right?"

She shook her head, returning to the present and blowing apologetic bubbles.

"No need to apologize," Maria said from my side. "No harm, no foul."

I nodded my agreement as Snips scuttled toward me and leaped into my arms. I held her out between the herbs, spices, and the fish, letting her season as she willed. I couldn't help but raise an appreciative eyebrow at her selection; she had clearly been paying attention to me when I was cooking. The flavors selected would pair well with what was arguably the most important ingredient.

As if reading my mind, Claws leaped into Maria's arm and gestured down at the honeycomb, unleashing a questioning chirp.

"Not yet," I said.

She crossed her arms and pouted, making Maria laugh and rub her head reassuringly.

"Have some patience, Claws," she said, stroking her softly. "If we rush the process, it might not work."

Letting out an aggrieved sigh, Claws finally nodded, accepting our words.

Completely unbothered, Snips had continued seasoning the fish, going back to add extra sprinkles here and there. I watched without adding my advice, content for this to be a collaborative effort. With any luck, the System might consider it another requirement for the quest I was on.

My oldest foe took that slight acknowledgment as an opportunity to strike out at me.

Quest: Group Project
Objective: [Error. Insufficient Power.]
Reward: [Error. Insufficient Power.]

"Uggghhh," I complained.

Snips froze, shooting me a worried glance.

"Sorry." I rubbed the top of her head. "Not you. I thought about that quest I'm on, and the System hit me with some error bullshit."

"I'm guessing it did so without you requesting it," Maria said. "Which reminds me, we never did speak about why you were so adamant about not reading your advancements."

"Oh, really? I'd completely forgotten," I lied, grinning and shooting her a wink.

"Riiight," she drawled. "The man with perfect recall somehow forgot that I wanted to talk about something he avoids."

"Weird, right?"

When I didn't continue yapping, she nudged me in the side. "Come on. Out with it." She held up a finger as an afterthought. "Unless it's going to give you some sort of awakening that leads to an explosion. In that case, I'd appreciate it if you let me go around the corner before you say it out loud."

I tried to give her a flat look, but it failed spectacularly; I couldn't help but join in with the beautiful smile she gave me.

If I was being honest with myself, I'd completely avoided thinking about the notifications and my subsequent aversion to them. The moment I brought them to mind, a familiar tightness appeared in my chest, feeling as though vines had wrapped themselves around my torso and squeezed. I was unaware of the cause, but this was the exact sensation that always came over me.

It was only natural that I tried to push System notifications away when this was how they made me feel, wasn't it?

Thinking back, though, that wasn't how it had always been. In the beginning, I'd been excited by the idea of the gamelike mechanic. It was new and novel, a reminder that I'd left Earth behind and arrived in a new world. But then the notifications had continued being, well, useless. *Insufficient power. Superfluous systems offline*, I quoted in my head, repeating the System's bothersome mantra for the first couple of months that I'd been here. That had been annoying, sure, but nothing like the sheer anxiety that seemed to constrict me now when the System spoke up.

"I think . . ." I said, verbally processing. "That they might be a confirmation of my power?"

"Hmmm." Maria rubbed her chin. "And acknowledging your power means you should take on more responsibility?"

I reeled back, her statement like a punch to my nervous system. "Uh, judging by the panic that just shot through me, I'd say yes."

"Oh, Fischer." In one smooth movement, she stepped in and slipped an arm around my back. The other went around my front, and when she clasped her fingers and pulled me tight, the squeeze she gave me was nothing like the lingering vines wrapping around my chest. A calm ease resonated from everywhere her body met mine, making the vines recede and my breaths come easier. "Even if it is a confirmation of your power, who cares what anyone else wants from you?" she asked. "Myself included."

"Tell that to Barry," I said, smirking.

"Barry can kiss rocks."

I barked a laugh that made the last vestiges of tightness leave me. "It's *kick* rocks," I corrected. "Barry can *kick* rocks."

"Yeah, well, he can kiss them too for all I care." She leaned back so she could look into my eyes, her hair falling away from her face. "Thank you for not exploding with that realization. It was much appreciated."

I laughed again, any memory of my anxiety gone. "You're most welcome, though the lack of a breakthrough could be because I haven't discovered a fix for it."

"You already have the solution, silly. It's that mindfulness you're always talking about. And if that doesn't work, just come talk to me so I can *squeeze* it out of you." She emphasized the point by pulling herself in and doing her best to crush me. My body was much too strong, so it just felt like a rather nice hug.

"Will do," I replied, wrapping my arms around her upper body.

Two creatures leaped up onto us, Claws perching atop my head and Snips clinging to my back. I closed my eyes, focusing on all the love they were offering. "I don't know what I'd do without you girls."

Claws let out a self-satisfied chirp as her upside-down head smiled at me, telling me she was all too aware I'd be lost without her.

Maria and I both laughed this time. Snips and Claws joined in, Snips with soft hisses and Claws with a maniacal cackle that would make any passersby assume she was evil.

"Okay," I said. "Let's get this meal started. If we wanna win over a new friend, we're gonna have to make something wonderful."

Claws's villainous chuckle immediately ceased. She leaped up onto the barbecue, staring at me as she awaited instructions.

"Now that Snips has applied her seasonings, we should cook the fish. If we add the honey too soon, it'll likely cook off and get diminished by the meat's juices, so I'm thinking we drizzle it over after. The scent will attract the bear. Also," I added, "we should add a tiny bit of Queen Bee's honey. Not too much, though."

"I was going to ask about that," Maria said. "Why don't you just smother it in Queen Bee's honey from the get-go? That would make the bear ascend immediately, wouldn't it?"

"It might sound weird, but that kind of feels like cheating? I'm sure he'd love it, and the smell of their chi-filled honey might have been what originally lured him in. That can be our backup plan if what we make here doesn't work."

Maria raised an eyebrow and gave me a smirk. "You made Bumblebro ascend with literal water in sugar. I don't think a backup plan will be necessary."

Claws, who had been growing visibly impatient as we conversed, chirped at us.

"Yeah, yeah." I rubbed her head. "We can start."

It only took a handful of minutes for us to get a fire roaring beneath the barbecue plate, and before long, the tallow smoked atop the cooking surface.

"Let's all do it at the same time," I said, gesturing at the fish. "As we place it on the barbecue, imagine chi going into it. I'll take the lead. Just do your best to follow along."

With a hand from Maria and me, a paw from Claws, and a firm pincer from Snips, we set the shore fish down on the barbecue plate. It immediately hissed and bubbled, soft vapors wafting up and filling the air with a delicious scent. I closed my eyes, picturing what I wanted from this creation.

As cliché as it was, especially coming from me, this was all about friendship. Contrary to what everyone assumed, none of my animal pals were my servants. I was as loyal to them as they were to me, and that was exactly what I desired from a potential bear companion.

I considered it further. Perhaps that wasn't being specific enough . . .

Though I considered Rocky a pal, the homie was a colossal prick. Our "friendship," if you could even call it that, was completely one-sided. He was entitled to his agency, but I didn't want another friendship like that. I wanted more bonds like what I had with the rest of my animal pals. Something deeper, even. My core buzzed its assent, agreeing with the sentiment. Then I pushed out with my will, pressing it toward the waiting ingredients.

As Maria, Claws, and Snips joined their wills to mine, I shifted my thinking toward how I would shape the fish's chi. I could infuse my essence into the meal, filling it with power. I could catch another fish and channel its chi into this one, distilling the essence into something stronger. Neither of these options felt right, though. My instincts screamed that the shore fish's natural state was correct. Leaning into this odd understanding, I was about to leave it at that when the world around us seemed to disagree.

Small wisps of chi floated up from the ground, coming forward of their own accord. I marveled at them as they curled through the air, condensing into thin lines of potential.

Startled as I was, it was nothing compared to how Maria, Snips, and Claws felt. I was aware of their attention from the moment I closed my eyes, and judging by the confusion radiating from them, they could sense the storm gathering around us. I sent soothing waves of reassurance out toward them, encouraging them to continue. Their shock slowly fell away, leaving only a profound curiosity about the anomalous event. When their wills rejoined with mine, one of them stood out among the others.

Likely because of Claws's recent advancement, her efforts were much more subtle. Whereas Maria and Snips were a blunt object, she was a precision tool, cutting through any spots that needed adjusting. She was clearly aware of me studying her movements, because she sent me what was best described as a solid wall of gloating. I could practically see her eyebrows wiggling at me, demanding praise. A small smile crossed my face before I returned to my mental efforts and left behind the sensations of my body.

The fish was almost cooked through, so without opening my eyes, I flipped it. Fat bubbled and spat, but I paid it no mind. The chi held within the fish told me that the last of its opaque flesh was turning white under the barbecue's heat. In response, the world's chi winding around us seemed to dance. Its condensed lines flared and sputtered like small flames.

It felt . . . *excited.*

I wasn't sure how to feel about the world itself being chuffed with our efforts, but

I didn't have the time to consider it. Following my instincts, I started leading the chi in toward us. Its lines still burgeoned like small flames, but they listened to my will, slowly winding in, getting closer. Maria, Snips, and Claws joined themselves to me, the former two like a hammer slamming nails into place, and Claws a guiding hand that helped me keep the strikes together.

The world grew even more content with our work, seeming to sing its approval.

Something atop the barbecue physically moved, distracting me for the barest of moments. It was part of the honeycomb. Engrossed as I was, I'd completely forgotten about the ingredient, but the condensing storm of chi hadn't. I added "the world adding ingredients without my intervention" to my mental list of things to consider later; I didn't have any more attention to spare.

The moment the honey touched the fish, we were in the endgame. I gave all my focus to molding the chi that whirled around us, its power now so strong that it was almost blinding to my senses. Maria and Snips wanted to get away from it, to flee, so I sent more assurance their way, telling them it was okay if they wanted to do so. I half expected them to take me up on the offer, but they both surprised me. Gritting their teeth, they doubled down, rejoining Claws and me and letting us shape their efforts.

An uncomfortable pressure started to build in my core, as if our undertaking was too grand. Too ambitious. I didn't understand. We were making food, something I'd done countless times. I'd experienced nothing like this before, and just as I was considering canceling the entire attempt, the strands of chi descended as one. Each passed through us and slammed into the fish.

It was like a flashbang going off inside my head, cutting off all of my senses. With everything going white, I felt myself falling.

CHAPTER FORTY-NINE

Loyalty

I felt myself falling to the floor but couldn't do anything to stop it. My entire body was numb, and I only barely registered my back striking the floor. Claws reached me first, clasping my arm. Snips and Maria were there a moment later, fussing over me.

"I'm fine," I tried to say, but I had no idea if the words actually made it out.

Despite losing the sensation of my, well, everything, I knew I was okay. I couldn't verbalize *how* I knew, but that didn't change the fact that I was safe.

"Fischer!" Maria's voice called, finally reaching my ears as some of my faculties returned.

"I'm fine," I repeated. Or tried to, anyway. I still had no idea if they could hear me. "I promise."

Judging by the way Maria pulled me into a hug, I guessed that the words had made it out. A few moments later, I could see again, only a thin blanket of numbness remaining over my senses.

"What happened?" she demanded, still hugging me tight.

I wrapped my arms around her, using my hands to pat both Snips and Claws. "I was hoping you could tell me. I feel like the sun hit me right in the brain."

She laughed, the sound filled with relief. "Well, that's no good. You need that."

"Right? Where would all my insightful thoughts come from without my noggin?"

Maria extricated herself from my grip then stood and helped me to my feet. Standing made a pulse of pain lance through my head, and I froze for a moment, rubbing my temples.

"Holy frack . . ." Maria said.

Peeking out through slitted eyes, I found her staring at the table beside the barbecue, and as I looked toward it, I understood. "Frack me," I agreed, gazing down at what I'd assumed would be a simple meal. The single shore fish had somehow either multiplied or grown. Its skeleton was nowhere to be seen, and entirely too many fillets for a single fish that size sat atop a plate. Steam rose from the glistening morsels, emphasizing the light brown of the perfectly cooked fillets.

The only thing that let me take all of this in was my enhanced awareness, because a fraction of a second after I first caught sight of our creation, words flashed in my field of view.

You have successfully taken part in a crafting ritual!

Quest updated: Group Project
Objective: [Error. Insufficient Power.]
Reward: [Error. Insufficient Power.]

I grinned, the excitement making me forget all about my headache. "Did you get that too?" I asked.

"Yeah . . ." Maria replied, accompanied by an affirmative chirp and hiss from Snips, both as awe-filled as each other.

I took a step forward, intending to get a better look. The moment I did, more words appeared.

Honeyed Fish Feast of the Communion
Mythic
Made of honey and a mature shore fish, this feast was created by the shared efforts of those possessing deep bonds with each other. Taking part in this feast will grant the consumer with the boon: Kindred Spirits.
Kindred Spirits effect: Permanent boost to Loyalty.

I shook my head, dismissing the words. Though they were gone from view, they remained firmly rooted in mind as they raced around my head, various implications unraveling. Loyalty was measurable?

"Whoa," Maria said, staring into space. "That's . . . *whoa.*"

"Uh-huh."

I glanced at Snips and Claws, finding both of their mouths parted and eyes focused on nothing in particular. I expected Claws to cackle with how successful our creation had been, but she appeared to be too shocked to—

Before I could even finish the thought, she raised her forepaws toward the sky and arched her back as she unleashed a maniacal cackle, her needle-sharp teeth reflecting the day's light. When her laughter crawled to a stop, she rubbed her paws together, hunching over as she started scheming. Snips blew thoughtful bubbles, and Maria wound a finger around strands of her hair, still staring into space.

I closed my eyes, focusing on the System message once more. There were numerous moral and ethical implications stemming from the wording, and the more I considered it, the more sure I became. I opened my eyes and watched Claws, unsure how I should broach the subject.

Maria let out a sigh, and when I looked her way, she gave me a wincing smile. "We can't use it, can we?"

I grimaced back. "I don't think so, no. Not yet, anyway."

What? Claws demanded with a sharp trill, staring up at us. *Why?*

"It's a little too mind-controlly, Claws. The way the 'loyalty' part is phrased makes it sound like anyone who eats it won't have a choice. It's one thing for you to eat it, because you understand the implications and can consent to them. A regular bear can't."

She flopped to her back dramatically, a single paw grasping toward the sky as despair took her.

I couldn't help but laugh, shaking my head at her performance. "Oh, shush, you little drama queen. I didn't say the bear could *never* eat it—I said he couldn't eat it *yet*."

She froze, then her head slowly drifted my way, hope sparking in her eyes when they met mine.

I grinned back. "I have an idea . . ."

Deep beneath the earth, a massive creature stirred. Far below the surface as he was, the surrounding dirt and rock held the heat of his body, wrapping him in a pleasant cocoon of warmth. Despite his comfort, something prodded at his awareness. A low rumble came from his throat as he stretched his limbs, not understanding what had woken him.

Still half asleep, the bear recalled the delicious feast of honey he'd had. It was as though he could still smell it on the air, its fragrance somehow potent enough to reach him all the way at the bottom of his den. He took a deep breath, imagining that the delicious comb was right in front of him. When air hit the back of his throat, his eyes flew open.

His bulbous nose sniffed away, and as the last vestiges of sleep left him, he realized that it wasn't just his imagination. There was honey nearby. He rolled over to his front and slowly stood, his muscles protesting after hours of disuse. He stretched his mighty body before he ambled up the tunnel, heading for the surface. With each length of tunnel he crossed, the luscious sweetness of the honey urged him on, making his mouth water. When he had traversed half the way out, he paused, lifting his head as he smelled the air.

Another scent had joined that of the honey, its promise just as enticing. He could smell *fish*.

It made even less sense than smelling honey from the depths of his den. His abode was high in the mountains, far from any water source. He remained there for a long moment, keenly aware of the possibility of danger. It was one thing to smell honey, but to find fish outside of his den? It reeked of trickery, and the bear instinctively knew who would be behind it: the two-legged creatures. Images flashed through his mind of the two-legged ones standing high above him, their faces fierce as they jabbed out with giant, painful sticks.

He hesitated, considering what to do.

Eventually, he looked back down the tunnel. He'd already passed numerous off-shooting passages that would take him to the other exits. Even if he followed the scents and found an ambush waiting, he could just retreat farther into his cave, leaving another way. The multiple openings were exactly why this was the perfect den, offering countless methods of escape if he was ever discovered.

If that was what happened, though—if the upright beings had trailed him back to his abode—he would have to abandon it.

This thought made a primal rage swell up from deep in his body, the hair around his neck bristling. This was *his* den, and if the numbers weren't too disadvantageous, he would defend it. Using his rage as fuel, he padded forward, moving silently along the hard-packed earth. At each branch in the tunnel he came across, he paused to sniff the air, carefully checking for the unmistakable stench of interlopers. When each alternative passage was deemed empty, he continued on, his fury building.

At the last curve in the tunnel, he forced himself to stop. It was no small feat; delicious scents pulled him forward, and towering rage urged him on. He tamped both instincts down as best he could. It wasn't too late for him to leave. He could turn and flee, departing through another exit before even spotting the trap. Whether it was the influence of his hunger and fury, or the possibility that it wasn't treachery that had brought the delicious-smelling foods to him, the bear made a choice.

He slunk forward, his shoulders hunched and head low as he went around the final bend. What he found there immediately confirmed his suspicions.

A whole fish sat before him, with trails of smoke coming from it that reminded him of the clouds flowing from his mouth during cold evenings. The fish was *smothered* in honey, the delicious goo dripping to pool on the object, which confirmed this food was presented by the two-legged creatures. It was on one of the flat white stones that he'd only seen around them. When he had still been a cub, only a fraction of the size he was now, he'd eaten off them countless times. More images flashed through his mind of a small upright creature leaving food where he could steal it.

He shook his head and released a low, rumbling growl. He had to focus on the surrounding forest. As the bear padded forward, every movement was fluid, testing. His head remained still, but his eyes darted, scanning every possible hiding place as he searched for pale skin or jabbing sticks. When he reached the cave entrance, he took multiple false exits, each time sending his head slightly farther out before withdrawing it. The entire time, he scoured everything visible, anticipating the ambush.

It never came.

With half of his body protruding from the safety of his den, he waited. He could see everything around him, and apart from the leaves slowly swaying above, there was no movement. He waited an excessive amount of time, expecting the attack to come at each passing moment. The longer he waited, the more he suspected it wouldn't come. Had the hairless creatures been so foolish as to leave their food unattended? It had happened countless times before. The images flashed again: a catalog of each meal he'd eaten from atop a flat stone, outsmarting the two-legged cub.

It took all of his self-control to not run forward and bite into the honey-covered fish. The memories of meals past made his hunger grow even more. It swelled into an irresistible urge, his mouth watering and breaths coming heavy. With his steps careless in comparison to earlier, he loped forward. His teeth bit down into the fish, saliva pouring as its sweet and savory flavors hit his tongue. He'd intended to sprint back to his den with the meal, but with his prize in his mouth, he was unable to stop himself.

He crunched down into the fish, its warm flesh falling apart. Some of it fell down to the white, unnaturally round stone, but he paid it no mind. His mind was completely occupied by the tastes assaulting him. He crunched through bone, grinding them to dust beneath his massive teeth. When no sharp bits remained, he swallowed. Heat radiated from the meal as it passed down toward his stomach. Though it was almost burning, the warmth was undeniably pleasant.

He lost himself as he devoured the rest of it, and when he licked the golden honey from the circular rock, his entire body shook. He had never tasted honey so wonderful—so *perfect*. The heat now spreading from his stomach crept out to encompass his entire body. Indescribable bliss washed over him, building and building as he sat on the grass, unable to stand any longer. Abruptly, the air pressure changed. As if a storm were brewing, it pressed down into his body. Opening his eyes, he expected to find dark skies and roiling clouds, but the afternoon was clear.

He tried to stand, but the weight was oppressive. All too late, the thought that this might be a trap crossed his mind, the idea not bringing the panic it should.

The heat of the eaten meal rose up within him, fighting off the outside pressure. When both forces collided, the world exploded in white.

Pop!

CHAPTER FIFTY

Misconceptions

My core radiated joy as I stared down at Kallis's newest spirit beast.

"Is . . ." Maria trailed off, searching for the right words. "Is he okay?"

"Yeah. Why?"

She smirked, raising an eyebrow at me. "Because he looks like he's having an existential crisis."

"It does look that way . . . Pretty adorable, though."

When the meal's chi had started running through the bear's body and forming a core, he'd sat down, entirely overwhelmed by the process. After the loud pop that always accompanied the start of a spirit beast's ascension, he hadn't moved. Well, not much, anyway. His jaw was slack, his row of bottom teeth exposed to the air. His eyes were wide and staring into space as knowledge flowed into him in an unstoppable stream. If I was being honest with myself, the expression was hilarious, and it took all of my willpower to not dash forward and rub my hands through his coarse fur.

"It's the same as when you ascended, Pelly," Maria said, turning to smile at her. "You were just as overwhelmed."

Pelly gave her some audacious side-eye, clearly not enjoying the comparison to the comatose bear.

"And just as cute," I added, running a hand down her neck.

Pelly preened, puffing her feathers out at the compliment.

"How long do you think it will take?" Maria asked, leaning against my side.

"Not too long, I don't think. Based on what all of our animal pals said, the process seems to have been sped up. It took you both days to receive all the knowledge, right?" I asked Claws and Snips, who were creeping closer to the bear.

They both turned to study me, cocking their heads.

"You have no idea what I said, do you?" I shook my head, laughing. "Never mind. Don't get too close to him, okay? We don't know how he'll react when he comes to."

Claws chirped defiantly and flexed, her tiny muscles bulging.

"It's not your safety I'm worried about, you goose. I just don't want to scare or overwhelm him."

She blew air through her lips, making a dismissive gesture with one paw.

Smiling at Claws's predictable behavior, Maria squeezed my arm. Her gaze drifted toward the bear. "What do you think he's experiencing right now?"

"I'm not sure." I put an arm around her. "But I hope the knowledge finishes streaming soon. I can't wait to meet him."

* * *

Trapped within the mire of his own consciousness, the bear watched the knowledge coming in, his mind somehow able to parse most of it the instant it arrived.

It was . . . wondrous.

The knowledge was of things that didn't seem important at face value, yet he couldn't help but yearn for understanding. He was aware of the two-legged being—no, the male *human*—that stood before him. It was the same person who had caught him raiding the beehive earlier in the day, and with a surety the bear couldn't put into words, he knew that their souls were linked.

Words . . . he thought.

It was a stunning realization that everything he had ever experienced could be so accurately conveyed with language. Before, he had thoughts, but now . . . there was structure to them. They weren't merely remembered images, smells, and emotions. He could understand them. *Process* them. Using this newfound method, he delved deep into his own awareness, the stream of information coming in now thin enough to be parsed by a portion of his mind.

When he revisited the pivotal scenes of his past, they were illuminated by an entirely new light.

His memory of humans being cruel tricksters wasn't necessarily wrong, but the species wasn't inherently evil. Far from it. They experienced a wide array of emotions that were much more complicated than those of an unawakened bear. When he recalled the fierce faces of the humans wielding what he now knew were spears, most of them were terrified. There was still anger and a hint of cruelty, sure, but they were just as afraid of his mother as she had been of them.

The ambush, the one that had killed his mother, wasn't an ambush at all.

She had been leading him through the forest in search of food when she paused and sniffed the air. Following her lead, he did the same. There was a delicious scent, one that called him forward. She had followed it of course, just as he had followed her. It had been a mistake—a fatal one. Instead of a free meal, they had found a pack of humans camping in a clearing.

Everyone, both animal and human, froze when they caught sight of each other. There was stillness for a tense moment. And then, she charged. They all followed their roles perfectly in the macabre play, doing exactly as their nature dictated. The mother bear sought to destroy, to eliminate anything that would threaten her cub. The humans fought for their lives, doing everything they could to survive. They'd tried to escape at first, tried to flee into the forest and outrun the threat. She chased them down, not able to understand that they'd happily leave her and her cub alone if she only gave them the chance.

When she caught one of them on the back of the leg with her mighty paw, their tactics had changed. And though he hated them for what they did to her, he could neither fault nor blame them. They were . . . He grasped for the word, having not yet mastered the language unfurling in his mind.

Loyal, he decided. *The humans were loyal.*

They could have left the caught man there, sacrificed him and escaped with their lives. Instead, they'd risked their own, coming back to fight his mother off. Again, she could have left, could have retreated. But that wasn't in her nature. She would defend her cub to her own detriment—even sacrificing her very body. Her very *life*.

Spears, fiery branches, and a thick net descended on her . . .

When they grew too visceral, the bear banished the thoughts. They were too painful.

Seeking to better understand humanity, his mind drifted toward the other times he'd interacted with them. Most obvious were all the times he'd stolen food from the flat, circular stones that only human ingenuity could create.

Plates. They were called plates.

Each time he'd encountered them, it hadn't been in a human home as one might expect. It had been in the middle of the forest, where neither food nor plates had any reason to be. He dove further into his memories, peeling back layers and layers of misconception until he came to the first time he'd met *her*.

It had been weeks since the fell encounter that led to his mother's demise, and he wasn't faring well. Young as he was, he hadn't yet learned where to get food. He found berries, roots, and even a few small mammals, but nowhere near enough to sustain his growing body. Overcome by exhaustion, he had hidden in a hollow tree, a place that would have likely become his grave . . . if not for *her*.

When she'd peered down into his hole the first time, he saw only a predator. Lacking the strength to do anything about it, he'd crawled as far back into the hollow as he could, hoping beyond hope that she would leave him alone. Now that he looked back on it, he saw only curiosity and sadness in her eyes.

They weren't the eyes of a predator; they were the eyes of a child.

"Poor little bear," she had said, then turned and ran, her wild hair trailing behind her.

He should have left and found a new place to hide, but he'd lacked the energy. Telling himself he would get up and flee in a moment, he fell asleep. When he woke again, it was to the smell of something delicious. Half asleep, he got to his feet shakily, the promise of a meal enough to move his body. Right before the entrance to his hollow, the end of a loaf of bread sat atop a plate. The little girl stood a few meters back, peering from behind a trunk. Thinking he was getting the better of her at the time, he'd snatched up the bread and retreated back beneath the tree.

He now knew it to be an old and stale bit of food, but in that moment, it had been the tastiest thing he'd ever eaten. He devoured it, even licking up the crumbs from the dirt. Only after he'd finished eating did the girl approach again. Once more, he got as far back into the hollow as possible. In his past, he saw a face with the same fury as those who had "ambushed" his mother. In truth, all she had done was smile down at him.

"Good little bear," she'd said, then picked up the plate and ran.

They repeated this countless times, the young girl progressively lingering a little longer. She brought him bread, fruit, and even spoiled meat, every meal slowly returning his vitality. The girl had to be at most six: old enough to feel compassion, yet too young to know fear. Because his only other experience with humans had been when they snuffed out his mother, if he had possessed more strength the first time the girl showed herself to him, he might have ended her life. Thankfully, he hadn't. He couldn't say whether it was because she was a source of food or whether it was divine providence that stilled his claw, but he was thankful nonetheless. He wasn't sure he could live with himself if he'd harmed her.

The last time he'd seen her, he was awake when she arrived. She skipped forward with a wide smile on her face, beaming down at him as she set down a plate absolutely *loaded* with food. Nuts, fruit, bread, and *unspoiled* meat, their scents combining to make his stomach growl.

"This will have to be the last time I bring you food, little bear," she said. "My parents aren't going to be happy when they find all this food missing. I might not be allowed out until you're fully grown."

In response, he had peeled back his lips and growled, the sound reverberating around the hollow he occupied.

"Hey!" she retorted with the petulance only a child could show a wild animal. "I brought you food!"

Not understanding at the time, he'd just stared, waiting for an attack to come. It never did, of course.

She spared him one last glance and another grin, then dashed away, hiding behind her usual tree. She watched him as he devoured the food, barely chewing it.

His eyes were pinned to her as she stepped out from behind the trunk and waved. "Bye, little bear!" she yelled, grinning. "Good luck!"

With that, she turned and ran, disappearing for the last time. She, a mere child, had saved his life.

His final interaction with humans had been only earlier today, and when he'd seen their faces, he once more saw the cruelty and anger of those who had attacked his mother. But now that his intelligence was burgeoning, he knew that to be false. They'd seemed shocked to see him, yes, but also overjoyed. Excited. It was the same with the animals, the crab and otter, who he now recognized as spirit beasts. They, too, had been only happy to see him. The otter reminded him of something, and after only a moment's thought, he realized what it was: the eyes of the otter contained the same light as the little girl's. They were both filled with boundless curiosity.

Despite how that look tugged at his emotions, it was nothing compared to the confusion boiling up from within when he considered the man standing there. His name was Fischer, and though he appeared ordinary, he was far from it. He was a little taller and broader at the shoulder than other humans, but it wasn't his physical size that was anomalous—it was the weight of his soul. Fischer felt like a king. An emperor, whose words alone would cause the planet to bend, perhaps to break. He held all this power, yet he was kind. He cared about those around him.

Though the bear wasn't aware how he knew, he was certain: Fischer, this benevolent leader, had caused his awakening. Their souls were somehow intertwined, and the more he felt of Fischer, the more confused the bear became. The man's soul didn't feel singular, for lack of a better word. At first, he assumed that Fischer had somehow stolen the souls of others, but that wasn't it. He could sense the color of Fischer's intentions—the man wasn't the type of person to do that. Also, the other souls felt attached, not owned. Suspecting that he wouldn't glean any more understanding with his awareness alone, the bear dismissed the thoughts.

As musings about Fischer and images of the past floated away in his mind's eye, he was left to consider it all. He'd encountered humans three times as an unawakened bear, and all had been drastically different. Because of the information still streaming into his awareness, he well knew how unique each human could be. But applying that knowledge to events he'd seen for himself was something else entirely. It made the encounters seem . . . profound.

Now that he was no longer lost in the past, he realized the information flowing in had almost crawled to a stop. The relative silence let him focus on his senses once more. Shaking his head, he blinked bleary eyes, the outside world slowly coming into focus. The entire time the universe's knowledge poured into him, he was aware of Fischer's physical presence before him.

What he hadn't felt was the rest of them.

As the blurred shapes sharpened into distinct beings, all the bear could do was stare. The woman from earlier was there, and the smile on her face matched the one Fischer was giving him. Beside them, the crab and otter waved, the former with a deadly looking claw, the other suspended in midair, Fischer holding her by the scruff of her neck.

"Stop struggling, Claws," Fischer said, shaking his head at the otter. "I know you want to ride him, but I'm not gonna let go."

Despite being detained, the otter only waved harder, displaying her needle-sharp teeth in what some would deem a smile and others would deem a threat.

Then, there were the creatures he'd never encountered before. A giant lobster that gave him a nod, its body thicker and longer than the surrounding tree trunks. A giant dog of nightmare, its skin darker than midnight, its tail wagging. On top of the dog, a cinnamon-colored bunny that shot him a wink and boxed the air when he looked her way. Two pelicans of similar size and different species, standing close to one another and staring at him with their intelligent eyes. A small cloud of insects that buzzed what was definitely a greeting. Just to the side of the dozens of bees, two distinctly different bees that bobbed up and down in acknowledgment.

With each of the spirit beasts he inspected, his suspicions were further confirmed. These creatures were the "souls" that he'd felt linked to Fischer, and their connections weren't forced—each bond was freely given. It was a stunning revelation, and the bear's head drifted back toward the human in question, unable to escape his pull.

When their gazes met, the bear froze. Fischer had shrunk . . . ? As the bear continued looking at him, though, he saw the truth: it wasn't just Fischer that had shrunk. It was *everything*. Even the world seemed to have gotten smaller, the giant trees no longer as grand as they once were. It could only mean one thing. The world hadn't shrunk at all—he had *grown*. The bear gazed down and extended his foreclaws, expecting the act to lift his body slightly. Instead, the earth cracked beneath him, splitting as if it were dried mud.

Confronted by his newfound strength, he lifted his paw, inspecting it. His claws, once blunted by use, had been enlarged and restored. Their tips were as deadly sharp as the otter's teeth, and because of the muscle behind them, he suspected he could swipe through rock.

"Pretty amazing, huh?" Fischer asked. "Everyone's body changes after they awaken. Well, all my animal pals did, anyway."

The bear, feeling more than a little weird about the gesture, nodded. It *was* amazing.

"Well, it's a pleasure to meet you, mate. Sorry to rush right into it, but there's something time-sensitive we need to take care of . . ." Grinning, Fischer brought the hand that wasn't grasping the otter from behind his back. He held a plate that was covered in food.

It looked to be fish, cut into small chunks and smothered in golden honey. The bear sniffed the air but couldn't smell a thing. Odd.

"I've been shielding it with my chi to keep it fresh," Fischer explained, smiling at him. "Before we eat it, though, there's one more formality . . ."

"There is?" Maria asked, curling an eyebrow at him. "Hang on. Don't tell me—"

"Yep," Fischer replied, giving her an amused look. He turned back toward the bear, his eyes sparkling.

"Would you like a name, mate?"

CHAPTER FIFTY-ONE

Names

G ods above," Maria said from beside me, shaking her head and rubbing the bridge of her nose. "Save us."

I barked a laugh. "Come on—you can't dread my names *that* much."

Maria looked up at the bear. "Sorry in advance."

As he glanced between us, our newest pal's brow furrowed.

"She's just being dramatic," I said. "All of my animal pals have names, and I'm pretty sure they love them."

A wave of agreement came from everyone around me, most emphatically from Corporal Claws, who I still had by the scruff of the neck. She nodded and chirped so loud that she almost broke free.

The bear considered it for a long moment, its giant head tilting side to the side. I'd thought he was big before, but now he was damned *massive*. He'd almost doubled in size. If he was any larger, he might not be able to fit between the surrounding trees. I started imagining how fun it would be to ride him into battle, but before I could get too lost in the fantasy, he nodded at me. There was no hesitance in his eyes, only trust.

I smiled, set down the plate of food, and strode forward. "Yes, Claws," I said, looking down at her before she could chirp the question. "You can say hello now. This is Corporal Claws," I said, holding her out. The bear nodded, half raising a paw. He paused for a moment, then extended the limb for Claws to shake. Rather than shake it, she grabbed one of his giant talons and inspected it, her eyes alight with excitement as she let out an appreciative coo.

While Claws continued gushing over the daggers attached to the bear's paw, I introduced everyone.

"We've got Corporal Claws here, espionage extraordinaire and wielder of lightning."

She chirped, still staring down at his paw.

"Sergeant Snips, my ever-reliable guard crab who shoots arcs of blue energy like an anime protagonist."

Snips nodded and blew greeting bubbles.

"Brigadier Borks, a hellhound with the abilities to teleport, store stuff like a sapient bag of holding, and go intangible."

Borks let out a loud bark, transforming into his golden-retriever form.

"Oh yeah, he also shapeshifts. Next, we've got Cinnamon, our resident karate-enthusiast bunny. She's small, but she makes up for her size with sheer technique and soft fur."

Claws let out an indignant chirp, pointing at herself.

"Yes, Claws—you also have soft fur."

Completely ignoring us, Cinnamon had launched into a shadow-boxing routine, sliding to and fro atop Borks's back.

"Then we've got the two pelicans, Private Pelly and Warrant Officer Williams, aka Bill. Pelly is Cinnamon's adopted daughter, and Bill is the one instructing Cinnamon in the martial arts."

Pelly fluffed her feathers out and honked, while Bill nodded, having stood a little taller when I mentioned his teachings.

"The leviathan before you is Private Pistachio. He is our keen-eyed sniper, with the ability to shoot long range blasts that also have devastating effects up close."

Pistachio, ever the stoic, gave a simple nod.

"The smallest of us are our insectoid pals. There's Bumblebro the bumblebee, who I may or may not have awakened by mistake. It was a happy accident, however, because he has proved to be the best of bugs. Queen Bee is, well, a queen bee. Her hive was attacked by some nasty wasps, and Bumblebro came to her rescue. In order to save her life, he fed her some of his special honey, which caused her to awaken. I was completely unaware of all this, so it was a double whoopsie. Still, a happy one."

They both buzzed, their affection for one another clear in their proximity and body language.

"Then we have their progeny. Again, without my knowledge, they reproduced. Oh, don't give me that look, you two. I'm glad you did!" I pointed at the cloud of bee hybrids. "These are the Buzzy Boys—most of them, anyway. The rest are off patrolling the surrounding lands, keeping their compound eyes peeled for threats."

They let out a droning sound, overjoyed to meet their newest pal.

"Last but not least, we have Maria, my girlfriend. I know she's not much to look at, but—" I dodged a stick thrown at my head. "Kidding! I was kidding!"

"I know," she replied, smirking. "Just wanted to test your reflexes."

I turned back toward the bear. "Truthfully, she's the most beautiful person I've ever met. Inside and out." I stole a glance, thoroughly enjoying the blush that came to her cheeks.

"There are a few more beings, but they're not here right now." Withdrawing Claws from her inspection of the bear's paw—and earning a squawked chirp in response—I held out my hand. "It's truly a pleasure to meet you, mate. I'm beyond glad that you've awakened."

With each person and animal pal I'd introduced, the bear had given a polite nod. This time, he dipped his head so low that his nose almost touched the ground.

"None of that," I said, grasping his paw and shaking it. "I appreciate the gesture, but we're equals."

He lifted his eyes to stare at me, and after only a moment, dipped his head again.

I laughed and reached out, ruffling the top of his head. "You're a polite fella for such a big creature." His coarse fur was remarkably soft, and as I felt how large his skull was, I got a new appreciation for his size. "Sorry," I said, suddenly withdrawing my hand. "I probably should have asked if that was all right."

He shook his head and let out a rumbling grunt that told me it was okay.

"Well," I said. "You've met everyone else. I suppose I should introduce you to them . . ." I turned my head and took everyone in, seeing anticipation covering their faces. "Everyone, meet our newest pal."

I let a silence stretch. After a few moments, Maria exhaled sharply. "Gods above, Fischer, just tell us and put us out of our miser—"

"Technical Officer Theodore Roosevelt!" I boomed, cutting her off.

Another silence stretched out, rolling over the forest.

"Fischer . . ." Maria said, pausing to move her mouth inaudibly. "I'm definitely missing something."

Claws chirped her agreement, her cute little brow furrowing as she tapped her chin.

"What do you mean?" I asked, cocking my head.

"Technical Officer Theodore Roosevelt?" she repeated.

"Yeah?" I fought to hide my smile. "What of it?"

"How does that have anything to do . . ." She trailed off, and in the next instant, her posture deflated. She gave me a stare flatter than any I'd received before. "Don't tell me . . ."

"Yep!" I spread my arms, gesturing at all of my animal pals. "Everyone, this is Technical Officer Theodore Roosevelt." I wiggled my eyebrows at Maria. "Teddy for short."

My spirit beast friends roared their approval, their myriad sounds combining into a cacophony.

In spite of her annoyance at me and my naming habits, Maria stepped forward and leaned down so she was eye to eye with Teddy. "It's lovely to meet you, Teddy. Welcome. I'm sure we'll become the best of friends in no time at all."

I leaned in, too. "Is it okay if I give you a good scratching?" I asked, unable to hold myself back any longer.

He gave me an odd look but nodded, and I reached out to scratch behind his ear. In retrospect, I should have seen the betrayal coming.

A deviant flew past me, beating me to the punch. Corporal Claws appeared on his neck, reaching up with both paws to dig in behind one of Teddy's ears and give him one heck of a scritching. His response was immediate. He tried to lean his entire body into it, his eyes rolling up involuntarily. Seeing weakness, I reached a hand behind his other ear and joined in, as did Maria, slinging one arm over his neck so she could get both sides of his soft jowls.

Appearing almost drunk, Teddy swayed back and forth, not knowing which way to lean as his eyes closed in bliss.

After a good scratch, I withdrew, taking a few steps back to give him some space.

"Okay, gang," I said. "I reckon it's time we get to the reason we rushed Teddy's ascension."

He gave me a growl that would have scared the strongest of humans, but I understood its meaning. He was curious.

"We prepared a meal for you, mate. Maria, Snips, Claws, and I made it together, but it was way more effective than any of us could have anticipated." I picked up the plate again and held it out. "Have a look at this—see if you can read the description."

His eyes immediately went distant, his brows slowly rising high. When he shook his head to dismiss the words, his eyes were wide.

"Right?" I asked. "I thought we shouldn't offer you this until you were awakened."

As Teddy peered around at all of us, I could practically see the thoughts racing through his mind. And because of how attuned I was to chi, I could feel his changing emotions. Unsurprisingly, he wasn't immediately thrilled with the idea. His consciousness had just been slammed with an indescribable amount of data, all of which expanded his inherent intelligence and wisdom. Based on the way his core shifted, Teddy well knew the implications of an unmeasured boost to something as ambiguous as "loyalty."

"What am I doing . . ." I whispered, shaking my head and withdrawing my awareness.

"What's wrong?" Maria asked, leaning in toward me.

I chanced a glance Teddy's way, but he was too preoccupied to listen to our conversation. "I was scanning his chi by accident," I replied, grabbing her hand. "We just need to wait for Teddy's decision."

Abruptly, he let out a great sigh, dipping his head.

I did my best to hide my disappointment, putting on a smile. "It's okay, mate. It was a lot to ask of you. Too much, really, when you've only just met us."

When his gaze met mine, there was a hint of confusion on his face, his eyes displaying countless sentiments. He took a deep breath, gestured toward the plate, and nodded.

Hope reignited in the pit of my stomach. "You . . . you want to eat it?"

He was completely still for a long moment. Then, with a single measured movement, he nodded again.

I couldn't hide my excitement as I dashed for the plate, wanting to release my shield around it before Teddy could change his mind. The second I withdrew my essence and exposed the feast to fresh air, its aromas exploded outward. Absent one second and all-encompassing the next, it slammed into me, strong enough to make my mouth water.

My reaction was potent, but it was nothing compared to Teddy's.

The bear, who had come across as the pinnacle of well-mannered so far, lumbered forward. His steps were shuddering, as if his desire to be polite warred with an insatiable need to taste the meal. His eyes turned predatory as he drew closer, like the plate of honeyed fish was cornered prey. When he opened his great mouth, his fangs glistened in the afternoon sun, wet with saliva. Seeing those features, there was no doubt about how deadly a creature he was. His canines were built for tearing through flesh, his molars designed to crunch through bone.

Completely undeterred, Claws zipped forward, her mouth agape and eyes twinkling as she inspected his pearly whites.

Mere centimeters from the food, he blinked, seeming to return to himself as he noticed Claws. With his lips drawn back and teeth exposed, his gaze drifted from Claws to everyone else. He slowly closed his mouth, hiding his finger-length canines. In a glacial movement, he sat back on his haunches, cleared his throat with a rumbling growl, and adopted a passive look. He extended a giant paw toward the plate of food and nodded differentially for us to go ahead, as if he hadn't just been about to ravage it.

The contrast between descending predator and well-mannered gentlebear was too much for me. A laugh flew free of my throat, making shame appear on Teddy's face. "Mate, please," I said, gesturing at the plate. "Help yourself."

He shook his head softly, averting his eyes and again pointing for us to go first.

"Okay," I said. "Everyone grab a piece, then. Quick."

It was done in the blink of an eye, the meat-eaters retrieving a chunk of fish, and Cinnamon and the bees collecting some of the honey from the plate. Only Teddy hadn't immediately gone along with it. I rectified his lack of fish by grabbing an extra fillet, smothering it in honey, and holding it out to him.

"At the same time?" I suggested, grinning.

Staring at the food and licking his lips, he extended a paw. I placed the fish there, and without further ado, held up my own. "To friendship," I said, raising it high.

The answering calls from Maria and all of my animal pals made my heart swell. Seeing that Teddy was just staring down at his portion, I lifted his paw toward his mouth, just as I lifted my food to mine.

Before I could bite down into the morsel, power swelled in the ground beneath us, encompassing a vast swathe of grass. It grew stronger as something approached, winding up from below at incredible speed.

"Uh-oh," I said, just in time for the forest floor to explode.

CHAPTER FIFTY-TWO

Becoming One

It was a beautiful afternoon in the forest surrounding Tropica. The sun shone down from above, the celestial body on its inexorable path toward the western mountains. I was surrounded by my animal pals, including Teddy, a bear who'd only awakened just minutes ago. Maria was at my side, her happiness as infectious as always.

And, almost completely unexpected, two more pals had just exploded up from beneath us.

I'd felt them coming at the last moment, and as Lieutenant Colonel Lemony Thicket and her yet-unnamed partner in crime erupted their roots from between us, I extended a patchy barrier of chi, protecting us and the food from the small chunks of earth flying in every direction.

"You came!" I said, grinning at Lemon.

Standing in opposition to my joy at her arrival, she radiated annoyance. Using a thick root, she grew the approximation of a stick body, then crossed her arms and tapped a foot, casting her displeasure over me.

"Whoa, what's with the hostility?" I asked.

She pointed around at everyone, the gestures growing more animated with each animal her little root hand was directed at. When she finally pointed at herself, she cocked her head. Even if her body language hadn't told me what she was asking, the simmering anger pulsing from her would have. She felt scorned, assuming I hadn't invited her.

"I did invite you, Lemon, you goose."

Her tapping foot halted, as did her growing resentment at being excluded.

Wait, what? her soul seemed to ask.

"Maria and I came by your grove when we were gathering everyone. We invited you, we called to you, and Maria even tried tickling your trunk. You didn't respond. We even swung by your body, our new tree friend," I said, gesturing toward the tree spirit that lived in the tree that had exploded from the old church's underground. "You didn't respond either."

"Which begs the question, Lemon . . ." Maria leaned in close, raising an eyebrow and smirking. "What were you two doing?"

If Lemon's roots were capable of perspiring, she would have started sweating bullets. She immediately panicked, and when I sent my chi her way, she retreated from it, concealing her emotions.

"Nothing to say, huh?" Maria asked, a grin slowly spreading across her face.

Her question only made Lemon and her tree spirit pal shrink further away, some of their roots subconsciously retracting back into the ground.

I barked a laugh. "Relax, you two. We're only teasing."

Maria let out a light giggle, covering her mouth. "Sorry, Lemon. You came in so hot that I couldn't help myself."

Lemon let out the mental equivalent of a sigh, her chi finally relaxing.

She had been mostly absent over the past month or so, her awareness always elsewhere. It was obvious that she was working toward something, and if it was anyone else, her secrecy would have troubled me. Considering it was Lemon, though, I wasn't the least bit worried. I trusted her implicitly, especially because I could feel a hint of her emotions. She was trying to be sneaky, but there was very clearly no malevolence in her actions. If it had been the younger tree spirit acting alone, I might have been suspicious. With Lemon leading the charge, they could do as they pleased.

"Whatever you two have been up to," I said, "I know it's going to be marvelous."

At these words, the last bit of tension knotted up in Lemon's core disappeared, and she sent me an almost-overwhelming wave of gratitude.

"Oh yeah." I snapped my fingers as if just remembering something. "Lemon, this is Technical Officer Theodore Roosevelt—Teddy for short. Teddy, this is Lieutenant Colonel Lemony Thicket—affectionately known as Lemon. And this . . ." I pointed at the other tree spirit's roots. "This is our tree spirit . . . pal. Lemon helped him awaken, and he doesn't want a name yet. Still, he's more than welcome on our shores."

Lemon, disgruntled as she had been, had somehow missed Teddy's giant form. Hesitantly, she reached a root out toward him. Just as cautiously, Teddy extended a paw and shook her offered limb. The sight filled me with joy.

"Wonderful. Now we've all been introduced. Well, excluding Rocky, but he's a different beast entirely."

Teddy cocked his head in question, but I shook mine. "Forget I said anything. I've already yapped enough. I can tell you all about our criminal crab after we take part in this feast. Speaking of . . ." I turned to Lemon and the other tree spirit. "You should inspect the food before you agree to eat it, especially you, tree spirit pal."

Lemon's constructed body flowed forward, as did a smaller tendril from the other spirit's root system. They leaned in close, peering at the bits of fish remaining on the plate. As one, they recoiled, both exuding entirely different emotions. Lemon was shocked, of course, but mostly excited. Her student was . . . hesitant. Caring more for his answer, I sent whispers of my awareness toward him, wanting to get more of a feel for his opinion. I got the sense that he was truly considering it, and just when I thought he'd grab a chunk, his disposition shifted. Fear washed out of him, and he drew back, shaking his head.

I smiled at him, trying to hide my disappointment. "That's okay, mate. I totally understand." Turning my attention on Lemon, my smile became much more genuine. "Are you in?"

She nodded fervently, spearing a chunk with a root and lifting it up.

"Okay," I said, looking around. "You've all been patient enough. Let's taste it at the same—"

Unable to wait a moment longer, Claws unleashed a deafening trill and bit down so hard that flakes of fish exploded over the grass. It started an avalanche of munching, and I didn't even have time to laugh before I ate my own, not wanting to ruin whatever Xianxia-land, System-made shenanigans made the meal's bonding properties work.

The moment the flesh touched my tongue, I was transported away, my awareness seeming to glide upward.

The entire outside of the fillet was crispy, as if deep fried and covered in invisible crumbs. The honey covering it, despite being hot, had kept its consistency. The sweet substance oozed throughout my mouth, enhanced by the savory flavors of the fish. The seasoning and herbs that Snips had used combined with the rest of the meal, making my consciousness soar as I was taken elsewhere. As I chewed, the tastes only grew more intense, somehow building.

It defied logic. Your taste buds should get more accustomed with each passing second, even if only a little. What was the cause? All the while, it felt as though I was rocketing upward, wind passing me by in a pleasant stream and trying to draw my attention from the meal. Even through this overwhelming sensation, the flavors built. My passage started to slow, a heat appearing from nowhere to pepper my skin. As it did, light sprouted from before me. I swallowed the mouthful of fish, opening my eyes and expecting to find myself back on the forest floor.

Instead, I was flying.

High above the clouds and beneath the slowly descending sun, I floated in a stunningly blue sky. I could see the curvature of the atmosphere, the cloud cover stretching out in every direction. There was a ghostly hand before me. My eyes darted to it, instinctively wary of anything getting so close without me noticing. But it was mine. I extended my arm, looking both at and through it. I thought that was pretty shocking in itself, but then more ghosts zoomed up through the wall of clouds below me.

When a light blue orb arrived lacking a body, I instinctively recognized it. Lemon was peering at the outside world, filled with wonder as she gazed up at the sun. The rest of my animal pals had the shape of their bodies, and when the Buzzy Boys started arriving, I couldn't help but raise an eyebrow. It wasn't only the ones who ate honey that came shooting up—*all* of them did. From different angles, they shot up to join the main body of insects. One by one, everyone else joined us. When they arrived, I had the pleasure of witnessing their initial reactions to the vista we found ourselves in. I could feel their amazement stronger than ever before, the link joining us enhanced by the honeyed fish.

Despite having already swallowed my mouthful of food, more sensations washed over me, as if I was still chewing. It made me focus on my senses, and as I gave them my full attention, I realized what was happening. I was tasting what everyone else was, our experiences somehow combined. Surprisingly, I felt an echo of chi connecting with the ground. Beyond curious, I sent my awareness downward, following it all the way back to my body. Our physical forms were all there still, and as I moved my ghostly arm around, my body mirrored the action.

With my curiosity blossoming, I raised my hand and took another bite of fish, returning to my place above the clouds. I crunched down on the layer of crisp skin, revealing the wonderfully flakey meat beneath. The sensations of it melting in my mouth rolled over me, spreading out toward everyone else as well. All of their expressions were rapturous as they peered around at the view we had of the afternoon sky.

The magic that connected us grew stronger with each passing moment, and as it did, I started getting glimpses into my companions' minds. In the blink of an eye, the glimpses solidified into something more. I could sense everyone's thoughts, and it felt almost as if they were just another aspect of me . . . but that wasn't entirely accurate. I wasn't the only one being exposed to these thoughts—*everyone* was. We were all enmeshed in a vast web, and they were just as connected to each other as they were to me.

The invisible ropes of magic that bound us began multiplying, slowly granting even more insight. It felt as though the connection was waning, so I sent out a pulse of chi, encouraging everyone to take another bite of the meal if they had any remaining. I got a wave of assent in response, and those of us with food left bit down into it. I fought down a laugh as I noticed Corporal Claws licking up her exploded flakes of fish from the grass.

Surprisingly, the sensations of multiple sets of taste buds were muted this time, not seeming as grand now that we also had access to the surface of each other's thoughts. When the essence reached our cores, it shot outward, empowering our connection. It made them all feel closer than before, and I got even stronger flashes of the thoughts they were having.

Fear, excitement, hesitation, joy, and everything in between. The myriad voices were overwhelming, all melding into a confusing chorus.

I tried to single out the individual sources, but the noise only increased as our connections built, deafening me. I closed my eyes, my forehead furrowing as I tried to parse the data streaming in. I couldn't say who it began with, but after the first person panicked, so did everyone else. The thoughts and voices grew frenzied, fighting one another to be heard. I tried to calm them, to reassure them that everything was going to be okay, but it was no use. They couldn't hear me.

Through the noise, I could feel my jaw clenching. I didn't believe we were in physical danger, but my pals were certainly at risk of some emotional turmoil, which was exactly the opposite of what this experience was supposed to be.

All at once, the noise ended.

And in the silence that remained, we truly became one.

CHAPTER FIFTY-THREE

Expansion

When I opened my eyes, I found our spiritual forms still high above the clouds. Though the susurration had disappeared all at once, our connection to one another remained. I peered around the circle, and as my thoughts ran through my companions' minds, they felt as if they were my own. There was a moment where we instinctively raised our mental walls, seeking to keep ourselves hidden. But then we threw the gates wide, inviting each other in.

Maria was right beside me, and her soul was just as beautiful as she was. Filled with light and life, she wanted the best for everyone around her. When I felt her love for me, I echoed it back toward her, delighting in the way it made her core seem to vibrate. There was a hint of something more within her, something she had pushed far down. She could have kept it from us if she wanted. Instead, she offered it up, baring her soul. It was a desire to be more useful—a need to contribute. We neither judged nor denied this aspect of her, simply acknowledging it as truth.

Claws was to the other side of Maria, and as her true intentions were revealed, I wasn't the least bit surprised. She felt an immeasurable amount of love and affection, and she wanted to share it with everyone. Some might call it an issue that she showed her affections by being a menace and pranking people, but not me. There were no hidden secrets deep within my favorite otter. She was exactly what she appeared to be.

Snips's presence called out to me next, her motherly instincts drowning out the other voices. Snips sought to protect everyone, to be the last line of defense should the worst come to our shores. More than anyone else, she wanted to defend *me*. Her opinion of me was . . . a lot. If presented with the choice, she would sacrifice her life ten times over to save mine. If I was my usual self, I might have told her I didn't want that. I might have denied her feelings. But as with all the revelations so far, I accepted it for what it was. Who was I to tell someone how to feel?

There was something else deep in her consciousness, an aspect of Snips that she was just discovering for herself. Instead of shoving it down, she offered it toward us all, letting understanding of it unfurl in our minds. It was a small bubble of loneliness, its source clear.

She missed Rocky.

He had transformed over the past months, becoming more and more of an issue. That wasn't the version of him that she longed for, though. She missed the troublesome crab who kept inviting himself into her tidal pond. Even his desire to be yeeted was a source of entertainment at first, one that had grown less and less endearing as they had to become punishments for his misbehavior. She had never voiced it, but she believed something was corrupting Rocky from the inside. More than anything, she hoped he would return without it, his time alone having banished that misguided part of himself. Even if he was still afflicted, however, she'd take that version of him over nothing. It was a raw truth, and I sent waves of love her way, as did everyone else, thanking her for her openness.

Cinnamon was next, and she didn't give a frack about anything other than sick martial arts moves and going for rides in the sky with her adopted daughter. The contrast was hilarious, and I sensed my body laughing involuntarily. Cinnamon loved everyone, of course—especially Pelly—but her true passions were aerial moves atop Pelly's back and perfecting the roundhouse kick.

Borks's sense of belonging called out next, and as he gazed around with puppy-dog eyes, his ghostly tail wagged. Before arriving on our shores, all he had wanted was to belong to a pack once more. He had found that and more. As each being offered their truths up to him, his sense of family only increased. He felt like he was a part of something bigger than himself, and his only desire was for our bonds to go deeper.

Unexpectedly, the next thing that drew me in came from two different creatures.

It was the pelicans, Bill and Pelly. They both called out to us for one simple reason: they shared the same hidden, non-romantic affection for one another. They stared at each other as their dual appreciation unfolded. They weren't ashamed of their feelings and had only kept their truths close to their hearts for fear of overstepping. Pelly saw Bill as a father, and Bill felt the same. Now that the depth of their platonic love was revealed, they offered it up freely, both to each other and the rest of us. It was beyond heartwarming.

A motherly pride radiated from Cinnamon, momentarily interrupting her imaginings of karate chops and flying kicks.

The Buzzy Boys were next, and they were just happy to be here. They got great satisfaction from being needed by their "hive," which included all of us. They would do everything they could to guard and protect our surrounding lands, even sacrificing themselves to do so.

Twin appreciations radiated out, louder than the rest of us. It was Queen Bee and Bumblebro. The two were family oriented, and they held equal love for both everyone present and the Buzzy Boys, their children. There was a dark bubble or wariness within them, and without more than a moment's thought, they offered it up. It was a fear of Teddy. They were aware of it and trying to challenge their preconceptions, but they couldn't deny its potency.

A strong reassurance came in response, Teddy both acknowledging and opposing their fear. He wasn't at all bothered by the insects' assumptions. If anything, he understood it better than most. He *loved* honey, but now that he was a sapient being, he would never harm even a single bee again. He was ashamed of his past actions and assumptions, yet didn't blame himself. Teddy had been a primal creature following his instincts when he'd destroyed hives in the pursuit of honey, just as the bees' primal instincts told them to be wary of him now.

When the bees felt this, their worry evaporated, leaving behind a healthy respect and a desire to learn more about the bear.

Pistachio's spirit nodded at them, appreciating their resolve. At first glance, his internal sentiments were just as strong as his outward-presenting stoicism. But buried deep down, there was a shadow of sadness there for his fellow lobsters' downfall, the ones that had been dispatched as part of Snips's vengeance against Sebastion and the Cult of the Leviathan all those months ago. Snips sent an apologetic pulse toward him, but Pistachio cut it off. He didn't blame her for her actions, and he reminded her that she had spared him. He felt a need to rectify the injustice, but he saw it as his responsibility, not hers. He didn't yet know how to do it, but now that he was fully aware of the desire, he would find a way.

Lemon, unable to suppress her feelings any longer, called out. She identified strongly with Claws's means of affection, finding joy in expressing her love by tricking and surprising those she cared about. Lemon had a root-deep desire to help everyone, but it stretched far beyond the connections present. She revealed it, making us raise our metaphorical eyebrows. She wanted to help the entire *world*. It was ambitious, to say the least. I noticed her delving deeper, intending to show us what she had been doing over the past weeks, but I sent out a pulse of my own. Telling us now would run contrary to her desire for surprise and trickery, so I told her to keep it to herself. Surprisingly, the rest of my companions did the same, echoing an identical sentiment.

All attention turned my way, and filled with gratitude for everyone's transparency, I unveiled my deepest thoughts. First, my love and appreciation of the surrounding souls flowed out, slamming into and resonating with their cores. Brighter than all the others, an image of Maria planted itself firmly in mind. The sun was behind her, illuminating her sandy hair as it fell from behind an ear. Without prompting, the image shifted. Hundreds of different scenes appeared, only vanishing when another took its place.

They were all of Maria.

Her blue eyes beneath the midday sun as she stared up at me. The way she flushed and averted her eyes when she was embarrassed, only making my affection for her grow. Her hugging Claws tight and giving the little otter a good scritching, delighting just as much as I did in the little miscreant's soft fur. Us walking hand in hand beneath the verdant forest, her gazing up at the shifting canopy and me gazing at her. On and on they went, none of a sexual nature, yet all managing to perfectly capture an aspect of her entrancing form.

It felt like it went on forever, yet it was over in the blink of a cultivator's eye. As the last of the images disappeared, I was left with my companions' emotions, all as happy as I was that I'd been able to make such a rare connection. Maria's love came through strongest, both giving me the mental equivalent of a hug and urging me to continue sharing.

With my core buzzing, a profound thankfulness for my new life came next. I knew it might be overwhelming, but out of respect for their own openness, I didn't hide a single ounce of the truth. As with some of the others, I had a patch of darkness coloring the depths of my awareness. Despite my willingness to share, it opened up slowly, like a black rose blooming.

I was all too aware of my deep-seated fear of taking control of the church, and now everyone else was too. There was a reason for that fear, of course. I was terrified of losing the freedom I'd gained when arriving in Tropica, and anything contributing to that, whether perceived or real, was immediately deemed a threat. Along with the fear of taking control, there was my worry of gaining too much power. Of being forced into the role of a god. I'd expressed my willingness to do so for everyone's sake, but that didn't make the idea of it any less unattractive.

With my deepest secret revealed for everyone present to see, I focused on *why* I was so afraid of changing the status quo. I'd told most of my animal pals of what had transpired in my previous life on Earth, but now that we were one, I *showed* them.

My privileged life as the son of a billionaire, and the way I was molded to inherit my father's business empire. The relationship with my father and mother, the former having cared only for his wealth and legacy up until the very end, the latter leaving when I was still a boy, likely unable to deal with my oppressive father.

It would have taken an entire day to explain all the intricacies if they were expressed by words. With their consciousnesses joined to mine, we relived the moments together, my companions reexperiencing the emotions with me. A hint of shock came from everyone, Maria included. I'd already told her about my past, opened up as much as one could with words. But hearing was different from seeing.

From there, I returned to my life here, showing how ecstatic, how blissful, my time on Kallis had been. The sun that rose every morning, casting its warming light over everything I could see. The joy I got from the simple parts of life, like fishing, cooking, or even just having a nice nap in the shade of a tree.

Finally, I let them see how I felt about all of them again. Because of the dark cloud of fear coloring my thoughts before, I hadn't unveiled the depths of my appreciation for them. This time, I let it all out. All the souls surrounding me, along with all the human pals I'd made since arriving in this world, were the seasoning of my life. The activities and scenery I enjoyed in Tropica were wonderful, sure, but without others to enjoy it with, it would have been bland. *Flavorless.*

Allowing this gratitude to flow out of me washed away the negative aftertaste of my previous life, cleansing our palates and leaving only love for one another behind. Adoration poured from each of them, feeling the same way. Even Teddy was there, already attached to us after becoming one with our thoughts and seeing the color of our souls with his own eyes.

Our fondness for one another built, each participating core resonating with the sentiment. As it climbed higher and higher, I sensed that a change was coming. The chi connecting us all shuddered, then expanded. In what could have only been the barest of moments, the interconnecting ropes flew out from us, their tendrils spreading across the sky. They sprawled out far into the distance, the kilometers-wide net slowly ceasing its expansion.

Through the affection and thankfulness for one another, a great curiosity sprouted. We all watched as the chaotic shamble of interconnected vines began sinking. Down and down they went, and rather than stopping on the ground when they landed there, they sank down through dirt, rocks, sand, and water. Only when they were deep, deep below did they come to a stop, seeming to find the right place.

Immediately, they called out for something—something that neither I nor my present companions could give them.

Now that the mesh was no longer connecting us, our knowledge of each other's internal state slowly receded. Though it was like losing a part of myself, I used the last of our "oneness" to thank them all. The emotion was echoed tenfold, washing over me until the very last moment.

As our spirits floated back down toward our bodies, my awareness once more singular, I bathed in the aftershocks of what we'd just experienced.

CHAPTER FIFTY-FOUR

Bear Hug

High in the mountains to the northwest, a lone alchemist was trapped in his thoughts. If he had a friend present, perhaps they could have helped him challenge his internal narrative and break out of the downward spiral he was currently engaged in.

Alas, Solomon was alone.

The echo of a long-departed god had destroyed his place of power, obliterating the means with which he was going to achieve ascension. Worse, the lightning-covered boulder had clearly been sent by a remnant fragment of Zeus. Of all the possible gods to attempt to strike him down, it just had to be the god of the sky.

Solomon looked upward, narrowing his eyes at the clouds above. More echoes could be up there this very moment, watching and waiting for the perfect time to strike. Solomon stared for a long while, part of his brain suspecting that another attempt would come the moment he looked away.

When nothing came, he let out a slow sigh, trying to calm his whirling mind. He was sitting on a wooden stool of his own design, having worked to rebuild the equipment that the falling meteor had destroyed. It'd taken him some time, but he'd managed to replace everything—well, the physical components, anyway. He'd not yet collected any more of the herbs and plants he would need to ascend.

If he was being honest with himself, he wasn't sure if he'd bother.

A shaking hand drifted to the pouch around his neck, and without thinking about it, he opened the drawstring to peer inside. The powdered bark of the blue tree was there, his last sample of the most important ingredient. He stared at it as he considered his options.

Though they were obvious, each possibility seemed untenable.

He could continue on with his plan, forging a new future for himself as the Alchemist of prophecy. He gritted his teeth, acknowledging that it wasn't so simple. Trying to do so could lead to another attack, one he might not survive this time. The other choice was to abandon his dream, to walk away from this place and never again aim for the heavens. He was close to ascension, so his body held more vigor than it had in years, but who could say how long that would last? He could pass in his sleep one night not long from now, a gnat in the cosmos that never amounted to anything.

The idea of being nothing, of not ascending to the heavens after coming so close to godhood, made fury build within him. Yet it did nothing to still his trembling hands.

Clenching his fists, Solomon stood, wanting to take his anger out on something. He was partial to shattering vials during fits of rage, but he was without equipment, forced high into the mountains to flee a fledgling cultivator back in Tropica. Left with nothing else to destroy, he grabbed his stool and raised it high above his head. Just as he'd gathered his strength and prepared to slam it into the trunk of a tree, a shift in the surrounding air brought him up short.

It was as though something passed through him, its overwhelming potential screaming out to him.

In a fraction of a moment, the sensation passed, traveling down into the earth beneath his feet. He tracked it as long as he could, eventually losing all sense of it as the phenomenon moved far below.

Solomon stood completely still, not even daring to breathe in the face of such power. When something clattered to the ground immediately behind him, he flew forward, instinctively moving for the door of his wooden hut. He peered over his shoulder as he went, and when he saw the source of the noise, he skidded to a stop, finally exhaling. A soft laugh escaped his throat, relief soothing his prickling skin.

It was the stool. He hadn't even felt himself dropping it.

Solomon had gone his entire life without hearing a peep from the gods prior to the meteor clearly sent by Zeus. And now, a second echo had called out.

His heart fluttered as he jumped to the most obvious conclusion: the remnant power of another god must have felt his plight. Rather than smack him down or attack him, it had sent a sign.

It had urged him on.

Solomon's blood pulsed, and his skin prickled once more, this time for an entirely different reason. He threw his head back and laughed, unable to believe his luck. Even if Zeus attacked again, Solomon now had the echo of another god watching his back, one that wanted him to reach for the heavens.

The next moment, Solomon took off, dashing for the forest.

He had ingredients to collect.

As I slowly settled back into my body, physical sensation returned. When I felt something tickling my cheeks, I wiped my face, my hands coming away wet. Though I was anything but sad following the rapturous experience in the sky, I found myself unable to halt the tears. I heard a whimper from my left, and a second later a form crashed into me, one I couldn't mistake.

Maria, her chest heaving with sobs and her own tear-streaked face pressing against my chest, hugged me tight. In swift succession, a series of animals slammed into us. Snips, Claws, and Cinnamon were first, all three nuzzling in as close as they could get. Pelly and Bill came next, looping their magnificent necks over Maria's back. When Borks arrived, he transformed into a Chihuahua and forced his way under Maria's arm, whimpering and hitting my chin with rapid-fire licks. Even Pistachio joined in, laying his overlarge antennae across my legs. Myriad roots shot from the ground around us, and before my still-swimming eyes, I watched countless flowers bloom from them, Lemon reassuring us in her own way.

Suddenly, something blocked out the sun. I blinked fresh tears away and gazed up, finding the source of the shade.

Teddy was standing above us, great rivulets of liquid running down his face to pool around his nose. Bumblebro, Queen Bee, and the rest of the Buzzy Boys were on his head, all peering down at us, even their compound eyes somehow leaking. Teddy leaned down, then paused, averting his gaze as he let out a soft, questioning growl.

"Of course you can join the cuddle puddle, you big goof." I sniffed and let out a half-hearted laugh. "Get down here."

He let out a great huff and flopped down on top of us, wrapping everyone up. Because of our experience in the sky only moments ago, he knew exactly how much pressure our bodies could take. He squeezed us tight, giving us a literal bear hug. The bees buzzed the entire time, their wings emitting a comforting tone that somehow made my core feel warm. I closed my eyes, enjoying the embrace.

Both figuratively and literally surrounded by love, my thoughts drifted toward the connecting mesh that had sunk deep into the ground beneath me. Though filled with potential, whatever power it would one day come to yield remained entirely unfulfilled. It had called out for something, and with our minds still linked, everyone present had known that we didn't have what it wanted. But now that I was alone with my thoughts, I had an idea, one that I dove into completely.

As future plans unfurled in my mind, I lost track of time.

What could have been seconds or minutes later, a rhythmic beating drew my attention. Maria's heart had been racing when she first slammed into me, but the longer we embraced, the slower her pulse became. Content with the extent of my planning, I focused on my body and all of my surrounding companions.

It was both a long time later and all too soon when I patted Teddy on the side. "Okay, big guy. Let's get up."

There was no response, and as I paid closer attention to him, incredulity washed over me. "Are you serious, Teddy?"

"What is it?" Maria asked lazily.

"He's fallen asleep!"

Teddy let out a loud snore in response, even our loud conversation not enough to wake him.

"What a shame," Maria said, squeezing me tighter and pressing the side of her face into my chest. "Guess we'll just have to stay here forever."

A muffled chirp of agreement came from somewhere to my side, accompanied by some happy bubbles popping against my torso.

"Girls," I said, "I'm enjoying myself as much as you are, but if we stay here all day, I can't explain the adventure I've just thought of . . ."

There was a moment of silence, everyone going completely still as my words sank into them. But that single blessed glimpse of calmness was short-lived, because absolute hell broke loose almost immediately. Every creature tried to flee the pile, scrambling over one another to escape. Their aggressive exits were enough to wake Teddy, who woke with a start and launched himself skyward, letting out a comical roar as he sailed up above the treetops.

"Huh," I said, sitting up and watching Teddy flip end over end, his roar taking on a confused tone when he realized he was in open air. "That's something."

"Look at him go," Maria added, craning her neck, her face unable to decide if she was impressed or amused.

As he reached the apex of his flight, Pelly and Bill appeared at his sides, swooping in to grab an arm each. As he made his descent of shame, Teddy dipped his head in apology, appearing more embarrassed than I'd ever seen another being look.

"My bad," I called. "That one was on me."

He looked around as he landed, his brow furrowing when he noticed none of the animals were looking at him, their attention locked on me. He cocked his head, trying to understand.

"You fell asleep, mate, and no one wanted to get up. So I mentioned that I had a plan for our next adventure."

Teddy cast aside his embarrassment and straightened, his ears perking up.

I grinned in response, looking around at my alert companions. "Here's what I was thinking . . ."

A half hour later, as we made our way back to New Tropica, I sighed and looked at Claws, whose arms were crossed as she somehow raised her nose at me from the ground. "I'm sorry, Claws," I said. "We can't all go."

She gave me a venomous dose of side-eye, not looking away. After a long moment, she snorted and raised her nose once more.

Though Snips wasn't so obvious with her dissatisfaction, her carapace dropped low, revealing how disappointed she was.

"We won't be gone long!" Maria tried.

In response, Cinnamon hopped up beside Claws and adopted the cross-armed posture. She raised her nose even higher than Claws, her neck stretching farther than I knew it could.

Hmph! she squeaked

Hmph! Claws agreed, beginning a competition between the two for who could appear more disgruntled.

Everyone else was more accepting of the endeavor, Borks and Teddy because they were invited, and the rest because they weren't as sassy. Knowing that trying to comfort Claws or Cinnamon might result in a lightning shock or a karate kick to the jaw, I scooped up Snips and cradled her in my arms.

"We'll be back before you know it." I rubbed my chin on the top of her carapace. "I promise."

Despite her obvious disappointment, she leaned in to me, letting me comfort her.

Claws's head swiveled our way, a dash of jealousy joining the annoyance in her eyes.

Maria giggled. "Come here, you goose."

Claws's jaw moved, her desire for scritches warring with her indignation. Seeing an opportunity, Cinnamon pounced. She leaped from the spot, sailing for Maria's outstretched arms before Claws could reach a decision.

It was, undoubtedly, a mistake.

The poor bunny wasn't even halfway there when lightning erupted. Claws unleashed a battle cry as she rocketed across the ground faster than Cinnamon could hope to see. Kicking off the sand, Claws slammed into Cinnamon, withdrawing her lightning chi at the last possible second.

Rather than punt the bunny skyward, Claws latched on to her. In a jumble of limbs, fur, and blurred strikes, the two soared upward. I shook my head, and Maria sighed.

"Seriously . . ." she said, rubbing the bridge of her nose.

I just laughed. "If they're already willing to have a practice bout, maybe they'll get over their exclusion relatively quickly."

Later that night, when I put my hand under my pillow, I was proven wrong.

I groaned, slowly getting up.

"What's wrong?" Maria called from the shower.

I lifted the pillow, frowning at what I'd touched. "There's a pile of sand under my pillow."

There was a moment of silence as Maria turned the shower off, followed by a loud giggle that echoed off the bathroom tiles. "I guess Claws is still bothered."

"When did she even find the time to put sand under my pillow?" I started scraping it into one hand.

"She must have snuck off when we were talking to Barry."

"I could have sworn she was there the entire time . . ."

Maria exited the bathroom, and I couldn't help but stare, the sand completely forgotten.

She'd gotten into her pajamas, her visible skin glowing from the hot shower. Despite this, I could still see her face flush when she noticed me staring.

"What?" she asked, twirling a wet strand of hair.

"What do you mean, *what*? Have you seen yourself? How am I supposed to look anywhere else?"

She tried to frown at me, but she couldn't completely hide her smile.

"Come here," I said, discarding the sand I'd been collecting. It scattered across the floor.

She raised an eyebrow at me. "That's very unhygienic, Fischer. Who knows where that sand has been—*oh!*"

Her hair blew back from her face as I appeared in front of her and wrapped my hands around her waist.

"I should really get going . . ." she said, her lips remaining parted as she stared up at me.

"You should," I agreed. "We've got a big day ahead of us tomorrow."

Her beautiful blue eyes reminded me of all the emotions I'd felt from her earlier. We had been joined as one only hours ago, able to see—to comprehend completely—the way we felt for one another. To some couples, such a baring of souls would have been a death sentence for their relationship.

To us, it was anything but.

We both leaned in, and as her velvet lips met mine, I stopped thinking about earlier.

CHAPTER FIFTY-FIVE

Adventure

When I woke the following morning, I could feel one of my animal pals nuzzling up against my chest. I smiled, taking a deep breath and stretching my arms.

"Good morning," I said, not particularly worried about which of them it was. Whoever they were, I was glad they were here.

There was no response, and when I opened my eyes a moment later, my smile froze.

Claws's face was only centimeters from mine, her ears pressed back in alarm. Blinking, I looked where I'd felt someone nuzzling up to me. My blanket had been peeled back, revealing my chest. Sitting atop it, Cinnamon held my shirt open with one paw. In the other, she was clutching something, paused midway through stuffing it into my pajamas. I glanced back at Claws, seeing her forepaws also hiding something she was doing her best to hide from me. Something yellow . . .

"Is . . ." I rubbed my eyes, clearing away the lingering vestiges of sleep. "Is that sand?"

Retreat! Claws trilled, turning and scrambling for the door.

Cinnamon panicked, jumping so hard from my chest that she slammed into the roof.

Thump!

Stunned, she fell back to the bed, wobbling as she tried to orient herself.

"What the frack?" I asked, my wits too addled to laugh at the instant karma. "Are you okay?"

When she straightened, she let out a panicked scream and kicked away from the bed again, ricocheting off the far wall before rocketing out my bedroom door. If the second thump was a trustworthy indicator, she'd collided with another wall out there. Corporal Claws's chittering laughter trailed off as they departed out the front door, skittering into the morning air.

When I sat up, a bucket of sand poured out of my shirt and pooled around me on the bed. I just stared down at it for a long moment, not even knowing where to begin. Deciding that a little sport would be a good way to start the morning, I stood, stretched, and sprinted outside. They'd had a good head start, but no matter how fast they were, the two little miscreants were no match for me.

The moment I stepped out into the morning rays, however, I found a menagerie waiting for me.

Every animal pal but Claws and Cinnamon were present, even half of the Buzzy Boys—those that weren't off scouting—coming to say goodbye. I extended my senses, searching for the missing two. When I located them, I shook my head, peering over my shoulder. Two distinct half-visible heads poked up over the headland.

"Come down here, you little rats. I'm not going to punish you."

Not trusting me, they retreated, ducking from view.

"What did they do?" Maria asked, smirking and raising an eyebrow.

"They graduated from putting sand under my pillow to putting sand under my everything." I shook a leg, causing sand to cascade down onto the porch and a laugh to pour from Maria.

She shook her head, her smile only growing. "So much for getting over it quickly. Claws seems to be holding a grudge."

"I'll forgive them if they clean it by the time we get back!" I yelled, loud enough for them to hear.

"Speaking of," Maria said, hefting the bag on her shoulder. "We're all ready to go. Need a hand packing?"

"Nope!" I grinned. "I packed after you went home last night—be back in a moment."

I had the quickest of showers, got dressed in my traveling clothes, and returned outside, my oversized travel pack slung over one shoulder. When I got there, I found two unexpected forms cradled in Maria's arms. Claws and Cinnamon, having apparently climbed down from the headland, averted their gazes from me.

"Girls . . ." Maria chided. "Did you have something you wanted to tell Fischer before we leave?"

Both sighed, their haughty postures deflating. Maria stepped forward, preparing to hand them over, when I held up a hand. I knew Claws all too well, and she was being entirely too forthcoming with an apology.

"Show me your hands," I said, pointing down at her.

Claws tilted her head to the side, then extended her paw pads, letting me inspect them. I thought I might be being too paranoid, so I opened my mouth to apologize, then narrowed my eyes at her as another possibility struck me. "Empty your pockets, missy."

Her smile grew tense, and she reached into the little pockets where she kept her favorite rocks and shiny baubles. From the left one, she produced an opalescent stone, smooth with use. And from the other . . .

Claws screamed a trill sound and threw her paw toward me, unleashing a spray of particles.

"Pocket sand!" I yelled, shielding my face. "I knew it!"

She made to escape, roaring with chittered laughter, but I caught her by the scruff of her neck. When I held her up to my face, she panicked, the whites of her eyes telling me she expected retribution. Instead, I pulled her into a hug. "I'm going to miss you. We won't be gone long."

She tensed but melted into my arms a moment later, letting out a soft coo.

Cinnamon came to join her, leaning her forepaws on my chest and giving me a little bunny kiss on the cheek.

I held them a while longer before passing them over to Maria. "Okay, gang. Maria, Teddy, Borks, and I are off. We leave the village in your capable hands. I'd love it if you could all come with us, but it's better to be safe than sorry."

Claws's bottom lip protruded, having one last crack at making me change my mind.

"I know it's sad, Claws," Maria said, using one hand to pet her head. "But Fischer knew Barry would request that most of you stay behind. Besides, on the off chance that someone is foolish enough to attack us, who would be better at defending the village? They say the best defense is a good offense, and you are, without a doubt, the *strongest* among us. Other than Fischer, of course."

With each word, Claws sat up a little straighter. By the end, her chest was puffed out, and her pout had been replaced by a proud grin.

"She's right," I said, not needing to bend the truth. "I have no doubt you could take out an entire army with your lightning boulders alone. I can't think of a more devastating offense than you and Cinnamon's combo attack."

They were both preening now, Cinnamon's mouth curling up, and Claws making little *oh, stop it* gestures with one paw.

With everyone as reassured as we could make them, we made our way down the line, saying goodbye to everyone in turn. When I reached the end, I took one last glance at the coast. The sun was just threatening to rise over the distant horizon, its rays casting a glow into the pink-and-purple sky. I could hear the softly lapping waves from here, their incessant murmurs filling my soul with a great calm. I took a deep breath of the salty air, locking the memory of its scent firmly in mind.

And with that, we were off, heading for the road leading west from Tropica. We took a path where no one would spot Teddy, and the sun finally breached the horizon as we strode through the forest, casting long shadows where it found gaps in the canopy above.

"No word from the other two?" I asked, shooting a questioning look Maria's way.

She shook her head. "Not a peep."

"That's a shame. I was hoping they took us up on the offer. Deklan in particular would have loved . . ." I trailed off as I sensed two cultivators ahead of us in the forest, and the moment I recognized them, a wide grin came to my face.

Maria leaned over in front of me, overtaking my field of view. "What would Deklan have loved?"

"The secret we kept from them." I shot her a wink. "Which he's about to learn firsthand."

"What do you . . . *Ohhh!*" Her head darted in the direction I was facing.

Right on cue, Deklan popped out from behind a tree, trailed by the other person I'd sensed.

"You guys came!" Maria said. "We thought you'd . . . Oh, Dom! Hi!"

Deklan smirked, raising an eyebrow. "What about me? Do I not earn a hello? And what's this about a secret?"

"Sorry! Hi to you, too!" She swept a loose strand of hair behind her ear. "I just didn't expect to see Dom, is all."

"She assumed you were Trent," I explained. "We invited him, too. You haven't heard from him, have you?"

"We did, actually," Deklan replied. "I dropped by and encouraged him to come along, but he wasn't feeling it." He gave us a slight shrug, then jolted straight as he remembered something. "Oh, I wanted to ask: Can Dom come along instead? It's fine if you say no, but I figured it couldn't hurt to—"

"Of course!" Maria and I both interrupted, sharing a delighted glance before returning our attention to the brothers.

"You're more than welcome, mate," I said. "We had to limit the numbers just because we don't want to leave New Tropica vulnerable, but you can definitely replace him."

"Honestly," Maria added, "we probably should have thought to invite you. Sorry."

"Not at all." Dom gave us a carefree smile that mirrored Deklan's. "I get it. As relaxing and calming as things have been since we arrived, they've also been kind of intense?" He shrugged. "I feel like you probably have a lot going on behind the—*bear!*"

Deklan leaped backward as he also caught sight of Teddy, scream-yelling, "*There's a giant fracking bear behind you!*"

Teddy, not anticipating their reactions, just lumbered casually from between the trees, followed by Borks. I laughed so violently that my legs immediately buckled, and as I looked at the incomprehension replacing the fear on the brothers' faces, I cackled even harder. After a few attempts at explaining myself that ended in choked fits of giggles, I could finally speak. "You asked about the secret, remember?" I wiped tears from my eyes as I sat up, shaking my head. "He's the secret. Deklan, Dom—this is Teddy. Teddy, meet Deklan and Dom."

As polite as ever, my newest animal pal dipped his mighty head in greeting.

"He's . . ." Deklan licked his lips as his eyes went wide. "You're a spirit beast, Teddy?"

"Of course he is," Dom answered, letting out a self-deprecating laugh. "Look at the size of him!"

Deklan stepped forward, his legs seeming to move of their own accord. His vision was locked on Teddy, and as he reached out a tentative hand, it came up just short. "Is . . . is it okay if I touch you, mate?"

Teddy, his head still slightly bowed, nodded.

Deklan ran a hand over Teddy's broad skull, amazement bubbling up into his core.

I marveled at the ever-increasing awe as Deklan continued petting him, finding the spot on the side of Teddy's neck that made the bear sway. It was the exact reaction I'd expected from Deklan, and Maria and I shared a knowing glance as we saw our plan coming together.

"Why didn't you tell anyone?" Dom asked, watching Teddy with only a little less amazement than his brother.

"Because we wanted to leave on this little excursion, mate. Do you think Ellis would have let us leave otherwise? I had to tell Theo because he would have seen through my subterfuge, but he agreed to keep it a secret. Until we're too far away for Ellis to come find us, at least."

The brothers laughed at this. "Yeah," Deklan said. "That makes sense. So what exactly is the plan, then? You mentioned fishing when we spoke last night."

I grinned, hefting my backpack and the rods within it. "That's right, mate. I only told Barry and the other leaders *why* we were going on a fishing trip. I guess now is as good a time as any to let you know." I held up a finger. "First, you know about the quest I'm on, yeah?"

Deklan nodded. "It doesn't tell you the details but keeps updating when you make things with others, right?"

"Exactly. It's called Group Project, and it's updated twice from cooking. I have a feeling that we'll get something cool when it's finally finished. Not that we know *when* that'll happen, given how the System just keeps saying, 'Insufficient power.'" I held up a second finger. "The next reason is because of what happened to us yesterday."

I'd only explained it in vague terms to everyone but Barry and Theo, knowing that revealing too much would make Ellis trail after us like a dog chasing a tire. I quickly ran through it in more detail, doing my best to put the transcendent experience into words. Deklan and Dom were suitably shocked, their eyes darting between Maria, Borks, Teddy, and me as I explained.

"We knew something sank into the ground," Deklan said.

Dom nodded. "Everyone felt it. Even I did, and my cultivation isn't that advanced."

"Right," I said. "Well, what I left out is that it felt like it wanted something from us. The more I considered it, the more I understood what it craved."

They both leaned in, their curiosity obvious.

"It wanted power, but not the power I, or anyone else for that matter, could give it. It doesn't want chi from our cores. And of all the things I've encountered in this world, there was one type of fish with way more chi than any other."

"The one we're going to fish for?" Deklan surmised.

"That's the one, mate. I reckon if we have a chance of powering whatever that weird latticework is, it'll be with a bunch of the giant fish we came across on our way to Gormona. The potent alligator gar are just as the name suggests. The chi filling their flesh is *potent*."

The brothers stole a meaningful look at each other.

"Let me get this straight," Deklan said. "We're fishing for what you've described as giant fish, doing so because it will possibly impact the very land, *and* it's effectively a secret mission?"

"A secret mission . . ." Dom repeated, a glint entering his eyes.

"I'm glad you're as excited as I am." I took a deep breath, then held up a third and final finger. "The last reason for us going is Teddy. He's only just awakened, and after our awareness was joined, I understand exactly how laid-back he is. I reckon you and he have similar personalities, Deklan, and I wanted to give him at least a few days of relaxation before Ellis starts harassing him for details about his entire, er, *everything*."

Deklan slung an arm over Teddy's neck again. "A laid-back bear, huh? I think we're gonna get along just fine."

Seeing the change in Deklan since his arrival in Tropica had been a constant source of joy, and watching him immediately click with Teddy made my core sing. Maria looped an arm through mine, also watching them.

"What are we waiting for, then?" Deklan asked, straightening and petting Teddy on the head. "The sooner we leave, the sooner we can fish, right?"

"Couldn't have said it better myself." I checked if everyone was ready, and after a series of nods and verbal confirmations, I turned to Borks. "Can we store our stuff in your dimensional space, buddy?"

Yes! he barked, his tongue lolling as he ripped a hole in space.

With our packs stowed, we were off, moving at a leisurely speed. Well, a leisurely speed for cultivators. Trees and grass sped by in a blur, adventure fueling each step.

CHAPTER FIFTY-SIX

Mischief

Unlike the last time we made our way from Tropica to Gormona, we didn't travel along the road for long. Less than a half hour later, we approached the first village. Veering off the road and into the forest, the temperature immediately dropped by a few degrees, some of the frosty night air remaining trapped beneath the canopy.

Without needing to talk, we unanimously decided to remain between the trees. It would take us longer to find our destination, but that was fine.

Though I'd listed Teddy's recent ascension as the third reason for this adventure, that didn't make it less important than the others. He'd been a regular bear yesterday, and I'd not even known of his existence twenty-four hours ago. In such a small span of time, he'd awakened, had the universe pour data into his mind, and then had an otherworldly experience above the clouds. It was a lot to take in, no matter how well-adjusted he may have seemed.

I shot a glance his way, unable to stop myself from grinning at his behavior. Just like Borks liked to sniff the air as we ran, Teddy was doing the exact same thing, his nostrils flaring and lips lifting periodically. I vaguely recalled something about bears having the keenest sense of smell of any animal back on Earth. I wasn't entirely sure if it was true, but the way his head twitched toward things that Borks didn't register made me inclined to believe it.

After a few hours, I was just considering lunch when Borks and Teddy both skidded to a stop.

I opened my mouth to ask what was going on, but then I noticed their ears alert and twitching. They slowly spun their heads, locating the direction of whatever sound they detected. I caught a hint of a deep tone, so faint that I might have imagined it. Borks and Teddy both went rigid, and without sharing a glance, they slipped off through the underbrush.

When I looked her way, Maria's eyes reflected the worry I felt within. We dashed after them, followed closely by Deklan and Dom. As we seemed to near our destination, the animals slowed, both hunching as low as they could while still creeping forward. I'd caught a few more tones on the wind, slowly growing loud enough that I knew they weren't a figment of my imagination. When I smelled the unmistakable scent wafting through the air, I finally understood what we approached.

My traitorous mouth watered of its own accord.

Maria sensed it too, because she raised an eyebrow at me, also curious about why Teddy and Borks approached as if expecting a battle. All at once, the buzz of wings bounced off the surrounding trunks, seeming . . . angry? A sense of urgency came over me and I moved forward, slipping through the trees just to the right of Borks. A moment later, the source of the cacophonous buzzing came into view.

I absorbed the sight in the blink of a cultivator's eye.

Before us sat one of the thickest trees I'd ever seen since coming to this world. Its branches closed most holes in the canopy, and the surrounding ground was free of other trunks, the leaves having stolen the sunlight others would need to survive. Occupying a hollow midway up the tree, a beehive of gigantic proportions was abuzz with activity. The bees were swarming out of their home, forming distinct clouds in the space between grass and canopy. Their purpose was immediately clear when I noticed the other insects smattered around the area.

The bees were defending their hive.

Giant wasps as big as beetles were on the attack, their mandibles biting through any bees that came too close. Undeterred, the defenders continued their darting maneuvers, attempting to exchange their lives for an attacker's. Before I even had the chance to consider helping, Teddy was on the move. He lumbered forward, slowly enough that any bees he hit just bounced off him, spiraling through the air before righting themselves once more. Each wasp was systematically dispatched by his mighty claws. In a matter of seconds, it was all over.

Rather than thank Teddy for the assist, the bees turned their ire on him. He was neither angry nor upset about the treatment. Teddy knew well that they were only doing as their nature dictated, using every tool they had to defend their hive, despite how relatively powerless they were. Teddy had a hint of satisfaction on his face as he retreated from their attacks, no doubt content he could help a hive rather than destroy it.

When he got back to us, he looked back at the clear section of grass. As his gaze roamed over where he'd ended the lives of a dozen wasps, a sense of uncertainty radiated from his core. I immediately knew the cause of his doubts.

"You did good, mate," I said, patting his large head. "On the good–bad scale, bees are the goodest of boys. You shouldn't feel bad about taking out a few wasps to save an entire hive."

The statement took a hint of his self-reproach away, but a shadow still remained. I rubbed his fur some more, knowing there was only so much I could achieve with words. He was sapient now. He would have to work out his morality for himself.

"I'm sure Queen Bee and Bumblebro would be proud. They'd have done the exact same thing."

This sentiment eased his conscience even more, and he dipped his head gratefully, as polite as ever. We remained there for a few minutes, watching the bees as they slowly calmed. Most returned to the hive, but some others came from it. Unexpectedly, these new arrivals started collecting the fallen. They dragged them across the grass, sometimes moving only centimeters at a time before having to pause, get a better grip, and try again.

"What are they doing?" Maria asked.

"Moving the bodies from the hive to stop the spread of disease. Before Queen Bee awakened, her hive threw all the dead workers out after they were attacked.

"Wow," Deklan said. "That's so interesting."

"They're like little undertakers," Dom added, his eyes watching the bees' efforts closely.

We stayed put, playing witness as the fallen were systematically deposited at the bases of other trees. Once the last was moved, the hive returned to business as usual, scores of insects flying away in search of nectar and pollen.

With the show over, we resumed our travel, everyone slipping into a comfortable silence that was only occasionally broken when Dom and Deklan messed with one another, causing the victim at the time to curse and chase after the offender. Our pace remained leisurely, staying that way until I couldn't contain my excitement any longer.

We were almost there.

With a hurried clip, I dashed ahead, leading the way for everyone else to follow. None of them backed down from the challenge, and I grinned. I kept stealing glances over my shoulder to see Maria's pumping arms, Borks leaping from tree to tree while changing forms, and the huffing forms of Teddy and the two brothers bringing up the rear. If he wanted to, Teddy could have charged through the trees unaffected, but he stepped gingerly around them, weaving his massive body so nary a branch was disturbed.

I smelled the water before I saw it, and I skidded to a stop as I entered the lake's clearing. I turned, waiting for everyone else to catch up. Maria and Borks, having been right behind me, landed at my side. Neither of them had broken a sweat.

Deklan and Dom came next, taking heaving breaths as they jogged from between the trunks. Their eyes went wide when they caught sight of the craterous lake. They ambled up to its very edge, peering down at the water as they leaned on their knees. Teddy's footsteps came into hearing range, his soft padding barely audible. When he emerged from the trees, he was trailing a black-and-blue butterfly, watching it with sparkling eyes as it flitted to and fro through the air.

With his eyes pinned to the beautiful insect, he didn't notice the rest of us. I saw exactly what was about to happen, the future unfolding in my enhanced mind as I took in his trajectory, speed, and mass. I had all the time in the world to stop it . . .

Instead, I glanced at Maria.

When her gaze met mine, there was mischief dancing in her eyes. I set a hand on Borks's shoulder, letting him know not to intervene. He darted a quick look my way, an unmistakable grin curling his lips. He'd already reached the same conclusion. It took all of my self-control to not laugh and give it away.

Deklan and Dom were still leaning over, their chests heaving as they fought to catch their breath. Being in such a vulnerable position, they had no hope of withstanding the force of a two-ton bear barreling into them. They both released yelps as they sailed into the air above the lake. Teddy skidded to a halt right at the edge of the crater, his ears pinned to his head as he snapped back to reality and realized what he'd done.

When the brothers hit the water, they skipped like thrown stones, their limbs outstretched with the force of their passage. With two gigantic splashes, their impromptu flight finally came to an end.

"Deklan skipped an extra time," Maria noted, amusement coloring her voice. "Does that mean he wins?"

"Hmm. Maybe?" I tapped my chin. "Dom's final splash was way bigger."

"A tie, then."

Ruff! Borks agreed, his wagging tail a blur.

In contrast to our enjoyment, Teddy was distraught. He bowed over and over as Deklan and Dom swam back to shore. A constant sound of apology came from Teddy, something partway between a groan and a whine. Rather than annoyed, however, the brothers were laughing and flicking water at each other as they crawled onto shore.

"Thanks, Teddy!" Deklan said. "My brother needed that—he'd worked up quite a lather from our run here."

"Agreed!" Dom nodded. "And my brother needed it more. He smelled like absolute shi—"

Dom didn't have a chance to finish his insult. Deklan slammed into him, wrestling him back into the lake. I smiled and shook my head as they fought like only brothers could, their grins never disappearing whilst they postured for dominance over the other.

Despite how happy they were, Teddy continued bobbing his head in apology. I grabbed him by the shoulder. "C'mon, mate. Wanna see how we set up the rods?"

A half hour later, the brothers had changed into dry clothes, and all the rods were set up. I hadn't told them anything about the bait needed to catch the potent alligator gar, wanting them to experience it firsthand. I was sitting between Borks and Maria on the shore, with Dom, Deklan, and finally Teddy to the right of us. The brothers held a finger to their lines, their breaths shallow and calm as they waited for a bite. At the same time, the tips of their rods twitched. Together, their posture shifted, going from relaxed to alert in an instant.

Because they were both experienced fishermen by now, they didn't strike too soon. They waited for the right moment, and their patience was rewarded a split second later when both their lines went taut.

The hooked fish did their best to escape, but they had no chance. With wide smiles, Deklan and Dom reeled them in to the shore. Before they could lift them from the water, though, I got up, facing Maria and gesturing for her to follow. She gave me a questioning look, and I shot her a wink, letting her know I was up to something. Mischief entered her eyes for the second time today, and she followed me down to the water.

I scooped up Deklan's when it got to the rocks, cupping it in my hands. The jungle mudminnow's weird little feet immediately pressed into my palms in an attempt to escape, but I didn't let the odd sensation bother me. Maria did the same to Dom's, and when we turned toward the two brothers, their attention was locked on our clasped hands.

"What . . . what are they?" Deklan asked, his core radiating suspicion.

Schooling my face, I locked eyes with him. "Do you trust me, mate?"

After a short pause, he nodded.

"Close your eyes and put your hands out," I instructed.

Only when their lids were firmly shut did I let my grin show. Moving together, Maria and I placed the jungle mudminnows—in all their horrific, multi-limbed glory—onto the brothers' open hands.

CHAPTER FIFTY-SEVEN

Monster

I *trusted* you!" Deklan yelled, his arms outstretched so the jungle mudminnow was as far from his body as possible. He pinched the crime against nature of a fish between his thumb and forefinger, all four of its legs undulating as they tried to find purchase.

Beside him, Dom stared down at his cupped hands. Not wasting the opportunity, the creature within stood upright and tried to run back to the water. Dom's face went pale.

"You all right, mate?" I asked.

He opened his mouth to reply, but dry-heaved instead. "Why does it—" He dry-heaved again, dropping the fish and wiping his hands on his pants. "Why does it feel so *wrong?*"

Maria and I cackled with laughter, leaning against each other.

"*I trusted you!*" Deklan repeated, looking both disgusted and amused.

The mudminnow Dom had dropped sprinted past Deklan on its way to the water, and he plucked it from the ground, scrunching his face at its humanlike legs as they kicked in the air. Peering at it must have drawn his vision in, because his gaze went distant. I focused on it too, making words appear in front of me.

Mature Jungle Mudminnow
Unique
This fish is a creation of the followers of Ceto. It is unknown how long the jungle mudminnow has existed within the Kallis Realm, but in that time, it has stabilized itself within the food chain. This fish has become the favored prey of the potent alligator gar.

When I shook my head and returned to the present, utter revulsion covered Deklan's face. "The alligator gars eat these? *On purpose?*"

His incredulity only made me laugh harder, my chest starting to ache as the air was forced from my lungs.

"Pass them here," I said, getting to my feet. "No need to let them suffer." After two swift movements, I set them down on a rock. "We need to swap out your fishing rigs for something bigger, then we should be good to go."

After washing their hands for an overly dramatic amount of time, shooting us judgmental looks all the while, the brothers rejoined us. When they noticed the giant hooks we'd attached, their eyes went wide.

"Trust me," I said. "The fish are big enough to justify it."

They nodded, anticipation radiating from their body language and cores both. Not needing guidance, they attached an entire mudminnow as bait each, then strode down to the water.

"In the middle?" Dom asked.

"Duh," Deklan said, playfully rolling his eyes. "Do you think giant fish live in the shallows?"

In response, Dom picked up a pebble and rubbed it between two fingers, scowling at his brother. I half expected him to flick it at Deklan's head, but he pretended to drop it, instead shoving it into a pocket. "You're lucky I'd rather fish than teach you a lesson."

I raised a brow at Maria, wordlessly asking if she'd noticed. But before I got her attention, the brothers cast out their lines. I watched as the rigs sailed over the water, Deklan's splashing down to the left and Dom's to the right, both in the deepest section of the lake.

As if in recognition of their perfect casts, the world froze. I hadn't even realized there was a breeze before, but now that it had vanished, the silence of the surrounding trees was deafening. Tiny ripples spreading from the brothers' lines were the only movement visible, the pattern beautiful and hypnotic.

When Deklan's reel screamed a moment later, I wasn't at all surprised.

"Poseidon's silty bottom!" he yelled, holding his rod high.

Its tip bent and bounced with each movement of the fish's head as it tried to escape, but as with every creature that had faced the brothers lately, it didn't stand a chance. When it swam toward Dom's line, I worried that they might become tangled. Before I could tell him to wind it back, he was already doing so, ensuring he didn't get in Deklan's way.

It had only traveled a few meters when the second fish struck.

"By Triton's stiff conch . . ." Dom uttered, his tone disbelieving. "It's *big* . . ."

Whilst Deklan hooted and hollered as he slowly reeled the fish in, Dom remained reserved, his eyes intense as he fought his to shore. When the potent alligator gars approached the shallows, their long, powerful tails made the water churn, giving the brothers their first sight of the fish.

Instead of dashing into the water to grab them, I reached out and grabbed the rods. "What are you waiting for? Go get 'em!"

Deklan dove—literally *dove*—into the lake, landing with the grace of a drunken starfish. He was wrestling his alligator gar above water a moment later, holding firm as it kicked its giant tail.

"Watch the mouth!" Maria winced, reaching out a hand as if she could help telekinetically. "The teeth are deadly!"

Dom was in the water now too, having walked instead of diving like his maniac brother. After a small battle, one which almost saw Dom get bitten by Deklan's fish when said maniac got too close, the brothers were walking up the shore.

I slipped forward, dispatching both alligator gar with my trusty spike.

As one, our eyes were drawn into them.

Mature Potent Alligator Gar
Unique
This species variation of the alligator gar has evolved through its predation of jungle mudminnows, an unnatural fish created by the followers of Ceto, over thousands of years. Through millennia of evolution, the potent alligator gar has managed to produce a unique kind of chi that only matures when exposed to heat.

"Unique chi?" Deklan asked. "Only after being exposed to heat?"

"How . . ." Dom licked his lips. "How potent are we talking?"

"One way to find out," I said, shooting them a wink.

Deklan's eyes were alight with expectation when they met mine. "Fire?"

"Fire," I confirmed.

Before I could even finish the word, Deklan and Dom were off, setting their fish down and dashing off in search of branches.

With the smell of smoke coming from the campfire and the flavor of potent alligator gar lingering in my mouth, I leaned back against a tree. I let out a soft groan.

"Agreed," Maria said, resting a hand on her stomach and leaning beside me.

Despite having caught two fish as long as a man was tall, we absolutely devoured them. Borks and Teddy had one of the frames each, meticulously removing every possible bit of meat. The brothers were sitting across from us, both looking just as full.

"You gonna eat that?" Dom asked, pointing down at the last bit of fish on Deklan's plate.

"Yes," Deklan replied.

"You sure?"

He gave Dom a suspicious look. "Yes, I'm sure. I'm just letting the rest settle."

The look wasn't misplaced, because a moment later, Dom made his move.

His hand darted out, grabbing the fillet with lightning-fast precision. Deklan, however, was prepared. They say the best defense is a good offense, which was probably why Deklan aimed his punch at Dom's head. Dom had to block with both arms, leaving the fish behind for Deklan to quickly scoop into his mouth.

Deklan gave him a smug grin as he chewed, taking his time to enjoy every—

Crunch.

Deklan froze. He furrowed his brow, tongued his cheek, then spat out . . . a rock? Tiny fractions of one, anyway. It had been crushed between Deklan's empowered molars. I stared at the small pile for a long moment. Had the rock been *in* the fillet? Had I somehow put it on his plate when I was dishing up the servings? If so, how would such a mistake slip past my enhanced awareness?

When I felt the victory radiating from Dom's core, I finally understood.

"Dom!" I barked a laugh. "That was *devious!*"

Deklan's eyes narrowed as he spun toward his brother. "What did you do?"

"The pebble," I said, shaking my head.

"Revenge is a . . . is a . . . cold dish," Dom said, completely butchering the phrase and making me giggle even harder.

Comprehension arrived in Deklan's eyes just as violence flowed from his core. He shot to his feet. "You put a pebble in my last bite? You *animal!*" He turned to Borks and Teddy. "No offense."

They both shrugged, but Deklan didn't see the gestures because he was busy flying through the air toward Dom.

"Dinner and a show," Maria remarked as the two men duked it out, fighting just as they had in the lake.

A smile graced her lips, making me watch her for a moment before returning my attention to the brothers.

Though Deklan was definitely annoyed by the betrayal, he was equally enjoying their little sparring session. We let them go for a few minutes. Teddy finally stepped in when Dom was thrown toward a tree. The man would have crashed through it, so Teddy caught him and pulled him into a bear hug.

"Truce?" Dom asked from a position of exactly zero power, his legs dangling above the ground as Teddy held him tight.

Deklan appeared to seriously consider the offer, tilting his head back and forth. "Fine. But only temporarily, and only because there's more fishing to do. I will avenge my meal."

"Deal," Dom said, straightening his clothes as Teddy set him down.

After resting a while as the brothers fought, my full stomach felt much more comfortable. I stood up and stretched, letting out a soft groan. "I think I have to do something regrettable," I said.

This immediately drew everyone's attention.

"Er, like what?" Dom asked, unruffling his last sleeve.

"So, you know how I can sense chi, right?"

"Right," Maria said, slightly raising a brow.

"Well," I continued, "I can technically search out fish that have chi in their bodies, right?"

"Ohhh," Maria said. "To make sure we don't fish up all of them?"

I grimaced. "Exactly."

"Wait, why is that regrettable?" Dom asked.

Deklan whapped him softly on the back of the head. "Because it's cheating. If you can sense exactly where fish are, and how many there are, Fischer could just throw the hook directly at them."

"I mean, it's not really cheating if he's using his power . . . is it?"

"He's not just cheating the fish, you goose," Deklan said. "He's cheating himself. Think about how it feels when your line is in the water. The unknown possibilities, knowing that at any moment, something massive could strike. The excitement that comes with it. *The anticipation.*"

"That's it, mate," I confirmed. "But in this case, I'll have to do it anyway. I don't want to catch all the alligator gar and make them effectively extinct. If I'm unlucky and there is a hidden species in here, scanning the water will spoil that surprise."

"Ohhh." Dom frowned. "Yeah, I don't like that at all."

"Don't worry." I laughed. "I won't tell you if there is." I walked over to the bank, letting out a slow sigh as I stared up at the waning afternoon light. I didn't want to do it, yet it had to be done. I hesitated a moment longer, gathered my chi, then sent my awareness snaking outward.

It went through the ground first, winding over rocks, earth, and sand. Surprisingly, I felt creatures there, each possessing the smallest hint of chi. Worms, insects, even tiny aquatic invertebrates living around the rocks of the shore. Their life forces were like stars in the night sky, lighting up the darkness behind my eyes. After pausing to appreciate their beauty, I pushed my awareness farther, extending into the lake's black waters.

The first species was something I'd seen before, but not in this lake. They were little guppies, only as large as the end of my pinky finger. Maria and I had spotted them in one of the creeks feeding into the river, and though I thought there were a lot of them then, it was nothing compared to the thousands occupying the lake. They swam all around the edge, schooling in large groups that occasionally split apart, only to rejoin once more.

When I saw why they separated, a shiver ran down my spine. From within the layer of silt on the lake's floor, a jungle mudminnow struck. It stood up on its weird little legs, then leaped and darted for the guppies. Each time I'd seen a jungle mudminnow walking, I'd been disgusted. Somehow, witnessing its fleshy legs trailing through the water as it swam was even worse.

I felt a moment of compassion for the guppies. I couldn't think of a more unnerving ambush predator to be targeted by.

My awareness sank into the silt where the rest of the mudminnows waited. There were *thousands* of them, all completely still and waiting for a school of bait to swim by. Another involuntary shiver came, running down my entire body. No matter which way you looked at it, there were entirely too many legs in this lake.

Seeking to banish that thought from my mind, I extended my senses farther. The bottom of the lake grew deeper at a steady gradient. There was a sudden drop-off, making me raise an eyebrow. It went down and down for meters, revealing a craterous hole within. When I sensed the life down there, I felt my body jolt.

"What's wrong?" Maria asked, her voice only barely making it through to me.

I lingered a moment longer at the bottom of the lake, my shock not fading. There were hundreds of the alligator gar, so we'd have no issue with supply. They sat almost completely still, their fins and bodies only occasionally moving. But they weren't what made me have such a visceral reaction. Deep below them, buried completely in the mud, something ancient sat. Its power was . . . old. *Really* old. The chi within its massive body tasted like the essence that suffused the world.

Maria squeezed my arm, tugging at my awareness. "Come back to us," she said, her voice soothing.

When I opened my eyes, I slowly turned her way, my body going numb. Borks and Teddy had been resting, but now they were up, keenly aware of my reaction.

"What did you see?" Maria implored, resting a hand on mine. "Is there no more of the alligator gar? I'm sure we can find something else to—"

"No," I interrupted. "There are hundreds of them."

"What is it, then?" Deklan asked, gazing at the lake's placid waters.

"I . . . can't tell you."

"What?" Hurt accompanied Maria's question, radiating from her core.

I immediately returned to the present, banishing the thoughts whirling through my mind. "I'm not keeping it a secret for a bad reason. It's . . ." I trailed off, wondering how to word it.

"You saw something else, didn't you?" Deklan asked, turning his attention to the others. "Fischer promised not to tell us if he found a bigger fish, remember?"

Dom shook his head. "I take it back. I wanna know."

"Aye," Deklan agreed.

Borks and Teddy agreed with assenting growls, their ears alert.

I looked at them all. "Are you sure?"

They gave a sharp nod, now staring right at me.

"Calling it a big fish doesn't really cut it." I swallowed, my mouth dry. "There is a *monster* at the bottom of this lake."

CHAPTER FIFTY-EIGHT

Frozen

Light slowly bled from the sky as the sun set farther to the west. It shone its orange rays over us, the trees on the other side of the lake casting long shadows that made the water appear almost black. Despite how beautiful a sight it was, all three of the people present were staring at me.

Teddy and Borks, perhaps sensing the danger through our connection, watched the lake's outwardly calm waters, their hackles raised.

"A monster?" Deklan asked, his eyes flicking to the water before returning to me. "What do you mean?"

"Just what I said, mate. There's a *monster* down there."

"Big enough to eat alligator gar?" Maria asked.

"It doesn't feed on anything," I replied. "It's alive but frozen in time, as if it's hibernating. That's the sense I got from it, anyway."

Dom's face had gone serious. "How big are we talking?"

I pursed my lips as I thought for a moment, then turned and paced out some steps. When I was around eight meters away, I faced them. "This long."

"How . . ." Maria swallowed. "How wide?"

I shrugged and walked back toward them. "The surrounding area is soaked with chi, so I couldn't tell where the actual body ends."

"Can you beat it?" she asked in a whisper.

"I think so, but I can't say for certain . . ."

As we all stared at the lake, we slipped into a solemn silence. My enhanced mind started working overtime, attempting to understand how such a creature could end up in the middle of a relatively small lake.

The jungle mudminnows, in all their horrifying glory, had come into being because of experimentation by the followers of Ceto. Did that mean the monster was of their creation? Or was it something much older, something they weren't even aware of? What if their experiments had been an attempt to wake it up?

As I tried to determine how long it had been sequestered here, I recalled the creature's chi. It *was* ancient. Its power was indistinguishable from the world's essence, making me believe it predated this time period and the machinations of Ceto's followers. With that information added to the equation, one answer leaped out at me.

"I think . . ." I paused and cleared my dry throat. "I think it's been here since the power disappeared from the world. The followers of Ceto were active thousands of years ago, right?" The same thoughts ran through my mind. No matter how many times I reconsidered, I reached the same conclusion. "I don't think this creature, whatever it is, will wake up until more power returns to the world."

Silence reigned, only broken by a soft wind rustling the leaves above us.

"But if more power *does* return . . . ?" Maria asked, voicing what everyone was thinking.

I nodded. "Then it will probably wake up."

I sent my awareness back down below the lake, bypassing the guppies, mudminnows, and alligator gars. The monster's existence drew me in. Understanding that I'd glean no more information, I withdrew once more. As I opened my eyes, I took a deep breath and let it out slowly.

"There's not much point in thinking about it, is there?" Maria asked, resting her head on my shoulder.

"Nope," I agreed. "It's a future problem. I don't see it waking up anytime soon."

She shook her head softly, her hair bouncing against her face. "True as that might be, I don't know if I'll be able to stop myself from worrying about it . . ."

I shot her a grin. "I might have just the thing to keep us occupied."

"More fishing?" Deklan asked, the prospect snapping him from his introspection.

"No." I laughed. "Well, not yet, anyway. Let me check something first." Without another word, I leaped up to the branches of the biggest tree I could see.

"Great," Maria said. "He's finally lost his marbles."

"To be fair, you could argue that I never had any marbles in the first place . . ." I climbed farther up the tree, clinging to it as I poked my head above the canopy. When I spied the giant mountain to the north, I couldn't help but smile.

That makes things easier, I thought, hopping down to the ground.

Still smiling, I faced the brothers. "So, fellas, have you had a chance to do any carpentry since you arrived in New Tropica?"

"Fischer?" Maria asked from behind me.

"What's up?"

"Why the frack did you bring a saw with you?"

I turned around from the tree I was cutting, raising an eyebrow at her. "We were camping. What if we needed to cut something?"

"Well, aside from your ability to flick a tree in half, we have Teddy and Borks with us. They could have just cut it down and made lengths of wood the same way that Corporal Claws does . . ."

"Yeah, but where's the fun in that?" I asked.

She squinted at me. I walked over and looped an arm around her back. "I want to saw the wood myself because it's going to be wet, so we'll need to rely on the System stepping in and transforming it. I thought the more involved I was, the better."

"Okay, that makes sense, but I still don't understand why you brought a damned saw."

"I'm prepared for any and all situations," I replied, wiggling my eyebrows at her. "It must be nice to have such a reliable and attractive boyfriend."

"And humble," she said, rolling her eyes at me.

"How could I forget?" I bent and kissed her on the forehead, earning a cute little smile from her. I called out to the brothers, who were back beside the lake, "I won't take long cutting all this."

"No rush!" Deklan yelled back, not bothering to look my way as he waited for a fish to bite.

Dom was too busy to reply. He pulled up a jungle mudminnow, made a disgusted look when its legs touched him, and swiftly dispatched it.

"It's kinda handy having resident bait catchers," Maria said, pulling me into a hug.

"Agreed," I said, rubbing her back. "I'd better get back to it, otherwise those two will fish up every mudminnow in the lake."

"Didn't you say there were thousands?" she asked as we separated.

"Don't underestimate them." I nodded toward the brothers, who were both pulling up another mudminnow. "They are fishing machines."

As I started sawing again, Maria was heading their way, likely going to ensure they didn't actually pull up every single one of the weird little fish.

A half hour later, I had all the wooden panels ready to go. They were wet, of course, but hopefully that wouldn't matter.

"What about wheels?" Deklan asked as he and his brother stared down at the plans.

I shot him a wink. "I'll be heavily relying on System shenanigans for those. If that doesn't work, it won't take too long to carve some. I just didn't want to chop down an old tree if I didn't have to. Don't give me that look, Borks. It's because most of the trunk would be wasted, not because I'm lazy."

When he wagged his tail in response, I narrowed my eyes at him. "You've been hanging out with Claws too much." The wagging only increased.

"Are you sure we need to do this?" Dom asked, scratching the back of his head as he continued studying the sheet.

Deklan gave him an odd look. "What do you mean?"

"Well, can't we just use Borks's dimensional space?"

I shook my head. "I don't think it's a good idea. Have you smelled how stinky fish can get after a while? What if we can't clean it out?"

"Oh . . ."

Borks gave a reassuring bark, making me laugh. "I know you're not bothered, but you enjoy the smell of stinky fish. I don't want everything we put in there to come out smelling like week-old eel."

"Yeah, I'm vetoing that idea, Borks," Maria said, reaching over to scratch his head as she triple-checked the plans. "Let's start— Wait, did you bring nails?" she asked me. "Or are we using joints?"

"Only someone extremely prepared, intelligent, and astoundingly handsome would go camping and think to bring a hammer and—"

"You brought them," she interrupted, sighing.

"Uh-huh," I replied, grinning as I retrieved a leather pouch from my back pocket.

"If we all do this together, we might even get lucky and have it count as another group project. Everyone ready?"

"Ready," they replied.

With Borks and Teddy helping brace wooden panels, the work began. We were a well-oiled machine, putting the project together in no time at all. As I picked up the last piece of wood, I focused on my intention. Planting it firmly in mind, I put the wood in place. Everyone reached out and touched it, and I could feel their wills extending and joining with mine.

I was getting used to the act of shaping people's wills as we made things together. With my enhanced awareness of chi, it was only natural that I slip into the role of support, assisting others to reach their fullest potential. This time, though, I found myself mostly unneeded. I still had to chip in and mold the brothers' essence a little. Maria, Teddy, and Borks, however . . .

Their intentions were perfect.

They'd been a little scattered at first, but as they felt my will, their chi readjusted. It was astounding, and after only a moment of consideration, I realized why they were so capable.

It was because of our experience yesterday, when our souls were connected as one. They had a bone-deep understanding of me, just as I understood them. Something about that bonding had made our joined crafting capabilities much, *much* more potent.

With our wills pouring out into the surrounding world, it happened. Power swelled from the ground, whirled around us, and rushed in toward the two wooden structures. We'd built the lid first and set it against a tree, but as the chi seeped into it, the large piece blurred. In the blink of a cultivator's eye, it melded with the base.

Power came from all of our cores, oozing into the wood and distorting it. It blurred, bulged, then snapped back into place. As I blinked rapidly, taking in the completed project, a smile spread over my countenance.

Just as planned, four wheels had appeared from thin air. They were as large as a wagon's, meaning they could easily traverse uneven terrain. They were attached to a base the size of a, well . . . it was also the size of a wagon. That's where the similarities ended, however. Its sides were short, only a meter or so tall. Now that I looked for something to compare it to, it reminded me of the pop-up campers people seemed so fond of back on Earth.

I stepped forward, running a hand over the wood. The panels were no longer visible, the entire body having transformed into a single structure as if it was carved from a giant tree. The lid was joined to the top somehow, and half worrying that it had sealed, I lifted it. The heavy lid came up slowly, the pieces fitting snugly together.

As I stared down into the space of my mobile esky—or cooler, as those heretical Americans would have called it back on Earth—I laughed. "It's perfect!"

"So the fish go in here?" Deklan asked, running his hand along the bottom of it.

"Exactly."

"Won't they go bad in here, too?" Dom scrunched up his face. "If this gets in the sun, it's effectively an oven . . . right?"

"They could go bad, but you're missing a vital piece of information."

I'd only told Maria the rest of my plan, and we both shared a grin as confusion colored everyone else's features.

"If you'll join me," I said, leaping up to the top of a tree.

A moment later, all of our heads poked above the canopy.

"See that mountain toward the—"

A sharp crack split the late-afternoon air.

Because of our enhanced cognition, we all turned in time to see the look of sheer terror on Teddy's face. With his ears pinned back and the whites of his eyes showing, he seemed to plead for help.

Like the moment you lean a little too far back on a chair and begin to fall, Teddy well knew that he was at gravity's mercy. After what was only a moment but must have felt like an eternity for my newest pal, his head disappeared from sight, plunging below the canopy.

There was a loud thump when he hit the forest floor, immediately overshadowed by our raucous laughter. Teddy's ears were still pinned back when he returned to the treetops, choosing a thicker branch this time.

"I'm sorry," I said, wiping tears from my eyes. "Are you okay?"

He nodded, abashment radiating from his core.

Seeking to change the subject, I pointed at the northern mountain once more. "What do you all see?"

"A mountain?" Deklan answered. "I don't see— *Ohhhh!*"

"What?" Dom demanded, his head darting back and forth. "What is it?"

I grinned. "What color is it?"

"It's white, but what does that— *Oh!* It's covered in snow!"

"That's right, mate. And chunks of ice, if we're lucky."

I pointed down toward the ground, where our makeshift esky on wheels sat.

"We haven't made an oven, fellas. We've made a fridge."

CHAPTER FIFTY-NINE

Downhill

As I sailed through the late-afternoon air, a frigid wind raced over me, biting deep into my skin. Before becoming a cultivator, it would have chilled me to the bone. Now, it just made me smile. I held my arms wide, enjoying the potent sensations that washed over my body.

Still skybound, I glanced back, spotting everyone else between the trees at the base of the mountain. I'd not been able to contain my excitement, so I raced ahead and leaped up into the air the moment we reached the slope. Not wanting to create an earthquake with my jump, I'd only used enough energy to get a third of the way up, and as the mountain approached from below, I grinned. Only touching down for a fraction of a second, I kicked off again, causing shale to fracture.

The next time I landed, it was atop a thin layer of snow. Filled with exhilaration, I launched myself again, getting high enough to see over the top of the mountain. What I found there took my breath away. It was a clear day, and despite the sun's fading light, I could see land all the way to the northern horizon. To the east, I spotted the ocean. From here, it was like a giant god had taken a bite of the continent, letting the sea rush in and claim the space.

When I reached the apex of my flight, gravity took hold. As it dragged me landward, I focused my attention on the snowy peak. With my enhanced awareness, I watched it come as if in slow motion, the icy wind a constant grounding presence. I braced my legs, expecting to crash through a knee-high layer of snow and hit the rocks below.

Instead, I sank up to my shoulders, finding myself completely encapsulated by ice.

"Huh," I said, wiggling my body.

It was like a cold hug, which, now that I thought about it, probably shouldn't be enjoyable. It was, though, the freezing touch of the snow invigorating. I waited there a moment longer before freeing myself, and as I peered down to find my friends, I realized my whoopsie. Apparently, crashing down into a snow-covered peak wasn't the best of ideas. I'd thought the whooshing sound was the howling wind. As it turns out, I might have created a little avalanche.

Well, maybe *little* wasn't the right word . . .

Tons and tons of snow raced down the slope, gathering more mass as it went. I spotted an anomalous color among the white vista, and when I squinted at it, I smiled. Borks, in his long-boi form, danced over the top of it. His empowered body made it look easy, despite the fact that a regular animal would have been buried beneath the frozen flood in the blink of an eye.

With his tongue hanging from his mouth, he made it to me in less than a minute. He unleashed a series of rapid-fire licks on my leg, and I fussed his neck with both hands, giving him a good scritching.

"Where's everyone else, buddy?"

I already suspected the answer, but it was confirmed when he ripped a hole in space.

"The frack, Fischer?" Maria asked, stepping through first. "What was that?"

I waved my hand, making a dismissive gesture. "Oh, just a little avalanche. Nothing to worry about."

"An *avalanche?* Why does your world have a word for a frozen landslide?"

"Iunno. We frack around with winter sports. Skiing and snowboarding are pretty fun . . ." I blinked and stared into space, realizing I might have just found Tropica's newest obsession.

Maria snapped her fingers in front of my face, yoinking me back to the present. "Good," she said. "I was worried that the cold might have frozen your brain for a second."

"There's nothing to freeze, I'm afraid," I joked, knocking the side of my head. "I just had a wonderful idea for a side quest, but it'll have to wait for another time."

She narrowed her eyes at me, but I just grinned. "Shall we?"

"Nope," Deklan said. "Details."

"Uh-huh." Dom nodded and fist-bumped his brother. "We demand more information."

"On . . . ?" I asked.

"Side quest," they both replied at the same time, then gave each other a sly smile and another fist-bump.

"Oh. Right."

I gave them a quick rundown of skiing and snowboarding, and with each word, they looked more and more like kids on Christmas morning.

"You're sure we can't give it a try?" Deklan asked.

"Wouldn't take long," Dom added, "and it would help us, uhhh, understand it better?"

"Right." Deklan nodded gravely. "We don't *want* to do it, per se, but if it's for the sake of knowledge . . ."

I expected Maria to be the voice of reason. In retrospect, that was a terrible assumption to make.

"I mean, it couldn't hurt to go downhill once . . . would it?" she asked.

I held up my hands. "You don't need to convince me to have a good time. It might take us too long to make the necessary equipment, but I have an idea . . ."

It only took Borks a few moments to dig more snow than we needed into his dimensional space, and now that we'd handled what we came for, everyone got into position.

"Riders, ready?" I asked.

Maria, Deklan, and Dom gave me a thumbs-up. Borks let out an affirmative ruff.

"How about you, sled?"

Teddy nodded vigorously.

"Okay! Here we go!"

Teddy was lying on his back, his body reclined so his head faced down the slope. Everyone else was riding him like a toboggan, with Borks up front, the brothers in the middle, and Maria bringing up the rear. I put both my hands on Teddy's back feet.

Showing great restraint, I only tickled his paws a little, stopping when he tensed up and let out a noise that was part warning growl, part giggle. I took slow steps at first, but after a few strides, I picked up the pace. Within a hundred meters, I was sprinting, and just as I reached max speed, I leaped onto Teddy's body, wrapping my arms around Maria's torso.

We were absolutely *flying*, and with our combined mass, we only got faster.

"Hold on tight!" I yelled, following my own advice and leaning into Maria.

I wouldn't be hurt if I fell off, but I wanted to be a part of this inaugural trip every step of the way. The landscape passing us by became a white blur, the wind growing to a howl as we absolutely tore down the slope. Unable to contain his excitement, Borks unleashed a howl, so loud that it cut through the gale.

I joined in, making a sound that was probably embarrassing but still felt good to release. The others joined in, howling at the setting sun as we rocketed down the mountainside. Acting like the love interests in some romantasy novel was rather intoxicating, so when Teddy hit a small lip of rock and careened into the air, we all followed suit.

As we cartwheeled, flipped, and spun chaotically above the slope, I occasionally locked eyes with another rider. One emotion was more prevalent than any other: sheer, unadulterated exuberance. I considered righting myself like the others were doing, but where was the fun in that? I careened wildly, my limbs splayed outward as I descended.

When I struck the snow again, I expected to sink into it, just as I had when landing on top of the mountain. Once more, I was incorrect. I mean, I did hit snow, but I also hit the solid rock directly beneath it only a fraction of a second later. It cracked beneath my body, the shale comprising the mountain obliterated by the force.

The rock absorbed most of the impact, so I didn't bounce again, instead sliding among a sea of pebbles as I slowly came to a stop a few hundred meters later.

When Maria landed by my side, she was crying with laughter. "You—" She cut off, wheezing. "Are you okay?"

"Physically? Doing great. Mentally? My ego might not recover."

I peered up behind me, finding a crater where I had landed. It looked like it was made by a siege weapon. Once more being ridden by Borks, Deklan, and Dom, Teddy slid around the hole, gliding over the mess of shale that my collision had caused. His head was upside down, and I didn't miss the way his eyes were locked on to me, the hint of a smile tugging at his lips.

As expected, he moved an arm, gliding toward me at incredible speed. I could have gotten out of the way, but instead, I reefed Maria's leg out from under her. She let out a startled noise as I pulled her into my lap.

Just in time, too.

Teddy hit us like a . . . well, like a multiple-ton spirit beast sledding downhill while being ridden by two cultivators and a hellhound. Teddy wrapped his powerful forelimbs around us, pulling us in to his chest. I accepted my hug, my stomach swimming with excitement as we skated toward the base of the mountain. Even when the snow ended, Teddy continued on, his enhanced fur sliding right over everything it came across.

All our cores radiated joy as snow became rock and rock became grass. Our passage slowed, and Teddy finally came to a stop against the trunk of a tree.

Deklan held his arms above his head and slid to the ground, crashing to his back. "You know, I think I like snowboarding."

The rest of us followed suit, sloughing off Teddy's torso and lying beneath the tree. My heart was thumping with the adrenaline running through me, and as the last light of day finally disappeared, I let out a contented sigh. "I suppose we should go catch those fish."

"We should," Maria agreed.

"Uh-huh," Deklan and Dom chorused.

Yet none of us moved.

We stared at the sky as the stars lazily came into view, shining their pin-prick light down upon us.

Deep beneath the ruined castle of Theogonia, liquid fire pulsed through the king's veins.

Augustus had thought he knew what it meant to burn. Decades had passed since the time of his awakening, and with each year, his understanding of fire only grew. It was the great destructive force, the element that reduced everything to ash. Some had argued that fire had natural counters, like water, earth, or wind. They were wrong. If a fire burned bright enough, none of these elements stood a chance. Water became steam, earth turned molten, and air only served to fuel the flames, increasing their heat.

Only days ago, he thought there was nothing more to learn about fire. What a fool he had been.

The chi oozing from Theogonia, the essence they had labeled as "corrupted," was nothing of the sort. With its help, Augustus finally understood the truth: he had known *nothing*.

Like a forest being burned to the ground so new vegetation could sprout, his vessel was being rebuilt from within. The blood in his veins boiled as the forbidden chi washed through him, forging his soul into something new. Something better.

There was a soft whimper from beside him, shattering his moment of tranquility. He opened his eyes, fighting down the urge to smite the offender from this plane.

Though he stared his hatred at Aisa, the woman who'd whimpered, another sound drew his attention.

His wife, Penelope, let out a sharp gasp, covering her mouth as she stared at him. "S-sorry! It's just." She swallowed, considering her words. "Your eyes, Augustus."

"Ooo," Tiberius cooed, peering down at him like a curious bird. "Red!"

The rest of the prisoners echoed his call. "Red." "Red?" *"Red!"* They cackled, making the fire burning through Augustus flare.

"Silence!" he screamed, cutting them off. "Fetch me a looking glass."

Princess Tryphena disappeared through the door, returning a moment later with a grave expression and a shard of glass. Augustus meant to stand by the torch to see what they meant, but there was no need. Twin orbs reflected back at him, like burning suns seen through a smoke-filled sky. His eyes were lit from within, the forbidden chi's changes to his body already visible. He threw his head back and laughed, letting the sound crawl out until his throat was hoarse.

"Do you want another shielding potion, Father?" Tryphena asked, a hint of . . . was that *worry* coloring her tone?

"I don't need protection, child," he spat, emphasizing the last word. "In fact, you should join me."

"But . . ." Tryphena's eyes drifted to Aisa.

The woman was pale and peppered with sweat. She and the rest of the handlers had opened themselves up to the forbidden chi, using it as a source of power to ascend. Unlike Augustus, they appeared too weak to handle it.

The king clenched his jaw, fighting the urge to strike someone down. "Suit yourself. If you don't have the spine to cultivate this chi, it would probably have been too much for you anyway."

Lines formed on Tryphena's forehead, and she opened her mouth to reply, but Penelope clamped a hand over it.

Augustus stared at them for a long moment, daring either of them to utter a word. When nothing came, he let out a slow breath. "Don't provide any more potions to the handlers. They need to embrace this power without any shielding if they wish to ascend."

All six of them paled at this, their eyes darting to his.

"Good," he said, giving them a vicious grin. "Use that emotion to serve your kingdom. Your *king*."

"Serve."

"Serve."

"Serve!" the prisoners echoed, breaking out into laughter once more.

This time, the king wasn't annoyed. He took joy in their calls. He closed his eyes and focused once more, drawing more of the chi in.

It was like pouring molten slag right into his veins, and it only made his smile grow.

With this power, he would avenge his honor.

CHAPTER SIXTY

Acidic

Within the dark confines of a wooden hovel, a lone man toiled.

Though Solomon had practiced his profession for tens of thousands of hours over his decades-long life, he had never undertaken a task so grand. It was the last concoction that the mortal known as Solomon would ever create. After he consumed it, he would become Solomon the ascendant. Solomon *the Alchemist*.

The coveted title of the prophesized alchemist . . . it was his to claim. All he had to do was grasp it.

He opened his eyes, peering out at the arrayed ingredients. It was all there, including the rare root he'd discovered and the last bit of bark from the blue tree. After a lifetime spent crafting while surrounded by the Cult of the Alchemist's proprietary haze, it felt . . . weird to work without it. The smoke let them manipulate the world's chi without being detected by the crown. Now that he was alone in the mountains, there was no need for such measures, especially because it could impact his awakening.

One might assume that the lack of a stinging throat and watering eyes would be a welcome reprieve, but to Solomon, it felt like something was missing.

Taking a deep breath, he gathered his resolve and swept his worries aside.

He had sculpted a cauldron from rock, slowly scraping away at the excess material over the span of a day. The water within it was now at a boil. It was time to begin. With but a moment's pause, Solomon threw the basic ingredients in. The first hour of crafting sped by, Solomon's body remembering exactly what to do. When it came time to add his self-named root, he gathered his will, just as the cult's secret texts advised.

Even if he hadn't been instructed on what to do, he'd have known.

Each subsequent step felt *right*, for lack of a better word. As if both his body and the universe wanted the same thing. It was like scratching an itch one wasn't aware of, and as he continued gathering his will and picturing what he wanted, a smile spread over his aged features. Without even looking at the root, he grabbed it in one hand and a sharpened rock in the other. His eyes were still locked on the roiling cauldron as he sliced down the length of the Solomon root.

He'd not opened one up before, and now that he had, he understood.

There was a hidden core within, its flesh soft and springy compared to the encasing fibers. That middle section, only a fraction of the root's width, called out to him. It was loaded with essence. Finally looking down, he collected the chi-filled center and threw it into the cauldron. The concoction within spat and hissed, urging him on.

The decaying bark of the blue tree was next, and when he sent his will toward it, he knew there was nothing to add. It was imperfect. In a state of decomposition. Yet it was all he had. Over the span of a few heartbeats, he imagined it falling into the cauldron and filling it with power. Without hesitation, he upended the pouch and shook.

The clumps of dust hit the surface, and the mixture reacted violently.

Foam bubbled up, threatening to spill over the side and take some of the dust with it. Knowing that the ingredient escaping could spell the end of this mixture, Solomon fought back. He pressed down on it with his will, the foam barely staying contained. It was like shoving down with invisible hands, and if not for his panic, he'd likely have enjoyed the sensation.

Thankfully, his efforts worked, and the bubbles slowly receded, revealing . . .

"What in Circe's loving wand?" he swore, blinking at the mixture.

It had been mostly opaque earlier, lacking all color. He'd added a green root and the blackened, formerly blue bark. Somehow, this had turned the concoction blood red. He swallowed, unable to miss the power flowing out of it. Even if it hadn't transformed so notably, he'd have known: this potion, when properly condensed, would lead to his awakening.

He was distracted, so he closed his eyes, focusing his intent on the end result. Without realizing it, he slipped into a trance. When he opened his eyes once more, he took a heaving breath, only to cough and sputter immediately. His shack was *filled* with a thick haze. It burned everything it touched, his eyes, mouth, nose, and throat on fire. He made to run, to flee from the agony, but stopped before he could take a step.

This was what he wanted, wasn't it? He'd missed the burn of his concealing smoke. Before the magnitude of his goal, this temporary discomfort was nothing. Even if he was to lose his vision, ascension would return it.

Though he had to blink nonstop, he forced his eyes to remain open as he waved a hand above the cauldron, dispersing the smoke. Expecting to find it much the same, he was pleasantly surprised to see the concoction mostly reduced. He'd thought that only a few minutes had passed, but it had been hours. Despite the acrid haze burning everywhere it touched, relief flooded him.

It was almost complete.

He took deep breaths that scorched his lungs, yet this did nothing to deter him. All the while, he continued picturing his ascension to godhood, clinging to that eventuality in order to push through the pain. After an agonizing stretch of time, something shifted in the air. Though his hovel was closed to the outside world, a breeze stirred. There was a moment of confusion, of not believing his senses. Then, all at once, the smoke flowed back into the cauldron in wispy streams, returning to the red concoction.

Before Solomon's very eyes, it started to glow. The red light seeped through the cauldron, even solid stone unable to contain its brilliance.

He dropped to his knees on the earthen floor, gazing up at the incandescent light. Now that the smoke was absent, the air tasted sweet. Before he knew it, he was cackling, his voice harsh and scratched from exposure to the concoction. Wheezing for breath, he got back to his feet, leaning on his bench for support.

The light was retreating, returning to the mixture which now had a shimmering quality. He dipped a finger in it, testing its heat. Somehow, the haze flowing into it had cooled the potion. His hands shook as he grabbed the lip of the cauldron and brought it to his mouth.

It was more magnificent than he could have imagined.

Rather than taste it on his tongue, his entire awareness seemed to drink in its essence, flooding him with warmth. He took massive gulps, not stopping until he'd consumed every last drop. He licked his lips and set down the cauldron, raising his arms toward the roof and the sky beyond, imagining a great pillar of light descending from the heavens to—

A sharp pain tore through him, like a knife plunging into his stomach. Groaning, he doubled over, clutching his abdomen. Just when the sensation faded, the knife twisted and tore. A choked sound came from his throat as he collapsed. As fast as it came, the searing agony disappeared, only to return a moment later. Though the warmth remained, it disappeared each time the knife came back.

Pulled back and forth between pain and bliss, an acidic aftertaste covered his tongue. It was . . . *wrong*.

The potion had failed.

With that knowledge afflicting him, the pain came stronger than ever before. He blacked out, his consciousness doing all it could to protect him from the suffering.

The following morning, I woke to a pleasant fluttering in my stomach. Still half asleep, I searched my muddied thoughts for the cause of my excitement. It took me a moment, but as I stared at the line of sunlight streaming in the front of my tent, I remembered.

"Fishing day!" I yelled, sitting bolt upright. "Wake up!"

There was no response, so I looked around, pouting. Neither Maria nor Borks, who'd both cuddled me to sleep, were anywhere to be seen.

A beautiful face poked into the tent and raised an eyebrow, making my pout turn into a grin.

"We're already awake, you goose," Maria said, giving me an amused look. "We're just about to start making breakfast."

"Be out in a moment."

I stretched, enjoying the movement of sleep-sore muscles before pushing the tent flap aside and stumbling into the light. We'd set up our campsite on the western side of the lake on Maria's instructions, meaning the morning sun could beam down on us. I mentally thanked Maria for her foresight as I stood beneath its warming rays, closing my eyes and facing it with my, uh . . . face.

"Good sleep-in?" Deklan asked.

"Yeah, mate." I took a deep breath and let it out slowly, a sense of calm flowing through me.

When I opened my eyes once more, I strode over to everyone else. They were surrounding a small fire, and I beamed at the nods, grins, and waves that came my way. "What can I do to help?" I asked, bending to pat Borks on the head. He licked me and wagged his tail in response.

"You can just sit there and look handsome," Maria said, shooting me a wink. "I've got this covered."

She was just arranging a bunch of unbaked croissants onto a tray, so I walked over and planted a peck on the top of her head, earning a cute little shimmy of her shoulders in return. I ambled over to Teddy and sat down beside him, covering a yawn. "How'd you sleep, big fella?"

He nodded and let out a rumbling growl that meant *good*. Despite the fact that his mere act of communicating sounded like tectonic plates shifting, he averted his eyes. I wanted to tell him he didn't have to be so deferential. I wanted to tell him that he was welcome as he was. Instead, I reached up and patted one of his giant shoulders. "I'm glad, buddy," I said.

We spoke about small things as Maria prepared breakfast, the blessed smells of coffee and cooking pastries slowly building and becoming irresistible. Just as the coffee pot was starting to hiss, a bubble of chi exploded far to the east. I jolted, my head darting in its direction. It was . . . *acidic*?

"What's wrong?" Deklan asked.

"Huh?" Maria spun, facing me. "What happened?"

I stood. "You don't feel that?"

"No?" She got to her feet, her face serious. "Feel what? You're worrying me."

"Someone or something just awakened to the east. Right outside of Tropica. It feels . . . wrong."

"Go," she said, already moving. "We'll follow."

I nodded. "With me, Borks."

He transformed into his Chihuahua form. I scooped him up in my arms, dashed to the end of the lake, and leaped. Trees sailed past below me as I took us toward the anomaly, a foreboding worry sprouting from deep within me.

CHAPTER SIXTY-ONE

Cleanse

The forest sailed by below us, countless colors blurring into a single blanket of green. Over mountains and across valleys, Borks and I flew, never once changing direction. I destroyed more than a few trees in my passage. Each time I landed, I carved through swaths of them like a scythe through so many stalks of wheat. I didn't spare them a second thought, the safety of my friends taking priority. At the speed I was traveling now, we'd get there in less than an hour.

"Not fast enough . . ." I muttered, wracking my mind for a solution. "Borks, can you teleport to the east without an exact destination in mind?"

A slight pulse of hesitation came from him, followed by a much stronger wave of determination.

I skidded to a stop, obliterating another dozen trees. Borks leaped down, and the air shattered as a black portal unfurled. Scooping him into my arms, I shot through it. We emerged high above the forest, and because of my connection to Borks, I could feel where we'd teleported from, a whisper of his chi coming from that direction. It had worked. We'd appeared kilometers closer to Tropica.

"Did you make the destination high so we didn't appear underground?" I asked Borks as we dropped to the ground.

He let out an affirmative *ruff.*

"Good boy. Bark at me whenever you can portal again."

Bracing himself in my arms, he nodded. His reserves were depleted due to how far we'd traveled, but even now, ambient chi refilled his core.

Taking turns leaping and portaling, we traveled faster than ever before. When I took us sailing over a hill, I spotted the source of the acidic-tasting chi.

It was impossible to miss.

A blackened circle of trees broke up the forest's monotony, every leaf on them having decayed and fallen. Our trajectory continued, and I crashed down only a few hundred meters away from the clearing. I'd noticed the acidic feeling the entire time we traveled, but now, I could smell it, too. Borks lifted his nose to test the air; he regretted it immediately. Shaking his head and letting out a series of snorts, he wobbled, seeming to lose all sense of balance.

"Whoa!" I stilled him with a hand. "You okay?"

He made a hacking noise, his balance only getting worse. Having seen enough, I grabbed him and jumped, crashing through and obliterating the canopy of a tree on my way clear of the area. When I landed on a distant hill, I cradled him in my arms, gazing down at him. Thankfully, his breathing eased and he sat up, his legs firm beneath him.

"What was that?" I asked. "Are you good?"

He nodded, staring down at the spot from which I'd leaped. He let out a low growl, its meaning obvious. *Poison.*

Whether because of my relative strength or comparatively weak sense of smell, I wasn't affected. "Are you okay if I leave you here, mate? I wouldn't ask otherwise, but—"

A sense of reassurance washed over me. Borks understood the urgency.

Smiling, I rubbed his head. "You're a good boy. Rest up, buddy. I'll be back before you know it."

Firming my jaw, I leaped for the circle of black marring the beautiful forest, and when I landed in the center, I covered my mouth, doing all I could to keep out the noxious smell. It hadn't been bad from afar. From here, it was like breathing in battery acid. An odd hint of something herbal accompanied it, only making the scent more pungent.

I released chi from my core, surrounding myself with a firm layer of shielding.

The relief was immediate, and I almost released a slow breath out of reflex. There was a makeshift shack in the center of the clearing. I reached out to grab the door, only for it to crumble within my grasp. Leaping back despite my protection, the door fell to the ground, shattering into uncountable fragments. I strode over them on my way to the entrance, the pieces crunching beneath my feet. As I peered into the squat building, I cringed. Everything within had been made of wood and was rotting before my very eyes.

I sent my awareness out toward it, feeling the decay happening in real time. There was a stone bowl on top of a warped bench, even its hardened body turning a sickly brown color.

Not a bowl, I realized. *A cauldron.*

Not at all caring for my moment of clarity, the table gave way dramatically, disintegrating to nothing as the cauldron fell through it and crashed to the floor. Before the roof could rain down on me like noxious confetti, I left the hovel, and the moment I was back outside, I firmed my jaw. Someone or something had awakened here. There was no doubt about it. If the toxic chi was any indication of their character, this person had to be found.

I shot thin strands of chi out, scouring every direction for any hint of a foreign core. I found Borks pretty quickly, and as he sensed my attention, I got the distinct impression that his tail was wagging ferociously. On and on, my chi stretched. Yet no matter how far I went, there was neither hide nor hair of anything suspicious. If whatever being had ascended here was present, I'd have known. Which left two possibilities: they'd left or they'd perished. Considering just how damaged the area was, I suspected the latter.

But it was better to be safe than sorry.

Gathering my strength, I leaped straight upward. The resulting shock wave made what remained of the shack, and more than a few rotted trees, fall to pieces. While skybound, I scanned the forest, seeking any hint of contamination. There was . . . nothing. Beyond the toxic clearing, all was well. Most of my worry fell away as I returned to the forest floor, bending my legs and landing much quieter than I'd left it. I raced toward Borks, and when I got there, I was happy to find him well.

"Feeling better, mate?"

Ruff! he replied, giving me a full-body wag.

"Good boy." I mussed the top of his head. "Can you go tell everyone that it's okay?"

He cocked his head at me, speaking a thousand words with that one expression.

I rubbed behind his ear. "I'm gonna go tell Barry and the gang about what I found here. As soon as I let them know, I'll meet you all back at the lake. Shouldn't be gone for more than an hour or . . ." I tapped my chin. "Actually, I might come back here to try cleanse it first, so I could take longer."

Showing complete trust in me, he licked my hand a few times in less than a second, then turned and fled, slipping into his long-boi form as he tore a portal in space and leaped through it. A few kilometers away, high in the air, he turned to face me. His entire body wagged once more when he caught me staring.

"What did I do to deserve such a good boy?" I asked myself with a smile.

When Borks finally disappeared from sight, I turned and ran, sprinting farther east. The sooner I told everyone of the potential danger, the sooner I could return to the lake and our day of fishing.

Hidden beneath the ground of what used to be his shack, Solomon's *everything* was wracked by another wave of pain.

He curled into a ball and held his legs close, praying for the agony to vanish. It wasn't supposed to be like this. He had succeeded in his ascension. He had made a potion that started the process of his awakening.

And now, he was dying.

Though he couldn't tell how he knew, he was certain. It might take days or even weeks, but his destruction was assured if he didn't do anything. Solomon would find a way out, though. He had to.

Each time his torment resumed, a part of him wished his life would end. But the episodes always passed, leaving him gasping for breath in his sealed-off compartment.

As soon as he'd regained consciousness and realized he'd ascended, he acted quickly. Solomon had dug a hole in the earth where he stood, only pausing when pain shot through him. He'd sealed the entry with wood and layers of earth. When the wood started to crumble, dissolving beneath the toxic chi of his creation, he used small punches to pack the earth tight.

As soon as he'd been enclosed and the walls were no longer threatening to cave in, he poked a tiny hole in his cavern, then started the small fire. He'd thrown the last of his herbs, those that were used by the Cult of the Alchemist to hide their manipulation of chi, in the flames. The leaves and stems had been mostly blackened, but when they caught fire, the smell that rose from them was familiar. Within moments, he'd been surrounded by a detection-dampening haze.

He was just getting over another wave of agony when the beast arrived.

He thought he imagined the vibration that ran through the surrounding soil, but then a great huffing sound came from nearby, making his blood run cold. Solomon froze, and in the silence that followed, a human voice breached his awareness. He couldn't make out the words, but it was definitely a male. As quietly as Solomon could, he sealed the hole to the outside world and went very, *very* still. Over the next few minutes, there were another series of vibrations and sounds, all building within to create a monolithic wall of anxiety.

A cultivator and a spirit beast had detected his awakening. They had come to end his life.

Though he hadn't heard the cultivator's words when he'd spoken to the beast, he was sure: it was *not* the voice of Tom Osnan Jr. The revelation that there was more than one uncollared cultivator on the loose should have set his mind to boiling, but with the echoes of anguish lingering in his bones, he didn't particularly care about the details.

Another wave of torment came, smothering him in misery. This was the longest yet, and when it finally ended, tears rolled down his face to pool on one cheek.

Clenching his jaw, Solomon focused on the outside world, trying to detect any hint of the cultivator. Blessedly, it appeared as though his ruse had worked; the cultivator hadn't found his place of hiding. Even if Solomon wanted to leave, to flee now that the coast was clear, he wasn't sure he could. When he'd first dug this hole, he thought it a temporary dwelling. A place he could hide until his body recuperated.

With every new wave of searing agony that arrived, he became less and less sure that he would live through this. Unless something changed, this place would be his tomb. He laughed bitterly, his cult's concealing haze making his throat sting when he inhaled.

"Not a cult," he croaked out, tears welling in his eyes. "A church."

He had become *the* Alchemist of prophecy, using a potion to awaken. And here, alone and trapped underground, his church's celebrated deity would perish. He would have laughed then, but the next wave of suffering came. Before his consciousness faded, he hoped—prayed—for his end.

What could have been hours or days later, Solomon opened his eyes when a shuddering vibration shook his burial chamber.

"Welp," came a muffled voice from above. "Smells just as bad as I remember."

There was an odd accent and inflection to the voice, tugging at Solomon's memories. A part of his mind sought to eke out the source.

"Wouldn't wanna ruin a good pair of pants," the voice continued conversationally, uncaring of Solomon's efforts.

Pants . . . ?

Solomon had a long moment to consider the confusing statement before an odd sensation washed over him, making his skin tingle. At first, he thought it was the next episode of torment—but the pain never arrived.

It's chi, he realized. The cultivator had found him.

Solomon should have been distraught. Should have railed and fought for his life. Instead, he squeezed his eyes shut, hoping that it would be quick and painless.

"What is that?" the voice asked, filled with curiosity.

The next moment, the stranger's chi drove *into* Solomon, washing through his entire body. All but paralyzed, Solomon's eyes went wide as the stranger's essence infiltrated his core.

CHAPTER SIXTY-TWO

Radiation

I furrowed my brow as I continued feeling the world with my chi, focusing it right on the spot where the shack had been.

All that remained of it now was a divot in the earth, covered by remnant . . . *Are they ashes? Rotten fibers?* I rubbed some of the decaying material between my fingers, the texture gritty, porous, and . . . oily? Whatever the toxic chi had turned the wood into, it was decidedly unpleasant.

I went to rub it off on my leg but caught myself just in time. "Wouldn't wanna ruin a good pair of pants."

It had only taken an hour or so to go back to Barry and let him know what I'd found in the clearing. Thankfully, Ellis had been running an experiment with the smiths, so I'd been able to make a clean getaway without too many questions. Even now, the former archivist might be on his way here.

I had better hurry, then, I thought, smiling despite my surroundings.

I sent my chi flooding out, dissipating the shield I had been covering my body with. I was ready to reform it at a moment's notice, but there was no need; the thick ropes of essence flowing from me were too strong for the toxic chi to get close to my body. I scanned the entire area in a fraction of a second, and as the results flooded into my awareness, I peered straight down, raising an eyebrow. The source of the corruption felt like it was below me, buried beneath the ground where the shack had been.

"What *is* that . . . ?" I asked, unable to contain my curiosity.

I honed in on it as a new fear emerged; had the cultivator or spirit beast retreated underground, burrowing their way to safety?

But . . . no. There was no core there, neither beast nor human present. There was, however, a disgustingly potent dose of the acidic chi, and I felt it lashing out at my pure essence, trying to consume it.

I snorted at its attempt. The little pocket of chi down there might be anathema to life, but it was pitifully weak. I poured a mere fraction of my core out. As I did, I pictured rays of light glowing from me, burning away all that was unwholesome. It was over in the blink of an eye, and a sense of unease I wasn't aware of fell away as the corruption was cleansed. With the blight gone, the forest air seemed to rush in, swirling into the vacuum left behind.

"Huh," I said after taking a deep breath of the now-sweet air. "That was easy. Should've done it earlier."

I looked around, smiling as the world seemed right once more. I turned, crouched, and leaped, soaring over the forest.

I had some fishin' to do.

When Solomon could breathe again, he took a shuddering gasp of air.

He expected it to sting. To burn as though his very lungs were aflame. His hole in the ground was still filled with haze, but inhaling it only made his throat tingle a little. The reality of the situation slowly settled over him as he felt his body's sensations.

He had been healed, if that word could even cover the extent of his transformation. It had all happened so fast. One moment, he had been poisoned from within, cursed with the knowledge that his own chi was destroying him. The next, a force of nature had forced its way into his core and cauterized the corruption. Now that he was fixed, Solomon could continue taking steps on the path of ascension. He could become the embodiment of the Alchemist of prophecy. But that didn't seem so important anymore, because he had just encountered a being that, given time, would become *true* divinity.

From that flash of power, something that could have only been seconds, Solomon had gleaned all he needed to know about the being that had purified him. Because of the haze filling the underground pocket of air that Solomon occupied, the stranger, an ascendent of unimaginable power, hadn't noticed him. Despite this, the stranger's chi had sought him out and . . . fixed him.

That was easy, the man had said. *Should've done it earlier.*

When Solomon recalled how the man's essence felt, a faint smile came to his face. It had been . . . *pure*. The antithesis of the acidic chi radiating from Solomon and poisoning the surrounding forest. He had been terrified when it first happened, but the longer he was exposed to the other man's light, the more certain he became that the man wished him no ill will.

Now that he was healed, he considered bursting up from the ground and pursuing the stranger. Part of him wanted to chase him down and thank him profusely, but the more primitive parts of his brain, those that were focused on self-preservation, urged caution. If the seemingly benevolent man was aware that Solomon had been the source of the corruption, would he be so kind?

Solomon shook his head softly. No. There was much more to consider before he did something so brazen. How did this man's existence slot in with Solomon's understanding of the long-departed gods and their lingering wills? All the signs that he had attributed to the residual power of beings long departed—was it possible that he had been wrong?

Beneath the now-cleansed forest, breathing a haze that no longer hurt his throat, Solomon's enhanced mind began unwinding the threads of all he knew, so numerous they were uncountable.

By the time I arrived back in the clearing it was almost midday, and I only had a single thought on my mind.

"Thank the gods," Maria said, hugging me. "What happened? Are you oka—"

"Howmanyfishdidyoucatchwithoutme?" I blurted, unable to contain the words.

Maria blinked up at me as I took a steadying breath, the rest of my brain catching up to the surroundings. Her lips formed a line and she slapped my chest, not hard enough to hurt me but enough to convey her annoyance. "Are you serious? You leave me behind to go chase some vague threat, then come back and ask about fishing?"

The corner of Deklan and Dom's mouths curled up, but when I narrowed my eyes at them, they became acutely interested in the surrounding trees.

I held up my hands as I returned my attention to Maria. "Okay, valid criticism, but you know I'm a simple man. Besides." I waved a hand. "It wasn't a problem." I quickly explained all that had happened.

Maria rested her head on my chest, a slight shiver running down her back. "I wonder what it was that ascended? Some poor beetle or something?"

I shrugged. "No clue. I couldn't find the faintest hint of any life. Whatever it was, I'm guessing it was immediately consumed by the acidic chi."

Maria shivered again, stronger this time. "That doesn't bode well for the rest of the world, does it?"

I rubbed her back. "It'll be fine. Barry is having the Buzzy Boys and our pelican pals scour the area for now. We can worry about it when we get back. Which means . . ."

"There's only one thing for us to do," Deklan said, shooting his brother a knowing look.

"I reckon you're right," Dom agreed, a grin slowly spreading over his face.

I nodded. "Whatever we do from here out, finishing my quest is the quickest path to improvement we have. And even if cooking a bunch of alligator gar doesn't help finish the quest, feeding everyone a bunch of chi-filled fish might lead to a breakthrough or two."

Maria cleared her throat and released me from her hug. "I *suppose* you're right . . ."

When I spotted the twinkle in her eye, I barked a laugh. "Don't play coy. You're just as keen as we are to do some fishing. Speaking of, you never answered me. Did you catch many while I was gone?"

She shook her head, loose strands of hair bouncing across her glowing cheeks. "No. It didn't feel right doing it without you, so we spent the morning getting your esky-wagon-whatever ready."

I raised an eyebrow, but she didn't elaborate, just pointed at yesterday's construction. I strode over and lifted the lid, finding the bottom absolutely covered in a layer of ice bricks. They fit together perfectly, only thin lines betraying that it wasn't a single sheet.

"Damn. How did you get them so flush?"

"Teddy and Borks," Maria answered, our bear pal blushing beneath his thick fur while Borks oozed pride. "They packed snow into bricks."

I grinned at my fuzzy pals. "You guys are the best. Thank you."

"So the esky is ready to go," Maria said, shooting a furtive glance toward the water. "All that's left is to catch the fish . . ."

Without another word, we raced for our rods, all keen on being the first with a line in the water.

The day sped by in a pleasant blur, and after only a few hours, I'd stopped counting how many I'd caught. The early afternoon had arrived, and as the sun beamed down on my lower legs, it seemed to warm my very soul. I closed my eyes and smiled at the world, only opening them when another fish tried to tear off with my bait.

The fight was over not long after, and as I passed the alligator gar off to Teddy so he could put it in the mobile esky, he gestured for me to follow him. Raising an eyebrow, I plodded behind him, the air growing cooler as I moved beneath the canopy. Teddy cracked the lid and I peered inside.

My jaw dropped open. "Whoa. It's already full?"

Teddy nodded, almost apologetically.

I reached out and rubbed his head, trying to reassure him despite the fact he had nothing to be sorry for. "We were even more productive than I thought. Thanks for letting me know, buddy."

Engrossed as everyone else was with fishing, they hadn't heard our conversation.

"Tools down!" I yelled, playing foreman. I got a series of confused looks in return, making me snort. "Don't catch any more fish! We don't have any more room in the esky."

This only deepened their confusion.

"Wait, you're serious?" Maria asked. "It's full?"

"As full as my heart when I spot an entrancing young lady on the streets of Tropica—" I went full Matrix, leaning backward to dodge the pebble pelted my way. "I meant you!" I laughed, shooting her a wink as she gave me an exaggerated pout.

"Fish on!" Deklan yelled, his rod bending in half.

"Bro . . ." Dom said, shaking his head. "Why did you leave your line in?"

"I was retrieving it!"

I rolled my eyes playfully, having already seen the slow retrieve Deklan was doing, my lackadaisical pal clearly hoping this exact scenario would play out.

"It's fine," I said. "Just don't catch any more after that one."

Deklan easily fought it back to shore, and without even removing it from the lake's water, he unhooked it and let it go, smiling to himself as it returned to the depths.

"Thanks, fishy," he whispered to himself, watching it go.

"Okay, gang," I said when I had their attention once more. "Looks like we're good to go. Should we head off now?"

"As keen as I am to spend another night camping," Maria said, "I'm even more excited to get back and cook up a feast for everyone."

The brothers both nodded, and as one, we started dismantling the basic camp. Within minutes, we were ready to go. After giving the area one last scan for anything we'd missed, I gazed out at the lake. Everyone came to join me, settling into a comfortable silence as the calm waters drew us in. A soft breeze blew, rustling the surrounding leaves.

"This was a lovely little trip," Maria said, resting a head on my shoulder.

The brothers grunted in agreement, and Borks let out an affirmative *ruff*, wagging his tail.

I cast a gaze Teddy's way. "Did you enjoy your first vacation, buddy?"

He'd been transfixed by the lake, and when he slowly swiveled my way, he gave me a slight nod, still entirely too polite.

I rubbed his massive head. "Good. There will be plenty more in the future." I turned, striding for the wagon. "Let's get going."

After an hour, we'd covered kilometers of ground, trees racing past as I maneuvered the wagon through them. With my power, I was able to match everyone else's pace. Surprisingly, I found it just as relaxing as when I was fishing earlier. I easily slipped into the rhythm, my body seeming to move of its own accord as I weaved to and fro beneath the trees. Seeking to stretch my capabilities, I sent my chi ahead of us, sensing where the trunks grew more sparse. I separated from the others for short distances, but I always returned, winding back toward them when the forest allowed.

"Stop showing off," Maria said, trying and failing to appear annoyed.

I just shot her a wink and gave her my best grin. We were halfway there now, and we'd be home well before dark. *Plenty of time to prepare and cook—*

Subtle as a hammer to the spine, a presence exploded into my awareness. I skidded to a stop, my eyes going wide as I faced the west. Within the blink of an eye, everyone came to my side.

"What is it?" Maria asked, her voice laden with worry as she looked around.

"Something far away," I said, my nostrils flaring.

If the acidic chi earlier was poison, whatever I felt now was the equivalent of nuclear radiation. I hoped that my initial reaction was wrong, and that it would resolve into something more benign. It didn't.

"It's . . . *evil*," I said, clenching my jaw and fighting off a wave of nausea.

Worse, it was powerful. I could feel it from so far away. Was it a person? A spirit beast? An—

A spear of terror jabbed my core as the anomaly appeared on the other side of me. I whirled, facing the east. Facing Tropica . . .

Everyone else felt it this time, because they spun at the same time as I did. My skin prickled with its proximity, beads of sweat sprouting from my forehead.

Whoever or whatever it was, they had come.

CHAPTER SIXTY-THREE

Preordained

Though there had been much to consider, it didn't take Solomon long to reach a decision. After less than an hour beneath the ground, filled with direction and determination, he raised a hand to the compacted earth. He'd thought the strength of his enhanced body was impressive when he created the cavern, but it didn't hold a candle to his power now. His arm passed through the soil like a knife through butter, easily carving a way out into the daylight.

Though the corruption had been cleaned away, the surrounding forest was still heavily damaged. No acidic chi remained, but their leaves, bark, and most of their branches were gone, having wasted away while his core was still leaking tainted essence. Despite this, his conscience was clean.

The early afternoon sun shone its warmth over his skin, banishing any lingering worries. He had a path forward, one that would lead to his ascension. He wasn't yet sure what to do about the cultivator he'd encountered, the man of pure chi who had cleansed his soul, but that didn't change his course.

Solomon's plan was simple. He was going to create potions. He was going to experiment. And he was going to gain *power*. Then, only once he had more strength, he could decide whether to approach the stranger. He took a single step forward, intent on finding his first batch of ingredients, but paused.

With the agony he'd been subjected to earlier, he'd been too distracted to truly notice how much his body had changed. Now that the pain was gone, he closed his eyes, focusing on his other senses.

The smallest of breezes blew, making the remaining leaves shift and sway in the surrounding trees. The sound was almost deafening as it built to a cacophonous roar, only partially muted when the air struck his skin, distracting him.

The scents of the forest came next. Solomon well knew what decaying plant life smelled like, but he'd never experienced it like this. The aroma was so potent that it dulled everything else, drawing him in. Following a hunch, he tried to reduce his sensitivity. Perhaps it was a skill he'd have to practice. He—

The air immediately behind him, right above where his shack had been, erupted into flames.

Though his body was improved, it was like standing next to the sun, and he dashed away. Well, he tried to. His legs failed him, and Solomon skidded across the recently healed grass, crashing against a dead tree. He'd not picked up enough speed to smash through the half-decayed trunk, so he lay against it, his limbs not doing what he ordered them to.

With his eyes wide and terror crawling up from his abdomen, he witnessed the impossible. A bonfire smoldered in midair, tendrils licking out unnaturally fast. They seemed to weave into a pattern, following invisible threads that made little sense . . . until they formed a circle. The moment the shape was noticeable, it burgeoned out, slowly burning larger and larger.

Foul wind poured from the gap in the sickly flames, even more rancid than the corruption that had previously tainted Solomon's core. A wave of nausea washed over him, yet he couldn't move. Couldn't escape. Try as he might, he was locked in place. Squinting against the turgid portal's unholy light, all he could do was watch as the first figure emerged.

A man leaped through, the withering grass combusting around his feet when he landed. He wore flames like a noble would don jewelry, rings, bracelets, and a necklace of flames all moving as unnaturally as the portal. And atop his head, extending into seven flickering points, a crown made the man seem even taller than he was. The air warped around it, the headpiece seeming to suck in its own light.

Solomon recognized the man.

"K—" His voice cut off, and he took a wheezing breath that ended in a wracking cough. "King . . . ?"

Augustus Reginald Gormona's eyes flicked to Solomon, and he took a step forward. "Fischer . . ." he said, his hatred burning even brighter than the flames.

Six people came through behind the king. Despite lacking the living fires he wore, the same nauseating aroma oozed from the women. He thought he recognized them from somewhere, but Solomon couldn't place it.

"No . . ." the king said, his jaw tensing and relaxing swiftly. "Not Fischer. But I *know* you . . . don't I?"

A jumble of people hopped through the rent in space next, moving chaotically and barreling into the six women. The women, whose identities were still tugging at part of Solomon's mind, turned and made to attack the latter group. They tittered and leaped away from the threat, separating around the clearing.

"Free?"

"Free!"

"*Freeee!*" they chorused, laughing as they hopped about.

"Now, now," one of them said, the voice like a punch to Solomon's frontal cortex. "My little birds are just happy that they can spread their wings. There is no need for violence, handlers."

"Francis?" he asked, already knowing it to be him. "High Alchemist Francis . . . ?"

"Little Solomon? Is that you . . . ?"

"Ah," the king said, recognition coloring his face. "Solomon the alchemist. I remember now."

"Gods above!" Francis yelled. "The king! Bow, little Solomon!"

Solomon just blinked. He'd heard Francis's madness had worsened, but what was going on? There was a sound like crackling tinder, and the king appeared right in front of Solomon. The next thing he knew, he was suspended in the air, his feet dangling.

"You became a cultivator." The king's eyes were inhuman as they seemed to stare through Solomon. "Foolish . . ."

"Oh," Francis said. "*Oh, oh, oh!* You aren't just an alchemist anymore, are you, Solomon?" He nodded to himself, the question apparently rhetorical. "Wonderful. I didn't think you had it in you." He made a waving gesture toward Solomon. "You should let him live, my king."

"Why?" Augustus Reginald Gormona ground out. "We're here to kill traitors. Why would I allow the existence of another?"

"Because he's useful. Just ask my birds."

"Yes!"

"Yes!"

"Yes!" the large group of . . . *birds?* chorused.

"No!" one of them said, causing the others' heads to swivel her way. "Kidding!" she sang. The silent accusations of the rest melted away, replaced by high-pitched cackles.

Solomon recognized them then, and the pieces clicked into place all at once. The sickly air. The strange power afflicting all those that had arrived. Francis's presence. The familiar faces . . .

"Theogonia," he said, barely able to believe it. "You've come from Theogonia."

"See?" Francis said, smiling and nodding toward Solomon. "He's useful! Yes, he's a cultivator, but so is everyone here! Well, except for me. Solomon is a senior member of the Cult of the Alchemist, so he's aware of the . . . *services* provided to the crown, Your Majesty. He is a loyal vassal."

"We will see . . ."

Solomon crashed to the floor, his limbs still not completely working. The king made a disgusted noise then turned, dismissing him. Another four people stepped through the portal. The moment they were clear, it fizzled out, the fire dying.

"*Tom,*" the king said, spitting the name. "You said we would find Fischer here."

Solomon had thought—*prayed*—that there would be no more surprises today. He was wrong. Lord Tom Osnan Sr., Queen Penelope, and Princess Tryphena had stepped through the portal, accompanied by an unknown man. Among them, only Lord Osnan oozed the corrupted chi, having drawn its essence into his core.

"I said Fischer is in Tropica," Lord Osnan said, looking around.

"And how do you know that?" the king demanded, his adorning flames flaring.

"He told me that he knew my son, who has been living in Tropica for the last few years." He gestured at the surrounding trees. "This isn't Tropica. This isn't the coastal town I pointed to on the map. You brought us to the wrong place."

The king's fire grew hotter as he took a step toward Osnan, who clenched his fists as vines rose from beneath him, writhing in the air. As with the king's flames, the power radiated corrupted chi.

"Ah, such chance happenings!" Francis said, broadcasting his voice. "Solomon, you were stationed in Tropica, were you not?"

As all eyes turned to him, Solomon nodded. "Yes. It's just east of here. Close."

A vicious grin came to the king's face. "Good. We can address your insubordination later, *Tom.*"

The roots rising from Osnan's feet creaked as they wound around one another, nauseating chi pouring from them. "Why don't we address it now?"

There was a madness in the two men's eyes, and the more chi they exuded, the worse it became. If Solomon did nothing, there was a good chance their clash would lead to his destruction.

"It's my fault!" he yelled, getting their attention. Both hate-filled gazes shot toward him, and he swallowed, his throat dry and scratchy. "I awakened here earlier today by creating a potion. Something went wrong with the concoction, and I . . . I barely survived." He nodded at one of the trees. "It wasn't your arrival that killed everything here. It was me. I'm guessing that's why you were drawn here instead of directly to Tropica. Neither of you are to blame."

"Ah, such humble words from this loyal servant. A mere accident, I say!" Francis said. "Nay, perhaps it was divine intervention that—"

Below them, something colossal stirred. The very ground shook, and as Solomon sent his new senses downward, he found it. There was a network down there, a net of sorts that ran in every direction. Though partially intangible, it sprawled out toward the west. Eastward, where Tropica sat and the king was headed, it grew more dense. Every cultivator present must have felt the same thing, because they all looked down, their brows furrowing. Even the "birds" grew serious, the odd network below the only thing that had broken their childlike behavior.

"You see?" Francis beseeched, staring at the king. "Tropica has defensive measures! A mesh of power that spans the distance of mountains! It might have led to our destruction—er, I mean, the destruction of those less powerful than you, my king. Our arrival here was preordained!"

When Solomon felt the pure essence that made up most of the underground object's power, his suspicions were confirmed. The man who had cleansed him, that being of such pure unrivaled power that had easily healed his poisoned body, was the same person that the king was hunting. He'd seen the man before, in line for coffee at Lena's Café, what felt like lifetimes ago. Solomon had noted his odd accent—the same one he'd heard earlier today. The chi held in the mesh below was *his*. It was Fischer's. Solomon couldn't forget how it felt if he tried.

In the silence that followed, none could have been more shocked than Solomon. That's what he had thought, anyway—up until the moment he spied Tom Osnan Sr.

The king noticed, too, because he narrowed his eyes on him. "What now, Tom? Thought of some new way to vex me?"

Solomon expected the lord to bite back, to instigate another fight. Instead, he simply shook his head, looking almost sick. "It's definitely him, Augustus. That power . . ." A shiver ran down Tom Osnan's spine. "Fischer is in Tropica, and whatever that thing is below us, he put it there. I'm certain."

The king started laughing, the sound . . . wrong. Like someone had thrown wet wood in a raging fire. The "birds" joined in, just happy for an excuse to giggle. "Good," the king finally said, then cleared his throat. "Fischer has thought to set up a defense, but all he's done is lead us directly to where he is. Follow the net, find the Fischer."

Without another word, he turned and faced the east. "Let us introduce ourselves. We wouldn't want to be ungracious guests . . ."

The king started walking, trees charring and smoking as he passed. Solomon stood and watched as most everyone fell into step, following his lead. Francis came to his side, a few of his "birds" remaining to cast sidelong glances their way.

"Hang on a second . . ." Francis said, frowning after them. "Is that the *king?*"

CHAPTER SIXTY-FOUR

Dark Clouds

Beneath a sky of pale blue and surrounded by verdant forest, a wave of nausea washed over me. I stumbled, the sensation so strong that it felt like a physical blow. I let go of the cart, and as I took another step forward, Maria caught me. Though she supported my weight, her face told me that whatever had come was affecting her, too.

I shook my head and tried to stand upright. Something was wrong. It was as if gravity had increased, but it wasn't impacting my entire body—just my lower half.

"What—"

I cut off as my chi was yanked from my core, channeling down into the ground. Maria let out a sharp gasp, and I felt some of her essence pass through me. Our intertwined power shot deeper and deeper. Heading for . . . the vast network of ropes that had connected my friends and me when we were skybound. Without my permission, my core had opened up and given freely. Maria had been touching me when it started, and I'd subconsciously requisitioned her power too.

"Fischer!" Maria half yelled, her voice panicked. "What was that? What's happening?"

"The . . ." I swallowed. "Our bond."

Her eyes widened a little, and despite my vague answer, she understood. Her gaze flicked down, and I felt her awareness extend, tracing my chi as it poured down into the thing we'd created together.

Instinctively, I knew that I could cut it off. If I truly wanted, I could rally my will and slam the floodgates closed. Doing so would leave me free to move, to go and confront whoever or whatever had arrived so close to home. So why did that feel like it was the incorrect move? Anxiety bubbled up, starting as a burbling stream and quickly becoming a swollen river.

My desire to go stamp out the threat warred with the bonds to those I held dearest. The network below us, the container that was both empty yet filled with potential, demanded that I let my chi flow into it. But my conscious mind couldn't fathom *why*.

I swore, gritting my teeth. "I need to power it. Frack me. I don't know why, but I *need* to. I might have to stay here . . ."

Seeing my distress, Borks dashed to me and nuzzled my leg. Only to let out a yelp and leap back, his tail between his legs.

"Nobody touch me," I said. "I'll steal your chi. I didn't mean to do that, Borks. I'm sorry. I—"

"Can you get in the pocket dimension?" Deklan cut in. "Borks's, I mean."

"No. That would stop my power from exiting. And don't ask me how I know that. I've got no clue."

"The cart!" Maria yelled. "Can you get on the cart?"

Suspecting it just might work, I spun, willing my body to move. I was barely upright, and when I tried to lift myself, I lacked the strength. I shook my head. "I can't—"

"On three!" Deklan said. "Lift him on three! Everyone ready?"

My eyes darted around, too overwhelmed to protest. They all nodded at Deklan's words and got into position.

"One. Two—"

Jumping the gun, Teddy lifted me with his mighty paws, lobbing me into the air. His reactive roar tore through the forest as I stole some of his core's power, so loud that it shook the surrounding trees. As I blinked up at the sky, my senses were only half focused on the small birds fleeing; they were mostly centered around the absolute torrent of chi being yoinked from my abdomen.

"Hold on tight!" Maria said, grabbing one of the handles as Dom grabbed the other. "We're going back to Tropica. Teddy—make us a path! We can replant the trees!"

I tried to shoot him an apologetic look, but Teddy was already barreling forward. Borks and Deklan joined him. Before their combined might, the forest might as well have been made of straw. Maria and Dom took off, and I felt a pang of regret for the chunks of splintered wood flying to land around us. I swept it aside. Now wasn't the time.

We had to get back to Tropica. We had to get back to our friends.

Within the Church of Fischer's headquarters in New Tropica, Barry shook his head, smiling at the debate being waged before him.

"Let it go, Ellis," Theo said. "They'll be back today or tomorrow."

"But the information is fresh *now*! Might I not go look at the site that Fischer said was corrupted? Why can't I just give it a glance—"

"Because you can't be trusted!" Danny replied, looking just as amused as Barry felt. "The moment you get there and see it for yourself, you'll find an excuse to go track Fischer down!"

"But what if the corruption spreads? It would be only prudent to go see if Fischer's plan to fix it worked, would it not?"

"One of the Buzzy Bros already reported that it's clear, Ellis," Barry stated, doing his best to hide his smile. "There is absolutely nothing to worry about."

As if the world wished to call Barry a liar, a wave of power rolled over them, seeming to force the air from the room.

They all shot to their feet, staring to the east where the horrific chi was coming from. Barry waited for it to disappear, the seconds that passed feeling like an eternity.

When it only grew stronger, he clenched his jaw, his momentary panic immediately swept away by duty.

"Evacuate Tropica," he ordered, marching for the door.

A man radiating chi sprinted into the room, his eyes as sharp as the essence he was releasing. "Something has come," Roger barked, his body stiff.

"We know." Barry led him outside. "We can all feel it. Can you rally the defenders at defense position three?"

"Aye," was all Roger said, knowing by heart what that simple sentence meant. He pulled a horn from his belt and let out three quick blasts of noise. Before the first had finished echoing off the surrounding buildings, people were emerging and moving for the meeting point.

Any other time, Barry would have stood and watched them go, soaking in how cohesive a force New Tropica had become. He still took pride in it, but he never stopped moving for even a moment. "Reservists!" he yelled through cupped hands, loud enough to be heard by every cultivator for at least a dozen kilometers. "Evacuate the citizens of Tropica!"

The facade of the citizens' sleepy coastal life might be about to come to an abrupt end. Barry wasn't happy about the emotional turmoil they could potentially experience, but if it meant they were kept safe, it was a small price to pay.

Barry shook his head. That was a problem for later. For now, he had tasks to do and people to evacuate.

Just over a half hour later, odd vibrations thumped the ground as Barry sped toward defense position three—the clear ground just west of Tropica.

He'd participated in the evacuation, which had gone surprisingly smoothly. With George and Geraldine's help, they'd managed to convince everyone that the evacuation was on order of the crown. That nebulous reason hadn't been enough for some of the nobility, but when George had added the detail that there might be cultivators on the loose—which was more accurate than the townsfolk knew—they had been all too happy with retreating to the north. Thankfully, the congregation hadn't needed to reveal their status as cultivators. Not yet, anyway.

It had been an oddly frustrating experience for him, but he didn't take the time to consider why. Shaking his head, he sped up, the surrounding crops racing past in a blur. When he stepped from between two rows of sugarcane, he skidded to a stop, a low whistle escaping his lips.

It had been less than an hour, yet the area between Tropica and the western mountains had been transformed. It resembled the training grounds that Roger had constructed by packing the earth. Even now, cultivators moved farther west in groups of ten, stomping the ground and flattening the battlefield, which was causing the vibrations Barry felt earlier. Every member of the congregation, each human present, wore their church robes, the black fabric with royal-blue embroidery of a fishing rod making them look like the cohesive force they were.

Ahead of them, Pistachio and Snips sliced through trees like a pair of bloodthirsty lumberjacks with a vendetta against all plant life. Pelly and Bill swooped down and picked up the felled trees, carrying them to either side of the packed field.

Beneath their chosen place of battle, Barry could feel Lemon and the other tree spirit doing . . . something. He didn't have the time to go and ask them, but he had complete faith in them and their intentions.

Barry couldn't spot Claws or Cinnamon, and for a moment, he worried they'd defied orders and gone to find Fischer. He whirled, scanning the area for them. A shrill chirp cut through the din of the preparations, demanding his attention. When he looked toward the source, he found a patch of gray and black on one of the surrounding mountain peaks. Standing atop a stack of gathered boulders, Claws and Cinnamon waved, their mischievous grins unmissable even from here.

Theo snorted from beside him. "They did ask permission first, for what it's worth. I said it was a good idea."

Barry grinned, not needing to fake his excitement. "I haven't seen Claws's electric boulders yet . . ."

Queen Bee and Bumblebro came darting through the air, both making a low drone with their wings. Barry held out his hand, giving them a spot to land. Queen Bee let out a questioning tone, her body laced with anxiety.

Barry nodded. "I agree, and I was about to say the same thing. Have the Buzzy Boys retreat. We don't need them to scout to know that the enemy approaches." The sickly scent of their chi had grown stronger since he'd first felt it, the enemy forces slowly coming closer to Tropica.

Queen Bee and Bumblebro nodded their thanks, then darted away. Barry expected them to go toward the west, but they flew for Bill and Pelly instead. Barry raised an eyebrow, but with a single gesture from Queen Bee, both Pelly and Bill shot skyward. With their necks extended, twin honks came from them, so loud that Barry wanted to cover his ears.

The sight eased some of his worry. It reminded him that although he was the de facto leader here, the other members of the congregation were more than capable of organizing themselves. Clearing the trees was Snips and Pistachio's idea. Claws and Cinnamon had taken it upon themselves to gather ammunition and find a place to fire it from. Lemon and the other tree spirit were doing something underground. And the bees and pelicans had been in communication, having prepared a way to recall the Buzzy Boys if the order was given.

The capabilities of everyone present were a soothing balm, yet it didn't quash all of his anxiety. He surveyed the field again, his lips forming a line. Was this really the best place to defend? It made sense from a tactical point of view; this was the only road that led into Tropica and was the path of least resistance. But would the enemy recognize that and choose a different approach?

Judging by how slowly the enemy was moving, the defensive force had time to reposition. He faced the south, toward New Tropica, then north, where the mountains weren't so prevalent. They'd discussed this time and time again. They'd decided if an enemy force came, *this* was the best place to hold the defense. Was there something they hadn't considered, though? More information that would lead to a different decision being reached? His thoughts started to spiral, building into a storm.

"Barry," Roger said, appearing before him in an instant and causing a wall of air to crash into him.

Barry shook his head, returning to the present. "Sorry, I was just wondering if—"

"Yeah, I know. Stop it."

" . . . What?"

"If you'll excuse my bluntness, you need to stop questioning yourself."

All Barry could do was blink.

"I could feel your unease from across the field," Roger continued, his tone matter-of-fact and not at all accusatory. "Now, only some of us have had the breakthrough that lets us sense emotions clearly, but a few of those that came from Gormona are rather . . . perceptive. I saw more than one head darting your way just now."

The words struck Barry like a gut punch, and a spear of guilt lodged itself firmly in his abdomen. "Sorry."

Roger shook his head. "It's fine. This is your first battle, if that's even what we'll call this when all is said and done. A little doubt is only natural. That's usually the commander's role. Here, though, with an army of superhuman thought detectors on your side? It might be best to push those doubts away. By all means, consider every angle, but don't let yourself slip into despair."

Barry blinked again. Abruptly, he barked a laugh. "Having superhuman thought detectors as friends really muddies the waters, huh?"

A wry smile crossed Roger's lips. "Aye. That it does. If anyone has to have cultivators, though, I'm glad they're on our side." Roger's eyes went distant for a moment, and as he chewed his upper lip, Barry got an intense feeling of melancholy, strong enough for even him to feel. Roger sucked air through his teeth. "Well, look at me, not following my own advice."

"You're fine," Theo said. "I wasn't there, but I've heard tell of the war you were in."

Roger ran a hair through his hair. "Better to get lost in thought now than when the enemy arrives, I suppose. I'd best go line up the troops." He turned and strode away, the air around him even sharper than the sword sheathed at his waist.

Barry took a slow breath, doing one of the exercises from Earth that Fischer had shown him. A minute later, his pulse had slowed. As the outside world returned to the forefront of his awareness, Barry heard Roger's barked orders. He had separated the congregation into two distinct groups: defenders and reservists. The former was larger by far, broken up into seven squads of eight to twelve based on complementary powers. They lined up as Roger instructed, moving to the places he pointed with his sword.

Barry's eyes were drawn to the weapon. It had been created by Roger and the smiths and looked like a normal sword. Well, it *would* have looked like a normal sword if it didn't have streaks of pitch-black metal running through it. It caught the afternoon sunlight, the silver metal reflecting it and the black metal drinking it in. He'd have to inspect it once this was all over.

Footsteps approached Barry, and he already knew who it was before turning. "Everything ready?" he asked.

"Just so," Keith replied.

Beside him, Trent's jaw was tense, his eyes watching the distant horizon. "Yes."

"Do you have any more insight?" Barry asked, searching Trent's face. "Do you still believe it's him?"

"I didn't learn anything new, and I couldn't tell you how I know . . . but I'm almost certain."

Suddenly, a flash of orange lit the back of the western mountains. Like a meteor flying toward the heavens, an orb of blazing fire came into view, soaring upward and flaring. When it reached the clouds, it exploded, the blast brighter than the setting sun. Though it had the color of normal fire, that sickening chi flew from it, the wave potent enough to make more than a few of the congregation clutch their stomachs. Barry held firm, watching the flames as they burned out, leaving black streaks in their wake.

Trent's upper lip twitched as he looked at the now-dull sky. "Never mind. I'm one hundred percent certain." He spat to the side, a dark cloud passing over his face. "It's my father. He has come."

CHAPTER SIXTY-FIVE

Doubt

From the rear of the procession, Solomon watched as the king knelt down and gathered power. Augustus Reginald Gormona had said he had a warning for Fischer and the rest of the traitors. When the king unleashed an uppercut faster than even Solomon's enhanced eyes could track, he cringed back from the flames, singed by even that small exposure. In an instant, the fireball was rocketing upward, the oppressive heat becoming a tolerable warmth the farther away it got. On and on it flew, heading toward the clouds.

"*Psst.*"

Solomon jumped, the sound having come from right beside him. Francis was there, standing between Solomon and the king. "I'm not mad," Francis said, watching the fireball.

"Okay . . ."

"No, really. I'm not mad, and I have no intention of following this false god." His eyes flicked to Solomon's. They were sharp and attentive, no longer appearing hazy. "Tell me. Did you truly awaken by creating a potion, Solomon? Are you *the* Alchemist?"

Solomon licked his lips, peering past Francis to look at the king. "They can hear your treachery . . ."

"No, they can't." Francis lifted the thurible he was holding—a small cage on the end of a chain. Incense burned within, causing wisps of smoke to fill the air. It had an oddly familiar smell. "A creation of my own making. It mutes sound."

Solomon had noticed the odd cage before, and he wasn't the only one. When the king had asked about it, Francis said, "I am burning it in anticipatory celebration of your swift victory," which had made the king roll his eyes and drop the line of questioning. Now that Solomon had been told, he realized that Francis was telling the truth. Anything beyond the wisps of smoke sounded as if it was far away, even to his enhanced hearing.

"How?" he asked, dumbfounded.

"Wrong question," Francis said, his back to the king. "What matters is what we're going to do about this situation. Keep your eyes peeled for a chance to escape. If you're truly *the* Alchemist, Solomon, we need you to gather more power and—" The fireball high above exploded, consuming the sky and casting an orange light over everything. Even from the ground, it was like standing next to a roaring bonfire, the flames singeing all they touched.

A hot wind washed over them, expelling the incense and returning sound to the world. Francis whirled, one shoulder dipping as he let out a loud, "Ooooh! How pretty!" He slipped toward his birds, singing, "Are you okay, my dears? Did any of your feathers get burned?"

"No?"

"No!"

"*Feathers?*" they called, cackling together as a warm breeze swept over them. Two of the former nobles had used their bodies to shield the merchant Marcus, the only non-cultivator present, from the blast. They hopped toward their fellows now, abandoning Marcus in favor of laughing with the others.

Despite the heat, a shiver ran through Solomon, goose bumps sprouting on his skin. How long had Francis been feigning madness? For a moment, Francis's deference crept into him, making a sense of self-importance propagate. But then the memory of Fischer's chi came slicing through, cutting all of Solomon's delusions off at the stem. Even with centuries to gather chi, would he ever hold a candle to Fischer's incandescence? If Solomon were to truly become the Alchemist that his cult—his *church*—spoke of, would he need to eclipse that blinding light?

The king, who had his hands held wide and his face bent skyward, abruptly roared. The sound was unnatural in both frequency and volume. It made every cell in Solomon's body wish to flee, but was nothing compared to the wave of sickly chi that hit him. He immediately crumpled, his arms only barely holding him up as he retched.

Instinctively, his eyes flicked toward the roaring figure, wanting to keep an eye on the threat that was the king's existence. Everyone but the cultivators who had channeled the corrupted chi were also on the ground, all being sick.

The king made a disgusted noise as he stared down at his wife and his daughter, both women holding themselves upright just as Solomon did. "Pathetic." His voice sounded like it came from a different direction, the corrupted chi warping Solomon's senses. The king continued, "This is your punishment for refusing to channel this wondrous essence. Keel over and repent."

Seeing such contempt for his own daughter made another layer of terror form atop Solomon's core. He'd been stationed in the capital and was one of the few cultivators trusted to deliver the royal family their medicine. Despite the man's reputation of grandeur and ruthlessness, Princess Tryphena had always softened his fist. Now, as King Augustus Reginald Gormona stared down at that same girl, the daughter whose presence always brought a smile to his face, his visage held disappointment and scorn. With the king's gaze still locked on his own flesh and blood, he pulled his fist back, gathering power.

Solomon knew in that moment that Augustus Reginald Gormona was beyond redemption.

Small flames sprouted from the king's fist, licking out with unnatural haste as they grew. The nausea returned, overwhelming Solomon, yet he didn't look away, expecting the blow to come at any second.

The king spat to the side, causing a patch of now-dead grass to catch flame. "I grow tired of waiting. I need to *hit* something." He clenched his fist, making a loud crack, as if he'd somehow shattered something within it. His flames rushed out in thin lines, winding through the air and surrounding everyone. In a matter of seconds, the lines formed a bubble around them.

The king snapped with the fingers of his other hand, and they lurched into motion. Solomon retched again, fragments of dirt and trees flying by in a blur as the king took them forward, obliterating everything outside of the protective bubble he'd created.

When the fireball exploded above the sky to the west, it was as though it went off within my skull. White circles swam through my vision, and I was only just barely able to hold on to the cart. A faint pain appeared behind my eyes. I squeezed them shut, willing it to disappear.

"Veer toward the explosion!" Maria yelled. Teddy roared in response, subtly changing trajectory through the trees. More of the sickly chi oozed out from up ahead. Despite my headache, the nausea, and the vast swaths of my power being drained from my core, I could tell that the enemy was racing away from us. All of a sudden, the incessant sounds of trunks cracking and wood splintering disappeared. I forced my eyes open, and in an instant, took in everything around me. There was a path of utter destruction before us, even worse than the one Teddy and the boys had created. Whereas we had only been crashing through trees, whoever had arrived had been tearing through *everything*.

Even the grass and a good half meter of the ground had been burned away, the remaining edges blackened. The path was completely straight, heading east and disappearing over the closest mountain.

Heading directly for Tropica . . .

Knowing what was at stake, we never stopped moving—up until the very moment I was struck by an invisible wall of force. I flew backwards, tumbling off the fish-filled cart and skidding along the ground. I recognized the chi that had assaulted me, and as I sat up on the decimated ground, I blinked into space, unbelieving.

"Fischer!" Maria called, at my side in a moment. "What was—"

"I need to stay here," I said, cutting her off.

"What? Why? We can carry you, it's—"

"No." I rubbed my temples, fighting off the pounding headache. "I was just hit by a wall of my own chi."

"You . . . *What?*" she demanded, her brow furrowing in confusion.

I was sure of it. The network of interconnected ropes below us—the thing created by the bonds between my friends, Maria, and me—had slammed me with a wall of my own essence. The unseen network had been siphoning my chi from me, only to expend a large portion of it to whack me in the face. It was an absolute waste, yet the mesh and whatever awareness it possessed had decided the act was necessary.

Just as I trusted it to draw from my core, I trusted it now. At any point, I could cut off the power flowing from me. Now that I knew it might create a physical wall to block me, I could smash through it if I wanted to. It might have caught me off guard, but it was *my* chi. I was in control of it if I put my mind to it. Soothing waves washed over me, an echo of my animal pals and Maria reassuring me that everything was going to be okay.

"We don't have the time," I said. "The mesh we created, the thing with all that latent potential . . . It wants me to stay here. I *need* to stay here. You guys need to leave me. It only needs me to stay. I'll join you as soon as I can."

"I am *not* leaving you!" Maria declared.

I didn't need to search her eyes to know that she wasn't lying. Knowing any objection would be a futile endeavor, I nodded. "Okay. Everyone else—please go back and help them. Go defend Tropica, just in case."

There was the faintest moment of hesitation, in which Deklan, Dom, Teddy, and Borks all stared at me. Reaching the same conclusion simultaneously, they nodded, and then they were off. I opened my mouth to call toward Borks, to tell him that he should go on ahead. His power was a stage above everyone else, and if he traveled alone, he'd get there faster. It wasn't necessary, however. Borks slipped through a portal, sparing me a glance and a slight wag of his tail before the crack in space closed behind him.

Maria knelt down beside me, and we watched as Teddy, Deklan, and Dom dashed away, the two brothers still dragging the cart. Despite the situation, I couldn't help but smile at their departure as they disappeared over the mountain, trailing the path of destruction. "They could have left the cart here . . ."

"And leave their precious catch behind?" Maria replied, amusement in her voice. "You'd sooner convince me to leave you behind." When she turned to me, her expression was severe. "Are you really okay?"

I nodded, not having to think about it. "This is where I need to be." I closed my eyes and focused on the chi pouring from me. As soon as I did, I understood. Here, with my core close to the ground and my body centered, my chi flowed out with ease. Buckets of it entered the underground network. The echoes of my friends' wills were in the periphery, urging me to continue feeding it. If not for their encouragement, I'd have cut my essence off long ago. From beside me, I felt Maria settle into the same cross-legged posture, and with her permission, the mesh drew from her core as well. It was a smaller stream, but still a significant amount for her less-advanced core.

I reached out and, sensing my presence, her fingers interlaced with mine. Hand in hand, we channeled our chi, slowly filling the network of interconnected lines below.

Barry clenched his jaw as the disgusting chi raced their way, traveling faster than anything he'd sensed before. A quiet settled over the defensive forces, more than a few struggling to stay upright against the onslaught of nausea that came with each pulse of power.

The sky to the west grew orange, the light having nothing to do with the setting sun. Tones of red joined in, bleeding from just over the closest mountain range and spreading out toward the horizon. It was like the very heavens were aflame.

Doubt spoke up from within Barry, rearing its ugly head as the skies turned maroon. He looked toward Roger, seeking reassurance. The sword-aspect cultivator was conversing with Anna, but when he noticed Barry's inner thoughts, he glanced over. He gave Barry a thumbs-up, which was about as sappy as Roger could get. Barry nodded. He clenched his jaw, his self-doubt dying down.

In its wake, excitement took hold. It had been there all along, an ember waiting to catch flame. Seeing Roger's confidence had cleared away Barry's worry, allowing oxygen to fuel the fire. His limbs tingled as his anticipation rose to a fever pitch.

Crimson waves of light came over the closest mountain, drawing all of Barry's attention. Judging by the strength of the corrupted chi, the enemy wasn't far off. In mere minutes, they would arrive, and the Church of Fischer would finally have a chance to test the efficacy of its—

The top half of the closest mountain exploded. A giant orb of flames tore through it, shattering the rock there as if it were made of glass. The sphere shot down the slope toward them, barreling directly for the front line of defenders.

CHAPTER SIXTY-SIX

The Heavens Descend

What Barry had first assumed was a giant fireball unraveled as it flowed down the slope, the thin ropes of burning flame that comprised it lashing out to destroy every bit of life they could touch. Though the surrounding trees were green and lush, that did nothing to stop them from combusting. Before the first fragment of shattered mountain hit the ground, most of the mountainside was ablaze. And all Barry could do was watch as the living conflagration descended.

The top of the raging orb was open now, revealing the figures within. They were more numerous than he'd expected, over a dozen people riding within the half sphere. Most of them were upright, but the rest were pinned to the back wall by the speed at which they traveled. Among those standing, one figure stood taller than the rest. The disgusting chi radiated from his core, winding out to fuel the myriad flames.

Augustus Reginald Gormona. The king.

"Fischerrr!" he screamed at the sky, his voice seeming to come from everywhere at once. His arms were held to the side, and as he lowered his gaze, he clapped his hands together. Everyone atop the bubble skidded to a stop, but the chi continued on. It flowed forward across the packed earth, becoming a two-meter high wall of flame. More of the sickly essence came oozing from the king, pouring out to increase the deadly wall. It grew in width, encompassing the entire length of the defending forces. Half of them, mostly those of the reservists, were crumpled to the floor, unable to stand as the king's corrupted chi sent waves of nausea crashing over them. They were defenseless as the flames raced forward like an orange and red tsunami, ready to extinguish their lives.

But the Church of Fischer was prepared.

A number of humans and creatures flew forward, appearing between the defenders and the encroaching flames. Chi flooded from them. Private Pistachio's claws slammed together, delivering twin blasts that tore a hole through the eastern section. Sergeant Snips flew forward with blue light streaming from her carapace, and she released rapid-fire arcs of energy that exploded when they hit, blowing that bit of wall backwards. On the left side, Ellis threw himself into the path of the fire. It flowed around the shining scaled armor of his own creation, the wall there scattering into separate streams that Private Pelly and Warrant Officer Williams beat back with flaps of their mighty wings.

Two men stood in the center, standing against the storm. Roger drew back his sword, and when he lashed out, the air split. A sound like metal on metal cut through the roar of the flames, slicing it in half. The wall exploded. Trent was on his right, his hands aglow. The rest of the approaching fires had been neutralized by the others, yet he waited, gathering his power. Roger drew back his sword again, preparing to unleash another cut, but there was no need.

Trent's fist punched out, twin infernos pouring from his core and out of his body. The columns slammed into his father's attack.

Boooom!

The explosion made air shoot outward, striking Barry a physical blow that was strong enough to knock a non-cultivator from their feet. Rather than neutralize the wall as others' attacks had, the violent reaction engulfed Trent, the blast large enough for Roger to have to leap back a few meters. Barry might have felt a moment of worry for Trent's well-being, but he could see a shadow of his form through the fire. The prince was relaxed, and when the flames finally died, he stood tall. His outer robe had been consumed, leaving behind an instantly recognizable item of clothing that they'd stolen from the king.

Indestructible Flame Suit of the Weaver
Rare
Woven of web from a core weaver, this suit is almost completely impervious to damage from all chi. It does not provide any resistance.
Bonus Effect: +30 percent effectiveness to fire chi.

It fit snug against Trent's body, revealing well-defined muscle that belied the portly state he'd possessed when first coming to Tropica. It wasn't just his awakening that had caused the transformation, but also months of hard work and physical training. The field was completely clear now, and hatred covered Trent's face as he stared his father down. The king, however, had eyes for someone else.

"You show yourself, Lizard Wizard!" Augustus Reginald Gormona spat, a manic hint in his tone. "Where is your master, foul sorcerer? Bring him to—"

A scream tore across the battlefield, shrill enough to cut off the king's monologue. Barry immediately knew who she was based on the descriptions he'd heard.

Penelope Francine Gormona tried to stand but fell back to her knees, her lower lip quivering. "Trent? Is that you?"

Any of the attackers that weren't already staring at Trent turned toward him, recognition flashing across their faces at the name, if not the face.

"Hello, Mother," he replied, his mask of hatred remaining.

A silence settled over everyone as Trent's father, the king, gaped. A wide smile formed, followed swiftly by spontaneous laughter. It climbed to a malevolent cackle that made Barry's skin prickle.

"Perfect!" the king declared, still laughing. "You have broken through the block and harnessed your chi! Come here, son. Fight by my side against your captors! I have much to tell you once we are finished here."

Trent spat on the ground. "I'd sooner burn myself alive."

"Trent . . ." his mother said, barely holding back a sob. "Are you well? Where have you—"

"*Silence!*" the king roared, shooting her a venomous glare. She deflated, her eyes darting between him and her son. Augustus turned his back on her. "You tread dangerous ground, son. You may be my blood, but I shan't stand for more disrespect."

Trent snorted. "You lost any chance of me respecting you when you poisoned me."

"Poisoned?" The king's brow furrowed. "I did no such thing."

Roger shot a glance Barry's way, the question clear: *Do we let this continue?* Barry held two fingers down, the signal to wait. Fischer would surely have felt the threat by now, and he would be on the way. The more time they wasted, the better.

Heat radiated from Trent, washing over the battlefield and causing more than a few defenders to take a step back. "Yes. You. Did." His skin danced with light as if flames were roiling beneath. "You gave me the pills that turned me into a hideous *moron!*" Fire erupted from his back. "And don't think I haven't seen you back there, *Solomon. Francis.*" He spat the names as if they were a curse and glared at the men. "I know it was you that made them. I remember *everything.*"

From the back of the group, Solomon stammered. "P-Prince, I . . ."

Barry's head rocked back when he sensed the man's essence—he could feel a hint of Fischer there. Combined with his newborn core . . . was this who had ascended and created the poisonous chi earlier today? But that surprise was nothing compared to the shock Barry felt when he spotted the man behind Solomon. They hadn't seen him in months, and now Barry knew why. Marcus, the merchant who always brought wares and a friendly smile to Tropica, was with the procession. He was curled into a ball, his face pale and body shaking.

Solomon swallowed and cleared his throat. "I was just doing my job as a member of the Cult of the Alchemist, Prince. It is what must be done to all male heirs of the Gormona bloodli—"

The king was on him in a flash, almost faster than Barry's eyes could register. He clutched Solomon by the neck and lifted him from the ground. "You blabber crown secrets." His entire body quaked with rage, his arms bulging. *"Die."*

Though Barry hadn't yet had a breakthrough, even he could feel the repulsive chi that poured out of the king's core. It traveled up his body, and when it flared to life against the alchemist's neck, the man's life would be over. With the amount of chi he was gathering, everyone nearby, including the king's wife and daughter, would be severely injured if not outright killed. They knew it, too. Their eyes were filled with panic.

Barry took a half step forward, but there was nothing he could do to save them. No one could get there in time. Steeling himself, he prepared to avert his gaze, not wanting to witness the carnage. But before the flames could erupt, a chaotic web of black lines split the air between Solomon and the king. The latter dashed backward, so when Borks flew from the portal, the king was off balance.

Borks let out a vicious growl and licked his teeth. He was in the form that Fischer had called a . . . was it a *Chi-wow-wow*? Still midair and not at all caring for Barry's musings, Borks shifted into a breed that was built like an anvil, its face smooshed and skin covered in rolls. Tucking his legs, Borks hit the king with the force of a fur-covered cannonball.

Augustus Reginald Gormona was sent flying. He crashed into the group of cor-rupted cultivators, each of them leaping forward to catch him and arrest his momen-tum. The moment Borks touched the ground, he shifted again. In his true form now, that of a hellhound of nightmare, he used the first ability that Barry had ever seen him utilize. Black vines of shadow erupted from the earth, wrapping the arms, legs, and torsos of everyone who had the disgusting chi in their cores.

Borks shifted for the third time in so many seconds. Now covered in golden fur, he appeared before Marcus and licked him on the cheek, wagging his tail.

The merchant, who had been assailed by the king's sickly chi since their arrival, blinked up at Borks from the ground. "Borks?" he croaked, his eyes unbelieving. Borks nodded, grabbed him by the collar, and flicked him into the air. A portal opened, and Marcus sailed through it.

When the other side appeared beside Barry, he was ready. He caught Marcus and gestured for a defender to come over. "Take him to safety!" The man nodded, col-lected Marcus with care, and took off toward Tropica. In the short time that took, Borks had already sent the rest through.

First came the queen, then the princess, followed by the alchemists, Solomon, and Francis. Now that they were close, Barry was even more sure. These people were no threat. Their cores were less powerful than his, and he was far from the strongest cultivator present. Peter, who had experienced a breakthrough, let his power wash out over everyone.

"The missing cook?" the queen asked, blinking up at the former royal chef.

"Hello, Your Majesty. Seems like you might have gotten yourself in over your head." He patted her on the shoulder, making her cringe back. "It's Peter, by the way. Don't do anything silly, and you won't be hurt." Whether because of his words or his innate power, she shrank back. Princess Tryphena reached for her chi, which was, as Fischer would say, an objectively bad move. Peter flicked her on the chin, knocking her out cold. The queen gasped but dared not make a move.

Borks had leaped through after them, and as he dismissed the portal, he wobbled, his legs shaking. He was spent. He reverted to his hellhound form and collapsed to the sand, his tongue lolling and chest heaving.

"Good boy," Barry said. Despite not stopping for a moment, Borks had accurately assessed the situation. Those he'd brought through weren't any sort of threat. If any-thing, they were in danger by remaining next to the king. Barry didn't feel any sort of allegiance to the people cowering on the ground before him, but from what he knew, they weren't deserving of death. He patted Borks's side. "You are *such* a good boy." Borks wagged his tail, and Barry stood, surveying the scene.

Borks's vines were still holding everyone down. They struggled against them, pulling at their limbs in a futile attempt at escape. The hellhound had gained even more power since joining them here in Tropica, and despite his exhaustion, he kept them constricted. Even the king was down, apparently still stunned by the earlier attack. They were all defenseless, yet no one had moved against them.

But there was a good reason for that.

Barry cast his eyes skyward, a small smile gracing his lips. "Odd weather we've been having lately, wouldn't you say, Peter?"

Peter nodded, his eyes reflecting blue light as he looked up. "I'd hate to be caught in that storm without an umbrella. Looks pretty, though."

Following their gazes, Solomon's jaw dropped open, and there it remained as he watched the heavens descend.

The first boulder, launched from a nearby mountaintop and wreathed in lightning, soared directly toward the still-dazed king. Behind it, dozens followed, looking like nothing so much as shooting stars.

CHAPTER SIXTY-SEVEN

Attack

A high-pitched whistle rang over the battlefield, growing louder by the second as it cut through the dying flames still crackling on the mountainside. The trees there were blackened and charred, their fibers having long been burned away.

Something deep within Barry's mind wanted to retreat from the approach of something large enough to be heard from hundreds of meters away. He set that instinct aside. It wasn't needed.

As the strike from above drew closer, he clicked his tongue. The lightning-covered boulder was slightly off target. It didn't really matter, though. It would land right beside the king, the monarch certainly within the blast radius. Besides, there were plenty more to come. At least one of them would be a direct hit. In the moments before the first one landed, Barry cast his vision upward, wanting to witness the beautiful barrage. The "stars" were brighter now, having gotten closer to the ground. He stared as long as possible, soaking in the sight.

Abruptly, he squinted and leaned forward, trying to get a better look. "Peter . . ."

"Yes, Barry?"

He pointed up. "Third boulder from the left, all the way at the back. Is that . . . ?"

Peter held up a hand to block out the setting sun. He searched for less than a second before his eyes went wide. He boomed a laugh. "What the frack is she doing?"

Pressed against the bottom of the boulder, with her needle-sharp teeth locked in a vicious smile, Corporal Claws launched herself. To a regular human, all they would have seen was a bolt of bright-blue lightning splitting the afternoon air. The skin of Claws's face rippled back, the force of her approach creating drag on even her enhanced body. In a fraction of a fraction of a second, she was on the off-target boulder. She struck it with great care, her limbs absorbing the landing only to extend them once more and course-correct the giant stone.

The boulder, now covered in even more lightning, rocketed directly at the king. It hit with sickening force, the ground shifting beneath Barry's feet.

Everything that followed happened in the blink of an eye. A crater appeared, the expelled air and dirt sending everyone around the king flying. Claws did a loop and crashed down after her boulder, hitting with enough force to make a second blast shake the world. All the spirit beasts attacked, their respective powers launched for the closest enemy. Roger drew his sword back and readied a strike, holding it as a defensive measure should any of the corrupted cultivators recover. Trent, with flames rocketing from his back, shot forward, heading for the crater his father and Claws were at the bottom of. Time seemed to freeze as the attacks flew.

Barry felt the wave of sickening nausea before he saw the flames. It was the foulest yet, and as it rolled over Barry's core, his vision spun. When the inferno erupted from the crater, he was blasted from his feet. Tendrils of flame wound from the hole as if they had their own wills, climbing over each other in search of prey. They shielded all the king's allies, consuming the attacks that the defenders had sent their way. Claws, the whites of her eyes showing as she glanced back in panic, rocketed out ahead of the conflagration. Even she couldn't withstand the heat . . .

It was all Barry needed to see. "Reservists!" he yelled, getting back to his feet. "Retreat to the citizens!" They'd have no issue dealing with this threat, and he didn't want to pointlessly risk anyone's life. Remembering that they had organized a signal for such a circumstance, he pulled the horn from his belt and let out two long tones, followed by a short one. The reservists fled, helping each other as they went.

The flames gave chase. As they flared in pursuit, Barry felt the king's will behind them. They weren't conscious at all; they were directed. They rushed to close the distance, heading for those that were closest.

In a single fluid movement, Roger got back to his feet and lashed out with his sword, the blade arcing through the air. The razor-sharp chi that shot from him, both literally and figuratively, sliced through the king's will, splitting the entire explosion in a crosscut pattern. The countless sections detonated, combining to rush past Barry as hot wind.

High above the ground, Claws latched on to Bill's back. Cinnamon was atop Pelly next to them. Together, they returned to the ground, landing amongst the reforming defenders. All eyes were on the crater as the king stirred within. Even Barry could feel the circulation of that disgusting chi as the monarch strode up the slope. As he came into view, Barry's stomach churned, and it wasn't only because of the essence coming from his core.

The boulder had done a number on him.

Sections of his skin were aflame, the fires slowly shrinking as his body regenerated. The entire right side of his face glowed an angry red, like the heart of a furnace. When it finally fizzled out, the king opened his eyes, and they contained madness and hatred in equal measure. His accomplices came to his side at an unnatural clip, their cores oozing the same corrupted chi.

Of all things, the enemies' posture confused him. There were three distinct groups. The first ten people, a mix of genders, peered at the defenders with their heads cocked to the side. Their expressions reminded Barry of a flock of seagulls eyeing up a potential meal. The next six were all women. They stood with straight backs and blank faces. The last two, Augustus Reginald Gormona and the man who had to be Tom Osnan Sr., appeared ready to murder anything that stood in their way.

As the two armies stared one another down, Claws loped forward. She chirped at the group of women, getting their attention and giving them one of Rocky's rudest gestures.

One of the women's eyes widened in recognition, then narrowed. "Where are the rest of your kin, *Fat Rat Pack*? And the other creatures?"

In response, Claws raised her other forepaw, doubling down. She gesticulated wildly, hitting them with the rude gesture from all angles.

The king's eyes roamed over the crowd, focusing on all the spirit beasts present. Finally, they landed on Ellis, who was in his Lizard Wizard regalia. "Ah. I see." His voice was emotionless, lacking any of the fury on his face. "It was all a ruse . . ." He opened his hand, flexing his fingers. "You're no sorcerer, *Ellis*. You are but a common traitor."

Ellis flicked up the hood of his armor, revealing his visage for all to see. "That is a matter of perspective, Augustus. With the chi running through your veins, some would say that you are a traitor to humanity."

The king's power flared in response, the nauseating essence washing over them. Before it could settle on their cores, a sharp chi sliced through it. Two fingers on Roger's sword hand had been pointed down this entire time, signaling to everyone to let this moment drag on as long as possible. Now, his hand shook, a physical manifestation of the bladelike fury coming from him. A shiver ran down his spine, his breaths coming heavy.

The king focused on him, but upon seeing Roger looking at someone else, he tracked his gaze, raising a single eyebrow. Roger stared at one of the cultivators that looked like birds.

The skinny man peered back, craning his neck. "Oh!" he called. "I know you!"

"Know?"

"Know."

"*Know!*" the others repeated, smiling and hopping around.

"Lucian," Roger ground out, his teeth bared and muscles tense. "You should be dead."

"Dead!"

"Dead?"

"*Dead*, dead?" They all laughed and resumed their hopping.

Roger's arm shook violently now, a soldier fighting back the urge to attack. "You tore through my men—your own troops—like a reaper through wheat, you insane piece of shit."

"Ah," the king said. "I understand now . . . you were a soldier in the campaign against Theogonia."

"Aye," Roger spat. "A captain."

"Unimportant." The king shrugged one shoulder, his disconcertingly calm voice still at odds with his expression. "Join us. Swap sides now. Your power feels deadly. *Useful.* Return to your kingdom. If you kneel before me, you can—"

"*Shut up.*" The two words from Roger held the weight of command, his metallic chi laced throughout.

The king closed his mouth, his body bowing to the threat before his mind could protest. When he realized he'd obeyed, flames literally burst from his body. The king snarled and opened up his core, making Barry and most of the defenders fight off another wave of nausea.

"Attack," the king said without inflection.

And the world erupted into chaos.

Both front lines lurched forward, power streaming from their cores. Before they could so much as finish their first step, the ground between them split, the top of a giant root breaching the surface. All around the battlefield, the same scene repeated itself, thick roots making chunks of dirt rise and fall aside. To the left of the tamped field, a patch of ground exploded. Two trunks of different shades of blue climbed toward the heavens. They wound around each other, branches and leaves unfurling when they were hundreds of meters above.

Lemon and the other tree spirit had arrived.

The air seemed to quiver as both tree spirits opened up their cores. The next thing Barry knew, clean chi washed over him. It was an amplification of the world's essence, and though it didn't completely nullify the odious power coming from the king, it took the edge away. Barry took a deep breath, and as he exhaled, his nausea was gone. Attackers and defenders both had leaped away from the ruptured ground, not knowing what appeared from below. As the defenders breathed the cleansed air, they straightened, their vitality returning.

Roger held his sword toward the sky, his fist clenched around the hilt. Knowing what was to come, Barry filled his lungs. A silence like the calm before a storm descended, the very world seeming to hold its breath.

"*Attack!*" they both roared, their chi fueling the words.

As one, New Tropica's forces charged.

CHAPTER SIXTY-EIGHT

Combo

Torrents of chi poured through me, the flow only increasing as time dragged on. A full quarter of my significant reserves were drained each second, and if left to my own devices, I'd have been completely drained in moments. But I wasn't alone. The world's chi assisted, bubbling up from deep beneath me, only to travel through my cores on its way back down to the network below.

Despite the amount traveling through Maria being only a fraction of what passed through me, it wasn't any less taxing on her. Tension radiated from her, her jaw clenched and shoulders hunched. I realized I was doing the same thing. I squeezed her hand to get her attention, then forced myself to relax. She followed suit, releasing a small breath and easing the tension in her coiled muscles.

Considering there was a battle playing out in our mind's eye, it was no small feat.

Since the enemy force had arrived in their blazing orb of misguided glory, Maria and I had been watching, the network beneath us somehow relaying sights, sounds, and to my great dismay, smells. I could have done without the latter, because the king's corrupted chi had the aroma of a love child from the unholy pairing of a septic tank and a fish left to rot in the sun. In short, the homie smelled like absolute shi—

Maria sent me a mental nudge, telling me off for getting distracted.

Sorry, I sent back, returning my attention to the battle.

The actions and competency of the defense force made my heart sing; Borks's arrival, Claws and Cinnamon's combo meteor attack, and the kindness shown to the alchemists and the royal family, people who had done terribly by most of the congregation. It made an immense sense of gratitude for my pals pour from me, joining the chi draining down into the network below.

It took me a moment to understand why Roger and Barry were stalling. They likely knew as well as I did that the attacking force didn't stand a chance against the combined might of the defenders. It was definitely a conscious choice, though—one that, I realized, was communicated to the others by holding two fingers down. They were stalling for my arrival, which, now that I considered it, was the smartest move with the information they had access to.

When the identity of Lizard Wizard was discovered, I felt a little miffed. I'd been hoping for a dramatic reveal, but the king's madness seemed too advanced to allow for fun hijinks. A smile came to my face as I recalled how our names had fooled him for so long. But my enjoyment evaporated when Roger revealed how he knew the weird little bird man. Sadness flowed from Maria, as did a desire to go to him. Sharon was at the rear of the field, and our omniscient point of view let us see the heartbreak wrought across her face. She, too, wanted to comfort him.

When the front lines finally launched toward each other, it was a welcome distraction from Roger's emotional devastation—even if the charge only lasted for the length of a single step.

Unlike everyone on the field, Maria and I had been well aware of Lemon and the other tree spirit's preparations, so we weren't at all surprised when the ground burst apart. They had been gathering power down there the entire time, a vast web of roots stretching out to gather the world's essence. My two wooden friends blasted it out over the battle, forcing most of the king's nauseating essence back toward him and his deranged followers.

When Barry and Roger bellowed in tandem for the counterattack to begin, a shiver ran through me. As one, the defenders flew forward, going on the offensive. I had a sense of everyone's power, and if we were only counting the humans, the enemy forces might have had the advantage.

But that didn't account for the immense strength of all my animal pals, who were first off the line.

Private Pistachio, as stoic as ever, channeled power into the hinges of his mighty clackers. Corporal Claws, wreathed in lightning and donning her trademark smirk, rocketed toward the handlers. Sergeant Snips, with blue chi jetting from her joints, prepared to unleash the first of a barrage of aura-blades. Bumblebro and Queen Bee, who had gone unnoticed thus far by the enemy forces, darted from under Roger's collar, their wings droning and compound eyes locked on two of the birdlike cultivators. Pelly and Bill spiraled down from above, picking up speed with each rotation. Borks, still recovering from his earlier expenditure, got to his feet. Cinnamon dashed toward him, and despite his exhaustion, he opened up a portal. The other side was behind the king, and as she flew for the hole in space, she was already winding up a devastating roundhouse kick. Roots shot up from beneath the enemy, coiling back and preparing to strike.

It all happened in slow motion. My enhanced awareness let me see even the smallest of details, so I was able to witness the precise moment their power was ripped from their very grasps. Simultaneously, their cores opened up, the chi held within pouring down into the network that my essence was also flowing into.

Somehow, the king also felt it. His eyes and grin turned vicious as those that were flying through the air lost momentum. His hands were a blur as they extended before him, the fire chi held within already flaring out. It would wash over my friends in less than a second, and with their power being sucked away, I wasn't sure they'd come out unscathed. Even the soothing chi that Lemon helped exude was gone, its power draining into the ground instead.

I jumped to my feet, preparing to leap away as I started forcing the floodgates of my core closed. I had to go there. I had to save them. I—

Trust! the echoes of my friends' souls called to me through the bond. *Trust! Trust! Trust!*

Such reassurance had been good enough before, but seeing my completely defenseless animal pals flying toward the king was too much. I continued slamming my will against the network draining my chi, and though it put up a fight, my strength was too immense. It would only take a moment longer, then I'd be off, racing toward Tropica at the speed of . . .

Huh?

Trent and Roger, at a clip faster than I was aware they could travel, straight-up zoomed in front of everyone else. They were immediately before the king, both men's arms drawn back as chi rushed from their cores toward their hands. Together, they swung. Roger's beautiful blade, its surface a ripple of silver and black, arced wide. Trent's chi rushed in, his flames billowing out and condensing right before Roger.

What was their goal? Roger could slice through Trent's chi, but what good was that? The resulting explosion would be nowhere near enough to counter the king's building corruption. It only steeled my decision to up and leave this place. But just before Roger's sword entered Trent's flames, he twisted his hand, weeping through the cloud of condensed fire with the flat of the blade.

Some of the flames were pushed aside from the sword, only to get caught up in the low-pressure wake of Roger's lightning-quick attack. Exposed to the heat, the weapon's black ripples glowed a hot red. Just as it looked like the sword would melt, bladelike chi shot out of it, cutting into Trent's essence.

My eyes flew wide. It was a fracking combo attack!

Fwooom!

The cone-shaped inferno that resulted engulfed the king, the mountainside, and the burned-out husks of trees that remained. The king's corrupted chi, condensed and not yet unleashed, backfired. The sound and detonation were so strong that my vision of the landscape flickered for a second, warping before coming back into view.

"Frack me . . ." I said, taking in the desolation.

The entire mountain was ablaze. Of the defensive forces, only Trent and Roger remained standing. Everyone had been knocked back a few meters, flung clear of any danger. It took me a moment to spot the king and his accomplices. They were halfway up the mountain within a sphere of sickly chi. Well, almost all of them were. There was a man missing, either incinerated or sent flying far enough for me to not sense him.

As the king dismissed his power, the sphere popped, his disgusting essence oozing back out over the battlefield. As if in answer, Lemon's soothing essence returned, as strong as before but with a hint of warmth. I sent my awareness that way, not understanding how she was doing it while her chi was still getting siphoned down below.

The answer was simple: it wasn't Lemon.

Peter sat at the base of the unnamed tree spirit's trunk, his legs crossed and eyes closed. He was acting as a relay, drawing up buckets of chi and sending it out. The warmth was coming from *him*, a reflection of his core's aspect. I breathed a slow breath, willing my pounding heart to calm.

A familiar hand reached up, lacing her fingers with mine. *Come,* Maria sent me. *Sit.*

Trust . . . the echoes of my pals repeated, urging me not to shut myself off.

I wanted to. I really did. Despite some of our strongest defenders being taken out of the fight, the others were proving that everything would be okay. It seemed like an almost sure thing . . . but that was just it. *Almost* didn't seem good enough. So why did my heart tell me to stay . . . ? I sought out a sign, expanding my awareness in search of something to reassure me that my heart could be trusted.

When I found the approaching group, I couldn't help but laugh. The fluttering chi coming from them was just what I had been looking for. Squeezing Maria's hand, I sat back down and opened up my core.

This was going to be interesting.

As Deklan glanced back at the almost-comatose Teddy, he was beyond glad that he and his brother had brought the cart. The bear had collapsed out of nowhere, seemingly unable to move of his own accord.

They were almost back at Tropica. Even if they hadn't been able to feel the mix of chi coming from just east, the godsdamned fireball that consumed a *mountain* ahead was a pretty good indicator. The moment Teddy had collapsed, the brothers leaped into action, lifting him up onto the cart. As a result, something within Deklan's core had buzzed. It was mirrored in Dom's, the twins experiencing something they'd only felt once before.

Last time, they'd been attacked. Ambushed by Nathan. Their cores had resonated with the desire to protect each other and the life they'd found, but the world's power had fled before their breakthrough could take place. They'd been defenseless as a result, and if not for the intervention of Snips, Claws, and Borks, they'd likely have lost their lives. This time, something felt different. What about putting Teddy on the cart had felt so . . . right?

They were at the base of the flaming mountain now, still trailing the dirt path made by the enemy's passage. What trees hadn't been destroyed were singed and smoking, their greenery not enough to completely fight off the explosion's heat. The air was steamy as they started climbing the hillside, moisture having been expelled from the earth. The sickly chi hit them like a sledgehammer, making both brothers miss a step. They stumbled, holding on to the cart's handles for balance.

A moment later, a cool breeze flowed over the mountain's destroyed peak. It brought the world's essence with it, and a warmth washed over Deklan's body that was nothing like the corrupted chi. Though it also brought heat with it, it was comforting, making him feel like he was lounging in the afternoon sun.

Deklan would have loved to sit in that moment, to embrace the coziness and forget all about the battle he could feel taking place. Before he could say no to that impulse, the battle came to him. A man flew from the forest, screeching like an owl as he rocketed toward Deklan. Corrupted essence streamed from his arms and trailed behind him, the mere touch of it causing trunks to wither and die. That alone made it clear that in their current state, the brothers had absolutely no chance.

Deklan reached for his core, trying to embrace the world's chi as had happened before. Dom did the same, the twins aware of each other as they searched for the meaning that would facilitate their breakthrough. It had to do with them. The life they had found. A profound desire to protect it had caused the chi to rush in the last time. They both felt that now. Yet the world's power wouldn't come to them.

Time crawled to a stop as the crazed man flew. His gaze flicked to the side, and at the last possible second, he swooped to the left. Like a bird in flight, his arms redirected his passage right past the brothers and toward Teddy, who was still only half conscious.

If the man were to strike him . . .

Both Deklan and Dom spun, tried to get in the way and shield Teddy in time. But the enemy's speed increased, air hissing as his outstretched limbs tore through it. Deklan extended a hand toward Teddy, trying to reach him despite knowing it was too far. The breeze flowing by slowed, then paused, halting in midair. Small bubbles of chi rose from the ground, each drop further muting the nauseating essence surrounding them.

Deklan gritted his teeth and he lunged further. Dom was right beside him, one hand raised and fingers grasping. They'd never make it. But Deklan didn't care. It didn't matter that he wasn't strong enough. It didn't matter that he lacked the power to defend his furry friend. Teddy was defenseless, and Deklan needed to *protect* him . . .

With only moments before the enemy cultivator hammered into Teddy, the world answered, and chi rushed into the brothers' cores faster than either of them could comprehend. It swelled there, pressing against their abdomens as it condensed. Deklan knew how this was supposed to go. After the power exploded out of them, they'd be rendered unconscious for a short time as their bodies and minds adjusted. That, too, was unacceptable.

Sickly essence extended from the assailant as he flew headfirst for Teddy's undefended back, now only centimeters away. The excess chi poured from the brothers. It scattered in every direction, assaulting Deklan's awareness. His vision already failing, he gathered his will and harnessed the fleeing essence. Dom did the same, and, both knowing what to do, they shot it toward Teddy. Rather than hit him, the chi molded to his body, forming a thin layer of prismatic light.

The cart exploded in a cloud of splinters, ice, and chunks of fish as the man flew into Teddy.

Before the carnage settled, Deklan was falling backwards, his vision going black.

CHAPTER SIXTY-NINE

Vengeance

As Deklan's consciousness stirred, a comforting weight settled over his body. To anyone else, it would be harder than forged steel. But as it flowed around him, it bent, conforming to his shape. He squeezed his hand, marveling at the strength it possessed. When had he become so powerful? He extended his senses, and the moment he discovered Dom beside him, also lost in his own musings, knowledge came rushing back in.

Teddy!

Though Deklan's vision refused to focus and his limbs tingled, he shot to his feet, looking for his pal. Their breakthrough had come, but what if it hadn't been enough? Teddy could have been injured, or worse, by the enemy cultivator's attack. Deklan could feel his and Dom's chi still wrapping their friend's body, but it told him nothing of Teddy's internal state.

"Teddy!" Dom yelled, panic tinging his voice as he shot upright. "Are you okay?"

Deklan stumbled forward, heading for the blur of brown in his view that had to be the bear. Ice crunched beneath his feet, and he fell to his knees before Teddy. Reaching out a hand, Deklan prepared for the worst. His hands moved through the protective barrier. He intended to search Teddy for any sign of a wound, but the moment he touched fur, a jolt ran through. Faster than the blink of an eye, something far below had stolen some of Deklan's chi, deemed it inadequate, and spat it back out.

All at once, Deklan's senses returned. The essence coursing through his and his brother's body snapped into place, making them both take a sharp breath. As they exhaled, they gazed down at Teddy, relief flooding them.

"Is . . ." Deklan licked his lips. "Is he *asleep?*"

Teddy snored in response, his impressive jowls flapping as he released a deep sigh. He lay atop a mound of shattered cart, chunks of ice, and bits of fish. Despite the destruction of their hard work, Deklan smiled. Teddy was perfectly fine.

"Whoa . . ." Dom said, peering down at the cultivator.

The man lay under one of Teddy's giant paws, his mouth ajar and eyes rolled into the back of his head. There was a large bump just below his hairline, which was, evidently, the bit of his body he'd tried to hit Teddy with.

"Yeah," Deklan agreed. "Looks like our chi is just as strong as it feels."

With the knowledge that Teddy was safe, Deklan surveyed what remained of the fish they'd harvested. Seeing the damage really hammered home how strong their shield-like chi was; the cultivator's attack had held almost-unfathomable power, and unlike Teddy, the cart hadn't stood a chance. Most of the fish were completely obliterated, even the scales and bones turned to paste.

It filled Deklan with a smoldering rage, one he'd not felt since discovering the king's lies.

To him, taking a life, even one of a non-sapient animal, was no small thing. Each fish caught was something to be cherished and thanked, for they were a source of sustenance for Deklan and those he held dear. This entire cartload of fish, which had been bound for the congregation, were now destroyed. Their lives had been taken, and for what? Just to be smashed by some birdbrained prick?

His lip twitched, and he averted his eyes, the sight only making his blood boil. One corner of the cart seemed to have mostly survived, and Deklan walked over to it, kicking a loose plank of wood aside. The object below it made his eyes fly wide. The lower half of a fish poked up, its head buried in chunks of ice and wooden splinters. He held his breath as he brushed away the debris, hoping beyond hope that it had somehow survived the impact. He grabbed it by the tail and lifted it gingerly. He must have instinctively wanted to protect it, because his chi rushed out, creating a shielding barrier around it. Deklan slowly turned it, praying that it was whole. As he twisted it this way and that, he couldn't find a spot of damage. He released his breath, a small smile coming to his face.

"Deklan!" Dom called, grabbing Deklan's attention and holding something up like a trophy—another fish, some scales missing but the flesh intact. Dom's was also covered in a protective shield, impervious to outside damage.

A strained groan came from behind Teddy. Holding his head with both hands, the enemy cultivator sat up, straining to move aside the giant bear paw holding him down.

Deklan and Dom shared a glance, a pair of devious grins coming to their faces.

I felt an immense sense of schadenfreude as Deklan and Dom smacked the absolute piss out of the cultivator. Their fish clubs swung down like unholy mallets, one connecting to the chest and the other to the head. Loath as I was to admit it, the evil prick had flown rather gracefully when he'd attacked Teddy earlier. Now, he careened through the air like a bug caught in a storm, his limbs splayed as he sailed back over the mountain whence he'd come.

The bloke had tried to take out my favorite bear, and that alone made him deserving of the strike. But his crimes didn't end there. He was also the one who had wronged Roger so long ago, only increasing my sense of pleasure at his fish-based punishment. When I saw his trajectory, I couldn't help but laugh. He'd be in for a world of hurt when he eventually landed. Maria watched closely, her core buzzing in delight at the dispensation of justice.

Dom's eyes were tracking the man's passage, but he tore them away, focusing on Teddy. He passed his fish to Deklan, then bent and tried to lift the bear. Just as when

Deklan had touched Teddy, the network below stole a bit of Dom's chi before spitting it back out violently.

"Frack me!" Dom said, leaping backwards.

Deklan grimaced. "Yeah. Seems like we can't move him."

Dom looked to the east, then shifted his gaze to his twin. "Go help them."

"You're sure?"

Dom nodded back, taking a step closer to Teddy. "I'll keep him safe. You protect the others."

That was all that needed to be said. Dual-wielding a pair of fish as tall as he was and running with a speed only possible because of his breakthrough, Deklan raced toward the mountaintop. His face was tight, an anger still burning deep within him at what had become of our fish-filled cart.

I completely understood how he felt. We'd made my mobile esky together, and seeing it destroyed felt like a personal attack. The fish going to waste was even more egregious. If not for my need to remain still as I channeled chi into the ground, I'd have rushed there and enacted a similar punishment. Thankfully, the process of filling the network below seemed to be coming to an end. It still demanded something else, some requirement that I couldn't yet identify, but I could worry about that when the time came. Hopefully it wouldn't take much longer.

Trust! the echoes reminded me, repeating themselves.

Reminded that I was stuck in place, I sent my awareness toward the battle, fighting off the desire to go assist my friends. The defenders were holding their own, but that didn't stop my guilt from bubbling up.

Because of my absence and the temporary incapacitation of my animal pals, the defenders were stretched thin. We had the numbers advantage, but the king's forces made up for it with the power of their corrupted chi. It took at least four of our regular cultivators to take on just one of the former prisoners or handlers. Trent was holding back the king by himself, the father–son duo clashing in midair above the battlefield like fire-spewing Super Saiyans. Roger had paired off against Tom Osnan Sr., whose power seemed to have increased tenfold. He grew massive vines from the ground that were laced with sickly essence. They lashed out at Roger with unending persistence, only to get cut down by Roger's blades.

Groups of spare defenders were moving around the battle in search of an opportunity to strike, but the attackers and their corrupted chi seemed to be unnaturally perceptive, even for cultivators. Each time a group found what seemed like the perfect position, their target would dash away before they could even attempt to flank them.

A familiar scent that I couldn't quite place rose from just beside the battle. I investigated, and when I didn't sense anything, I gave it a quick visual scan before returning my attention to the—

What the?

I did a double take.

Two men were crouched in the shrubs there, feeding what looked like herbs into a fire. Suddenly, I recognized the smell. It was the scent that had lingered in the clearing I'd cleansed earlier today. The moment I'd sensed the chi of the alchemist Solomon, I was almost certain that he was the one who'd been behind the poisonous patch. Now, I was sure that it was him. But what were he and Francis, the "high alchemist" or whatever, doing?

They started talking, and I listened intently.

"You're sure this will help, Solomon?" Francis asked.

"Positive. It would be impossible for you to tell, but . . ." He trailed off as he reached into his pocket. Finding what he was looking for, he fed it into the flames. "But the king and his forces seem to be able to sense the cultivators here. If we can dull their senses, even just a little . . ."

Francis grabbed his sleeve, and when Solomon looked his way, Francis's gaze was fervent. "We can use it as cover to leave." Francis's eyes widened, and he dipped his head. "If it pleases you, I mean. Sir."

Solomon should have been elated at the deference from the High Alchemist Francis. It was a symbol of his ascension, his status as *the* Alchemist. But all Solomon felt was worry for the safety of the people here. They were cultivators, people who were reputed to be vile. According to the Church of the Alchemist's doctrine, only the medicinal herbs that their deity consumed would stop their heart from becoming that of a rabid dog.

Yet the people here, some who had been chained in the capital, seemed anything but. Hades's scraggly beard, there was a literal *hellhound* with them, and even he seemed nice. It went against everything Solomon thought was the truth. And there was another reason that Solomon wanted to help them.

"The man that leads this place, the one named Fischer that the king is after . . . he saved me, Francis."

"A chance encounter! One that we should thank the heavens for! But *not* one that you should lose your life over!"

"It's more than that. Fischer's chi . . ." Solomon gestured for Francis to follow him, who did so after only a little hesitation.

They moved through the bushes, taking care not to be spotted by any of the attacking force. After going around ten meters, Solomon started building another fire. Moments later, the kindling was aflame, and they fed herbs into it.

"His chi is pure, Francis," Solomon continued, not knowing any other way to describe it. "*He* is pure. From that alone, I was inclined to trust him, but seeing how his followers act . . ." Solomon shook his head. "There's no doubt in my mind. He's a good person, and there's no reason we can't coexist. For that to happen, though, they need to win."

Francis's disappointment with that answer was clear on his face, but he said nothing.

An odd whistling sound cut through the din of battle, and Solomon chanced a look, expecting to see another of the meteors that were apparently a result of a spirit beast. Instead of a spherical shape zooming through the air, he spied the silhouette of a man. It arced directly to the center of the battle. When they noticed it, almost everyone froze, scanning for a possible attack. Upon spotting the man sailing their way, the moment dragged on, the witnesses likely as confused as Solomon by the events.

All but one man, anyway.

"Lucian!" the soldier with the sharp chi—was it Roger?—bellowed, drawing back his sword. Moving so fast to Solomon's senses that it looked like he teleported, Roger appeared in the air right before one of Francis's birds. He lashed out with the flat of his blade. It connected with a horrifying crack, which sounded more like a splitting mountain than metal on flesh. Lucian, still somehow in one piece, slammed into Tom Osnan Sr. The men tumbled end over end, landing in a tangle of limbs.

"Er . . . I'm sorry?" Solomon whispered to Francis, not knowing what else to say.

"Don't be. That one is too far gone."

Solomon shook his head. He didn't have the power to join this fight. The best way for him to help was to blind the enemies' senses. He reached into his pocket, searching for the last herb this fire needed.

High above the battle, Trent crossed his arms before him, absorbing a blow.

"Useless!" his father screamed, sickly chi shooting from his fist.

Trent had to shield his body with flame. Even so, his father's heat was almost too much, the king's essence seeking to burn him away. They gazed at each other, both men's eyes filled with hatred.

Augustus Reginald Gormona shook his head. "You are my greatest mistake."

"Good," Trent replied, sending flames roaring from his arms.

His father flew backwards, coming to rest in midair with fire streaming from his bare feet, his shoes having long been incinerated. "You could have been the next ruler. Instead, you'll just be a lesson for generations to come. A reminder of what happens when you betray your *family*."

Trent snorted, amusement warring with his fury. "*I* betrayed *my* family? You fed me *poison*!"

"Don't be dramatic. It had to be done, just as it was done to me."

A conversation replayed in Trent's mind, a memory that he recalled with unerring accuracy. They were within the throne room, the late-afternoon light streaming in through the stained-glass windows above. Trent was only a child, barely old enough to form a coherent sentence.

"This new recipe is stronger, my king," Solomon said, opening his bag. "I recommend a half dose."

The king tugged at his beard in thought. He didn't have to consider long. "Give him the full dose. I still harbored fantasies of overthrowing my father when I was a boy—I never did, of course, but I won't risk having my own son plot against me."

Trent's mother, at least, hesitated a little. "Perhaps we could start with a smaller dose. If that doesn't work, we can—"

"Do not speak out of turn." Though the king's words were quiet, the threat in them was clear.

She averted her gaze and dipped her head in supplication.

Looking back now, Trent could see the hesitation on Solomon's face. The alchemists knew what would happen. And neither of them said a thing. Instead, they'd poured their concoction into a cup and given it to Trent. He recalled the taste. The sickly sweet flavor mixed with underlying wrongness that only a child could willingly ingest without asking questions. The light streaming through the colored windows above gave a bloodred tint to the clear potion.

It all flashed before him in an instant, and as Trent returned to the present, he made no effort to hide his disgust with everyone involved. "I remember everything, *Father*," he spat. "You could have killed me with the dose you gave me. You put my own life at risk because you were scared of a child." He leaned forward, getting closer. "All because you're a *coward*."

The king snarled, flames curling from between bared teeth. Without a word, he flew forward, cocking his arm back and suffusing it with chi. It was exactly what Trent had been waiting for. He raised his left hand, only sending enough essence there to block the vicious blow. Hiding his right hand from sight, he prepared the rest of his power in his core, gathering it for use.

Trent was going to counterattack. With any luck, he'd end the fight in one move.

He forced a serious expression, not wanting to give away the ruse he'd been working toward since their battle began. His father drew closer by the second, and as the king punched out with his closed fist, Trent finally smiled. The king was committed, and it was too late for him to pull back. Trent's chi burst from his core, overjoyed to be let free. It shot down his arm and into his fist, the power swelling there almost too much for him to handle. His grin growing wider, Trent's right hand rocketed forward, propelled by jets of flame.

He craved the surprise that would be wrought over his father's face, his gaze boring into his father in anticipation of the moment the king recognized defeat.

But the moment never came.

His father's face only grew elated, a hint of undeniable madness coloring his features. When he felt and saw the power swelling from his father's closed hand, Trent immediately recognized his mistake. His father had been holding back, too. And as the punch approached, leveled directly at Trent's abdomen, it was his own defeat that he foresaw. Just as he'd laid the trap for his father, his father had laid a trap for him, one that it was too late for him to retreat from.

When his obliteration was only a fraction of a second away, an odd calm settled over Trent, caressing his body. He didn't look away, instead choosing to witness the deathblow from his own father as it descended. Before the fist physically struck, the corrupted fire shot forward as a never-ending torrent of flames that assailed his body. He closed his eyes then, accepting his fate. A second passed, then two. By the time the flamethrower ended, he still felt no pain.

Trent cracked an eye, peering out at the world, just in time to see two massive silvery clubs slam right into his father's head. The king shot to the ground as a blur, making a crater when he landed with a sickening thud.

"It's just like I told you," Deklan said, resting a giant—*are those fish?*—on each shoulder.

" . . . What?" was all Trent could say, blinking at the massive creatures that Deklan had used as blunt-force weapons.

"Remember?" Deklan tilted his head, giving him a friendly smile. "I said that you should learn to rely on the people around you." He pointed at Trent's arm with one of his humongous fish clubs. "I've got you covered, and I mean that quite literally."

Trent lifted his hand, holding it before his face and twisting it in the light. There was a silvery sheen covering his skin, and now that he focused on it, he could tell where his sense of calm had come from earlier. It wasn't his at all. It was an extension of Deklan's power. Just as Roger's chi felt like a blade ready to cut, Deklan's was a soothing barrier, willing to shield you from danger.

A boulder deep within Trent's mind cracked. As the surface fractured, the inside crumbled, falling away like so many grains of sand. He took a shuddering breath as emotions rushed up from nowhere, hitting him harder than Deklan had smacked his father. Tears welled in his eyes. But before the first had a chance to fall, a sense of dread pooled beneath them, swiftly rising up to become a tidal wave.

Trent glanced down.

From the crater his father had made, the nauseating chi returned, strong enough to wash away the clean essence being released by Peter and the spirit tree. At the same time, apocalyptic flames spread over the battlefield, consuming all they touched and forcing the defenders back.

CHAPTER SEVENTY

Pride

As I witnessed Trent's eyes welling, I almost shed a tear of my own. Deklan had arrived just in time, giving me my second dose of schadenfreude for the day when he whapped the king upside the head with dual-wielded fish. Even better, the network below was done draining us, its mesh of interconnected ropes filled to the brim with chi. I'd had to empty my entire core, but it worked.

I breathed a sigh of relief and tried to stand. My body didn't answer, my subconscious still listening to the echoed urging of my pals' wills to remain connected. I tugged at the connection, not understanding what still needed to be done. Before I got a concrete answer, the king attacked. He released so much power that his core strained at the seams, threatening to break. The flames were hot enough to burn everything they touched. Packed earth cracked and blistered, warping beneath the assault.

The defenders retreated from him in droves. The attackers held their ground, which I assumed to be a foolish move. I was wrong. Rather than hurt them, the flames seemed to bolster their strength and double the madness in their eyes. The king was engulfing most of the area now, his chi's expansion slowing but not coming to a stop. He railed against the limitations of his body, not at all bothered by the fact that his core was threatening to detonate.

As the defenders regrouped, they turned toward the flames and awaited the attackers' advance. Now that my animal pals' chi was no longer being drained, they got to their feet. A sharp pang of worry drove into me. If they were as drained as I felt, they wouldn't be able to do much more than move around. But then the same network they'd been feeding power into sent essence streaming back to them. In an instant, their cores were refilled, their chi returned. Despite how much it had to expend, it didn't even put a dent in the network's reserves.

Beside me, Maria let out a hiss, shocked by the sensation of essence running through her.

I was the only one still drained, the network not giving me a single drop of power. "Go," I said. "Help them." Though my eyes were still closed, I felt her attention roam over me.

She gasped. "It didn't give you anything?"

"No. I still have to do something."

"I'm not leaving you." Her resolve washed over me, telling me any complaint was useless.

"But . . ." I tried anyway.

"No." She sat back down beside me. "I'm not leaving you undefended."

I reached over and rested a hand on her leg, her touch a welcome comfort. If I was completely honest with myself, I was happy about her staying. As selfish as it was, I didn't want to expose her to the danger the king represented. The network below sent me a mental nudge, delivering a pulse of chi directly to my core. It wasn't just mine. The trickle held a hint of me, Maria, and each of my animal pals. After being deprived of chi, the feeling of it coursing through my body was like the first cup of coffee in the morning, making endorphins rush through me. As fast as the power came, it was whisked away, draining down into the ground and leaving me empty.

Truth . . . the echoes whispered.

"You want more truth?"

The response was immediate. *Yes,* the echo of everyone responded.

"In that case, I want you to give me my chi back so I can go help my friends. That's the truth."

There was a long silence, nothing coming in reply. While I waited, I watched the battle.

Sergeant Snips, back at full strength and beating back the flames with her arcs of energy. Private Pistachio unleashing blast after blast, only pausing long enough to gather more power in his joints. Corporal Claws and Cinnamon riding atop the pelicans' backs, the former chirping as she spotted an outcropping of stone. Bill and Pelly locking on to it, diving groundward with their violently inclined passengers. Borks, ears alert and eyes darting, saving his abilities to be used defensively. Bumblebro and Queen Bee, steering clear of flames and waiting for an opportunity to strike. Lemon, once more joining Peter and the other tree spirit, flooding pure chi out into the world.

No, the voices finally answered, giving me a bigger taste of chi before tearing it away again. *Truth.*

Why was it slowly increasing the dose of power before taking it away again . . . ?

Yes, the echoes called. The process was repeated, an increased burst coursing through me before being dragged away, returned to the network.

I thought I understood now. It would return my power, flooding me with chi until I was full . . . but only once I did what it wanted. What was the goal here? Was it trying to make me have another breakthrough?

Yes! it answered, the echoes seeming exasperated.

I considered just getting up anyway. I'd likely be able to draw a fair bit of chi back into my core, especially if I went to the battlefield and ate one of the fish Deklan was currently smacking a woman over the head with, the handler having the audacity to leave the protective area of the king's flames.

No, the echoes replied, growing increasingly annoying despite sounding like those I loved. *Trust. Trust. Trust.*

Frustratingly, I believed it. I clenched my jaw and took a steadying breath. "This is some bullshit, you know that?"

Yes, they answered, holding a hint of Claws's mischievous grin.

It might have made any other person up and leave immediately. To me, though, it was like a warm hug. I barked a laugh, then turned to Maria. "Sorry," I said. "I promise I'm not going insane. I'm talking to—"

"I know," she interrupted, squeezing my hand again. "I can feel it, too."

I opened my eyes, leaving behind the vision of a lightning-wreathed boulder just as things were about to get interesting. I stared into Maria's eyes, searching for an answer. "What do I do?"

"What you've always done, silly." She gave me her cutest smile, the one that was somehow both shy and filled with confidence. She lifted my hand and rested it against her cheek, leaning on me. "The right thing. Stop questioning yourself and do whatever you think is right."

It was a simple statement, yet it struck me to my core. I was getting so caught up in the minutiae of what I *should* do that I wasn't listening to what I felt was correct. I let out a slow breath, mentally laying out the facts.

Now that my animal pals were no longer incapacitated, I didn't believe that the enemy's forces as a whole presented a threat—not one that the defenders couldn't overcome, anyway. The only thing that gave me pause was the king. His core was increasingly unstable, and it was clear that he lacked the self-preservation that any sane individual should possess.

Because of the numerous conversations that had taken place since the battle began, I'd managed to work out that Theogonia was the source of the king's corruption. So . . . what would happen if he straight-up exploded? Would my beloved Tropica become my new world's equivalent of Chernobyl? A place that was anathema to life? Such an eventuality would be devastating, but we could rebuild. The real threat was that the king detonating like a nuclear bomb would endanger my pals.

But . . . I trusted my friends. Even if something like that were to occur, I *knew* that they'd find a way to nullify it or get everyone to safety. The air around me vibrated, as if the very world agreed.

Trust, the network echoed. It, too, believed that the defenders would be fine.

Maria still rested her head on my hand, so I stroked her cheek with my thumb. "Thank you," I said.

"For what?" She tilted her head to the side, a strand of hair falling from behind her ear.

I didn't respond for a moment, soaking in as much of her beauty as possible. "For always knowing just what to say." I gave her a smile that she returned, her cheeks rosy. Closing my eyes and crossing my legs, I adopted a meditative stance. "If this thing wants truth, I'll give it some bloody truth."

The moment I rejoined my awareness to the network below, the battlefield returned in my mind's eye. A lot had changed in a short time. A never-ending barrage of boulders crashed down on the king's position, the ground thumping and fires flaring with each strike. Enemy cultivators kept leaving the king's flames, only to retreat after they got whacked by a fish or blasted by the onslaught of attacks launched their way. I searched the surrounding forest, finding a total of fifteen small campfires burning. Even the oldest of them still spewed out the alchemists' numbing haze, the clouds drifting over the field, suffusing the air.

Barry had just finished telling five defenders what the herbal smell was, and at his instruction they split up, dashing around from group to group and repeating the words in hushed whispers.

A bone-chilling roar cut across the field, bringing terror to the hearts of the masses and a smile to my face. Teddy and Dom had arrived. Deklan's brother was riding Teddy like a horse with the build of a . . . well, a bear. Somehow, he held on as Teddy charged down the mountain. One of the enemy cultivators spotted the threat and left the safety of the king's inferno, the misguided handler assuming she could easily quash them. She was, of course, wrong. And unfortunately for her, Teddy had no qualms with hitting a woman whose core was corrupted. Teddy's paw, impervious to any of the damage she could inflict, lashed out and struck her torso with the force of a runaway Truck-kun. He slammed her into the ground, and she went completely still.

She was alive, though . . . I think.

On the other side of the blaze, the rest of the attackers had regrouped. Sick of being thrown back and too insane to know that it was a terrible idea, they formed a flying wedge and forced their way out of the inferno. I wasn't sure if it was intentional, but as they raced from the king's still-expanding zone, the flames came with them. It wreathed their bodies, and when Snips sent an arc of energy their way, the barrier lashed out and blunted the attack. Pistachio's blast came next, and though the flames absorbed some of the force, it didn't get all of it. The formation rocked backwards, two men at the rear shoved out of the protecting flames.

Because of the awareness-dulling haze now covering the battlefield, they didn't feel the portal that Borks opened up behind them.

Two squads of defenders, all former slaves of Gormona, stepped through space. Scratch that—they weren't just former slaves. A defender struck out with an open fist, and instead of a chi blast, two insects flew forward. Queen Bee and Bumblebro's wings were silent as they slammed into an attacker's jaws, the man spinning around like a beyblade before falling to the ground, unconscious. The other man, similarly unaware, was punched in several places at once by the former slaves. Instead of spinning, his head rocked back, his eyes rolling. Both knocked-out men were left there, the flying wedge of enemies not even aware it had happened.

A sense of ease washed over me. The enemy force was being picked apart, meticulously dismantled by the defenders. I shook my head and grinned as I checked on Solomon, who was fist-pumping at his successful contribution to the battle.

Next, it was Roger's turn to attack. His blade arced out, cutting a crisscross pattern into the entire right flank. The attackers reeled back as Tom Osnan Sr. dashed forward, raising vines that absorbed the myriad slices. At the rear of the wedge, another three cultivators were expelled from the protective zone. Before they knew what was happening, silent blows landed across their bodies, taking them out of the fight.

Unlike his followers, the king was well aware of his force's diminishing numbers. Even through his madness, his fury burned, flaring bright each time an ally was eliminated. His core had small rips in it now. Despite the damage, he continued forcing his flames outward.

A pulse of chi dragged me away from my contemplation of the king. Nestled within the defensive forces, Barry's core was also fluctuating.

"Seriously, Barry," Danny said, his eyes locked on the fight. "Your battle tactics have proved incredible. If I didn't know better, I'd have assumed you were a seasoned soldier."

"Agreed," Ellis said, not looking up from the notepad he was scribbling in. "Because of your plans, we are only needing to utilize a fraction of our forces."

The defenders close by nodded and voiced similar sentiments, heaping the praise on him. My brow furrowed, confusion rolling over me. Barry should have been preening under their commendations.

So why did he appear so troubled?

CHAPTER SEVENTY-ONE

Smoke and Mirrors

With each person that praised Barry's actions, his soul vibrated. If he were the older version of himself, the one without an enhanced awareness of his own being, he'd have preened like a proud rooster. Now, though, he was all too aware of his ego and its inflation. It wasn't a problem in and of itself—an ego was only natural. He was human, after all.

The discordance came when that ego clashed with the version of himself that he wanted to be.

Barry was the stand-in leader of the Church of Fischer. As such, he should be the person who Fischer's followers could look to for guidance. A paragon of virtue. Yet here he was, reveling in the praise. It was . . . *fickle*. For him to derive his self-worth from others' perception of him was to put his happiness in their hands. He tried to deny it. Tried to push it down and pretend it didn't exist. But it wasn't working anymore.

Unfortunately, this wasn't a new development. He hadn't consciously admitted it before, but this shameful inclination of his was why he'd been pushing Fischer to take control of the church. Barry gritted his teeth, tuning out the outside voices heaping more accolades on him.

I don't feel worthy of my position . . .

His core hummed, something deep within him resonating with that acknowledgment.

I don't feel worthy of being a leader . . .

Something sloughed away as he admitted that truth, a weight he hadn't known was there. The world's chi felt alive around him, gathering and dancing as Peter and the tree spirits sent ever more flowing over the battlefield. Voices called out to him, trying to get his attention and yank him back to the present. Barry ignored them. He had to get to the bottom of this cognitive dissonance.

Was he truly unworthy of being a leader? If he was a little too proud—a little too vain—what did that matter? Even if failing those present would bring him discomfort, it would be temporary. He would never give up. He would strive nonstop, fighting to get back to a position where people were proud of his actions.

If his pride was a motivator, though, did that mean he would betray his comrades? If there was a choice to make, one that would hurt those he cared about in order to boost people's perception of him, would he take the self-serving option?

His answer was as immediate as it was true. No, he wouldn't. His ego might chafe, but he'd still choose the well-being of others every time. His core shook, as did the surrounding clouds of chi, urging him on.

Oh . . . Barry realized, possessing unwavering clarity. *I* am *a good leader* . . .

It wasn't his vanity talking, either—it was fact. In spite of his pride, Barry would readily sacrifice his happiness if it meant improving the well-being of others.

The world agreed.

All at once, the surrounding essence slammed into him, filling his core to the brim. His body seemed to soak up all it could, his muscles swelling and skeleton changing. The next moment, excess power exploded out of his core as its bounds increased.

Even though I wasn't physically there, I recoiled from the explosion, instinctively backing away. The blast was different from the bladelike chi of Roger's ascension, yet it was just as deadly for anyone caught in the detonation.

Luckily for the surrounding defenders, everyone now knew what a breakthrough looked like. Danny had tried to get Barry's attention at first, even giving him a little shake for good measure. But the moment the world's chi started gathering, he ordered everyone to back up. Just in time, too, because it had slammed into Barry a moment later.

I'd been keenly aware of Barry's thought process, the network I was connected to relaying his deepest thoughts in real time. I had no idea that Barry was dealing with such doubt, and now that he'd overcome it, I was beyond happy for him. The explosion that resulted from his breakthrough had thrown up a cloud of dust, and as it settled, I raised a mental eyebrow at Barry's body. The homie was absolutely *jacked*. Like ten years of weight training and a healthy dose of anabolics jacked.

"Frack me," Danny said, shaking his head in disbelief as Barry sat up. "What has Helen been feeding you, buddy?"

Barry blinked down at his glistening arms, which had literally torn their way out of his shirt. He opened and closed his fists, testing his new strength. The surrounding defenders gaped at his new form, their faces ranging from stunned, awed, and everything in between. Which wasn't really surprising considering he looked like a Greek god. Though all of their reactions were positive, another person on the battlefield was far from happy about the event.

An inhuman scream came from the flames, leaving no doubt as to who the sound came from. The king's hatred was reaching new heights. Most of the flying wedge had been taken out by now, only three of them still standing. As the scream slowly tapered off, the inferno raging atop the field ebbed. Thick strands of corruption flowed from around the defenders still standing. When their protective flames were gone, the streams continued.

"What the . . . ?" Roger said, his eyes wide as he gaped at the downed enemies. Despite none of the king's protective chi surrounding them, torrents of power still flowed from their cores. Their patriarch wasn't just retrieving his own power. He was also stealing theirs.

It poured into his outstretched hands, flowing through his body and down into his core. There, his nexus of power expanded, the walls stretching to accommodate the vast swaths of essence coming in. Though his eyes still held indescribable madness, there was a hint of bluster there, too.

He planned this, I realized.

I'd assumed he'd gone completely insane, spewing so much power that the lining of his core stretched to such a degree that it ripped. But it had been intentional. He had damaged himself so that his core could hold more power. As I sent my awareness closer, inspecting the king's nexus, new tears appeared along its surface. Just as quick as they came, the wounds were cauterized, his sickly chi sealing them shut. It was an unending process, yet his core remained stable.

A silence settled over the defenders as the flames continued shrinking. It was late now, the sun having almost fully set over the western mountains. The burning fires had made the scene bright, but now that they were disappearing, darkness crept in. As the last of the streams left the attackers, they collapsed, their leader having sucked them dry.

In that gloom, all eyes turned to the king.

Barry stepped forward, his new muscles bulging enough to give even the most confident of men a little body dysmorphia. "Wave-break formation!" he bellowed, his voice possessing a rich timbre.

I had no idea what that meant, but as the defenders shifted, I swiftly understood. Only a select few stepped forward, the rest falling back into a defensive position. Roger, Trent, the twins, and Barry were the first to the front, followed by Snips, Borks, and finally Claws, who zapped there from the rock outcropping in what may as well have been called an instant. Peter was the only one absent, still helping the tree spirits radiate clean chi over the battlefield. It was all those who had experienced a breakthrough—the strongest of our forces.

They were to be the shoreline, the immovable force that broke any foe foolish enough to crash into it.

Barry turned to Borks and Claws, using one hand to point at the unconscious attackers. "Please retrieve them."

My two furry pals were a blur of enthusiasm as they darted forward and collected everyone, temporarily storing them in Borks's dimensional space, then removed them to the rear of the field. Only a handful of seconds had passed before they returned to the front lines. Those few seconds were all it took for the king to finish absorbing his flames. Fire danced across his skin, weaving unnatural lines that flared and sputtered each time a new tear appeared on the surface of his core.

Without warning, the king attacked. He was a living flame, and a blazing trail marked his passage. Deklan and Dom flew forward, manifesting a shield that covered the air. The former was still wielding his fish clubs, using them as an extension of himself. Roger stood just behind them, his sword drawn back and waiting. Barry crouched and spread his arms, chi gathering in his core. I focused on him, the network I was connected to urging me to watch.

The king released a spinning kick against the shield that would make Cinnamon proud. It sounded like ten concurrent lightning strikes, the force of it pushing the brothers back a meter. Roger, faster even than most cultivators could see, slashed upward. Deklan and Dom opened up a gap in the shield, instinctively knowing just how much room the strike would need. It slammed into the king's chest, cutting him from left hip to opposite shoulder. Despite breaking skin, no blood flowed from the wound, his fire burning to heal the damage in an instant.

The king reeled back only long enough for him to bend his legs and spring forward again, this time delivering a right hook to Deklan's side of the shield. Before it connected, Barry's chi burst from him. I expected him to have some flashy specialty, a finishing move worthy of his ego. I was wrong. Barry's essence joined the twins', reinforcing the shield and giving it a reflective surface that reminded me of a mirror. When the king's punch connected, his own power was turned against him, his feet leaving the ground.

And it wasn't just the twins that'd had their chi reinforced. Roger's sword, also possessing a mirrorlike quality, whistled through the air. A wall of invisible blades slipped through a gap in the shield, and with Barry's power enhancing them, they cut into the king and sent him flying backward across the battlefield. His body skipped over the ground like a stone on water, divots getting cut from the blackened earth each time he made contact.

The king whirled and skidded to a stop on all fours, his entire torso ablaze as his wounds sealed themselves. A snarl split his face, but it was almost immediately hidden when a meter-wide portal opened right before him. Forked lightning, a pillar of flame, and countless energy blades—all empowered by Barry and possessing a reflective sheen—slammed into the king, forcing him to the ground. Roger drew his arm back, the tip of his sword held forward. When he jabbed toward the king, his movement was a blur, holding every ounce of chi he could muster.

The strike was so potent that it manifested as a spearpoint, and it drove right for the enemy cultivator's abdomen. I believed cores to be a metaphysical structure, something that couldn't be hurt by physical blows, but that didn't stop Roger's strike from piercing the king's. Given how thin he'd stretched his nexus of power, the reflective spearpoint shot right through it, impaling him to the ground.

Sections of scar tissue riddled his core in each place he'd cauterized, and they all ruptured at once. As sure as I was that the sun would rise each morning, I could tell that the king's core was damaged beyond repair. There was no coming back from this.

To call the resulting blast an explosion was to rob it of its magnitude. The king was consumed from within as each stream of corrupted chi he'd retrieved was expelled, creating a fireball taller than the surrounding mountains. The frontline of defenders was cast away, the twins' shield holding and forcing everyone back. They skidded into the other defenders. Barry put a hand to Deklan's and Dom's shoulders, pouring his power into them. Their shield became a great metallic sphere, covering everyone present.

When the inferno started shrinking, I breathed a sigh of relief. It was finally over.

No, the echoes from the network urged.

"What?" I asked. "What do you mean, no? There's no way he could survive—" I cut off when I felt it.

Deep below me, running adjacent to the thick mesh that was now filled with the chi of my friends and me, something burrowed. It was the sickly chi that the king used, the same corrupting force that fueled his flames, and it was barreling toward him.

It emerged from the ground beneath his feet, immediately shooting up to refill his core. As it flowed into him, the king seemed to return to himself, his will oozing out over the battlefield. There was a distorted noise, like the static from a thousand TVs at full volume. The air warped as the flames shrank, condensing until they were the shape of a man.

The king, now tapped directly into the power that had corrupted him, flicked a single finger.

A train-sized cylinder of flame spewed from him, hammering into the defenders. Deklan and Dom restored the shield just in time. The entire defensive force, sequestered beneath the semicircular barrier, was thrown backward. The king extended his arm again, ready to flick another pillar of corrupted chi their way.

My stomach sank as a possibility—that I'd made the wrong choice by remaining here—reared its ugly head. Instead of pushing it away, railing against it, I took a deep breath and let the thought pass by like a cloud high above. I'd already decided to trust in my friends, and there was no point in doubting them now.

I focused on the defenders, channeling my worry into curiosity about how they would overcome the obstacle. And within the shield, a series of breakthroughs took place, each of them contained by individual bubbles of the twins' power.

Anna, the former slave of Gormona who had shown her loyalty time and time again, exploded with dangerous chi. It was like Roger's in that it felt like a threat, and despite the lack of a cutting edge, it felt just as deadly. She focused her blunt-force power on the king, stumbling but somehow remaining conscious.

Danny, who'd spent most of his life as a quartermaster in the capital, collapsed. He shook his head and came to a moment later, an odd essence radiating from his core. It felt almost like Peter's and Barry's—a supportive power.

Keith, in a move that I didn't find surprising, caught fire. Thankfully, it was nothing like the corrosive flames that the king was releasing, and extinguished the moment he passed out.

They were all potent, but nowhere near as powerful as the last.

Teddy's entire body glowed red, his face contorting in anger. Unlike Anna, his legs never wavered, a palpable torrent of injustice coming from every one of his pores as he stared at the king. His was the rage of a sleeping bear, awoken too soon by some foolish invader. Like a den mother that saw every defender as one of her cubs, Teddy was furious at the king's actions.

Barry absorbed each of their transformations in an instant. "Drop the shield long enough for us to exit."

"No need." Deklan shrugged nonchalantly, as if they were discussing what to eat for dinner. "You guys can pass through it."

"Good," he replied, the timbre still in his voice but his tone cold. "Tsunami formation."

The response was immediate.

All those who had experienced a breakthrough, other than the two brothers, strode forward and left the shield. Teddy took up the vanguard position next to Roger and Trent, everyone gathering their chi. The king, seeing their approach, paused. He looked like an elemental spirit, only his shape now reminiscent of the human he had once been. Orbs of bright-white flame watched everyone, his sickening chi oozing out to feel their power.

He laughed, then. At least, I thought it was a laugh. His head rocked back, and a sound like a house fire came from his throat, casting heat into the night sky that distorted the air. He cocked his arm back, holding it there as he gathered an unbelievable amount of power.

Before another cloud of doubt could cross my mind, the voices of the network below shifted to an elated chorus. They directed my sight toward the east, and though it made the impending clash leave my mind's eye, I let my vision shift. I needed to know why the remnant copies of my pals felt victorious.

When I found the being flying over the sand, my jaw dropped open. Though he was already moving at an incredible clip, the little deviant unleashed a blast from one claw, rocketing even faster. His core was almost empty, but the power he possessed . . . it had changed. He was *strong*.

"What the frack is he carrying?" Maria asked, her attention on the woven basket nestled against his darkened carapace. "And where did he get it?"

"No idea what it is," I replied, daring to hope that he could turn the tides of battle. "And if I had to guess where he got it, I'd say it's stolen. Probably from a small child. Or a puppy."

Unaware of the incoming reinforcement, the king unleashed his blast. If the earlier attack was train-sized, this one was the size of an aircraft carrier. Wider than the battlefield, his flames roared forward like a vengeful spirit, seeking to consume everything in their path. Though his human features were hidden by flame, I could sense the arrogance radiating from him. He believed that his attack would tear right through the party of defenders charging his way.

Busy unleashing hellfire as he was, the king didn't notice the sapient creature sailing in from the east. The defenders were similarly occupied, gathering their chi and preparing to unleash it against the king's inferno.

Only one being noticed. Perhaps it was their connection that made her look back and search the sky. Maybe it was her longing for him, her desire to see him once more. Or, possibly, it was just chance that made Sergeant Snips turn and look up, scanning the sky with a lingering gaze. Whatever caused it, the result was the same. Her visible eye went wide, her mouth parts undulating in disbelief as she spotted the Xianxia-land equivalent of a stealth bomber.

Rocky, playing it way cooler than I knew he could, simply shot her a wink and tipped an imaginary hat as he sailed over the defenders.

He landed before the incoming death sentence, set his woven basket down, and reached in to retrieve something. He withdrew a slender item just as the wall of corrupted chi slammed into him. Though his chi now felt like an active volcano, I still held my breath as Rocky's core absorbed the king's flames. He would be fine against fire, I was sure of it, but what about the corruption . . . ?

It was over in seconds, Rocky's body parched of power and all too happy to soak up the ship-sized conflagration. I hadn't noticed before, but he was covered in red lines that seemed to glow from within, standing in stark contrast to his now-black carapace. Was it reflective of how much chi he held? Before I could consider it further, he shook violently.

I honed in on him, sending my awareness down toward his core. Just as I'd suspected, it was the corrupted chi. It was seeking to infect him. Seeking to *change* him. Snips flew forward, tears streaming as she scuttled to his side. Rocky's eyes were closed, his entire awareness focused on fighting back against the corruption. What was he . . . ?

With what felt like practiced ease, he cast the corruption out. Just like that, he simply . . . released it. A cloud of dark green vapor flowed from his mouth. Waving a claw through it, he dispersed the sickly smell, making a displeased face.

In his other claw, he held the slender thing that he'd removed from the woven basket. One end was glowing, the king's flames having caused it to catch fire.

"You've gotta be kidding me . . ." I said, not believing my eyes.

Rocky held the stick to his mouth, giving Snips a reassuring pat with his other claw as she burst into tears.

"What is that?" Maria asked, her attention also on Rocky. "And what is he doing with it?"

I shook my head, struggling to find the right words. I'd seen inside the basket—it was filled to the brim with the same objects. The little prick had hundreds of them.

"Where the *fuck* did Rocky find cigarettes?"

CHAPTER SEVENTY-TWO

<small>◦</small>

Trust

I watched as Rocky took a deep drag, holding it in as he gazed down at Snips. Though not an expert on crab anatomy, I was pretty sure he wasn't supposed to have lungs. I shook my head at the smell; it was definitely tobacco. When he exhaled, a colossal cloud of smoke flew from his mouth. It billowed over the darkened field, lit from within as it surrounded the flaming form of the king.

Rocky's arrival had temporarily hit the man's reset button, but being surrounded by smoke snapped him out of it. His body flared, burning the smoke away. Despite having the appearance of a mindless elemental, incandescent fury spewed from his core, almost as repugnant as his sickly chi. He pulled his fist back again and gathered power, his connection to the source of corrupt chi growing stronger.

It took much less time to charge up this aircraft-carrier-sized blast.

As the inferno raged forward, racing across the battlefield toward Rocky, I held my breath. He'd dismantled it once, but had it been a fluke? Was Rocky incapable of weathering multiple hits? The deviant crab scuttled forward, stepping into the space between his beloved Snips and the flames. Again, he sucked it in with ease, the lines covering his body going so bright that they illuminated the area when the fire was extinguished.

This time, it wasn't only the sickly chi that he expelled from his core. Rocky sent a great gout of flame tearing over the battlefield. It contained the same power as the king's, but the essence was condensed, making it burn significantly hotter. The attack flowed over the king and into the base of the mountain behind him, drilling a hole into the earth. When the last of the chi dispersed, all I could do was raise an eyebrow at the carnage.

A trench had formed in a straight line from Rocky and past the king, its base covered in what looked like molten slag. If the old version of the crab had wielded such power, I might have launched him into the sun for the well-being of every life on this planet. He wasn't the same crab, though. The hint of human that had been within him as I flung him over the ocean was nowhere to be seen. Instead of paranoid and self-aggrandizing, he felt as stalwart and reliable as the rest of my animal pals. Whatever had happened to him, Rocky was truly a changed man.

Er, crab, I amended in my head.

See? the echoes within the network gloated, radiating vindication. *Trust.*

They grabbed my hand and urged me downward, but I told them to wait, pausing to consider.

On the surface, it seemed like the king had met his perfect match in Rocky, but that wasn't necessarily the case. The deviant crab could absorb his strongest attacks, sure, but the king's connection with the corrupted source grew by the minute. That underground tunnel was growing wider, ever more essence flowing through it. If I let the spirits lead me away, what if I was gone for too long? What if the king became a force too strong for even Rocky to handle?

The network reached out, and I already knew what it was going to say.

"He knows," Maria said, letting out a small laugh and squeezing my hand. "Trust. He heard you the first time."

The echoes seemed to narrow their collective eyes at her. *Yes*, they sent with a pout, Claws's personality once more shining through. *Trust.*

I laughed, shaking my head as the king fired off another wall of flame. "Okay. Let's go."

I gave Maria's hand a squeeze in parting, then allowed myself to be drawn below. I passed different layers of soil on my way down, slowly settling within one of the giant chi-filled ropes that comprised the network. Though I could still see the battle in my mind's eye, it was different. Before, it was like physically being there, my senses absorbing sights, smells, and even temperature. Now . . . it was like viewing the battle on a screen. I could still feel the aura radiating from the cores of every cultivator and spirit beast, but that was all.

Rocky absorbed another fire blast, his body filling with chi before expelling a torrent of flame at the king. The monarch's attack had been stronger than before, but Rocky easily handled it, filling me with a sense of calm. Suddenly, the mesh I was within forced my vision onto itself. I didn't understand . . . until I saw the tendrils of chi shooting up from below. There was one for each of my pals and Maria, the invisible vines slowly attaching to their cores.

All at once, their awareness was there beside me. Realization washed over them, the echoes' memories rejoining with their own. Terror reigned in more than a few hearts when they first arrived, but it swiftly bled away. The strength of our bond soothed any lingering doubt, bringing us to a place of understanding.

In that serene mindset, something monolithic appeared in our midst. Despite never having felt it before, I immediately recognized it as an aspect of the network that we were within. It wasn't quite a sapient being, but . . . a shadow of one? The possibility of one? It continued forming, rising from so far down that it may as well have been the planet's core. We had some big personalities among us, but compared to the mountain of potential still climbing, we were ants.

It was, to my astonishment, almost within my grasp. This ancient thing's power, older than I could even fathom, was on offer . . . . If only I could satisfy whatever requirements it demanded.

Lacking the subtlety of the polite urging my friends' echoes had used, the monolith forced my vision inward, my awareness sent spiraling down into my own consciousness. It was trying to show me something.

My life on Earth, I realized.

It zoomed by at mind-bending speed, sharing my experiences with those connected to me. When we'd been in the sky, I'd shared visions of my life as a CEO. Of my relationship with my parents and the turmoil it had wrought. This wasn't just snippets; it was a recounting of everything.

With their emotions soothing me, I felt neither pain nor despair. I saw it with complete clarity. When the timeline reached my encounter with Truck-kun, we snapped back to the present. I expected a moment of rest, one that I could use to search for the truth I needed to find.

No such luck. We were immediately catapulted into different memories, the scenes flashing by like the saddest montage ever.

It started with the times I'd lied to myself about everything being okay, culminating in my accidental obliteration of a tree when Maria and I were camping. Next, it was my avoidance of Maria. Each time I'd pushed her away, terrified of the idea that I would ascend to the heavens and she would stay behind, choosing her life on Kallis over eternity with me. As expected, that chapter ended with my breakthrough atop the sands, where I'd finally admitted the truth to myself and blasted a crater in the shore.

When the next act arrived, I instinctively knew it was the last. Each flash was a time I'd rejected leadership, both within my mind and externally to Roger and Barry. When the visions came to an end, the moment seemed to drag, signifying that, unlike the other two acts, there wasn't yet a conclusion. Again, before I could ponder overlong, we were skull-dragged elsewhere.

Barry's recent breakthrough. The first time I'd experienced it, I had been aware of his internal state and the doubt that wracked him. As I witnessed it again, this time from his point of view, it was like holding up a mirror to my own subconscious.

Back on Earth, my time leading my father's empire had been an utter failure. When presented with the choice of doing right by a business or its employees, I chose the employees every time. And I didn't regret it. Not one bit. There were consequences, of course. I'd been ousted from the corporations, my actions deemed "problematic" by shareholders. It had sent me on a downward spiral, one that made me question . . . well, everything.

After arriving in Tropica, I'd told myself that I didn't want to take up the mantle of leadership because I wanted to live an idyllic life, one where I could just spend every day fishing and exploring, surrounded by good company and a certain freckled cutie. It was the easiest kind of lie—one that wasn't a lie at all. Of course I wanted those things for myself. I'd have to be mad to choose responsibility and meetings over fishing and sunshine.

But it wasn't the full truth. It wasn't what made anxiety harden in my core. How could it be?

The monolith vibrated softly, urging me on.

I was no longer just some random bloke. I didn't need to sit and deliberate in an office on the fortieth floor, losing hair and sleep because I received backlash from the board. I was absolutely surrounded by capable people, all of whom were the equivalent of superheroes back on Earth. Unlike fictional characters, though, my friends were real. If I truly wanted, I could just sit on the beach and have any hard decisions brought to me, Maria's hand in one hand and one of my animal pals under the other. By process of elimination, it wasn't the fear of responsibility causing me doubt.

The monolith shook, steering me toward Barry's breakthrough again.

Barry had been concerned about his ego, worried that he was a terrible leader because it was others' opinions of him that he derived his self-worth from. I was similar, yet entirely different. I was terrified that I would make the wrong decision, and those I loved would leave me. Just as the board of directors, some of whom I'd considered friends, turned their back on me.

It wasn't just my close circle, either. I was also scared of the average person's opinion. After the corporation ousted me, my public lambasting had been relentless. Overnight, I had gone from a respected business prodigy to just another nepo baby who tried to nose-dive their predecessor's empire. The media had dragged me for months, making the derisive voices inescapable.

It was weird looking back on it, because I truly didn't give a shit about the position anymore. Leaving 'business' behind had led me on a path of self-discovery, and I'd come out on the other side happier than I could have ever imagined. I thought I had conquered my past, not caring about the perceived betrayal and the public derision.

Apparently, I was wrong. It had left a web of trauma, one that my subconscious was trying to protect me from experiencing again. I imagined a black bubble of self-doubt in my mind, anchors extending from its body and locking it in place.

The monolith shuddered, my surroundings seeming to move with it. I was close now. I was almost there.

Trust, the network sent as a feeling, its gigantic body incapable of speech. *TRUST!*

With that final word, realization bloomed like a wildflower.

I needed to trust my friends. I needed to believe in the family I had formed. Pulses of affection came along the ropes that connected us, telling me that their love wasn't conditional. They weren't empty reassurances. Far from it. They were warm, glowing truths, each a declaration that shone brighter than the midday sun.

More, the network demanded.

I needed to believe in my instincts. I needed to have confidence in the decisions I made as a leader, because no matter what, my friends—my family—had my back.

They all sent affirmation, agreeing.

And public sentiment? It could get fracked. As with Barry, the opinions of others might hurt. No one wants to be a public punching bag. But who cared? I'd prefer to be liked—I was only human, after all—but as long as I had my circle around me, other people's opinions of me were an afterthought.

Now that I realized what had been plaguing me, it seemed so obvious that I wanted to laugh. A sense of inevitability set in, the monolithic presence leaning in and oozing anticipation.

I opened my eyes in the real world, clearing my throat. I took a deep breath, prepared myself for what was about to occur, and spoke the words.

"I need to trust myself and those I love."

I intended for only Maria and me to hear it. Instead, the network below seemed to scream the words, throwing them over every bit of land it stretched beneath. The ground shook, and this time, it wasn't metaphorical. Still connected to the network, I felt the shift. Starting right in the center where the monolith had stood, a single mote of light appeared. One became ten, and ten became a hundred, the spread exponential as each branching section became illuminated. A moment later, the light left its confines. It radiated up through the earth and breached the surface.

Radiating brilliant beams of white from our bodies, Maria and I looked at each other, twin smiles crossing our faces as we realized the extent of the network's power. Though we both shone with light, mine was twice as bright as hers.

"Wow," she said, squinting at me. "I knew our futures were bright, but damn."

I barked a laugh as she covered her mouth and let out an intoxicating giggle. "Are you ready?" she asked, tilting her head.

"Come on," I said, extending my hand.

She laced her fingers with mine, and hand in hand, we flexed our will and moved to the battlefield in a silent flash of light, the network's vast power transporting us. It wasn't anything like Borks's ability. There was no portal to step through—no expenditure of chi to facilitate the transfer of our bodies. We simply appeared.

Hovering ten meters above the ground, we shone like incandescent stars. As fast as we had come, our animal pals joined us in the sky, every spirit beast except Rocky floating up to stand in midair. Each of them, and also the ground, shone with the same light as Maria. We turned to face the east, wanting to see the transformation we could sense coming.

"Hey, uh, Fischer?" someone called from below.

"What's up, Barry?" I replied, glancing down.

"Uh, yeah, I was just curious—it was you that yelled about trusting yourself and those you love earlier, right? And what's up with the whole—"

"Why are you glowing like Apollo's shiny sphincter?" Deklan demanded, cutting him off.

"Oh, that? Long story."

"Fischer . . ." an inhuman voice growled. I spun, finding the king blazing with heat and rage. Both his arms were held behind him, gathering power in what was likely going to be some kind of double-punch move.

"Oh. My bad." I pinched two fingers together, raising a solid wall of the network's light across the tunnel that channeled corruption into him. "I forgot you were there, mate. Give us a moment, yeah?"

He fell to his knees, his fire dwindling as his source of power vanished.

The change was almost here, the network's chi condensing beneath Tropica at an increased rate. I focused on the defenders below and raised a single hand. As I did so, pillars of light lifted each of them to the same height as us. I brought Rocky over to stand by Snips, and the deviant crab gave me a thankful nod.

With my other hand, I grasped toward Tropica and pulled it toward us. The reservists that had retreated came flying on wisps of chi, and I deposited them atop the light next to the other defenders, smiling at their wonderment. With one more flick of my wrist, I collected the two alchemists. They'd retreated far away into the forest from the king's chi, but despite Francis's constant suggestion of fleeing Tropica for good, Solomon had remained.

I placed them next to Barry, who gave the two men an appreciative nod, then looked at the ground, peering past his ridiculously muscular chest. "So, Fischer, what are we doing up—"

"Look at Tropica, mate," I replied, cutting him off. "It's about to happen."

As if my words were the permission it was waiting for, the world transformed. Tropica's buildings morphed into light, shifting around to make room for the energy approaching from the southwest. As tendrils of incandescence, the buildings of New Tropica flowed into the village. Everything twisted this way and that, seeking the correct configuration. I worried about the prisoners for a moment, those who had been confined back in New Tropica, but I felt them before me, being transported safely to the new village.

When the buildings had decided on their places in the world, they grew. Some gained new floors. Others acquired basements, new rooms, and even balconies, the powerful network somehow knowing what each construction needed. It was all over in a matter of moments. Happy with its work, the network's light solidified once more, locking each building into place.

As the glow receded and I caught sight of Tropica's new layout, I let out a soft whistle. "Hot damn. Now that's a village worthy of a fantasy world."

It wasn't just the functionality of the buildings that had been improved. Each was a unique piece of art, possessing little flares and flourishes that distinguished them from the others. A decorative beam here, an elaborate cornice there—so much had changed that I wondered how many months it would have taken to do it ourselves. Though the additions were prevalent, they were neither gaudy nor overbearing. The touches were delicate, somehow making the entire village seem like a cohesive piece.

I could have looked at it for hours; the world had other plans.

In an instant, the light flowed back underground, depositing us back on the packed earth and taking part of my awareness further beneath it. I dissociated from my body, watching the network as it drew uncountable strands of chi into the center of its mass. The ball condensed in stages, each taking only a fraction of a second. Then, just when I thought it could get no smaller, the underground star exploded.

The resulting blast was anything but destructive. The power rushing past me made a sense of joy and contentment flood every part of my awareness. I smiled at everyone around me. It was the purest of chi, a concentrated version of the world's. And it was spreading.

It didn't stop at the edge of the network's outer reaches, not even slowing a little in its expansion. In my mind's eye, I tried to comprehend the scope of it, tried to imagine just how far it would reach. Sensing my attempt, the network jumped in, dragging my awareness away to soar over the land. So high that I could see the planet's curve, I was reminded of the time I saw Lemon's memories and was shown leagues of cultivator-made destruction.

The landscape below me had been transformed since then. Hints of the millennia-old scars remained on the planet's surface, but they had been reclaimed by nature. Craters became valleys, upturned bedrock became mountains, and long gouges became riverbeds. Everywhere I could see, life had won. And the bubble of condensed chi still expanding from the network seemed to bolster it.

Leaves looked greener, water looked bluer, and the very land hummed in satisfaction. Chi had returned to this little part of the world, and might just return to all of it, given time. I glanced down, seeing my friends, their posture unbelieving as they felt how the world was supposed to feel. How it had felt thousands of years ago before the gods fled. I beamed down at them, my contentment overwhelming.

Before returning to my body, I sought the thing I'd felt underground, the guiding force that had helped build the network. There was nothing, not even a whisper remaining of that monolithic presence.

Shrugging, I opened my eyes—only to be met with an absolute wall of text.

An Absolute Wall of Text

Y ou have successfully taken part in a crafting ritual!

Quest complete: Group Project
Objective: You have discovered the importance of crafting as a group! Complete four crafting rituals within the territory of Tropica.
Progress: 4/4
Reward: Upgrade Tropica Village from Tier 1 to Tier 2.
Tropica has evolved!

Domain has evolved!
Effect: 40% Suppression, 40% Bolstering, 40% Growth, 500% Range.
Evolution: All effects doubled.
Warning! Foreign Domain detected.
. . .
Foreign Domain has been destroyed.

New Quest: In Defense of Tropica Village
Objective: Tropica Village has become a Tier 2 village. The evolution brings many benefits, which others will yearn for. Defend Tropica against ten external threats.
Progress: 0/10
Reward: Variable

New Quest: Hidden Knowledge
Objective: Because of the combined efforts of Tropica Village, chi has returned to part of the world. Discover three long-forgotten secrets.
Progress: 0/3
Reward: A History of the Kallis Wars, Seventh Edition

CHAPTER SEVENTY-THREE

A Time of Great Change

Silence reigned as my vision cleared, everyone staring either into space or at each other. Given how well I knew my pals, I was acutely aware of who would give the best reaction. As was almost everyone else, apparently. As one, our heads swiveled toward Ellis.

"Seventh edition . . ." he said, his hand shaking as he slowly closed his notepad.

I opened my mouth to respond, to make some no-doubt *hilarious* and timely quip, but nothing came out. "Damn," I said instead. "That's a lot to take in."

"Uh-huh," Maria agreed, staring at the far distance.

Barry cleared his throat. "Well done, everyone. I—" He cut off as power bloomed behind us, its corrupted nature undeniable.

Rocky leaped into action, putting himself between us and the threat.

Perhaps the king thought he stood a chance now that the network's power had been distributed. Perhaps he was too mad to gauge his position accurately, reduced to base instincts as the chi he embraced destroyed more and more of his body. Or perhaps he was aware of his doom and had decided to make one last desperate attempt.

Whatever the reason, the result remained the same: another wave of flame flew toward us, unleashed from the king's extended hands.

I appeared beside Rocky in a flash of light and flicked my wrist. The inferno simply disappeared, there one second and gone the next. I took a step toward the king, then paused and turned to the side. "Rocky, mate, I'm glad you're back and all, but where the frack did you find those?"

The moment I'd made the threat vanish, the deviant little crab had taken a deep drag of his fantasy cigarette, which, now that I was up close, I saw was an artisanal version of the mass-produced ones we'd had on Earth. He exhaled slowly, making a vague motion toward the sea with a nonchalant air.

"You know what," I said, "never mind. That's a story for another time. Don't give those to anyone else, okay? It's a bad habit."

Of course, he hissed, even his bubbled speech somehow sounding cooler.

Talk about a glow-up, I thought, returning my attention to the king.

He was gathering more power, still sucking up corrupted chi through his underground tunnel to Theogonia.

"*Fischer* . . ." he croaked, sounding like his lungs were burning away.

"Yeah, mate. That's me."

He let out a scream—at least that's what I thought it was supposed to be. It was more akin to wind racing down an ablaze hallway. He released his gathering power, letting out his strongest attack yet. Before it traveled so much as a few centimeters, I poured incandescent light from my body, the network providing it in abundance. His corrupted chi was cleansed, the fire dying out in a puff of smoke.

My light shot through it and into the king. It shone through him, penetrating down to his core and cleaning all the remnant corruption out. I'd instinctively known that I could destroy the sickly essence, but I was unaware of just how powerful it would be. The chi shone from my entire body, finding and destroying every last imperfection. When it hit the king's forces behind me, they were roused from unconsciousness, shooting upright. The cleansing chi shot into their cores, just as it had the king's.

They were offered a choice, and not all of them reacted the same way.

They could relinquish their corruption, let the purifying light lancing through them cleanse it away. All but one of the king's allies immediately let go, and as the poison was burned off, their cores started to heal. It was miraculous to watch. Tears welled in all of their eyes, having nothing to do with pain or despair.

I could feel their awareness of the process, their understanding that the corruption they had embraced was being washed away. The restoration of their bodies was so potent that even the king's ruptured core could be fixed. One ally, the one that had caused Roger unending grief and subsequently been on the receiving end of a fish-related beatdown, denied the light. The king, too, turned away, holding on to his corrupted power with everything he had.

I understood what would happen then. If they didn't let go of the chi within their cells, it wouldn't just be the corruption that was burned away. I forced my will down on them, making them understand the consequences of their choice. They acknowledged it. They were completely aware. And yet they denied my extended hand, choosing instead the evil power stemming from Theogonia.

The two men combusted in a flash, burning away in a pyre of their own making. Not even a mote of ash remained.

If it had happened even a day ago, I might have blamed myself for the duo's demise. I might have thought that my friends saw me as a monster for facilitating the event that led to their souls' departure, then projected that view onto myself. The word I'd heard uncountable times in the last few hours echoed in my mind, a single syllable that held immeasurable weight.

Trust . . .

I was not to blame. Any person who embraced that power would eventually die. Each time they channeled it, they were further condemned. As the last of the corruption was forced from the king's former allies, those who had readily relinquished the chi afflicting them, I breathed a slow sigh. My conscience was clear.

Now that there was nothing left to clean aboveground, I focused my attention below. The network's light raced along it, using each disgusting bit of essence as fuel. At the literal speed of light, it traced a path back to the heart of the corruption.

When it arrived in Theogonia, it exploded up from beneath the castle, ballooning into a radiant orb of light that covered kilometers of land. The only thing holding up some of the gnarled trees was the corruption lacing them, and as it was burned away, they collapsed in a pile of plant matter. It was a horrific level of destruction. Something about the swaths of forest just evaporating before my eyes made me angry, but a spark of hope also came to life.

Just as had happened to the scarred landscape created by long-departed cultivators, life would return to Theogonia. It was just a matter of time. Holding on to that eventuality, my awareness was dragged back through the tunnel.

As I returned to my body, I noticed how tired I was. It wasn't the bone-deep weariness of physical labor. It was like the foggy-brained feeling after a day spent at a computer beneath fluorescent lighting, but cranked up by orders of magnitude. I teetered, Maria grabbing my arm and steadying me before my face could become acquainted with the ground. "Thanks," I muttered, my mouth sluggish.

Though I'd closed my eyes, I could sense the approach of my animal pals, our bond having grown even deeper than it once was. Maria's presence was unignorable, her core feeling like an extension of my own. If it were any other human, I'd have worried about the implications. With Maria, all I felt was a deep thankfulness for her presence. I chanced a glance her way. She could sense my affection for her, causing tears of joy to well in her eyes.

"Oh no," I mumbled. "Are you . . . breaking up with me?"

"What?" Her head jarred backward, her eyes narrowing in suspicion. "What are you talking about?"

I waved a hand in Barry's general direction. "I know Barry has a rockin' bod now, but I can work out. I can change."

She rolled her eyes so hard that I thought she might get vertigo. "I'm over here worrying about you, but you're clearly fine." She lifted me in a princess carry and plopped me on Teddy's back, which was as emasculating as it was deserved. She leaped up behind me, hugging me around the waist and keeping me steady. "Would you carry us home, Teddy?" she asked. "Please."

Despite being a vision of wrath and spitting fury like ten minutes ago, he nodded politely and lumbered off, heading for my home. As he took through the rows of sugarcane, I wondered about what the future would bring.

When the villagers returned, there would be no way to hide Tropica's transformation. Heck, from their position at the northern headland, they for sure would have seen the king's flames. They might have even felt the heat. A time of great change was about to come to Tropica, and I had just declared myself the leader of it.

With that thought lingering in my mind, Teddy's swaying steps lulled me to sleep.

CHAPTER SEVENTY-FOUR

A Question

As I walked through the streets of Tropica the following morning, I marveled at the buildings. The sun was just peeking over rooftops to the east, casting its glorious rays on the new day. The entire time I'd lived in Tropica, the south side had been riddled with squat, crudely constructed dwellings that didn't hold a candle to the houses up north. Today, the sun's light shone down, illuminating how much that had changed. A demarcation no longer existed, even the dodgiest of homes now boasting architecture that could win awards back on Earth.

It was a heartwarming sight, one that was only moderately ruined by the man walking beside me. Roger's core was uncontrolled, his bladelike chi pouring out and filling the street we traversed. It was partially my fault and partially Sharon's, me because of a question, and her because of a statement.

"Lovely day for it . . ." I said, pointedly not looking his way.

All I got was a grumble in return, which I supposed was better than nothing.

"I love the new place, by the way," I tried again. "I can't believe Sharon found decorations for it already."

"They came with the transformation," he ground out, still staring forward.

"Ahhh, that makes sense."

I let a silence creep up on us as we strode toward the center of the village. My hopes that Roger would calm down were repeatedly dashed, his frustration seeming to build the closer we got. As we passed the smithy, which now had some wrought-iron decorations that were damned aesthetically pleasing, Fergus and Duncan came running out.

"Morning!" Fergus said, beaming a smile. "How are you feeling, Fischer? Mind if we tag along with—" He cut off, his eyes going wide as he entered the range of Roger's roiling chi. "Er, now that I think about it, I left something inside . . ." He backed away, dragging Duncan with him.

I forced my lips into a line, not letting even a hint of my amusement show. Annoyingly, Roger felt it coming from my core anyway, his sharp chi pulsing in response.

"There you are!" a familiar voice called from ahead, poking her head around a corner. "I worried that you two might have killed each other!"

I breathed a sigh of relief, thinking if anyone could make Roger calm down, it was his wife.

Nope.

When he caught sight of her, I instinctively pressed back against his flaring aura with some of the village's light, worried that he'd cut through a building or something. He felt my will pressing against it, paused, and took a deep breath. Exhaling slowly, his power receded. "My apologies," he stated, not sounding at all sorry. "I find myself out of sorts this morning."

I could have let my purifying light out completely, using it to wash away Roger's fury and make both of us feel better, but it wasn't time yet. Revealing it too soon would ruin Barry's plans.

Roger's eyes were still closed as he composed himself, so Sharon gave me a grimace and mouthed, *Sorry.*

In retrospect, I should have expected her arrival to make him even worse after what she said a half hour ago. Thankfully, her physical presence made Roger actively shrink his out-of-control aura, not wanting to hurt her despite the information she'd revealed to him.

I shook my head, recalling her words.

Oh, dear, Sharon had said as she patted his arm. *I've been helping Maria sneak out for weeks.*

If looks could kill, the glare he'd given me would have sliced me into small strips, put me on the longest sabiki rig ever, and cast me out to sea. Sharon had quickly departed, making up some excuse about needing to get back to Tropica and help prepare the theater while we hashed it out.

As we traversed the last few streets, I fidgeted with an object in my pocket, seeking to distract myself. It didn't work. We rounded a corner, and Barry's voice boomed out, carrying despite his conversational tone. "I know it may be hard to accept," he said, "but I think Tropica's transformation should be proof enough."

"Not to mention your transformation, Barry," George said, not drawing the amount of laughter I thought his joke deserved.

I stepped up to the edge of the theater and peered down, finding an absolute sea of people staring at George as he poked one of Barry's biceps. Trent was up there, too, his fireproof artifact cutting a figure almost as impressive as Barry's. Judging by the white pallor of some of the people sitting in the stands, I guessed that they'd already learned of everything. Scattered throughout the crowd, sitting as if they were just regular citizens, were the rest of the congregation. My spirit pals and Maria were off to the side, none of the unascended having the courage to sit anywhere near spirit beasts.

It was a stark contrast to the initial meeting we'd had with the freed slaves of Gormona before they joined the ranks of the Church of . . . well, *me.*

Back then, we'd had to put on a show of force, presenting an unwavering front to convince them they should join us. This time, Barry was just laying everything out, stating the facts as they had happened. Rather than an unspoken threat, the congregation, including all my animal pals, were sitting with the rest. It was a declaration that all were equal, and that just because we were cultivators, that didn't make us better than the regular citizens of Tropica.

But despite the calmness of the people sitting in the stands, I was under no illusion that there wouldn't be problems. There would still be people who assumed we were all mad. Maybe they'd run off to the capital, intent on selling us out to a monarchy that no longer existed. Perhaps they'd flee, heading for distant lands in an attempt to escape the changes coming to the world. Which they were free to try, of course. Whatever Tropica had become, it was no dictatorship.

It only took my enhanced mind a moment to consider all this. Unfortunately, it didn't distract me enough to calm my racing heart. I took a deep breath, and just as I was about to slink down the steps, Sharon grabbed my arm.

"Good luck," she whispered, giving me a bright smile.

Before I could respond, she jabbed an elbow into Roger's side, who grunted softly. He tensed his jaw, let out a long sigh, and locked eyes with me. "Good luck," he grumbled, looking like he'd rather have swallowed a boulder than speak those words.

"Thank you," I said, giving them a genuine smile. Then, I turned and descended the steps. Following Barry's instructions, I channeled my power. Light shone from my skin, a pure brilliance that didn't cast any shadows. It lit the entire area, bringing an immediate silence to the theater. All eyes turned my way, and as the last gaze landed on me, I released more chi.

It was only a fraction of mine and the village's purifying aura, but the effect was immediate.

Panic and shock melted away from everyone's faces as they took me in. I clenched my jaw, and sweeping aside my misgivings, I let them see me. Let them truly know my soul and its motivations. It was only for a second, but that was all that was needed. I smiled around the stands, seeing familiar faces, some that I'd met and even more that I'd merely exchanged pleasantries with on the streets of Tropica since arriving here. Blessedly, the light I was radiating also made *me* feel as though everything was going to be okay.

I eased my way down the steps and up onto the stage, traveling as slowly as Barry had suggested. Unlike him, I hated the attention on me. But considering the effect it had on the villagers of Tropica, it was a small price to pay. I stood beside Barry, the light coming from me making his muscles gleam . . . which he probably loved.

That thought made me smile, and I used it, casting it out toward the hundreds of faces still staring at me. Nodding at them, I released my chi. The light died out, the world returning to normal.

Barry whistled softly, shaking his head as the sound bounced around the theater. "Well, there you have it, everyone. As I told you earlier, the rest of the leadership and I will handle the day-to-day of the Church. Although Fischer will probably spend most of his time by the water, he is the *true* leader of Tropica. The one that will, eventually, become our god."

I was thankful that Barry let me be absent from his speech about my importance, power, and all that, but it did nothing to stop a pang of doubt and worry from crawling into me.

With my soothing aura now gone, my subconscious waited for the looks of awe to become glares of horror, terror, and derision. Seconds that felt like minutes passed, but the glares never came. The color had returned to every face, and no one made a sound as they watched the stage. I sought out the person I'd antagonized the most, expecting at least *her* to cast disdain my way. Lena, the patron of the north-side café I'd spent many of my first months in Tropica getting into barbed exchanges with, looked at me with naught but reverence.

As the moments passed, I finally believed Barry. I'd been hoping—praying—his words would come true, and that no one would despise me for who I was. He was right. I was neither hated nor feared.

As I'd discovered in last night's breakthrough, I didn't need their approval. But it felt good to have it anyway. That bubble of darkness within me, the metaphorical representation of the trauma from my old life, was uprooted and banished before the brightness of the faces watching me.

I didn't have to fake the smile that came over me, and the skin around my eyes bunched as I looked back at the sea of people, grateful for their trust.

There was a dash of movement to the side as Corporal Claws jumped on top of Teddy. She let out a loud whistle and clapped her forepaws together, trilling in delight as she beamed a full-toothed grin down at me and tried to start a round of applause. When no one joined in, she chirped indignantly, clapping even harder as she glared at everyone. A smattering of polite claps joined in, those who contributed still watching me with wide-eyed gazes.

I leaned toward Barry. "We good, mate?" I whispered. "This is getting a little weird for me."

He grinned and reached over, patting me on the back with one of his annoyingly toned arms. "Well done. That's all we needed. You can go now if you want—"

"Thanks!" I replied, cutting him off. "Sorry for the deceit, everyone!" I called toward the crowd as I marched off the stage. "If you'll excuse me, it's wonderful weather for fishing." I was at Maria's and my animal pals' side in a moment, not hiding the relief on my face. "To the shore, Borks!"

Ruff! he barked, his entire body wagging as he opened a portal.

Giving a small wave to the theater of people still watching me, I hopped through it, appearing on the patch of sand next to my headland. Maria came through next, followed by a flood of furred and carapaced pals. Borks was last, and he closed the portal behind him.

Before I could get a word out, Maria slammed into me, her arms going around my waist. "I'm so proud of—*oof!*"

She was hit on all sides, every creature coming to join the cuddle puddle. Snips clung to my back, as did Claws. Cinnamon leaped onto Maria's head. Bill landed on one of my shoulders, and Pelly landed on one of Maria's. Bumblebro and Queen Bee clung to my upper chest, buzzing with pride. Borks, in his golden-retriever form, wound around our legs. Even Lemon was there, one of her roots waiting for our arrival. She wound around us, squeezing softly. And Teddy, as patient as ever, waited until last, his giant arms wrapping us in a hug.

Of the animals present, only Rocky didn't partake. He lit his cigarette on one of the red lines covering his body, took a drag, and gave me a respectful nod.

Despite the impromptu cuddle puddle, now that I was free of the villagers' stares, my heart started thundering. Standing up on stage before them had been a daunting prospect, but it was nothing compared to what I was about to do. Claws, who had squirmed her way between Maria and me, cocked her head. She let out a questioning coo, rapidly glancing between my pounding heart and the anxiety written across my face. I took a steadying breath as adrenaline coursed through me.

Sensing something was up, my animal pals extricated themselves from the hug, their expressions worried as they gazed up at me from the ground.

"Fisher?" Maria asked, stepping back. "What's wrong?"

I swallowed, my mouth feeling dryer than the sand I stood atop. "I . . ." I shook my head, closed my eyes, and let out a slow sigh. Gathering every ounce of courage I could muster, I reached into my pocket, grabbing hold of the object I'd been fidgeting with earlier. It was cold and hard, and with a shaking hand, I removed it.

I stared into Maria's eyes, taking in the beautiful blue color of her irises, the sun making them shine. She was everything I could ever want and more.

"Maria," I said, dropping to one knee on the sand. "Will you marry me?"

She gasped, her eyes going wide and tears welling within them. She froze there for a long moment that felt like an eternity. Holding out her hand, she nodded, covering her mouth as a tear ran down her cheek.

"Yes," she said, her voice trembling, and I slid the ring onto her finger.

A roar of noise erupted from my animal pals, loud enough that a regular human might have been deafened. I shot to my feet and lifted Maria by the waist, my own eyes wet with tears as I held her tight.

"I love you," she said, sobbing.

"I love you, too."

Everyone else rejoined us, the cuddle even more fervent than before. Overwhelming emotions crashed over me like waves on the shore, and if I could have stayed in that moment forever, I would have.

"Also," I said, unable to help myself, "your dad might want to kill me."

"What?" she asked, cry-laughing into my shoulder. "Why?"

"Because I asked him for permission to marry you this morning."

She shook her head. "I don't care if he said no, Fischer. He has no say in our lives."

"Oh, no, he totally said yes. Though he wasn't exactly ecstatic about it . . ."

"What?" She leaned back, her eyes wet with joy and a confused smile lingering on her lips. "Then why would he want to kill you?"

I winced. "Because when he said it was still too soon to move in together, Sharon told him she's been sneaking you out for weeks . . ."

Her laughter bubbled up like a mountain spring, as beautiful as it was delicate. "We might have to go into hiding," she eventually said, the words coming out through fits of giggles.

"Whatever it takes."

We stared at each other for a long moment, reveling in our love for each other. We might have continued doing so, but a polite yet insistent hiss came from beside us.

Every head spun, turning to look at Rocky. He blew a single congratulatory bubble, ate the butt of his cigarette—which I suppose was better than littering, if a little gross—and locked his eyes on Snips. He made a complicated series of hisses and bubbles. The meaning was, unfortunately, clear.

I find myself overwhelmed with emotion, Mistress, he said, spinning to face the ocean. *I desire to be launched.*

Sergeant Snips, either happy to oblige the request or furious at him for ruining the moment, exploded forward. Water chi flowed from every hinge in her carapace, and with a smooth swing of her claw, she flung him out to sea. It was her best throw yet, rivaling the one I'd used to banish him.

Instead of his usual squeal of surprise, he removed another cigarette from gods knew where, lit it on his carapace, and took a deep, ponderous drag, his body tumbling end over end out toward the horizon.

Maria intertwined her fingers with mine, leaning her head on my arm as we watched him become a mere speck of black against the rising sun.

Epilogue

Tens of kilometers to the west, a long-forgotten power flowed across the land. It had been millennia since chi of this magnitude suffused the air, such potency not seen since the time before the gods fled. The world seemed to rejoice, both flora and fauna reacting to the shift, even if they weren't aware of the cause.

Leaves swayed in a nonexistent breeze. Sleeping creatures were roused from their rest, experiencing unexplainable bouts of energy. Insects called out, making whatever noise their small bodies could. Such were the minds of the unascended.

Some, however, knew what the chi meant. Or at least, they would when they regained their power.

Deep within a muddy bed of its own creation, a spirit beast stirred. The being had lain dormant for millennia, existing in a self-imposed stasis since the gods had departed this plane. Its mighty tail twitched, synapses within its enhanced mind firing of their own accord. It would take days, weeks, or perhaps even months before its awareness and body were restored. Until such a time, it would be a creature of base instincts, operating on the bare minimum requirements to keep it alive.

One such instinct rushed to the forefront of its consciousness, making its massive jaw hinge open.

Hunger . . . it thought, all of its mind needed to find the correct word.

The spirit beast lifted itself from its muddy prison, heading off in search of food. Luckily, it didn't have far to go.

About the Author

Haylock Jobson is the author of the Heretical Fishing series, originally released on Royal Road. He lives on the beautiful shores of Australia's Gold Coast and spends his days writing in local cafés, drinking what some might refer to as "too much" coffee and annoying strangers by asking if he can pet their dogs.

Podium

DISCOVER MORE

STORIES UNBOUND

PodiumEntertainment.com